Simon Kerl

A Comprehensive Grammar of the English Language

Simon Kerl

A Comprehensive Grammar of the English Language

Reprint of the original, first published in 1868.

1st Edition 2022 | ISBN: 978-3-37504-454-1

Verlag (Publisher): Salzwasser Verlag GmbH, Zeilweg 44, 60439 Frankfurt, Deutschland
Vertretungsberechtigt (Authorized to represent): E. Roepke, Zeilweg 44, 60439 Frankfurt, Deutschland
Druck (Print): Books on Demand GmbH, In de Tarpen 42, 22848 Norderstedt, Deutschland

A

COMPREHENSIVE GRAMMAR

OF THE

ENGLISH LANGUAGE.

FOR THE USE OF SCHOOLS.

By SIMON KERL, A.M.

"Fungar vice cotis, acutum
Reddere quæ ferrum valet, exsors ipsa secandi."
Horace.

NEW YORK:
IVISON, PHINNEY, BLAKEMAN & CO.,
CHICAGO: S. C. GRIGGS & CO.

1868.

KERL'S
SERIES OF ENGLISH GRAMMARS.

Kerl's Elementary English Grammar.—In the rapidity of its sales, this little treatise, according to its age, has surpassed every similar book ever published in this country. It contains, in a very compact and systematic form, about as much grammar as the majority of children have time to learn in our common public schools. It is, at the same time, so nearly identical with the first part of the large Grammar, as to enable the pupil to begin that book at Part Second, or even on p. 122. Pages, 164; well printed and bound.

Kerl's Comprehensive English Grammar.—This book is designed to be a thorough Practical Grammar, for the use of Common Schools. Nearly all that it contains beyond what the generality of Grammars have, will be new and useful. To its sections on VERBS, PREPOSITIONS, CONJUNCTIONS, PARSING, ANALYSIS, VERSIFICATION, PUNCTUATION, CAPITAL LETTERS, RHETORICAL FIGURES, and FALSE SYNTAX, particular attention is directed; and also to the arrangement of matter and to the copious ILLUSTRATIONS and EXERCISES. 375 pp., 12mo.

Kerl's Common-School Grammar.—This book is of an intermediate grade between the two foregoing ones; and it contains, besides, the most important historical elements of the English language. It is, however, so elementary, and yet so comprehensive, that it does not require either of the other books. Great care has been taken to make it, in matter, method, arrangement, and typography, as good as it can be made. About 300 pages. *Nearly ready.*

Kerl's Treatise on the English Language.—This book is designed for High-Schools, Colleges, and Private Students. Large 8vo. *In preparation.*

Entered according to Act of Congress, in the year 1861,
BY SIMON KERL,
In the Clerk's Office of the District Court for the Southern District of New York.

Entered according to act of Congress, in the year 1862,
BY SIMON KERL,
In the Clerk's Office of the District Court for the Southern District of New York.

Electrotyped by SMITH & McDOUGAL, 82 & 84 Beekman-street.

PREFACE.

It is generally admitted, at least by those persons who frequently have occasion to write the English language, that the knowledge of this subject, obtained in our schools, is not sufficient for the various requirements of life. In the following pages I therefore offer to the public an English Grammar that is designed to be, for practical purposes, more thorough than any other I have seen, the very largest not excepted.

In its *matter*, it does not differ much from other grammars, except that it has more, and that much of it is fresh from the original sources of the science. Whatever has been written on the subject by other grammarians, I have endeavored to ascertain; though I trust I have treated them less piratically and censoriously than most of them have treated their predecessors. The incidental remarks on grammar, made by reviewers, philologists, and other writers, have been diligently sought and considered. The best grammars of foreign languages have also been consulted; especially those of Becker, Vivier, Andrews, Crosby, and Kühner. Of the exercises to be corrected, about one half are the best of those which form the common inheritance of the science; and for the others I have read some work or works from every State in the Union, in order that the book may show all the various kinds of errors which are now current, like undetected counterfeit money, in the various parts of our country. If children imbibed no errors at home, it were well to exclude such exercises from grammars; but when a person has already caught a disease, I suppose it is best to convince him of his condition, and show him how to get rid of it. Errors in spelling, and errors manufactured by grammarians, are of course objectionable; but errors that are gathered from the usage of good writers, are a very different thing. Besides, parsing and analysis, when used alone, become too monotonous and wearisome, and hardly suffice to teach the correct use of the language.

In regard to the *arrangement* of matter,—an important item,—I venture to claim for the book a superiority over every other of its kind. It is well known that science and literature languished, until Bacon and Shakespeare emancipated them from the thralldom of ancient opinions; and, as Latin Grammars were first made, and English Grammars modeled after them, the latter have probably suffered from a similar dominion. A language that has many inflections, may well have its etymology taught as a separate branch; but a language, like ours, whose actual inflections might all be printed on two or three pages, needs no such treatment. Besides, words have etymology because they have syntax—the very existence of the one implying the other; and to stop with etymology, is to leave the work half finished. The greatest stickler for separating them in our language, has failed to draw the dividing line; and much of the etymology taught in our grammars—as in the cases of nouns—is sheer syntax. Every teacher of experience, too, must have observed how wearisome to pupils is the long desert of etymology, before they see its application in syntax; and then they often do not get the full benefit of this, because they have but a faint and confused recollection of the other. Moreover, by the usual system, almost the whole grammar must be learned before any practical benefit is derived from it; and, as children in many parts of the country can attend school only a part of each year, the consequence is, that they begin their grammar anew from year to year, get tired of its technical jargon, and derive, at last, but little benefit from the study. By the arrangement in this treatise, each section bears its own fruit, and will be, if learned, of permanent value, whether any further progress is made or not. The book, too, can be more conveniently resumed at the beginning of any section,

Parsing and Analysis have not only been made full, but stripped of much superfluous machinery. Doctrines and classifications have, in many places, been simplified and abridged; and for some of the insufficient articles in our grammars have been substituted others that are altogether more substantial. The book comprises both a Primary and a Higher Grammar, and is, in the highest sense, progressive and philosophical. It is built up, in Part First, by a regular synthesis, from the Alphabet to Analysis; in Part Second, from Pronunciation to Versification; and closes with a thorough and well-authorized section on Punctuation, as teaching the finish to the whole. In other grammars, most of the doctrine is printed in small type, and the exercises are printed in larger. This may be more agreeable to the teacher, but it is less so to the learner. I have given the main principles first, in large type, and apart from the examples; then the exercises in type sufficiently large; and, lastly, the unimportant doctrine in smaller type, under the head of Observations, and at the end of each section. The best modes of teaching and learning have been constantly kept in mind; but, of course, no reasonable teacher or learner will imagine, that the grammar of a mighty language—of a language that reaches into every fibre of human knowledge—can be learned without labor, or in "six lessons!" A full preface, explanatory and defensive, would require many pages. I therefore leave the work, without further remark, to the candor, judgment, and research of the reader.

TO TEACHERS.

Since almost every teacher has his own views about teaching, it is probably needless to add any suggestions. It may be proper, however, to state, that the pupil should learn, of the irregular verbs, only those forms which are in good present use; the others having been inserted merely for reference. The exercises from p. 36 to p. 44, should be used constantly with the recitations on the parts of speech. While the pupil is engaged in the parsing exercises, pp. 47—57, it may be well for him to strengthen himself by reviewing several times what precedes them. Indeed, while the pupil is passing through the exercises near the end of each section, he should repeatedly review the principles of the same section over which he has just passed; so that the principles and the exercises may act and re-act upon each other, till both are mastered. The numbers over words show the Rules of Syntax. The section on the Derivation of Words may be omitted, if taught in some other book. For a few of its words, the pupil will have to consult his dictionary. It would be a useful exercise for the pupil to copy the sentences given as examples in Part Second. He would thus learn to spell, to punctuate, to use capital letters, and would become familiar with all the various sentences which make language. The exercises for correction, it is probably best for the pupil to write off corrected, and bring them to school as a part of his evening task. If they be corrected orally, I would recommend that it be not done with too much ceremony or mechanical mannerism. In the sentence, "Him and me are of the same age," for instance, the pupil may simply say, "Incorrect: *him* and *me*, in the objective case, should be *he* and *I*, in the nominative case, because 'A pronoun, used as the subject of a finite verb, must be in the nominative case.'" For additional examples in analysis and parsing, may be used the numerous examples from p. 291 to the end. The section on Analysis should be reviewed frequently; and especially in connection with Punctuation, to which it is of the greatest value. A Key to the Exercises will be furnished, if it should be found necessary. It was my design to add an article on Composition; but, as this is not necessarily a part of grammar, and as it would have much enlarged the size of the book, I have omitted it. Should the present work be favorably received, however, I may add, as a sequel to this book, a small but adequate treatise on Composition; so that the two books will make a course of Grammar, Rhetoric, and Composition.

INDEX.

	PAGE		PAGE
Abbreviations,	337, 341	Nouns, Principles,	123-50
Accent,	92, 93; Poetic, 311, 312	Nouns, Exercises,	151-65
Adjectives,	10, 181-96	Nouns, Observations,	166-72
Adjectives, Principles,	181-83	Numbers, 6, 137-44; of Verbs,	209-12
Adjectives, Pronominal,	185-7	Observations, General,	283-9
Adjectives, Exercises,	189-93	Orthography,	90, 97-113
Adjectives, Observations,	193-6	Parsing,	47-57
Adjuncts,	33, 249, 250	Participles, 12, 21, 22, 197, 214-8
Adverbs,	30-2, 240-49	Parts of Speech,	2, 112
Adverbs, List of,	31, 32	" " "Words of Different, 274, 275
Adverbs, Principles,	240-43	Pauses, 97; Poetic,	310
Adverbs, Exercises,	243-7	Period,	336-8
Adverbs, Observations,	247-9	Persons, 6, 136, 137; of Verbs, 209-12
Analysis of Sentences,	58-87	Phrase,	3, 69, 86
Arrangement,	294, 295	Pleonasm,	246, 267
Articles,	9, 172-81	Poetry,	308-34
Articles, Principles,	172-4	Predicates,	2, 3, 58-60, 68-87
Articles, Exercises,	174-8	Prefixes,	114-6
Articles, Observations,	179-81	Prepositions,	32, 33, 249-62
Articulation,	96	Prepositions, Principles,	249, 250
Brackets,	362	Prepositions, Illustrations,	251-55
Cases,	7, 144-51	Prepositions, Constructions,	255-8
Clauses,	3, 58, 59, 70	Prepositions, Exercises,	258-61
Colon,	338-41	Prepositions, Observations,	261, 262
Comma,	343-50	Pronouns,	4, 5, 126-72
Comparison, Degrees of,	11, 182-5	Pronouns, Principles,	126-51
Conjugation,	23-9, 219, 220	Pronouns, Exercises,	151-65
Conjunctions,	33-5, 262-72	Pronouns, Observations,	166-72
Conjunctions, List of,	34, 35	Pronunciation,	90-97
Conjunctions, Principles,	262-4	Prepositions,	3, 58, 85, 87
Conjunctions, Illustrations,	264-7	Prosody,	90
Conjunctions, Exercises,	268-71	Punctuation,	335-74
Conjunctions, Observations,	271, 272	Quantity,	311
Curves,	360, 362	Questions for Review, 120, 121, 290-3
Dash,	355-9	Quotation-marks,	366, 367
Declension,	8, 9	Rhetorical Devices,	294-8
Derivation of Words,	113-20	Roots of Words,	113-9
Discourse,	3, 58, 85, 86	Scanning,	315-32
Ellipsis,	296	Semicolon,	341-3
Emphasis,	96	Sentences,	3, 58-87
Equivalent Expressions,	294, 295	Spelling,	108-13
Etymology,	90	Subjects,	2, 3, 58-60, 68-87
Exclamation-point,	352-4	Suffixes,	117-20
Exercises, General, 36-44, 68-85, 275-92	Syllables,	107, 108
Figures, Rhetorical,	298-307	Syntax, 44, 90; Rules of, 45-7
Forms of the Verb,	20, 24-9, 219	Tenses,	18, 19, 203-8
Genders,	5, 6, 133-6	Tones,	96
Grammar,	89	Underscore,	365, 866
Hyphen,	363-5	Verbs,	12-30, 196
Infinitives,	12, 21, 22, 197, 214-8	Verbs, Auxiliary,	22, 23, 212-4
Interjections,	35, 36, 272-4	Verbs, Irregular, List of,	13-16
Interrogation-point,	50, 351, 352	Verbs, Principles,	196-220
Letters, 1, 90-92; Capital,	97-107	Verbs, Exercises,	221-36
Marks, Miscellaneous,	371-74	Verbs, Observations,	236-40
Members of Sentences,	68, 86	Versification,	308-34, 87
Moods,	17, 18, 200-3, 207, 208	Voices,	17, 199, 200
Nouns,	4, 123-72	Words,	1, 2, 87

For any thing not found among the general principles, see the Observations at the end of the section.

SYNOPSIS OF PART FIRST.

1. Introductory View, or an *Outline.*—Letters, syllables, words, subjects, predicates, phrases, propositions, clauses, sentences, discourse.

2. Nouns and **Pronouns.**—CLASSES: *nouns,*—proper and common; *pronouns,*—personal, relative, and interrogative. PROPERTIES: *genders,*—masculine, feminine, common, and neuter; *persons,*—first, second, and third; *numbers,* — singular and plural; *cases,*—nominative, possessive, and objective. Declension. Exercises.

3. Articles.—KINDS; definite and indefinite. How *a* and *an* should be used.

4. Adjectives.—CLASSES: descriptive and definitive; definitive, with sub-classes. *Degrees of comparison;* positive, comparative, superlative. List of adjectives irregularly compared.

5. Verbs.—CLASSES: verbs finite, participles, infinitives, regular verbs, irregular verbs, list of irregular verbs; transitive or passive, intransitive or neuter. PROPERTIES: *voices,*—active, passive; *moods,*—indicative, subjunctive, potential, imperative, infinitive; *tenses,*—present, past, future, perfect, pluperfect, future-perfect, with *forms*—common, emphatic, progressive, passive; *persons* and *numbers.* Participles and infinitives. Auxiliary verbs. Conjugation. Exercises.

6. Adverbs.—Their chief characteristics. Full list, carefully classified.

7. Prepositions. — Their chief characteristics. Adjuncts. List of prepositions.

8. Conjunctions.—CLASSES; coördinate, subordinate, corresponding. List of conjunctions, classified according to their meanings.

9. Interjections.—List, classified according to the emotions.

10. Exercises on all the Parts of Speech.

11. Rules of Syntax.—The relations of words to one another, in the construction of sentences.

12. Parsing.—Formulas, models, and examples.

13. Analysis of Sentences. — Principles, with exercises. Sentences analyzed. Exercises. Observations. Summary of analysis and description.

PART FIRST.

1. INTRODUCTORY VIEW.

What is a letter?

A **letter** is a character that denotes one or more of the elementary sounds of language.

EXAMPLES: A, b, c; *a* ge, *a* t, *a* rt, *a* ll; *bubble*; cent, cart.

☞ Always read the examples carefully, reflecting upon each, so that you may learn clearly and fully what is meant by the definition or description.

How many elementary sounds has our language, and how many letters to represent them?

About *forty* elementary sounds, and *twenty-six* letters to represent them.

Into what two classes are the letters divided?

Into *vowels* and *consonants*.

Which are the vowels?

A, *e*, *i*, *o*, *u*, and sometimes *w* and *y*.

What is a syllable?

A **syllable** is a letter, or two or more combined, pronounced as one unbroken sound.

Ex.—A, I, on, no, not, stretched, barb'dst, a-e-ri-al, pro-fu-sion.

What is a word?

A **word** is a syllable, or two or more combined, used as the sign of some idea.

Ex.—Man, tree, world, sky, pink, beauty, strikes, well, fair, alas, because.

An *idea* is the picture or notion of a thing, in the mind.

How are words classified according to the number of syllables composing them?

Into *monosyllables, dissyllables, trisyllables,* and *polysyllables.*

Define these classes.

A *monosyllable* is a word of one syllable; a *dissyllable*, of two; a *trisyllable*, of three; and a *polysyllable*, of four or more.

Ex.—I, song; baker, railroad; ornament, commandment; customary, incomprehensibility.

How are words classified according as they are formed, or not formed, from one another?

Into *primitive, derivative,* and *compound.*

☞ Use the exercises on pp. 36-44, with each lesson.

Define these classes.

A *primitive* word is not formed from another word; a *derivative* word is formed from another word; and a *compound* word is composed of two or more other words.

Ex.—*Primitive:* Breeze, man, good, build, up. *Derivative:* Breezy, manful, goodness, builder, rebuild. *Compound:* Sea-breeze, mankind, dewdrop, newspaper, upon, sewing-machine.

How are words divided according to what they denote?

Into nine classes, called PARTS OF SPEECH.

Name them.

Nouns, Pronouns, Articles, Adjectives, Verbs, Adverbs, Prepositions, Conjunctions, and *Interjections.*

FAMILIAR EXPLANATION.—I might present to your mind, by words alone, all that I have ever seen or experienced. To do this, I should have to use *nouns* and *pronouns,* to denote objects; *articles,* to aid the nouns; *adjectives,* to express the qualities, conditions, or circumstances of objects; *verbs,* to express their actions, or states of existence; *adverbs,* to describe their actions, or to show the nature or degree of their qualities; *prepositions,* to express their positions or relations to one another; *conjunctions,* to continue the discourse, or to connect its parts; and *interjections,* to give vent to any feeling or emotion springing up suddenly within me.

Ex.—*Nouns:* "In *spring,* the *sun* shines pleasantly upon the *earth, leaves* and *flowers* come forth, and *birds* sing in the *woods.*"

Pronouns: "Roses encircle *my* window, and the roses adorn the window." *they* adorn *it.*"

Articles: "*The* church stands on *a* hill."

Adjectives: "*Ripe* strawberries are *good.*" "*That* man owns *two* farms."

Verbs: "Rivers *flow,* stars *shine,* men *work,* and boys *study* and *play.*"

Adverbs: "Below us, a *most* beautiful river flowed *very smoothly.*"

Prepositions: "There are cedars *on* the hill *beyond* the river."

Conjunctions: "John *and* James are happy, *because* they are good."

Interjections: "We all seek for happiness; but, *alas!* how few of us obtain it."

SUGGESTION TO THE TEACHER.—Take a walk with your class, during some leisure interval, and teach them the parts of speech, from the surrounding scenery.

Since the world furnishes thousands and thousands of objects for us to consider, or think about, and since we never speak without having something in mind, what is essential to every thought or saying?

A SUBJECT and a PREDICATE.

What is meant by the *subject?*

The **subject** denotes that of which something is said or affirmed.

Ex.—"*The cannons* were fired." "*The leaves and flowers in the garden* have been killed by the frost."

What is meant by the *predicate?*

The **predicate** denotes what is said or affirmed.

Ex.—"The cannons *were fired.*" "The leaves and flowers in the garden *have been killed by the frost.*"

How are subjects and predicates classified?

Into *simple* and *compound.*

Define simple subjects and compound subjects

A *simple* subject has but one nominative to which the predicate refers; a *compound* subject has more than one.

Ex.—*Simple:* "The boy learns;" "The boy who is studious, learns." *Compound:* "The boy and his sister learn." "The boys and girls who are studious, learn."

Define simple predicates and compound predicates.

A *simple* predicate has but one finite verb referring to the subject; a *compound* predicate has more than one.

Ex.—*Simple:* "Boys study;" "Boys study the lessons which are given to them." *Compound:* "Boys study, recite, and play;" "Boys study and recite the lessons which are given to them."

Subject, from *subjectus*, thrown under, because viewed as being the foundation on which the proposition or sentence is based. *Predicate*, from *prædico*, I speak or say.

What is a phrase?

A **phrase** is two or more words rightly put together, but not making a proposition.

Ex.—"In the next place." "To show you the fragrant blossoms of spring."

What is a proposition?

A **proposition** is a subject combined with its predicate.

Ex.—"Stars shine." "Even if my hopes should perish."

A *proposition* may be a clause, or not; or it may be a sentence, or less than a sentence. It is not necessarily either a clause or a sentence.

What is a clause?

A **clause** is any one of two or more propositions which together make a sentence.

Ex.—"The morning was pure and sunny, the fields were white with daisies, the hawthorn was covered with its fragrant blossoms, the bee hummed about every bank, and the swallow played high in air about the village steeple."—*Irving.* This sentence has five clauses, separated by the comma.

What is a sentence?

A **sentence** is a thought expressed by words, and comprised between two full pauses.

Ex.—"Every man is the architect of his own fortune." "Happy is he who finds a true friend, and happy is he who possesses the true qualities to be a friend."

How are sentences classified?

Into *simple* and *compound.*

What is a simple sentence?

A *simple* sentence contains but one proposition.

Ex.—"Wasps sting." "No man knows his destiny." "Return (thou) quickly."

What is a compound sentence?

A *compound* sentence contains two or more clauses.

Ex.—"As every thread of gold is precious, so is every moment of time; and as it would be folly to shoe horses (as Nero did) with gold, so it is to spend time in trifles."—*Mason.*

What is discourse?

Discourse is any series of properly related sentences, expressing continuous thought.

2. NOUNS AND PRONOUNS.

What is a noun?

A **noun** is a name.

EXAMPLES: God, Mary, man, men, George Washington, instructor, sky, sun, stars, clouds, town, St. Louis, street, flock, flower, soul, feeling, sense, motion, behavior.

Names are given to persons, to spiritual beings, to brute animals, and to things. The word *objects* may be used as a general term for all these classes.

Tell me which are the nouns in the following sentences:—
Lions and ostriches are found in Africa.
John and Joseph drove the horses to the pasture.
Pinks and roses are blooming in the garden.
Apples, peaches, melons, corn, and potatoes, are brought to market.

A **proper** noun is the name given to a particular object, to distinguish it from other objects of the same kind.

Ex.—George, Susan, William Shakespeare, London, New York, Mississippi, Monday, January; the *Robert Fulton;* the *Intelligencer;* the *Azores.*

A **common** noun is a name that can be applied to every object of the same kind.

Ex.—Boy, tree, house, city, river, road, horse, chair, ink, bird, blackbird.

Briefly: A *common* noun is a *generic* name; and a *proper* noun, an *individual* name. The former rather tells *what* the object is; and the latter, *who* or *which* it is.

Generic means belonging to a class; and *individual,* belonging to one object or group only, as distinguished from others of the same kind. All the objects in the world may be divided into a limited number of classes; as, rivers, valleys, hills, cities, leaves, flowers. A few of these classes—namely, persons, places, months, days, ships, boats, horses, oxen, rivers, mountains, and some others—are of so much importance to us in our daily affairs, that we have an extra name for each object of the class; as, *Thomas, Smith, Chicago, Missouri.* The names of the former kind are *common* nouns; those of the latter, *proper* nouns. A proper noun begins with a capital letter.

How many kinds of nouns are there, and what are they?

What is a pronoun?

A **pronoun** is a word that supplies the place of a noun.

Ex.—" William promised Mary that William would lend Mary William's grammar, that Mary might study the grammar," is expressed with greater facility and more agreeably, by saying, " William promised Mary that *he* would lend *her his* grammar, that *she* might study *it.*"

Pro means *for,* or *in stead of;* hence *pronoun* means *for a noun.* The word *substantive* is often used as a general term to denote either a noun or a pronoun, or whatever is used in the sense of a noun.

What is a personal pronoun?

A **personal** pronoun is one of that class of pronouns which are used to distinguish the three grammatical persons.

Ex.—" *I* told *you he* was not at home." " *We* told *him you* were not at home."

Persons, in grammar, are properties of words to distinguish the speaker, what is spoken to, and what is spoken of, from one another.

Which are the personal pronouns?

I, my, mine, myself, me; we, our, ours, (ourself,) ourselves, us;—thou, thy, thine, thyself, thee; you, ye, your, yours, yourself, yourselves;—he, his, him, himself; she, her, hers, herself; it, its, itself; they, their, theirs, them, and *themselves.*

What is a relative pronoun?

A **relative** pronoun is one that makes its clause dependent on another clause or word.

Ex.—"There is the man *whom* you saw;" "From the side of a mountain gushed forth a little rivulet, *which* lay like a silver thread, across the meadow." "I do not know *who* took your hat"; "No one knows *what* ails the child." Observe that the Italic words with what follows each, can make sense only in connection with the other words, and hence they are said to be *dependent*.

Which are the relative pronouns?

Who, whoever, whosoever; whose, whosever, whosesoever; whom, whomever, whomsoever; which, whichever, whichsoever; what, whatever, whatsoever; that; and as.

Whoso and *whatso* are sometimes found as shortened forms of *whosoever* and *whatsoever*.

What is an interrogative pronoun?

An **interrogative** pronoun is one used to ask a question.

Ex.—"*Who* took my hat?" "*Which* is yours?" "*What* ails the child?"

Which are the interrogative pronouns?

Who, whose, whom; which; and what.

What other words are frequently used as pronouns?

One, ones, oneself, none; other, others; that, those; each other, one another.

Which of the foregoing pronouns are compound, or what is a compound pronoun?

A **compound** pronoun is a simple pronoun with *self, selves, ever, so,* or *soever,* annexed to it; or it is a pronoun consisting of two words.

Ex.—My, *myself;* your, *yourself;* them, *themselves;* who, *whoever;* each *other.*

How many chief kinds of pronouns are there, and what are they?

What properties have nouns and pronouns?

Genders, persons, numbers, and **cases.**

Just as every apple, for instance, must be of some size, have some kind of color, have some kind of flavor, be hard or mellow, &c.

R. The pupil should constantly bear in mind, that language is made to suit the world, and not the world to suit language. The properties of words arise generally from the nature or relations of objects.

We can readily observe that the objects around us are either males, females, or neither; and to enable us to be sufficiently definite in these respects, words have what grammarians call *genders*.

When is a noun or pronoun of the masculine gender, or what does the masculine gender denote?

The **masculine** gender denotes males.

Ex.—Man, Charles, brother, horse, ox, drake, instructor, he, his, him.

When is a noun or pronoun of the feminine gender, or what does the feminine gender denote?

The **feminine** gender denotes females.

Ex.—Woman, Susan, niece, cow, duck, instructress, she, her.

NOUNS AND PRONOUNS.

When is a noun or pronoun of the common gender, or what does this gender denote?

The **common** gender denotes either males or females, or both.

Ex.—Parent, child, friend, cousin, people, bird, animal, I, we, our, your, who.

Common means applicable to either sex; neuter means applicable to neither sex.

When is a noun or pronoun of the neuter gender, or what does the neuter gender denote?

The **neuter** gender denotes neither males nor females.

Ex.—Book, rock, rose, wisdom, vice, cloud, happiness, it, what.

How many genders are there, and what are they?

---

b. In speaking, we may refer either to ourselves, to something spoken to, or to something spoken of, and there are no other ways of speaking; hence words have what grammarians call *persons*.

When is a noun or pronoun of the first person, or what does the first person denote?

The **first** person denotes the speaker.

Ex.—"*I Andrew Jackson, President* of the United States." "*I Paul* have written it." "*We*, the *people* of these colonies."

When is a noun or pronoun of the second person, or what does the second person denote?

The **second** person represents an object as spoken to.

Ex.—"*Thomas*, come to me." "*Gentlemen* of the jury." "O *Happiness!* our being's end and aim." "*Thou, thou,* art the man." "Wave *your* tops, *ye pines.*"

When is a noun or pronoun of the third person, or what does the third person denote?

The **third** person represents an object as spoken of.

Ex.—"*Experience* and *hope, pleasure* and *pain, life* and *death, money* and *power,* have a mighty *influence* on the *actions* of *mankind.*" "*He* knew *it* was *what she* wanted *him* to buy."

How many persons are there, and what are they?

---

c. There are more than one of almost every kind of objects; and in speaking we are continually referring either to one object or to more, of the different kinds with which we have to do; hence words have what grammarians call *numbers*.

When is a noun or pronoun of the singular number, or what does the singular number denote?

The **singular** number denotes but one.

Ex.—Desk, key, leaf, boy, Arthur, deer, sheep, swarm, army, I, my, me, thou, thee, thyself, yourself, he, him, she, her, it, itself.

When is a noun or pronoun of the plural number, or what does the plural number denote?

The **plural** number denotes more than one.

Ex.—Desks, keys, leaves, boys, deer, sheep, ashes, swarms, armies, we, our, us, ye, they, them.

How is the plural number of nouns generally formed?

By adding *s*, sometimes *es*, to the singular.

Ex.—Glove, *gloves;* chair, *chairs;* church, *churches;* bush, *bushes;* fox, *foxes;* chimney, *chimneys;* negro, *negroes;* nation, *nations.*

What is a collective noun?

A **collective** noun is a noun denoting, in the singular form, more than one object of the same kind.

Ex.—Family, army, swarm, crowd, multitude, congregation, pair, tribe, class.

How many numbers are there, and what are they?

NOUNS AND PRONOUNS.

d. If I say, "Your brother's friend sent James to me;
Your friend's brother sent me to James;
My brother's friend sent James to you;
James sent your brother's friend to me;
I sent your friend's brother to James;
You sent James to my friend's brother;" you can easily see that all these sentences differ much from one another in meaning. The difference of meaning arises from the different relations of the words to one another, and these different relations are called *cases*. That objects exist or act, that objects are owned, or make parts of other objects, and that objects are acted upon, are the three chief conditions of things, on which *cases* are based.

When is a noun or pronoun in the *nominative* case, or what does the *nominative* case denote?

The **nominative** case denotes the condition of a noun or pronoun that is used as the subject of a predicate.

Ex.—"*John* strikes James." "*Joseph* swims." "The *field* is ploughed." "The *rose* is beautiful." "*Fishes* swim in the sea, and *birds* fly in the air." "Mary's *bunch* of flowers is fading."

A noun or pronoun is also in the *nominative case*, when it is used *independently* or *absolutely*.

Ex.—*Independently:* "*John*, come to me;" "Alas, poor *Yorick!*" "The Pilgrim *Fathers*,—where are they?" "Merchant's *Bank*." *Absolutely:* "The *tree* having fallen, we returned;" "*Bonaparte* being banished, peace was restored;" "To become a *scholar*, requires exertion."

Independently; used in addressing persons or other objects, in exclaiming, or in simply directing attention to an object. *Absolutely*; used before a participle, or after a participle or an infinitive, without being governed by it or controlled by any other word.

When is a noun or pronoun in the *possessive* case, or what does the *possessive* case denote?

The **possessive** case denotes possession.

Ex.—"*John's* horse;" "*My* slate;" "The *children's* books;" "The *girls'* room."

What is the regular sign of the possessive case?

An apostrophe, or comma above the line, followed by the letter *s*.

Ex.—"*Mary's* slate;" "*Burns's* poems;" "The *soldier's* grave;" "*Men's* affairs."

Is the possessive *s* always expressed?

It is omitted from plural nouns ending with *s*, and sometimes also from singular nouns ending with *s*, or an *s*-sound.

Ex.—"The *pigeons'* roosting-place;" "The *soldiers'* camp;" "For *conscience'* sake."

When is a noun or pronoun in the *objective* case, or what does the *objective* case denote?

The **objective** case denotes the condition of a noun or pronoun that is used as the object of a verb or preposition.

Ex.—"The horse EATS *hay*;" "This stream TURNS a *mill*." "The water flows OVER the *dam*;" "I SAW *her* WITH *him*;" "He SAW *me* WITH *her*."

The object of a transitive verb or of a preposition, is the noun or pronoun required after it to make sense; as, "I rolled a *stone* down the *hill*." Here *stone* is the object of the verb *rolled*, and *hill* is the object of the preposition *down*.

How many *cases* are there, and what are they?

When must a noun or pronoun agree in case with another noun or pronoun?

When it is but a repetition of the other, or when it denotes, by way of explanation, the same thing.

Ex.—"I, *I*, am the *man*." "Friends, false *friends*, have ruined me." "Smith is a *barber*." "Smith the *barber* is my *neighbor*."

How can the different cases of nouns be distinguished?

By their meanings : or, the *nominative* may be found by asking a question with *who* or *what* before the verb ; the *objective*, with *whom* or *what* after the verb ; and the *possessive* is known by the apostrophe.

Ex.—"Mary plucked flowers for John's sister." Who plucked?—plucked what?—for whom?

---

e. Having now shown you what properties nouns and pronouns have, I shall next show you, briefly and regularly, how the different nouns and pronouns are written to express these properties. This process is called *declension*.

What, then, is it, to *decline* a noun or pronoun?

To **decline** a noun or pronoun, is to show, in some regular way, what forms it has to express its grammatical properties.

Observe that nouns sometimes remain unchanged, and that pronouns are sometimes wholly changed, to express their properties.

DECLENSION OF NOUNS AND PRONOUNS.

Nouns.

	SINGULAR.			PLURAL.	
Nominative.	*Possessive.*	*Objective.*	*Nominative.*	*Possessive.*	*Objective.*
Boy,	boy's,	boy ;	boys,	boys',	boys.
Man,	man's,	man ;	men,	men's,	men.
Lady,	lady's,	lady ;	ladies,	ladies',	ladies.
Fox,	fox's,	fox ;	foxes,	foxes',	foxes.
John,	John's,	John.			

Pronouns.

	SINGULAR.			PLURAL		
	Nom.	*Poss.*	*Obj.*	*Nom.*	*Poss.*	*Obj.*
1st PERS.	I,	my *or* mine,	me ;	we,	our *or* ours,	us.
2d PERS.	Thou *or* you,	thy *or* thine, your *or* yours,	thee *or* you ;	ye *or* you,	your *or* yours,	you.
3d PERS. *Mas.*	He,	his,	him ;			
Fem.	She,	her *or* hers,	her ;	they,	their *or* theirs,	them.
Neut.	It,	its,	it ;			

	Nom. or *Obj.*			*Nom.* or *Obj.*		
1.	Myself (*or* ourself) ;			ourselves.		
2.	Thyself *or* yourself ;			yourselves.		
3.	Himself, herself, itself ;			themselves.		

	Nom.	*Poss.*	*Obj.*	*Nom.*	*Poss.*	*Obj.*
	One,	one's,	one ;	ones,	ones',	ones.
	Other,	other's,	other ;	others,	others',	others.

	Nom.	Poss.	Obj.
Sing. or Plur.	Who,	whose,	whom. (—ever or soever.)
	Which,	whose,	which. "
	That,	whose,	that.
	What,	———	what. "
	As,	———	as.
	None,	———	none.

Decline *John, man, boy, lady, fox, farmer, Benjamin, city.*
Decline *I, thou, you, he, she, it, myself, thyself, yourself, himself, herself, itself, as, other, who, whoever, whosoever, which, what, that, as, none.*

Tell me the gender of each of the following words, and why:—
Theodore, Theodora, he, hers, she, I, they, it, who, which, what.

Tell me the person of each of the following pronouns, and why:—
I, we, my, myself, thou, thyself, she, he, it, its, himself, one, other, that, who.

Tell me the number of each of the following pronouns, and why:—
I, you, he, me, we, my, us, thee, yourselves, them, herself, themselves, it, she, hers, which, what, others.

Tell me the case of each of the following pronouns:—
I, me, we, us, thou, thee, thyself, they, them, who, whom.

Of what gender, person, number, and case is each of the following pronouns?—
Him, his, its, he, them, it, I, you, thy, their, she, thou, me, your, us, they, my, mine, thine, yours, it, hers, theirs, we, thee, our, ours, ye, them, myself, ourself, themselves, ourselves, thyself, yourselves, yourself, himself, itself, herself, one, none, one's, ones', other, others', who, what, which, whatever.

3. ARTICLES.

If I say, "Give me *a* book," you understand that any book will answer my purpose; but if I say, "Give me *the* book," you understand that I want some particular book. If I say, "Missouri is north of Arkansas," I mean States; but if I say, "*The* Missouri is north of *the* Arkansas," I mean rivers. These little words, *a* and *the*, which often have so important an effect on the sense of nouns, are called *articles.*

What, then, is an *article?*

An **article** is a word placed before a noun, to show how the noun is applied.

Ex.—"Man is made for society; but *a* man naturally prefers *the* man whose temper and inclinations best suit his own."

How many articles are there, and what are they?

Two: **the,** the *definite* article; and **a** or **an,** the *indefinite* article.

What does the *definite* article show?

The **definite** article shows that some particular object or group is meant.

Ex.—"*The* horse, *the* horses, *the* stage, *the* Connecticut, *the* lion; *the* green meadows; *the* iron-bound bucket; *the* brave Pulaski."

What does the *indefinite* article show?

The **indefinite** article shows that no particular one of the kind is meant.

Ex.—"*A* bird, *a* mouse, *an* apple, *a* cherry, *a* carriage; *an* idle boy."

How do *a* and *an* differ?
In application only; in meaning, they are the same.

Where is *an* used?
Before words beginning with a vowel sound.

Ex.—"*An* article, *an* enemy, *an* inch, *an* urn, *an* hour; *an* honest man."

Where is *a* used?
Before words beginning with a consonant sound.

Ex.—"*A* banquet, *a* cucumber, *a* dunce, *a* fox, *a* horse, *a* jug, *a* king, *a* lion, *a* youth, *a* university, *a* eulogy; *a* one-horse carriage."

Place the proper indefinite article before each of the following words or phrases:—
Razor, house, knife, humming-bird, chicken, ounce, insult, unit, ox, ball, hundred, African; interesting story; humble cottage.

4. ADJECTIVES.

The nouns and pronouns, as you remember, denote objects. But our regard for objects depends not a little on their qualities and circumstances; and hence there is a large class of words to express these, for all the various purposes of life. The word *river*, for instance, denotes something that may be *cool, deep, clear, swift, broad, winding*. *Apple* denotes something that may be *red, large, ripe, mellow, juicy*. And when I say, "*that* apple, *this* apple, *every* apple, *four* apples, the *fourth* apple," the slanting words show, without expressing quality, more precisely what I mean. These qualifying and designating—these descriptive and definitive words, which generally *add* an idea to that of the noun, are therefore called *adjectives*.

What, then, is an *adjective*?

An **adjective** is a word used to qualify or limit the meaning of a substantive.

Ex.—White, green, good, lazy, tall, shrill, religious. "A *bay* horse; a *sharp* knife; a *sharper* knife; a *bright* day; a *stormy* night; *golden* clouds; a *gold* watch; *Missouri* apples; a *quivering* aspen; *that sun-tipped* elm; a boy *nine* years *old*."

What is a *descriptive* adjective?

A **descriptive** adjective describes or qualifies.

Ex.—"A *rapid* river; the *blue* sky; a *modest* woman." "She is *beautiful, amiable*, and *intelligent*." "The *rippling* brook; the *twinkling* stars; *waving* woods; a *roaring* storm; a *broken* pitcher." The last five adjectives, and others like them, are usually called *participial* adjectives.

What is a *definitive* adjective?

A **definitive** adjective merely limits or modifies.

Ex.—"*Four* peaches; *all* peaches; *some* peaches; *this* peach; *yonder* peaches."

Which are the principal definitive adjectives?

All, any, both, certain, each, every, either, else, few, many, many a, much, neither, no, one, other, own, same, some, such, that, this, very, what, which, and *yon* or *yonder. One, two, three, four,* etc.; *first, second, third,* etc.

Nearly all the adjectives of the first class are usually called *pronominal* adjectives, some of them being occasionally used as pronouns; and those of the second class are called *numeral* adjectives. Since we may refer to objects *definitely, indefinitely,* or *distributively*, the pronominal adjectives are accordingly, some of them, *definite* or *demonstrative*, as *this, that, yonder;* some, *indefinite*, as *any, some, other;* and some, *distributive*, as *each, every, either, neither, many a*. And since we may either *count* or *number*, some of the numeral adjectives are called *cardinal*, as *one, two, three;* and the others, *ordinal*, as *first, second, third*.

ADJECTIVES.

Since the same quality may exist in different objects, and in the same degree or in different degrees,—as, "*red* cheeks, *red* roses, *red* hair, *redder* cheeks, the *reddest* roses,"—adjectives have what grammarians call the *degrees of comparison;* the *positive*, the *comparative*, and the *superlative*.

How does the *positive* degree describe an object?

The **positive** degree ascribes to an object the quality simply, or an equal degree of it.

Ex.—High, strong, rocky, polite, black, prudent; "as *white* as snow."

How does the *comparative* degree describe an object?

The **comparative** degree ascribes to an object the quality in a higher or a lower degree.

Ex.—Higher, stronger, rockier, politer, better, more prudent, less prudent.

How does the *superlative* degree describe an object?

The **superlative** degree ascribes to an object the quality in the highest or the lowest degree.

Ex.—Highest, strongest, rockiest, politest, best, most prudent, least prudent.

How are adjectives of one syllable, and some of two syllables, compared, when we wish to express *increase* of the quality?

By adding *er* or *est* to the word in the positive degree.

Ex.—Pos. *wise*, comp. *wiser*, superl. *wisest;* great, *greater*, *greatest;* lovely, *lovelier*, *loveliest;* serene, *serener*, *serenest;* thin, *thinner*, *thinnest*.

Final *y* is often changed to *i*, final *e* is always omitted, and a single final consonant is often doubled, before the ending *er* or *est*. See pp. 108, 109.

How are all adjectives of more than two syllables, and some of two syllables, compared?

By *more* and *most*.

Ex.—Pos. *beautiful*, comp. *more beautiful*, superl. *most beautiful; active*, *more active*, *most active; unlucky*, *more unlucky*, *most unlucky*.

How are adjectives compared when we wish to express decrease of the quality?

By *less* and *least*.

Ex.—Wise, *less wise*, *least wise;* arrogant, *less arrogant*, *least arrogant*.

Some adjectives are not compared according to the foregoing rules, and are therefore said to be *irregular*. The following is a list:—

Positive.	Compar.	Superl.	Posit.	Compar.	Superl.
Good,	better,	best.	Hind,	hinder,	hindmost.
Bad, ill, *or* evil,	worse,	worst.	Far,	farther,	farthest.
Much *or* many,	more,	most.	Near,	nearer,	nearest, *or* next.
Little,	less,	least.	Late,	later,	latest, *or* last.
Fore,	former,	foremost, *or* first.	Old,	older, *or* elder,	oldest, *or* eldest.

Can all adjectives be compared?

Some can not be compared with propriety.

Ex.—Eternal, straight, dead, equal, square, perpendicular, two-edged, speechless.

Is the word which the adjective qualifies or limits, always expressed?

It is not; but, in parsing, it must be supplied.

Ex.—"These apples are better than those" [apples]. "The idle [persons] are generally mischievous."

5. VERBS.

If we look into the world, we shall find, that, to the many different beings and things denoted by nouns and pronouns, belong not only many different qualities, denoted by adjectives, but also many different motions, actions, and states of existence, which are expressed by certain words called *verbs;* as, John *reads, writes, runs,* and *plays.*

What, then, is a *verb,* or what is its chief use in language?

A verb is a word used to affirm something of a subject.

Ex.—"The wind *blows.*" "The rose *blooms.*" "There *is* an endless world." "The tree *is* dead." "If I *should go.*" "Brutus *stabbed* Cæsar." "Cæsar *was stabbed* by Brutus." "*Do* you not *study?*" "*Do* (you) *study* diligently."

Verb means *word,* or, pre-eminently, *the word.* Grammarians have called this part of speech so, because it makes the chief part of every grammar, or because it is the chief word of language.

Every verb denotes some kind of action or state. And *affirmations,* with grammarians, mean all kinds of assertions; also commands and questions.

Tell which are the verbs in the following sentences, and why:—

Birds sing. Mother sews, knits, and spins. Columbus discovered America. Jesus wept. The dew glistens. Go where the men are reaping. The problems should have been solved. The water is frozen.

When verbs are actually used to express affirmations, they are called *finite* verbs; but there are two forms of the verb which do not express affirmations, and are called the *participle* and the *infinitive:* as, *Writing, written, being written, having written, having been written; to write, to have written, to be written, to have been written.*

What, then, is a *participle?*

A participle is a form of the verb, that merely assumes the act or state, and is construed like an adjective.

Ex.—"A tree, FULL of fruit;" "A tree, *bending* with fruit." "He said few things INDICATIVE of wisdom;" "He said few things *indicating* wisdom." "The man was found DEAD;" "The man was found *murdered.*"

Construed like an adjective—arranged in the same way with other words of the sentence.

What is an *infinitive?*

An infinitive is a form of the verb that begins generally with *to,* and expressing no affirmation.

Ex.—"An opportunity *to study.*" "He is obliged *to sell.*" "He seems *to have been disappointed.*"

Of how many words may a verb consist?

Of as many as four.

Ex.—"Eagles *soar.*" "The house *was built.*" "The mail *may have arrived.*" "These lessons *should have been learned.*" "*Having written.*" "*To have been writing.*"

———

Almost every verb may be expressed in a great variety of ways or forms; thus, from WRITE we have *writing, wrote, written, writes, writeth, writest, to write, to have written, to be written, to have been written, is writing, to have been writing, having written, having been written, is written, was written, should be written, is writing, was writing, can write, must write, will write, shall write, would write, should write, could write, may write, might write, may be written, may be writing, may have been writing, might have been written, might have been writing, mightst have been writing,* &c., &c.

Now, that we may be enabled to master all these different forms,—understand their meaning, and thus be enabled to use them correctly,—grammarians have found it best to divide verbs into certain *classes,* and also to regard them as having certain *properties.*

How are verbs classified?

Into *regular* and *irregular*, with reference to their form.

Into *transitive* and *intransitive*, with reference to their meaning or use; and the former are often used as *passive*, and some of the latter are always *neuter*.

What is a regular verb?

A **regular** verb takes the ending *ed*, to form its preterit and its perfect participle.

Ex.—Present *play*, preterit *played*, perfect participle *played; move, moved, moved*.

E, at the end of a word, is dropped before an ending that begins with a vowel.—In stead of *preterit* the pupil may also say *past*, a less appropriate but more euphonic word.

What is an irregular verb?

An **irregular** verb does not take the ending *ed*, to form its preterit and its perfect participle.

Ex.—Present *see*, preterit *saw*, perfect participle *seen; speak, spoke, spoken*.

Which are the *principal parts* of the verb, or those from which all the other parts are formed?

The **principal parts** are the *present*, or the simplest form given in a dictionary; the *preterit*, or the simplest form that affirms a past fact; and the *perfect participle*, or the form that makes sense with the word *having* or *being*.

Ex.—Pres. (to) *walk, write;* pret. (I) *walked,* (I) *wrote;* perf. part. having *walked,* being *written.*

List of Irregular Verbs.

The following catalogue shows the principal parts of all the irregular verbs. Having learned these, the student also knows the principal parts of all the other verbs, which must be regular. He must not infer, however, from the word *irregular*, that these verbs are a mere straggling offshoot of the language; for they are really the very core or pith of it.

In using irregular verbs, we are liable to error for the most part only in the use of those whose preterit and perfect participle are not alike. These verbs have therefore been given first, and separate from the rest, that they may be learned perfectly. R. denotes that the regular form may also be used in stead of the others. * denotes that the form under it is seldom used, being either ancient, poetic, or of late introduction. The form supposed to be of the best present usage, is placed first. The second form of some verbs is preferable, when applied in a certain way; as, "*freighted* with spices and silks," "*fraught* with mischief;" "*thunderstruck*," "*sorrow-stricken*."—Memorize the unmarked forms only.

1. THE TWO PAST FORMS DIFFERENT.

Present.	Preterit, or Past.	Perfect Participle.	Present.	Preterit, or Past.	Perfect Part.
Arise,	arose,	arisen.	Beget,	begot, begat,*	begotten, begot.
Awake,	awoke, r., awaked,	awoke.*	Begin,	began, begun,*	begun.
Be,	was,	been.	Bid,	bid, bade,	bid, bidden.
Bear (*bring forth*),	bore, bare,	born.	Bite,	bit,	bitten, bit.
Bear (*carry*),	bore,	borne.	Blow,	blew, r.,*	blown, r.*
Beat,	beat,	beaten, beat.	Break,	broke,* brake,*	broken, broke.*
Become,	became,	become.			
Befall,	befell,	befallen.			

VERBS.

Present.	Preterit, or Past.	Perfect Participle.	Present.	Preterit, or Past.	Perfect Part.
Chide,	chid,	chidden, chid.	Ride,	rode,	rode, ridden.
Choose,	chose,	chosen.	Ring,	rang, rung,	rung.
Cleave (adhere),	cleaved, clave,*	cleaved.	Rise,	rose,	risen.
			Rive,	rived,	riven, r.*
Cleave (split),	cleft, clove, clave,	cleft, cloven.	Run,	ran, run,*	run.
			Saw,	sawed,	sawn, r.
Come,	came,	come.	See,	saw,	seen.
Crow,	crowed, crew,	crowed.	Seethe,	seethed, sod,	seethed, sodden.
Dare (venture),	dared,b durst,	dared.	Shake,	shook,	shaken.
(Dare—challenge,	dared,	dared.)	Shape,	shaped,	shaped, shapen.*
Dive,	dived, dove,*	dived.	Shave,	shaved,	shaved, shaven.
Do (principal verb),	did,	done.	Shear,	sheared, shore,*	shorn, r.
Draw,	drew,	drawn.	Show,	showed,	shown, r.
Drink,	drank,	drunk, drank.*	Shrink,	shrunk, shrank,	shrunk, shrunken.*
Drive,	drove,	driven.	Slay,	slew,	slain.
Eat,	ate, ĕat,	eaten, ĕat.*	Slide,	slid, r.,	slidden, slid, r.
Fall,	fell,	fallen.			
Fly,	flew,	flown.	Smite,	smote,	smitten, smit.
Forbear,	forbore,	forborne.			
Forget,	forgot,	forgotten, forgot.	Sing,	sung, sang,	sung.
			Sink,	sunk, sank,	sunk.
Forsake,	forsook,	forsaken.	Sow (scatter),	sowed,	sown, r.
Freeze,	froze,	frozen.	Speak,	spoke, spake,*	spoken.
Freight,	freighted,	freighted, fraught.	Spit,	spit, spat,*	spit, spitten.*
Get,	got,	got, gotten.	Spring,	sprung, sprang,	sprung.
Give,	gave,	given.			
Go,	went,	gone.	Steal,	stole,	stolen.
Grave,	graved,	graven, r.	Stride,	strode, strid,	stridden, strid.
Grow,	grew,	grown.			
Heave,	heaved, hove,	heaved, hoven.*	Strike,	struck,	struck, stricken.
Hew,	hewed,	hewn, r.	Strive,	strove, r.,*	striven, r.*
Hide,	hid,	hidden, hid.	Strow,	strowed,	strown, r.
			Swear,	swore, sware,	sworn.
Hold,	held,	held, holden.c*	Swell,	swelled,	swollen, r.
Know,	knew,	known.	Swim,	swum, swam,	swum.
Lade (load),	laded,	laden, r.			
Lean,	leaned, lĕant,	leaned, lĕant.	Take,	took,	taken.
			Tear,	tore,	torn.
Leap,	leaped, lĕapt,*	leaped, lĕapt.*	Thrive,	thrived, throve,	thrived, thriven.
Lie (repose).	lay,	lain.	Throw,	threw, r.,*	thrown, r.*
(Lie—speak falsely,	lied,	lied.)	Tread,	trod, trode,*	trodden, trod.
Mow,	mowed,	mown, r. proved,	Wax,	waxed,	waxed, waxen.
Prove,	proved,	proven.*	Wear,	wore,	worn.
Rend,	rent,	rent, rended.d*	Weave,	wove, r.,*	woven, r.*
			Write,	wrote, writ,*	written.

(a.) "My tongue *clave* to the roof of my mouth."—*Dickens.* (b.) "This line he *dared* not cross."—*Macaulay.* (c.) Beholden; withholden.* (d.) "Come as the winds come when forests are *rended.*"—*W. Scott.*

VERBS.

2. THE TWO PAST OR THE THREE FORMS ALIKE.

Present.	Preterit, or Past.	Perfect Participle.	Present.	Preterit, or Past.	Perfect Part.
Abide,	abode, r.,*	abode, r.*	Lay,	laid,	laid.
Behold,	beheld,	beheld.	Lead,	led,	led.
Belay,	belaid, r.,	belaid, r.	Learn,	learned,	learned,
Bend,	bent, r.,	bent, r.		learnt,	learnt.
Bereave,	bereft, r.,	bereft, r.	Leave,	left,	left.
Beseech,	besought,	besought.	Lend,	lent,	lent.
Bestead,*	bestead,*	bestead.*	Let,	let,	let.
Bet,	bet, r.,	bet, r.	Light,	lighted,	lighted,
Betide,	betided,	betided,		lit,	lit.
	betid.*	betid.*	Lose,	lost,	lost.
Bind,	bound,	bound.	Make,	made,	made.
Bleed,	bled,	bled.	Mean,	meant,	meant.
Blend,	blended,	blended,	Meet,	met,	met.
	blent,*	blent.*	Pass,	passed,	passed,
Bless,	blessed,	blessed,		past,*	past.b
	blest,	blest.	Pay,	paid,	paid.
Breed,	bred,	bred.	Pen (fence in),	penned,	penned,
Bring,	brought,	brought.		pent,	pent.
Build,	built, r.,	built, r.	(Pen—write,	penned,	penned.)
Burn,	burned,	burned,	Plead,	pleaded,	pleaded,
	burnt,	burnt.		plead,	plead,
Burst,	burst, r.,*	burst, r.*		pled,	pled.
Buy,	bought,	bought.	Put,	put,	put.
Cast,	cast,	cast.	Quit,	quit, r.,	quit, r.
Catch,	caught, r.,*	caught, r.*	Rap,	rapped,	rapped,
Cling,	clung,	clung.		rapt,	rapt.c
Clothe,	clothed,	clothed,	Read,	read,	read.
	clad,	clad.	Reave,	reft, r.,*	reft, r.*
Cost,	cost,	cost.	Rid,	rid,	rid.
Creep,	crept,	crept.	Say,	said,	said.
Cut,	cut,	cut.	Seek,	sought,	sought.
Deal,	dealt, r.,*	dealt, r.*	Sell,	sold,	sold.
Dig,	dug, r.,	dug, r.	Send,	sent,	sent.
Dwell,	dwelt, r.,	dwelt, r.	Set,	set,	set.
Dream,	dreamed,	dreamed,	Shed,	shed,	shed.
	dreamt,	dreamt.	Shine,	shone, r.,*	shone, r.*
Dress,	dressed,	dressed,	Shoe,	shod,	shod.
	drest,*	drest.*	Shoot,	shot,	shot.
Feed,	fed,	fed.	Shred,	shred,	shred.
Feel,	felt,	felt.	Shut,	shut,	shut.
Fight,	fought,	fought.	Sit,	sat,	sat.
Find,	found,	found.	Sleep,	slept,	slept.
Flee,	fled,	fled.	Sling,	slung,	slung.
Fling,	flung,	flung.	Slink,	slunk,	slunk.
Gild,	gilded,	gilded,	Slit,	slit, r.,	slit, r.
	gilt,	gilt.	Smell,	smelt, r.,	smelt, r.
Gird,	girt, r.,	girt, r.	Speed,	sped, r.,*	sped, r.*
Grind,	ground,	ground.	Spell,	spelled,	spelled,
Hang,	hung, r.,	hung, r.a		spelt,	spelt.
Have (principal verb),	had,	had.	Spend,	spent,	spent.
			Spill,	spilt, r.,	spilt, r.
Hear,	heard,	heard.	Spin,	spun,	spun.
Hit,	hit,	hit.	Split,	split, r.,*	split, r.*
Hurt,	hurt,	hurt.	Spoil,	spoiled,	spoiled,
Keep,	kept,	kept.		spoilt,*	spoilt.*
Kneel,	knelt,	knelt,	Spread,	spread,	spread.
	kneeled,	kneeled.	Stay,	staid, r.,	staid, r.d
Knit,	knit, r.,	knit, r.	String,	strung, r.,	strung, r.

(a.) Hang, hanged, hanged; *to suspend by the neck with intent to kill*: but the distinction is not always observed. (b.) *Past* is used as an adjective or as a noun. (c.) Rap, rapt, rapt; *to seize with rapture*. (d.) Stay, stayed, stayed; *to cause to stop*.

Present.	Preterit, or Past.	Perfect Particip.	Present.	Preterit, or Past.	Perfect Part.
Stave,	stove, r.,	stove, r.	Work,	worked,	worked,
Stand,	stood,	stood.		wrought,	wrought.
Stick,	stuck,	stuck.	Wring,	wrung, r.,*	wrung, r.*
Sting,	stung,	stung.			
Stink,	stunk, stank,*	stunk.	Beware,	———	———
Sweat,	sweat, r.,	sweat, r.	Can,	could,	———
	swet,	swet.	Do (auxil'y),	did,	———
Sweep,	swept,	swept.	Have (auxil'y),	had,	———
Swing,	swung,	swung.	May,	might,	———
Teach,	taught,	taught.	Must,	must,	———
Tell,	told,	told.	Ought,	ought,	———
Think,	thought,	thought.		quoth,	———
Thrust,	thrust,	thrust.	Shall,	should,	———
Wake,	woke, r.,	woke, r.	Will (auxil'y),	would,	———
Wed,	wedded,	wedded,	(Will—*wish*,		
	wed,*	wed.*	*bequeath*, }	willed,	willed.)
Weep,	wept,	wept.	Wit,		
Wet,	wet, r.,	wet, r.	Wot,* }	wot,* }	
Win,	won,	won.	Wis,* }	wist,* }	
Wind,	wound, r.,*	wound, r.*	Weet,* }	wote,* }	

What are the last few verbs usually called?

Defective, because some of the parts are wanting; and verbs having more parts than are absolutely necessary, are termed *redundant*, as *bereave, slide, swim*.

How are formed the principal parts of verbs derived from others by means of prefixes?

Generally in the same way as those of their primitives.

Ex.—Take, *took, taken*; mistake, *mistook, mistaken*.

What is a *transitive* verb?

A **transitive** verb is a verb that has an object.

Ex.—"John *struck* JAMES." "Cats *devour* RATS and MICE." "I *know* HIM." "I *know* the LESSON."

Transitive means *passing over:* there is generally an act passing from the doer to what is acted on. *Intransitive* means *not passing over*. *Passive* means *suffering* or *receiving*. *Neuter* means *neither*; and neuter verbs were so named because they are neither *active* nor *passive*.

What is a *passive* verb?

A **passive** verb is a transitive verb so used that it represents its subject as acted upon.

Ex.—"John struck James." "James *was struck* by John."

When is a verb *intransitive*, or what is an *intransitive* verb?

An **intransitive** verb does not have an object.

Ex.—"John *walks*." "The child *cries*." "The rose *blooms*." "Webster *was* eloquent." "Webster *was* an orator." "Alice *reads* and *writes* well."

What is a *neuter* verb?

A **neuter** verb is an intransitive verb that does not imply action or exertion.

Ex.—"Troy *was*." "There *is* a land of every land the pride." "The spurs *lay* on the shelf." "It *stood* near." "The plants *look* green and fresh."

What properties have verbs?

Voices, moods, tenses, persons, and numbers.

a. A transitive verb can generally be expressed in two different ways; as, "Farmers *raise* corn," "Corn *is raised* by farmers": and hence transitive verbs are said to have two voices,—the *active* and the *passive*.

When is a verb in the *active* voice, or what does this voice denote?

The **active** voice represents the subject as acting, or the verb as relating to an object.

Ex.—"David *slew* Goliath." "John *resembles* his father." "They *owned* this farm."

When is a verb in the *passive* voice, or what does this voice denote?

The **passive** voice represents the subject as acted upon, or the verb as having the object for its subject.

Ex.—"Goliath *was slain* by David." "This farm *was owned* by them."

b. If I say, "I *write*," I express a matter of fact; "I *may* or *can write*," I express what is not matter of fact, yet may become so; "If I *were writing*," "If I *had written*," I express a mere supposition; "*Write*," I request it to be done; "*To write*," "*Writing*," I simply speak of the act. These different modes of expressing the verb in reference to its subject, may give you some idea of what grammarians call *moods*.

When is a verb in the *indicative* mood, or what does the *indicative* mood express?

The **indicative** mood affirms something as an actual occurrence or fact.

Ex.—"John *has caught* some fish." "God *created* this beautiful world." "Cork *floats*." "The guilty *are* not happy." "Far away in the South *is* a beautiful isle."

Indicative means declaring; *subjunctive*, joined to; *potential*, having power; *imperative*, commanding; and *infinitive*, left free.

How does the *subjunctive* mood express the act or state?

The **subjunctive** mood affirms something as a future contingency, or as a mere supposition, wish, or conclusion.

Ex.—"If it *rain* to-night, our plants will live." "Beware lest he *deceive* you." "He talked to me as if I *were* a widow." "*Were* I a lawyer, I should not like to plead a rogue's case." "O, *had* I the wings of a dove."—*Cowper.* "But if I *asked* your papa, he would only say you *had* better [to] stay at home."—*Bulwer.* "But I should wrong my friend, if I *concealed* it."—*Id.* "If conscience *had had* as strong a hold on his mind as honor, he *had* still *been* innocent."—*British Essayists.*

What words often precede this mood, or indicate it?

If, though, that, lest, except, unless, provided, &c.

What does a verb in the subjunctive mood suggest, when it refers to present or past time?

That the contrary of what is supposed, or something different, is the true state of the case. See above.

What other mood does the subjunctive resemble in its form, and what one in its meaning?

In its form, the indicative; but in meaning, the potential, with which it is also most frequently associated in sentences. See above.

How does the potential represent the act or state?

The **potential** mood affirms merely the power, liberty, liability, necessity, will, duty, or a similar relation of the subject, in regard to the act or state.

Ex.—"God *can destroy* this world." "You *may play.*" "Youth *may be trifled* away." "They who *would be* happy, *must be* virtuous." "Children *should obey* their teachers."

How can this mood be known, or what words are used to express it?

May, can, must, might, could, would, and *should.*

When is a verb in the imperative mood, or what does the imperative mood express?

The **imperative** mood expresses command, exhortation, entreaty, or permission.

Ex.—"John, *study* your lesson." "*Go* where glory waits thee." "Oh! then *remember* me." "*Return* to your friends."

We *command* inferiors, *exhort* equals, *entreat* superiors, and *permit* in compliance with the will of others.

What is the subject of every verb in the imperative mood?

Thou, you, or *ye,* usually understood.

Ex.—"Know thyself"—Know *thou* thyself. "My young friends, be pure and cautious"—My young friends, be *ye* pure and cautious.

When is a verb in the infinitive mood, or how does this mood express the act or state?

The **infinitive** mood does not affirm the act or state. It comprises the participle and the infinitive.

Ex.—"Corn *to grind.*" "The clouds *dispersing.*" "Be careful *to avoid* the danger."

Which of the moods can be used interrogatively?

The indicative and the potential.

Ex.—"*Shall* we *slight* this decisive moment?" "Who *is* the culprit?" "How *can* I?"

How are they made interrogative?

By placing the subject after the verb, or after some part of it.

Ex.—"Thou art he;" "ART *thou* he?" "You can help us;" "CAN *you* HELP US?"

How many moods, and what are they?

C. Time may naturally be divided into *present, past,* and *future;* and we may consider an act or state as simply taking place in each of these periods, or as completed: thus, "I *write,* I *have written;*" "I *wrote,* I *had written;*" "I *shall write,* I *shall have written.*" Hence verbs have what grammarians call *tenses.*

When is a verb in the present tense, or what does this tense express?

The **present** tense expresses the act or state in present time.

Ex.—"I *write.*" "I *am writing.*" "It *snows.*" "You *may commence.*" "*Let* me *see* your new book." "St. Louis *is* situated on a plain *bordering* on the Mississippi."

In what peculiar sense is this tense sometimes used?

To express what is always so from the very nature or condition of things.

Ex.—"Heat *melts* ice." "A fool and his money *are* soon *parted.*" "Moles *burrow* in the ground." "Traveling *is* expensive." "People *must die.*" "Man *is made to mourn.*"

When is a verb in the past tense, or what is the meaning of this tense?

The **past** tense refers the act or state simply to past time.

Ex.—"God *created* the world." "Troy *was*, but is no more." "Away *went* Gilpin." "Bonaparte *was banished* to St. Helena." "She *died* this morning." "I soon *saw* that he *could* not *see.*" "The ship *arrived* before day."

This tense is usually called the *imperfect* tense, but inappropriately. It may be well to call it the *aorist* tense, in the subjunctive and the potential mood, whenever it does not denote past time.

When is a verb in the future tense, or what is the meaning of this tense?

The **future** tense refers the act or state simply to future time.

Ex.—"The cars *will come* this evening." "Merit *will be rewarded.*" "The trees *will shed* their leaves." "There *will be* a final judgment day."

When is a verb in the perfect tense, or what does this tense express?

The **perfect** tense represents something as past, but still connected with present time.

Ex.—"This magnificent city *has been built* within one hundred years." "He *has practised* law two years." "I *have* just *sold* my horse." "The mail *may have arrived.*" "This house appears *to have been* a church." "Though severely *wounded*, he still lives."

When is a verb in the pluperfect tense, or what does this tense express?

The **pluperfect** tense represents something as finished or ended by a certain past time.

Ex.—"I *had* already *sent* my trunk to the river, when I received your letter." "A fish *had been* on the hook." "A fish *might have been* on the hook."

When is a verb in the future-perfect tense, or what does this tense express?

The **future-perfect** tense represents something as finished or ended by a certain future time.

Ex.—"The flowers *will have withered*, when winter returns."

GENERAL ILLUSTRATION.—I write (now). I have written (just now). I wrote (at some past time). I had written (by or before a certain past time). I shall write (at some time hereafter). I shall have written (by or before a certain future time). So, The tree blossoms—has blossomed—blossomed—had blossomed—will blossom—will have blossomed. The three perfect tenses are sometimes called the *relative* tenses, because they relate from one point of time to another; and the other three tenses, which have not this relation, are called the *absolute* tenses.

Every perfect tense, except sometimes a participle, must have what two parts?

Have, or some one of its variations, and the perfect participle of some verb.

Ex.—Have written; having written; to have written; may have written; has been writing; should have been writing; had written; shall have written; shall have been written.

How does the present, the past, or the future tense, sometimes express an act or state?

As something habitual or customary in present, past, or future time.

Ex.—"He *chews* tobacco." "People *go* to church on Sunday." "The dead *are put* into the ground." "There *would* he *spend* his earnings." "The wolf also *shall dwell* with the lamb, and the leopard *shall lie* down with the kid."

When the act or state is expressed as ideal rather than real, as in the subjunctive mood, and frequently in the potential, what may be observed of the tenses, in respect to the time of the event?

That they move forward, one tense or more, in time.

Ex.—"If I *am*"—now; "If I *be*"—hereafter. "If I *was*"—at any past time; "If I *were*"—now. "I *had been* there"—before that time; "*Had* I *been* there"—at that time. "I *am paying* you"—now; "I *may* or *can pay* you"—next Christmas. "I *paid* you"—then; "I *might* or *could pay* you"—now. "I *had paid* you"—before a certain past time; "I *might have paid* you"—at a certain past time. "Such governments *could* not *last*, if they *contained* ever so much wisdom and virtue."—*P. Henry.* At any time. See 2d def. of present tense.

In most of the tenses, a verb may be expressed in several different ways: as, "He *strikes*;" "He *does strike*;" "He *is striking*;" "He *is struck*;" "He *striketh*." These, grammarians usually distinguish, by calling them, emphatically, the **FORMS** *of the verb.*

When is a verb in the *common* form, or what is the *common* form?

The **common** form is the verb expressed in the most simple and ordinary manner.

Ex.—"He *went* home." "Time *flies.*" "No man *has* ever *been* too honest."

When is a verb in the *emphatic* form, or what is the *emphatic* form?

The **emphatic** form has *do* or *did* as a part of the verb, to give it greater force.

Ex.—"I *did say* so." "Really, it *does move*." "*Do come* to see me."

When is a verb in the *progressive* form, or what is the *progressive* form?

The **progressive** form is *be*, or some variation of it, combined with the participle that ends in *ing*. It denotes continuance of the act or state.

Ex.—"I wrote;" "I *was writing.*" "She goes to church;" "She *is going* to church."

When is a verb in the *passive* form, or what is the *passive* form?

The **passive** form is *be*, or some variation of it, combined with the perfect participle. It is generally passive in sense.

Ex.—"The oak *was shattered* by lightning." "The melancholy days *are come*."

When is a verb in the *ancient* form, or *solemn* style, or how may this form be known?

The **ancient** form has the ending *t*, *st*, or *est*, and *th* or *eth*, and generally uses *thou* or *ye* in stead of *you*.

Ex.—"Thou *barb'dst* the dart that wounds thee." "Adversity *flattereth* no man."

How many tenses, and what are they?—how many forms, and what are they?

---

d. When I say, "I *am*, thou *art*, he *is*;" "I *write*, thou *writest*, he *writes*;" you see that the verb varies with the *person* of its subject: and when I say, "I *am*, we *are*;" "He *is*, they *are*;" "He *writes*, they *write*;" you see that the verb varies with the *number* of its subject. Hence the verb is said to have *person* and *number;* that is, it is so expressed as to indicate the person and number of its subject, and thereby the subject itself.

What, then, is meant by the *person* and *number* of a verb?

The **person** and **number** of a verb are its form as being suitable to the person and number of its subject.

The term "*a form of the verb*," signifies, in its widest sense, any mode of expressing it.

When is a verb *singular*, and when *plural?*

It is *singular*, when its form is proper for predicating of a singular subject; and *plural*, when proper for predicating of a plural subject.

Ex.—"The NIGHT *was* serene, and the STARS *were twinkling* most brilliantly in their blue depths."

Define *singular* subjects and *plural* subjects.

A *singular* subject denotes one object, or more objects taken singly or separately; a *plural* subject denotes more than one, but not taken as one single thing.

Ex.—*Singular:* "*The boy* is studious;" "*Every tree* is known by its fruit;" "*John, James, or Joseph,* is studying;" "*Neither John, James, nor Joseph,* is studying." *Plural:* "*The boys* are studious;" "*John, James, and Joseph,* are studious;" "*The people* are fickle."

In correct discourse, of what person and number is the verb always said to be?

Of the same as its subject, or nominative.

Ex.—"I *am*." Here *am* is said to be of the first person and singular number, because its subject, *I*, is of this person and number.

PARTICIPLES AND INFINITIVES.

What is a participle? What is an infinitive? See p. 12.

How many and what participles are there, and how many and what infinitives are there?

Two of each,—the *present* and the *perfect;* and also a third participle, the *compound.*

How does the *present participle* represent the act or state?

The **present** participle represents the act or state as present, but oftener as future, at the time referred to.

Ex.—"We saw the moon *rising*." "Who goes *borrowing*, goes *sorrowing*."

How does the *present infinitive* represent the act or state?

The **present** infinitive represents the act or state as present at the time referred to, but oftener, as future.

Ex.—"He seems *to study*." "Man never is, but always *to be*, blest."—*Pope.* "I intended *to say* less, and certainly expected *to hear* more liberal sentiments offered on the other side."

How does the *perfect* participle or infinitive represent the act or state?

The **perfect** participle or **infinitive** represents the act or state as past or ended at the time referred to.

Ex.—"A fox, *caught* in a trap." "The river appears *to have risen*." "The Indians are supposed *to have come* from Asia or Siberia,"

The perfect participle is sometimes *present* in sense; as, "He lives *loved* by all." The present infinitive sometimes denotes simply the act or state; and the perfect infinitive, the completed act or state.

What is a *compound* participle?

A **compound participle** consists of two or more participles; and it is in sense generally a *perfect*, but sometimes a *present*, participle.

Ex.—"*Having purchased* a farm, he retired to the country." "The terms *being settled*, he produced the cash." "He, *having been* previously *engaged*, and *being then engaged*, in making surveys of the country, was the most suitable man we could find."

How is the participle sometimes used?

As an adjective, and then called a *participial* adjective.

Define a *participial adjective*.

A **participial adjective** ascribes the act or state to its subject as a quality.

Ex.—"A *leaping* and *murmuring* rivulet;" "*Written* laws."

Participles and infinitives are frequently used as what other parts of speech?

As **nouns**, and then often called **verbal** nouns.

When should a participle or an infinitive be considered a noun?

When it evidently takes the place, and is used in the sense, of a noun.

Ex.—"*To live* without *being annoyed*, is pleasant." What is pleasant? without what?—*Life* without *annoyance* is pleasant. "Successful *studying* requires exertion." "*To have learned* so beautiful an art, will be ever a pleasure to me." "My *knowing* him was of great advantage to me." "His *having been* there, was the ground of suspicion." "*To live* temperately, *to avoid* excitement, and *to take* alternate exercise and rest, are essential to health"—*Temperance, tranquillity*, and alternate *exercise* and *rest*, are essential to health. "Boys like *to play*." (Boys like apples.) "He began *to work*." (He began his *work*.) "*To love* is *to obey*." "*To be* —or not *to be*,—that is the question!" (*Life*—or *death*,—that is the question!)

AUXILIARY VERBS.

No complete verb in our language can express all its properties, or be expressed in all its forms, without the aid of certain other little verbs. Thus, to express "strike" in future time, we say, "*shall* or *will* strike;" in the potential mood, "*may, can, must, might, could, would*, or *should* strike;" in the passive voice, "*is* struck, *was* struck, *being* struck," &c. These little *helping* verbs are therefore called *auxiliary* verbs. *Auxiliary* means *helping*.

How, then, would you define an *auxiliary* verb?

An **auxiliary** verb helps another verb to express its meaning in a certain manner or time.

Which are the auxiliary verbs?

Be, and all its variations; *do, did; can, could; have, had; may, might; must; shall, should; will, would*.

For what are the auxiliaries *be* and its variations used?

They are used to express the verb progressively or passively.

Ex.—"The farmer *is ploughing* his field." "The field *is ploughed*."

For what are the auxiliaries *do* and *did* used?

They are used to express the verb with emphasis, or with greater force.

Ex.—"I *do assure* you, I shall be here in time." "He *did say* so."

What do *can* and *could* imply?

Power or ability.

Ex.—"I *can lift* the stone." "I *can learn* the lesson." "I *could* not *give* my consent."

What do *have* and *had* imply, and for what are they used?

They imply possession, and are used to express the act or state as finished or ended at the time referred to.

Ex.—"I *have gathered* the plums which the wind *had blown* down."

What meaning is conveyed by *may* and *might*?

Permission, possibility, or probability; sometimes reasonableness.

Ex.—"You *may go* to play." "But remember the horse *may die*." "It *may rain* this evening." "But the question *might be asked*, whether the tax is legal."

What do *must*, *shall*, and *should* denote?

Duty or injunction: but *shall*, more frequently compulsion; and *must*, generally necessity.

Ex.—"We *should care* for others' feelings." "Thou *shalt* not *swear*." "You *must* not *look* for me before next week." "Pupils *must obey*." "Naughty boy! you *shall be punished*."

What do *will* and *would* denote?

Willingness, adaptation, or tendency.

Ex.—"He *would pay* if he could." "This *will do*." "Weeds *will grow* where there is no cultivation." "Roses *will fade*."

For what purpose are all the auxiliaries more or less used?

To express the verb interrogatively. For this purpose, they are placed before the nominative.

Ex.—"You are wounded." "*Are* you wounded?" "*Does* he know you?"

CONJUGATION AND SYNOPSIS.

What is it, to *conjugate* a verb?

To **conjugate** a verb is to show, in a regular way, how some or all of its parts are correctly expressed.

Ex.—*Be* and *write* in the present tense, indicative mood.

	Singular.		Plural.
First Pers.	I am,	First Pers.	We are,
Second Pers.	You are,	Second Pers.	You are,
Third Pers.	He, she, or it, is;	Third Pers.	They are.
	1. I write,		1. We write,
	2. You write,		2. You write,
	3. He, she, or it, writes;		3. They write.

Conjugation probably signified, in old times, the joining of various endings and prefixes to the chief parts of verbs, called the roots; but, with us, the word rather signifies the joining of the various forms to their different nominatives.

24 VERBS.

What is it, to *give the synopsis* of a verb?

To **give the synopsis** of a verb, is to express it correctly, in a single person and number, or in a particular form, through some or all of its moods and tenses.

Ex.—Synopsis of *write*, with *I*, through the indicative mood: Present, *I write*; past, *I wrote*; future, *I shall* or *will write*; perfect, *I have written*; pluperfect, *I had written*; future-perfect, *I shall* or *will have written*.

The word *synopsis* means a *look at the whole*; and as we are apt to see only the chief or most striking parts, by looking at all at once, the word has come to signify the chief parts or the outline of the whole of a thing.

CONJUGATION EXEMPLIFIED.

I have here presented to you the very irregular verb *be*, the regular verb *move*,* and the irregular verb *take*, in all the forms in which they can be expressed. Like them, or by their means, may all other verbs be expressed in all their forms; and for *I, you, he, she, it, we, you,* and *they*, can be used any other nominatives having the same person and number, that is, all nominatives whatsoever; so that the following conjugation is sufficient to teach all the correct forms of all the verbs, for all the propositions that have been spoken or written, and all that can be spoken or written, in the English language.

Recite the following paradigm, across the page; and the synopsis with *thou*, down the page. *C*. stands for Common Form; *E.*, for Emphatic; *Pr.*, for Progressive; and *P.*, for Passive.

Observe that the verb, like the nouns and pronouns in their declension, remains sometimes unchanged, is sometimes partly changed, and is sometimes wholly changed, to express its different properties; and that it sometimes calls in the help of the auxiliary verbs.

Be.	Move.	Take.
	Principal Parts.	
Present.	*Preterit, or Past.*	*Perfect Participle.*
Be,	was,	been.
Move,	moved,	moved.
Take,	took,	taken.

INDICATIVE MOOD.

ABSOLUTE TENSES.

Present Tense.

	Singular.				*Plural.*	
	First Person.	*Second Person.*	*Third Person.*	*1st Pers.*	*2d Pers.*	*3d Pers.*
	I	You	He, She, or It,	We	You	They
	am,	are,	is;	are,	are,	are.
C.	move,	move,	moves;	move,	move,	move.
E.	do move,	do move,	does move;	do move,	do move,	do move.
Pr.	am moving,	are moving,	is moving	are moving,	are moving,	are moving.
P.	am moved,	are moved,	is moved;	are moved,	are moved,	are moved.
C.	take,	take,	takes;	take,	take,	take.
E.	do take,	do take,	does take;	do take,	do take,	do take.
Pr.	am taking,	are taking,	is taking;	are taking,	are taking,	are taking.
P.	am taken,	are taken,	is taken;	are taken,	are taken,	are taken.

* Since *love* can not be used in the progressive form, and is objectionable also for other reasons, *move* has been preferred. It is very difficult to find a suitable verb. The next best that occur to me, are *row, call, tend, aid, rule.*

VERBS.

Past Tense. (IMPERFECT.)

Singular.   *Plural.*

1.	2.	3.	1.	2.	3.
I	You	He, She, or It,	We	You	They
was,	were,	was;	were,	were,	were.
C. moved,	moved,	moved;	moved,	moved,	moved.
E. did move,	did move,	did move;	did move,	did move,	did move.
Pr. was moving,	were moving,	was moving;	were moving,	were moving,	were moving.
P. was moved,	were moved,	was moved;	were moved,	were moved,	were moved.
C. took,	took,	took;	took,	took,	took.
E. did take,	did take,	did take;	did take,	did take,	did take.
Pr. was taking,	were taking,	was taking;	were taking,	were taking,	were taking.
P. was taken,	were taken,	was taken;	were taken,	were taken,	were taken.

Future Tense. (FIRST-FUTURE.)

Singular.   *Plural.*

1.	2.	3.	1.	2.	3.
I	You	He, She, or It,	We	You	They
		shall or *will*—			
be,	be,	be;	be,	be,	be.
C. move,	move,	move;	move,	move,	move.
Pr. be moving,	be moving,	be moving;	be moving,	be moving,	be moving.
P. be moved,	be moved,	be moved;	be moved,	be moved,	be moved.
C. take,	take,	take;	take,	take,	take.
Pr. be taking,	be taking,	be taking;	be taking,	be taking,	be taking.
P. be taken,	be taken,	be taken;	be taken,	be taken,	be taken.

RELATIVE TENSES.

Perfect Tense.

Singular.   *Plural.*

1.	2.	3.	1.	2.	3.
I	You	He, She, or It,	We	You	They
have—	*have*—	*has*—	*have*—	*have*—	*have*—
been,	been,	been;	been,	been,	been.
C. moved,	moved,	moved;	moved,	moved,	moved.
Pr. been moving,	been moving,	been moving;	been moving,	been moving,	been moving.
P. been moved,	been moved,	been moved;	been moved,	been moved,	been moved.
C. taken,	taken,	taken;	taken,	taken,	taken.
Pr. been taking,	been taking,	been taking;	been taking,	been taking,	been taking.
P. been taken,	been taken,	been taken;	been taken,	been taken,	been taken.

Pluperfect Tense.

Singular.   *Plural.*

1.	2.	3.	1.	2.	3.
I	You	He, She, or It,	We	You	They
		had—			
been,	been,	been;	been,	been,	been.
C. moved,	moved,	moved;	moved,	moved,	moved.
Pr. been moving,	been moving,	been moving;	been moving,	been moving,	been moving.
P. been moved,	been moved,	been moved;	been moved,	been moved,	been moved.
C. taken,	taken,	taken;	taken,	taken,	taken.
Pr. been taking,	been taking,	been taking;	been taking,	been taking,	been taking.
P. been taken,	been taken,	been taken;	been taken,	been taken,	been taken.

Future-perfect Tense. (SECOND-FUTURE.)

	Singular.				Plural.	
1.	2.	3.	1.	2.	3.
I	You	He, She, or It,	We	You	They

shall or *will have—*

	been,	been,	been;	been,	been,	been.
C.	moved,	moved,	moved;	moved,	moved,	moved.
Pr.	been moving,	been moving,	been moving;	been moving,	been moving,	been moving
P.	been moved,	been moved,	been moved;	been moved,	been moved,	been moved.
C.	taken,	taken,	taken;	taken,	taken,	taken.
Pr.	been taking,	been taking,	been taking;	been taking,	been taking,	been taking.
P.	been taken,	been taken,	been taken;	been taken,	been taken,	been taken.

SUBJUNCTIVE MOOD.
Present Tense.

	Singular.				Plural.	
1.	2.	3.	1.	2.	3.
If I	If you	If he, she, or it,	If we	If you	If they

	be,	be,	be;	be,	be,	be.
C.	move,	move,	move;	move,	move,	move.
E.	do move,	do move,	do move;	do move,	do move,	do move.
Pr.	be moving,	be moving,	be moving;	be moving,	be moving,	be moving.
P.	be moved,	be moved,	be moved;	be moved,	be moved,	be moved.
C.	take,	take,	take;	take,	take,	take.
E.	do take,	do take,	do take;	do take,	do take,	do take.
Pr.	be taking,	be taking,	be taking;	be taking,	be taking,	be taking.
P.	be taken,	be taken,	be taken;	be taken,	be taken,	be taken.

Past Tense. (IMPERFECT.)

	Singular.				Plural.	
1.	2.	3.	1.	2.	3.
If I	If you	If he, she, or it,	If we	If you	If they

	were,	were,	were;	were,	were,	were.
C.	moved,	moved,	moved;	moved,	moved,	moved.
E.	did move,	did move,	did move;	did move,	did move,	did move.
Pr.	were moving,	were moving,	were moving;	were moving,	were moving,	were moving
P.	were moved,	were moved,	were moved;	were moved,	were moved,	were moved.
C.	took,	took,	took;	took,	took,	took.
E.	did take,	did take,	did take;	did take,	did take,	did take.
Pr.	were taking,	were taking,	were taking;	were taking,	were taking,	were taking.
P.	were taken,	were taken,	were taken;	were taken,	were taken,	were taken.

Pluperfect Tense.

	Singular.				Plural.	
1.	2.	3.	1.	2.	3.
If I	If you	If he, she, or it,	If we	If you	If they

had—

	been,	been,	been;	been,	been,	been.
C.	moved,	moved,	moved;	moved,	moved,	moved.
Pr.	been moving,	been moving,	been moving;	been moving,	been moving,	been moving
P.	been moved,	been moved,	been moved;	been moved,	been moved,	been moved.
C.	taken,	taken,	taken;	taken,	taken,	taken.
Pr.	been taking,	been taking,	been taking;	been taking,	been taking,	been taking.
P.	been taken,	been taken,	been taken;	been taken,	been taken,	been taken.

We can also say, "Were I," "Had I been," "Be it ever so fine, I would not buy it;" for, "If I were," "If I had been," "Though it be ever so fine, I would not buy it."

VERBS.

POTENTIAL MOOD.

Present Tense.

Singular.   *Plural.*

	1.	2.	3.	1.	2.	3.
	I	You	He, She, or It,	We	You	They
	\multicolumn{6}{c}{*may, can,* or *must*—}					
	be,	be,	be;	be,	be,	be.
C.	move,	move,	move;	move,	move,	move.
Pr.	be moving,	be moving,	be moving;	be moving,	be moving,	be moving.
P.	be moved,	be moved,	be moved;	be moved,	be moved,	be moved.
C.	take,	take,	take;	take,	take,	take.
Pr.	be taking,	be taking,	be taking;	be taking,	be taking,	be taking.
P.	be taken,	be taken,	be taken;	be taken,	be taken,	be taken.

Past Tense.   (IMPERFECT.)

Singular.   *Plural.*

	1.	2.	3.	1.	2.	3.
	I	You	He, She, or It,	We	You	They
	\multicolumn{6}{c}{*might, could, would,* or *should*—}					
	be,	be,	be;	be,	be,	be.
C.	move,	move,	move;	move,	move,	move.
Pr.	be moving,	be moving,	be moving;	be moving,	be moving,	be moving.
P.	be moved,	be moved,	be moved;	be moved,	be moved,	be moved.
C.	take,	take,	take;	take,	take,	take.
Pr.	be taking,	be taking,	be taking;	be taking,	be taking,	be taking.
P.	be taken,	be taken,	be taken;	be taken,	be taken,	be taken.

Perfect Tense.

Singular.   *Plural.*

	1.	2.	3.	1.	2.	3.
	I	You	He, She, or It,	We	You	They
	\multicolumn{6}{c}{*may, can,* or *must have*—}					
	been,	been,	been;	been,	been,	been.
C.	moved,	moved,	moved;	moved,	moved,	moved.
Pr.	been moving,	been moving,	been moving;	been moving,	been moving,	been moving.
P.	been moved,	been moved,	been moved;	been moved,	been moved,	been moved.
C.	taken,	taken,	taken;	taken,	taken,	taken.
Pr.	been taking,	been taking,	been taking;	been taking,	been taking,	been taking.
P.	been taken,	been taken,	been taken;	been taken,	been taken,	been taken.

Pluperfect Tense.

Singular.   *Plural.*

	1.	2.	3.	1.	2.	3.
	I	You	He, She, or It,	We	You	They
	\multicolumn{6}{c}{*might, could, would,* or *should have*—}					
	been,	been,	been;	been,	been,	been.
C.	moved,	moved,	moved;	moved,	moved,	moved.
Pr.	been moving,	been moving,	been moving;	been moving,	been moving,	been moving.
P.	been moved,	been moved,	been moved;	been moved,	been moved,	been moved.
C.	taken,	taken,	taken;	taken,	taken,	taken.
Pr.	been taking,	been taking,	been taking;	been taking,	been taking,	been taking.
P.	been taken,	been taken,	been taken;	been taken,	been taken,	been taken.

IMPERATIVE MOOD.
Present Tense.

Singular.   *Plural.*
2.   2.

C. Be, *or* be thou;   be, *or* be ye.
E. Do be, *or* do thou be;   do be, *or* do ye be.

C. Move, *or* move thou;   move, *or* move ye.
E. Do move, *or* do thou move;   do move, *or* do ye move.
Pr. Be moving, *or* be thou moving;   be moving, *or* be ye moving.
P. Be moved, *or* be thou moved;   be moved, *or* be ye moved.

C. Take, *or* take thou;   take, *or* take ye.
E. Do take, *or* do thou take;   do take, *or* do ye take.
Pr. Be taking, *or* be thou taking;   be taking, *or* be ye taking.
P. Be taken, *or* be thou taken;   be taken, *or* be ye taken.

You is used in the singular, as well as *thou;* and in the plural it is quite as common as *ye.* When the imperative is to denote gentleness and entreaty rather than harshness and authority, *you* is perhaps preferable to *thou.*

INFINITIVE MOOD.

Present Infinitive.   **Perfect Infinitive.**
To be.   To have been.
C. To move.   To have moved.
Pr. To be moving.   To have been moving.
P. To be moved.   To have been moved.
C. To take.   To have taken.
Pr. To be taking.   To have been taking.
P. To be taken.   To have been taken.

Present Participle.   **Perfect Participle.**
Being.   Been.
Moving.   Moved.
Taking.   Taken.

Compound Participle.
Neuter. Having been.
Passive. Being moved.
Active. Having moved.
Passive. Having been moved.

Passive. Being taken.
Active. Having taken.
Passive. Having been taken.

To, the sign of the infinitives, is omitted after *bid, make, need, hear, | let, see, feel,* and *dare,* in the active voice.

ANCIENT FORM, OR SOLEMN STYLE.—THOU.
INDICATIVE MOOD.

	Present.	Past.	Future.	Perfect.	Pluperfect.	Future-perfect.
	THOU	THOU	THOU	THOU	THOU	THOU
			shalt or *wilt*—	*hast*—	*hadst*—	*shalt* or *wilt have*—
	art;	wast, *or* wert;	be;	been;	been;	been;
C.	movest,	movedst,	move,	moved,	moved,	moved,
E.	dost move,	didst move,				
Pr.	art moving,	wast moving,	be moving;	been moving,	been moving,	been moving,
P.	art moved,	wast moved;	be moved;	been moved;	been moved;	been moved;
C.	takest,	tookst,	take,	taken,	taken,	taken,
E.	dost take,	didst take,				
Pr.	art taking,	wast taking,	be taking,	been taking,	been taking,	been taking,
P.	art taken.	wast taken.	be taken.	been taken.	been taken.	been taken.

SUBJUNCTIVE MOOD.

Present.	Past.	Pluperfect.
If THOU	If THOU	If THOU hadst—
be;	wert, or were;	been;
C. move,	moved,	moved,
E. do move,	did move, or didst move,	
Pr. be moving,	wert moving,	been moving,
P. be moved;	wert moved;	been moved;
C. take,	took,	taken,
E. do take,	did take, or didst take,	
Pr. be taking,	wert taking,	been taking,
P. be taken.	wert taken.	been taken.

We can also say, "Wert thou," "Wert thou moved," "Hadst thou been," "Hadst thou moved;" for, "If thou wert," "If thou hadst been," etc.

POTENTIAL MOOD.

Present.	Past.	Perfect.	Pluperfect.
THOU	THOU	THOU	THOU
mayst, canst, or must—	mightst, couldst, wouldst, or shouldst—	mayst, canst, or must have—	mightst, couldst, wouldst, or shouldst have—
be;	be;	been;	been;
C. move,	move,	moved,	moved,
Pr. be moving,	be moving,	been moving,	been moving,
P. be moved;	be moved;	been moved;	been moved;
C. take,	take,	taken,	taken,
Pr. be taking,	be taking,	been taking,	been taking,
P. be taken.	be taken.	been taken.	been taken.

The Ancient Form has the ending *eth*, in stead of *s* or *es*, in the third person singular; and *ye* in stead of *you*, in the second person plural.

Ex.—"Who *chooseth* me must give and hazard all he *hath*."—*Shakespeare*. "Ye are the salt of the earth."—*Bible*.

Doth is used for the auxiliary *does*, and *doeth* for the verb *does*. *Hath* and *saith* are contractions of *haveth* and *sayeth*.

How many and what tenses has the *indicative* mood?—the *subjunctive*?—the *potential*?—the *imperative*? What *participles* are there?—what *infinitives*?

In what mood and tense do you find *do?*—*did?*—*have?*—*had?*—*shall* or *will?*—*shall* or *will have?*—*may, can*, or *must?*—*may, can*, or *must have?*—*might, could, would*, or *should?*—*might, could, would*, or *should have?*

Does the subjunctive mood vary in its forms, through the different persons and numbers? Can you show how some of its forms differ from the corresponding forms of the indicative mood?

Tell of what mood and tense; then conjugate throughout the tense, beginning with the first person singular:—

I imagine. He suffered. We have gained. I had been ploughing. I will visit. Were I. Had I been. If he were. Were I invited. Had I been invited. If I be invited. They shall have finished. I lay. We read. It may pass. You should have come. We may have been robbed. I was speaking. It is rising. You might be preparing. She had been singing. Had you been studying. Do you hope? Did she smile? If I do fall. If thou rely. Thou art. Art thou? He forgiveth. Dost thou not forgive? It must have happened. They are gone. Thou art going. We were proceeding.

Predicate each of the following verbs correctly of THOU; *then of* HE, *and of* THEY:—

Am, was, have been, would have been, are deceived, had been, do say, did maintain, gave, touched, cast, amass, recommend, be discouraged, shall have been, will pardon, may have been rejoicing, was elected, should have been elected, wrapped, consider, considered, have been loitering.

Change into the other tenses of the same mood?—
I write, I may write, If I write, If I be writing, To write.

Give the synopsis of the verb BE, *with the nominative* I;—*with* YOU;—THOU;—HE;—WE—THEY;—THE MAN;—THE MEN.

In like manner give the synopsis of each of the following verbs:—
Bind, arrest, have, do, be known, be proved, be conversing.

Give THOU *with each auxiliary except* BE *and its variations;—give* HE.

6. ADVERBS.

If I say, "He reasons *correctly,* speaks *fluently,* and persuades *earnestly;*" "Walk *up,* walk *down,* walk *in,* walk *out,* walk *slowly,* walk *not;*" "*Very* tall, *horribly* ugly, *sternly* inquisitive, *surprisingly* abrupt, *more* ingenious, *most* eloquent, *very powerfully, quite fast;*" you see that the Italicized words tell *how, when, where,* or *to what degree,* a thing is done; also *how* or *in what degree* a quality or property exists; and being most generally applied or added to *verbs,* they are called *adverbs.*

What is an *adverb?*

An **adverb** is a word used to modify the meaning of a verb, an adjective, or an adverb. See above.

Some entire phrases, as *long ago, in vain, to and fro, by and by, the more, the less, sooner or later,* are generally used as adverbs, and called *adverbial phrases.* Perhaps they may as well be called simply *adverbs.*

We have said that adverbs modify verbs, adjectives, and adverbs; but what other parts do they sometimes affect?

Phrases, entire sentences, and sometimes perhaps nouns or pronouns.

Ex.—"He sailed NEARLY *round the world.*" "The murdered traveller's bones were found FAR *down a narrow glen.*"—*Bryant.* "*Do you know him?*—No." "Can you not go?" "Can *not* YOU go?" "The immortality of the soul has been evinced to *almost* a DEMONSTRATION."—*Addison.* "And the FAME *hereof* went abroad."—*Bible.*

Whether an adverb, as such, may ever be said to modify a substantive, is questionable. But there is a difference, for instance, between "Can you not go?" and "Can not you go?" And sometimes the adverb seems to relate to the verb lurking in the noun. Perhaps it is best to parse such words, sometimes as adjectives, and sometimes as adverbs modifying the VERB *with reference to the subject, the object, the adjunct, or whatever part is affected.*

If adverbs describe or limit as well as adjectives, can they also be compared?

Yes.

How do they differ from adjectives in comparison?

A smaller portion of them can be compared; and they are more frequently compared by *more* and *most.*

Ex.—Thus, we can say, "*Slow, slower, slowest; lively, livelier, liveliest*"; but we must say, "*So, more so, most so; wisely, more wisely, most wisely.*"

What do most adverbs express?

Manner, Place, Time, or **Degree.**

Ex.—Elegantly, well, merrily, gayly; here, there; now, then; very, more, most.

List of Adverbs.

Since it is not unfrequently difficult to determine whether a given word is an adverb or not, or to what class of adverbs it should be referred, a full catalogue is given below, which must be carefully and thoroughly studied. The classification, too, is more minute than it usually is; because it is supposed that the nature and various powers of the adverbs may be better learned by this means.

MANNER, MODE, or QUALITY. *How?*

So, thus, well, ill, how, wisely, foolishly, justly, slowly, somehow, anyhow, however, howsoever, otherwise, else, likewise, like, alike, as, extempore, headlong, lengthwise, crosswise, across, aslant, astride, astraddle, adrift, amain, afloat, apace, apart, asunder, amiss, anew, fast, together, separately, aloud, accordingly, agreeably, necessarily, in vain, in brief, at once, in short, foot by foot, so so, so and so, helter-skelter, hurry-skurry, namely, suddenly, silently, feelingly, surprisingly, touchingly, trippingly, lovingly, hurriedly, mournfully, sweetly, proportionally, exactly, heavily, lightly; and many others ending in *ly*, and formed from *adjectives* or *present participles*.

PLACE. *Where? Whence? Whither?*

Of place absolute: Here, there, yonder, where, everywhere, somewhere, universally, nowhere, wherever, wheresoever, anywhere, herein, therein, wherein, hereabouts, thereabouts, whereabouts, hereabout, thereabout, abed, aground, on high, all over, here and there.

Of place reckoned FROM *some point:* Whence, hence, thence, elsewhere, otherwhere, away, far, afar, far off, out, remotely, abroad, above, forth, below, ahead, aloof, outwards, about, around, beneath, before, behind, over, under, within, without, from within, from without.

Of place reckoned TO *some point:* Whither, thither, hither, in, up, down, upwards, downwards, inwards, backwards, forwards, hitherward, thitherward, homeward, aside, ashore, afield, aloft, aboard, aground, nigh.—The forms *upward, downward, backward*, &c., are also used as adverbs.

Of order: First, secondly, thirdly, &c., next, lastly, finally, at last, in fine.

TIME. *When? How long? How often? How soon? How long ago?*

Of time absolute: Ever, never, always, eternally, perpetually, continually, constantly, endlessly, forever, incessantly, everlastingly, evermore, aye.

Of time relative, i. e., *reckoned with, to, or from some other time:* When, whenever, then, meanwhile, meantime, as, while, whilst, till, until, otherwhile, after, afterward, afterwards, subsequently, before, ere, late, early, betimes, seasonably.

Of time repeated: Again, often, oft, oftentimes, sometimes, occasionally, seldom, rarely, frequently, now and then, ever and anon, daily, weekly, hourly, monthly, yearly, annually, anew, once, twice, thrice, four times, etc.

Of time present: Now, to-day, nowadays, at present, yet (—heretofore and now), as yet.

Of time past: Yesterday, heretofore, recently, lately, of late, already, formerly, just now, just, anciently, since, hitherto, long since, long ago, erewhile, till now.

Of time future: Hereafter, henceforth, henceforward, soon, to-morrow, shortly, erelong, by and by, presently, instantly, immediately, straightway, straightways, directly, forthwith, not yet, anon.

DEGREE. *How much? How little? To what extent?*

Adverbs of degree are not easily classified; for adverbs from several other classes may sometimes be used to express degree. The following adverbs, to the dash-line, are not all strictly adverbs of degree.

Adverbs showing how much, to what extent, or in what degree: Much, more, most, greatly, far, further, very, too, little, less, least, extra, mostly, entirely, chiefly, principally, mainly, generally, commonly, usually, in general, fully, full, completely, totally, wholly, perfectly, all, altogether, quite, exceedingly, extravagantly, immeasurably, immensely, excessively, boundlessly, infinitely, inconceivably, clear, stark, nearly, well-nigh, partly, partially, intensely, scarcely, scantily, precisely, enough, exactly, even, everso, just, equally, sufficiently, adequately, proportionately, competently, as, so, how, however, howsoever, somewhat, at all.

Of exclusion or emphasis: Merely, only, but, alone, simply, barely, just, particularly, especially, in particular.

Adverbs implying something additional to what has been mentioned, or something beyond what might be expected: Also, besides, else, still, yet, too, likewise, withal, moreover, furthermore, however, extra, eke, even, nevertheless, anyhow.

Adverbs implying cause or means: Why, wherefore, therefore, hence, thence, consequently, accordingly, whereby, hereby, thereby.

Of negation: Not, nay, no, nowise, noway, noways, by no means.

Of affirmation or admittance: Truly, doubtless, undoubtedly, unquestionably, forsooth, indeed, well, very well, well then, yes, yea, ay, verily, surely, certainly, really, assuredly, certes, amen, of course, to be sure.

Of doubt or uncertainty: Perhaps, probably, possibly, perchance, peradventure, haply, mayhap, may-be.

The adverbs of the last three classes are sometimes termed *modal* adverbs. They are said to show "the manner of the assertion." They have a more direct reference to the mind of the speaker than the others have. We may deny or refuse, hesitate, consent; disbelieve, doubt, believe; pass from strong negation through doubt into strong positive assertion, and *vice versa.*

EXPLETIVE ADVERBS. *These serve merely to begin sentences, in order to render them less blunt or more sprightly; as,* There, well, why.

CONJUNCTIVE ADVERBS. *These connect as well as modify. They are usually adverbs of time, place, or manner; as,* When, where, while, till, as, etc.

INTERROGATIVE ADVERBS. *These are those adverbs of the foregoing classes, which are used to ask questions; as,* Why? where? how? whither?

From the foregoing list, it may be seen that the same word may sometimes be referred to one class of adverbs, and sometimes to another, according to its meaning.

Ex.—"I have *just* come." (*Time.*) "It is *just* full;" i. e., neither more nor less, (*Extent or degree.*)

It is supposed that the student, after having carefully studied the foregoing catalogue, will be able to refer any adverb not in it to its proper class. In parsing, when an adverb can not be easily referred to some special class, it may be more convenient to refer it to the general class to which it belongs,—to call it simply an adverb of *manner, place, time,* or *degree.*

Will you mention six adverbs of manner?—three of place where?—three of place whence?—three of place whither?—three of order?—three of time absolute?—three of time relative?—three of time repeated?—three of time present?—three of time past?—three of time future?—six of degree?—three implying exclusion?—three implying something additional?—three of cause?—three of negation?—three of affirmation?—three of doubt?—three expletive adverbs?—six conjunctive adverbs?—one interrogative adverb of manner, one of place, and one of time?—six adverbial phrases?

7. PREPOSITIONS.

When I say, "The horses are *in* the ferry-boat, the ferry-boat is *on* the river, and the river is *between* the hills; you see that the words *in, on,* and *between,* show how different objects are relatively situated. These little words are called *prepositions;* for *preposition* means *placing before,* and prepositions must generally be placed before nouns, to make the latter capable of being used as descriptive words.

What is a *preposition?*

A **preposition** is a word used to govern a noun or pronoun, and show its relation to some other word.

Ex.—In, on, under, above, over, round, at, from, to, through.

Two prepositions are sometimes combined, and some phrases are constantly used in the sense of prepositions. The former expressions may be called *complex prepositions;* the latter, *prepositional phrases;* or both may be termed simply *prepositions.* See the List.

PREPOSITIONS.

What does a preposition usually join to some other word or part of the sentence?

A substantive denoting the place, time, doer, possessor, cause, means, manner, or some other circumstance.

Ex.—"The apples hang ON the *tree*." "We have snow IN *winter*." "He was stabbed BY a *volunteer*, WITH the *sword* OF a *Kentuckian*." "To write WITH *ease* and *rapidity*."

What is an *adjunct*?

An **adjunct** is a preposition with its object, or with the words required after it to complete the sense. See above.

Is the preposition always expressed?

It is sometimes understood.

Ex.—"Give him his book"—Give his book *to* him. "I stood near him"—I stood near *to* him. "He is like his father"—He is like *to* or *unto* his father.

List of Prepositions.

A,	bating,	ere,	respecting,	up,	atween,
aboard,	before,	except,	round,	upon,	atwixt,
about,	behind,	excepting,	save,	versus,	cross,
above,	below,	for,	saving,	with,	dehors,
across,	beneath,	from,	since,	within,	inside,
after,	beside,	in,	through,	without.	maugre,
against,	besides,	into,	throughout,		minus,
along,	between,	notwith-	till,	Not Common.	outside,
amid,	betwixt,	standing,	to,		plus,
amidst,	beyond,	of,	touching,	Abaft,	sans,
among,	but,	off,	toward,	adown,	than,
amongst,	by,	on,	towards,	afore,	thorough,
around,	concerning,	over,	under,	aloft,	via,
aslant,	despite,	past,	underneath,	alongside,	withal,
at,	down,	pending,	until,	aloof,	withinside.
athwart,	during,	per,	unto,	aneath,	

Aboard of,	as to,	from betwixt,	from out of,
according to,	because of,	from beyond,	from under,
along with,	from among,	from off,	out of,
as for,	from before,	from out,	round about.

Can you repeat the prepositions that begin with a?—b?—c?—d?—e?—f?—i?—n?—o?—p?—r?—s?—t?—u?—w?

8. CONJUNCTIONS.

When I say, "John *and* James write;" "John writes *and* ciphers;" "John writes fast *and* well;" "John spilt his ink on the desk *and* on the floor;" "John writes twice every day, *and* I generally look at his writing;" you see that the word *and* brings on something more to what has been said, or joins together two *words*, two *phrases*, or two *propositions*; and as *conjunction* means *joining together*, this word, and others like it, have been called *conjunctions*.

What definition, then, may be given of a *conjunction*?

A **conjunction** is a word used to connect other words, and show the sense in which they are connected.

Ex.—"Grain will be cheap, *and* perhaps unsalable." "Grain will be cheap, *for* the harvest is abundant." "Grain will be cheap, *if* the winter continue mild." "Grain will be cheap, *but* now it is dear." "He rides, *if* he is sick." "He rides, *though* he is sick." "He rides, *because* he is sick."

Two conjunctions are sometimes combined, and certain phrases are sometimes used in the sense of conjunctions: as, "His health, *as well as* his estate, is ruined; *and yet* he still persists in his course." The former expressions may be called *complex conjunctions;* and the latter, *conjunctive phrases;* or both may be termed simply *conjunctions.*

What is a *coördinate* conjunction?

A **coördinate** conjunction connects parts of equal rank.

Ex.—And, but, or. "The woods are sprouting, *and* the dove is cooing." Here *and* connects clauses that do not depend on each other, and therefore they are said to be *coördinate,* which means *of equal rank.*

What is a *subordinate* conjunction?

A **subordinate** conjunction connects parts of unequal rank.

Ex.—If, that, since, because. "I will work for you, *if* you pay me." Here *if* connects two clauses, of which one depends on the other, and therefore the dependent one is said to be *subordinate,* which means *ranking under.*

What is a *corresponding* or *correlative* conjunction?

A **corresponding** conjunction suggests another conjunction, and assists it in connecting the same parts.

Ex.—"I will *neither* buy NOR sell." "*Though* he reproves me, *yet* I esteem him."

Can you mention the chief ideas conveyed by the different conjunctions in reference to the parts connected?

Addition, separation, contrariety, cause, consequence, purpose, condition, concession, and comparison.

By examining the beginning of this section, what words would you infer may be connected by conjunctions?

Words of almost any part of speech.

Where are conjunctions mostly used?

In connecting the parts of compound sentences.

Are conjunctions ever understood?

Sometimes they are; and other words are generally understood after them.

Ex.—"Rout, [and] ruin, [and] panic, seized them all." "I knew [that] he had lost it." "You may first read this sentence, and then [you may] parse it."

How may adverbs, prepositions, and conjunctions be distinguished, or what is the chief characteristic of each class?

Of the *adverb,* to modify or limit; of the *preposition,* to govern a substantive in the objective case; and of the *conjunction,* to connect.

Ex.—"He took *but* one apple." "I saw all *but* him." "I saw him, *but* he would not come."

List of Conjunctions.

1. *Conjunctions implying continuance or addition, simply or emphatically:* And, as well as, again, also, besides, both, moreover, furthermore, even, nay, so (—also). (*Copulative conjunctions.*)

2. *Separation or choice:* Or, nor, either, neither, or else. (*Alternative or disjunctive conjunctions.*)

3. *Contrariety, restriction, or reservation:* But, yet, still, however, howsoever, nevertheless, notwithstanding, unless (—but not... if), except that, save. (*Adversative or restrictive conjunctions.*)

4. *Comparison:* Than, as. (*Comparative conjunctions.*)

5. *Concession:* Although, though, even if, even though, notwithstanding, albeit. (*Concessive conjunctions.*)

6. *Condition or doubt:* If, unless (—if not), whether, provided, provided that, in case that, so, except, lest. (*Conditional or contingent conjunctions.*)

7. *Cause or reason:* Because, for, since, as, seeing, inasmuch as, forasmuch as, whereas. (*Causal conjunctions.*)

8. *Consequence or inference:* Then, so, therefore, wherefore. (*Illative conjunctions.*)

9. *Purpose, motive, or statement:* That, so that, in order that, lest, so as.

10. *Corresponding conjunctions:* Either—or; neither—nor; whether—or; if—then; though, or although—yet; both—and; as—so; as—as.

Conjunctions are sometimes accumulated, or take adverbial particles, merely to strengthen or to modify slightly the connection between the parts. Sometimes, phrases even, or adverbial particles, may be treated simply as conjunctions, unless great accuracy is required; or else they may be analyzed more rigidly otherwise, especially by supplying such words as may be reasonably supposed to have been omitted.

The conjunctions of the first three classes are chiefly *coördinate;* the others, to the tenth class, *subordinate.* The former rather indicate the movements and turns of thought; the latter subjoin parts that are used more or less in the sense of parts of speech.

Can you mention two copulative conjunctions?—two alternative? (Pass thus through the List.)

9. INTERJECTIONS.

In every language, there are certain words used when the mind is suddenly or greatly excited, in order to give vent to some strong feeling or sudden emotion; as, *Oh! alas!* These words are called *interjections,* a word that means *thrown among;* for they are so loosely combined with the other words of a sentence, that they seem *thrown among* them.

What is an *interjection?*

An **interjection** is a word that expresses an emotion only, and is not connected in construction with any other word.

Ex.—Alas! fie! O! oh! ah! hurrah! hail! adieu! "*O* Grave! where is thy victory?" "Those were happy days; but, *alas!* they are no more!" "*Pshaw!* never mind it."

Where are interjections most frequently found, and what may aid us in discovering them?

In poetry and in oratory: they are generally followed by the exclamation-point.

As the heart is susceptible of many different emotions or feelings, the interjections may be divided into various classes.

List of Interjections.

1. *Of sorrow, grief, or pity:* Oh! alas! ah! alack! hoo! welladay!
2. *Of earnestness or joy:* O! eigh! hey! eh! ha!
3. *Of surprise, wonder, or horror:* Hah! ha! what! h'm! heigh! strange! indeed! hey-dey! la! whew! zounds! eh! ah! oh! hoity-toity!

4. *Of contempt or aversion:* Pshaw! pish! tut! tush! poh! foh! bah! humph! faugh! whew! off! begone! avaunt!
5. *Of exultation or approbation:* Aha! ah! hey! huzzah! hurrah! good! bravo!
6. *Of attention or calling:* Ho! lo! behold! look! see! hark! la! heigh-ho! soho! hollo! halloa! hoy! hold! whoh! halt! 'st!
7. *Of silence:* Hush! hist! whist! 'st! aw! mum!
8. *Of interrogating:* Eh? hem, or h'm? (The opposite of the preceding class.)
9. *Of detection:* Aha! oho! ay-ay!
10. *Of laughter:* Ha, ha, ha! he, he, he!
11. *Of saluting or parting:* Welcome! hail! all-hail! adieu! good-by! *and perhaps* good-day! good-night! good-morning! good-evening!

It is difficult to make a satisfactory classification of interjections. Most of them are used with great latitude of meaning; that is, in various senses. When the learner meets with an interjection, it is perhaps best that he should determine its meaning from the spirit of the sentence or discourse.

If a man cultivates the earth, he may be styled a *farmer;* if the same man should engage in the business of buying and selling goods, a *merchant;* if in preaching the gospel, a *preacher:* even so the same word, according to its use, is sometimes of one part of speech, and sometimes of another.

Ex.—" A *black* horse ;" " To *black* boots ;" " *Black* is a color."
The first *black* is an adjective ; the second, a verb; and the third, a noun.
Can you mention two interjections of grief?—two of joy? (Pass thus through the List.)

10. EXERCISES ON THE FOREGOING PAGES.

1. *Tell which of the following letters are vowels, and which are consonants:—*
A, b, c, d, e, f, g, h, i, j, k, l, m, n, o, p, q, r, s, t, u, v, w, x, y, z; bar, bed, kind, fond, turn, Baltimore.

Tell which are monosyllables, dissyllables, trisyllables, polysyllables, and why:—
Pink, lily, daffodil, ordinary, gold, silver, golden, silvery, book, grammar, grammatical, grammatically, arithmetic, geography, behavior, punishment, recitation, teacher, home, mother, relative, relatives, unassisted.

2. *Whether primitive, derivative, or compound, and why:—*
Play, playing, play-day, playfellow, snow, snowy, ball, balls, snowball, snowballs, noble, nobly, nobleness, ignoble, noble-minded, plant, replant, transplanted, planter, plantation, tea-plant, water-melon, nothing, nevertheless.

Tell which is the subject, and which is the predicate, and why:—
Birds sing. Flowers bloom. Cats catch mice. The dew refreshes the flowers. The stars gem the sky. The Indians' tents stood along the river. John caught a fish. William studies his lesson. A guilty conscience needs no accuser. The grass is growing. The bird has been singing. The clothes will have been dried. Farmers raise corn. Corn is raised by farmers.

3. *The subject and the predicate, and why; whether simple or compound, and why:—*
The stars twinkle. The sun and moon shine. The sun rises and sets. Emma was gathering roses. Trees and flowers grow, flourish, and decay. The troubled ocean roars. Honey-suckles and roses overspread our portico. Laura brought a fresh rose, and gave it to me. A dark cloud hides the sun. The sun is hidden by a dark cloud. You and he may go and recite. The soldiers' horses were in the pasture. The cannons which the soldiers brought, were captured in the battle. Do well, but boast not.

Whether a phrase or a sentence, and why:—
Far away. The dark storm approaches. John's slate. Many small pieces. John's slate is broken into many small pieces. The rising sun. The sun is rising. A large red apple. Give me a large red apple. To write a letter. I wish to write a letter.

Whether a simple sentence or a compound, and why; and if compound, mention the clauses:—
Hope gilds the future. True praise takes root and spreads. Fishes swim in the sea, and birds fly in the air. The sun illuminates the distant hills. As we were coming home, we saw a most beautiful rainbow. I wish I were a child again. Billows are murmuring on the hollow shore. Gold can not purchase life, nor can diamonds bring back the moments we have lost. God has robed the world with beauty. From flower and shrub arose a sweet perfume. The rose seemed to weep for the buds it had left. We mourn in black, because the grave is a place of darkness and dread; the Chinese mourn in white, because heaven, whither their friends are supposed to have gone, is a place of perfect purity; the Egyptians mourn in blue, because that is the color of heaven; and the Abyssinians mourn in yellow, because falling leaves remind us of death. Hark! they whisper, angels say, Sister-spirit, come away.

4. *The nouns, and why:—*
A green tree. A house of marble. There are lilies and tulips in our garden. The farmer ploughs his field. The groves were God's first temples. Love and kindness go together. Col. Thomas H. Benton died in the year 1858. There was much Indian fighting in the settling of this country. I like apples. I like to skate. Learn the *how* and the *why*. *You* is a pronoun. Why he did not go, is obvious. Oranges and lemons grow, like apples, on small trees, but in warm climates.

The pear and quince lay squandered on the grass;
The mould was purple with unheeded showers
Of bloomy plums;—a wilderness it was
Of fruits, and weeds, and flowers!—*Hood*.

The nouns, and why; whether proper or common, and why:—
Girl, Susan, boy, George, country, day, Europe, Saturday, month, September, holiday, Christmas, bird, blackbird, parrot, Polly, river, Mississippi, mountains, Andes, island, Cuba, chain, Jane, Louis, Louisa, Louisiana, state, city, New York, year, 1860, soil, mind, hope, army; Mrs. Amelia Welby; General Alexander Hamilton; the prophet Jonah; Cape Lookout. Ferdinand and Isabella, the king and queen of Spain, enabled Columbus, a Genoese, to discover America. Tea is the dried leaves of a shrub which grows chiefly in China. The clamor of most politicians is but an effort to get the *ins* out and the *outs* in.

The pronouns, and why; what kind, and why:—
He saw me. We love them. She deceived herself. Know thyself. When a dandy has squandered his estate, he is not apt to regain it. The lady who had been sick, received the peaches which were ripe. This is the same marble that you gave me, and it is the best one that I have. Who came? Who is he? Which is he? What is he? We bought only such mules as we needed. (—*those mules which*—) Love what is worthy of love. (—*the thing which*—) This apple is neither yours nor mine, but hers. (—*your apple nor my apple, but her apple.*) By others' faults, wise men correct their own. (*By other men's faults, etc.*) None are completely happy. (*No persons are, etc.*) He loves no other land so much as that of his adoption. (—*as the land*—) Whatever comes from the heart, goes to the heart. Do you know who he is? Teach me what truth is.

Put nouns for the pronouns:—
John knows his lesson. Mary has lost her bonnet. He met her. I saw him and you. He showed them the lesson, that they might learn it. The girl

went with her father, and the boy went with his mother, and they were good children. Who knows who he is? (*What person * * * that man, etc.*) Bad boys spoil good ones. Take what you like.

5. *The gender, and why :—*
Brother, seamstress, Julius, Julia, parent, father, mother, son, daughter, child, duck, gander, robin, snow, book, mouse, he, him, hymn, she, it, they, we, I, eye, you, it, its, himself, herself, themselves, nature, game, person, corpse, spirit. *John* is a noun, and *she* is a pronoun.

Give the feminine to each masculine term, then the masculine to each feminine term:—
Boy, *girl;* brother, *sister;* beau, *belle;* bridegroom, *bride;* buck, *doe;* hart, roe; stag, *hind;* bull, *cow;* bullock or steer, *heifer;* drake, *duck;* father, *mother;* friar or monk, *nun:* gander, *goose;* gentleman, *lady;* lord, *lady;* horse, *mare;* husband, *wife;* king, *queen;* lad, *lass;* male, *female;* man, *woman;* master, *mistress;* master, *miss;* nephew, *niece;* ram or buck, *ewe;* sir, *madam;* uncle, aunt; wizard, *witch;* youth, *damsel* or *maiden;* Charles, *Caroline.*

Abbot, *abbess;* actor, *actress;* ar'biter, *ar'bitress;* bar'on, *bar'oness;* benefac'-tor, *benefac'tress;* count or earl, *countess;* duke, *duch'ess;* emperor, *empress;* enchant'er, *enchant'ress;* gov'ernor, *gov'erness;* heir, *heiress;* hōst, *hōstess;* hunter, *huntress;* instructor, *instructress;* Jew, *Jewess;* lion, *lioness;* marquis, *mar'-chioness;* negro, *negress;* patron, *patroness;* peer, *peeress;* poet, *poetess;* priest, *priestess;* prince, *princess;* prior, *pri'oress;* prophet, *prophetess;* protector, *protectress;* shepherd, *shepherdess;* sor'cerer, *sor'ceress;* tiger, *tigress;* tutor, *tutor ess;* vis'count, *vis'countess;* widower, *widow:* administra/tor, *administra'trix,* exec'utor, *exec'utrix;* testa'tor, *testa'trix;* he'ro, *her'oine;* Joseph, *Josephīne;* don. *donna;* sign'or, *signo'ra;* sultan, *sulta'na;* tzar, *tzarī'na;* Augustus, *Augusta.*

He-goat, *she-goat;* buck-rabbit, *doe-rabbit;* cock-sparrow, *hen-sparrow;* man-servant, *maid-servant;* male descendants, *female descendants;* Mr. Reynolds, *Mrs. Reynolds, Miss Reynolds.*

6. *The person, and why :—*
I, you, he, we, my, us, thee, yourselves, mine, thine, thyself, himself, themselves, it, she, hers; a drooping willow; my dictionary; your grammar; her slate; Washington's birthday. I am the captain, sir. We passengers have poor fare. Then said I to him, "Well, my little friend, how fare the schoolboys?"
My mother! when I learned that thou wast dead,
Say, wast thou conscious of the tears I shed?
Hovered thy spirit o'er thy sorrowing son,
Wretch even then, life's journey just begun?
I heard the bell tolled on thy funeral day,
I saw the hearse that bore these slow away,
And, turning from my nursery window, drew
A long, long sigh, and wept a last adieu!—*Cowper.*

Change into the other persons :—
John writes. The girls study. Henry, you may play. I William Ringbolt hold myself responsible. Shall Hannibal compare himself with this half-year captain?

The number, and why :—
Book, books, rose, roses, partridge, partridges, friends, geese, lilies, family, families, scissors, ashes, letters, love, swarm, hay, honey, molasses, I, we, you, thou, him, they, his, several, one, ones, none, one another, our, ours, my, a, an, each man, either man, every man, neither road, two, a two, two twos, a twin, twins, a pair, two pair, is, was, reads, scales.

Spell the plurals of the singulars, then the singulars of the plurals :—
Man, *men;* woman, *women;* child, *children;* ox, *oxen;* foot, *feet;* goose, *geese;* tooth, *teeth;* mouse, *mice;* louse, *lice;* cow, *cows* or *kine;* this, *these;* that, *those;* I, *we;* thou, *ye;* he, *they;* is, *are;* was, *were.*

THE PARTS OF SPEECH.

Brother, *brothers* (of the same family), *brethren* (of the same society); die, *dies* (stamps for coining), *dice* (small cubes for gaming); fish, *fishes* (individuals), *fish* (quantity, or the species); penny, *pennies* (pieces of money), *pence* (how much in value).

Beef, *beeves*; calf, *calves*; elf, *elves*; half, *halves*; knife, *knives*; leaf, *leaves*; life, *lives*; loaf, *loaves*; self, *selves*; sheaf, *sheaves*; shelf, *shelves*; thief, *thieves*; wife, *wives*; wolf, *wolves*.

(To *s, x, z, sh,* and *ch* soft; and to *i, o. u,* or *y,* preceded each by a consonant,—add *es: y* is changed to *i.*) Atlas, *atlases*; fox, *foxes*; to'paz, *to'pazes*; dish, *dishes*; church, *churches*; monarch, *monarchs*; al'kali, *al'kalies*; negro, *negroes*; gnu, *gnues*; story, *stories*; money, *moneys*; larva, *larvæ*; lam'ina, *lam'inæ*; minu'tia, *minutiæ*; alum'na, *alum'næ*; alum'nus, *alum'ni*; ma'gus, *ma'gi*; ar-ca'num, *arca'ni*; da'tum, *da'ta*; memoran'dum, *memoran'da*; phenom'enon, *phenom'ena*; sta'men, *stam'ina*; ge'nus, *gen'era*; axis, *axes*; anal'ysis, *anal'yces*; antith'esis, *antith'eses*; basis, *bases*; crisis, *crises*; ellip'sis, *ellip'ses*; em'phasis, *em'phases*; hypoth'esis, *hypoth'eses*; paren'thesis, *paren'theses*; synop'sis, *synop'ses*; syn'thesis, *syn'theses*; append'ix, *append'ices*; beau, *beaux*; monsieur, *messieurs*; cherub, *cherubs* or *cher'ubim*; seraph, *seraphs* or *ser'aphim*; bandit, *bandits* or *banditti*; brother-in-law, *brothers-in-law*; sister-in-law, *sisters-in-law*; court-martial, *courts-martial*; aid-de-camp, *aids-de-camp*; billet-doux, *billets-doux*; cupful, *cupfuls*; spoonful, *spoonfuls*; man-servant, *men-servants*; Miss Warner, the *Misses Warner*; Mr. Hunter, the *Messrs. Hunter*; Dr. Hunter, *Drs. Hunter*.

7. *The noun or pronoun, and why; then the case, and why:—*

John found Mary's book. Lucy's lamb nips the grass. Fair blooms the lily. He wrote his name in his book. John shot some squirrels in your father's field. Sweet fountain, once again I visit thee. The Greeks were more ingenious than the Romans [were]. In peace, he was the gale of spring; in war, the mountain-storm. The plough, the sword, the pen, and the needle,—how mighty! To venture in was to die. I know that you can learn. Why he went, is plain. Promising and performing are two different things. James does what is right, to them whom he loves. I myself hurt myself. A piece of candy, ten inches long, is worth a dime.

On that day of desolation,
Lady, I was captive made;
Bleeding for my Christian nation,
By the walls of high Belgrade.—*Campbell.*

8. *Gender, person, number, and case:—*

My, he, she, it, they, us, our, your, yours, them, we, you, hers, its, yourself, yourselves, ourselves, themselves, who, what, one's, ones', none, others.

What is the objective corresponding to—

I?—thou?—we?—ye?—he?—she?—it?—they?—you?—who?

What is the nominative corresponding to—

Me?—us?—thee?—him?—whom?—her?—hers?—them?—themselves?—herself?—it?—which?

Form the compound pronoun:—

My, our, thy, your, him, her, it, one, them, who, which, what.

Spell the possessive singular; then the possessive plural, if the word can have it:—

Sister, (thus: S-i-s-sis—t-e-r-apostrophe-s-ter's—Sister's,) John, day, Sparks, prince, horse, St. James, John Henry Thomson, he, one, who, other, she, it, court-martial, brother-in-law, book-keeper; the duke of Northumberland; Allen and Baker; Morris the bookseller; Morris, the bookseller.

Tell which are the pronouns, and their antecedents when it can be determined; also dispose of both nouns and pronouns in regard to case:—

The tree has shed its leaves. Liberty has God on her side. Let every man take care of himself. John, you, and I, must water our garden. John and James know their lesson. Neither John nor James knows his lesson. Henry, you must study. And there her brood the partridge led. The best throw with the dice is to throw them away. If you will not take pains, pains will take you. He who says what he likes, shall hear what he does not like. Promises may get friends, but it is performance that keeps them. He who created me, whose I am, and whom I serve, is eternal. His praise is lost who waits till all commend. Said William to Joseph, "I will go with you." The two brothers love each other. All our pupils are kind to one another. Your situation is not such a one as mine. Is the book yours, or mine? Take my advice, or that of your father. It is easy to spend money. It rained the whole night. It was Henry that said it. You are very sick, and I am sorry for it. You wrote to me, which was all you did. Whoever violates this rule, shall suffer the penalty. Who is he? Can you tell which is which? Whom do you take me to be? Whatever he undertakes, he performs. Whatever is, is right. Whatever I am, I tremble to think what I may be. I hope what I say will have an effect upon him, and prevent the impression which what he says may have upon others. Select whatever man is most suitable.

Heaven hides from brutes what men, from men what spirits, know.—*Pope.*

Insert the nouns and pronouns that will preserve the sense, and make the expression full:—

I have lost the letter you wrote. Who bets, should be willing to lose. The door opens to whoever knocks. I want such as hear me, to take warning. I want those to take warning, who hear me. Whom she loves so much I never could fancy. Here are the marbles: take which is yours.

9. *The article, and why; whether definite or indefinite, and why; and to what it belongs:—*

The roses in the garden. The rose is a beautiful flower. A fish from the river. A daughter of a duke. The daughter of a duke. The daughter of the duke. A daughter of the duke.

10. *The adjective, and why; whether descriptive or definitive, and why; and to what it belongs:—*

The blue sky. The sky is blue. An aspiring man. A modest and beautiful woman, with eyes bright, blue, and affectionate. The night grew darker and darker. That field has been in cultivation four years. The first car is not full, having but one man in it. The landscape was fresh with dew and bright with morning light. The rosy-fingered Morn. The star-powdered galaxy. The apples boiled soft. Now fairer blooms the drooping rose. His hammock swung loose at the sport of the wind. He is asleep. The fear of being awkward makes us awkward. To be indolent in youth, is ruinous.

11. *Compare, of the following adjectives, those which can be compared:—*

Wise, studious, near, good, evil, melodious, high, tuneful, saucy, eloquent, expressive, lovely, nimble, late, many, much, few, little, old, glowing, accomplished, expert, half-finished, full, counterfeit, graceful, meagre, worthless, bottomless, fundamental, ornamental, vernal, green, sluggish, sunburnt, free, first.

Mention and spell the three degrees of comparison:—

Strong, weak, light, gay, rough, nice, coarse, fierce, white, ripe, thin, slim, dim, fit, hot, fat, glad, big, droll, dry, sprightly. (Dissyllables ending in *y* or *le*, or accented on the second syllable, are compared like monosyllables.) Manly, gentle, feeble, able, idle, sereno, discreet, polite, sublime, intense, profound.

THE PARTS OF SPEECH. 41

Compare by using LESS *and* LEAST :—
Broad, convenient, confident, oily, troublesome, thick, joyful, sorrowful, exorbitant, exact, indulgent, handsome.

Join suitable adjectives to each of the following nouns :—
Moon, field, fountain, trees, garden, horse, willow, man, woman, mule, pen, ink, day, wood, boys, thoughts, feelings, actions, conduct.

12. *The verbs, and why :—*
The sun rises. Saddle your horse. Bees collect honey. Honey is collected by bees. The bird flutters. The trees wave. The workmen have built the house. Pinks are fragrant. The thunder was rolling. The mill can not grind with the water that has passed. Riches are got with pain, kept with care, and lost with grief. Drunkenness makes a man's eyes red, bloats his face, empties his purse, wastes his property, poisons his blood, destroys his digestion, blunts his feelings, corrupts his body and mind, disgraces his family, and shortens his life.

The participles and the infinitives, and why :—
Planting, planted, to plant, having planted, to be planted, to be planting, having been planted, to have planted, to have been planting, to have been planted. Columbus became wearied and disheartened by impediments thrown in his way. The Indians fled, leaving their mules tied to the bushes. We saw the sun rising. We saw the sun rise.
When my eyes shall be turned to behold, for the last time, the sun in heaven, may I not see him shining on the broken and dishonored fragments of a once glorious Union; on States severed, discordant, and belligerent; on a land rent with civil feud, or drenched, it may be, with fraternal blood.—*Webster.*

13. *Give the principal parts; and tell whether the verb is regular or irregular, and why :—*
Form, attack, strip, deny, bow, sow, grow, sew, sin, win, spin, rise, despise, moralize, skim, swim, heal, steal, fling, bring, spread, dread, twit, sit, fit, hit, die, lie, fold, hold, uphold, close, lose, choose, blind, find, fine, spurn, burn, reel, feel, blend, send, tend, lend, loan, tent, need, feed, blight, fight, wink, drink, slink, squeak, speak, steep, sleep, cleave, weave, leave, reach, teach, fret, get, let, whet, smut, put, agree, free, see, flee, fly, cry, spite, bite, write, take, make, bake, bare, dare, stray, pay, slay, may, trick, click, stick, call, fall, fell, bind, bound, grind, ground, heat, eat, roam, come, welcome, hive, strive, live, give, forgive, undo, undergo, counteract, say, gainsay, will, till, shall, cull, have, shave, land, stand, am, be, rise, raise, tell, toll, quell, lie, lay, sit, seat, set.

23. *Give, in the order of the conjugation, the participles, then the infinitives :—*
Move, rise, spring, degrade, drown, invigorate, overwhelm, bleed.

16. *The verbs, and why; whether transitive, passive, intransitive, or neuter, and why :—*
The horse carries his rider. The horses are hitched to the wagon. The water turns the wheel. The wheel is turned by the water. Mary reads. Mary is reading her book. The book is read. The man kicked the horse. The man was kicked by the horse. The horse kicks. Such as I am I have always been, and always shall be. To teach, having taught, having been taught, to have been taught, to have been teaching. He talks well. He talks nonsense. Since these men could not be convinced, it was determined to persecute them. He seated himself. He sat in a corner. He set a trap for a rat. Lay the book where it lay before. The workmen are building the house. The house is building. Green maple saws well. He was never heard of afterwards.

17. *Change the following sentences so as to make the active verbs passive, and the passive verbs active:—*

The sun adorns the world. Indolence produces misery. My neighbor has planted some apple-trees. The dog bit the stranger. The distance was measured by a surveyor. Morse invented the telegraph. The boat was built by Ericsson. Can the river be forded, at this place, by a man on horseback? He paid for the carriage. The ministers speak of peace. He was expected to strike.

22—9. *The verb, and why; then the auxiliary, what it implies, and what mood and tense it expresses:—*

John can read. Mary may write. Die I must. He does improve rapidly. Do you know him? The sun has risen. The thief had left the tavern when his pursuers came. I have a knife, and it is sharp. You shall obey me. Ye will not come that ye may have life. I will come if I can. He would not remain, if he were sent. Whoever would desert, should be hanged. Did not you go too? May God ever protect the right.

17. *The verb, and why; then the mood, and why:—*

William is writing. The rosemary nods on the grave, and the lily lolls on the wave. He caught a fish. It will rain this evening. I may command, but you must obey. He could and should have assisted us, but he would not. Do not value a gem by what it is set in. If William study, he will soon know his lesson. If wishes were horses, beggars would ride. Train up a child in the way he should go; and when he is old, he will not depart from it. The violet soon will cease to smile, the whippoorwill to chant. May you be happy. O, that he were wiser! If you are disappointed, blame not me. If you be disappointed, blame not me. This government will fall, if it lose the confidence of the people. This government would fall, if it lost the confidence of the people. This government would have fallen, had it lost the confidence of the people. Let us now turn to another part. Turn we now to another part. Somebody call my wife. (Imperative.)

18. *The verb, and why; then the tense, and why:—*

The moonlight is glimmering on the water. Hushed now are the whirlwinds that ruffled the deep. The storm had ceased before we reached a shelter. The storm ceased before we reached a shelter. He who is a stranger to industry, may possess, but he can not enjoy. Men must be taught as if you taught them not. How bright yon pearly clouds reposing lie! He sank exhausted on the bloody field. It would have pleased me to have heard from you. Strike! for the green graves of your sires. I may have made some mistakes. I had heard that the spirit of discontent was very prevalent here; but with pleasure I find that I have been grossly misinformed. Had the whole Turkish empire risen in opposition, it could not, at that moment, have deterred them. Your character will have been formed at the age of twenty. She seems to study. He is supposed to have written the book. As soon as I have learned my lesson, I will play with you.

20. *The verbs, and why; then the forms, and why:—*

Twilight is weeping o'er the pensive rose. It fell instantly. It does amaze me. Ye know not what ye say. Learning taketh away the barbarity of men's minds. Our chains are forging. The improved rifles are being introduced into the army. Thou art the man.

21. *The verbs, and why; then of what person and number, to agree with———:—*

I study. We write. He stutters. Grass grows. They were. You might improve. Thou art he. It is. It is I. It is they. Is it he? Thou hast been. The wind has risen. Cows are lowing. The cricket chirps. Sing, heavenly Muse. Seek we the shade. I myself saw him. The general himself was slain.

Down went the ship and her gallant crew. Down went the ship, with her gallant crew. The public are respectfully invited. The country was harassed by civil war. Many a man has been ruined by speculation. To complain is useless. It is useless to complain. What signifies your complaining? Either your horse or mine is gone. Neither the woman nor her child was hurt. Thou or I am to blame. He, as well as I, is to blame.

23. *Conjugate each of the following verbs, beginning with the first person singular, and stopping with the subject:—*

The boy learns. (Thus: SINGULAR, 1st person, *I learn*; 2d person, *You learn*; 3d person, *He*, or *the boy*, *learns*.) The leaves are falling. Flowers must fade. Jane reads. Jane and Eliza read. Jane or Eliza reads. The lands may have been sold. The horse has been eating. The horses have been fed. Had they been there.

24—9. *Conjugate fully the verbs* RULE, PERMIT, CARRY, STRIKE, SEE.

The verbs; regular or irregular; transitive, passive, intransitive, or neuter; mood, tense, and form; person and number,—and why:—

He reads. We have slept. She died. Were we surpassed? Were we surpassed. You had seen him. Had you seen him? Take care, lest you lose it. My time might have been improved better. The strawberries are ripening.

Let me read in good books, and believe and obey,
That, when Death turns me out of this cottage of clay,
I may dwell in a palace in heaven.—*Watts.*

30—2. *The adverbs, and why; of what kind, and what they modify:—*

Wisely, now, here, very. The horse runs swiftly. God is everywhere. Never before did I see her look so pale. These things have always been so. I have been too idle heretofore, but henceforth I will study more diligently. Your book is more beautiful, but mine is more useful. He was lately here. You do not know him as well as I do. The hall was brilliantly illuminated, and densely crowded with hearers. Play is good while it is play. The cooler the water, the better I like it. There was nothing there that I wanted. Can not you help us? Secondly, there were no means of transportation. I consulted him once or twice; not oftener. You have perhaps not noticed quite all the adverbs in the sentence which I have just read.

Compare:—

Late, soon, early, much, little, well, ill, long, far, proudly, heroically.

Mention the corresponding adverb:—

True, new, sure, good, (well,) glaring, studious, ardent, bad, patient, noble, lazy, profuse, slavish, richer, (more richly,) richest, plainer, severest, necessary, graphic, critic, order, grammar, history, arithmetic, geography.

With vigor; in a careless manner; without care; in what place; from what cause; in this place; in that place; at all times; at the present time; as occasion requires; in the lowest degree; at that time; one time; in the second place; from instinct; by the year.

32—3. *The prepositions, and why; and between what they show the relation:—*

Flowers are growing along the rivulet. I saw him, through a window. The bear was attacked by the dogs, and chased through a cane-brake into the river. My dinner is in my basket under the bench. Beneath the oak lie acorns in abundance. The hog never looks up to him who threshes down the acorns. By assisting me you will confer a favor on me. It happened since morning, and before eleven o'clock. He came from beyond Jordan. The affectation of unattainable graces, only adds distortion to clownishness. They were rowing up the river; but we, down.

33—5. *The conjunctions, what they imply, and what they connect:—*
Him and her we know; but who are you? It ran around the house, and under the floor. You must study, if you would be wise. He is neither educated, nor naturally wise. I will either come or send. Unless you are economical, you will never be rich. 'Tis true, but yet in vain.

35—6. *The interjections, and why; then of what kind:—*
O! oh! alas! welcome! ho! ah! tush! hurrah! Deluded hopes!—oh, worse than death! Tut! such aristocracy! Aha! caught at last. Adieu! adieu! dear native land.

Tell of what part of speech each word is, and show its relation to the other words:—
A saucy sparrow got into a martin's nest while the owner was abroad; and when he returned, the sparrow put his head out of the hole, and pecked at the martin with open bill, as he attempted to enter his own house.
   'Tis the star-spangled banner! O, long may it wave
   O'er the land of the free and the home of the brave.—*Key.*
   And there lay the rider distorted and pale,
   With the dew on his brow and the rust on his mail.—*Byron.*

Supply the words omitted:—
A man and woman were drowned. You may write, and then cipher. Give him his book. He is like you. A book of my sister's. John knows more than Rufus. The first tree and the fourth are dead. I shall call for you at Smith's. You have the horse I want. Let it be. Arm, soldiers! How now, Tubal; what news from Genoa? Sweet the pleasure, rich the treasure. Strange indeed. Will you go there?—I go there? Never. Soon ripe, soon rotten.

Change the position of the words without changing the meaning:—
After a painful struggle, I yielded to my fate. Sweet songs were heard the leafy dells along. Me glory summons to the martial scene. Various, sincere, and constant are the efforts of men to produce that happiness which the mind requires. Gone, for ever gone, are the happy days of youth.

☞ For additional exercises, if wanted, use the examples on pp. 48—57.

11. RULES OF SYNTAX.

THE RELATIONS OF WORDS TO ONE ANOTHER, IN THE STRUCTURE OF SENTENCES.

Words are used to express thoughts; but every thought requires two or more words to be associated or grouped together, in order to express it. Almost every word, therefore, is so made or modified, or is of such a nature, that it looks to some other word for complete sense, and would be as unmeaning and useless by itself as a detached piece of a steam-engine.

Ex.—"The white house gleaming on yonder hill, was built long ago for me and my family to live in it." *The* relates to *house,* showing that some particular one is meant; *white* relates to *house,* describing it; *house* relates to *was built,* the thing said of it; *gleaming* relates to *house,* describing it; *on* relates to *gleaming* and *hill,* showing where; *hill* relates to *on,* showing on what; *was built,* relates to *house,* showing what is said of it; *long ago* relates to *was built,* showing when; *for* relates to *was built* and *me and my family,* showing the purpose; *me and my family* relates to *for;* and connects *me* and *family,* showing that the two are to be taken together; *my* relates to *family,* showing what family; *to live* relates to *me* and *family,* showing what we do; *in* relates to *it* and *to live,* showing where; and *it* relates to *house* as the thing meant, and to *in* as denoting where. This illustration may teach you, to some extent, what the following Rules mean.

☞ To illustrate the relations or offices of words still better, the teacher may do well to write on the blackboard, in connected or detached order, the foregoing sentence, and the most suitable of the sentences which accompany the following Rules; and then join the related parts by connecting lines drawn above or below.

RULE I.—*A **noun** or **pronoun** used as the subject of a finite verb, must be in the nominative case.*

I am; not, *Me* am. *We* are. (*Who* are?) *He* is. *They* are. *Thou* dar'st not. The *m.n who* is industrious, can earn what *he* needs. (*Man* is the subject of *can earn.*) *I* have less than *he* (has). *To lie* is disgraceful. *That honesty is the best policy*, is generally admitted.

RULE II.—*A **noun** or **pronoun** used independently or absolutely, must be in the nominative case.*

Independent.—*By direct address:* Go, *Tubal,* go. *Plato,* thou reasonest well. *By exclamation:* Three thousand *ducats!* 'tis a good round sum. *To be—or not to be,—that is the question!* (*Life—or death,—that is the question!*) *By pleonasm or specification:* The Pilgrim *Fathers,*—where are they? My *banks* they are furnished with bees. Worcester's *Dictionary,* Unabridged. (Title.)

Absolute.—*Before a participle:* The *rain* having ceased, the sun reäppeared. The *steed* [being] at hand, why longer tarry? (*Being* is often understood.) *After a participle or an infinitive:* The vanity of being a *belle.* To be a good *Christian,* was his highest ambition. No one suspected his being a *foreigner.*

RULE III.—*A **noun** or **pronoun** that limits the meaning of another by denoting possession, must be in the possessive case.*

John's horse. (That is, not any horse, but the one that belongs to John.) *Sir Walter Scott's* works. *Whose* book is it, if not *mine* [—*my* book]? *My* new one. *Smith's* [store] and *Barton's* store. *Smith, Allen,* and *Barton's* store. Call at *Smith's,* the bookseller. (That is, at Smith's house or store.) The *captain* of the Neptune's wife. There is no evidence of *their* having quarreled.

RULE IV.—*A **noun** or **pronoun** used as the object of a transitive verb, must be in the objective case.*

We caught *them;* not, *they.* The soil produces *cotton, rice,* and *sugar.* I saw *him,* and he saw *me.* "*Whom* did you hit?—*John.*" (Supply "I hit.") I hid *myself.* Having made the *law,* enforce *it.* By reading good *books,* you will improve. To see green *fields,* is pleasant. Most children like *to play*—like *skating.* Do you know *when to send?* No one knows *how much the fellow is in debt.*

RULE V.—*A **noun** or **pronoun** used as the object of a preposition, must be in the objective case.*

It was sent by *me* to *him.* (That is, we could not say, when speaking correctly, It was sent by *I* to *he.*) A melon on a *vine.* Lend *me* your knife. (Supply *to.*) "Of *whom* did you buy it?—*Jones.*" By *reading* in good *books,* you will improve. She does nothing except *to scold.* The question of *what are to be the powers of the crown,* is superior to *that* of *who is to wear it.*

RULE VI.—*A **noun** or **pronoun** used without a governing word, but limiting like an adjunct or adverb some other word, must be in the objective case.*

The street is a *mile* long. (Long to what extent?) He remained five *days.* (*During* five days. A preposition can generally be supplied. These objectives are abridged adjuncts without the preposition, just as *in vain, in short,* etc., are abridged adjuncts without their objects.) The horse ran six *miles.* It is a *ton* heavier. I do not care a *straw.* The milk is a *little* sour. The knife is well

worth a *dollar*. He went *home*. I was taught *music*, and she was taught *it*. "He has been here five *times*." And perhaps, "Five times *four* are twenty."
Most nouns under this Rule denote some estimate of *space, time, weight*, or *value*.

RULE VII.—*A **noun** or **pronoun** used for explanation or emphasis, by being predicated of another, or put in apposition with another, must be in the same case.*

This Rule embraces two kinds of construction: SAME CASE, by *predication*; and SAME CASE, by *apposition*. When two substantives refer to the same person or thing, and an intransitive or passive verb joins them, the latter or explanatory substantive is said to be predicated of the other, and is called a *predicate nominative* or *substantive*; as, "Jackson was the *general*." When no verb joins them, the substantives are said to be in *apposition*, or the latter is called an *appositive*; as, "Jackson, the *general*."

Miscellaneous: Taxes, endless *taxes*, are the *consequences* of corruption. She looks a *goddess*, and she walks a *queen*. They made him *captain*. He was made *captain*. *Feet* was I to the lame. Ye *scenes* of my childhood. Explain the terms *reason* and *instinct*. They bore *each* [*one*] a banner. They regard winter as the *season* of domestic enjoyment. By a frith, or *firth*. His friend and *partner* is dead. I *myself* went. It was *I*. What is he? *Whom* do you take me to be? IT is easy *to spend* money. It is not known *how the Egyptians* embalmed *their dead*.

RULE VIII.—*The relative **what**, or a like term when its form allows them, may supply two cases.*

I took *what* suited me. *Whoever* sins, shall suffer. I will employ *whomsoever* you recommend. I am not *what* I have been. Take *whichever horse* you like.

This Rule is merely a convenience: it can be dispensed with, by applying two other Rules.

RULE IX.—*A **pronoun** must agree with its antecedent, in gender, person, and number.*

Thomas found *his* dog with Henry's dogs; and *they* were all chasing a deer *which* had leaped out of the wheat-field. (The *antecedent* is the substantive in reference to which the pronoun is used; as, "Mary has lost her book." Here *Mary* is the antecedent of *her*.) Who *that* knows him, would trust him?

RULE X.—*An **article** or an **adjective** belongs to the noun or pronoun to which it relates.*

Articles.—Bring *a* rose from *the* garden. *A* gardener's wages. Once upon a summer's *day*. *A* | *noun* and pronoun. The | *house* and *lot*. An | *industrious people*, having *a* | *great many curious inventions*. See p. 173.

Adjectives.—*This* apple is *ripe*. The truly *good* [people] are *happy*. The apples boiled *soft*. To live comfortably, is *desirable*. (What is desirable?)

RULE X.—*An adjective is sometimes used absolutely after a participle or an infinitive.*

To be *good* is to be *happy*. (Goodness is happiness.) The way to be *happy*, is to be good. The dread of being *poor*. (This Note can often be dispensed with, by regarding the phrase as a noun, or by supplying a noun. See p. 188.)

RULE XI.—*A **finite verb** must agree with its subject, in person and number.*

I *am*; not, I *is*. He *is*. They *are*. Thou *art*. Tea and silk *are brought* from the East. A week or a month soon *passes* away. Our people *are* enterprising. No nation *is* at war with us. *Believe* [thou]. To write ten lines a day, | *is* sufficient. That so many *are ruined* in large cities, | *is* owing to bad examples.

NOTE XI.—*In a few peculiar expressions, finite verbs are used without a suitable subject, or without any subject.*

Ex.—"*Methinks*." And perhaps, "God said, *Let* us make man in our image."
"Forthwith on all sides to his aid *was run*
By angels many and strong."—*Milton's P. L., B. VI.*

RULE XII.—*A **participle** relates to the noun or pronoun which is the subject of the act or state.*

RULES OF SYNTAX.

*An **infinitive** relates to an expressed or indefinite subject; and it may besides modify the meaning, or complete the construction, of some other part of the sentence.*

The last clause of this Rule often applies also to participles. The subject of a participle or an infinitive, is the noun or pronoun denoting the object to which the act or state belongs; and it may be in the objective case, as well as in the nominative.

Columbus became *wearied** by impediments *thrown* in his way. The water came *foaming* over the rocks. The Passions oft, *to hear* her shell, thronged around her magic cell. (*To hear* relates to *Passions* for its subject, and also limits *thronged*.) We walked out *to see* the moon *rising*. Now is the time *to sell*. A mountain so high as *to be* perpetually *covered* with snow.

NOTE XIII.—*A participle or an infinitive is sometimes used absolutely or independently.*

To go *prepared*, is necessary. Generally *speaking*, wealth demoralizes. To go about, *seeking* employment, is irksome. But, *to proceed:* It has been remarked, etc. Every man has, so *to speak*, several strings by which he may be pulled. (Suitable words can generally be supplied, to avoid the necessity of using this Note.)

[The infinitive is the most irksome element in syntax. I therefore offer to teachers the following Rule for trial, as one that will reach all constructions of participles and infinitives.

RULE XII.—*A **participle** or an **infinitive**, being a part of the verb, relates to an expressed or indefinite subject; and it may besides have the sense of a noun, an adjective, an adverb, or a clause.*]

RULE XIII.—*An **adverb** belongs to the word or words which it modifies.*

A *most* beautiful horse galloped *very* | *rapidly* up the road. *There* was nothing *there* that I wanted. *When* will you go? *The* cooler the water, *the* better I like it.

NOTE XIII.—*A conjunctive adverb joins on something that usually expresses the time, place, or manner; or that is used in the sense of an adverb, an adjective, or a noun.*

Ex.—"Go *when* you please." "The grave *where* our hero was buried." (What grave?) "I know *how* you got it." (Know what?) "He did *as* I said." (How?) In stead of this Note, the Rule can generally be applied, by parsing the adverb as relating to the verbs in both propositions.

REMARK XIII.—*An adverb appears to be sometimes used independently.*

Ex.—"*Well*, I really don't know what to do." "*Why*, that is a new idea." Adverbs thus used partake somewhat of the nature of both conjunctions and interjections. *Yes, nay, amen*, etc., are usually parsed as being independent, though they nearly always relate to the preceding sentence or discourse.

RULE XIV.—*A **preposition** shows the relation between two terms, and governs the latter in the objective case.*

The *antecedent term* may be a *noun*, a *pronoun*, an *adjective*, a *verb*, an *adverb*, or even a *phrase;* the *subsequent term* must be a *substantive*. Sometimes the terms are inverted. *Analysis* will always help to show which are the related terms.

A man | *of* | wisdom spoke. The man spoke | *of* | wisdom. Parrhasius stood gazing *u p o n* the canvas. (What upon what?) A brook, clear | *at* | its *source*.

RULE XV.—***Conjunctions*** *connect clauses or sentences; and also words or phrases in the same construction.*

Weeds | *a n d* | briers now grow in the field, *because* it is not cultivated. But a long *and* cordial friendship had existed between him *and* me.

As or *than* sometimes joins an infinitive to a clause, in stead of uniting two clauses.

RULE XVI.—***Interjections*** *have no grammatical connection with other words.*

Can you repeat Rule 1st?—2d?—3d?—4th?—5th?—6th?—7th?—8th?—9th?—10th?—11th?—12th?—13th?—14th?—15th?—16th?

12. PARSING.

General Formula.—The part of speech, and why; the kind, and why; the properties, and why; the relation to other words, and according to what Rule.

Articles.

Formula.—An *article*, and why; *definite, indefinite,* and why; to what it belongs, and according to what Rule.

"The river."

" *The* " is an *article*,—a word placed before a noun to show how it is applied; *definite*, it shows that some particular river is meant; and it belongs to " *river*," according to Rule X : " *An article belongs to the noun to which it relates.*"

ABRIDGED.—*The* is the definite article; and it belongs to *river*, etc.

" *River* " is a noun, it is a name; *common*, it is a name that can be applied to every object of the same kind; *neuter gender*, it denotes neither a male nor a female; *third person*, it represents an object as spoken of; *singular number*, it means but one.

ANALYSIS.—*The river* is a phrase. The principal word is *river*, modified by the article *The*. (All the following exercises may be first analyzed, and then parsed, if the teacher deems it best to do so.)

In like manner parse the following phrases :—

The man.	The men.	A rose.	An arrow.
The horse.	The horses.	A melon.	An island.
The child.	The children.	A university.	An uncle.

" A man's hat."

" *A* " is an *article*,—a word placed before a noun to show how it is applied; *indefinite*, it shows that no particular man is meant; and it belongs to " *man's*," according to Rule X. (Repeat it.)

ABRIDGED.—*A* is the indefinite article; and it belongs to *man's*, etc.

" *Man's* " is a *noun*, it is a name; *common*, it is a name common to all objects of the same kind; *masculine gender*, it denotes a male; *third person*, it represents an object as spoken of; *singular number*, it means but one ; and in the *possessive case*, it limits the meaning of " *hat*," according to Rule III. (Repeat it.)

" *Hat* " is parsed like " *river*."

ABRIDGED.—*Man's* is a common noun, of the masculine gender, third person, singular number; and in the possessive case, governed by *hat*, according to, etc.

ANALYSIS.—*A man's hat* is a phrase. The principal word is *hat*, modified by *man's*, showing what hat; and *man's* is modified by *A*, showing that no particular man is meant.

In like manner parse the following phrases :—

A neighbor's farm.   The boy's book.
An Indian's hatchet.   The boys' books.
The sun's splendor.   Women's fancies.

Adjectives.

Formula.—An *adjective*, and why; *descriptive, definitive,* and why; whether compared or not, and how ; the *degree*, and why ; to what it belongs, and according to what Rule.

* It is not necessary, in parsing, to repeat more of a Rule than the example requires.

PARSING.

"A beautiful morning, with a refreshing breeze."

"*Beautiful*" is an *adjective*,—a word used to qualify or limit the meaning of a noun ; *descriptive*, it describes or qualifies the morning ; *compared* pos. *beautiful*, comp. *more beautiful*, superl. *most beautiful ;* in the *positive degree*, it expresses the quality simply ; and it belongs to "*morning*," according to Rule X. (Repeat it.)

ABRIDGED.—*Beautiful* is a descriptive adjective, in the positive degree (pos. *beautiful*, comp. *more beautiful*, superl. *most beautiful*) ; and it belongs to *morning*.

"*Refreshing*" is an adjective,—a word, etc. * * * *participial*, it ascribes the act to its subject as a quality ; and it belongs to "*breeze*," according to Rule X.

ABRIDGED.—*Refreshing* is a participial adjective, from the verb *refresh ;* and it belongs to *breeze*, according to Rule X. (Repeat it.)

ANALYSIS.—*A beautiful morning, with a refreshing breeze*, is a phrase. (Give definition.) The principal word is *morning*, which is modified by the article *A*, the adjective *beautiful*, and the adjunct *with a refreshing breeze*. *Breeze* is modified by the article *a*, the adjective *refreshing*, and joined to *morning* by the preposition *with*.

Descriptive Adjectives.

A[a] ripe melon.	A whiter rose.	The black-winged redbird.
A dark night.	The fairest lady.	The red-winged blackbird.

Flowery meadows.
Purling streams.
Mahogany[b] furniture.
The best gift.
The worst condition.
A good boy's mother.

A most[o] ingenious story.
The least[o] troublesome servant.
Webster's most[o] eloquent speech.
The obedient and industrious pupil.
A man bold, sensible, sensitive, proud, and[o] ambitious.

"All men."   "Five dollars."

Formula.—An *adjective*, and why ; the *kind*, and why ; to what it belongs, and according to what Rule.

"*All*" is an *adjective*,—a word used to qualify or limit the meaning of a noun; *definitive*, it limits or modifies the meaning of "*men ;*" and it belongs to "*men*," according to Rule X. (Repeat it.)

ABRIDGED.—*All* is a definitive adjective ; and belongs to *men*, according to, etc.

"*Five*" is an adjective,—a word, etc. * * * *numeral*, and of the *cardinal* kind, because it expresses number and shows how many ; and it belongs to "*dollars*," according to Rule X. (Repeat it.)

ABRIDGED.—*Five* is a numeral adjective, of the cardinal kind ; and belongs to *dollars*, according to Rule X.

Definitive Adjectives.

Yonder house.   These trees.   Every fourth man.
This tree.   Each pupil.   Those two benches.
That barn.   Such a person.   The lawyer's own case.

Twelve Spartan virgins, noble, young, and[o] fair,
With[o] violet wreaths adorned[o] their[o] flowing hair.—*Dryden.*

(a.) "*A*" shows that no particular "ripe melon" is meant. (b.) Say, in stead of comparison, "It can not be compared with propriety." (o.) To be omitted in parsing.

Nouns.

Formula.—A *noun*, and why ; $\left.{proper, \atop common,}\right\}$ and why ; *collective*, and why ; *gender*, and why · *person*, and why ; *number*, and why ; (declension ;) *case*, and Rule.

"Snow is falling."

"*Snow*" is a *noun*, it is a name ; *common*, it is the common name of a substance; *neuter gender*, it denotes neither male nor female; *third person*, it represents an object as spoken of; *singular number*, it means but one; and in the *nominative case*—it is the subject of the verb *is falling*—according to Rule I. (Repeat it.)

ABRIDGED*.—*Snow* is a common noun, of the neuter gender, third person, singular number; and in the nominative case. to *is falling*, according to Rule I.

ANALYSIS.—*Snow is falling*, is a simple declarative sentence. *Snow* is the subject, and *is falling* is the predicate.

Parse the articles, the adjectives, and the nouns:—

David slew Goliath[a].
Cattle eat grass.
In golden ringlets[b].
Edward Everett's[c] orations.
Allen's[d] and Brown's store.
Allen and Brown's store.

Jones[e] the saddler's[f] wife.
The Duke of Wellington's[g] forces.
Mr. Smith taught Ida[a] music[a].
Give John[h] the book.
James the coachman[i] is sick.
George is a gentleman[j].

Alice[k], bring your books, slate, and paper.
The boy[l]—O! where was he?
My mother[m] being sick, I remained at home.
The canal is 4 feet[n] deep, and 36 feet wide.
To advance[r] was now utterly impossible.
Thou shalt not steal[s], is the eighth commandment.

(a.) "*Goliath*" is a noun, it is a name; *proper*, it is the name of a particular person, to distinguish him from other persons, etc. * * * and in the objective case—it is the object of the verb "*slew*"—according to Rule IV. (b.) "*Ringlets*" is a noun, etc. * * * and in the *objective* case—it is the object of the preposition *In*—according to Rule V. (c.) "*Edward Everett's*" is a proper noun. (d.)—and in the possessive case—it limits the meaning of *store*, understood—according to Rule III. (e.)—and in the *possessive case*—it limits the meaning of "*wife*," by showing whose wife she is—according to Rule III. (f.)—and in the *possessive* case, to agree with "*Jones*," according to Rule VII. (g.)—and in the *objective* case—it is the object of the preposition "*of*"—according to Rule V. (h.)—and in the *objective* case—it is the object of the preposition *to*, understood—according to Rule V. (i.)—and in the *nominative* case, to agree with "*James*," according to Rule VII. (k.)—and in the *nominative* case independent, by direct address, according to Rule II. (l.) Rule II. (m.)—and in the *nominative* case absolute, according to Rule II. (n.)—and in the *objective* case, limiting "*deep*," according to Rule VI. (r.) "*To advance*" is an infinitive, used here as a noun of the n. g., 3d p., s. n.; and in the nominative case to "*was*," according to Rule I. (s.) *Thou shalt not steal*, is a clause, used here as a noun of the neuter gender, 3d p., s. n.; and in the nominative case to *is*, according to Rule I. Now parse each word.

Pronouns.

Formula.—A *pronoun*,—definition; *personal, relative, interrogative,* and why; *gender*, and why; *person*, and why; *number*, and why; (declension;) *case*, and Rule.

"I myself saw John and his brother."

"*I*" is a *pronoun*,—a word that supplies the place of a noun; *personal*, it is one of the pronouns that serve to distinguish the three grammatical persons; of the *common gender*, it may denote either a male or a female; *first person*, it denotes the speaker; *singular number*, it means but one; and in the *nominative case*—it is the subject of the verb "*saw*"—according to Rule I. Nom., *I*; poss., *my* or *mine*, etc.

ABRIDGED.—*I* is a personal pronoun, of the common gender, first person, singular number; and in the nominative case to the verb *saw*, according to Rule I.

"*Myself*" is a *pronoun*,—a word that supplies the place of a noun; *compound*, it is compounded of *my* and *self ; personal*, etc. * * * and in the *nominative case*, to agree with "*I*," according to Rule VII.

ABRIDGED.—*Myself* is a compound personal pronoun, of the common gender, etc.

"*His*" is a *pronoun*,—a word used in stead of a noun; *personal*, it is one of

* Parsing is usually abridged, by simply omitting the reasons.

the pronouns that serve to distinguish the three grammatical persons; of the *masculine gender, third person,* and *singular number,* to agree with "*John,*" according to Rule IX; (repeat it;) nom. *he,* poss. *his;* and in the *possessive case*—it limits the meaning of "*brother*"—according to Rule III. (Repeat it.)

ABRIDGED.—*His* is a personal pronoun, of the masculine gender, 3d pers., s. n., to agree with *John,* according to Rule IX; (repeat it;) and in the possessive case, governed by *brother,* according to Rule III.

ANALYSIS.—This is a simple declarative sentence. The entire subject is *I myself; I* is the subject-nominative, which is modified by the emphatic appositive *myself. Saw John and his brother,* is the entire predicate; *saw* is the predicate-verb, which is modified by the objects *John* and *brother,* which are connected by *and,* and the latter of which is modified by *his.* (For Analysis, henceforth, see pp. 64–7.)

Parse the articles, the adjectives, the nouns, and the pronouns :—
Personal Pronouns.

We caught him.*
Albert dressed himself⁹ & ⁴.
With me⁹.
Thou² majestic Ocean⁷.
Art thou¹ the man⁷ ?

Martha and Mary have recited ⁹their² lessons.
A dutiful son is the delight⁷ of his parents.
John, ⁹you¹ are wanted.

* In these and all future parsing lessons, a number placed over a word, indicates the Rule to be applied to it; and a caret (∧) shows where words are to be supplied.

"Read thy doom in the flowers, which fade and die."

"*Which*" is a *pronoun,*—a word that supplies the place of a noun; *relative,* its clause relates to and describes a preceding word, and is dependent; of the *neuter gender, third person,* and *plural number,* to agree with "*flowers,*" according to Rule IX; (repeat it;) and in the *nominative case*—it is the subject of the verbs "*fade*" and "*die*"—according to Rule I.

ABRIDGED.—*Which* is a relative pronoun, of the neuter gender, third person, and singular number, to agree with *flowers,* according to Rule IX; and in the nominative case to the verbs *fade* and *die,* according to Rule I.

"James reads what pleases him."

"*What*" is a *pronoun,*—a word that supplies the place of a noun; *relative,* it makes its clause dependent on another; of the *neuter gender,* it denotes neither a male nor a female; *third person,* it represents an object as spoken of; *singular number,* it means but one; and it is here used as the object of "*reads*" and the subject of "*pleases,*"—because it takes the place of *that which* or *thing which,*—according to Rule VIII. (Repeat it.)

ABRIDGED.—*What* is a relative pronoun, of the neuter gender, third person, singular number; and it is here used as the object of *reads,* etc.

"Nature deigns to bless whatever man will use her gifts aright."

"*Whatever*" is an *adjective,*—a word that qualifies or limits the meaning of a substantive; *definitive,* it limits or modifies the meaning of "*man;*" and it belongs to "*man,*" according to Rule X.

"*Man*" is a *noun,* it is a name; *common,* it is a generic name, etc. * * * and it is used here as the object of "*to bless*" and the subject of "*will use,*"—because the phrase *whatever man* takes the place of *any* or *every man that,*—according to Rule VIII.

ABRIDGED.—*Man* is a common noun, of the m. g., 3d p., s. n.; and it is here used as the object, etc.

"I do not know what he is doing."

"*What he is doing,*" is a clause used in the sense of a noun, of the neuter gender, third person, singular number; and in the objective case—it is the object of "*do know*"—according to Rule IV.

"*What*" is a *pronoun,*—a word that supplies the place of a noun; *relative,* it makes its clause dependent on another; *responsive,* it is used as if in answer to a question; of the *neuter gender*, it denotes neither a male nor a female; *third person*, it represents an object as spoken of; *singular number*, it means but one; and in the *objective case*—it is the object of the verb "*is doing*"—according to Rule IV.

ABRIDGED.— *What* is a responsive relative pronoun, of the n. g., 3d p., s. n.; and in the objective case, governed by *is doing*, according to Rule IV.

Relative Pronouns.

I saw your brother[4], who[9 & 1] was well.
She [9]who[1] studies her[2] glass, neglects her heart.
He was such a talker [9]as[1 a] could delight us all[10].

It was I[7] [9]that[1 b] went.
What[8] costs nothing, is worth[10] nothing[6].
Take whatever[8] you like.
We shall leave what is useless.
I am his[3] [9]who[1 c] created me.

(*a*.)—"was such a talker as"—was a talker *that*, or *who*—. (*b*.) *That*—*who*; hence a *relative* pronoun. (*c*.) That is,—"*his property*, who created me;" or, "the property of *him who*," etc.

"Whom did you see?"

"*W h o m*" is a *pronoun*,—a word that takes the place of a noun; *interrogative*, it is used to ask a question; of the *common gender*, it may denote either a male or a female; *third person*, it represents an object as spoken of; *singular number*, it means but one; and in the *objective case*—it is the object of the verb "*did see*"—according to Rule IV.

ABRIDGED.— *Whom* is an interrogative pronoun, of the common gender, third person, singular number; and in the objective case, governed by *did see*, etc.

"The Gaul offered his own head to whoever should bring him that of Nero." "The old bird feeds her young ones." "These horses I received for the others."

"*W h o e v e r*" is a *pronoun*,—a word that supplies the place of a noun; *compound*, it is compounded of *who* and *ever* ; *relative*, it makes its clause dependent on another; of the *common gender, third person, singular number*, to agree with "*person*," or "*any person*,"—understood before it,—according to Rule IX; and in the *nominative case*—it is the subject of the verb "*should give*"—according to Rule I.

ABRIDGED.— *Whoever* is a compound relative pron., of the c. g., 3d p., s. n., etc.

"*T h a t*" is a *pronoun*,—a word that supplies the place of a noun; it is here used in place of "*the head*," and is therefore of the *neuter gender, third person, singular number* ; and in the *objective case*—being the object of the verb "*should bring*"—according to Rule IV. ("*Ones*" and "*others*" are parsed in a similar way.)

ABRIDGED.— *That* is a demonstrative pronoun, used here in place of the phrase *the head*, and is therefore of the n. g., 3d p., s. n.; and in the objective case, governed by *should bring*, etc.

Interrogative Pronouns.

[a]Who[7] was Blennerhasset[1] ?
[b]Who[1] is my neighbor[7] ?

Who[1] can tell what[7] democracy[1] is ?

Miscellaneous Examples.

Your horse trots well, but mine[c] paces. Others may be wiser, but none[1] are more amiable, than she is. Whoever[8] gives to the poor, lends to the Lord. From their love of each other[d].

I hope[e] what[8] I say will have an effect upon him, and prevent the impression which[4] what[8] he says may have upon others.

(*a*.) "Who was Blennerhasset?"—Blennerhasset was who? (*b*.) To apply Rule VII to "*who*," would give a different meaning to the sentence. (*c*.) Say, "*Mine*" is here used for "*my horse*." *My* is a pronoun, etc. (Parse the two words as usual.) (*d*.) "*Each other*" is a *pronoun*,—a word that supplies the place of a noun ; *compound*, it consists of two words ; of the com. gen., etc. (*e*.) "*Hope*" has the entire member after it as its object. (Hope what?)

Verbs.

Finite Verbs.

Formula.—A *verb*, and why; *principal parts;* regular, irregular, } and why; *transitive*, with *voice*, *intransitive* or *neuter*, } and why; the *mood*, and why; the *tense*, and why,—with *form* (emphatic or progressive), and why; (conjugation;) the *person* and *number*, to agree with its subject ———, according to Rule XI.

"My father is ploughing the field which was bought last year."

"*Is ploughing*" is a *verb*,—a word used to affirm something of a subject; *principal parts*,—pres. *plough*, past *ploughed*, perf. part. *ploughed* ; *regular*, it assumes the ending *ed ; transitive*, it has an object (*field*),—and in the *active voice*, because it represents its subject as acting ; *indicative mood*, it affirms something as an actual occurrence or fact ; *present tense*, it expresses the act in present time,—and progressive form, it represents it as continuing; (singular number—first person, I *am ploughing ;* 2d p., You *are ploughing ;* 3d p., He, or my father, *is ploughing ;*) and in the *third person* and *singular number*, to agree with its subject *father*, according to Rule XI. (Repeat it.)

ABRIDGED.—*Is ploughing* is a regular transitive verb, from the verb *plough;* (principal parts,—pres. *plough*, past *ploughed*, perf. part. *ploughed ;*) in the indicative mood, present tense, progressive form ; and in the third person and singular number, to agree with its subject *father*, according to Rule XI.

"*Was bought*" is a verb,—a word used to affirm something of a subject; *principal parts*,—pres. *buy*, past *bought*, perf. part. *bought; irregular*, it does not assume the ending *ed ; transitive*, but in the *passive voice*, because it affirms the act of the object acted upon ; *indicative mood*, it asserts something as an actual occurrence or fact ; *past tense*, it refers the act simply to past time ; *third person* and *singular number*, to agree with its subject *which*, according to Rule XI.

ABRIDGED.— *Was bought* is an irr. pass. verb, from the verb *buy ;* (principal parts,—pres. *buy*, past *bought*, perf. part. *bought ;* in the ind. m., past t., and c. f. ; and in the 3d p., s. n., to agree, etc.

Parse the articles, adjectives, nouns, pronouns, and verbs :—

Regular Verbs.
Columbus discovered America.
John regretted his loss.
Fortune worries men.

Irregular Verbs.
They struck me.
Birds fly. It was I[7].
Joseph has lost his hat.

Transitive Verbs.
Horses eat corn.
The Indians shunned us.
We armed ourselves.

Voices.
She broke the pitcher.
The pitcher is broken.
They named her[4] Mary[7].
She was named Mary[7].

Intransitive Verbs.
Bright leaves quivered.
Rivers flow, and winds blow.
John will become rich.
Horace struts a dandy[7].

Neuter Verbs.
The rose is beautiful.
Fierce was the conflict.
The house stands firm[10].

Moods.
Robert sold his horse.
Did you see him ?
Were he rich, he would be lazy.
Every living creature must die.
Can you spell "*phthisic*" ?
Be sincere. (Be thou sincere.)
Man is made to mourn.

PARSING.

Tenses.

The distant hills look blue.
The soldiers will be attacked.
Your coat will have been finished.
You must write a composition.
We should love our neighbors.
The apples might have been eaten.
The lady may have been handsome.
Had I but known it.
Do you venture a small fish, to catch a great one.

Forms.

The tall pines are rustling.
I do protest against it.
Thou hast a heart of adamant.

Persons and Numbers.

Reckless youth makes rueful age.
How are the mighty[c] fallen!
Time and tide wait for no man.
Monday or Tuesday was[b] the day.
Neither labor nor money was spared.
Yonder lives a hero and patriot.
His family is large.
The multitude pursue pleasure.
Every house has a garden.
You or he is in fault.
You, he, and I, are invited.
I say, be your own friend.
To scorn meanness, is heroic.
That weak men should seek strength in cunning, is natural.

(*a.*) Say,—" and in the third person, plural number, to agree with *Time* and *tide*, a plural subject, according to Rule XI." (*b.*) Say,—" and in the 3d p., s. n., to agree with *Monday* or *Tuesday*, a singular subject, according to," etc (*c.*) Supply *men*, or parse *mighty* as a noun.

Participles and Infinitives.

Formula.—A *participle*,
An *infinitive*, } and why ; *transitive*, with *voice*,
intransitive or *neuter*, } and why ;
present,
perfect, } and why ; with *form*, and why ; to what it relates, and according to what Rule.

In parsing a present participle, omit *form* ; and in general omit of the Formulas whatever is not applicable.

"The traveler, having been robbed, was obliged to sell his horse."

"*Having been robbed*" is a *participle*,—a form of the verb, that merely assumes the act or state, and is generally construed like an adjective ; *compound*, it consists of three simple participles ; *passive*, it represents its subject as acted upon ; *perfect* in sense, it expresses the act or state as past and finished at the time referred to ; and it relates to "*traveler*," according to Rule XII. (Repeat it.)

ABRIDGED.—*Having been robbed* is a compound, passive, perfect participle, from the verb *rob, robbed, robbed ;* and it relates to *traveler*, according to Rule XII.

"*To sell*" is an *infinitive*,—a form of the verb that begins usually with *to*, and expresses no affirmation ; *transitive*, it has an object ; *active voice*, it represents its subject as doing something ; *present*, it denotes the act simply ; and it relates to "*traveler*," and completes the sense of "*was obliged*," according to Rule XII.

ABRIDGED.—*To sell* is a transitive, active, present infinitive, from the verb *sell, sold, sold ;* and it relates to *traveler* as its subject, and limits *was obliged*, showing as to what, according to Rule XII.

"To betray is base."   "I insist on writing the letter."

"*To betray*" is an *intransitive, active, present infinitive*, from the verb *betray, betrayed, betrayed*. It is here used also as a noun of the *neuter gender, third person, singular number ;* and in the *nominative case*—being the subject of the verb *is*—according to Rule I.

"*Writing*" is a *transitive, active, present participle*, from the verb *write, wrote, written*. It is here used also as a noun of the *neuter gender, third person, singular number ;* and in the *objective case*—being the object of the preposition *on* —according to Rule V.

"It affords us pleasure to have seen the rising sun attended by so many beautiful clouds."

"*To have seen*" is a *transitive, active, perfect infinitive*, from the verb *see*, *saw, seen.* It is here used also as a noun of the *neuter gender, third person, singular number;* and in the *nominative case,* to agree with "*It,*" according to Rule VII.

"*Rising*" is an *adjective,*—a word used to qualify or limit the meaning of a substantive ; *participial,* it is a participle—from the verb *rise, rose, risen*—ascribing the act or state to its subject as a quality; and it belongs to "*sun,*" according to Rule X.

"*Attended*" is a *participle,*—a form of the verb, that merely assumes the act or state, and is generally construed like an adjective; *passive,* it represents its subject as acted upon ; *perfect* in form, but present in sense, for it represents the act or state as present and continuing at the time referred to; and it relates to "*sun,*" according to Rule XII.

ABRIDGED.—*Attended* is a passive participle, from the regular verb *attend, attended, attended;* it is perfect in form but present in sense, and relates to, etc.

☞ The second Rule for participles and infinitives, which is given on page 71, can be applied to all the foregoing and all the following participles and infinitives.

Parse all except the adverbs, prepositions, conjunctions, and interjections:—

Participles.

The Indians fled, leaving their mules tied to the bushes. Singing thou dost soar, and soaring ever singest. The war' being ended, prosperity revived. Time and thinking tame the strongest grief. - Of making many books, there is no end.

Infinitives.

And fools, who came to scoff, remained to pray. We are never too old to learn. Here was an opportunity to grow[a] rich. I ordered him[b] to be brought. She is wiser than to believe it. I ought to have written. To err[1] is human ; to forgive, divine. I forgot to mention[4] it. It is knowledge enough for some people, to know[7] how far they can proceed in mischief with impunity.

Miscellaneous Examples.

Let[d] Love have[d] eyes, and Beauty will have ears.

It had been[e] useless, had he done[e] it.

Accordingly, a company assembled[11] armed[12] and accoutred[12], and, having procured[12] a field-piece, appointed[11] Major Harrison commander[7], and proceeded[11] to accomplish[12] their design.

(*a.*) That is,—"an opportunity *for him* or *any one* to grow rich." (*b.*) Logically, the phrase, "*him to be brought,*" is the object of "*ordered ;*" grammatically, *him* is the object. (*c.*) "*How far they can proceed,*" etc., is the object of "*know.*" See p. 51. (*d.*) Supply *you* or *thou,* and *to. Do you let,* etc. See p. 28. (*e.*) Subjunctive mood. See p. 17 or 201.

Adverbs.

Formula.—An *adverb,* and why ; if it can be *compared,* say so, and how; of *what kind ;* to what it belongs, and according to what Rule or Note.

"The trees are waving beautifully."

"*Beautifully*" is an *adverb,* it modifies the meaning of a verb ("are waving") ; it can be compared,—pos. *beautifully,* comp. *more beautifully,* superl. *most beautifully ;* it is an adverb of manner or quality ; and it belongs to the verb "*are waving,*" according to Rule XIII. (Repeat of the Rule as much as is applicable.)

ABRIDGED.—*Beautifully* is an adverb of manner, can be compared, modifies the verb *are waving,* and belongs to it according to Rule XIII.

"Gather roses while they bloom."

"*While*" is an *adverb,*—a word used to modify the meaning of a verb, an adjective, or an adverb ; it is a *conjunctive* adverb of time; and it belongs to both the verb "*gather*" and the verb "*bloom,*" according to Rule XIII. Or say,—

"*While*" is an *adverb*,—a word used to modify the meaning of a verb, an adjective, or an adverb; *conjunctive*, it connects its own clause to another to express the time, according to Note XIII.

ABRIDGED.— *While* is a conjunctive adverb of time, modifying the verbs *gather* and *bloom*, and belonging to them according to Rule XIII. Or say,— *While* is a conjunctive adverb of time, that joins a dependent clause to another clause adverbially, or to express the time, according to Note XIII.

"Can not you go too?"

"*Not*" is an *adverb*,—a word used to modify the meaning of a verb, an adjective, or an adverb; it is an adverb of negation; and it modifies the verb "*can go*" with reference to "*you*," and therefore belongs to them, according to Rule XIII.

ABRIDGED.—*Not* is a negative adverb, modifying the verb *can go* with reference to its subject *you*, and therefore belonging to them, according to Rule XIII.

Parse the articles, adjectives, nouns, pronouns, verbs, and adverbs :—

1. *Adverbs Modifying Verbs.*

The horse galloped gracefully.
The birds sung sweetly.
Mary sews and knits well.
Our roses must soon fade.
Lofty mountains successively appear.
Here will I stand.

2. *Adverbs Modifying Adjectives.*

Her child was very young.
The music rose softly sweet.
John is most studious.
He is perfectly honest.
My hat is almost new.
The wound was intensely painful.

3. *Adverbs Modifying Adverbs.*

Some horses can run very fast.
He stutters nearly always.
You must come very soon.
Thomas is not very industrious.
The field is not entirely planted.
She had been writing very carefully.

4. *Miscellaneous Examples.*

Smack went the whip, round went the wheels. Flowers come forth early. Sadly and slowly we laid him down.[13] We carved not[a] a line, we raised not a stone. He lay like a warrior[b] taking his rest. Even[c] from the tomb the voice of nature cries. These scenes, once so[d] delightful, no longer please him. As[e] you sow, so[e] you shall reap. When will you come? The dew glitters when the sun rises.

(*a.*) "*Not*" limits the meaning of "*carved*" in respect to "*a line.*" (*b.*) Or Rule VI. (*c.*) "*Even*" modifies the adverbial adjunct "*from the tomb;*" or, rather, it modifies the verb "*cries,*" with reference to the phrase "*from the tomb.*" Adjuncts— adverbs or adjectives; hence adverbs can modify them, and not, as some grammarians teach, the preposition only. (See p. 30.) (*d.*) Degree. (*e.*) Manner.

Prepositions.

Formula.—A *preposition*,—definition; between what it shows the relation; Rule.

"The water flows over the dam."

"*Over*" is a *preposition*,—a word used to govern a noun or pronoun, and show its relation to some other word; it here shows the relation of "*flows*" to "*dam*," according to Rule XIV. (Repeat it.)

ABRIDGED.—*Over* is a preposition, showing the relation between *flows* and *dam*, according to Rule XIV.

Parse all the words except the conjunctions :—

I found a dollar in the road. In spring, the leaves come forth. We should not live beyond our means. He struggled, like a hero, against the evils of fortune. An eagle rose near *the city, and flew over it far away beyond the distant hills. We went from New York to Washington City, by railroad, in eight hours. As to the policy of the measure, I shall say nothing. The river is washing the soil from under the tree. I caught a turtle in stead of a fish.

Conjunctions.

Formula.—A *conjunction*, and why; its peculiar nature; what it connects; Rule.

"The meadow produces grass and flowers."

"*A n d*" is a *conjunction*,—a word used to connect other words, and show the sense in which they are connected; it implies simply continuance, or that something more is added; and it connects the words *grass* and *flowers*, according to Rule XV.

ABRIDGED.—*And* is a copulative conjunction, connecting *grass* and *flowers*, according to Rule XV.

"You must either buy mine or sell yours."

"*Either*" is a conjunction, a word, etc. * * * it corresponds to "*or*," and assists it in connecting two phrases according to Rule XV.

"*O r*" is a conjunction, etc. * * * it is *alternative*, or allows but one of the things offered, to the exclusion of the rest; it here corresponds to "*either*," and connects two phrases according to Rule XV.

Parse all the words:—

Words Connected.

Learning refines and elevates the mind. Cultivate your heart and mind. She is amiable, intelligent, and handsome. The silk was light-blue, or sky-colored: it should have been white or black.

Phrases Connected.

Through floods and through forests he bounded away.
Death saw the floweret to the desert given,
Plucked it from earth, and planted it in heaven.

Clauses or Sentences Connected.

Eagles generally go alone, but little birds go in flocks. Italian music's sweet because 'tis dear. If it rain to-morrow, we shall have to remain at home. Whether my brother come or not, I will either buy or rent the farm. Though he is poor, yet he is honest. He was always courteous to wise and gifted men; for he knew that talents, though in poverty, are more glorious than birth or riches [are].

Interjections.

Formula.—An *interjection*, and why; of what kind; Rule.

"Alas! no hope for me remains."

A l a s is an interjection of grief; and it is used independently. Rule XVI.

O, young Lochinvar is come out of the West. Ah! few[10]ₐ shall part where many[10]ₐ meet! O Desdemona[2]! Desdemona! dead? Dead! Oh! oh! oh! (Supply *art thou* and *thou art*.)

14. ANALYSIS OF SENTENCES.

Discourse is a general word denoting either *prose* or *poetry.*
Discourse is composed of propositions.
A *proposition* consists of a subject combined with its predicate.
The *subject* denotes that of which something is affirmed.
The *predicate* denotes what is affirmed.

Discourse may be divided into paragraphs.
Paragraphs are composed of sentences.
A *sentence** is a thought expressed by words.
Sentences are either *simple* or *compound.*
A *simple sentence* contains but one proposition.

A sentence may still be called *simple*, when its nominative is a proposition; but not so when it contains a subordinate proposition in any other relation. Some grammarians supply words so as to make with each finite verb a proposition or simple sentence; but, whenever we can conveniently do so, it is best to regard a series of finite verbs as but one predicate. See pp. 68, 85.

A *compound sentence* contains two or more propositions, or simple sentences. If one of the propositions modifies another, the sentence is, by some grammarians, called *complex.* See p. 68.

A *clause* is any one of two or more propositions which together make a sentence.

Exercises.

Tell whether the sentences are simple or compound, and why; mention the propositions or clauses, and why; mention the subjects and the predicates, and why; and whether simple or compound, and why:—

The flowers are gemmed with dew. The maple on the hill-side has lost its bright green, and its leaves have the hue of gold. As you come near, they spring up, fly a little distance, and light again. Suspicion ever haunts the guilty mind. Hard things become easy by use; and skill is gained by little and little. The weight of years has bent him, and the winter of age rests upon his head. He touched his harp, and nations heard entranced. The union is the vital sap of the tree; if we reject the Constitution, we girdle the tree; its leaves will wither, its branches drop off, and the mouldering trunk will be torn down by the tempest. The good times, when the farmer entertained the traveler without pay; when he invited him to tarry, and join in the chase; when Christmas and Fourth of July were seasons of general festivity,—have passed away. "Thy worldly hopes," said the hermit, "shall have faded, thy castles of ambition crumbled, and thy fiery passions subdued, ere thou hast reached the meridian of life." Read this Declaration at the head of the army, —every sword will be drawn from its scabbard, and the solemn vow uttered, to maintain it, or to perish on the bed of honor. (Construe both the infinitive phrases with each of the two clauses just before them in the same member.) What

---

* A *sentence* is merely so much of discourse as makes a complete thought in the view of the person uttering it; a *proposition* is a single combination of such words as make a predication, judgment, or thought; and a *phrase* is merely two or more words rightly put together for thought, without expressing a predication.

costs nothing, is worth nothing. That he must fail, is certain. 'Tis liberty alone that gives the flowers of fleeting life their lustre and perfume. Go, and assist him, that the work may be finished. He who is false to God, is not true to man. Though thy slumbers may be deep, yet thy spirit shall not sleep; there are shades that will not vanish, there are thoughts thou canst not banish. To dress, to visit, to gossip, and to thrum her piano, are the chief employments of the modern belle.

Every proposition is either *declarative, interrogative, imperative*, or *exclamatory*. Every sentence is the same, or a composite of these.

A *declarative* proposition expresses a declaration; an *interrogative* proposition, a question; an *imperative* proposition, a command; and an *exclamatory* proposition, an exclamation.

Ex.—"John rides that wild horse." "Does John ride that wild horse?" "John, ride that wild horse." "John rides that wild horse!" An *exclamatory* sentence is merely a declarative, an interrogative, or an imperative sentence, uttered chiefly to express the emotion of the speaker.

Exercises.

The propositions; and whether declarative, interrogative, imperative, or exclamatory, and why:—

A waving willow was bending over the fountain. Rise, and defend thyself. Shall I assist you? How beautiful is yonder sunset! If James has a hundred marbles, why does he never show us any of them? Men may, I find, be honest, though they differ. Now Twilight lets her curtain down, and pins it with a star. Green be the turf above thee, friend of my better days. What shall I say? What a piece of work is man! She is busy in the garden, among the posies. The spreading orange waves a load of gold. Hear him! hear him! There can be no study without time; and the mind must abide, and dwell upon things, or be always a stranger to the inside of them. The fly sat upon the axle-tree of the chariot-wheel, and said, "What a dust do I raise!"

Every proposition is either *independent* or *dependent*.

An *independent* proposition makes complete sense by itself.

A *dependent* proposition depends on another for complete sense.

The clause of a complex sentence on which the other clauses depend, is often called the *principal* or *leading clause;* its subject and predicate, the *principal* or *leading subject* and *predicate;* and the dependent clauses, *subordinate clauses.*

Exercises.

The propositions; and whether independent or dependent, and why:—

The morning dawns, and the clouds disperse. The dew glistens, when the sun rises. I would not enter, on my list of friends, the man who needlessly sets foot upon a worm. Stillest streams oft water fairest meadows; and the bird that flutters least, is longest on the wing. The path of sorrow leads to the land where sorrow is unknown. If the mind be curbed and humbled too much in children,—if their spirits be abased and broken much by too strict a hand over them,—they lose all their vigor and industry. Come ye in peace here, or come ye in war? In one place we saw a gang of sixty-five horses; but the buffaloes seemed absolutely to cover the ground. "Come," says Puss, "without any more ado; 'tis time to go to breakfast: cats don't live upon dialogues."

Every proposition may be divided into the *entire subject* and the *entire predicate.*

The *entire subject* must have one or more *subject-nominatives* to the same verb or verbs.

The *entire predicate* must have one or more *finite verbs* agreeing with the same subject, which may be called the *predicate-verbs.*

Hence both subjects and predicates are either *simple* or *compound.*

The subject-nominative may be a *word*, a *phrase*, or an *entire clause;* the predicate-verb is simply a *verb*, or a principal verb with its auxiliaries.

Most grammarians call the entire subject the *logical subject;* the entire predicate, the *logical predicate;* the subject-nominative, the *grammatical subject;* and the predicate-verb, the *grammatical predicate.* This mode of naming is not so simple as the one we have given.

Exercises.

The propositions; the entire subjects, and then the subject-nominatives; the entire predicates, and then the predicate-verbs:—

Men work. Most men work daily. The leaves rustle. The leaves rustle in the passing breeze. Leaves and flowers must perish. Flowers bloom and fade. Leaves and flowers flourish and decay. Poplars and alders ever quivering played, and nodding cypress formed a fragrant shade. In youth alone, unhappy mortals live; but, ah! the mighty gift is fugitive. The same errors run through all families in which there is wealth enough to afford that their sons may be good for nothing. Depart. In concert act, like modern friends, since one can serve the other's ends. That it is our duty to be kind and obliging, admits of no doubt. The division and quavering which please so much in music, have a resemblance to the glittering of light, as when the moonbeams play upon the water. It is often the fault of parents, guardians, and teachers, that so many persons miscarry. (Here either "It" or the clause "that so many," etc., may be considered the subject of "is," and the other term may be parsed as agreeing with the subject in case.) It is hardly practicable for the human mind to obtain a clear and familiar knowledge of an art, without illustrations and exemplifications. Ah me! the blooming pride of May, and that of beauty, are but one.

The parts into which sentences are divided in analysis, are called *elements.* Subject-nominatives and predicate-verbs are the *principal elements;* and they may be modified by *words, phrases,* or *clauses.*

A part that *modifies* another, adds something to its meaning, or takes away something.

What modifies, is either explanatory or restrictive.

Ex.—" The town lay at the foot of a hill, *which we climbed.*" "The town lay at the foot of the hill *which we climbed.*"

Whatever modifies a substantive, is an *adjective element.*

Ex.—"*Solomon's* Temple." What temple? "David, the *king* and *psalmist.*" What David? "The land *of palms.*" What land? "A hill *crowned with majestic trees.*" What kind of hill? "A proposition *to sell the farm.*" What proposition? "The store *which is on the corner.*" What store? "A request *that you will go with us.*" What kind of request?

What modifies, may itself be modified.

ANALYSIS OF SENTENCES.

A NOUN may be modified—
1. By an *article*. "The MAN is intelligent."
2. By an *adjective*. "A *beautiful* ROSE;" "A ROSE, *red* and *beautiful*."
3. By a *possessive*. "*John's* HORSE;" "*My* SLATE."
4. By an *appos'itive*. "JOHN *the saddler*;" "The POET *Milton*."
5. By a *participle*, with what belongs to it. "A LAW *relating to taxes*."
6. By an *infinitive*, with what belongs to it. "A PATH *to guide us*."
7. By an *adjunct*. "A MAN *of wisdom*."
8. By a *clause*. "The WILLOW *which stands by the spring*;" "A REQUEST *that you will go with us to-morrow*."

A PRONOUN may be modified in the same ways, except not by a *possessive*.

A modified word has frequently several modifications at once.

Exercises.

The nouns and pronouns, and by what they are modified:—
A dewy rose. The land of oranges. Lurking evils. Evils lurking near. Evils that lurk near. A house situated on the river. An opportunity to study. The sun's beams. Milton the poet. The deer which ran out of the field, and which I shot. A bright morning, fresh and balmy, that refreshed us all. The calumet was produced, and the two forlorn powers smoked eternal friendship between themselves, and vengeance upon their common spoilers, the Crows. The silence of the night; the calmness of the sea; the lambent radiance of the moon, trembling on the surface of the waves; and the deep azure of the sky, spangled with a thousand stars,—concurred to heighten the beauty of the scene. With loss of Eden, till one greater man restore us, and regain the blissful seat. Numerous small lakes lie inland, round which, on beaten trails, roam herds of red deer. Sweet day, so cool, so calm, so bright, the bridal of the earth and sky.

Whatever modifies a verb, an adjective, or an adverb, or may be given in answer to an interrogative adverb, or as the complement of a predicate, is an *adverbial element*.

Ex.—"The house was sold *yesterday*." When? "The house contains *much furniture*." Contains what? "The house was a *mere cabin*." Was what? "The house fell, *crushing its inmates*." Fell how? "The house was sold *to pay the owner's debts*." Why? "The house was sold *because the owner was in debt*." Why?

A modified verb may be a finite verb, a participle, or an infinitive.

A VERB may be modified—
1. By an *objective*. "Men BUILD *houses*." "I KNEW *it* TO BE *him*."
2. By a *predicate-nominative*. "John HAS BECOME *a farmer*."
3. By an *adjective*. "To BE *wise*;" "James IS *idle*."*
4. By an *adverb*. "The horse RAN *fast*."
5. By a *participle+*. "The stone ROLLED *thundering down the hill*."
6. By an *infinitive+*. "I HAVE CONCLUDED *to remain with you*."

* Owing to a slight radical difference in the modes of classifying, there is sometimes an apparent incongruity between Parsing and Analysis. Thus, in parsing, *idle* is referred to *James*, because *James* denotes the object to which the quality belongs; but, in analyzing, it is referred to *is*, because it makes with *is* the predicate.

7. By an *adjunct.* "Apples GROW *on trees.*"
8. By a *clause.* "She THINKS *he is rich;*" "He STUDIES *that he may learn.*"

Exercises.

The verbs, and by what modified:—

A light beaming brightly. He writes with ease. Cast not pearls before swine. He became a partner. She is industrious. I intend to go. I believe he will succeed when he makes a vigorous effort. Among the flowering vines is one deserving of particular notice. Each flower is composed of six leaves about three inches in length, of beautiful crimson, the inside spotted with white. Its leaves of fine green are oval, and disposed by threes. This plant grows upon the trees without attaching itself to them. When it has reached the topmost branches, it descends perpendicularly, and, as it continues to grow, extends from tree to tree, until its various stalks interlace the grove like the rigging of a ship. Nature from the storm shines out afresh. Not even a philosopher can endure the toothache patiently. There never yet were hearts or skies, clouds might not wander through. Chaucer said, "If a man's soul is in his pocket, he should be punished there."

An ADJECTIVE may be modified—

1. By an *adverb.* "She is *foolishly* PROUD."
2. By an *infinitive.* "The fruit is GOOD *to eat.*"
3. By an *adjunct.* "He is CAREFUL *of his books.*"

Exercises.

The adjectives, and by what modified:—

She was uncommonly beautiful. He is poor in money, but rich in knowledge. Be quick to hear, but slow to speak. The visions of my youth are past—too bright, too beautiful to last. How dear to my heart are the scenes of my childhood! That father, faint in death below, his voice no longer heard. Wise in council and brave in war, he soon became the most successful leader.

An ADVERB may be modified—

1. By an *adverb.* "The horse ran *very* FAST."
2. By an *adjunct.* "He has acted INCONSISTENTLY *with his professions.*"

Exercises.

The adverbs, and by what modified:—

It is very badly done. She studies most diligently. You can not come too soon. He has written agreeably to your directions.

When a dependent clause is abridged into a phrase, having a nominative absolute, the phrase retains the modifying sense of the clause.

Some grammarians call such also independent phrases, though perhaps needlessly.

Exercises.
The absolute phrases, and what they modify:—

My trunk being packed, I sent for a carriage. (Sent why or when?) The sun having set, we returned home. His father having been imprisoned, he went to rescue him. Along he sauntered, his musing fancies absorbing his whole soul.

Nominatives independent, or the phrases containing them, and interjections, are *independent elements.*

Exercises
Point out the independent words or phrases:—

O Liberty! can man resign thee, once having felt thy glorious flame! Weep on the rocks of roaring winds, O maid of Inistore! O Milan! O the golden bells which oft at eve so sweetly tolled! Alas, alas! fair Inès, she's gone into the West. The land of the heart is the land of the West; oho boys! oho boys! oho! Hist, Romeo, hist! My stars! what a fish! Ha, ha, ha! a fine gentleman, truly.

Connecting words are conjunctions, prepositions, relative pronouns, and some adverbs. Sometimes phrases.

Sometimes connectives are omitted, or the connection is sufficiently obvious by the position of the parts.

Exercises,
Point out the connectives, tell of what kind, and what they connect:—

The sun has set, and the moon and stars begin to appear. He took the horse, which was neither his nor mine. When I behold a fashionable table set out, I fancy that gouts, fevers, and lethargies, lie in ambush among the dishes. He that knows not how to suffer, has no greatness of soul. Though deep, yet clear; though gentle, yet not dull. The moment I touched it, down it fell. The deeper the water, the smoother it flows. (Connected by the correlative sense of the clauses.) To be happy is not only to be free from the pains and diseases of the body, but also from the cares and diseases of the mind.

Who steals my purse, steals trash; 'tis something, nothing;
'Twas mine, 'tis his, and has been slave to thousands:
But he who filches from me my good name,
Robs me of that which not enriches him,
And makes me poor indeed!

Propositions are sometimes *elliptical* or *inverted.*

Exercises,
Point out the elliptical parts, supply the omitted words, and restore the logical arrangement:—

And jokes went round, and careless chat. No mate, no comrade, Lucy knew. Oh, how damp, and dark, and cold! "Then, why don't you go," said I. Pride costs us more than hunger, thirst, and cold. The woman (strange circumstance!) remained obstinately silent. Out of debt, out of danger. On the cool and shady hills, coffee-shrubs and tamarinds grow. Alas for love, if thou wert all, and naught beyond, O earth! Of all the thousand stirs not one. "Sir, I can not.—What, my lord?—Make you a better answer."

Sentences, propositions, and phrases, may be analyzed according to the following

Formulas.

A *sentence*, and why; *simple, complex,* or *compound,* and why; *declarative, interrogative, imperative, exclamatory,* or a composite of, and why.

—— is a phrase;   the chief word
     an independent phrase; the independent substantive is ——, modified by ——.

—— is the entire subject;   the subject-nominative is ——, modified by ——.
                 predicate;   predicate-verb

—— is the entire subject;   the subject-nominatives are——, connected by——, and modified by——.
                 predicate;   predicate-verbs

ANALYSIS EXEMPLIFIED.
Simple Sentences Analyzed.

"Sin degrades."

This is a *sentence*, it is a thought expressed by words; *simple,* it contains but one proposition; *declarative,* it expresses a declaration.

Sin is the subject, because it denotes that of which something is affirmed; and *degrades* is the predicate, because it denotes what is affirmed of sin. *Sin* is also the subject-nominative; and *degrades,* the predicate-verb.

"My friend, were these houses and lands purchased and improved by our old senator, David Barton?"

This is a *sentence*, it is a collection of words making complete sense; *simple,* it contains but one proposition, or but one subject and one predicate; *interrogative,* it asks a question.

My friend is an independent phrase, because it has no grammatical connection with the rest of the sentence. *Friend* is the principal word, and it is modified or limited by the possessive *My.*

The phrase *these houses and lands,* is the subject, because it denotes that of which something is affirmed.

The phrase *were purchased and improved by our old senator, David Barton,* is the predicate, because it denotes what is affirmed of the subject.

Houses and *lands* are the subject-nominatives, connected by the word *and,* and modified by the adjective *these.*

Were purchased and [*were*] *improved* are the predicate-verbs, connected by *and* and modified by the phrase *by our old senator, David Barton. Our old senator* is modified by *David Barton; old senator* is modified or limited by the possessive *our;* and *senator* is modified by *old.*

Or thus: *Was* is the copula; *purchased* and *improved* are the attributes, modified by —— (as before).

Compound Sentences Analyzed.

"A man who saves the fragments of time, will accomplish much in the course of his life."

This is a *sentence*, it is a complete thought expressed by words; *compound,* it contains more propositions than one; (or, *complex,* it contains two propositions, of which one modifies the other;) *declarative,* it expresses a declaration.

A man who saves the fragments of time, is the entire subject of the principal clause, because it denotes that of which something is affirmed; and *will accomplish much in the course of his life,* is the entire predicate, because it denotes what is affirmed of the subject. *Man* is the subject-nominative; and it is modified by the article *A*, and the clause *who saves the fragments of time: will accomplish* is the predicate-verb, and is modified by the object *much* and the adjunct *in the course of his life*.

Who saves the fragments of time, is a proposition connected to *man*, by the relative *who*, as a subordinate clause performing the office of an adjective.

Who is the entire subject and the subject-nominative: *saves the fragments of time*, is the entire predicate; *saves* is the predicate-verb, and is modified by its object *fragments*, which is itself modified by the article *the* and the adjunct *of time*.

"What pleases the palate, is not always good for the constitution."

This is a *sentence*, it is a collection of words making complete sense; *compound*, consisting of two propositions; (or, *complex*, it contains two propositions, of which one modifies the other;) *declarative*, it expresses a declaration.

What is equivalent to *that which*. *What*, or *that which*, *pleases the palate*, is the entire subject of the principal clause; and *is not always good for the constitution*, is the entire predicate. *That* is the subject-nominative, and is modified by the clause *which pleases the palate; is* is the predicate-verb, and is modified by the adjective *good*, which is itself modified by the adjunct *for the constitution* and the adverb *always*, and *always* is modified by the adverb *not*.

Which pleases the palate, is a proposition connected to *that*, by the relative *which*, as a subordinate clause performing the office of an adjective.

Which is the entire subject and the subject-nominative; *pleases the palate*, is the entire predicate; *pleases* is the predicate-verb, modified by the object *palate*, which is itself modified by *the*.

["Who were the robbers of the house, has not yet been ascertained."

This is a *simple* sentence, (or *complex*—see pp. 63 and 71,) having the incorporated clause, *Who were the robbers of the house*, as the entire subject and the subject-nominative. *Has not yet been ascertained*, is the entire predicate, etc.

Who were the robbers of the house, is a subordinate clause incorporated into the sentence as a substantive in the nominative case. *Who* is the entire subject and the subject-nominative, etc.]

"My son, if thou wouldst receive my words, and hide my commandments with thee, so that thou mayst gain wisdom; yea, if thou wouldst seek it as silver, and search for it as hidden treasure,—then live in the fear of the Lord, and find the knowledge of God."

This is a *sentence*, it is a collection of words making complete sense; *compound*, it consists of several propositions; a composite of *declarative*, or *conditional declarative*, and *imperative* clauses, or rather an *imperative* sentence, for its chief aim is to express a command or an exhortation. (Or *complex*.—See p. 68.)

"*My son*,"—

This is an independent phrase, because it has no grammatical connection with the rest of the sentence, etc. (Proceed as before.)

"*If thou wouldst receive my words, and hide my commandments with thee*,"—

ANALYSIS OF SENTENCES.

This is a proposition connected as a dependent clause, by the conjunction *if*, to the last clause of the sentence, etc. (Analyze these clauses in the same way as the clauses and sentences above were analyzed.)

"*So that thou mayst gain wisdom;*"—
This is a clause dependent on the clause preceding it, to which it is connected by *so that*, etc.

"*Yea, if thou wouldst seek it as silver, and search for it as hidden treasure;*"—
This is a clause coördinate with the member preceding it, to which it is connected by the emphatic *yea;* and dependent on the last clause of the sentence, to which it is connected by *if*.

"*As silver,*"—   "*As for hidden treasure;*"—
As silver is put for *as you would seek for silver*, and is therefore a clause connected to the preceding predicate by *as* as a subordinate clause, performing the office of an adverb of manner, etc.

"*Then live in the fear of the Lord, and find the knowledge of God.*"
This is the principal or independent clause, connected by *then* to the rest of the sentence. *Thou*, understood, is the entire subject and the subject-nominative, etc.

NOTE.—Long sentences are generally most easily analyzed, by commencing at the beginning of the sentence, and taking not more than one clause, independent word or phrase, at a time, and proceeding thus until the entire sentence is exhausted. It is generally better to defer dependent clauses, till their principal clauses are analyzed.

"There is strong reason to suspect that some able Whig politicians, who thought it dangerous to relax, at that moment, the laws against political offences, but who could not, without incurring the charge of inconsistency, declare themselves adverse to relaxation, had conceived a hope that they might, by fomenting the dispute about the court of the lord high steward, defer for at least a year the passing of a bill which they disliked, and yet could not decently oppose."—*Macaulay.*

ANALYSIS.—This is a *complex* declarative sentence, or a *compound* declarative sentence, of which some of the clauses are *dependent*. *There is strong reason to suspect*, is the principal clause, of which *strong reason to suspect*, is the entire subject; and *There is*, the entire predicate; *reason* is the subject-nominative, modified by the adjective *strong*, and by the infinitive *to suspect* performing the office of an adjective; *is* is the predicate-verb, modified by *There*.

That some able Whig politicians had conceived a hope, is the next simple declarative clause, performing the office of a noun in the objective case governed by *to suspect*, to which it is connected by *that*. *Some able Whig politicians*, is the entire subject; and *had conceived a hope*, is the entire predicate: *politicians* is the subject-nominative, modified by the adjectives *some*, *able*, and *Whig;* and *had conceived* is the predicate-verb, modified by the object *hope*, which is itself modified by the article *a*.

Who thought it dangerous, etc., (read to *but*,) is a subordinate relative clause, connected to *politicians* by *who*, and performing the office of an adjective. *Who* is the entire subject and subject-nominative; *thought it dangerous*, etc., is the entire predicate, of which *thought* is the predicate-verb, modified by the object *it*, which is modified by *dangerous*, and the appositive *to relax*, etc., of which *to relax* is modified by the adjunct *at that moment*, an adverbial element whose principal word is *moment*, modified by *that*, and connected to the verb by *at*; *to relax* is further modified by the object *the laws*, and *laws* is modified by the adjunct *against political offences*, performing the office of an adjective.

But who could not, without, etc. (read to *had*), is a relative clause also modifying *politicians*, and connected as a coördinate clause to the clause before it, by the adversative conjunction *but*. *Who* is the entire subject and the subject-nominative; *could not, without incurring*, etc., is the entire predicate, of which *could declare* is the predicate-verb, modified by the negative adverb *not*, the adverbial adjunct *without incurring the charge of inconsistency*, the object *themselves*, which is modified by the adjective *adverse*, and *adverse* is modified by the adverbial adjunct *to relaxation*.

That they might, etc. (to *which*), is the next simple clause,—dependent, connected to *hope* by *that*, and performing the office of an adjective. *They* is the entire subject and the subject-nominative; *might defer*, etc., is the entire predicate, of which *might defer* is the predicate-verb, modified by the adverbial elements *by fomenting the dispute about the court of the lord high steward* (means), *for a year* (time), and the objective element *the passing of a bill*; *fomenting* is joined to *might defer* by *by* and modified by *dispute*, *dispute* is modified by *the* and *about the court*, *court* is joined to *dispute* by *about* and modified by *the* and *of the lord high steward*, *lord* is joined to *court* by *of* and modified by *the* and the appositive *high steward*; *for a year* is modified by the adverbial phrase *at least*; *passing* is modified by *the* and the adjunct *of a bill*.

Which they disliked, etc. (to the end), is a relative clause,—declarative, dependent, connected to *bill* by *which*, and performing the office of an adjective. *They* is the entire subject and the subject-nominative, *disliked* and *could oppose* are the predicate-verbs, connected by *and yet*, and modified, both, by the objective *which*, and the latter verb by the adverb *decently*, which is itself modified by the negative adverb *not*.

The sentence consists of six clauses, very finely bound together, of which the subject of the principal clause is branched out into a cluster of dependent clauses. —The student will seldom find a sentence more difficult to analyze.

Paragraphs or sentences may be briefly analyzed by simply pointing out the clauses or propositions in their logical order. Parsing, also, may be much abridged.

 Ex. "Man hath his daily work of body or mind
   Appointed, which declares his dignity,
   And the regard of Heaven on all his ways;
   While other animals inactive range,
   And of their doings God takes no account."—*Milton*.

Man hath his daily work of body or mind appointed.
Which declares his dignity, and the regard of Heaven on all his ways.
While other animals range inactive.
And God takes no account of their doings.

Man is a common noun, in the nominative case to *hath*; *hath* is an irregular transitive verb agreeing with *Man*; *his* is a personal pronoun, relating to *Man* as its antecedent, and possessing *work*, etc.

☞ For exercises, use the phrases and sentences on pp. 48—57.

COMPLEX AND COMPOUND SENTENCES.

Note.—The ideas entertained about Analysis are so various that they have not as yet settled down into a uniform system. What we have said on this subject from page 57 to 67, forms a very simple system that is perhaps sufficiently exact for ordinary purposes. We have not there insisted on *complex* sentences; or, rather, we have regarded all complex sentences as compound, but not all compound sentences as complex, or used *compound* as a generic term to *complex*. The following views, however, which now prevail most in Great Britain, are more exact and philosophical, and will probably give better satisfaction to those who are in the habit of thinking closely upon the structure of language.

There runs through discourse, more or less, a serial sense, and also a modified sense. The former gives us *compound* structure; and the latter, *complex* structure.

All sentences that have two or more distinct predicates, are either *complex* or *compound*.

A *complex sentence* contains but one principal clause, with one or more dependent clauses.

The DEPENDENT CLAUSE is combined with the principal clause, in the sense of a *NOUN,* an *ADJECTIVE,* or an *ADVERB,* or else simply depends on it for complete sense. The subordinate or dependent clauses which make with other clauses complex members or sentences, comprise the *relative clauses,* the *adverbial clauses,* the *correlative clauses,* and generally the *conjunctive clauses* that express *comparison, condition, concession, exception, cause, consequence,* or *purpose.* See p. 35.

For a thorough understanding of the foregoing paragraph,—and, indeed, of this whole page,—the student should consult the rest of this section, especially the following Exercises.

What is grammatically dependent, may be logically principal; that is, the dependent clause or word in construction may be the most important in sense; as. "*When the sun rises,* the birds sing;" "To think *a l w a y s accurately,* is a *great* accomplishment."

A *compound sentence* contains two or more principal coördinate clauses.

Such clauses are generally connected by conjunctions of the first three classes (see p. 34), or they have no connective.

Complex and *compound,* as here used, are entirely distinct: so that a sentence may be complex without being compound, or compound without being complex.

A *complex member* consists of two or more clauses combined like those of a complex sentence, and forms only a part of a sentence.

A *compound member* consists of two or more coördinate clauses, and forms only a part of a sentence.

A phrase whose chief word is modified by another phrase, may be called *complex.*

The **subject** is the nucleus of the sentence, round which every thing else clusters, and which is, in fact, modified by every thing else, even by the predicate-verb itself, with all its appendages. Now, if we regard dependent clauses always as modifying clauses, we shall have the strange anomaly, when clauses are used as subjects, of making the subject modify the predicate. (See p. 58.) But the above definition of a complex sentence and of dependent clauses, avoids the difficulty.

In another sense, the **predicate** is the main part of the sentence. For what is to be said or communicated, is naturally of the greatest concern both to him that speaks and to him that hears, and is the cause that there is any speaking at all. Besides, the predicate may embrace quite a volume of thinking, as thought upon thought flows out from the subject. See p. 72.

The skeleton of thought which underlies the full-robed sentence, may be briefly exhibited thus:—

Which one?
How many?
Of what kind?
} Subject. {
Is what?
Does what*?
Suffers what*?
When*?
Where?
How?
Why?
As to what?

So great a power of expression has the predicate-verb, that it expresses, to a great extent, along with the affirmation itself, the parts we have marked with stars.

EXERCISES IN ANALYSIS.

Suppose we could have a sentence that comprises all the various parts and modes of construction, which can be found in the whole compass of literature. By teaching this one sentence, we should teach all the elements of discourse. But, since no such sentence can exist, let us present in detail, from good writers, such a circuit of expressions as will embrace the body and all the outbranchings which together would make up this ideal sentence. After having thus exhibited, as fully as our space will allow, *the sentence* (from page 70 to 83), we may next show *the kinds of sentences;* and the whole will then furnish a comprehensive view of the construction of all sentences.

In the search for sentences to illustrate the construction of language according to the foregoing plan, I have been struck with this remarkable fact: The great and most admired authors of our literature—such as Shakespeare, Milton, Addison, Goldsmith, Irving, and Macaulay—have readily furnished me the various kinds of sentences which I sought; while inferior writers have generally exhibited an abundance of certain types only. I have therefore come to the conclusion that one of the great secrets of that imperial excellence of style which confers immortality, is variety of construction; and one of the great causes which prompt us to condemn the inferior writer as wearisome, is monotony of construction. If this is true, surely nothing else can be of greater importance than to store the learner's mind with the various types of construction, that they may lie in his mind like seed, ready to spring up afterwards in a luxuriant style, as rich, diversified, and harmonious as the creation itself.

It is often a convenience to name phrases and clauses according to their leading or principal words, or according to their sense.* Hence we have—

Substantive phrases. "*For me to go,* is impossible."
Adjective phrases. "A tree, *dead at the top.*"
Participial phrases. "A tree, *stripped of its leaves.*"
Infinitive phrases. "A few boxes, *to be sent to the depot.*"
Adverbial phrases. "He came *early in the morning.*" "*To and fro.*"
Appositive or explanatory phrases. "Athens, *the capital of Attica.*" "It is not always prudent *to rely on promises.*"
Absolute phrases. "*The cars having arrived,* we departed."
Independent phrases. "*My friend,* let us return."
Idiomatic phrases.† "*By and by,* you will not go *at all.*"
Adjuncts. "A statue *of marble* stood *in the public square.*"

---
* This classification of phrases and clauses is not taken from any recent writer, but from Kerl's Treatise on the English Language, published in 1859, and now out of print.
† An *idiom* is a mode of expression peculiar to a language, and sometimes to several languages, without admitting of analysis in the usual way; so that it must often be taken as a whole, the sense running through it somewhat like the grain through a knot of wood.

Adjuncts have been called, by two or three recent writers, *prepositional phrases*, and then *adjective* or *adverbial phrases*, according as they are used in an adjective or in an adverbial sense; but this use of the terms seems not altogether commendable, since they are also often applied to such phrases as *according to, from betwixt, ever and anon*, etc. In such sentences as "My hopes,—their starry light is gone," *My hopes* has been called a *pleonastic phrase*; but, since it is, in some form, indispensable to the sentence, we should perhaps rather regard *their* as the pleonastic word. The fact is, that the phrase, by the usual parsing, becomes superfluous, and may, in *that sense*, be considered *grammatically independent*; but, *logically* considered, *their* is the superfluous word. The *construction*, however, may be called *pleonastic, for the sake of emphasis;* and, in most instances, it seems not improper to regard it as a species of *apposition;* for, as a general rule, we should not regard as independent what can be otherwise disposed of, nor apply an extraordinary principle where an ordinary one will answer as well.

Substantive clauses. "*That I should go*," is impossible.
Adjective clauses. (Relative and other clauses qualifying substantives.)
Relative clauses. "The man *who came yesterday*." "I know *who he is*."
Correlative clauses. "*The farther I went, the worse I fared.*" "*As the one dies*, so dies the other."
Appositive or explanatory clauses. "It is evident *that he must soon fail*." The opinion *that the stars are inhabited*," etc.
Adverbial clauses. "*When sinners entice thee*, consent thou not."
Conjunctive clauses. "We turned back, *for we knew not the way*."
Conditional clauses. "*If you fail*, you will be disgraced."
Causal clauses. "He is economical, *because he is poor*."
Comparative clauses. "I have more *than you have*, etc. See p. 85.

☞ In arranging the following exercises, I have, in general, passed from *words* to *phrases* and from *phrases* to *clauses*, from *unmodified* to *modified*, from *simple* to *compound*, from *full construction* to *elliptical*, and from *simple* and *logical arrangement* to *complicated* and *inverted* or *poetical*. To make the simplest classification, it has been necessary to give sentences beyond the pupil's present ability. The latter paragraphs or the more complicated sentences should therefore be deferred for a second or third course.—Superior (ˢ), over the end of a sentence, shows that it is *simple;* (·), *complex* ; and (ᶜ), *compound* ᶜ.
The examples of this section will also be found unsurpassed as a series of Parsing Exercises.

Principal Elements.

Simple Subjects and Predicates.—I went.* Stars shine. It snows. Lights were shining. He was dismissed. Could they have gone? He should have been rewarded. Write.† Who sang? Singing had commenced. To whisper is forbidden.

* This is a simple declarative sentence. The subject is *I*, and the predicate is *went*. † This is a simple imperative sentence. The subject is *thou* understood; the predicate is *write*.

These roses are very beautiful.* Lies have short legs.† Virtuous youth brings forth accomplished and flourishing manhood.ˢ One sword keeps another in the scabbard.ˢ Too much fear is an enemy to good deliberation.ˢ Milton, the author of Paradise Lost, is the sublimest of poets.ˢ In every grove warbles the voice of love and pleasure.ˢ Let § nothing frighten you but sin.ˢ Give me the horse.ˢ Come, nymph demure, with mantle blue.ˢ| The inquisitive are generally talkative.ˢ To what expedient wilt thou fly?ˢ How wonderfully are we made!ˢ To the left, the Dunderberg reared its woody precipices, height over height, forest over forest, away into the deep summer sky.ˢ**
    No hive hast thou of hoarded sweets.ˢ††
    When first thy Sire to send on earth,
    Virtue, his darling child, designed.ˢ—*Gray*.
    For contemplation he, and valor, formed;
    For softness she, and sweet attractive graceᶜ.—*Milton*.

* This is a simple declarative sentence. The entire subject is *These roses*; the subject-nominative is *roses*, which is modified by the adjective *These*. The entire predicate is *are very beautiful;* the predicate-verb is *are*, which is limited by the adjective *beautiful*, or combines with it in making a descriptive assertion of the subject. *Beautiful* is modified by

EXERCISES IN ANALYSIS. 71

the adverb *very*, expressing degree. † This is a simple declarative sentence. *Lies* is the subject. *Have short legs*, is the entire predicate; *have* is the predicate-verb, which is modified by the object *legs*, which is itself modified by the adjective *short*. ‡ *Is* combines with *enemy*, to make an explanatory assertion of the subject. § *Let* is modified by the phrase after it as the entire object, and by *nothing* as the simple object. *Frighten* modifies *nothing*, —or refers the act to it,—and also depends on *Let*. "We saw the ship *sink*"; I heard the bell *tolling*; "She called him a *knave*"; "The storm turned the milk *sour*": in each of these sentences the Italic word modifies the substantive, and depends also on the verb. ‖ (*Thou*) *nymph demure*, etc. may be considered the entire subject. ** You may supply *rising*, after *height* and *forest*; and dispose of these absolute phrases as adverbial, modifying *reared its woody precipices*, by showing *how*. †† This is a simple declarative sentence. The prose or logical arrangement of the words would be, *Thou hast no hive of hoarded sweets*. (Now analyze the sentence.)

They who are set to rule over others, must be just.* We found, in our rambles, several pieces of flint which the Indians had once used for arrow-heads.ˣ The disputes between the majority which supported the mayor, and the minority headed by the magistrates, had repeatedly run so high that bloodshed seemed inevitable.ˣ

The bounding steed you pompously bestride,
Shares with his lord the pleasure and the prideˣ.—*Pope*.

* This is a complex declarative sentence that has a dependent clause used in the sense of an adjective. *They who are set to rule over others*, is the entire principal subject; *they* is the subject-nominative, modified by the relative clause *who are set to rule over others*. *Must be just*, is the entire principal predicate; *must be* is the predicate-verb, which is modified by the adjective *just*, or combines with it in making a descriptive assertion of the subject. *Who are set to rule over others*, is a dependent clause, joined to *they* by the relative *who*, and used in the sense of an adjective. *Who* is the subject; *are set to rule over others*, is the entire predicate; *are set* is the predicate-verb, which is modified by the infinitive phrase *to rule over others*; and *to rule* is modified by the adjunct *over others*.

To relieve the poor, is our duty.* To pay as you go, is the safest way to fortuneˣ. To return to sup at some of the palaces of the nobility, was then the customᵃ To have advanced much farther without wagons or supplies, would have been dangerousᵃ. The enemy's deceiving him was the cause of his failure. (*Better:* That the enemy deceived him, was the cause of his failure.)

To be at war with one we love,
Doth work like madness in the brainᵃ.—*Coleridge*.

Unknown to them, when sensual pleasures cloy,
To fill the languid pause with finer joyˣ.—*Goldsmith*.

ᵃ This is a simple declarative sentence, having the infinitive phrase, *To relieve the poor*, as the entire subject, and *To relieve* as the simple subject. *To relieve* is modified by the object *people* (understood), and *people* is modified by the adjective *poor* and the article *the*. *Is our duty*, is the entire predicate; *is* is the predicate-verb, which combines with *duty*, to make a descriptive assertion of the subject. *Duty* is modified by the possessive pronoun *our*.

That the earth is round, is now well known.* Whether we should go, was next discussedˣ. Why he said so, is now obviousˣ. Who was the author of Junius's Letters, is not yet provedˣ. What became of Sir John Franklin, is still a mysteryˣ. How many and what enormous lies have been published in the newspapers, must have astonished every honest reader.ˣ Let us stick to the common highway, and do our best there, was the instinctive feeling of the man.ˣ "Dust thou art, to dust returnest," was not written of the soul.ˣ

"*My fan*," let others say, who laugh at toil;
"*Fan! hood! glove! scarf!*" is her laconic style.º—*Young*.

* This is a complex declarative sentence, with a dependent clause used in the sense of a noun in the nominative case. *That the earth is round*, is the principal subject. *Is now well known*, is its entire predicate. *Is known* is the predicate-verb, and is modified by the adverbs *now* and *well*. *That*, commencing the dependent clause, is the connective; or, rather,

it serves as a sort of handle to the clause, showing that all its words are to be taken together as one thing. *The earth* is the entire subject; and *earth* is the nominative, modified by the article *the*. *Is round*, is the entire predicate; *is* is the predicate-verb, and is modified by the adjective *round*, or combines with it in making a descriptive assertion of the subject. (Some grammarians would say, *is* is the copula, and *round* is the attribute.)

Observe that the dependent clauses in the last paragraph of exercises, are used in the sense of nouns in the nominative case.

A *dependent clause* or *member*, used in the sense of a *noun*, generally begins with *that*, or with *but* or *but that* (not elegant); with the responsive relative *who*, *which*, or *what* ; or with the word *how*, *why*, *when*, *whence*, *where*, *whither*, *whether*, or *wherefore*. Sometimes it is simply an imperative clause or member; and sometimes it is a sentence introduced as a direct quotation.

Compound Subjects and Predicates.—John and I went.º Either James or Henry is talking.ªt   Lead, iron, and coal, were foundª. Every door, window, and balcony, was filled with spectators.ªt   Can pleasures, or riches, or honors cure a guilty conscience ?ª t   Never did a single encouraging remark, a bright hope, or a warm wish cross my path.ªt   Day after day, and hour after hour, passed heavily away.t His magnificence, his taste, his classical learning, the grace and urbanity of his manners, were admitted even by his enemies.ª

War, famine, pest, volcano, storm, and fire,
Intestine broils, oppression with her heart
Wrapt up in triple brass, besiege mankind.ª—*Young.*

Read and write.‡   He rose, reigned, and fellª.   Slowly and sadly they climb the distant mountains, and read their doom in the setting sun.ª §

The rose had been washed, just washed in a shower,
  Which Mary to Anna conveyed ;
A delicate moisture encumbered the flower,
  And weighed down its beautiful head.º—*Cowper.*

He tried each art, reproved each dull delay,
Allured to brighter worlds, and led the wayª.—*Goldsmith.*

ª This is a simple declarative sentence, with a compound subject. *John and I* is the entire subject; and *John* and *I* are the nominatives, connected by *and*.   † When the subject is distributive, some grammarians prefer to call the sentence compound, and then repeat the predicate with each nominative.   It is generally best, however, to dispose of sentences as we find them; and to regard sentences compound that have compound subjects, only when a predicate must be supplied in order to parse them.   ‡ This is a simple imperative sentence, with a compound predicate. The subject is *thou* or *you* understood ; and the verbs are *read* and *write*, connected by *and*.   (By supplying *thou* with each verb, the sentence would become compound.)   § Such sentences as this one, some grammarians would call *compound*, and with much good ground for their opinion. A compound predicate usually implies a much greater transition in thought than a compound subject. A compound predicate can generally be conceived as consisting of two or more distinct thoughts ; but a compound subject can seldom be so regarded. To make the analysis of sentences, however, as little intricate as possible, it may be best to follow the mode of analysis shown in the exercises.

To hope and strive is the way to thrive.ª*   To be liberal, and to be benevolent, are often two different thingsª.†   To be wise in our own eyes, to be wise in the opinion of the world, and to be wise in the sight of our Creator, are three things that rarely coincideˣ.   That he should take offense at such a trifle, and that he should then write and publish an article about it, surprised us all.ˣ

That secrets are a sacred trust,
That friends should be sincere and just,

EXERCISES IN ANALYSIS. 73

<blockquote>
That constancy befits them,
Are observations on the case,
That savor much of common-place,
And all the world admits them[c].[†]—*Cowper.*
</blockquote>

The wit whose vivacity condemns slower tongues to silence, the scholar whose knowledge allows no man to fancy that he instructs him, the critic who suffers no fallacy to pass undetected, and the reasoner who condemns the idle to thought and the negligent to attention, are generally praised and feared, reverenced and avoided[x].—*Johnson.*

Glass is impermeable to water, is capable of receiving and retaining the most lustrous colors, is susceptible of the finest polish, can be carved or sculptured like stone or metal, never loses a fraction of its substance by constant use, and is so insensible to the action of acids that it is employed by chemists for purposes to which no other substance could be applied[x].

* *To hope and strive* is the entire subject and the subject-nominative. *To hope* and *to strive* are each, in part, the subject of *is*. *Is* agrees with *to hope* and *to strive* conjointly, taken as one thing. Perhaps it may be well to consider such subjects as a distinct species of compound subjects,—to call them subjects that are compound in form, yet singular in construction, because grouped as one thing, or consisting of a cluster of attributes that represent but one object. To this head may then be referred such expressions as, "Yonder *lives* a great *scholar* and *divine*."

† This is a simple declarative sentence, with a compound subject. *To be liberal, and to be benevolent,* is the entire subject. *To be* and *to be* are the simple subjects, connected by *and*, and modified, the former by *liberal*, and the latter by *benevolent*. *Are often two different things,* is the entire predicate; and *are* is the predicate-verb, etc.

‡ This is a compound declarative sentence, consisting of a complex member and a clause. (Though compound in form, it is really, in sense, wholly a complex sentence; for the clause comprising the last line—equivalent to *and that are admitted by all the world*—is but a continuation of the dependent sense commenced by the relative clause before it; and has been expressed like a principal clause of a compound sentence, merely for the sake of rhyme and measure.) The entire subject of the complex member is compound, and consists of the three dependent clauses, *that secrets are a,* etc., (read to *are,*) used in the sense of nouns in the nominative case, and connected by simple succession. *That,* at the beginning of each clause, shows that the words of the clause are to be taken together, and referred as a whole to something else. The subject of the first clause is *secrets;* the entire predicate is *are a sacred trust,* and the predicate-verb, or copula, is *are,* etc. *Are observations on the case, That savor much of common-place,* is the entire predicate of the complex member, and *are* is the predicate-verb, which makes with *observations* an explanatory assertion of the subject. *Observations* is modified by the adjunct *on the case,* and the relative clause *that savor much of common-place,* used both in the sense of adjectives, etc. *And all the world admits them,* is a principal clause, joined to the complex member by the conjunction *And. All the world,* is the entire subject, etc.

Adjective Elements.

1. Articles.—A church.* The mail. A swift horse. The swiftest horse. Peter the Great.† A nation's traditions. A winter's storm. A house and lot.‡ A boy and girl.§ The singular and the plural number.

* This is a phrase. The principal word is *church*, modified by the article *A*. † Peter the Great—Peter the Great Emperor; or, The Great Peter. *Traditions* is modified by the possessive *nation's*, and *nation's* is modified by the article *A*. *Storm* is modified by the article *A* and the possessive *winter's*. ‡ This is a phrase. The principle words are *house* and *lot,* connected by *and,* and modified conjointly by the article *A*. § This is a phrase. The principal words are *boy* and *girl,* connected by the conjunction *and,* and modified, the former by the article *A*, and the latter by the article *a* understood.

2. Adjectives.—One man.* The first man. Shining clouds. This apple. This large apple. This large red apple. These two large red apples. Green fields and forests. A swift and limpid rivulet. A virgin lovely as the dewy rose.† He used very forcible but courteous language.‡ A bright and handsome young lady she was[s]. All men agree to call vinegar sour, honey sweet, and aloes bitter[s].§ The whole world swarms with life, animal and vegetable*. His life might be compared to an anthem on his own favorite organ,—high-toned, solemn, and majestic*. Then followed a long, a strange, a glorious conflict of genius against power*.‖ Vigilant, industrious, and economical, he could not fail to become rich*.** Lofty and sour he was to them that loved him not; but to the hearts that cherished him, mild as summer°. †† So necessary and excellent a faculty to the mind is memory, that all other faculties borrow from it their beauty and perfection*. There is something more sprightly, more delightful and entertaining, in the living discourse of a wise, learned, and well-qualified teacher, than in silent reading*

    Deep in the grove, beneath the secret shade,
    A various wreath of odorous flowers she made;
    Gay mottled pinks, and jonquils sweet, she chose,
    The violet blue, sweet thyme, and flaunting rose°.‡‡—*Collins.*

  * This is a phrase. The principal word is *man*, modified by the adjective *One*. † This is a phrase, or a phrase combined with a dependent clause. *Virgin* is the principal word, modified by the article *A* and the adjective *lovely;* and *lovely* is modified by the dependent clause *as the dewy rose (is lovely)*, used in the sense of an adverb. ‡ This is a simple declarative sentence. The subject is *He*. The entire predicate is, *used very forcible but courteous language;* *used* is the predicate-verb, modified by the object *language;* *language* is modified by the adjectives *forcible* and *courteous*, which are connected by the conjunction *but*; and *forcible* is modified by the adverb *very*, expressing degree. § *To call* is modified by *vinegar sour, honey sweet*, etc., (to the end,) as the entire object, and by *vinegar, honey*, and *aloes* as the simple objects, which are respectively modified by the adjectives *sour, sweet*, and *bitter*, and these are themselves affected by the verb *to call*. ‖ *Conflict* is understood after *long*, and the others are put in apposition with it. ** *He*, with the adjectives *vigilant, industrious*, and *economical*, is the entire subject. *He* is the subject-nominative, modified by the adjectives *vigilant, industrious*, and *economical*. †† The dependent clause, *as summer (is mild)*, limits, determines, or completes the comparison. *As* is understood *before mild*. ‡‡ Here it is doubtful whether the first line should be taken with the subject or with the predicate. It should probably be a part of the predicate; for its chief sense is, to tell *where* the wreath *was made*. The adjective phrase and the adjunct can be said to modify the rest of the predicate, by showing *where*. See pp. 61 and 87.

3. Possessives.—John's horse.* Our Redeemer. Simpson's Playfair's Euclid. India's coral strand. The Duke of Wellington's forces. Gen. George Washington's residence. Lewis and Raymond's factory. The sea is His, for He made it.

  * This is a phrase. *Horse* is the principal word, which is modified by the possessive *John's*. *Euclid* is modified by *Playfair's*, and the phrase *Playfair's Euclid* is modified by *Simpson's*. *Forces* is modified by *Duke* ('s), and *Duke* is modified by *the* and *of Wellington*.

4. Appositive or Explanatory Expressions.—The poet Young.* Young the poet. The words *fancy* and *taste*. A cove, or inlet. To regard him as the ablest minister.† As a mathematician, he had few equals*. My duty as her instructer. At Mason's, the bookseller. At Mason the bookseller's. King David the psalmist. Thou sun, both eye and soul of the world. They named him John*. Madame de Stael calls beautiful architecture frozen music*.

Up soars the lark, the lyrical poet of the sky*.‡ But they—the poor, the helpless—had lost in him their friend, almost their father.⁷ In pronouncing the words⁴ lilies,⁷ roses,⁷ tulips, pinks, jonquils, we see the things themselves,⁷ and seem to taste all their beauty and sweetness*. John, John, John! you lazy boy! One honest John Tomkins, a hedger⁷ and ditcher,⁷ although he was poor, did not want to be richer*. There is but¹³ one God, the author, the creator, the governor of the world; almighty, eternal, and incomprehensible*.

EXERCISES IN ANALYSIS. 75

O Music², sphere-descended maid,⁷
Friend⁷ of pleasure, wisdom's aid,
Why, goddess,¹ why, to us denied,
Lay'st thou thy ancient lyre aside°.—*Collins.*

° This is a phrase. The principal word is *poet*, which is modified by the article *The* and the appositive *Young*. † This is a phrase. The principal word is the verb *To regard*, which is modified by the phrase *him as the ablest minister*, as the entire object, and by *him* as the simple object. *Minister* is affected by the verb, put in apposition with *him*, connected to it by the conjunction *as*, and modified by the article *the* and the adjective *ablest*. (In the analyzing of phrases, look out constantly for the chief words; mention them, then the modifications before them, and then those after them.) ‡ This is a simple declarative sentence, made highly rhetorical by inversion. The prose or logical arrangement of the words would be, *The lark, the lyrical poet of the sky, soars up. The lark, the lyrical poet of the sky,* is the entire subject; *lark* is the subject-nominative, modified by the article *the*, and the explanatory phrase *the lyrical poet of the sky; poet* is put in apposition with *lark*, and modified by the article *the*, the adjective *lyrical*, and the adjective adjunct *of the sky; sky* is modified by the article *the*, and joined to *poet* by *of*. *Soars up* is the entire predicate; *soars* is the predicate-verb, modified by the adverb *up*. § This is an independent phrase, because it expresses merely an address. The first *John* is the principal word, which is modified by *John, John*, and perhaps *you* rather than *boy*. *You* is modified by *boy*, and *boy* by *lazy*. See sentences beginning with *it*, next paragraph.

It is mean to divulge the secrets of a friend¹.* It would be difficult to persuade ourselves that the rose is not very beautifulˣ. It is our duty to be friendly toward mankind, as much as it is our interest that mankind should be friendly toward usˣ.† This you should engrave upon your heart, rather to suffer wrong than to do wrong°. To bake, to boil, to roast, to fry, to stew; to wash, and iron, and scrub, and sweep; and, at our idle intervals, to repose ourselves on knitting and sewing,—these, I suppose, must be feminine occupations for the present°.‡

It is not all of life to live; nor all of death, to die°.

O, it is excellent
To have a giant's strength; but it is tyrannous
To use it as a giant°.—*Shakespeare.*

° This is a simple declarative sentence. *It*, with the explanatory infinitive phrase *to divulge the*, etc., is the entire subject; and *It* is the subject-nominative. *It* is modified by the phrase *to divulge the*, etc., as the entire appositive or explanatory phrase, and by *to divulge* as the simple appositive. *To divulge* is modified by the object *secrets*, and *secrets* is modified by the article *the* and the adjunct *of a friend;* and *friend* is modified by the article *a*, and joined to *secrets* by the preposition *of*. † *Is mean* is the entire predicate, etc. † The phrase *as much* modifies the phrase *is our duty*. ‡ Some grammarians would consider this group of infinitives independent, by pleonasm; but it is probably best to regard them as being in apposition with *things*, understood after *these*.

It is an old saying, that an open admonition is an open disgraceˣ.* It is scarcely to be imagined, how soon the mind sinks to a level with its conditionˣ. It matters very little¹² what² spot may have been the birthplace of such a man as Washingtonˣ. The story is perhaps too delicate for thy ear; suffice it, that I came, saw, and loved°. The opinion that the soul is immortal, has been almost universally entertainedˣ. (That the soul is immortal, is an opinion that has been almost universally entertained.) He took a dram every morning before breakfast,—a habit which soon overpowered him, and made him a drunkardˣ.† She then told me—what I had suspected before—that she was to be shortly married.ˣ‡ It seems proper that I should conclude my preface with the following sentence from Montaigne: "*I have here made only a nosegay of culled flowers, and brought nothing of my own but the string that ties them*ˣ."

She knows, and knows no more, her Bible true—
A truth the brilliant Frenchman never knewˣ.—*Cowper.*

4*

76 EXERCISES IN ANALYSIS.

* This is a complex declarative sentence, consisting of a principal clause, and a dependent clause in apposition with the subject of the principal clause. *It* is introduced into the sentence, and made the principal subject in stead of the appositive clause, for rhetorical effect, or that the sentence may assume a more impressive form. *It*, with the appositive or explanatory clause, *that an open admonition*, etc., is the entire principal subject; and *It* is the subject-nominative. *It* is modified by the appositive clause, which explains it. *That* is a sort of handle to the appositive clause, showing that its words relate, as a whole, to something else. *An open admonition*, is the entire subject of the dependent clause, etc. *Is an old saying*, is the entire principal predicate, etc. † *Habit* is in apposition with the clause before it, and is therefore in the nominative case; for a substantive should be considered in the nominative case, when there is no word to determine its case. ‡ The clause *that she*, etc., is the object of *told*; and *that*, comprehended in *what*, is put in apposition with it. It would be the reverse, were the dash omitted after *me*.

5. Participles. — Snow falling.   The army having retreated. Our horses being much fatigued.   An humble cottage, thatched with straw.   Who, seeing me, fled*.   To have a dagger concealed.*

Having reached the bridge, we opened fire upon the enemy*.† He had a beautiful daughter, betrothed to a chief*. The wolf, exasperated by the wound, sprang upon the horse*. The mind, soothed into a hallowed melancholy by the mystery of the scene, listened with pensive stillness, to catch each sound vaguely echoed from the shore*. There are twenty-six senators, distinguished for their wisdom, not elevated by popular favor, but chosen by a select body of men*.

> Meanwhile[13] the Son of God, who yet some days
> Lodged[11] in Bethabara where John baptized,
> Musing[12] and much revolving in his breast
> How best the mighty work he might begin
> Of Savior to mankind, and which way first
> Publish his godlike office now mature,
> One day* walked[11] forth alone, the Spirit[2] leading,
> And his deep thoughts,[2] the better to converse
> With solitude, till far from track of men,
> Thought[2] following thought, and step by step led on,
> He entered now the bordering desert wild[x].‡—*Milton.*

> Exulting, trembling, raging, fainting,
> Possessed beyond the Muse's painting,
> By turns they felt the glowing mind
> Disturbed, delighted, raised, refined*.§—*Collins.*

* This is a phrase. The principal word is *To have*, which is modified by the object *dagger*; and *dagger* is modified by the article *a* and the participle *concealed*. † This is a simple declarative sentence, containing with a participial phrase that is equivalent to the dependent clause of a complex sentence. *We*, with *Having crossed the bridge*, is the entire subject. *We* is the subject-nominative, modified by the participial phrase *Having crossed the bridge*; *Having crossed* is modified by the object *bridge*, and *bridge* is modified by the article *the*. *Opened fire upon the enemy*, is the entire predicate; *opened* is the predicate-verb, which so blends with its object *fire* as to make an idiomatic phrase with it, that is modified by the adverbial adjunct *upon the enemy*, showing *whither*. ‡ The compound absolute phrase, *the Spirit leading, and his deep thoughts (leading)*, is here used adverbially, in the sense of a dependent clause, modifying *walked*, or the phrase *walked forth alone*, by showing *how* he went or *why* alone. § *They*, with the participles *Exulting, trembling, raging, fainting*, and the participial phrase, *Possessed beyond the Muse's painting*, is the entire subject. *Felt, By turns the glowing mind Disturbed, delighted, raised, refined*, is the entire predicate. *Mind* is modified by the participles *Disturbed, delighted, raised, refined*, which are also affected by the verb *felt*.

6. Infinitives.—A task to be learned.*   A house to let.   Contributions to relieve the poor.

Let us have some of these clams cooked for supper*.† The book, to be fully appreciated, should be compared with others of the same kind*. Is there no way to bring home a wandering sheep, but by worrying him to death? The king felt an earnest desire to heal old grievances, to secure the personal rights and property of the colonists, and to promote their prosperity*.

One word is too often profaned
For me to profane it*.—*Shelley.*

Quick let us rise, the happy seats explore,
And bear oppression's insolence no more*.—*Johnson.*

* This is a phrase. The principal word is *task*, modified by the article *A* and the infinitive *to be learned.* † This is a simple imperative sentence. The subject is *thou* or *you* understood. The entire predicate is *Let us have*, etc. *Let* is the predicate-verb, which is modified by the phrase *us have*, etc., as the entire object, and by *us* as the simple object. *Have* relates to *us*, and is modified by the object *clams* understood; *clams* is modified by the adjective *some*, and the adjective adjunct *of these clams*; *clams*, of the adjunct, is modified by the adjective *these*, the infinitive (*to be*) *cooked*, and joined to *some*, or *clams* understood, by *of*; and *cooked* is affected by the verb *have*, and modified by the adverbial adjunct *for supper.* ‡ *For me to profane it*—For my profaning, or profanation; therefore *to profane* is also affected by *For*.

7. Adjuncts.—The roar of the lion.* Laws against corruption. A house with its furniture. The spirit within us. The large elm between the garden and the river. A procession round and through the park. The gold in a piece of quartz from the mines of California. Is there not a display of infinite goodness, in the vicissitudes of the seasons?*† There is a flower about to bloom*.‡ The sailors did not exactly like the idea of being treated so*.§ The question of who is to lead them, is now under discussion*. In large cities, the many temptations to vice from bad examples, are another argument against the educating of children there*. A Gothic cathedral is a blossoming in stone, subdued by the insatiable desire of harmony in man*.∥ Brazil is regarded as a land¶ of mighty rivers and virgin forests, palm-trees and jaguars, anacondas and alligators, howling monkeys and screaming parrots, diamond-mines, revolutions, and earthquakes*.** But what¶ are lands, and seas, and skies, to civilized men, without society, without knowledge, without morals, without religious culture? and how can these be enjoyed, in all their extent and all their excellence, but†† under the protection of wise institutions and free government?*

'Tis the sunset of life gives me mystical lore,
And coming events cast their shadows before*.‡‡—*Campbell.*

* This is a phrase. The principal word is *roar*, which is modified by the article *The* and the adjective adjunct *of the lion;* and *lion* is modified by the article *the*, and joined to *roar* by the preposition *of*. *Elm* is modified by the adjective adjunct *between the garden and the river*, which is compound in its object. *Procession* is modified by the adjective adjunct *round and through the park*, which is compound in its prepositions. *Gold* is modified by the complex adjective adjunct, *in a piece of quartz from the mines of California.* † This is a simple interrogative sentence. The entire subject is, *a display of infinite goodness; display* is the simple subject, modified by the article *a* and the adjective adjunct *of infinite goodness; goodness* is modified by the adjective *infinite*, and joined to *display* by the preposition *of*. *Is there not, in the vicissitudes of the seasons,* is the entire predicate, and *is* is the predicate-verb, modified by the adverb *there*,—which is a somewhat demonstrative word, and enables the sentence to assume a more impressive form,—and by the complex adjunct *in the vicissitudes of the seasons,* used in the sense of an adverb of place. *Vicissitudes* is modified by the article *the* and the adjective adjunct *of the seasons*, and connected to the verb *is* by the preposition *in*, etc. ‡ *Flower* is modified by the adjunct *about to bloom.* § *Idea* is modified by the adjective adjunct, *of being treated so;* and *being treated*, a verbal noun, is modified by the adverb *so*, and joined to *idea* by the preposition *of*. So, *of who is to lead them*, is an adjective adjunct, describing *question.* ∥ By the *insatiable desire of harmony in man*, is a complex adverbial adjunct, because it modifies a verb (*subdued*); *of harmony* and *in man* are adjective adjuncts, because they describe or modify nouns. ** *Of mighty rivers*, etc., is an adjective adjunct that describes *land*, and is compound and grouped in its objects. †† *But*, equivalent here to *except*, may be considered a preposition governing the clause (*that we must enjoy them*), *under the protection,* etc. ‡‡ Supply *them* after *before*.

The chief adjective adjunct is that which begins with *of.*

8. Clauses.—The honeysuckles which bloom round our portico.* A limpid rivulet that purled over the pebbles. Such laws as those by which he was tried. The flowers and gems which he brought. The land where the orange and citron grow. Plain proof that he is guilty. He who said nothing, had the better of it, and got what he wanted[x].† The taxes, of whatever kind they may be, must be collected[x].‡ Conversation unfolds and displays the hidden treasures of knowledge, with which reading, observation, and study, had before enriched the mind[x]. As one that runs in haste, and leaps over a fence, may fall into a pit, on the other side, that he did not see; so is the man who plunges suddenly into any action before he sees the consequences[x]. How strange it seems that the passion of love should be the supreme mover of the world; that it is this which has dictated the greatest sacrifices, and influenced all societies and times; that to this the loftiest and loveliest genius has ever consecrated its devotions; that *but for*[14] love there were no civilization, no music, no poetry, no beauty, no life beyond the brute's[x] !

The lamb thy riot dooms to bleed to-day,
Had he thy reason, would he skip and play[x]?—*Pope.*

* This is a phrase combined with a clause. *Honeysuckles* is the principal word, modified by the article *The;* and by the relative clause *which bloom,* etc., used in the sense of an adjective. See p. 71. † *He who said nothing,* is the entire principal subject, and *He* is the subject-nominative, etc. *Had the better of it, and got what he wanted,* is the entire predicate, and compound ; *had* and *got* are the predicate-verbs, connected by *and,* and modified, the former, by the object *part* understood, which is itself modified by the article *the,* the adjective *better,* and the adjunct *of it ;* and the latter, by the object *that* (comprehended in *what*), which is itself modified by the relative clause *which* (comprehended in *what*) *he wanted,* etc. ‡ *Of whatever nature they may be,* is a dependent clause, connected with *taxes* through the relative adjective *whatever,* and describing it like an adjective. *Of whatever nature,* is an adjunct combining with *may be* like an adjective, to make an explanatory assertion of the subject *they.*

A *clause* that is used in the sense of an *adjective*, generally begins with the relative *who, which, that, as, whoever, whichever, whatever,* etc., with the adverb *where, when, why,* or *till ;* or with the conjunction *that.*

Adverbial Elements.

1. Objectives.—To catch fish. Having entertained the company. Glad to have seen you. After having written his letter.

Birds build nests.* Touch me if you dare[x]. She gave what she could not sell[x]. A friend exaggerates a man's virtues; an enemy, his crimes[e]. The soil produces corn, tobacco, hemp, and grass remarkably well[s]. Here he brought her the choicest food, the finest clothing, mats for her bed, and sandal-oil to perfume herself with[s]. The hurricane even tore down enclosures that had been lately made, trees that had stood for ages, and mansions that had been built of stone.† O eloquent, just, and mighty Death! whom none could advise, thou hast persuaded; what none hath dared, thou hast done; and whom all the world hath flattered, thou only hast cast out and despised[e]!

Him the Almighty Power
Hurled headlong flaming from the ethereal sky,
With hideous ruin and combustion, down[13]
To bottomless perdition, there to dwell
In adamantine chains and penal fires,
Who durst defy the Omnipotent to arms[x].—*Milton.*

EXERCISES IN ANALYSIS. 79

I like to study*. He knew not what to say*.‡ We preferred to remain at home, and learn our lessons*.§ Never expect to govern others, unless you have first learned how to govern yourself ˣ. She taught me to read, to write, and to sing*. He intended to go to the West, to purchase him a farm, and to end his days on it in peace and happiness*. After such a hint, I could not avoid offering her my assistance, and regretting my apparent want of gallantry*.

Teach me to love and to forgive;
Exact¹ˢ my own defects to scan;
What⁷ others are, to feel; and know myself a man'.‖—*Gray.*

I believe that he is honest and industrious.** She saw that we were tired, and needed something to eat ˣ. Tell us not, sir, that we are weak, unable to cope with so formidable an adversary ˣ. Who¹ can tell who⁷ he is ˣ ? He now learned what it is to be poor ˣ. Every one must have noticed how much more amiable some children are than others ˣ. "Trifles," said Sir Joshua Reynolds, "make perfection; but perfection is no trifle ˣ." They said that Halifax loved the dignity and emolument of office, that while he continued to be president it would be impossible for him to put forth his whole strength against the government, and that to dismiss him would be to set him free from all restraint ˣ.

Stern, rugged nurse! thy rigid lore
With patience many a year she bore;
What sorrow is thou bad'st her know,
And from her own she learned to melt at others' woe.°—*Gray.*

Observe that most of the *dependent clauses* of this section, are used as *nouns* in the objective case.

* This is a simple declarative sentence. The subject is *Birds;* the entire predicate is *build nests,* and *build* is the predicate-verb, which is limited or modified by the object *nests.*
† This is a complex declarative sentence, with a compound object. *Tore* is limited by *enclosures that,* etc., (to the end,) as the entire object : and by *enclosures, trees,* and *mansions,* as the simple objects, which are connected by *and,* and modified each by a relative clause performing the office of an adjective. ‡ In parsing, *what* is governed by *to say;* and *what to say,* is governed by *knew.* § This is a simple declarative sentence, with a compound object. *We* is the subject ; *preferred to remain,* etc., is the entire predicate ; *preferred* is the predicate-verb, modified by the compound infinitive phrase *to remain,* etc., as the entire object ; and by *to remain* and *to learn* as the simple objects, connected by *and,* and modified, etc. ‖ Say first that it is a complex imperative sentence, consisting of a clause and a long compound infinitive expression as the entire object ; and then show what the prose or logical arrangement of the words would be. *Teach* is modified by the double object *me* and the infinitive phrase. ** This is a complex declarative sentence that has a dependent clause used in the sense of a noun in the objective case. *I* is the principal subject. *Believe that,* etc., is the entire principal predicate ; *believe* is the predicate-verb, which is modified by the objective clause *that he,* etc., *That* is the connective used formally to incorporate the dependent clause, in the sense of a noun, with the other words of the sentence. *He* is the subject of the dependent clause, etc.

2. Predicate-Nominatives.—To be a soldier. He has become a farmer*. He was styled a hero*. She was appointed governess*. He was a friend to us.* Man is a bundle of habits and relations*. We know not who⁷ he is ˣ. He is not the man whom⁷ you take him to be ˣ. We stand the latest, and, if we fall, the last, experiment⁷ of self-government°. He is, in every respect, a statesman and a soldier*. A poor relation is the most irrelevant thing in nature, an odious approximation⁷, a haunting conscience, a perpetually recurring mortification, a drawback on your rising, a stain in your blood, a drain on your purse, and a more intolerable drain on your pride*.

All nature is but art unknown to thee;
All chance, direction which thou canst not see;

All discord, harmony not understood;
All partial evil, universal good[c].—*Pope.*
Of thousands, thou[1] both sepulchre and pall,
Old Ocean,[2] art[s]! †—*Dana.*

To venture in was to die.‡ The plan was, to outflank the enemy and cut off his supplies[e]. The best way to preserve health is, to be careful about diet and exercise[e]. His only wish was, to die in a foreign land, to be buried by strangers, and to sleep in obscurity[e].

No more—where ignorance is bliss,
'Tis folly to be wise[c].—*Gray.*

My impression is, that you will succeed.§ The law should be, that he who can not read should not vote[x]. The excuse was, that the army had not been well enough equipped, that the roads were too bad, and that the supplies were insufficient[x].

It is not that[15] my lot is low,
That[9] bids the silent tear to flow;
It is not grief that[9] bids me moan,
It is that[15] I am all[13] alone[c].—*H. K. White.*

Observe that most of the *dependent clauses* of this section have the sense of *nouns* used as predicate-nominatives.

[*] This is a simple declarative sentence. The subject is *He*; the entire predicate is, *was a friend to us*; *was* is the predicate-verb, which combines with *friend*, as a predicate-nominative, in making an explanatory assertion of the subject. *Friend* is modified by the article *a*, and limited by the adjective adjunct *to us*. † Some grammarians would take *thou* and *Old Ocean* together as the entire or logical subject. ‡ This is a simple declarative sentence. *To venture in* is the entire subject, and *To venture* is the simple subject, which is modified by the adverb *in*. *Was to die*, is the entire predicate: *was* is the predicate-verb, which combines with the infinitive *to die*, used in the sense of a predicate-nominative, and makes with it an explanatory assertion of the subject. § This is a complex declarative sentence, with a dependent clause used in the sense of a predicate-nominative. *My impression* is the entire principal subject, etc. *Is that you will succeed*, is the entire principal predicate; *is* is the predicate-verb, which combines with the clause *that you*, etc., to make with it an explanatory assertion of the subject.

3. Adjectives.—To be studious. Being studious. To burn blue. He became rich[e]. She was considered beautiful[e]. Cold blew the wind[e].

Roses and violets are fragrant[e].* Her countenance looked mild and beautiful[e]. Large, glossy, and black hung the beautiful fruit[e]. The question now before Congress is practical as death, enduring as time, and high as human destiny[x]. Envy is so base and detestable, so vile in its original, and so pernicious in its effects, that the predominance of almost any other passion is to be preferred[x]. Not to do evil is better than the sharpest sorrow for having done it; and to do good is better and more valuable than both[c].

Continuous as the stars that shine
And flash along the Milky Way,
They stretched in never-ending line
Along the margin of a bay[x].†—*Wordsworth.*

* See p. 70. † They (the daffodils) stretched *how* along the margin of the bay?

4. Adverbs.—To march boldly. Never decaying. Not to be expected. Severely handled. He spoke eloquently[e] The bird flew rapidly away[e]. The net was curiously woven[e].

Adjectives Modified.—Not slow. Highly useful. Deep enough. The fellow is constitutionally lazy[e]. How various, how animated, how full of interest is the survey![e]

Adverbs Modified.— Rather slowly.   Not often.   Very generally.
Altogether too soon.   Not quite fast enough.
The boy has studied his lesson very faithfully indeed*.   He thought he had never seen any thing quite so beautiful before*.   What he did, he did patiently, accurately, and thoroughly*.   Here, all is confusion; there, all is order† and beauty°.   We will remain wheresoever you wish*. Remember, while you are deliberating, the season now so favorable may pass away, never to return*.   Surely, never, never, shall we again behold so magnificent a spectacle !*   Thus he went on till the sun approached his meridian, and the increased heat preyed upon his strength.*   A young chief discovered the cave accidentally, while diving after a turtle*.   Use books as bees use flowers*.   As a veil enhances beauty, so does modesty throw a charm over virtues and talents*.   Not many generations ago, where you now sit, lived and loved another race of beings*.

When I call back to my mind the grandeur and beauty of those almost uninhabited shores; when I picture to myself the dense and lofty summits of the forests, that everywhere spread along the hills, and overhung the margins of the streams; when I see that no¹³ longer¹³ any aborigines are to be found there, and that the vast herds of elks, deer, and buffaloes, which once pastured on these hills and in these valleys, have ceased to exist; when I reflect that this grand portion of our Union is now more or less covered with villages, farms, and towns, where the din of hammers and machinery is constantly heard—that the woods are fast disappearing under the axe by day and the fire by night, that hundreds of steamboats are plying to and fro over the whole length of our majestic rivers; when I remember that these extraordinary changes have all taken place in the short period of twenty years,—I pause, wonder, and, although I know all to be true, can scarcely believe its reality.†—*Audubon.*

The blessed to-day is as completely so,
As who began three thousand years ago*.‡—*Pope.*

* This is a complex declarative sentence, consisting of a principal clause and a dependent member.   *Thus he went on,* is the principal clause.   *He* is the subject; *went* is the predicate-verb, modified by the adverbs *thus* and *on.*   *Till the sun,* etc., is the dependent member joined to the principal clause by the conjunctive adverb *till,* to express the time; and it is compound, consisting of two coördinate clauses, which are connected by *and.*   (Now analyze the clauses.)   † This is a complex declarative sentence, with a long compound or serial dependent member, whose parts are respectively connected with the principal clause by the conjunctive adverb *when,* to express the time, and have, some of them, secondary dependent clauses.   The sentence has the periodic form.   ‡ Supply *man* before *blessed. Three thousand years ago,* an adverbial phrase.

5. Participles.—To die fighting.   To lie concealed.   She appeared well dressed*.   He went on his way rejoicing*.   She sat enthroned¹² in her imperial beauty*.   These, and millions more, came flocking*.   Our recruits stood shivering, and rubbing their hands, in groups on the decks of the boats*.

Nine times⁶ the space⁶ that measures day and night
To mortal men, he with his horrid crew
Lay vanquished, rolling in the fiery gulf,
Confounded though immortal*.—*Milton.*
Now the bright morning star, day's harbinger,
Comes dancing from the east.*—*Milton.*

This is a favorite construction with Milton, and occurs often in Paradise Lost.

* This is a simple declarative sentence.   *The bright morning star, day's harbinger,* is the entire subject, etc.   *Now comes dancing from the east,* is the entire predicate.   *Comes* is the

predicate-verb, which is modified by the adverb *Now*, showing *when;* by the participle *dancing*, showing *how;* and by the adverbial adjunct *from the east*, showing *whence.*

6. Infinitives.—The child seemed to sleep. He was supposed to be rich. He was known to have assisted the editor. To regain the pass, to send off an adequate detachment, and to hold his position against any force that could be brought against him, he needed twenty additional regiments[x].

> Here jasmines spread their silver flower,
> To deck the wall or weave the bower[*].

Adjectives Modified—Rather young to go to school. Too old to be whipped. Good to eat. A thing not easy to be done. Pope was not content to please; he desired to excel, and therefore always did his best[c]. We are as prone to make a torment of our fears, as to luxuriate in our hopes[x].

Adverbs Modified.—It is too badly done to last[*]. It was so bright as to dazzle our eyes.[*] He proceeded too cautiously to fall into such a trap[*]. Do not let them return to be overwhelmed by a superior army[*]. Each should be careful to perform his part handsomely,—without drawling, omitting, faltering, stopping, hesitating[*], etc. I have yet three miles to walk by noon, to tell some boarding-school misses whether their husbands are to be captains in the army or peers of the realm; a question which I promised them to answer by that time[x].—*Goldsmith.*

> Night is the time for toil,
> To plough the classic field;
> Intent to find the buried spoil
> Its wealthy furrows yield[o].—*Montgomery.*

[*] The infinitive phrase, *to dazzle our eyes*, modifies the phrase *so bright*, to which it is joined by the conjunction *as*. Or else say, *To dazzle our eyes* is the entire subject of a dependent clause that has *was bright* understood as the predicate. Sometimes the former mode, and sometimes the latter, seems the better way of disposing of such expressions. † This is a complex declarative sentence. *To walk* is modified by the infinitive phrase after it; or, rather, this phrase with its clause modifies all the predicate before it, being itself equivalent to a complex member. *To tell* is modified by the indirect object *misses*, and the direct object the clause *whether their*, etc. *Question* is put in apposition with the dependent clause immediately before it. ‡ Supply, *The time for us to be*, before *Intent*.

7. Adjuncts.—To be in trouble. Annoyed by musquitoes. Delivered from evil. Suspected of having been negligent. The papers are in the drawer[*]. The house stood within a little grove of timber[*]. Parrhasius stood gazing forgetfully upon the canvas[*].

Adjectives Modified.—Dutiful to parents. Watchful of our liberties. Indolent about every thing. Inflexible in faith, invincible in arms.

Adverb Modified.—Agreeably to nature.

Religion dwells not in the tongue, but in the heart[c].[*] We had traveled a whole day, without seeing a single human being[*].† My hope was too much like despair for prudence to smother[*].‡ Much will depend on when and where such a poem is read[x].§ One hot summer's morning[*], a little cloud rose out of the sea, and glided lightly, like a playful child, through the blue sky, and the wide earth, which lay parched and languishing from the long drought[x]. Created thing naught valued he, nor feared[*].—*Milton.*

> By the brook the shepherd dines;
> From the fierce meridian heat
> Sheltered by the branching pines,
> Pendant o'er his grassy seat[*].—*Cunningham.*

They sat in silent watchfulness, the sacred cypress tree about;⟦
And from the wrinkled brows of age their failing eyes looked out*.— *Whtr.*
None knew thee but to love thee, none named thee but to praise°.**—*Hlk.*
Turn, gentle hermit of the dale, and guide my lonely way
To where you taper cheers the vale with hospitable ray°.— *Goldsmith.*

* This is a compound declarative sentence, consisting of a negative and an affirmative proposition. (Supply *it dwells* after *but.*) *Dwells not in the tongue*, is the entire predicate of the negative proposition. *Dwells* is the predicate-verb, modified by the adverb *not*, and the adverbial adjunct *in the heart*, showing *where*, etc. Or call the sentence simple, with a compound adverbial adjunct of place, whose parts are connected by the correlative words *not* . . . *but*, of which adjunct a part is denied by the former connective, and the other part affirmed by the latter. † *Traveled* is modified by the abridged adverbial adjunct *a whole day*, expressing time, and the extended adverbial adjunct *without seeing a single human being*, expressing manner. ‡ *Like* is modified or limited by *despair*, which represents the adverbial adjunct *to despair;* and the entire adjunct *for prudence to smother*, modifies *too much*, or, rather, the entire predicate before it, being equivalent to a dependent clause. *To smother*, relates to *prudence*, and is also affected by the preposition. (Too much *for smothering*, or, too much *to be smothered*.) § *On when and where such*, etc., is an adverbial adjunct that has a double clause for its object. ∥ An inverted adverbial adjunct, showing *where* they sat. ** *But to love thee*, an adverbial adjunct, showing *how* he was known and loved.

8. Clauses.—I came that I might assist you^x.* Be assured that I shall always keep your welfare at heart^x. When a person laughs at mischief, he tells us that he is pleased it is done, though he is sorry he had no hand in it^x. I am afraid that he will not return^x. It was done so ingeniously that we could not understand it. See pp. 79–81.

* This is a complex declarative sentence, consisting of a principal and a dependent clause. The principal clause is *I came;* the dependent clause is, *that I might assist you*, which is adverbial because it answers to the adverb *why;* and it is joined to *came* by the conjunction *that*, expressing purpose. † Adjectives and adverbs are sometimes modified by clauses.

A *clause* that is used in the sense of an *adverb*, generally begins with some one or some part of the following connectives :—

Words.—*Where, when, whence, while, whilst, whither, wherever, whereas, wherefore, whenever, whithersoever, since, before, after, ere, till, until, if, as, for, because, that, then, lest, unless, except, provided, though, although, notwithstanding* (=*though*), *yet, still, nevertheless, without* (=*unless*); also *whoever, whatever, however, whichever,* carrying with them the sense of *notwithstanding*. **Phrases.**—*As far as, so far as, as long as, as soon as, as often as, just as, as much as, inasmuch as, as if, so that, provided that, the instant*, etc. **Correlatives.**—*As—as, so—as, so—that, such—that, if—then, though—yet,* (comparative)—*than, the* (comparative)—*the* (comparative), etc.

Connecting Elements.

The connectives in the following sentences are Italicized ; tell of what kind they are, and what they connect:—

In that season *of* the year *when* the serenity *of* the sky, the various fruits *which* cover the ground, the discolored foliage of the trees, *and* all the sweet *but* fading graces of autumn, open the mind *to* benevolence *and* dispose it *for* contemplation, I was wandering *in* a beautiful *and* romantic country, *till* curiosity gave way *to* weariness; *and* I sat down *on* the fragment *of* a rock overgrown *with* moss, *where* the rustling *of* the leaves, the dashing *of* waters, *and* the hum *of* the distant city, soothed my mind *into* the most perfect tranquillity, *and* sleep insensibly stole *upon* me, *as* I was indulging the agreeable reveries *which* the objects *around* me naturally inspired.—*Aikin.*

Independent Elements.

Well, sir, let me know what merit you had, to introduce you into good company[x]?[*] But the daughter—alas, poor creature!—she is "accomplished," and can not do household work[x]. And then for company, doesn't she see the butcher, the baker, and the dustman—to say nothing of the sweep? In a word, is it not Pliny, my lord, who says that the most effectual way of governing is by example?[†]

Triumphal arch! that fill'st the sky when storms prepare to part,
I ask not proud philosophy to teach me what thou art[c].[‡]

* *Well* and *sir*, as used in this sentence, are both grammatically independent, though important to the meaning of the sentence. † *In a word* is used elliptically for the grammatically independent phrase *To speak in a word;* and it is, in fact, an emphatic connective, joining what follows to what precedes it. The phrases *in short, in brief, upon the whole, to wit,* etc., and the clause *that is*, are often used as a sort of emphatic coördinate connectives. ‡ The first line is an independent expression, consisting of a phrase that is independent by address, and whose principal word is modified by an adjective relative clause, which is itself modified by an adverbial clause.

Simple Sentences.

A hollow tree sheltered us from the storm.* Heaven lies about us in our infancy. Bad education and bad example increase greatly our natural depravity. All vice infatuates and corrupts the judgment. The surest way to lose power, is to abuse it. London, the capital of England, is the largest and richest city in the world. Italy is noted for its delightful climate, its beautiful scenery, and its historical recollections. George Washington was born in Virginia, on the 22d of February, 1732. True politeness is modest, unpretending, and generous. To be without wants, is the prerogative of God only. It is too often the fate of labor, to be oppressed by capital. O blessed Health! thou art above all price. Generally speaking, large bodies move slowly.† Cats and dogs catch and eat rats and mice.‡ A patriot, he impoverished the people.§

* This is a simple declarative sentence. The entire subject is *A hollow tree;* the entire predicate, *sheltered us from the storm,* etc. See p. 70. † This is a simple sentence: the phrase *Generally speaking* is rather independent, though it stands as the remnant and representative of a clause. ‡ This is a simple sentence; notwithstanding it has a compound subject, and a compound predicate with a compound object. § This should perhaps rather be considered an elliptical complex sentence; because the sense is, *Though he was a patriot, yet he impoverished the people.*

Complex Sentences.

Ah! who can tell how hard it is to climb
The steep where Fame's proud temple shines afar?*

No pleasure can be innocent from which our health suffers. When all is composed and quiet within us, the discharge of our duties is easy. A writer on physic, of the first rank, asserts that our diet is the chief cause of all our diseases. Be not discontented if you meet not with success at first. Beware lest thou sin. Show not your teeth, unless you can bite. I were to blame, were I to do so. As the flower springs and perishes, so does man. The deeper the well, the cooler the water. The value we set upon life, is seen by what we do to preserve it. Whatever is done skillfully, appears to be done well. There is not a more pleasing emotion than gratitude. I went because I was invited. To chirp is the first sound a young bird utters. To be weak is miserable, doing or suffering. What that principle of life is which we call soul; how it is distinguished from mere animal life; how it is connected with the body; and in what state it subsists when its bodily functions cease,—are inscrutable mysteries.

EXERCISES IN ANALYSIS.

Who noble ends by noble means obtains,
Or, failing, smiles in exile or in chains,
Like good Aurelius let him reign, or bleed
Like Socrates, that man is great indeed[x].†—*Pope.*

[That man is great indeed, who, let him reign (though he should reign) like good Aurelius or bleed like Socrates, obtains noble ends by noble means, or (who), failing (to obtain them so), smiles in exile or in chains]

* This is a complex interrogative sentence. The interjection *Ah* is independent in construction. *Who can tell*, is the principal clause; *how hard it is to climb the steep*, is the primary dependent clause, which modifies the verb *can tell*, in the sense of a noun in the objective case; and *where Fame's proud temple shines afar*, is the secondary dependent clause, modifying *steep*, in the sense of an adjective. † See p. 85.

Clauses of Complex Sentences abridged into Phrases.

Dependent clauses can frequently be abridged into *absolute phrases, participial phrases, infinitive phrases,* or *adjuncts*. It is, to a great extent, a characteristic of the complex sentence, that its parts can fold or draw up till they become the elements of a mere simple sentence.

When Cæsar had crossed the Rubicon, Pompey prepared for battle[x]. Cæsar having crossed the Rubicon, Pompey prepared for battle[x]. Since I had nothing else to do, I went[x]. Having nothing else to do, I went[x]. When I had eaten my dinner, I returned to the store. Having eaten my dinner, I returned to the store. She did not know what she should say. She did not know what to say. It was requested that he should stay. He was requested to stay. You will suffer from cold, if you remain here. You will suffer from cold, by remaining here. As we approached the house, we saw that the enemy were retreating. On approaching the house, we saw the enemy retreating.

Compound Sentences.

What in me is dark, illumine; what is low, raise and support.*
Times change, and we change with them. If we must fail, be it so; but we shall not fail. He said nothing more, nor did I. To be content with what is sufficient, is the greatest wisdom: he who increases his riches, increases his cares. The son, as well as the father, is expert in business. Strong proofs, not a loud voice, produce conviction. They all escaped; some plunged into the river, and others hid in the woods. Well—I don't know—what if I should be too late? The slothful man is a burden to himself; he loiters about and knows not what to do; his days pass away like the shadow of a cloud, and he leaves behind him no mark for remembrance; his body is diseased for want of exercise; his mind is darkened, and his thoughts are confused; he wishes for action without the power to move, and longs for knowledge but has no application.

Eternal Hope! when yonder spheres sublime
Pealed their first notes to sound the march of Time,
Thy joyous youth began, but not to fade:
When all the sister planets have decayed;
When wrapt in flames the realms of ether glow,
And Heaven's last thunder shakes the world below,—
Thou, undismayed, shalt o'er the ruins smile,
And light thy torch at Nature's funeral pile.†—*Campbell.*

* This is a compound imperative sentence, consisting of two complex members. The subject of the first member is *thou* understood; the entire predicate is *illumine what in me is dark*, and the predicate-verb is *illumine*, modified by *what in me is dark*, as the entire object, and by *that*, comprehended in *what*, as the simple object; *that* is modified by the adjunct *in me*. *Which*, comprehended in *what*, is the subject of the dependent clause, and *is dark* is the predicate. (Thus analyze the rest.) † Two complex members.

OBSERVATIONS.

Language can be studied *practically*, *historically*, or *metaphysically*. In our schools, there is time for the *practical* only, and for so much of the others as will contribute to this. Analysis belongs mainly to the metaphysical, and is yet comparatively in its infancy. It is, however, but an offshoot from those dazzling and captivating speculations of the Schoolmen, which proved so barren in the end that the disappointed world revenged itself by naming all *dunces* from *Duns Scotus*, one of the greatest Doctors of the creed. Analysis is highly useful for giving a comprehensive insight into the construction of language. But Analysis itself, and the correction of False Syntax, depend directly on Parsing. Analysis can therefore never justly supersede parsing. In fact, the parts of speech should be well understood before analysis is commenced; for otherwise there are no handles to sentences by which the learner can catch hold of their parts to analyze them; and it is certainly easier for him to see the sense of a noun or an adjective in a word, than in the complexity of thought which runs through a clause. In the foregoing pages we have endeavored both to simplify Analysis and to extend it.

About the word *subject*, writers differ but little. *Predicate* is applied by some to the verb only; by others, to the whole assertion made of the subject. We prefer the latter sense, which not only simplifies analysis, but is better sustained by writers on logic. The word *copula* is not altogether commendable: the verb *be* not only connects, but also asserts. (See p. 197.) The division of subjects and predicates into simple and compound, is also an improvement. According to Brown and other old grammarians, the sentence, " Dogs and cats catch and cat rats and mice," for instance, is compound, and must be resolved into eight simple sentences. This process would make analysis a disgustingly plethoric and voluminously prolix affair. Language tends constantly to brevity, and is often elliptical, especially in dialogue; but it must not be supposed that there was once a perfect and ponderous language from which everso much has dropped out, or that we always think first in the full form, and then express ourselves elliptically. We are quite as apt to think in one way as in the other. " *The work being done*, we returned," is brief. If I wished to attach greater importance to the subordinate idea, I would lift it out into greater prominence by greater fullness of expression, and would say, " *When the work was done*, we returned."

The division of sentences into *simple*, *complex*, and *compound*, is a beautiful one; but it is attended with some difficulties. These, however, may nearly all be referred to two heads: first, what words we suppose necessary to be supplied; secondly, whether we are to be governed by the *form* or the *sense* of the expression, that is, by the grammatical sense, or by the logical. Dismissing simple sentences, let us consider the other two classes, which comprise the chief part of literature. Of these, complex sentences seem at first view the more numerous; but, on closer inspection, it will appear that the two classes pervade our literature nearly in the proportion of half and half. It will often be found, however, that the whole sentence is compound; while its members are complex. Of books well known to the public, Young's Night Thoughts is one of the best types of compound sentences; and Milton's Paradise Lost, of complex. A sentence sometimes has the form of one class, yet the sense of the other; as, " Deny us recreation, and you unfit us for business "— If you deny etc.

"Is man a thief who steals my pelf,—
How great a one who robs himself?"—*On Idleness.*

These sentences have assumed, for the sake of emphasis, the compound form, though they are complex in sense. Emphatic conditional clauses sometimes take the imperative or interrogative form; for these forms are two of the most forcible. It is generally better to analyze sentences simply according to their form; for it is the province of Grammar to treat of the *forms of language*. In some few cases, however, it may be better to yield to the sense; or to say that the sentence is one thing in form and another in sense. In general, the compound sentence implies *additional thought;* the complex sentence, some *limitation or modification* of thought already expressed, or to be expressed. Compound sentences can generally be broken, at their loose joints, into two or more sentences; especially when we wish to give greater prominence to the latter part. Sentences that imply cause or inference,—the latter part beginning with *for* or *therefore* after a semicolon,—may also be often thus broken. Hence many grammarians call them compound too; and those expressing inference should often be called so. Critics have too generally condemned long sentences. Some of the long sentences in our old English writers carry rich clusters of thought with them, and are like bomb-shells in effect. Grammars, too, are generally filled with such sentences as, "The sun shines," and "The sky is blue;" while long and difficult ones seem to be studiously avoided.

SUMMARY OF ANALYSIS AND DESCRIPTION.

[This section is designed for reference only.]

A perfect or entirely satisfactory analysis of speech has never been made; and it is perhaps even less possible than a perfect analysis of the material world. Yet our knowledge of either may be much extended by such analyses as can be made.

Analysis is the separating of a whole into its parts.

Synthesis is the combining of parts into a whole.

The analysis of sentences with reference to the entire thoughts expressed by them, is called *Analysis;* and the analysis of words with reference to their ideas in the structure of sentences, is called *Parsing.*

Language is any series of words or signs by which we express or communicate thoughts.

Discourse is the embodying of thought with language, or it is some train of thought embodied in language. Discourse is to language what buildings are to building-materials.

Discourse, according to its subject-matter, to the manner in which is developed, or to the end in view, has been variously divided. The most obvious division is into *prose* and *poetry.*

The chief divisions of *prose* are *science, philosophy, history, travels, novels, essays, addresses, critiques,* and *letters.*

The chief divisions of *poetry* are *epic poetry, dramatic poetry* (*tragedies* and *comedies*), *lyric poetry* (*odes, songs,* and *sonnets*), *satires, epistles, epigrams,* and *epitaphs.*

Discourse is either *direct, indirect,* or *representative.*

Direct discourse represents the speaker as giving his own thoughts in his own language.

Indirect discourse represents the speaker as relating in his own language what he ascribes to another.

Representative discourse, or dialogue, enables the author to represent, by assumed characters, either his own sentiments or those of others.

The great advantage of *representative discourse*, and also to some extent of *indirect discourse*, is, that it enables the author to conceal or disguise his own opinions. Who shall say, for instance, to what extent Shakespeare is morally or critically responsible for his writings? See also Dr. Franklin's account of what a wise old Indian chief thought of the whites.

Perhaps the most rational division of discourse is the following:—

a. That which depends chiefly on *place,* and is termed *description.*

b. That which depends chiefly on *time,* and is termed *narrative.*

c. That which aims to unfold or exhibit the *nature* or *rationale* of things, and prevails in works of science and philosophy.

d. What accompanies each of these for the sake of illustration, or to render the speaker's meaning more intelligible or impressive.

Any of the first three mentioned, may predominate in the discourse, but they are not unfrequently combined.

1. *Discourse* may usually be divided into *paragraphs.*

2. A *paragraph* is a portion distinct in form and sense. Paragraphs often consist of two or more sentences.

3. A *sentence* is a thought expressed by words. A sentence must comprise words sufficient to be of itself complete in sense and grammatical construction. (A nominative in one sentence, for instance, can never be the subject of a verb in another sentence.)

The beginning of a sentence is denoted by a capital letter; and the end, usually by a period, an interrogation-point, or an exclamation-point.

4. Sentences are either *simple, complex,* or *compound ;* and their constituent parts are *words, phrases,* and *propositions.*

5. A *proposition* may be either *declarative, imperative, interrogative,* or *exclamatory ; actual* or *contingent ; positive* or *negative ; independent, principal, subordinate,* or *coördinate ;* it comprises but *one subject* and *one predicate,* though either or both may be *compound* or *modified* to any extent whatsoever.

6. A *phrase* consists of two or more words rightly put together, but not making a proposition; and it generally depends on something else for complete sense.

7. A word without grammatical relation to other words, or a phrase in which such a word is the principal one, is said to be *independent;* and, if it implies an address, it is sometimes called a *compellative,*—a word that means *forcing attention.*

ANALYSIS OF SENTENCES.

8. A *simple sentence* contains but one proposition; a *complex* or a *compound sentence*, two or more propositions, termed *clauses*.

9. Two or more clauses, forming a distinct part of a compound sentence, may be termed a *member;* and so may the remaining words, or group of clauses.

10. A member or a sentence that has a dependent clause, may be termed a *complex* member or sentence.

11. A sentence not making sense before it is read to the end, is said to be *compact* or *periodic* in structure; a sentence making sense before it is read to the end, is said to be *loose* in structure; and parts too closely connected to admit even the comma, may be said to be *close* or *restrictive* in structure.

12. The distinct, consecutive sentences of discourse are *coördinate;* that is, they stand on an equal footing, or are not conceived as modifying one another.

13. The *words, phrases,* or *clauses* of sentences, may be viewed as *principal, subordinate,* or *coördinate* parts.

14. *Principal* parts do not modify; *subordinate* or *dependent* parts modify; *coördinate* parts are generally the same in kind, and do not modify one another—or they perform the same office, are construed alike, and have a common dependence on something else.

15. Coördinate parts are generally construed in pairs or series, and connected by such words as *and, or, but*.

16. A phrase without a connective, or word to show its dependence, may be said to be connected by its *position;* a sentence or clause, by *simple succession;* and a clause so intimately connected with a finite verb—(as a subject-nominative, predicate-nominative, objective)—that it must be read with it in order to analyze the clause, may be said to be *incorporated* into the sentence.

17. The compellative, subject, or predicate, taken with its modifications, grammarians usually call the *logical* compellative, subject, or predicate; without them, the *grammatical* compellative, subject, or predicate.

Every proposition or clause should be separated, as soon as possible, into its *grammatical* subject and predicate; and all the dependent parts should then be referred, according to the sense, to the one or to the other.

18. The *syntax* of sentences is best considered under four heads; *relation, government, agreement,* and *position*.

19. The *relation* of words is their reference to one another according to the sense.

20. *Government* is the power which one word has over another in determining its case, person, number, or some other property.

21 *Agreement* is the correspondence of one word with another in case, person, number, or some other property.

22. *Position* refers to the place which a word occupies in reference to other words.

THE SIX ELEMENTS.

23. Discourse may be most conveniently analyzed, by resolving it into *six* elements; *two principal elements, two modifying elements,* a *connecting element,* and an *independent element.*

24. The two *principal elements* are the subject-nominatives and the predicate-verbs; both of which are easily distinguished, by their form and sense, from the other parts.

25. Subject-nominatives may even be clauses, but predicate-verbs can never be clauses.

26. The *modifying elements* are either *adjective elements* or *adverbial elements.*

27. Any word, phrase, or clause, that modifies a substantive, is an *adjective element.* It shows of what kind or nature the object is.

28. Any word, phrase, or clause, that modifies a verb, (participle, infinitive,) adjective, adverb, or entire predicate, is an *adverbial element.* It generally shows the place, time, manner, degree, condition, cause, effect, purpose, reason, inference, consequence, object, kind, quality, respect wherein, etc., or expresses affirmation or negation. Its chief use is, to make with the predicate-verb the predicate. For the sake of greater precision, the *objective elements* may be discriminated, as such, from the other adverbial elements.

29. The *connecting elements* are the conjunctions, the prepositions, some adverbs, and the relative pronouns. Connectives may perform, additionally, some office in the parts to which they belong; they may be expressed or omitted; they may be used singly or in pairs; they may consist of one word each, or of a phrase.

30. The *independent element* may be a substantive denoting what is addressed, or what is the mere subject of thought; or it may be an interjection; or it may be something that represents an entire sentence, or stands as the fragment of a sentence.

31. A part used singly, is called a *simple element;* a pair or series of parts is called a *compound element;* and a part that is modified by another, makes with it a *complex element.*

32. What is inverted or elliptical, should generally be analyzed as if it stood in its logical order or fullness.

33. It is sometimes not easy to determine whether an adjunct, an adjective, or an adjective phrase; a participle or a participial phrase; an infinitive or an infinitive phrase,—should be referred to the subject or to the predicate. Consider carefully what constitutes the whole of that of which the affirmation is made; next consider what constitutes .he whole of that which is strictly affirmed. When even this mode of judging is inadequate, it will probably be a matter of little consequence, to which part the modification is referred.

ANALYSIS OF SENTENCES. 87*

GENERAL DIRECTIONS FOR ANALYSIS AND DESCRIPTION.

1. Read a paragraph, and be sure that you clearly and fully comprehend it. If it is expressed not in the most ordinary manner, show how it has been raised (by equivalent expressions, arrangement, ellipsis, repetition, expansion, &c., figures, versification.—See pp. 294–334,) from the plain, logical sense and order, to the rhetorical. Next show how the sense has been brought out to the best advantage by the aid of punctuation and of capital letters.

2. Read the first sentence. Is it *simple, complex,* or *compound?* Is it *declarative, interrogative, imperative, exclamatory,* or a composite of these? consisting of what members, and how connected? Find the *compellative;* find the *principal clause,* by considering carefully what it was that was *chiefly* to be said; (in exclamatory, imperative, or interrogative sentences, the principal clause is generally more easily found by imagining them to be declarative;) and *dispose of all the rest of the sentence as adverbial or adjective modifications.* Every clause that can not be treated as a modifying element, must be considered a coördinate clause; and when two clauses so modify each other that it can not be told which is the principal, the two may be treated as *mutually dependent,* or as *correlative.*

Begin with the distinct clauses or independent phrases; take not more than is sufficient for one analysis; invert parts, if necessary, and supply whatever words are needed; and then state what kind of clause it is, connected by what —(word, simple succession, incorporated into the sentence)— to what, as a coördinate or as a subordinate element; and, if subordinate, whether it performs the office of a substantive, an adjective, or an adverb.

3. Next proceed according to the Formulas on p. 64.

4. Analyze the sub-parts; then take the next clause, and proceed in a similar manner, and so on until the sentence is exhausted. A series of finite verbs, however long or modified, should generally be treated as *one* predicate, if not parted by a nominative expressed. By doing so, the process of analysis will be much simplified. The same remark applies to a series of nominatives. When the sentence is analyzed, *parse* the words according to the Formulas heretofore given; that is, mention the part of speech, the kind, the properties, the relations to other words, the Rule. This is the analysis of words, viewed as *constructive elements of sentences.* They may, after they are parsed, be further analyzed and described as follows:—

Tell whether primitive, derivative, or compound; from what derived, of what compounded; the radical, the prefix, the suffix, their meaning, euphonic changes; the primary meaning, and thence by what figure or figures the meaning of the word as used in the paragraph before you; mention the conjugates; the synonyms, and how it differs from them; tell, if compound, why it is hyphened or consolidated. Is the word the best the author could have used?

5. Tell whether a monosyllable, dissyllable, etc.; which syllable has the chief accent, and which the weaker; whether the word is of Saxon origin, of Latin, Greek, French, etc.; whether it is harsh, soft, imitative, familiar, uncommon, popular, technical, etc.

6. VERSE, *as such, may be analyzed and described thus:*—

Say that it is *verse,* and why; tell whether it is *blank* verse or *rhyming* verse, and why; whether composed in couplets, triplets, or stanzas; how many lines to the stanza, how they rhyme together, and—if it has a name—what is the stanza called; of how many and what feet does each line consist, and to what does it rhyme, with what sort of rhyme; what licenses or deviations.

When any word or expression of such a mongrel or peculiar nature occurs, that no principle of grammar applies directly to it, it will be sufficient simply to show its use in the sentence; that is, its meaning, and its relation to the other parts.

SYNOPSIS OF PART SECOND.

1. Introductory View.—Grammar; English Grammar; its parts.

2. Pronunciation.—Letters and elementary sounds; accent; exercises; observations.

3. Orthography.—Capital letters, with exercises; syllables; rules of spelling, with exercises.

4. Derivation of Words.—Prefixes and suffixes, with exercises.

5. Nouns and Pronouns.—Classes of each; properties; exercises; observations. See Synopsis of Part First.

6. Articles.—Principles; exercises; observations.

7. Adjectives.—Classes; degrees of comparison; pronominal adjectives defined; exercises; observations.

8. Verbs.—Classes; properties; auxiliary verbs; participles and infinitives; conjugation; exercises; observations. See Synopsis of Part First.

9. Adverbs.—Principles; exercises; observations.

10. Prepositions.—Principles; illustrations; constructions; exercises; observations.

11. Conjunctions.—Principles; illustrations; exercises; observations.

12. Interjections.—Principles; exercises; observations.

13. Rhetorical Devices.—Equivalent expressions; arrangement; ellipsis; pleonasm; exercises.

14. Rhetorical Figures.—Definitions and illustrations; exercises; observations.

15. Versification.—Principles; more than one hundred and fifty different specimens of verse, scanned; observations.

16. Punctuation.—Period; colon; semicolon; comma; interrogation-point; exclamation-point; dash; curves; brackets; hyphen; underscore; observations; miscellaneous marks.

PART SECOND.

1. INTRODUCTORY VIEW.

Grammar treats of *language*. Taken in its widest sense, the Grammar of a language shows how its words are formed, modified, and arranged, to express thoughts, either in speaking or in writing, according to established usage.

<small>The word GRAMMAR means *marks* or *writing* ; because mankind did not feel the necessity of studying language, till they came to write it, and so first devised the science of writing. SCIENCE is knowledge put together in some proper order.</small>

Language, so far as Grammar is concerned with it, pertains to *words*, and is either *spoken* or *written*. Objects, actions, and sounds not articulate, may also be occasionally used as language, which is sometimes termed *natural* or *symbolic* language.

Language not only exists, but lives, grows, and decays. It is not a dead mechanism, but a living organism. Words, and modes of expression, are constantly coming into use; others, passing out of use; and others, assuming new burdens of meaning, and perhaps losing their old.

Not only Grammar, but also Logic and Rhetoric treat of language. Grammar looks to the vehicle, Logic and Rhetoric regard rather what is conveyed: these, learned in one language, generally suffice for any other; but it is not so with Grammar. Logic, with reference to language, teaches how thoughts are rightly expressed in regard to truth and reason; Rhetoric, how they are expressed so as to make the most vivid and effectual impression. A geometry displays most logic, and a book of poems most rhetoric.

English Grammar teaches how to speak and write the English language correctly. This is the *practical* view.

It is a thorough analysis, or anatomy, of the language, completely laying open its nature in *general principles*, and especially teaching those properties in respect to which we are liable to misuse it, or at least those on which its right construction depends. This is the *philosophical* view.

ENGLISH GRAMMAR may be divided into *five* parts; *Pronunciation, Orthography, Etymology, Syntax*, and *Prosody*.

<small>PRONUNCIATION means *uttering forth aloud* ; ORTHOGRAPHY, *correct writing* ; ETYMOLOGY, the *true nature of words* ; SYNTAX, *placing together* ; and PROSODY, *tone added*, and thence, whatever is added to the least adorned language, to make it clearer or more expressive.</small>

What is said of Grammar? English Grammar? Into how many parts divided?

Pronunciation treats of the sounds of the letters, and of the sounds and stress of syllables in the utterance of separate words.

Orthography treats of the forms of letters, and teaches how to spell words correctly.

Etymology, in its popular sense, is the history of words; but in grammar it merely denotes the part which classifies words, and teaches those properties and modifications which adapt them to the formation of sentences.

Syntax treats of the relations and proper arrangement of words in the formation of sentences.

Prosody, in its narrowest sense, treats of versification; in its widest sense, of figures, versification, utterance, and punctuation.

2. PRONUNCIATION.

Our language has about forty elementary sounds, which are represented by twenty-six letters, called the *alphabet*.

The Phoneticians make *forty-three elementary* sounds. LONG VOWELS: *eel, ale, arm, all, ope, food*. SHORT VOWELS: *in, ell, an, odd, up, foot*. SHADE VOWELS: *earth, air, ask*. DIPHTHONGS: *isle, oil, owl, mule*. COALESCENTS: *yea, way*. ASPIRATE: *hay*. EXPLODENTS: *rope, robe, fate, fade, etch, edge, lock, log*. CONTINUANTS: *safe, save, wreath, wreathe, buss, buzz, vicious, vision*. LIQUIDS: *full, for*. NASAL LIQUIDS: *seem, seen, sing*. If we regard the foregoing "diphthongs" as composite, equivalent to *ā-ee, ŏ-i, ā-oo*, and *ī-oo*, our language will have but *thirty-nine* simple sounds. If we regard *c* as a more slender sibilant than *s*; and if *o*, as heard in *form*, is broader or more orotund than *a*, as heard in *all*,— then there are *forty-one* simple sounds in all.

The parts of the throat and mouth, by means of which the letters are pronounced, are called the *organs of speech*. These are the *glottis, palate, tongue, teeth,* and *lips*.

The **elementary sounds** are either *inarticulate* or *articulate*.

The *inarticulate* sounds are simple sounds formed by keeping the organs of speech more or less apart or open.

The *articulate* sounds are simple sounds that begin or end in a closing of some of the organs of speech.

Articulate means "jointed;" *inarticulate*, "not jointed." These words are applied to speech, from a fancied resemblance of the syllables in a word to the parts of a jointed plant: thus, *in-im-ic-al, en-ter-tain-ment*. Here the sound, like the pith, is broken or stopped at certain points; and s, m, c, l, and t, serve as partitions in the sound, like the joints in the pith of a reed or stalk.

A **letter** is a character used to represent one or more of the elementary sounds of language; or it is the least distinct part of a written word.

A letter generally has for its name one of the *sounds*, or *powers*, which it represents.

Sometimes two or more letters represent but one elementary sound.

Ex.—*Ph—f*, as in *phleme; eau—o*, as in *beau; ch*, in *church; th*, in *thou*.

What is said of Pronunciation? Orthography? Etymology? Syntax? Prosody? What do you know of the original meaning of these terms? Our language has how many elementary sounds? Elementary sounds are of what two kinds? What is an inarticulate sound? An articulate sound? A letter?

PRONUNCIATION.—LETTERS AND THEIR SOUNDS.

The **letters** are divided into *vowels* and *consonants;* the consonants into *mutes* and *semivowels;* and some of the semivowels are called *liquids*.

This division of the letters not only distinguishes them according to their nature, but is the basis of many valuable rules.

The **vowels** are *a, e, i, o, u;* also *w* and *y*, when not followed by a vowel sound in the same syllable.

They can be sounded alone, and represent each several inarticulate elementary sounds. (Except *w*.)

Ex.—F*a*te, f*a*re, f*a*t, f*a*r, f*a*ll; m*e*, m*e*t; f*i*ne, f*i*n, f*a*tigue; n*o*, n*o*t, d*o*ve, pr*o*ve, b*oo*k; *u*se, *u*s, f*u*ll; c*i*ty, cr*y*; br*ow*, d*ew*, b*oy*.

The **consonants** are all the letters except the vowels.

They are so called because they can not be sounded alone; or, rather, when they are uttered alone, the sound of a vowel is always heard with them.

B, c, d, f, m, k, are pronounced as if written *be, se, de, ef, em, ka.*

W or *y* is a consonant when a vowel sound follows it in the same syllable; as in *water, young, year, Iowa, Bunyan.*

U and *i* are consonants when equivalent to the consonants *w* and *y;* as in *persuade, poniard.*—*X*— *ks, gz,* or *z;* as in *tax, exalt, Xerxes.*

The **mutes** have no sound whatever without the aid of a vowel, and at the end of a syllable stop the voice entirely.

They are *b, q, d, t, k, q*u (=*k*w); also *c* and *g* when hard, as in *lac, gig.*

The **semivowels** are all the consonants except the mutes. They are so called, because they are, in their nature, between vowels and mutes; having some sound by themselves.

The **liquids** are *l, m, n, r,* and perhaps *s;* so called from their soft sound, which easily flows into and unites with that of other letters.

Ex.—Lily, million, brilliant, Albion, Columbia, mammon, Alps, pearl, stamp, bring, volleying.

"Lull with Amelia's liquid name the Nine."—*Pope.*

A **diphthong** is two vowels joined and blended in one sound.

Ex.—Bl*oo*d, d*oo*m, b*oy*, r*ou*nd, *ea*rn, cr*ow*, n*ow*, v*ai*n, pl*ay*.

A diphthong is *proper,* if the two vowels are heard, or form a sound different from that of either; *improper,* if only one vowel is heard.

Ex.—*Oi*l, gr*ou*nd, r*oo*m, j*oy*, br*ow*, fr*au*d. *Ea*gle, h*ea*rt, m*ou*rn, f*ai*r, sl*eigh*t, dec*ei*t.

A **triphthong** is three vowels joined and blended in one sound.

Ex.—B*eau*ty, bur*eau*, v*iew*, b*uoy*.

How are the letters classified? What can you say of vowels? Consonants? *W* and *y*? Mutes? Liquids? Diphthongs? Triphthongs?

Triphthongs are also divided, like diphthongs, into *proper* and *improper*, according as the vowels are all sounded or not all sounded.

A letter is said to be *silent*, when it is suppressed in pronunciation.

Ex.—Wa*l*k, kil*n*, ni*gh*t, fore*i*gn, vi*c*tuals, *h*our.

The pronunciation of discourse by means of letters, may be compared to music from a flute or a similar instrument. The vowels are analogous to the different notes or tones: they afford the sound. The consonants resemble the stoppages by means of the fingers. Not any or every arrangement of letters makes language; nor will any or every mode of playing produce music.—In singing, vowel sounds are made most prominent.

Mention the vowels, consonants, mutes, semivowels, liquids, silent letters; also the diphthongs and triphthongs, and of what kind:—

O, b, d, e, i, f, a, m, u, r, s, f, l, q, y, g, z, announcement, analytical, history, czar, revolution, youthful, years, gorgeous, colorings, clang, oyster, weight, sleight, streak, steak, phthisic; sparkling fountains.—Rome was an ocean of flame. Height and depth were covered with red surges, that rolled before the blast like an endless tide.

Letters are formed into *syllables*, and syllables into *words*.

The simple or obvious sounds of language as we hear it spoken, are *syllables*.

When more syllables than one make a word, we admit into the pronunciation what is called *accent*.

ACCENT.

Accent is a distinguishing stress on some syllable of a word having two or more syllables.

Ex.—Ba′-ker, a-muse′, con′-ti-nent, con-tent′-ment, coun-ter-act′, tem′-per-a-ment, ge-o-graph′-ic-al; to con-tract′, a con′-tract. "Not the les-sor′, but the les-see′." "An au-gust′ procession, in the month of Au′-gust."

The common or word accent seems to have been introduced into language to distinguish syllables that are themselves words, from those which are only parts of words. An accented syllable at once indicates, that there are other syllables about it forming a part of the same word. Accent, moreover, contributes to euphony, and to ease of utterance. It also serves to distinguish words from others in some way related to them; and sometimes, to show the most important part of the word. An eminent German grammarian says, "As soon as language proceeds from mere articulation to coherency and connection, accent becomes the guide of the voice."

Words of three or more syllables generally have a chief accent, called the *primary* accent; and one or more inferior accents, called the *secondary* accent or accents.

Ex.—Lu′-mi-nà-ry, coùn-ter-act′, àn-te-ce′-dent, èp-i-gram-mat′-ic, ìn-dèm-ni-fi-ca′-tion, in-còm-pre-hèn-si-bil′-i-ty.

Some words, mostly compounds, have two accents of nearly equal stress.

Ex.—A′-men′, fare′-well′! down′-fall′, knit′ting-nee′dle, e′ven-hand′ed, lin′-sey-wool′sey.

To pronounce well, it is important to know the elementary sounds and their combinations, to divide words accurately into syllables, and to know which syllable

What can you say of triphthongs? When is a letter silent? What is said of letters, syllables, and accent? What is accent? What are some of its advantages? What is said of primary and of secondary accent? What of two equal accents? What is needed, to pronounce well?

of a word has the chief accent. To know where the chief accent should be placed, is sufficient; for the others then naturally fall into their places.

Most words used in our language have the chief accent either on the *penult* or on the *antepenult;* that is, on the second or the third syllable from the end.

Ex.—Val'-ley, con'-quest, at-tor'-ney, tem'-per-ate, mu-ta-bil'-i-ty.

Latin, Greek, or Scriptural names, always have the chief accent on the *penult* or on the *antepenult.*

Ex.—Cor-i-o-la'-nus, Ar-is-toph'-a-nes, Jer-e-mi'-ah, Je-ru'-sa-lem.

Ordinary English words sometimes have the chief accent as far back as on the fourth or even the fifth syllable from the end.

Ex.—Co-tem'-po-ra-ry, ob'-li-ga-to-ry. But when on the fifth syllable from the end, the pronunciation becomes so difficult that there is a strong tendency to throw the chief accent on some syllable nearer the end; and hence we often hear *ob'-li-ga-to-ry,* for instance, pronounced *ob-lig'-a-to-ry.*

Words ending in the sound of *shun, zhun,* or *chun,* or in any kindred sound, have the chief accent on the *penult.*

Ex.—Conven'-tion, popula'-tion, posses'-sion, combus'-tion, complex'-ion, ambro'-sia, musi'-cian, politi'-cian, pertina'-cious, circumstan'-tial, artifi'-cial, coura'-geous, insuffi'-cient.

Words ending in *cive, sive, ic, ics,* or *tive* preceded by a consonant, have the chief accent on the *penult.*

Ex.—Condu'-cive, eva'-sive, hero'-ic, sulphu'-ric, characterist'-ic, philanthrop'-ic, phonet'-ics, harmon'-ics, calisthen'-ics, consump'-tive.

Exceptions: Arith'-metic, ar'-senic (noun), ad'-jective, bish'-opric, cath'-olic, chol'-eric, ephem'-eric, her-etic, lu'-natic, pol'-itic, pol'-itics, rhet'-oric, sub'-stantive, tur'-meric, and perhaps pleth'-oric and splen'-etic.

Words ending in *acal, acy, athy; e-al, e-an, e-ous; efy, ety, erous; fluous, fluent; gonal, graphy; i-a, i-ac, i-al; i-an, ical, i-ous; inous, ify, ity; logy, loquy, lysis; meter, metry; orous, ulous; phony, tomy,* or *thropy,*—have the chief accent on the *antepenult.*

Ex.—Heli'-acal, theoc'-racy, sym'-pathy, empyr'-eal, or'-deal, Heron'-lean, ceru'-lean, sponta'-neous, stu'-pefy, sati'-ety, armig'-erous, aurif'-erous, super'-fluous, circum'-fluent, diag'-onal, orthog'-raphy, lithog'-raphy, rega'-lia, amino'-niæ, armo'-rial, trage'-dian, astronom'-ical, contume'-lious, om'-inous, volu'-minous, person'-ify, anal'-ogy, col'-loquy, paral'-ysis, barom'-eter, trigonom'-etry, o'-dorous, carniv'-orous, sed'-ulous, eu'-phony, anat'-omy, misan'-thropy.

Exceptions: Adamante'-an, antipode'-an, colosse'-an, cano'-rous, empyre'-an, Epicure'-an, hymene'-al, hymene'-an, pygme'-an.

Words of three or more syllables, ending in *ative,* have the accent on the *antepenult,* or on the preceding syllable.

Ex.—Ab'-lative, demon'-strative, commu'-nicative, op'-erative, pal'-liative, spec'-ulative.

Exceptions: Crea'-tive, colla'-tive, dila'-tive.

Some words may be pronounced in different ways, with good authority for each pronunciation.

Ex.—Adver'-tisement, or advertise'-ment; deco'-rous, or dec'-orous.

On what syllables are most of our words accented? How are Latin, Greek, or Scriptural names accented? What is said of words ending in the sound of *shun,* etc.? In *cive,* etc.? In *acal,* etc.? In *ative,* etc.? What is said of words pronounced in different ways?

Exercises in Pronunciation.

The following exercises may serve to guard the student against the chief current faults of Pronunciation. The words are those most frequently mispronounced in the different parts of the United States.

1. Give to every syllable its proper sound.

Pronounce the following words correctly: Been, were, of, for, nor, and, catch, caught, shut, bleat, such, get, can, little, end, gather, rather, cart, cow, sky, new, view, attitude, Tuesday, girl, gird, guise, garden, regard, where, there, bear, daughter, heärth, again, against, hinder, James, general, learn, sauce, saucy, saucer, touch, pert, because, umbrella, district, lord, God, dog, scarce, boil, spoil, join, joist, point, disappoint, my, myself, thy, thyself, earth, pretty, brethren, children, into, covered, roof, hoof, good, to, tassel, nature, future, once, hundred, image, twice, natural, national, rational, nothing, husband, different, whole, drove, stone, kettle, rinse, wince, liquorice, enthusiast, tune, gratitude, beauteous, immediate, unctuous, tedious, guardian, crystal, disticsh, pronunciation, since, yes, ear, are, another, cross-wise, chewing-tobacco, passage, steady, spectacle, stretch, education, speculation, contributed, diminutive, calculate, either, creature, parent, sword, daunt, haunt, hurricane, leisure, geography, extraordinary, often, soften, hasten, raspberry, subtle, disfranchise, sacrifice, auxiliary, irradiate, ignoramus, philosophy, diploma, divert, divest, dilemma, dilapidate, stupendous, tremendous, mountainous, proposal, verbatim, apparatus, afflatus, your, tour, going, after, parson, parse, yon, yonder, yours, theirs, his, ours, half, calf, certainly, sudden, suddenly, yellow, meadow, widow, window, shallow, hollow, Africä, Asiä, Americä, magnoliä, fought, might, Indians, negro, onions, have, boiler, engine, service, when, what, where, whet, which, while, sit, set, sat, liberty, Saturday, daguerreotype, stereotype, haven't, ask, asked, women, Ath'ens, Themis'toclês, method, records, attacked, continually, interest, latent, patent, chimney, bayonet, cupola, fiend, shook, books, inquiries, search, sort of, kind of, give me, draught, reïterated, isolated, acorn, vermin, precede, prevent, predict, perhaps, only, prairie, personage, potatoes, coquet, fortune, massacred, helped, curds, mercy, drowned, partaker, iniquities, heinous, violent, extremities, recoil, in stead, instrument, thousands, tremble, sarcasm, chasm, prism, film, elm, audacious, kitchen, foreigners, spirits, heard, beard, decisive, drain, figure, gibber, designate, Italian, stamp, sleek, flake, sieve, verdigris, does, dost, doth, feminine, masculine, clandestine, genuine, crystalline, favorite, respite, hostile, fertile, mercantile, profile, cav'alry. The English often say *hit* for *it*, and *orse* for *horse*, etc.

2. Be careful not to omit any letter or letters of a syllable, nor any syllable or syllables of a word, that are not silent.

Pronounce correctly: Kept, slept, nests, lists, costly, conquests, consonants, door, floor, and, idea, first, worth, months, clothes, sixths, old, must, guests, texts, adopts, bounds, minds, perfectly, shred, shrewd, shrub, shriek, shrink, shroud, shrill, strength, length, something, fold, child, held on, hands, stand, grinds, object, transcript, tempests, worse, curse, nursling, real, poem, horses, history, hickory, victory, several, emperor, salary, artery, separate, believe, temporarily, general, particular, nursery, boundary, flattery, governor, nominative, usually, excellency, purity, government, expect, suppose, attend, against, esteem, surface, astonished, waistband, waistcoat, according, clothing, morning, evening, entering, playing, Washington.

3. Place the accent on the proper syllable.

Dif'ficulty, oppo'nent, compo'nent, fanat'ic, her'etic, to'wards, in'to, ab'stractly, in'teresting, in'terested, ar'abic, or'chestra, contem'plative, super'fluous, ex'-quisite, indis'solubly, def'icit, dis'cipline, inex'orably, mis'chievous, al'abaster, im'petus, mis'cellany, sep'ulchre, condo'lence, manda'mus, quinine', or qui'nine,

What is the first direction in regard to pronunciation? The second? The third?

panthe'on, hori'zon, prec'edents, prece'dence, discourse', con'course, dessert', inqui'ry, ide'a, an'cestor, artif'icer, post'humous, burlesque', chagrin', placard', recess', di'versely, in'dustry, interfer'ence, retrib'utive, hos'pitable, compu'table, indis/putable, hos'pital, the'atre, muse'um, lyce'um, or'deal, com'promise, com'- missary, compla'cence, complaisance', gigan'tic, camel'opard.

4. Bear in mind that derivatives are not always accented or pronounced like their primitives.

Pronounce correctly: Pyr'amid, pyrăm'idal; revoke', rĕv'ocable; repair', rĕp'arable, rĕpara'tion; converse', con'versant; oblige', ob'ligatory; compare', com'parable, incom'parable; Eu'rope, Europe'an; Her'cules, Hercu'lean; or- gan'ic, organiz'able; dēpose', dĕposi'tion; rĕspire', rĕspir'atory, rĕspira'tion; cir'culate, cir'culatory; refer', rĕf'erable; lament', lăm'entable; metal'lic, mĕt'- allurgy; prĕserve', prĕserva'tion; dĕpute', dĕp'uty, dĕputa'tion; dĕtest', dĕtesta'- tion; sagā'cious, sagăc'ity; tenā'cious, tenăc'ity; crys'tal, crys'tallizable, crys- tallīza'tion, crys'tallurgy; prĕsent', prĕs-enta'tion; per'forate, per'forative; paral- lelopī'ped, parallelopĭp'edon; cal'culate, cal'culatory; sac'rifice, sacrif'icatory; confer', con'ference; il'iac, ill'acal; dĕfal'cate, dĕfalca'tion; aspire', as'pirate, aspir'ant; cyan'ic, cy'anate, cyā'nean; colos'sus, cŏlosse'an; comment', com- men'tative, com'mentaries; sup'plicate, sup'plicatory; assign', assign'er, ăs- sīgnēe'; lith'ograph, lithog'raphy; apos'trophe, ăpostroph'ic; philan'thropy, phil- anthrop'ic; sup'plement, supplement'al; condemn, condem'ner, condem-na'tion; damn, dam'ning; sol'emn, sol'em-nize; chastise', chas'tisement, advertise', ad- ver'tisement; ag'grandize, ag'grandizement; chiv'alry, chival'ric, chiv'alrous; allop'athy, allopath'ic; homœop'athy, homœopath'ic; hydrop'athy, hydropath'ic.

A change in the part of speech, often requires a change in the pronunciation; as, To pro-duce', the prod'-uce, prod'-ucts; to pro-gress', the prog'-ress; to uṣe, the use. Such words, when used as nouns or adjectives, generally have the accent on the first syllable; and when used as verbs, on the second or last.

Pronounce correctly: To absent',—to be ab'sent, ab'ject; to abstract',—an ab'stract, ab'stract qualities; to accent', affix', augment',—the ac'cent, af'fix, aug'ment. To colleague', collect', compact', complot', compound', compress', concert', concrete', conduct', confine', conflict', conserve', consort', contest', con- tract', contrast', convert', converse', convict', convoy', countercharge', counter- march', countersign', etc.; a col'league, col'lect, com'pact, com'plot, com'pound, com'press, con'cert, con'crete, the con'duct, con'fines, a con'flict, con'serve, con'- sort, con'test, con'tract, con'trast, con'vert, con'verse, con'vict, con'voy, coun'ter- charge, coun'termarch, coun'tersign, etc. To desert', descant', digest', discount'; a des'ert, des'cant, dī'gest, dis'count. To escort', essay', export', extract', exile'; an es'cort, es'say, ex'port, ex'tract, ex'ile. To ferment' forecast', foretell', fore- taste', frequent'; a for'ment, fore'taste, with fore'cast, fre'quent notices. To im- port', impress', incense', increase', inlay', insult', interchange', interdict'; an im'- port, im'press, in'cense, in'crease, in'lay, in'sult, in'terchange, in'terdict. To ob- ject', outlaw', overcharge', overflow', overthrow', etc.; an ob'ject, out'law, o'ver- charge, o'verflow, o'verthrow, etc. To perfume', permit', prefix', prelude', pre- mise', presage', present', project', protest'; a per'fume, per'mit, pre'fix, pre'lude, prĕm'ise, prĕs'age, prĕs'ent, prŏj'ect, pro'test. To rebel', record', refuse', retail', reprimand'; a reb'el, rĕc'ord, the rĕf'use, by re'tail, a rĕp'rimand. To subject', suffix', survey' a sub'ject, suf'fix, sur'vey. To torment', transfer', transport'; a tor'ment, trans'fer, trans'port. To undress', upstart'; an un'dress, up'start.

Prec'edents, prece'-dent statutes; with ar'-senic, arsen'-ic acid; to be su- pine', mi-nute', au-gust', com-pact', to be in-stinct' with life, to be inval'-id, gal'-lant,—an in'-valid, a gal-lant', in Au'-gust.

To ălly', an ălly'; to rĕlease', a rĕlease'; to dĭscourse', a dĭscourse'; to dĕ-sign', a design'; to intrigue', an intrigue'; to prĕf'ace, a prĕf'ace; to dĕscend', ascend',—the descent', ascent'; to assĕnt', consĕnt',—my assent', consent'.

The following are some of the governing principles of Pronunciation:—
1. Pronounce words according to their spelling, or according to analogy, unless custom is decidedly against such a pronunciation.
2. Indicate difference in meaning by difference in pronunciation.
3. Use accent in such a way that it may contribute to ease of utterance, or serve to distinguish and enforce the meaning.

English pronunciation has a hasty air, tends to brevity, and slides its accents toward the left. An *omnibus* has become a mere '*bus*; a *balco'-my* has become a *bal'-cony*. *Worcester* is pronounced *Wŭster; Brougham, Brōm;* and *Michilimackinac* loses its serpentine length in *Măk'-e-năw*. The verbal ending *ed* is yet heard in the speech of some very old people; but, unless the word is used adjectively, this ending is now generally blended with the preceding syllable, when it will coalesce with it in sound. Most of our final *e's* are but the remains of syllables that were once pronounced.

In regard to Utterance, it may be well to notice the following particulars:—
1. Articulation; 2. Degree of Loudness; 3. Degree of Rapidity; 4. Inflections; 5. Tones; 6. Emphasis; 7. Pauses.

1. Good *articulation* requires the words to be uttered with their proper sounds, clearly, fully in all their syllables, and distinctly from one another. It is opposed to mumbling, mouthing, mincing, muttering, slurring, drawling, clipping, lisping, hesitating, stammering, miscalling, and recalling.
"Words should drop from the lips as beautiful coins newly issued from the mint,—deeply and accurately impressed, perfectly finished, neatly struck by the proper organs, distinct, sharp, in due succession, and of due weight."—*Austin.*
That we have many words nearly alike in sound, yet widely different in meaning, is alone a sufficient reason for exact articulation. Thus, *cheer* and *jeer; pint* and *point; borne, born; genus, genius; imminent, eminent; satire, satyr; burst, bust; beer, bear, pear; close, clothes; false, faults; idle, idol; gluten, glutton; critic, critique; antic, antique; just, jest; real, reel; rear, rare; turnip, turn up.*

2 and 3. The *degree* of *loudness* or *rapidity* must depend on the speaker, the hearer, the discourse, the place, or other circumstances. Scarcely any thing else is so disagreeable as utterance too rapid, low, and jumbled, to be intelligible, and rather suggesting that the speaker is ashamed to let others know what he is saying.

4. *Inflections* refer to the passage of the voice from one key or pitch to another. There are three: the *rising* inflection, which implies elevation of the voice; the *falling* inflection, which implies a sinking of the voice; and the *circumflex,* which combines the other two. "Was it *you,* or *hè?*" "Madam, *yoú* have my father much offended."

5. The *tones* are voice as modulated by feeling. They should be adapted to the general discourse, and also to its distinct sentiments. Tones aim to awaken, by sympathy, the intended emotions in the hearer; and they may also give a favorable opinion of the speaker's heart and feelings.
"In *exordiums,* the voice should be low, yet clear; in *narrations,* distinct; in *reasoning,* slow; in *persuasions,* strong: it should thunder in *anger,* soften in *sorrow,* tremble in *fear,* and melt in *love.*"—*Hiley.*

6. *Emphasis* is an elevation of the voice on some words, word, or part of a word, by which the meaning is brought out more precisely or forcibly. Emphasis, properly used, adds greatly to the vigor of discourse. It tends to impress on the hearer how clearly and fully the speaker comprehends the meaning of his discourse, or the importance of the subject. It gives a favorable opinion of the speaker's understanding. A judicious union of emphasis and tone has sometimes a powerful effect. Emphasis: "We *must* FIGHT; I repeat it, sir, we MUST *fight.*"

What are some of the governing principles of Pronunciation? What is the tendency of English pronunciation? What can you say of articulation? Degree of loudness or rapidity? Inflections? Tones? Emphasis? Pauses?

7. *Pauses* are of three kinds: *sentential* or *grammatical* pauses, which show the grammatical sense; *rhetorical* pauses, which are used for emphasis, or for effect on the hearer; and *harmonic* or *metrical* pauses, which are used in poetry. The last two kinds are essentially the same. An emphatic pause is made before or after the utterance of something of great importance; and it may sometimes be far more eloquent than the most expressive words.

3. ORTHOGRAPHY.

The letters are used in various styles; as,—

Roman, *Italic*, *Script*, 𝔒𝔩𝔡 𝔈𝔫𝔤𝔩𝔦𝔰𝔥, Ornamental, **Full-face,** Clarendon.

The letters are printed in types of various sizes; as,—

Great Primer,   Small Pica,   Minion,
English,   Long Primer,   Nonpareil,
                Bourgeois,   Agate,
Pica,   Brevier,   Pearl,
                               Diamond.

The letters are used either as capital letters or as lower-case or small letters.

CAPITAL LETTERS.

1. Capital letters should not be used without good reason, or when small letters will express the sense as well or better.*

In the German language, every noun begins with a capital letter; and in Old English, capital letters are used about as often, and less definitely.

Capital letters seem to have been at the highest flood-mark in the time of Queen Elizabeth; at the lowest ebb, in the time of Queen Anne; and they rose again amazingly with the German notions of Carlyle, Wordsworth, and similar writers. I have seen pages of our periodical literature so full of these letters, or so disfigured with them, as to have almost a hieroglyphic appearance; and I have also noticed that illiterate people are apt to put a capital letter wherever they think it will look well, especially when it is one that they can make well.

A **capital letter** should begin—

2. The first word of any writing whether long or short.

Ex.—"Know all men by these presents," etc. "Of man's first disobedience, and the fruit," etc.

3. The first word of every complete sentence; and the first word after a ., ?, or !, denoting a full pause.

Ex.—"It must be filled up,—this terrible chasm. But how? Here is a list of proprietors. Choose from the wealthiest, in order that the smallest number of citizens may be sacrificed. But choose! Strike! Immolate, without mercy, these unfortunate victims!"—*Mirabeau.* But a parenthetic word that explains an initial capitalized word, is not therefore capitalized. "Guerillas [bands of robbers] infest the mountainous districts of Mexico."

* The numbers at the left are used as a convenience for future reference. What is to be memorized by the student, is generally distinguished by being printed in larger type, by being numbered, or by being indented, at the beginning of the paragraph, more than is usual. It would be well for each student of the class to procure a blank copy-book, and write in it at least one original example to illustrate each important principle.

4. The first word of the latter part of a line broken to begin anew, and even the first word after an inferior point,—to show more definitely the beginning of something to which the writer means to draw particular attention.

Ex.—"*Resolved*, That we approve," etc. "*Be it enacted by the Legislature of New York*, That a tax," etc. "One truth is clear: Whatever is, is right."—*Pope*. "Capital letters should be used in the following instances: At the beginning," etc.—*Epes Sargent*.
"I am, Sir, with sincere esteem,
"Your faithful servant,
"ROBERT PEEL."

5. The first word of every separate or independent phrase, especially in enumeration, or when used for a complete sentence.

Ex.—"The gunpowder overboard. Out with the boat! Here." "The friendship of Holland! The independence of Spain."—*Grattan*. "Indeed! What then?" "Select Poems of Mrs. Sigourney. 8vo. Philadelphia, 1842. Price $1.00." "To Joseph E. Brown, Esq." "Very respectfully, yours." "For Rent or Sale." "Total, $25." "Balance, $9.25." "Strata and laminæ may be distinguished from joints: 1. By the alternations of different material in the former. 2. By a difference of organic remains in the latter. 3. By ripple-marks and tortuosities. 4. By a difference in color of successive portions of rock."—*Hitchcock's Geology*.

"To Schools, ... $5,785.50;
To Bridges, ... 2,120.25."

A series of elliptic questions, implying intermediate answers, may be put into one sentence with but one capital; as, "Will you repeat the prepositions beginning with *af*—with *b*?—with *c*?—*Goold Brown*. But when the dash cannot well be used, as in mathematics, it may be better to use capitals; though some writers do not use them. "What is ¼ of 5? Of 11? Of 15? Of 7? Of 9?"—*Greenleaf*. "What are the factors of 20? of 21? of 22?" —*Davies*.

6. The first word of every line of poetry, written as such, unless the line is viewed as being but a part of the preceding line.

Ex.— "Now the smiles are thicker,
Wonder what they mean?
Faith, he's got the Knicker-
Bocker magazine!"—*J. G. Saxe*.

"Go to the isle whose green, beautiful border is girdled by Ocean's sonorous white waves."

Whether verse written in the form of prose should retain its capitals, usage has not positively determined. Mr. Goold Brown sometimes retains them, and sometimes not; as, "For whom, alas! dost thou prepare The sweets that I was wont to share."—*Cowper*. "To spin and to weave, to knit and to sew, were once a girl's employments; but now to dress, and to catch a beau, are all she calls enjoyments.—*Kimball*. But most other writers do not retain them. It is generally better, unless we wish to save space, or to present verse in the form of prose, to avoid such arrangement of poetic lines altogether.

7. Every word, phrase, or sentence, comprising an entire saying of some other person, when quoted and introduced at once as it was said by him, or so as to imply a change of speakers.

Ex.—"Solomon said, 'Pride goeth before destruction.'" "Remember this ancient maxim: 'Know thyself.'" "He shouted, 'Victory.'" "They sent back the reply, 'Independence or death!'" "And, 'This to me,' he said."—*Sir. W. Scott*. "Every tongue shall exclaim with heart-felt joy, Welcome! welcome! La Fayette."—*Everett*. "Cæsar cried, 'Help me, Cassius, or I sink.'" "Jesus answered them, Is it not written in your law,—I said, Ye are Gods?"—*Bible*. "The jury brought in a verdict of Not guilty."—*Macaulay*. "He answered, No." "The question, then, will naturally arise, How is the desired improvement to be effected? how are the theory and practice of the art to be obtained? We answer, By the most simple means; by the very means which are so well adapted to other subjects of learning."—*Wilson's Punctuation.* "Thus Cobbett observes, that 'The French, in their Bible, say *Le Verbe* where we say *The Word.*'"—*Goold Brown.* "Christianity does not spread a feast before us, and then come with a 'Touch not, taste not, handle not.'"—*Bishop Porteus.*

8. It is perhaps unnecessary to add, that indirect quotations or questions, resumed quotations, and quoted words or phrases that were not initial, should not begin with capitals.

Ex.—"Solomon says, that 'pride goeth before destruction.'" "That there must be some such relation, is obvious; but what is it? and how is it to be known?" "With Mr. Headley, an event always 'transpires.'"—*E. A. Poe.* "This indeed is, as Chatham says, 'a perilous and tremendous moment.'"

As to words, phrases, or sentences, introduced for illustration, usage is unsettled. Professors G. W. Gibbs and Gessner Harrison use small letters. "To denote the second complement; as, 'the Bible teaches us *that God is love.*'"—*Gibbs.* "E. g., *non poterat effugere,* he could not escape.'"—*Harrison.* But the practice of most modern writers is otherwise. Professor Harrison seems to use capitals wherever he quotes, out of the literature, parts from their beginning; but not if he quotes otherwise, or draws from his own invention. "So, *Ita est,* 'it is even so.'"—*Harrison.* "These are called *active* or *transitive* verbs; e. g., *multa verba dixit,* 'he spoke many words.'"—*Id.* Worcester, in his Dictionary, uses capital letters. "Any covering; as, 'The *coats* of an onion;' 'A *coat* of paint.'"—*Worcester.* "To carry or possess as a mark of authority or distinction; as, 'To bear the sword;' 'To bear a date or name.'"—*Id.* Professor Fowler also prefers capitals; but Mr. Goold Brown sometimes uses them, and sometimes not. It is evident that much depends on the unity or compactness the writer means to give to his sentences, and also on what prominence he means to give to his illustrations. Distinct sentences, even when not separated by a full point, should generally begin with capitals. When words or phrases are given as altogether from the writer himself, and merely to complete his sentence, or when they are rather suggested incidentally than formally quoted, capitals are unnecessary, though sometimes used. "Such are irregular verbs; as, *see, saw, seen; write, wrote, written.*"

9. Every term or appellation denoting the Deity.

Ex.—"God; the Supreme; the Most High; the Infinite One; Providence; Divine Providence; great Parent of good; the Lord of Sabaoth; the Savior; the Messiah; the Son of man; our Lord Jesus Christ; the Holy Spirit; in Christ, our Lord; the Father, the Son, and the Holy Ghost." "I turn to Thee." "Watched by the Divine eye." "Oh, give relief, and Heaven will bless your store."

An ordinary adjunct, used as a part of a name denoting the Deity, usually has no capital; as, "the Savior *of sinners,*" "the author *of all good.*" When a word denotes something as merely pertaining or belonging to the Deity, it does not usually need a capital; as, "Thy *wisdom* and *power* made them all: they are the works of Thy *hand.*"

10. When a pronoun, denoting the Deity, occurs in connection with its noun, it needs no capital, and seldom has one in American books; as, "Thy ownership and workmanship are God's; and thou art *his,* and *he* made thee."—*Greenwood.* When the words *god, goddess, deity, divinity,* and similar terms, are applied to the heathen deities, they do not begin with capitals.

11. Every proper name, or each chief word of a proper name; also the title, if any, preceding or following, especially when this stands as a part of the name.

Ex.—"John Henry Bolton; George Washington; General George Washington; Judge Wells; Dr. Jno. B. Johnson; Mrs. Elizabeth B. Browning; the Countess of Blessington; R. G. Woodson, Esq.; Arthur Price, Jun., Esq.; the Rev. Mr. Brooks; Washington City." "So Master Dick went off on his travels."—*O. W. Holmes.* "'You are old, Father William,' the young man replied."—*Southey.*

12. Common words denoting, in the same way as personal proper names, personified objects, or used as permanent individual

names; and phrases so used, as the titles of books, associations, or other objects,—are proper nouns in sense, and written accordingly.

Ex.—"Hail, Liberty!" "O Happiness! our being's end and aim." "The entrance into the garden of Hope, was by two gates; one of which was kept by Reason, and the other by Fancy." "Thy name is *Hasty Pudding!*—thus our sires were wont to greet thee fuming from the fires."—*Barlow.* "There lay Madam Partlet, basking in the sun, breast-high in sand."—*Dryden.* "This struck the Oak with a thought of admiration, and he could not forbear asking the Reed how he came to be so secure," etc.—*Æsop's Fables; best Edition.* "They went to the Butterfly's ball and the Grasshopper's feast." "The Commons, the Central Park, the Bay of Biscay"—*Worcester;* "the Pacific Ocean"—*Everett;* "in Westminster Hall"—*Macaulay;* "Baffin's Bay, Bristol Bay, the White Sea, the Sea of Japan, the Isle of Man, Hudson's Strait, the Gulf Stream, the Gulf of Guinea, on Lake Tchad"—*Oxford Professor;* "Oloffe the Dreamer, Alexander the Great, the Lake of Nicaragua, to Long and Staten Islands, in Long Island Sound, on Bunker Hill, to Mount Vernon, near the Cape of Good Hope, near the Five Points, the Rocky Mountains, the East River"—*Irving;* "from Prospect Hill, on Breed's Hill, at Moultrie's Point, beyond Charlestown Neck"—*Bancroft;* "to Pilot's Knob, to Council Bluffs, Fort Charles, Vancouver's Island, near Great Bear Lake, the White Sulphur Springs, on the Fourth, on New-Year's Day, the dissensions between the North and the South, the Know Nothings, the Radicals, the Friends, the Sisters of Charity, the Union Literary Society, the Milky Way, Scott's Lady of the Lake, Campbell's Battle of Hohenlinden, Milton's Paradise Lost and Paradise Regained, the first Number of the New Monthly, Dr. Mitchell's Popular Astronomy"—*Sundry Authorities.* Such Scotch or Irish names of mountains or lakes as *Ben Lomond, Loch Gyle,* etc., should always be written as two words, and capitalized. A letter or a word used as the name of itself, is not usually commenced with a capital. Mr. Goold Brown capitalizes letters so used, but not words; as, "*Tee, Tees; Ess, Esses;*" "The pronoun *who*."

13. It is worthy of notice, that not every personified noun is written with a capital, but only those which have the sense of proper names.

Ex.—"Wave your tops, ye pines."—*Milton.* "Ye eagles, playmates of the mountain storm."—*Coleridge.* (Ye men of Altorf.) "Thus liberty, partially, indeed, and transiently, revisited Italy."—*Macaulay.* (?)

14. Words derived from proper names, should begin with capitals.

Ex.—"American, Americanize, Americanisms, Columbian, French, Genoese, Latinize, Grecian, Italicize, Italics, (these two words are frequently not capitalized,) Christians, Christianize, Gallicisms, Hebraisms, Jesuits, Franciscans, Jacobites, a Cherokee, Wesleyan, Roman, Frenchman, Pole, Scotchman." "A Southern man as well as a Northern man."

15. But when such a word has lost its reference to the proper name, and has taken its place and a meaning among the common words of the language, it is not written with a capital.

Ex.—"In academic halls;" "champagne, china-ware, cashmere-shawls, colossal, daguerreotype, damask cheeks, godlike, a guinea, sandwiches, a good bilboa, to galvanize, to hector, hymeneal, jalap, laconic, laconicism, prussic acid, solar, lunar, turkey;" "most socratically"—*Irving. Unchristian,* and similar words, can not receive neatly a capital within.

16. Words of special emphasis or importance, or words peculiarly or technically applied, and not sufficiently definite if written otherwise, should begin with capitals.

Ex.—"The General Assembly; the excellence of our Constitution; our State; the Coal Measures, lying next; William Penn with several Friends; the War Department; the Auditor of Public Accounts;" "the Reform Bill"—*London Times;* "the Missouri Compromise"—*Congressional Globe.* (See also above, 12.)

"Education is the great business of the Institute."—*O. W. Holmes.* "The other member of the Committee was the Reverend Mr. Butters, who was to make the prayers before the Exercises of the Exhibition."—*Id.* "Every American-born husband is a possible President of the United States."—*Id.* "The Medical College in Mason Street."—*Everett.* "The disasters which this little band of Pilgrims encountered."—*Id.* "The Provincial Congress of Massachusetts."—*Id.* "The Governor of the Cape."—*British Quarterly.* "The guests were entertained by Mayor Rice, at his residence, No. 84, Union Place."—*A Boston Journal.* In a draft written by an intelligent gentleman, I see that the sum of money is capitalized—"Five Hundred and Fifty-five Dollars." A large banner floats over Broadway, with this motto: "The Union, the Constitution, and the enforcement of the Laws."—H. CLAY.

17. Writers often take greater liberty in designating by capitals the chief objects of their own science, art, or profession, than is allowed to other persons treating of such things only incidentally.

Ex.—"The Blue Bird [*better*—Blue-bird] of America," etc., says Audubon; because birds made his business of life, and so in treating of each he capitalizes the name. An astronomer, in treating of the solar system, says, "The Sun is the centre of the System." Fowler records his phrenological speculations thus: "His musical talent is great; for Time, Order, Calculation, and Tune, are largely developed." And merchants over all parts of our country do and may capitalize, in their accounts, the names of those things which constitute their business. It seems to be also becoming rather fashionable, to capitalize words in stead of Italicizing them; and we often see the peculiar vocabulary of school-books and scientific treatises, made particularly prominent in this way. Perhaps the printers, to whom this mode of distinction gives less trouble than any other, are those who have chiefly introduced it. The practice is apt to run to excess, and is then akin to that of using the dash excessively.

18. Names, titles, mottoes, or other expressions, when very emphatic, or when designed to catch the eye from a distance, are frequently printed or painted wholly in capitals. And in Advertisements and Notices, the liberty of capitalizing is carried to a great and almost indefinite extent.

Ex.—*Advertisement:* "Just published. A Collection of Songs, Duets, Trios, and Choruses. Together with a New and Complete Course of Elementary Instruction, and Lessons in Singing, for the School-room and the Social Circle. Price 6¼ cents."

19. The pronoun *I* and the interjection *O* should always be capitals.

Finally, the following rule may aid in deciding doubtful cases generally.

20. Whenever any term or terms of a certain import in the language, are employed as a title, or merely to designate a particular person or thing rather than to characterize the same by their meaning, capitals are used; otherwise not.

Ex.—"The Infinite One;" "the design of an infinite Creator, the law of the Almighty God."—*John Wilson.* "Either the world had a creator, or it existed by chance."—*Prof. Gibbs.* "The Green-Mountain Boys were allowed to choose their own officers."—*Bancroft.* "To Professor Longfellow, that is, to the poet Longfellow." "In his Public Despatches."—*Macaulay.* Whether I should write, "Webster's Speeches" or "Webster's speeches," "Burns's Poems" or "Burns's poems," depends altogether on whether I am thinking of the title or simply of the speeches or poems. "Gray hardly took more pains with his Elegy," not *elegy.* "I do not know, sir." "I am, Sir, very sincerely. your friend." "The Doctor now heard the approach of clattering hoofs."—*O. W. Holmes.* "In the preface of his work, he says," etc.—*G. Brown.* "In his Preface, he says," etc.—*Id.*

"The Coast Survey Company of the United States; the Hudson Bay Company; the Secretary of the Interior; New England; Mount Vernon; Fort Riley; Cape May; Sandy Hook; Long Island Sound; Little Egg Harbor; Lake Erie, Lake Ontario; along lakes Erie, Ontario, and Superior; a house in Laurel Grove—at Harpers's Ferry (*towns*); the Senate, and the House of Representatives; earth to earth; the productions of the earth; the planets, Mercury, Venus, Earth, Mars, etc.; the sun and the moon; robed in Luna's silver mantle; the vault of heaven; a heaven of bliss; protected by Heaven; my brother John; John Bull to Brother Jonathan; scenes of nature; according to nature;——and Nature sighed that all was lost." "I have hope;" "Eternal Hope! thy joyous youth began." "We had much pleasure;" "My name is Pleasure." "I reside at a French village—at a place called French Village." "See Rule 8th, and the Notes under it."

Familiar Illustrations and Critical Remarks.—A chapter in your *history* refers to your life; but a chapter in your *History* refers rather to a book written and so named by you. The new *Lucy* is not so old a boat as the *old Lucy*, but the *New Lucy* may be an old boat. When I speak of the *principal* of a school, I refer to his duties; but when I speak of the *Principal* of a school, I refer to his title. The *Monticello academy* is an academy, in Monticello, that bears the name of *Montrose Academy*. A person may be educated at a *university*, and, while in Virginia, may visit the *University*. The *punctuation* of a book refers to its sentential points, but its *Punctuation* is one of the subjects of which it treats. *Callaway county* is usually called *Callaway*, but *Kansas City* is not usually called *Kansas*. The *Ohio river* is as well denoted by the *Ohio*, which is a sufficient name to call it by: but the *Red River* is not usually called the *Red*, nor is the *Blue Ridge* ever called the *Blue*; for it takes both words to make the name. (This, I was told in the Globe Office at Washington City, is the distinction observed there; and I see but this objection to it, namely, that the phrases "the Ohio river," "the Mississippi river," for instance, might be understood as meaning, like the phrase "the Virginia militia," simply the river belonging to Ohio or Mississippi.) "And it continues to be called Hudson river unto this day."—*Irving.* Mr. Geo. Bancroft writes, inconsistently, "in Mystic river, on the Nouse River, the Savannah River, within the limits of the present Greene county." The *city of New York* or *New-York ci'y* is generally called *New York;* but *Jersey City* or *Jefferson City* needs both words to make the name. The Indian always says, "Great Spirit," or uses both words to denote God; but when Pope wrote, "Thou great First Cause," he used *great* in its ordinary descriptive sense. The *King of kings* shows preëminently God's relation to worldly *kings;* but the *Angel of Death* does not show the relation of any *angel* to *death.* The *Devil* denotes *Satan;* but a *devil* may be simply a bad person or spirit. Macaulay writes, "They have coined out of Machiavelli's Christian name a nickname [Nick] for the Devil;" also, "The Tempter, or the Evil Principle." " 'Will you walk into my parlor?' said the Spider to the Fly," denotes the two as if they were Mr. A and Mr. B, or as the chief subject of the composition. But Æsop's *foxes, lions, mice, crows,* etc., are not, in all books, honored with capitals. A *Methodist*, a *Republican,* a *Mussulman,* or a *Roarer,* belongs to some religious, political, or social sect or party. "William Penn with a few Friends," is very different from "William Penn with a few friends." "The First and the Second Sandstone," implies scientific distinction. Prof. Lyell, of England, writes, "the Old Red sandstone," "the Secondary series;" because, I suppose, in these capitalized words lies the technical distinction, and no other capitals are needed. The *gospel* denotes the Christian doctrines; but the *Gospels* and the *Revelation* denote parts of the New Testament. The phrase "Divine assistance" refers directly to God, but the phrase "divine beauty" does not. Missouri is a part of the *South,* though it is *west.* Such is the *union* of the *States,* that they are often called the *Union* or the *United States. Van Diemen's Land* is not the *land* belonging to Van Diemen. *Crabbe's Prairie* once was *Crabbe's prairie. Sutter's Mill* is now a little town, and the *mill* is washed away. *Bolton's Ferry* is a place on the Osage at which there is now no *ferry*. The *London Times* is a newspaper; *London times* are something else. The *Planter's House* is a hotel; the *planter's house* is noted for hospitality. "Monthly Meetings" are sometimes held by large and important religious societies; and are considered, I suppose, more definite, formal, and important than "monthly meetings." When I speak of the *Company* or the *Convention*, I mean to guard you against thinking of the wrong one, or to make you think of a particular one. The *Battle of the Books* refers to a celebrated literary controversy. The *Insurrection* was printed with a capital letter, only while the excitement lasted; but the *Revolution* and the *Reformation* are still matters of interest, and retain their capitals.

So, as the world advances, and new and stirring events are continually thrown up to the surface, any common word or phrase may yield itself up as a sort of temporary proper name; and, when no longer needed as such, be deprived of its capital, and returned to the common arsenal of speech.

Philadelphia has a *mint* and several *colleges*. I visited the *Mint* this morning, and also the *College* [Girard's]. "The city contains an Asylum for the Deaf, Dumb, and Blind, a Mint, and a City Hall," was written as if the names had been transcribed from the buildings themselves. The *Lunatic Asylum* is a particular and distinguished institution in our State, but there are *lunatic asylums* in most parts of the world. "The expulsion of our first parents from the Garden;" *i. e.*, from *Eden*. I went with him to visit the *Lakes*; *i. e.*, a celebrated group of *lakes*. The "lake of the Woods" is a lake in some famous woods, the "Lake of the woods" is a famous lake in woods, but the "Lake of the Woods" is simply a lake so called. "The Erie Canal" is wholly a name; but the "Erie and Ohio canal" is understood as being the canal between Lake Erie and the Ohio river. The *Missouri railroad* is a railroad in Missouri; but the *Missouri Railroad* could be located anywhere. We can see *white mountains* in almost any mountainous country; but the *White Mountains* are in New Hampshire. The *South Pass* denotes not only a *pass*, but is extended in application to the surrounding country, so as to denote a locality besides. *Niagara Falls* means not merely a *fall* of water. Lord Jeffrey, in stead of saying, "Shakespeare," says, "the Poet." The phrase *Old Dominion* is put for the proper name *Virginia*. Macaulay writes, "The mercenary warriors of the Peninsula," applying the word in a specific sense, or to Spain and Portugal. The phrase "Elegy in a Country Churchyard" is as much the proper name of a poem as *John* may be the proper name of a boy. "I saw his Excellency the Governor at the party;" *i. e.*, I saw *Mr. A.* there. Were I, however, to call Goldsmith's *Deserted Village* Goldsmith's *great poem*, I would not capitalize the latter phrase. (See 20.) "To the honorable legislature" is a less definite and complimentary phrase than "To the Honorable Legislature." The *London Times* says, "Her Majesty, the Prince Consort, the Bride, the Prince of Wales, and the other members of the Royal Family were there." Common folks would not have been thus honored with capitals. I should rather speak of myself as the *author* than as the *Author*, for fear people should think I set too high a value on my production, or on the class of persons to which I belong. But, if I were *president* of the United States, I should, considering the great and admitted dignity of the office, speak of myself as the *President*. I should begin my letter with this address,—"My dear Friend," "My dear Sir," "Dear Sir," "Dear Uncle," or "My dear Aunt Mary," &c. Judge Story writes, "My dear Sir:", "My Dear Sir:", "My dear Wife:"; Dr. Holmes, "My dear Professor,—"; Sydney Smith, "Dear Jeffrey," "My dear Mr. Jeffrey,"; the *Quarterly Review* has, "My Dear Friend,".

A Cambridge Professor speaks of his *Essay* in referring to a book called *Cambridge Essays*; and, having introduced Captain Marryatt, he afterwards speaks of him as the *Captain*, and not as the *captain*. Our Club, President, Secretary, and Treasurer, are such in title as well as in fact. "Book I, Part

Second, Etymology, Remark, Observation, Names of Deity, Rules concerning Examples and Quotations," refer to particular parts or headings of the book. An accurate grammarian writes, "Murray, in his Grammar, says, &c.—*The Critic, a Newspaper.*" An *Act of Congress* is not like an *act of a rope-dancer*, and of greater importance. A governor is not necessarily a Governor; nor a supreme court, a Supreme Court; nor the fifth street, Fifth Street. "Our Constitution" does not refer to our health, nor does "our State" refer to our condition. We may speak, however, in general terms, of the states, empires, and kingdoms of the earth; and dukes, kings, emperors, queens, consuls, presidents, judges, mayors, directors, commissioners, councilmen, etc., are all subject to the same rules in respect to capital letters. I am aware that it is rather dangerous to admit the principle of capitalizing words merely because they are deflected in sense; but, to some extent, the principle must be admitted, or, I should rather say, is already established. I find, in my reading, " the cane-brakes of the state of Louisiana"—*Bancroft;* " the union of the States"—*Everett;* " used in Louisiana and some neighboring states"—*Worcester;* " the people in his own state"—*Bryant;* " the States of Italy"—*Macaulay;*" " in the service of a single state"—*Id.:* but, if the *North, South, East,* and *West,* make the *United States,* I think one of these states is a *State,* being derived from a proper name; and because "the state of Virginia," for instance, may mean how Virginia is. I find also,—when the idea is universally considered, or "unified,"—"He is a member of the bar"—*Worcester:* " For the Bar or the Pulpit"—*Mandeville;* " He that killeth with the sword, must be killed with the sword"—*Bible;* " the Song is in poetry, what the Essay is in prose"—*Atl. Monthly;* "In ancient times the State supported the Oracle" —*Oxford Professor;* "These contemplative views of Nature and Man"—*Id.:* but such capitalizing should be indulged in very sparingly. "Have we lifted up our eyes to Him who is Love, Light, and Truth, and Bliss"—*Prof. Wilson.* (See also 9.) Mr. Hawthorne says, of an Italian statue, "Here, likewise, is seen a symbol (as apt at this moment as it was two thousand years ago) of the Human Soul, with its choice of Innocence or Evil close at hand, in the pretty figure of a child clasping a dove to her bosom, but assaulted by a snake." (See also 12.) Prof. Silliman writes, " The Flora of Australia has justly been regarded the most remarkable in the world;" " The European and Australian floras seem to me to be essentially distinct." I find, furthermore, " from Catharine-street"—*London Times;* "near William-street, in Mulberry-street"—*Irving;* " in Chatham-street"—*Greeley;* " in Grand street"—*Bryant;* " at the corner of Union street and Hanover street"—*Everett;*· " No. 22, School Street"—*John Wilson, of Boston;* " at a lawyer's office, in Nassau Street, New York"—*Atlantic Monthly.* The compounding of the two words makes the most exact term; the use of two capitals is more in accordance with analogy; (see 12;) but the last mode of expression is becoming perhaps most common. What I have shown and said in reference to streets, may also be noticed in reference to several other kinds of not very important objects, especially when the ordinary meaning of the word is still prominent. "We passed the Antelope hills, Gray creek, and Rocky Dell creek."—*U. S. Survey of R. R. Route to the Pacific.* (?) In English newspapers I generally find such words compounded; as, *Spring-gardens, Leicester-place, Hampden-street, Fourth-street;* "*Arklow-house, Connaught-place, June* 18*th.*" There seems to be a tendency to consider what figure the object makes in the writer's composition, or in the great affairs of the world; and, if it is not a matter of much interest or importance, to use small letters, or not more capitals than are absolutely necessary to distinguish the object from others of the same kind.

When *earth, heaven,* and *hell,* are spoken of as habitations, small letters generally begin the words; though some writers urge that when the latter two places denote the abodes of the blessed and of the miserable, they are always proper names, and should begin with capitals; and I find, in my reading. "Sleep on, and dream of Heaven a while;" " Frail child of earth! high heir of heaven!" *Heaven* and *Hell*, and some other such terms, as used by Milton, in Paradise Lost, should doubtless begin with capitals, being used in a somewhat unusually specific sense: they form a part of his "machinery." When Muses, Graces, Naiads, etc., are conceived in the splendor of ancient imagination, they are generally favored with capitals; but our own fairies, fays, gnomes, sylphs, hobgoblins, etc., are rather too puny in idea to be thus distinguished. The words *spring, summer, fall, autumn, winter, time, eternity, seasons, morning, evening, noon, day, night*, and many other terms denoting individual objects—such as *earth, heaven, hell, sun, moon, world, universe, nature, space, equator, zodiac, north, south, east, west*, etc.,—when used in their most ordinary sense, or when their meaning predominates, are not usually capitalized; but when they are used in a somewhat technical or peculiar sense, when they are personified, or when the objects are to be honorably distinguished, the words are capitalized. The terms *Pandemonium, Tartarus, Elysium, Gardens of the Hesperides, Elysian Fields*, are of course proper names. *Lord's Day* is equivalent to *Sunday*. *New-Year's Day*, the *Fourth*, *Good Friday*, or any other holiday, is as much a particular day as *Sunday, Monday*, or any other day of the week.

After all, something must be left to taste, or to the nice intuitive perceptions of the writer; and the two extremes of custom in regard to capital letters, may be briefly summed up thus:—

a. Any particular place, time, object, office, officer or functionary, association, writing, building, science, art, or great event, should be distinguished by capital letters.

b. Only initial words, *I* and *O*, titles and proper names, or what is used in the same way, should be thus distinguished.

The following principles may be added in regard to phrases and sentences:—

21. A new proper name made from an old one, by the addition of some common word. Capitals.

Ex.—"Orleans, *New Orleans;* Cambridge, *East Cambridge;* New Hampshire; Governor Clinton; Jefferson City; Rhode Island; Miller's Landing; Upper Canada; Astor House; Mount Mitchell; Kansas Territory; Japan Sea; Lisle Town; the Gulf of Mexico." This and the following are ruling principles, and fail to hold good only when the objects are rather insignificant.

22. One or more common words,—usually, a noun and an adjective, a noun and an adjunct, a noun and a possessive, a noun and its appositive, a phrase or a sentence,—raised to the dignity of a proper name for a particular object. Capitals.

Ex.—"The Park; Salt River; Salt Lake; Big Sandy; Sandy Hook; Land's End; the Cape of Good Hope; the Mountains of the Moon; the Laurel Hills; a hill called Cedar Crest; the United States; the Western States; the Little Belt; the Old South Church; City Police; Post Office; the Know Nothings; a book called—The Temple of Truth."

23. In capitalizing entire sentences or Italic head lines, distinguish, by capitals, the nouns; for the sake of greater distinction, the nouns, the qualifying adjectives, the participles, and other prominent words, and always write the mere particles small.

Ex.—"Our observations may be comprised under the following heads: *Proper Loudness of Voice; Distinctness; Slowness; Propriety of Pronunciation; Emphasis; Tones;* and *Mode of Reading Verse.*"—R. G. PARKER. "*Episcopal Innovation; or, the Test of Modern Orthodoxy in Eighty-seven Questions, imposed as Articles of Faith, upon Candidates for Licenses and Holy Orders, in the Diocese of Petersborough; with a Distinct Answer to each Question, and General Reflections relative to their Illegal Structure and Pernicious Tendency.*"—SYDNEY SMITH.

GENERAL DIRECTION FOR CORRECTING.—*First, read distinctly, as it is, what is to be corrected; condemn it; take a convenient erroneous portion, say what it should be, and give the reason by stating the principle violated; and, finally, read the corrected example.* For greater fullness, say, when convenient, that the erroneous part with such properties or such a meaning, should be so with such properties, such a meaning, or for such a purpose; because, etc.

Examples to be Corrected.

FORMULA.—Incorrect: the word ———, beginning with a small ———, should begin with a capital ———; because ———. (Give the precept violated, as presented on some preceding page; and vary the Formula when a variation is needed.)

Congress authorized gen. Washington to appoint an officer to take charge of the southern district. When Laud was arraigned, "can any one believe me a traitor," exclaimed the astonished prelate.—*Bancroft.* The blood of those who have Fallen at concord, lexington, and bunker's hill, cries aloud, "it is time to part." Three cheers were given for the "champion of the south." The bible says, children, obey your parents. A hundred presbyterian ministers preached every sunday in Middlesex. There was no Church to-day at middle grove. In Benton's thirty years you can find this Statement. All these pleas are overruled the moment a lady adduces her irrefragable argument, you must. Daniel Webster, secretary of state. At fort black Hawk. He Knew general la Fayette and captain Phipps. He was first a Captain and then a General. This Chief had the sounding appellation of white thunder. Washington city, the Capital of the United States, is in the district of Columbia. He is now president of Westminster college, and was formerly principal of Montrose academy. While every honest tongue "stop thief!" resounds. To this I answer, no. The answer may be, yes or no. The president lives in the white house. These Birds go South in Winter, but return in Spring or Summer. I saw, at the same time, a person called fraud, behind the counter, with false scales, light weights, and scanty measures. Falsehood let the arms of sophistry fall from her grasp, and, holding up the shield of impudence with both her hands, sheltered herself among the passions.—*id.* The first melting of Lead Ore, in this county, was in a rude log furnace. This is especially true of Elm and Hickory land. *Dum spiro, spero;* while I breathe, I hope. The question is, which of them can best pay the penalty? *Be it enacted by the legislature of Ohio,* that the taxes, etc. Lindley murray says, "when a quotation is brought in obliquely after a comma, a Capital is unnecessary; as, solomon observes, 'That Pride goeth before destruction.'"—*octavo grammar,* P. 284. At length, the comprehension bill was sent down to the commons. To the honorable the president and the house of convention. He was President of the massachusetts historical society, the Editor of a few volumes of its historical collections, and a contributor to the Boston daily advertiser. The author of the Task was a good Poet. Some welsh emigrants, who were zealous christians. The mexican leader was don antonio de lopez de santa anna. She is gone to him that comforteth as a father comforteth. The hand that made us, is divine. Here is the village of beaver meadow; also mauch chunk, or bear mountain, broad and spring mountains, bald ridge, and pine hills, are here. This swamp was called the shades of death, by the sufferers from wyoming. There dwelt a sage called discipline. He flattered himself that the tories might be induced to make some concessions to the dissenters, on condition that the whigs would be lenient to the jacobites. Some of the Bottom Prairies of the Missouri are sixty miles long.

Monroe house; Martha's vineyard; lake Champlain; little Peedee; Cook's inlet; Penobscot bay; mount Zion; mount Vernon; east indies; the white sea; the Indian ocean; Bunker hill; Harper's ferry; Jersey city; Charleston City; the

City of Cincinnati; in the County of La Grange; Apollo garden; Lafayette place; Boone County; the Prophet Isaiah; King Solomon; the Evangelist Matthew. The Gulf stream; the New-york Fire insurance Company.
The work is admirably adapted to the use of common schools,—
by thorough and varied exercises;
by frequent and complete reviews;
by simplicity of terms and arrangement.
See art's fair Empire o'er our shores advance.
I hate when vice can bolt her arguments,
and virtue has no tongue to check her pride.—*Milton.*
Our Clifford was a noble Youth.—*Wordsworth.*

SYLLABLES.

What is a syllable? A word? A monosyllable? A dissyllable? A trisyllable? A polysyllable? See p. 1.

24. Every **syllable** must consist of one or more vowels, or of one or more vowels enclosed on one or both sides by one or more consonants.

Ex.—*O, i-dle, au-ger, ba-ker, broil; an, ants; dot, shrill, breasts, shat-tered.*

25. What is put to the beginning of a word to modify its meaning, is termed a *prefix;* to the end, a *suffix;* and the part which receives the prefix or the suffix, is called the *root,* or *radical.*

Ex.—*Plant, re-plant, trans-plant, im-plant; act, act-or, act-ive, act-ivity; great, great-est; friend, friend-ship; form, re-form-ation.*

26. In dividing words into their syllables, the ear is the best guide. We should give to every syllable precisely those letters which the correct pronunciation of the word gives to it.

Ex.—*Su-prem-a-cy, il-lit-er-ate, pro-cras-tin-ate, mil-li-ner-y, pref-ace, as-tron-o-my, rev-e-la-tion, oth-er, es-quire, val-e-tu-di-na-ri-an, ma-ter-nal, bas-ket, bar-ber, bur-nish, twin-kle, ho-ri-zon, men-tal, Hel-en, Rob-ert, E-liz-a-beth.*

To write *burn-ish, blank-et, e-squire, sold-ier,* as Webster sometimes divides these and similar words, might suggest that the words are derived from *burn, blank, squire,* and *sold.*

27. Words should generally be divided according to their prefixes, suffixes, or grammatical endings, if they have any; and compound words should be divided into their simple ones.

Ex.—*Re-new, ring-let, great-er, wis-est, sin-ful, ful-ly, skil-less, rock-y, rent-ed, drill-ing, weav-er, mill-wheel, boat-swain, fore-most, whos-ever, wher-ever, an-other.*

28. When derivation and pronunciation conflict, the division must be made according to the *pronunciation.*

Ex.—*Ap-a-thy,* not *a-path-y; rec-ol-lec-tion* (remembrance), *big-a-my, as-cribe, pred-i-cate, in-def-i-nite, ap-os-tol-ic-al, ther-mom-e-ter.*

Vowels.—*Diphthongs and triphthongs,* not severed; as, *loy-al, buoy-ant: vowels making different syllables,* separated; as, *a-e-ri-al, co-op-e-rate: vowels changed to consonants,* to their own syllables; as, *un-ion, liq-uid, brill-iant.*

Consonants.—*Single consonant between two vowels, and not shortening the former nor sounded with it,* to the latter syllable; as, *re-bel', ha-zy, ea-sy: shortening the former vowel or joined to it,* to the former syllable; as, *reb'-el, heav-y, fraud-u-lent: mute and liquid not shortening the syllable preceding,* joined to the latter; as, *pa-trol: shortening it,* separated; as, *cit-ron: liquid and mute, blending with former vowel,* joined to it; as, *post-age: not both blending with former vowel,* separated; as, *dan-ger, pas-tor: two consonants, in other cases,* generally separated; as, *sup-per, mem-ber, mos-sy, col-lec-tive,* etc. *Ch, sh, th, gh, ph, wh, tch,* are treated as single letters; and *tion, sion,* etc., as single syllables.

29. A word having more syllables than one, may be divided at the end of a line, but only at the close of a syllable.

The part in either line should consist of at least more letters than one, and be of such a nature that it is not likely to be misconceived at the first impression.

Such words as *a-long, a-gain, o-lio, craft-y, read-y, curve-d, curv-ed, give-n, safe-r,* and *rhyme-r,* should rather stand wholly in one line; and such words as *accomplice-s, accompli-ces, advantage-s,* should rather be divided *accom-plices, advan-tages.*

30. Two or more words expressing but one conception, or habitually used together as the term for one object or idea, should be compounded.

Ex.—Steamboat, railroad, starlight, beehive, knitting-needle, spelling-book.
Tell whether primitive, derivative, or compound; also whether a monosyllable, a dissyllable, a trisyllable, or a polysyllable:—
Man, manhood, man-eater, management, confidential, uninformed, uninflammable, penitentiary, nevertheless, horseman, Mussulman, nightingale, whereabout.
From what derived:—
Lilies, knives, greater, authorize, farthest, speaks, speaking, applied, written, frosty, inequality, unprepared, happiest, personification, insensibleness.
Mention the prefixes and the suffixes:—
Unbought, unworthy, imperfect, artist, artful, reconstruct, fortify, fortification, overflow, bespattering, fascination, disproportionably, unpremeditated.
Divide into syllables:—
Another, luscious, varnish, tickle, musket, extraordinary, possession, monkey, western, paternal, reformation, recollect, recreate, impetus, impotence, grafter, rafter, charter, chanter, waiter, traitor, colony, felony, pitcher, lounger, noisy, sorcery, gallery, artery, knitting, shilling, willing, azure, nation, siren, brisket, associate, pronunciation, athwart, Ariadne, Diana.
Correct the following:—
Plan-ting, un-loa-ding, ma-keth, sto-ring, or-ga-ni-zing, e-squire, syst-em, might, swif-test, go-vern, cons-ti-tu-tion, va-le-tu-di-na-ri-an, mark-et, stor-my.
A white washed house. Double entry book keeping. I saw a humming bird on a slippery elm. Interest bearing notes. Glass-houses are made in glass houses.

SPELLING.

Spelling is the art of expressing words by their right letters, properly arranged. This art must be learned chiefly from spelling-books, dictionaries, and observation in reading.

Our language having been formed from several others, its words are often spelled very irregularly, and sometimes differ widely from the pronunciation; so that scarcely any useful rules can be given, except a few for derivative words.

Rule I.—Doubling.

31. Words of one syllable, ending in a single consonant preceded by a single vowel; and words of more syllables, ending in the same way, with the accent fixed on the last syllable,—double the consonant before a vowel in the derivative word.

In other cases, no doubling takes place.

Ex.—1. Sad, *sadder, saddest;* rebel, *rebelled, rebelling, rebellion, rebellious;* fop, *foppish, foppery;* quit, *quitting, acquittal;* in, *inner;* up, *upper;* wit, *witty, witticism;* quiz, *quizzed.* *Exception:* Gas, *gases* or *gasses.*

2. Seal, *sealed;* call, *called;* gild, *gilded;* hard, *harder, hardest;* infer, *inference;* travel, *traveled, traveling, traveler;* bias, *biased;* worship, *worshiping;* tax, *taxed, taxes.* *X* final — two consonants, *ks* or *gz;* therefore it is never doubled.

Tell the difference between—
Robed and *robbed; striped* and *stripped; hoping* and *hopping; bared* and *barred; doting* and *dotting; sparing* and *sparring; futed* and *futted; pining* and *pinning; puling* and *pulling; raged* and *ragged; waging* and *wagging; planing* and *planning; hater* and *hatter; spiting* and *spitting; spited* and *spitted; scared* and *scarred; biding* and *bidding.*

Some good writers double *l* in the derivatives of the following words:—
Apparel, bevel, bowel, cancel, carol, cavil, channel, chisel, counsel, cudgel, dishevel, drivel, duel, embowel, enamel, empanel, equal, gambol, gravel, grovel, handsel, hatchel, impanel, imperil, jewel, kennel, label, level, libel, marshal, marvel, model, panel, parcel, pencil, peril, pistol, pommel. quarrel, ravel, revel, rival, rowel, shovel, shrivel, snivel, tassel, trammel, travel, tunnel, unravel, victual. "Traveller"—*Prescott, Bryant;* "marvellous, carolled"—*Irving;* "worshipping"—*Bancroft.* These writers were so taught in youth; hence their practice: but such doubling is against analogy, and generally unnecessary.

Sometimes, however, *l,* and perhaps *p,* may be doubled, to prevent the liability of mistaking the word for some other; as, *Gravelly* from *gravel,—gravely* from *grave; kidnapper* from *kidnap.*

A few words from the Latin are derived according to the Latin primitive, and not according to the English; as, Metal (Lat. metallum), *metallic, metallurgy;* inflame, *inflammation;* excel, *excellent;* appeal, *appellant.*

Rule II.—Final Y.

32. **Y** final, preceded by a consonant and followed by any letter except *i,* is changed into *i* in the derivative word.

Ex.—Fly, *flies;* glory, *glories, glorify, glorified, glorifying, glorification;* try, *trial;* bury, *burial;* merry, *merrily, merriment;* pity, *pitiable;* ivy, *ivied.*

Exceptions: The derivatives of *sly, dry,* and *shy;* as, *slyly, dryly, shyness.* But Noah Webster and Goold Brown prefer to make these conform with the Rule.

33. **Y** final, preceded by a vowel, or followed by *i,* remains unchanged in the derivative word.

Ex.—Boy, *boys;* gay, *gayer, gayest, gayety;* cry, *cried, crying, crier;* allay, *allayed, allaying;* buoy, *buoyant, buoyancy;* destroy, *destroyer, destroying;* annoy, *annoyance;* chimney, *chimneys;* joy, *joyful.*

Exceptions: Pay, *paid;* say, *said;* lay, *laid;* day, *daily;* stay, *staid* (remained), *stayed* (checked).

Rule III.—Final E.

34. **E** final, when silent, is rejected before a vowel in the derivative word.

Ex.—Bite, *biting;* force, *forced, forcing, forcible;* grieve, *grievance, grievous;* blue, *bluish;* rogue, *roguish;* rattle, *rattling;* but *be, being.*

35. But when necessary to preserve the pronunciation or identity of the word, it is retained.

Ex.—Flee, *fleeing;* agree, *agreeable;* singe, *singeing;* trace, *traceable;* swinge, *swingeing;* courage, *courageous;* mile, *mileage;* glue, *gluey;* sue, "*sueing.*" Better,—"*suing,*" for we always write *construe, construing.*

Tell the difference between—
Dying and *dyeing; singing* and *singeing; swinging* and *swingeing.*

36. Words ending with *ie* change *i* into *y*, before *i*, to prevent the doubling of *i*.

Ex.—Die, *dying;* vie, *vying;* tie, *tying;* lie, *lying.*

37. E final is retained before a consonant in the derivative word.

Ex.—Base, *baseless, basement;* rue, *rueful;* definite, *definitely, definiteness;* eye, *eyelet;* shoe, *shoeless;* perverse, *perversely;* whole, *wholesome, wholesomely, wholesale;* release, *releasement.*

38. But when not necessary to preserve the pronunciation of the word, it is sometimes rejected.

Ex.—Due, *duly;* true, *truly;* awe, *awful:* also 'judge,' *judgment;* lodge, *lodgment,* etc.; because the *d* always softens the *g,* and renders the *e* unnecessary.

Rule IV.—Whether Ize or Ise.

39. If the word has a kindred meaning without the ending, or with a different ending, add *ize;* if not, add *ise.*

Ex.—Author, *authorize;* civil, *civilize;* theory, *theorize;* dramatist, *dramatize;* organ, *organize. Revise, compromise, enterprise, surprise.*

This Rule has some exceptions, as *criticise, exercise, assize;* yet I think it may well be applied to all words of this class still unsettled in orthography, and to such as may be formed hereafter. Some respectable modern British authors, perhaps to show their learning, generally use *ise,* which occurs often in Old English.

Rule V.—No Trebling.

40. The final letter may remain or be doubled, but not trebled, in the derivative word.

Ex.—Harmless, *harmlessly;* odd, *oddly;* possess, *possession,* not *possesssion;* full, *fully,* not *fullly;* stiff, *stiffness;* chaff, *chaffinch;* bliss, *blissful;* ill, *illness;* dull, *dullness;* tall, *tallness.* We find *treeen* and *gallless;* but these words should have the hyphen,—*tree-en, gall-less.*

Rule VI.—Compounds.

41. When simple words form compounds, they generally retain their own letters, especially if a hyphen still separates them.

Ex.—Barefoot, housewife, lady-like, party-spirit, well-grounded, hasty-pudding, thereabouts, juryman, whereby, wherein, whereunto, wherefore, wherewith, whereon. But 'where,' *wherever;* whose, *whosoever;* sheep, *shepherd;* feet, *fetlock;* pass, *pastime;* newly made, *new-made.*

42. One *l* from *ll* is frequently omitted; and the apostrophe from possessives always, when there is no hyphen.

Ex.—*Always, welcome, handful, fulfill, heartshorn, boatsman:* and according to Dr. Worcester, and some of the best of our old living writers, *wilful, skilful, fulness, dulness, chilness, thraldom, instalment;* but I should rather be governed here by analogy, and prefer, as Dr. Webster does, *skillful, willful, fullness, dullness, chillness, thralldom, installment.* See the preceding Rule.

Rule VII.—Final F, L, or S.

43. Monosyllables that end with *f, l,* or *s,* preceded by a single vowel, double the final consonant. Words that end with any other consonant in the same way, do not.

Ex.—Skiff, off, hill, shall, bliss, grass; car, drug nod, mob.

ORTHOGRAPHY.—SPELLING.

Exceptions: As, gas, has, was, yes, his, is, this, us, pus, thus, if, of, clef, nil, sol, sal (salt), bul (flounder).

Exceptions: Abb (yarn), ebb, add, odd, egg, jagg, ragg (stone), inn, err, burr, purr, butt, buzz, fuzz, yarr; and some proper names, as *Dodd*, *Hogg*, *Pitt*, *Prescott*. The verbs *mimic*, *physic*, and *traffic*, must assume *k* with an ending that needs it to preserve the sound; as, *Mimicked, trafficking*.

F is sometimes changed into *v*, in derivatives; as, Knife, *knives*; mischief, *mischievous*.

An apostrophe prevents the effect of a Rule; as, Fancy, *fancied, fancy'd;* Mary, *Mary's;* fly, *fly's.*

Always *c-ei*, never *c-ie*; always *c-ian* for the *person who;* eleven *e-fies—arefy, calefy, defy, humefy, liquefy, madefy, putrefy, rarefy, stupefy, tabefy, torrefy;* all the others are *i-fies;* and as to *a-bles* and *i-bles*, look sharply and remember.

Some words may be spelled in two or more different ways, with good authority for each.

Ex.—Keg, cag; plough, plow; inquire, enquire; flection, flexion; connection, connexion; hight, height; centre, center; metre, meter; hominy, homony, hommony; moccasin, moccason; musquito, mosquito, muscheto, &c.

44. Some letter or letters of a word are sometimes omitted, and what is left is sometimes changed and combined with another word. Such shortening is called *contraction*.

An apostrophe (') is usually put in the place of the letter or letters omitted.

Ex.—Th' or t', for *the;* 'm, *am;* 'rt, *art;* 're, *are;* 's, *is, us,* or *has;* 've, *have;* 'd, *had* or *would;* 'll, *will;* ma'am, *madam;* n't, *not;* don't, *do not;* won't, *will not;* doesn't, *does not;* shan't, *shall not*—ADDISON; can't, *can not;* 't, *it;* 'tis or it's, *it is;* 'tis n't, *it is not;* 'gan, *began;* pr'ythee, *I pray thee;* couldn't, *could not;* 'cause, *because;* e'en, *even;* e'er, *ever;* ne'er, *never;* o'er, *over;* whate'er, *whatever;* 'em, *them;* 'gainst, *against;* 'bove, *above;* 'midst, *amidst;* 'neath, *beneath;* wi', *with;* i', *in;* o', *of;* o'clock, *of the clock*.

45. A word is sometimes severed by an intervening word. Such separation is called *tmesis*.

Ex.—" *To* us *ward*"—Toward us. " On *which* side *soever*"—On whichsoever side. " The *live* day *long*"—The livelong day.

Generally speaking, spelling and pronunciation are the better, the better they agree, and serve to distinguish words that differ in meaning.

Exercises in Spelling.

Most of the following words are those which I have found spelled erroneously in the compositions of students, on sign-boards, in letters received, and in the newspapers and other hasty literature of our country. The exercises may also teach the student where the dangers of spelling lurk.

Spell the following words, and occasionally give the Rule where one applies:—

Skating, sliding, striving, druggist, forcible, pottage, quarries, rubbed, equaled, hoarseness, agonized, profited, benefited, allotted, gayety, witticisms, confessedly, valuable, usage, chastisement, steadily, steadfast, laziness, till, until, ruling, dreaded, truly, recurred, recurrence, conferred, conference, preferred, preferable, preference, embodiment, Whiggery, fulfilled, lodging, listlessly, dronish, almost, very, welcome, villain, vilify, shipped, paid, ceaseless, daily, servilely, irreconcilably, affiance, denial, syllabic, parallelogrammic, parallelogrammatic, improvements, moneyed, chillness, referred, reference, Italicize, modernized, wagon, offered, colonized, hackneyed, movables, desirable, baptized, valleys, wearisome, seated, quizzed, galloped, civilization, runner, useful, intermittent, realize, vying, unshrubbed, salable, aggregate, indispensably, belligerent, plausible, privilege, accompaniment, buzz, hum, replied, loneliness, portrayed, regretted, getting, transferable, transferee, messmate, parish, snappish, millinery, slavish, curable, tunable, tamable, welfare, thereby, wherever, thereafter, pastime, sometimes, something, opportunity, misstate, misspell, misspend, gemmed, webbed, haggard, sinner, snobbish, terseness, fringing, corselet, fusible, sedgy, smoky, ridgy, swimmer, dragged, bluish, stylish, gluing, blurred, smutty, hedge-row, festering, disbursement, piquant, obliquely, propeller, pommel, remittance, revival, contrivance, rehearsal, debatable, communing, pennyweight, perversely, alcoholize, generalissimo, clergyman, personification, thriftily, fortieth, whetted, demurrer, sluggish, grievous, proselytism, parallelism, vandalism, galvanize, magnetize, anglicize, knobby, liquefiable, charmer, visitor, realist, squatter, broad-brimmed, dullness, pitiable, penniless, likelihood, handicraft, merchandise, organization, worshipers, cities, jockeys, dizziness, gruffly, scaly, solely, wholly, doublings, hying, spied, spy-glass.

Equivalent Sounds.

In orthography, we are most liable to err wherever a different spelling would produce the same sound, or nearly the same sound.

Different vowels or different vowel combinations frequently produce the same sound.

Different consonants are sometimes equivalent in sound.

The single and the doubled consonant are often equivalent in sound.

Spell the following words: Brier, friar, actor, instructor, arbiter, parlor, survivor, fibre, inventor, cellar, elixir, proprietor, scholar, martyr, mortar, receiver, conqueror, regulator, grammar, brazier, grasier, beverage, porridge, selvage, dependent, defendant, tranquillity, gentility, vitiate, vicious, ancient, transient, noxious, musician, conscious, cetaceous, provincial, prudential, inured, encroaching, incumbent, encountered, inculcate, include, entirely, intrude, enjoyment, gem, jet, dressed, distressed, chest, assessed, relinquish, extinguish, bombasin, magazine, submarine, mandarin, chancellor, shalloon, control, enroll, patrol, appellant, membranous, tyrannous, herring, harass, embarrass, sense, pence, defense, license, district, description, sacrifice, criticise, conducive, defensive, intercede, supersede, fleece, geese, idiosyncrasy, secrecy, hypocrisy, nutritious, delicious, sententious, reflection, complexion, chronology, crystal, chocolate, saccharine, kitchen, martin, curtain, payment, raiment, separate, degenerate, exhilarate, dereliction, predilection, irreligious, sacrilegious, repentance, dependence, succeed, precede, secede, proceed, regale, prevail, prepare, impair, despair, compare, sneak, shriek, brevier, veneer, revere, buccaneer, financier, shote, float, dote, naught, groat, sought, awkward, though, through, tough, slough, cough, hiccough, miscellaneous, ceremonious, weasel, weevil, extirpate, foeman, yeoman, nuisance, sieve, receive, mien, relieve, seize, receipt, lien, ceiling, genteel, repeal, tearful, cheerful, screech-owl, lurched, perched, searched, gauge, business, gourd, hoard, horde, sword, brew, glue, labor, error, deposit, composite, dactyl, ductile, chlorite, formula, anomaly, paroxysm, causable, vendible, feasible, seizable, boisterous, disastrous, incumbrance, protuberance, cemetery, cerulean, ethereal, grandeur, nucleus, odious, analysis, paralysis, soothe, smooth, blowze, chouse, rheumatism, diphthong, public, monastic, logic, click, target, braggard, exaggerate, refrigerate, garrison, orison, partisan, partisanship, visible, admissible, copy, poppy, radish, reddish, declamatory, inflammatory, pontiff, pontifical, retaliate, palliate, diligence, intelligence, ballad, salad, balance, bilious, billiards, postillion, vermilion, rebellion, battalion, fallacy, policy, millennial, iniquity, impanel, innuendo, cabin, cabbage, reconnoiter, recommend, centre, theatre, horrid, florid, crystallize, immortalize, satellite, tyrannize, drizzly, grisly, tansy, frenzy, buttress, mattress, matrass, caterpillar, rapper, rapid, bigot, maggot, garret, claret, stopper, proper, copper, fodder, soder, valid, pallid, dissyllable, trisyllable, tussle, rustle, tenant, pennant, tiny, finny, gizzard, wizard, threshold.

The most ludicrous blunders are usually made by the missapplication of those words which agree in pronunciation, but differ in spelling and meaning.

FORMULA.—Incorrect: the word——(*spell, pronounce, and define*), is here mistaken for ——(*spell, pronounce, and define*).

Correct the errors: The Roman augers pretended to foretell future events. He sold all his manners for a small sum. Miners are not allowed to vote here. The weather may be easily distinguished by a small belle. The benches were all in tears, one above another. My boots are well-souled, and full of tax. We intend to start a weakly paper here. I used my toe for wadding. The oar was completely melted. The wind blue away the blew smoke. His bier was to him, not only drink, but food and lodging. The apothecary sold him six pains for fifty cents. Hawks pray on other birds. The beach stood on the beech. The flour was kept fresh in a pitcher of water. Cleaning and dying done here, according to order. The cobbler put his all into his pocket. My dear Ant. She had many airs to inherit the estate. She went with her bow to church. Do you like currents with cream and sugar? He sewed all the seed. They drank all the champaign. The judge immediately baled the prisoner. The martial had a very marshal look. He put the whole prophet into his pocket. The capital is always situated in the capitol. The bridal was in the barn. The desert was brought in by a sprightly mulatto. His reward was greater than his dessert. The principle is sick. I will right the write word. His chin was soon heeled. She rung all the close. The quire sung very well. Every boll on the place is filled with milk. His vices were all bought by some other blacksmith. The veins are governed by the wind. All these barrels are for sail, at ten o'clock. He was bread for the church.

4. DERIVATION OF WORDS.

This section belongs partly to Orthography and partly to Etymology, or lies between them.

Words are either *primitive* (or *radical*), *derivative*, or *compound*.

The elements of words, in regard to meaning, are *roots, prefixes,* and *suffixes*.

Roots are either native or foreign, and sometimes much disguised.

We have not room in this book to treat of the roots of our language, except to define incidentally and briefly about two hundred of the most common.

46. The same root may frequently be combined with several different prefixes or suffixes, or have more than one at the same time, or be combined with some other root.

Ex.—*Struct* (build), in-*struct*, con-*struct*, re-con-*struct*; *thermos* (heat), *metron* (measure), *thermometer*.

Prefixes usually modify the sense, without changing the part of speech.

Suffixes usually modify the part of speech, without materially affecting the sense in other respects.

Ex.—*De* (from, separation), *de*-stroy, *de*-stroy-*er*, *de*-struct-*ive*, *de*-struct-*ive-ly*, *de*-struct-*ive-ness*, *de*-struct-*ion*, *in-de*-struct-*ive*, *in-de*-struct-*ible*, *in-de*-struct-*ibil-ity*.

47. There are different prefixes capable of expressing the same sense, and there are also different suffixes capable of expressing the same sense; because the choice is to be determined not merely by the meaning of the appendage, but also by euphony, analogy, and the character of the root.

Ex.—Generous, *un*-generous; accurate, *in*-accurate; throne, *de*-throne, *un*-throne; confess, confess-*ion*; acknowledge, acknowledg-*ment*.

48. The meaning of a prefix is sometimes very obvious, sometimes obscure, and sometimes it has faded altogether.

Ex.—*Up*-hold, *trans*-plant, *in*-correct; *trans*-act, *per*-fect, *under*-stand; com-plete, *be*-stir.

49. In making a combined form, some of the parts frequently undergo a change for the sake of euphony or analogy. This consists in the *change, omission,* or *insertion* of some letter or letters. The initial consonant of the root often requires the final letter of the prefix to be like it.

Ex.—Con-lect, *col-lect*; dis-fer, *dif-fer*; in-moderate, *immoderate*; con-operate, *co-operate*; dis-vulge, *di-vulge*; a-archy, *an-archy*; mucilage-ous, *mucilag-inous*.

PREFIXES.

The prefixes in Roman letters are Latin; in Italic, Greek; in black, Saxon or native.

A; *on, in, at, to.* In a few words it is merely intensive.

Form, spell, and define:—

Bed, ground, shore, cross, sleep, pace, slant, field, side, wake, rise.

Thus: A*bed*; a—b-e-d-bed—abed; on or in bed.

A, AB, ABS; *from, separation.*

Vert (turn); solve (loosen), rupt (broken), sorb (suck); tract (draw), tain, (hold).

AD, A, AC, AF, AG, AL, AN, AP, AR, AS, AT; *to, at.*

Join, judge; mount, scend (climb); cord, cuse (charge); fix, fusion (pouring); gress (step), gravate (heavy); lot, luvial (washing); nex (join), nihilate (nothing); portion, preciate (price); rogate (lay claim); sure, sail (leap); tract (draw), tribute (give).

A, AN; *without, privation.*

Theist (God), chromatic (color), pathy (feeling), tom (cut); archy (government).

AMPHI; *two, double.* Theatre, bious (living).

ANA; *up, throughout, parallel, back, again.*

Tomy (cutting), lysis (separation), logy (discourse), gram (letter), baptist.

ANTE; *fore, before.* Chamber, date, meridian (noon), cedent (going).

ANTI, ANT; *against, opposition.*

Bilious, febrile, pathy (feeling), dote (given); arctic, agonist (contend).

APO, AP; *from, off.*

Gee (earth), strophe (turning), logy; helion (sun).

DERIVATION OF WORDS.—PREFIXES. 115

Be; *action directed to an object; intensity; by, near.*
Daub, dew, moan, lie, set, siege, cloud, spatter, take; side, fore, cause.
BENE; *good, well.* Fit (deed), volent (wishing), factor (doer), diction (saying).
BIS, BI; *twice, two.*
Cuit (baked); angular, valve, gamy (marriage), sect (cut), ped (foot).
CATA, CAT; down, against, throughout. (The opposite of ANA.)
Ract (flowing), strophe, chresis (use); hedral (seat), holic (whole).
CIRCUM, CIRCU; *round, about.*
Navigate, jacent (lying), spect (looking), stance (standing); late (borne), itous (going).
CIS; *on this side.* Alpine, Atlantic.
CON, CO, COG, COL, COM, COR; *with, together, jointly.*
Join, tract, fuse (pour), vene (come), ceive (take), flict (strike); extent, heir, operate; nate (born); league, lect (gather); press, mingle, pose (place); respond, relative.
CONTRA, CONTRO, COUNTER; *against, in opposition, answering to.*
Dict (say), vene, distinguish; vert; part, pressure, feit (make), act, plead.
DE; *from, down, destruction.*
Tract, press, throne, scend, tect (cover), tach (tie), spise (look), moralize.
DIA, DI; through, across. Meter, logue (speech), gonal (angle).
DIS, DI, DIF; *away, apart, undoing, negation.*
Join, organize, appear, ease, sect, tract, cover, perse (scatter), please, inter, order; verge (incline), stance, gress; fer (bear), fuse (pour).
E, EX, EC, EF; *out, out of, from.*
Ject (throw), lect (pick), vade (go), mit (send); pectorant (breast), press, pand (spread), tort (twist), pire (breathe); centric (centre), stasy (standing); fuse, fect (done), fulgence (shining).
EN (Greek or French), *EM; in, into, upon.*
Tangle, shrine, rage, gulf, large, grave (scrape), tomb; broider, blazon, bark, bitter, brace (arm).
EPI, EP; upon, after. Taph (tomb), demic (people), logue; ode.
EXTRA; *beyond.* Ordinary, vagant (going), mural (wall).
For, fore; *from, against, the contrary.* Bid, get, sake (seek), give, swear; go.
Fore, for; *before.*
Tell, run, see, know, taste, man, father, noon, arm; ward.
HYPER; beyond, over, excess. Borean (north), critical, meter (measure).
HYPO; under. Thesis (placing), sulphuric, crite (thoughts).
IN, IG, IM, IL, IR; *not, privation, the contrary.*
Human, discreet, elastic, consistent; noble; modest, mortal, patient; legal, liberal; reverent, regular, resolute.
IN, IM, IL, IR; *in, into, upon.*
Flame, struct, lay, here (stick), flect (bend), wrought; plant, pearl, print, press; luminate or lustrate (throw light); radiate (throw rays).
INTER; *between.* Weave, line, cede, regnum (reign), mix, marriage.
INTRO: *inwards, within.* Duce (lead), mission (sending).
META, METH; over, beyond, with, change.
Thesis, morphose (form), physics, phor (convey); od (way).
Mis; *wrong, ill.* Apply, call, deed, use, spell, take, fortune.
NON; *negation.* Conductor, conformity, sense, resident, payment.

OB, OC, OF, OP; *in the way, to, against.*
Trude (thrust), ject (throw), tain; cur, casion (falling); fer; pose, press.

Out; *beyond, not within.* Bid, grow, last, live, let, skirt, side, law, cast.

Over; *above, beyond, excess.*
Balance, hang, top, leap, spread, do, flow, look, wise, load, shoot, value.

PARA, PAR; *beside, against, from.*
Dox (opinion), graph (writing), phrase, site (food); helion, ody (song).

PER, PEL; *through, by.*
Use, form, ennial (year), ceive, sist (stand), fect, chance, cent (hundred); lucid (shining.)

PERI; *around, about, near.*
Patetic (walking), helion, od, phery (bearing), cranium, style (pillar).

POST; *after.* Script (writing), humous (ground), pone (place), mortem (death), meridian.

PRE; *before.*
Judge, mature, engage, dispose, sentiment, fer, sume (take), vent (come), side (sit), text (weaving).

PRETER; *past, beyond.* Natural, imperfect, mission.

PRO, PROF; *for, forth, forwards, before.*
Noun, ceed (go), gress, tect, pel (drive), spect (look), logue; fer.

RE; *again, back.*
Build, call, enter, new, view, pel, sonant (sounding), strain (draw), bound.

RETRO; *backwards.* Cede, vert, spect, grade (walk).

SE; *aside, apart.* Cede, clude (shut), cant (cutting), duce (lead), lect.

SEMI, DEMI, HEMI; *half.*
Annual, circle, colon, diameter, vowel; god, cannon; sphere.

SINE; *without.* Cure (care).

SUB, SUC, SUF, SUG, SUP, SUR, SUS,—SUBTER; *under, underneath, inferior.*
Soil, divide, marine; cor (run), cumb (lie down); fer, fuse; gest (bring); plant, press; rogate (ask); tain; fuge (fly), fluent (flowing).

SUPER, SUPRA, SUR; *above, over and above.*
Cargo, crescent (growing), fluous, natural; mundane; pass, charge.

SYN, SYL, SYM; *with, together.*
Thesis, tax (placing), opsis (view), agogue (lead); lable (taking), logism (counting); phony (sound), pathy (feeling).

TRANS, TRAN, TRA; *through, across, over, on the other side of.*
Act, plant, gress, Atlantic, pose, form, it (going); scribe (write), scend; dition (giving).

TRI; *three.* Colored, angular, meter, foliate (leaf), ennial.

Un; *not, negation, privation, undoing.*
Able, aided, bar, chain, happy, truth, wise, ship, do, twist, horse.

Under; *beneath, inferior.*
Agent, brush, current, ground, rate, sell, hand, go, mine, sign.

UNI; *one.* Corn (horn), form, florous (flowering), parous (producing), valve.

Up; *motion upwards, above, subversion.*
Turn, raise, rise, hold, land, hill, right, start, set, root.

With; *against, from, back.* Hold, draw, stand.

SUFFIXES, OR AFFIXES.

The derivatives of this class consist almost entirely of *nouns, adjectives, verbs,* and *adverbs.*

NOUNS.

Person or Instrument: Ard, ary, ee, ess, ine, ist, ite, ive, ix, n, nt, r.

Thing, Act, or State: Ade, age, al, dom, hood, ice, ics, ion, ism, ment, ness, nce, ncy, ry, ship, t, th, ude, ure, y.

A derived noun may denote either a *person,* a *thing,* an *act,* or a *state;* or it may denote the *abstract* of any of these. The "person who" must be either a doer of an act, a recipient of an act, or simply one in some way related to or concerned with that from which the name is formed. From the *thing,* the mind naturally passes to whatever is obviously related to it; and the meaning of the word is also extended accordingly. From the *act,* the mind and the meaning readily pass to what caused the act,— often a concrete object, or an abstract, or some faculty, skill, or principles, —or else to the result of the act, or to the manner. From the *state,* the passage is as easy to what causes it, to what follows from it, to what sustains it, or to what necessarily accompanies it. The same ending is not usually confined to one meaning, but ranges with the principles given under the head of Figures. See p. 299.

Form and spell, making the requisite euphonic changes; and define:—

Ard.—Drunk,* dote, slug, dull, cow (verb), Spain, Savoy.

Ary.—Adverse, statue, note, mission.

Ee. (Generally passive; the person to whom.)—Indorse, pay, patent, as sign, consign, trust, commit, legate, mortgage, lease, *less;* absent, refuge.

Ess, Ine, Ix; female.—Lion, heir; hero, Joseph; administrator.

Ist.—Copy, tour, journal, natural, novel, algebra, drug, duel, art, violin, pian-o; drama, *-tist;* enthusiasm, *-ast,* encomium.

Ite.—Favor, Israelite, Moab, Jacob.

Ive.—Capture, operate.

N.—America, Africa, Virginia, Kentucky, college, music.

Nt.—Claim, *-ant,* account, inhabit, combat, dispute, confide, protest, assist, assail, appeal; study, *-ent,* preside; oppose, *-ponent;* act, *-gent;* receive, *-cipient.*

R.—Oversee; lie, *-ar,* beg, school; farm, *-er,* hunt, make, plaster, settle, pipe, widow, hat, foreign; visit, *-or,* edit, profess, survive, speculate; conspire, *-ator;* compete, *-itor;* auction, *-eer,* mountain, gazette, pamphlet, chariot; cash, *-ier,* cannon, finance, cloth, glaze; save, *ior;* law, *-yer,* saw; team, *-ster,* web; poke, *-er* (thing), revolve, shut, boil, read, speak.

Diminutives. (These often imply endearment or contempt.)—Man, *-ikin;* lamb, *-kin;* ring, *-let,* stream, leaf, cover; lock, *-et,* mall; lord, *-ling,* hire, suckle. Globe, glob*ule;* grain, gran*ule;* ball, bul*let;* cat, kit*ten;* island, *isle;* isle, *islet.*

---

* Throughout the following exercises, the student should spell and define, from his dictionary, each word given; and then the derivative word in like manner. Thus: D-r-u-n-k-drunk, *intoxicated with liquor;* d-r-u-n-k-drunk-a-r-d-ard-drunkard, *one who is habitually drunk, a sot* A-d-ad-v-e-r-s-e-verse-adverse, *opposing, contrary;* a-d-ad-v-e-r-ver-adver-s-a-sa-adversa-r-y-ry-adversary, *one that opposes, an enemy.* So comprehensive is the collection of words here presented, that the defining of the words in the manner indicated, will amply repay the labor of using the dictionary.

118 DERIVATION OF WORDS.—SUFFIXES.

Ade.—Gascon, stock, lemon, baluster; stamp, -*ede*.
Age.—Use, marry, mile, post, equip, folium (leaf), bond, pupil, parson, hermit, anchor.
Al.—Peruse, remove, recite, requite, deny, propose, refuse, dismiss.
Dom.—Free, wise, martyr, king, duke.
Hood.—Child, brother, man, woman, boy, sister, hardy, lively.
Ice.—Serve, just, lath, *lat-tice*.
Ics.—Poet, harmony, mechanic, statist (state), phys (nature).
Ion.—Commune, precise, act, reflect, possess, expand; and many other words, in which the ending shows itself in the form of *tion* or *sion*.
Ism.—Fanatic, despot, critic, hero, baptize, heathen.
Ment.—Move, pave, content, case, punish, acquire, agree, arm, battle, complete, refresh.
Nce, ncy.—Acquaint, -*ance*, concord, resist, observ-e, convey; innocent, -*ence*, resident, differ, precede; pliant, -*ancy*, constant; despond, -*ency*, ascend.
Ness.—Good, bad, white, bold, happy, busy, comprehensive.
Ship.—Partner, scholar, town, workman, hard, friend, lord, court. See -HOOD.
T, th.—Constrain, join, restrain; warm, wide, long, strong.
Ude.—Disquiet, serve, solitary, right, *rect-*.
Ure.—Please, depart, moist, architect, seize, legislate, sign-*ature*, nourish, *nur-*.
Y.—Honest, modest, discover, grocer, injure; lunatic, -*acy*, private, pirate; secret, -*cy*; hypocrite, -*sy*; pedant, -*ry*, gallant, revel, bigot, master; brew, -*ery*, witch, mock, fish, crock; null, -*ity*, dense, pure, opportune, secure, elastic.

Words ending with *y* or *ry*, are often collective in sense, denoting groups of objects or acts; as, Orange-*ry*, shrub-*bery*, soldier-*y*, sorcer-*y*, trigonometry. So is the ending *ing* not unfrequently collective in sense; as, Bed, *bedding*; shop, *shopping*; *bagging, carpeting, hedging, gunning* (elements of science, or science as drawn from a multitude of acts or experiments).

ADJECTIVES.

Al, an, ar, ate, ble, en, ern, ful, ic, (ific,) ile, ine, ish, ive, nt, ous, some, ward, y, (ly, ary, ory).

Derivative adjectives generally signify—

Having of or having the nature of, more or less; or that the object described, in some way belongs or is related to that from whose name the adjective is formed.

The same word may frequently be used either as an adjective or as a noun.

Form and spell, making the requisite euphonic changes; and define:—

Al.—Nature, nation, origin, parent, ornament, music, autumn; senator, -*ial*, manor, matter, part, commerce; spirit, -*ual*, sense, habit; consequence, -*tial*, influence, essence; benefit, -*cial*; nose, *nas-*, pope, *pap-*, feast, *fes'-*.
An.—Europe, epicure, Italy, Africa, America, suburbs.
Ar.—Column, pole, consul; globe, -*ular*, circle, muscle, title, particle.
Ate.—Rose, globe, affection, consider, compassion.
Ble. (Passive, if from a transitive verb.)—Detest, -*able*, cure, eat, change, honor, tolerate, utter, value, fashion; corrupt. -*ible*, resist, sense, destroy, *destruct-*, accede, *access-*, perceive, *percept-*, divide, *divis-*.
En. (Of what substance made.)—Beech, hemp, silk, gold, wood

Ern.—North, south, east, west.

Ful. (Opposed to -LESS.)—Mind, peace, hope, brim, care, waste, cheer, youth, play, sin, wake, law, mourn, truth.

Ic.—Angel, hero, poet, sphere, lyre; vertex, *-ical*, dropsy; sympathy, *-etic*, pathos, theory; barometer, *-etric*, diameter; emblem, *-atic*, problem, system, drama; color, *-ific*, dolor; science, *-tific;* romance, *-tic;* pharisee, *-saic;* tragedy, *-gic;* Plato, *-nic.*

Ile.—Infant, serve, merchant, *mercant-*, puer (boy).

Ine.—Serpent, adamant, alkali; crystal, *-line.*

Ish.—Salt,, black, yellow, boy, fop, wolf, snap, scare, *skit-*, Spain, Ireland.

Ive. (Generally active.)—Create, abuse, progress, retain, *retent-*, attend; perceive, *-ceptive;* presume, *-sumptive;* produce, *product-;* disjoin, *disjunct-*; adhere, *-hesive*, corrode, intrude, decide; expel, *-pulsive*, repel.

Nt. (Generally active.)—Tolerate, *-ant*, please, buoy, triumph, luxury; solve, *-ent*, consist, abhor; compose, *-ponent.*

Ous.—Bulb, pore, pomp, fame, joy, ruin, peril, murder, mountain; bile, *-ious*, perfidy, malice; pity, *-eous*, beauty, duty; tempest, *-uous*, contempt; enormity, *-mous;* merit, *-orious;* mucilage, *-inous.*

Some.—Toil, tire, dark, glad, quarrel, weary. See -ISH.

Y.—Grass, hill, shade, swamp, meal, flower, mud, cloud, wealth, grease, sleep, pearl, wire; friend, *-ly*, beast, brother, heaven, man, time; residue, *-ary*, imagine, element; subsidy, *-iary;* contradict, *-ory*, conciliate, declare, satisfy.

Up*ward*, out*ward*, b*u*lb*iferous*, arm*igerous*, glob*ose*, spher*oid*, Arab*esque*, sta*tuesque*, grot*esque.*

VERBS.
Ate, en, fy, ish, ize, ise.

Derivative verbs generally signify—

To make or become; to impart the thing or quality to, or to exercise it; to make the ordinary use of; an act or state consisting of some common or permanent relation between the subject of the verb and the thing.

Form and spell, making the requisite euphonic changes; and define:—

Ate.—Alien, origin, germ, populous, luxury, fabric, facility, spoil, *spoli-*, grain, *granu-*, stimulous, office, vacant, circular.

En.—Black, white, sharp, red, soft, moist, less, sweet, bright, strength, haste, glad, sad, ripe, quick, thick, fright.

Fy.—Beauty, pure, just, simple, glory, class, sign, clear, *clari-*, right, *recti-*, peace, *paci-*, special, *speci-*, example, *exempli-*, fruit, *fructi-;* prophet, *-esy.*

Ish.—Brand, bland, public, famine, languid.

Ize, ise. (These generally signify *to make, to apply, to act the part of*.)—Legal, theory, modern, moral, organ, botany, tyrant, melody, familiar, character, apology; critic.

Sharp ending to flat or rough.—Cloth, breath, wreath, bath, price, advice, grass, excuse, abuse, grief, half, thief.

Accent changed.—Abstract, conflict, absent, frequent, rebel.

Word unchanged. (To make that use of which mankind generally make; some customary or habitual act or state; some active relation to.)—Hoe, shoe, shovel, plane, chisel, hammer, smoke, garden, farm, weed, plant, coop, soap, shear, gem, fire, lance, and the names of instrumental things generally.

ADVERBS.
Ly, ward or wards, wise or ways.
Form, spell, and define:—

Ly; *like, manner, quality.*—Bitter, strange, bright, plain, faint, fierce, swift, playful, studious, mere, scarce, in, one, on-, spiral, fearless, infallible.

Ward, wards; *direction.*—Back, in, out, up, down, home, heaven, east, lee, wind.

Wise, ways; *manner, way.*—Length, cross, other, side, edge; straight.

Errors are sometimes made in deriving words; as, *Maintainance, preventative, wroposial,* for *maintenance, preventive, proposal,* from *maintain, prevent, propose.* *Write down all the words you can think of as being derived from* FORM.

QUESTIONS FOR REVIEW.
☞ The numbers show the pages on which the answers are found.

Introductory View.
89. What is said of Grammar? What is said of language, as the medium for conveying thoughts? What is said of language, as to its growth and decay? How does Grammar differ from Logic and Rhetoric? What is said of English Grammar? Into how many and what parts may it be divided?
90. What is said of Pronunciation? Of Orthography? Of Etymology? Of Syntax? Of Prosody?

Pronunciation.
90. About how many elementary sounds has the English language? and how are they represented? What is said of the organs of speech? Of elementary sounds? Of inarticulate sounds? Of articulate sounds? What is a letter? What is meant by the powers of the letters? and how are they related to the names of the letters? The English alphabet is both deficient and redundant: explain how it is so.
91. How are the letters classified? What is the advantage of this classification? What is said of vowels? Of consonants? Of *w* and *y*? Of *u, i,* and *x*? Of mutes? Of semivowels? Of liquids? Of diphthongs? Of triphthongs?
92. When is a letter said to be silent? What sounds are made most prominent in singing? What is said, in the same connection, of letters, syllables, words, and accent?
92. Accent.—What is accent? What are some of its advantages? What is said of primary and of secondary accent? Give some examples. (Always give examples or illustrations with the answer, where such things are given in the book.) What is said of two equal accents on the same word? What is needed, to pronounce well?
93. On what syllables are most of our words accented? Which syllable is the penult? and which is the antepenult? How are Latin, Greek, or Scriptural names accented? What is said of English words that have the chief accent far removed to the left? What is said of words ending in the sound of *shun,* etc.? In *cive,* etc.? In *acal,* etc.? In *ative,* etc.? What is said of words pronounced in different ways? **94.** What is the first direction in regard to pronunciation? The second? The third? **95.** The fourth? What is said of the accent of words that are used as different parts of speech?
96. What are some of the governing principles of Pronunciation? What general remark is made about English pronunciation? What is said of utterance? What is said of articulation? Degree of loudness or rapidity? Inflections? Tones? Emphasis? **97.** Pauses?

Orthography.

97. In what styles are the letters used? In what sizes of type are they printed?
97. Capital Letters.—Letters are divided, according to their form, into what two great classes? What says rule 1st, to caution us against the excessive use of capital letters? How were capital letters used in Old English? What says rule 2d about commencing pieces of writing? What says rule 3d of sentences, or about the first word after a full pause?
98. What says rule 4th of important beginnings in sentences? What says rule 5th of phrases? Rule 6th of poetry? Rule 7th of direct quotations?
99. What says rule 8th of indirect quotations? What is said of examples? What says rule 9th of names of Deity? What important remarks under the same head? What says rule 11th of proper names and titles? What says rule 12th of the names of personified objects, and of common words and phrases applied to objects like proper names?
100. What says rule 13th of personification? What says rule 14th of words derived from proper names? What says rule 15th on the same subject? What says rule 16th of chief words? **101.** What says rule 17th of chief words? Rule 18th? Rule 19th of *I* and *O*? Rule 20th about doubtful cases?
105. What is said of taste as a guide to the use of capital letters? What seem to be the two extremes of custom, in regard to the use of capital letters? What says rule 21st of proper names that assume common words to make new proper names? What says rule 22d of phrases applied to objects like proper names? What says rule 23d of phrases and sentences that are to be used as headings?
107. Syllables.—What is a syllable? Of what must every syllable consist? What is a word? How are words named according to the number of their syllables? What is a prefix? A suffix? A root, or radical? By what are we to be chiefly guided, in dividing words into their syllables? What letters should be given to every syllable? What is said of *burnish, blanket,* etc.? How should words be divided according to their prefixes, suffixes, etc.? Where derivation and pronunciation conflict, which should be followed? **108.** How may words be divided at the ends of lines? When should words be compounded?
108. Spelling.—What is spelling? How is this art to be acquired? Why is it difficult to learn to spell the words of our language accurately? What says Rule 1st of doubling the final consonant? (Always give examples.)
109. What is said of the *l* which ends such words as *duel, equal,* etc.? Spell *gravelly;* and state why you spell it so. Why is *metallic* or *excellent* spelled with two *l's?* What says Rule 2d of final *y?* What exceptions? What is said of *y* unchanged? What exceptions? What says Rule 3d of final *e?* Exceptions?
110. What is said of final *ie?* Of *e* before consonants? What exceptions? What says Rule 4th of the endings *ize* and *ise?* Give some exceptions. What says Rule 5th of trebling the final letter? What says Rule 6th of compounds? What is said of *l* in such words as *willful, thralldom,* etc.? What says Rule 7th of final *f, l,* or *s?* **111.** What exceptions? What is said of *mimic, traffic,* etc.?
111. What is said of *f* changed to *v?* Of the apostrophe? Of *cei?* *cian?* and *efy?* Of words spelled differently? Of contractions? Of tmesis? What general remark is made about spelling and pronunciation?
112. What is said of equivalent sounds? **113.** In the spelling of what words are we liable to make the most ludicrous errors?

Derivation of Words.

113. How are words classified under this head? Define each kind. (See pp. 1 and 2.) What is said of the elements of words? What is said of roots? Of prefixes?
114. What is said of suffixes? What is said of different prefixes, as capable of expressing the same meaning? Of different suffixes? What is said of the meanings of prefixes? What euphonic changes are frequently made in forming derivative words? What is the meaning of the Saxon or English prefix *a?* Examples. Of the Latin prefix *a, ab,* or *abs?* Examples. (Pass thus through all the prefixes.) **117-20.** What kinds of words are generally formed by means of suffixes? What is said of derived nouns? Derivative adjectives? Derivative verbs? Derivative adverbs? Of words improperly derived?

PARTS OF SPEECH.

Nearly all that we shall say from this page to page 288, belongs to Etymology and Syntax.

A **Part of Speech** is a class of words, made according to their meaning and use in the construction of sentences. The English language has nine PARTS OF SPEECH; *Nouns, Pronouns, Articles, Adjectives, Verbs, Adverbs, Prepositions, Conjunctions,* and *Interjections.*

To this list, some grammarians would add the Participles, separating them from the Verbs; and some would reject from it the Articles, classing them with the Adjectives. But participles seem to have no better claim to being ranked a separate part of speech than infinitives have; and the two articles, considering that they can not be always construed like adjectives, that they are used at least as much as all the adjectives, that they are liable to as many errors, that they are recognized in other languages, and that they merely aid nouns somewhat in the direction of their distinction into proper and common, are worthy of being made a separate class.

Language, as we shall see, is a most ingenious instrument; wonderfully adapted to the myriad-minded human race, and enabling them to lay hold of the world and manage it intellectually in every conceivable way. The above classification of words, however, exhausts it, and all its capabilities. The *substantives* and the *verbs* are the chief classes, and next to them are the *adjectives* and the *adverbs.* These four classes have, to some extent, what are called *inflections;* that is, they are sometimes changed in form to express a modification in the idea.

Inflections abound most about the core or most ancient part of a language. In the course of time, they are often dropped, or detach themselves, their meaning being assumed by new and small words; so that the language becomes *collocative* rather than *inflected.* Such is the case with our language. It is properly the office of Grammar to treat of the *classes* of words, and of their properties which produce *inflections;* but, as the properties of words must also be regarded in the collocation of words, we usually treat of all those properties necessary to be regarded in the construction of sentences, whether they cause an entire change, a slight change, or even no change at all in the form of the word. Inflections, especially ancient ones, consist sometimes of a *vowel change* in the word; as *man, men; goose, geese; mouse, mice; cling, clung:* sometimes of a *different ending;* as, *fox, foxes; ox, oxen; great, greater; send, sent; write, written:* sometimes of *something prefixed;* as, *beautiful, more beautiful; write, may write, did write, to write:* and sometimes of two or more of these combined; as, *weave, woven; write, was written, to be writing; break, to have been broken.*

Words have sometimes been divided into *substantives, attributives,* and *particles.* Dr. Becker divides all words into *notional words* and *form words.* The former denote our notions, conceptions, or rather somewhat independent ideas; and virtually take up the gross of the world. They are the *nouns,* the *principal verbs,* and most of the *adjectives* and *adverbs.* The latter rather denote the ligatures, substitutes, and appendages,—the relations of our conceptions or notional ideas, —the various turns and windings of thought,—and give to language its adequate flexibility and force. They are *articles, prepositions, conjunctions, pronouns, interjections, auxiliary verbs,* and some *adjectives* and *adverbs.* Briefly, the former comprise conception-words,—thing-words, quality-words, and action-words; and the latter, substitutes and auxiliary words in general.

5. NOUNS AND PRONOUNS.
Nouns.

50. A **noun** is a name.

Ex.—George, Martha, Columbus, water, river, air, wind, farm, farmer, angel, world, mind, judgment, thought, joy, fitness, labor, laborer, laboriousness, Mary Jane Porter. "The *signs* +, —, ×, and ÷." "The *pronouns* he and *who*." "*Moll* or any other *she*." "To study *reading, writing*, and *ciphering*." "To attack the *enemy* being resolved upon." "I prefer *green* to *yellow*." "The clause, '*that man is born to trouble*.'" "With his '*How do you do?*' and '*What can I do for you?*'" "It would be improper, for us to do so." (What would be improper?) "That ll things good and beautiful must pass away, is a sorrowful reflection." (What a sorrowful reflection?)

Words from almost every other part of speech, also phrases and clauses, are sometimes used in the sense of nouns, and should then be parsed accordingly.

51. When two or more words form but one name, or are habitually used so, they may all be parsed together as one noun.

Ex.—Henry Hudson, Juan Fernandez, New Orleans, Jefferson City, Brigadier General Commandant, Messrs. Harper, Misses Lewis, Gen. George Washington; and perhaps as well, Duke of Northumberland, Charles II, Alexander the Great. "*Lord Bacon, Sir Walter Raleigh, Dr. Samuel Clarke,* and the *Duke of Marlborough,* were not brought up in public schools."—*Sydney Smith.*

Classes.

Nouns are divided into two classes,—*proper* and *common*; and a part of the common nouns may be divided into *collective* nouns, *abstract* nouns, and *material* nouns.

PROPER means *one's own*; COMMON, *belonging to several or many*; COLLECTIVE, *gathering into one*; ABSTRACT, *drawn from something else*; and MATERIAL, *pertaining to substance or matter.*

52. A **proper** noun is an individual name.

Ex.—Mary, Alexander Hamilton, California, Washington City, St. Petersburg, Missouri, Paradise Lost; the *Missouri;* the *Iliad;* the *Alleghanies;* the *Azores*. And according to some authorities, "The *Romans;* the *Cherokees;* the *Messrs. Harris.*"

When we find plural capitalized names that distinguish **groups** in the same way as singular proper names distinguish individuals, it is perhaps best to parse them always as proper nouns.

Proper nouns do not admit of definition. When first applied to objects, they are generally given at pleasure; and they serve to distinguish one individual of a kind, from others of the same kind. Most of the names on maps, and the names of persons, are proper nouns. The number of proper nouns is almost unlimited: that of places alone is said to exceed 70,000.

Most proper nouns had originally some meaning, which, however, was not designed to make the word applicable to all other similar objects, but to distinguish and exclude the object named, from all others. EXAMPLES: Jerusalem, *habitation of peace;* Christ, *anointed;* Margaret, *pearl;* Thatcher, Harper, Smith, *occupation;* White, Long, Stout, *quality;* Brooks, Woods, Hill, Dale, *locality;* Westcott, Westcote, Northcutt, *west cottage, north cottage;* Mississippi, *all the rivers;* Minnesota, *sky-tinted;* Shenandoah, *daughter of the stars;* Winnipiseogee, *smile of the Great Spirit.* The meaning of most proper nouns is lost, or is not taken into consideration in applying them

53. When a common noun denotes an object in the sense of a proper noun, it becomes a *proper* noun.

Ex.—The Park; the Commons; the Blue Ridge; Niagara Falls; Mammoth Cave. "And *Hope* enchanting smiled." These words are viewed as merely denoting particular objects rather than as characterizing them by the ordinary meanings of the words.

54. A common noun is a generic name.

Ex.—Man, boy, engineer, hunter, woman, horse, foxes, hill, oak, white-oak, apple, steamboat, anger, happiness, reason, sun, moon, earth, winter.

Common nouns have meaning, and admit of definition. They distinguish different kinds or sorts from one another, by reference to their nature. A common noun is applied to more objects than one on account of something in which they resemble, and from which the same name is given to them all. Those nouns in a dictionary which are defined, are common nouns. Of these, our language is said to have about 30,000.

55. When a proper noun assumes a meaning, or implies other objects having the same name, rather than similar objects having different names, it becomes a *common* noun.

Ex.—"He is neither a *Solomon* nor a *Samson*." "Bolivar was the *Washington* of South America." "No *Alexander* or *Cæsar* ever did so." "Some mute, inglorious *Milton* here may rest." "*Alps* on *Alps* [great difficulties] arise." "Massachusetts has produced her *Demosthenes*." "I saw the *Russians*, and also a *Turk* and several *Persians*, at the Astor House."

It is sometimes very difficult to determine whether a given noun is proper or common. The same word is sometimes a proper, and sometimes a common, noun.

Ex.—*Proper:* "*Sunday* precedes *Monday*." "*B* follows *A*." "*I* is a pronoun." "The planets are *Mercury, Venus, Earth*," &c. *Common:* "We have preaching on every *Sunday*." "The *b* is followed by an *a*." "An *I* or a *you*." "The sun shines upon the *earth*." When a word is used to name itself, universally considered, Mr. Goold Brown calls it a common noun, similar to such words as *water* and *virtue* denoting the objects universally; but when a letter is used to name itself, he calls it a proper noun. The distinction is *very nice*,—perhaps too much so.

A proper noun can not, as such, be extended in its application to any other similar objects: it is *designative* and *exclusive*. But a common noun is *descriptive* and *inclusive;* that is, when we have once named an object by it, we are ready to give the same name to any other similar object as soon as it appears to us; as, "Jupiter has four *moons*." According to Mr. Mills, the former *denotes;* the latter, "*connotes*." The ordinary household names that denote the objects which permanently and necessarily make the world, are considered *common* nouns, even when the word can denote but one object, or the thing universally; as, The sun, the earth, the moon, the stars, the angels; time, space, spring, winter, grass, virtue, beauty, man. Such plurals as *Alps, Alleghanies, Andes, Orkneys*, denoting contiguous parts rather than similar individuals, are undoubtedly proper nouns, analogous to the common nouns *ashes, scissors, assets, minutiæ*. Such terms as "the *Comanches*, the *Mohawks*, the *Gauls*, the *Belgians*, the *Spaniards*, the *Mexicans*, the *Jews*, the *Israelites*, the *Janizaries*, the *Mamelukes*, the two *Adamses*, the *Marshalls* of Virginia, the *Muses*, the *Sirens*, the *Sibyls*, the *Graces*, the *Naiads*, are considered *proper* nouns by some grammarians; and *common* nouns by others, who argue that whenever a proper noun is so used as to imply more objects than one having the same name, it becomes *common*.

56. A collective noun is a noun denoting, in the singular form, more than one object of the same kind.

Ex.—Assembly, swarm, flock, crowd, pair, family; "a hundred *head*."

57. But a noun in the singular number, that denotes a collection of things resembling in their general character, but differing in their particular character, is not a collective noun.

Ex.—Furniture, jewelry, machinery, finery, baggage, clothing.

An **abstract** noun denotes a quality, an action, or a mode of being.

Abstract signifies *drawn from*, and these nouns are so termed because they are not the names of certain substantive objects or things in the world, but the names of certain notions which the mind has drawn from them, or conceived concerning them. Thus, as we advance from childhood, in our acquaintance with the world, we form some idea of what is meant by *time, space, life, death, hope, virtue, wisdom, magnitude, disease, war, peace, government, goodness, youth, happiness, beauty, sorrow, murder, revenge, cold, heat, whiteness, softness, hardness, brightness, darkness, motion, rest, flight, silence, existence, height, depth, growth, custom, fashion, strife, honor, glory, industry, economy, indolence, grandeur, religion, knowledge, honesty, deception, drunkenness, poverty, destiny, ambition, power.* These and such nouns are *abstract*.

58. Most abstract nouns readily pass into concrete nouns.

Ex.—" The sisters were famous *beauties.*" " *Pride, Poverty,* and *Fashion,* once undertook to keep house together." *Concrete,* including the substance with its qualities.

59. A **material** noun denotes some kind of matter or substance.

Ex.—Bread, meat, water, wood, stone, wheat, flour, metal, gold, cabbage.

Abstract nouns and material nouns have a universal, indivisible application, and generally also special applications. Some writers consider them abstract or material, only when used in the former sense.

Ex.—1. " Beauty is attractive ;" " Rain moistens the ground ;" " Vice, fire, whiteness." 2. " The beauty of the rose ;" " The whiteness of snow ;" " The rain that fell last night ;" " A vice, a fire, vices, fires."

60. To the classes of nouns already given, some grammarians add *verbal* nouns,—participles and infinitives used in the sense of nouns, the former of which are sometimes called *gerundives*, or *participial nouns ; correlative* nouns,—such as *father* and *son, husband* and *wife, master* and *servant ;* and *diminutive* nouns,—or such as *gosling* from *goose, hillock* from *hill, lambkin* from *lamb, floweret* from *flower.*

The foregoing classification is in accordance with the teachings of grammarians generally. The two following classifications are perhaps more philosophical.

1. Nouns are either *concrete* or *abstract.*

Concrete nouns denote self-existent objects, or objects having attributes; as, *God, earth, rose.*

Abstract nouns denote attributes; as, *Goodness, power, wisdom, color, fragrance, motion, existence.*

2. Nouns may be divided into the following classes: *proper, abstract, material, verbal,* all of which imply unity or oneness, and *common* including *collective,* both of which imply plurality.

A *proper* noun is such a name of an object or a group, as is not applicable to every other similar object or group.

An *abstract* noun denotes an attribute universally considered · as, *Truth, duration.*

A *material* noun denotes a kind of substance universally considered · as, *Water, corn.*

A *verbal* noun is a participle or an infinitive used as a noun. The abstract nouns include the verbal nouns.

A *common* noun is such a name given to one or more objects, as is applicable to any others like them.

Collective nouns denote *groups* of similar objects, as other nouns denote *single* objects. The *common* nouns include the *collective* nouns.

The common nouns come near to the other classes in such expressions as, "The *lion* is courageous;" "The *oak* is an emblem of strength."

Abstract or *material* nouns denoting objects *personified*, and *common* nouns *deprived* of "*connotation*," generally become *proper*.

Proper, abstract, material, or *verbal* nouns, when *modified*, become *common.* The modification at once suggests plurality of objects. The modification may be effected by pluralizing the noun, or by using an article, adjective, adverb, adjunct, or other modifying expression.

Ex.—"There were Macphersons and Macdonalds." "The hauling of the stones and other materials, was a heavy expense." "The honors of the society." "To think always correctly, is a great accomplishment." "The Hudson, the Pyrenees," &c.—The river Hudson, or the Hudson river, &c. ; or they may be deemed exceptions.

Pronouns.

61. A **pronoun** is a word that supplies the place of a noun.

Ex.—"The father and *his* son cultivated the farm *which they* had purchased."

There are three great classes of names in all; *pronouns, common nouns,* and *proper nouns*. The *pronouns* are the fewest in number, only about sixty-six, and the most comprehensive in application; the *common nouns* are the next greater in number and less comprehensive in application; and the *proper nouns* are the most numerous and least comprehensive. It seems not improbable that *pronouns* were the *first names*, being the simplest words for denoting, under all circumstances, whatever was about the persons conversing; and that they were afterwards adopted almost wholly as substitutes for nouns. Their nature and very irregular declension indicate great antiquity, and sometimes pronouns—especially the personal pronouns of the first and second persons, the neuter pronoun *it*, and the relative pronoun *what*—are even yet so used as to refer, not so much to the names of objects, as to the objects themselves.

To avoid tiresome and disagreeable repetition of nouns, pronouns are used to represent persons or things already mentioned, inquired after, or easily recognized by them.

Ex.—Alexander told Elizabeth that Elizabeth might write Elizabeth's name in Elizabeth's book with Alexander's pen—"Alexander told Elizabeth that *she* might write *her* name in *her* book with *his* pen." "*Who* was *it?*" "*He* is a fine scholar."

62. The **antecedent** of a pronoun is the substantive in reference to which the pronoun is used. It usually precedes the pronoun, but sometimes follows it.

Ex.—"John obeys his instructor." Here *John* is the antecedent of *his.*
"Can storied urn or animated bust
Back to its mansion call the fleeting *breath?*"—*Gray.*

63. The antecedent may be a different pronoun, a phrase, or a clause, as well as a noun.

Ex.—"*He* WHO is well, undervalues health." "*Who* THAT is strictly honest, would flatter?" "I wished *to return*, but IT was impossible." "*It* is the novelty and delicacy of the design, THAT makes the picture so beautiful." "IT is dangerous *to wake a sleeping lion.*" "*He sold his farm*, and now he regrets IT."

It is worthy of notice, that when a pronoun has a modified antecedent, it represents it with all its modifications.

Ex.—" The largest tree of the grove spread its shade over us." Here *its* represents not *tree* merely, but *The largest tree of the grove.*

When a pronoun is used, we may nearly always put some noun in its place. It is not, however, customary to regard this word as its antecedent, but the corresponding word elsewhere used, which it represents. To a pronoun having an antecedent, Rule 9th, of page 46th, should be applied in parsing. When a pronoun is applied directly to the object itself; when the speaker can not be thought to have the supposed antecedent in his mind; and when the supposed antecedent does not *first* present, in the order of the sense, the object meant,— I doubt the necessity or even the propriety of applying Rule 9th. Hence the Rule may generally be dispensed with, in parsing *interrogatives*, *pronominals*, *responsives*, and frequently, *personal* pronouns and *relative* pronouns. Even in such sentences as, " *Who* knows himself a braggart, let *him* fear this ;" "*Whomsoever* you can not manage, *him* you need not send ;" " *Whatever* you do, do *it* well,"—*him* and *it* are probably not antecedents: the relatives do not refer to them; but more directly, or as directly as they, to the objects themselves.

Classes.

Pronouns are divided into three chief classes ; *personal, relative,* and *interrogative.*

64. The **personal** pronouns are those whose chief use is, to distinguish the different grammatical persons.

65. They are *I, thou* or *you, he, she,* and *it,* with their declined forms, and their compounds. See p. 8.

66. *You, your, yours, yourself,* are now preferred, in familiar or popular discourse, to the other forms.

67. *Thou, thy, thine, thee, thyself,* and *ye,* may rather be regarded as antiquated forms. They generally have an antique, scriptural, or poetic air. They are much used in the Bible, and frequently in other sacred writings and in poetry. They are also habitually used by the Friends, or Quakers. They seem, too, at one time, to have occasionally carried with them something of a blunt or insulting air; of which use, traces are still visible in our literature.

Ex.—" *Ye* are the salt of the earth."—*Bible.* " *Thou* Almighty Ruler, hallowed be *thy* name."—*Book of Prayers.* " *Thy* words had such a melting flow." "*Ye* winds, *ye* waves, *ye* elements !"—*Byron.* " All that Lord Cobham did, was at *thy* instigation, *thou* viper ! for I *thou thee, thou* traitor !"—*Lord Coke: Trial of Essex.*

" I have no words, my voice is in my sword ; *Thou* bloodier villain than terms can give *thee* out ! "—*Shakespeare.*

68. *He, she,* and *they,* sometimes refer to persons indefinitely.

Ex.—" *He* who trifles away his life, will never be rich in honors." " *She* who knows merely how to dress, dance, and flirt, will never make a good wife." "*They* who deserve most blame, are apt to blame first."

69. The pronoun *it* is sometimes used to denote what the speaker can not well designate in any other way, or what he deems sufficiently obvious when thus mentioned; and often to introduce at once what is more definitely denoted by some following word or words.

Ex.—" *It* rains." " *It* thunders." " *It* was moonlight on the Persian sea." " Who is *it* ?" " Who is *it* that calls the dead ?" " *It* ran into a hollow tree, but

I do not know what *it* was." "Lo! there *it* comes!"—*Shakespeare's Hamlet*. "How goes *it* with you?" "*It* is not well with me to-day." "Come and trip *it* as you go." "*It* is he." "*It* is I." "*It* was you." "*It* was they." "*It* is idleness that leads to vice." "*It* is now well known that the earth is round." "*It* is mean to take advantage of another's distress." The following remark tells the truth in many instances: "*It* denotes the state or condition of things."

70. The **compound personal** pronouns are used to denote persons or things as emphatically distinguished from others.

Ex.—"I will go *myself*; you may stay." "I spoke with the man *himself*." "I once felt a little inclined to marry her *myself*."

"Hereditary bondsmen! know ye not,
Who would be free, *themselves* must strike the blow?"—*Campbell*.

71. These pronouns are further used, when that which is denoted by the subject of the verb, is also that on which the act or state terminates.

Ex.—"They drew *themselves* up by ropes." "She saw *herself* in the glass.' "He killed *himself*." "Said I to *myself*, 'I am *myself* again.'"

72. A **relative** pronoun makes its clause dependent on another clause or word.

Ex.—"There is the man | *whom* you saw." "Nobody knows | *who* invented the letters." "I have *what* you need." "I can not tell *what* ails him." "Spirit *that* breathest through my lattice, thou," &c.—*Bryant*. Here, "whom you saw," for instance, can not stand by itself, and make sense.

73. The relative pronoun stands at or near the head of its clause, and the clause itself generally performs the office of an adjective or of a substantive.

Ex.—"The boy *who studies*, will learn"—The *studious* boy will learn. "I know *who he is*." (Know what?) "I will do *what* I promised to do"—I will do *the thing which* I promised to do.

The relative pronouns are *who, which, what, that*, and *as*, with their declined forms and their compounds. See p. 9.

74. *Who* is applied to persons, and to other objects when regarded as persons.

Ex.—"The MAN *who* feels truly noble, will become so." "And AVARICE, *who* sold himself to hell."—*Spenser*. "Now a faint tick was heard below, from th PENDULUM, *who* thus spoke."—*Jane Taylor*.

"'Dear Madam, I pray,' quoth a Magpie one day,
To a MONKEY, *who* happened to come in her way."—*Sargent's Speaker*.

75. *Which* is applied to things, or to what we regard so, to brute animals, to groups of persons denoted by collective nouns when all the individuals of the collection are viewed together as one thing; and frequently to children.

Ex.—"The ROSE *which*;" "The BIRD *which*;" "The ELEPHANT *which*;" "The WORLD *which*;" "The ARMY *which*." "He was the soul *which* animated the party." "The NATIONS *which* encompass the Mediterranean." "CONGRESS, *which* is a body of wise men." "The CHILD *which* we met."

76. *Which* is used in connection with some word denoting the object referred to, or when the object is present, or has been already mentioned or brought to mind.

Ex.—"The MISFORTUNES *which* crushed him." "I can not tell *which is which*." "I do not know *which* you mean."

77. *What* is applied to things, and sometimes to other objects when regarded as things.

Ex.—"I will take *what* you send." "There is in my carriage *what* has life, soul, and beauty."

78. *What* is used when the objects spoken of may be represented by the indefinite term *thing* or *things* and *which*. It represents them both, and does not have, in modern usage, the word *thing* or *things* understood before it. See *Language*, p. 89.

79. *That* is used in preference to *who* or *which* when both persons and other objects are referred to; nearly always when the relative clause is *restrictive*—especially after the superlative degree, after *who*, *same*, *very*, *no*, *all*, *any*, *each*, *every*, and frequently after the personal pronouns, or after predicate-nominatives referring to *it*; and generally where *who* or *which* would seem less proper, or would not sound so well.

Ex.—" The SHIP and PASSENGERS *that* were lost at sea." "In WORDS *that* breathe, and THOUGHTS *that* burn." "This is the HARDEST LESSON *that* we have yet had." "WHO *that* respects himself, would tell a lie ?" "The SAME STAR *that* we saw last night." "No MAN *that* knows him, would credit him." "And ALL *that* wealth or beauty ever gave." "IT is selfishness and vanity, *that* makes a woman a coquet."

80. The relative pronoun or relative clause is *restrictive*, when it makes the word to which it refers denote only such objects as are described by the relative clause: in the *restrictive* sense, it modifies an idea; in the other, it adds an idea.

Ex.—" RICHES *that* are ill gotten, are seldom enjoyed." Of course not all riches. "Read thy doom in the FLOWERS, *which* fade and die." Not restrictive. "He was a MAN *whom* nothing could turn aside from the PATH *which* duty pointed out." Restrictive. "God must be conscious of every MOTION *that* arises in the material UNIVERSE, *which* he thus essentially pervades." The first relative is restrictive; the other is not. "They enacted such LAWS *as* were needed." "Catch *what* comes."

It is often difficult to determine whether *that* should be preferred to *who* or *which*. Sometimes either may be used with equal propriety. When the antecedent is so fixed or definite by itself, or so limited by other definite words,—such as *the*, *that*, *those*,—that the relative clause can not vary its meaning, *who* or *which* may be allowable or even preferable; when the antecedent is an indefinite term, or is made indefinite by such modifying words as *a*, *some*, *any*, *every*, &c., *that* may be preferable, or even necessary to make the meaning sufficiently definite, or to show precisely what objects are meant.

"He is engaged in speculations *which* are very profitable," might suggest that all speculations are very profitable: say, "in *speculations that*." "He is a man *who* cheats everybody," may be understood to mean, that rascality is the essential quality of a man or of a gentleman: say, "*a man that*." "It is the thought or sentiment *which* lies under the figured expression, *that* gives it its merit." Here no change could be made without injuring the sentence: *which* and *that*, as here used, (though both restrictive,) well show the subordinate character of the middle clause, and the restrictive character of the last clause. "I don't doubt you'll like my friend, *whom* I have sent with a most trusty and faithful servant, *who* deserves your friendship and favor." This sentence is not so clear as it might be: had the author said, "*and* who deserves," the reference would have been clearly to "friend;" had he said, "*that* deserves," to "servant."

81. *That* is often used as an adjective or as a conjunction; so that you must regard it a pronoun, only when *who* or *which* can be put for it without destroying the sense.

Ex.—"That[10] man said that[18] he knows your father." "The ablest man that [who] spoke on the subject." " The same horse that [which] I rode."

82. *As* is generally a relative pronoun, when it is used after *such, many,* or *same.*

Ex.—"He pursued such a course *as* ruined him." "He deceived as many *as* trusted him." "The daughter has the same inclinations *as* the mother."

As, at bottom, is perhaps a conjunction; but since a relative must then be always supplied to complete the sense of the following clause, it may as well be parsed as a relative. Some grammarians maintain that it is never a relative, others, that it is always a relative after *such, many*, or *same.* The truth lies perhaps between the two extremes. *As* is used in two different senses. It may recall the *identical* objects mentioned before, or it may present only *similar* objects. When, by supplying the necessary words, the meaning would be changed, *as* should certainly be parsed as a relative. " I bought, at the auction, such mules *as* were sold—as many mules *as* were sold"=I bought the mules *that* were sold—all the mules *that* were sold; but, "I bought, at the auction, such mules *as* the mules were that were sold—as many mules *as* the mules were that were sold," suggests rather that there were two distinct parcels of mules, or that I bought other mules than those which were sold at the auction. Observe also, that, above, some other relative can be substituted for *as*, especially by changing the preceding *such* or *as many* into *the, those,* or *all.* So, "He took *as many as* he could get"=He took *all that* he could get. "He took such apples *as* pleased him." "She played such tunes *as* were called for." "He was the father of all such *as* play on the harp and organ." "As many *as* came, were baptized." "I will come at such an hour *as* I can spare." But when I say, "I bought such mules *as* you have for sale;" "We do not want such men *as* he is;" *as* should perhaps be considered a conjunction. In the last example, if parsed as a relative, it can not agree, as a predicate-nominative, with *he:* we can not say, "He is such men." Locke, however, has the following sentence: "There be some *men whom* you would rather have your *son* to be, with five hundred pounds a year, than some other with five thousand pounds." *Whom* is here used very much like *as* in the previous example.—This latter sense of *as* is also analogous to that of *than* in such sentences as, " I have more money than you have;" "He wanted more than he got." In these sentences, *than* should never be parsed as a relative, for it never expresses, when so used, the *identity* sometimes denoted by *as*. Most teachers, to avoid difficult distinctions, deem it best to parse *as*, construed after *such, many,* or *same*, always as a relative pronoun.

83. The **compound relative** pronouns are preferred to the simple ones, when the speaker means to indicate more forcibly that he refers to an object considered as general or undetermined. Sometimes they are almost equivalent to the simple pronouns.

Ex.—" *Whoever* [any person that] despises the lowly, knows not the fickleness of fortune"—Who despises the lowly, etc. "Take *whichever* [any one that] you like." " I'll do *whatever* [any or every thing that] is right." " *Who* steals my purse, steals trash."

These pronouns are parsed like the corresponding simple pronouns; but, as they never refer to a definite or particular object, they have rarely or never an expressed antecedent. The indefinite *ever* or *soever* partly represents the antecedent, by being a sort of substitute for the indefinite adjective which must precede the antecedent; hence when the antecedent is expressed or supplied, the *ever* or *soever* must generally be dropped; as, " *Whoever* cares not for others, should not expect their favor"—*Any person who* cares not for others, should not expect their favor. *Ever*, from denoting *time* indefinitely, was naturally extended to *place* and *time*, and thence of course to *objects.*

---

84. An **interrogative** pronoun is used to ask a question.

Ex.—" *Who* came with you?" " *What* do you want?" " *Which* is yours?"

The interrogative pronouns are *who, which, what,* and their declined forms.

Each of them may be applied to any person or thing whatsoever; except *who*, which is applicable to persons only.

85. *Who* inquires for the name or some other appellation, and when the name is in the question, it inquires for the character or some description of the person.

Ex.—" *Who* wrote the book?" " *Whose* glory did he emulate?" " *Whom* do you take me to be?" " *Who* was Blennerhasset?"

86. *Which* supposes the name known, or disregards it, but seeks further to distinguish a certain individual from others.

Ex.—" *Which* of you will go with me?" " *Which* is the Governor?" " *Which* is the tigress? *Which* must I take? *Which* is your daughter?" " *Which* is which?"

87. *What* goes still further, and inquires into the character or occupation.

Ex.—" *What* is that fellow?"

Briefly, *who* seeks to designate; *which*, to distinguish; and *what*, to describe.

Ex.—" *Who* is that gentleman?—Mr. Everett.— *Which* one?—Edward Everett.— *What* is he?—An eminent scholar and statesman."

Sometimes either *who* or *what* may be used in speaking of persons: but in most such instances, *who* is perhaps a little more respectful.

88. When *who*, *which*, or *what*, occurs in a clause that is in answer or apparently in answer to the same clause used interrogatively, it is neither an interrogative pronoun, nor a relative pronoun in the sense of other relative pronouns; but, according to some grammarians, it is a *responsive* or an *indefinite* pronoun. It may, however, be considered a *relative* pronoun; for it makes its clause *dependent* as the common relatives do.

Ex.—*Interrogative:* " *Who* broke the window?" *Responsive relative:* "I do not know *who* broke it." " Do you know *who* broke it?"

The following sentences illustrate the different uses of *who*, *which*, and *what:*—

Interrogative.	Responsive Relative.	Common Relative.
Who came?	I do not know *who* came. Do you know *who* came?	I do not know the man *who* came.
Which is the lesson?	I remember *which* is the lesson.	I remember the lesson *which* I recited.
What did he buy?	I know *what* he bought.	I admire *what* he bought.
What is truth?	Teach me *what* is truth. *Better:* Teach me *what* truth is.	Teach me *what* is true.

Hence, when these words are *interrogative* pronouns, they must stand at or near the beginning of the question; when *responsive relative* pronouns, the verb or preposition (usually preceding) governs the entire clause, or depends on it; and when *common relative* pronouns, it relates only to what is denoted by them.

———♦———

89. The chief other words used occasionally as pronouns, are *one, oneself, none, other, another, each other, one another,* and *that,* with their declined forms.

Ex.—"Some *one* has said, 'A blush is the color of virtue.'" " The best *ones.*" " Several *others.*" " *One* should not think too highly of *oneself.*" " The old bird feeds her young *ones.*" " The brother and sister love *each other.*" " The girls love *one another.*" " Wives and husbands are, indeed, incessantly complaining of *each other.*"—*Johnson.* " Put the dozen cups within *one another.*" " *None* [no persons] are completely happy." " The age of modest, industrious, and meritorious yeomanry is gone; and *that* [the age] of pining, office-seeking aristocracy is at hand."

Dr. Whately writes "*oneself*" in a form analogous to *herself, himself,* and better, I think, than "*one's self.*"

90. *One* often refers to mankind indefinitely, or to a class of objects already brought to mind, or obvious from the modifying word or words.

91. *Each other* and *one another* are often called *reciprocal pronouns.* They have a reflexive sense, and represent the relation between any two of the objects as being that between any and every other two of the entire series.

Some grammarians, by supplying words, parse each of the foregoing terms as two words, the first one in apposition with the whole group, and the other as an objective; as, "The two girls love *each* [one⁷] loves the] *other*" [one⁴]. But "The bad boys threw stones at *one another,*" may mean, *each one at the others,* as well as, *each one at the other one.* The Greek language expresses *one another* by one word, and the German also by one *inseparable* word that is precisely analogous to our phrase.

"Wie zwei Flammen *sich* ergreifen, wie
Harfentöne in *einander* spielen."—*Schiller.*

Here *einander* could not be parsed separately; for *ein in ander* would be a solecism.

There are several other words, of the pronominal or definitive adjectives, which are also frequently parsed as pronouns, especially when they refer distributively or emphatically to what has been already introduced. "They fled; *some* to the woods, and *some* to the river." "They had two horses *each.*" "Peace, order, and justice, were *all* destroyed." "I like *neither.*" It will be best to consider such words *pronouns,* when they can not be so well disposed of in any other way ; but they are frequently parsed as *pronouns* or *adverbs* when they might as well or better be parsed as *adjectives.*

The last group of pronouns which we have considered, do not fall within any one of our three great classes of pronouns. If deemed necessary, they may be called *reciprocal, indefinite, distributive,* or *demonstrative* pronouns, according to their sense.

---

92. In the place of a pronoun, we may frequently put a noun with the same pronoun, or with a word of the same class or nature, placed as an adjective before the noun.

Ex.—" *Who* is he?"—*What person* is he? "Show me *what* it is"—Show me *what thing* it is. " *Which* of the horses will you take?"— *Which horse* will you take? "I will ride one horse to drive the *others;*" *i. e.,* the *other horses.* " The pleasures of vice are momentary; *those* of virtue, everlasting"—The pleasures of vice are momentary; *the pleasures* of virtue, everlasting.

93. The pronoun is sometimes omitted.

Ex.—"'Tis Heaven [*that*] has brought me to the state [*which*] you see." "There is the man [*whom*] I saw." [*Thou*] "Thyself shalt see the act."

94. An antecedent may be supplied, when it is needed for the sake of other words, or even when it can be easily supplied, and without producing harshness.

Ex.—" Give it to whoever [*any one that*] needs it;" or, "Give it to [*any person*] who (ever) needs it." "Let such [*persons*] as hear, take heed." [*He*] "Who lives to fancy, never can be rich."

Properties.

NOUNS and PRONOUNS have **genders, persons, numbers,** and **cases.**

95. PRONOUNS agree with their antecedents, in *gender, person,* and *number.*

Genders.

The **gender** of a word is its meaning in regard to sex.

There are four genders; the *masculine*, the *feminine*, the *common*, and the *neuter*.

GENDERS meant originally *kinds* or *sorts*; thence, *kinds* in reference to *sex*; and thence, the sense and *form* of words as adapted to distinguish objects in regard to sex.

96. The **masculine** gender denotes males.

Ex.—Uncle, father, son, governor, Mr. Robertson, executor, dog, he, himself.

97. The **feminine** gender denotes females.

Ex.—Aunt, mother, daughter, girl, hen, goose, heroine, seamstress, she, herself.

98. The **common** gender denotes either males or females, or both.

Ex.—Persons, parents, children, cat, insects, I, you, they, who.

99. The **neuter** gender denotes neither males nor females.

Ex.—Tree, house, city, heaven, beauty, body, size, manhood, soul, it, what. The neuter gender pertains chiefly to things, and to qualities or other attributes.

Common gender of course does not imply *common sex*, but is the characteristic of those substantives which denote living beings, without showing in themselves whether males or females are meant, being equally applicable to both. The sex may, however, be sometimes ascertained from some other word in the sentence; and then the words should be parsed accordingly.

Ex.—" The child and his mother were in good health." Here *child* is masculine, as shown by *his*.

Some grammarians reject the "common gender," and would parse such words as *parents* and *friends*, as "of the masculine and feminine gender," "of the masculine or feminine gender," "of the masculine gender," or "of the feminine gender," according to the sense. I see no valid objection to the term *common gender*, provided *gender* and *sex* be not, as they frequently are, confounded. They are distinct in meaning: *gender* is a property belonging to *words* only; and *sex*, to *objects*.

100. Nouns strictly applicable to males only, or to females only, are sometimes used to denote both. This usually occurs when the speaker aims at brevity of speech, and when the sex is not important to his design. The masculine term is generally preferred.

Ex.—"*Horses* are fond of green pastures;" *i. e., horses*, and *mares* too. "The *Jews* are scattered over the whole world." "*Heirs* are often disappointed." "I saw *geese* and *ducks* in the pond." "The *poets* of England." But in connection with a proper name, only the appropriate term will harmonize in sense; as, "The *poet* Homer;" " The *poetess* Sappho."

101. Sometimes animals are regarded as male or female, not from their sex, but from their general character—from having masculine or feminine qualities.

Ex.—" The *lion* meets *his* foe boldly." " The *fox* made *his* escape." " The *spider* weaves *her* web." " The *dove* smooths *her* feathers." " The timid *hare* leaps from *her* covert." " Every *bee* minds *her* own business."—*Addison*. " The *ant* is a very cleanly insect, and throws out of *her* nest all the remains of the corn on which *she* feeds."—*Id*. Had these bees and ants appeared to Addison as uninteresting, ordinary things, he would probably have used "it" and "its;" but their *attractive, amiable*, and almost *rational* qualities made the adoption of the femine gender peculiarly elegant.

102. So, *inanimate* objects are sometimes regarded by the imagination as *living* beings, and have then a suitable sex ascribed to them. The objects, in such cases, are said to be *personified*, that is, endowed with *personal* qualities; and the nouns denoting such objects, may be parsed as masculine or feminine by *personification*.

Ex.—" The *sun* rose, and filled the earth with *his* glory." " The *moon* took *her* station still higher, and looked brighter than before." " The *boat* has lost *her* rudder." " There lay the *city* before us, in all *her* beauty." " Behold the *Morn* in amber clouds arise; see, with *her* rosy hands *she* paints the skies."—*Lee.* " Then *Anger* rushed—*his* eyes on fire."—*Collins. See his Ode on the Passions.*

103. A *collective* noun, when used in the plural form, or when it represents the collection as an aggregate or a whole, is of the neuter gender; when used otherwise, its gender corresponds with the sex of the individuals composing the collection.

Ex.—" Six *families* settled on this river." " Every *generation* has *its* peculiarities." " The *audience* were much pleased."

104. Some words may vary much in gender, according to the very different meanings which they have.

Ex.—" A *game* at ball;" " I saw no *game* in my hunt." " A brilliant *genius;*" " He has *genius.*" " The same man *that*—woman *that*—person *that*—apple *that.*"

The English language has three methods of distinguishing the two sexes.

105.   a. *By different words.*

Bachelor,	maid, spinster. }	Gander,	goose.	Nephew,	niece.
Beau,	belle.	Gentleman,	lady.	Papa,	mamma.
Boy,	girl.	Hart,	roe.	Rake,	jilt.
Boar,	sow.	Horse,	mare.	Ram,	ewe.
Bridegroom,	bride.	Husband,	wife.	Sire,	madame.
Brother,	sister.	King,	queen.	Sire (a horse),	dam.
Bull,	cow.	Lad,	lass.	Sir,	madam.
Bullock,	heifer.	Lord,	lady.	Sloven,	slut.
Cock, Rooster, }	hen.	Male,	female.	Son,	daughter
		Man,	woman.	Stag,	hind.
Colt,	filly.	Master,	mistress.	Steer,	heifer.
Dog,	bitch.	Master,	miss.	Swain,	nymph.
Drake,	duck.	Mr.,	Mrs.	Uncle,	aunt.
Earl,	countess.	Milter,	spawner.	Wizard,	witch.
Father,	mother.	Monk,	nun.	Youth,	damsel, maiden. }
Friar,	nun.	Monsieur,	mademoiselle.		
		Monsieur,	madame.	Charles,	Caroline.

106.   b. *By difference of termination.*

Most words of this class are appellations of office, occupation, or rank, and the feminine generally ends in *ess* or *trix*.

Ex.—Abbott, abbess. *Add* ess: Baron, heir, host, priest, count, poet, peer prophet, tutor*, mayor, prior, shepherd, sultan*, deacon, giant, dauphin, prince, (see Rules for Spelling,) ogre, patron, god, (see Rules for Spelling,) cit, Jew, hermit, archer, viscount, author, canon, diviner, doctor*, tailor, Hebrew, Jesuit, regent, soldier, warrior. *Change* ter *or* tor *into* tress, *and* der *into* dress : Actor, doctor, arbiter, benefactor, auditor, enchanter, elector, instructor, chanter, songster, conductor, embassador, hunter, mister, protector, traitor, commander, demander, detractor, victor, suitor, director*, proprietor, seamster, idolater, edi-

* Words marked with a star, have also some other form to denote the female.

tor, progenitor, fornicator, porter, painter, orator*, mediator*, offender, solicitor, rector, spectator*, creator, emulator, exactor, founder, tutor, huckster, sempster, inhabiter, minister, waiter, monitor, deserter*, inheritor*, inventor, competitor, executor*. *Change* TOR *into* TRIX: Administrator, executor, adjutor, testator, prosecutor, inheritor, director, arbitrator. *Change* RER *into* RESS: Adulterer, adventurer, caterer, cloisterer, huckesterer, murderer, sorcerer.

WORDS NOT SO REGULAR.

Emperor,	empress, emperess.	Carl, Landgrave,	carline. langravine.	Don, Infant,	donna. infanta.
Negro,	negress.	Margrave,	margravine.	Tzar,	tzarina.
Governor,	governess.	Palsgrave,	palsgravine.	Sultan,	sultana.
Votary,	votaress.	Joseph,	Josephine.	Augustus,	Augusta.
Tiger,	tigress.	Tragedian,	tragedienne.	Cornelius,	Cornelia.
Eagle,	eagless.	Chamberlain,	chambermaid.	George,	Georgia.
Launderer,	laundress.	Goodman,	goody.	Henry,	Henrietta.
Duke,	duchess.	Widower,	widow.	Julius,	Julia, Juliet.
Tyrant,	tyranness.	Lover, Love,	love.	Louis,	Louisa.
Pythonist,	pythoness.	Signore,	signora.	John,	Joanna.
Anchorite, Anchoret,	anchoress.	Marquis, Marquess,	marchioness.	Frank, Francis,	Frances.
Hero,	heroine.				

107. When, for either sex, the appropriate term is so seldom used as to be uncouth, the other term may be preferred; and wherever there is a term for but one of the sexes, it may be used for the other, if necessary.

108. Words derived or compounded from others, usually express gender in the same way.

Ex.—"Coheir, *coheiress*; archduke, *archduchess*; grandsire, *grandam*; landlord, *landlady*; schoolmaster, *schoolmistress*; schoolboy, *schoolgirl*; merman, *mermaid*; grandfather, *grandmother*; step-son, *step-daughter*; peacock, *peahen*."

109.   c. *By using a distinguishing word.*

Ex.—*He*-bear, *she*-bear; *he*-goat, *she*-goat; *buck*-rabbit, *doe*-rabbit; *cock*-sparrow, *hen*-sparrow; *man*-servant, *maid*-servant; *male* descendants, *female* descendants; *Mr.* Barton, *Mrs.* Barton; *Mr.* Reynolds, *Miss* Reynolds.

110. For some very common objects we have a common-gender term, as well as a masculine term and a feminine.

Ex.—*Parent*, father, mother; *child*, son, daughter; *person*, man, woman.

111. Some descriptive terms are so rarely needed to denote women, that they have no corresponding feminine terms.

Ex.—Printer, carpenter, robber, baker, brewer, hostler, lawyer, fop, drummer, colonel.

112. Others have rarely or never corresponding masculine terms.

Ex.—Laundress, seamstress, brunette, coquet, jilt, dowdy, vixen, termagant, hag.

Genders of Pronouns.

The speaker, and the person addressed, being mutually present, or generally known to each other in regard to sex, it was not thought necessary, in the formation of speech, to make different pronouns for distinguishing them in regard to sex. The personal pronouns of the first or the second person should therefore be parsed as of the *common* gender, unless the sex becomes more definitely known by some other word in the sentence. In the third person singular, however, the different sexes are distinguished by personal pronouns adapted in gender to each. See p. 11.

113. The pronoun *it*, usually regarded neuter only, is, I suspect, also of the common gender, when it stands for nouns of this gender, and sometimes when it denotes objects slightly personified.

Ex.—"The *tiger* broke *its* chain." "The *child* has singed *its* frock." "The *mouse* ran back when *it* saw me." "*Sleep* never visits sorrow; when *it* does, *it* is a comforter."—*Shakespeare.*

114. Indeed, it seems that the three pronouns *he, she,* and *it*, may sometimes refer to objects without special regard to sex; *he* being preferred for what is large, bold, or preëminent; *she*, for what is effeminate or dependent; and *it*, for what is small, unimportant, or imperfectly known. I think I have noticed this principle often, especially in our mode of speaking of laboring animals and of pets.

Ex.—"The *elephant* writhed *his* lithe proboscis." "The *swan* with *her* beautiful curving neck." "The *sea-bird* with *its* wild scream." "*Her* young the *partridge* led."—*Bryant.* In this last sentence, the other words make the feminine pronoun preferable.

Persons.

The **person** of a word shows whether the word refers to the speaker, the object spoken to, or the object spoken of.

There are three persons; the *first*, the *second*, and the *third*.

The word PERSONS is borrowed from stage-playing, and meant originally *masks, characters, actors,* or *speakers* on the stage; and thence is derived its sense as used in grammar.

115. The **first** person denotes the speaker.

Ex.—"*I William Jones* here certify, that," &c. "*I who* command you, am the general." "Many evils beset *us mortals.*"

116. The **second** person represents an object as spoken to.

Ex.—"*Henry*, shut the door." "*Friends, Romans, countrymen!* lend me *your* ears." "O *thou* Almighty *God, who* didst create this wondrous world." "Forbid it, *Justice.*" "O *Liberty!* what crimes are committed in *thy* name!"—*Mad. Roland.* When inanimate objects are addressed, they are of course personified.

117. The **third** person represents an object as spoken of.

Ex.—"The *city* is in a *bowl* of *mountains.*" "I have read *Webster's reply* to *Hayne.*" "I am the *man whom* you wish to see." "*To fail* is disgraceful."

The naming of the different persons as shown above, *first, second,* and *third*, is in accordance with the natural order of full discourse; as, "*I James Bennett* certify to *you, William Morrison,* that *Timothy Flint* is the legal *owner* of this *farm.*" It is also obvious, that we can refer, in speaking, only to ourselves, to something spoken to, or to something spoken of.

118. When a noun comes after a verb to explain the nominative, it is of the third person, though the nominative may be of the first or the second person.

Ex.—"We are the *patrons* that will support you." "You are the *person* wanted." "I am *sheriff* of the county." "We are *strangers* here." "You are *heroes.*"

Person rather disappears from the words *sheriff, strangers,* and *heroes,* as here used without an article. *Sheriff*, for instance, does not seem to denote the speaker as such, nor a person spoken of as such, but is simply descriptive somewhat like an adjective.

119. A word used in *speaking of* one or *of* a part of the persons speaking or addressed, is in the third person.

Ex.—"Each *one* of us is studying *his* lesson." "Every *one* of you knows *his* duty." "*Some* of you have lost *their* places." (Speaking to a spelling-class.) "*Some* of you have lost *your* places," sounds perhaps better to some ears; yet the former is the correct expression according to principle.

120. The third person is sometimes elegantly used for the first or the second.

Ex.—"The king is always willing to listen to the just complaints of his subjects;" for, "I am always," &c. "Surely, my mother does not mean to marry me to such an old miser;" for, "Surely, mother, you do not," &c.

Persons of pronouns.

121. The pronouns of the first person plural, *we, our, ours,* etc., are used when the speaker includes others with himself; and sometimes, to represent two or more persons as uttering the same thing together.

Ex.—"Let *us* go." "John, Mary, and I, must learn *our* lessons." "*We*, the people," &c.—*Constitution of the U. S.* "*We* are going to the mountains."—*Rocky-Mountain Song.*

122. The pronouns of the second person plural, *you, your*, etc., are used to denote two or more persons addressed, or one only with others included.

Ex.—"My countrymen, I appeal to *you.*" "*You* boys may go and play." "*You*, sir, *you* are the boys that threw rocks through the windows." "*You* mechanics [speaking to one only] are required to work only ten hours per day."

123. Hence it is, perhaps, that *we* and *you*, as well as *they*, sometimes refer to mankind generally.

Ex.—"*We* are apt to love those who love us." "*You* may as well seek honey in gall, as happiness in vice." "Shakespeare presents to *you* the universal world." "*They* say that Buchanan will be elected." "*They* say that free governments will ultimately be established in all parts of the world."

When a pronoun refers to two or more substantives taken together, and of different persons, it prefers the first person to the second, and the second to the third.

Ex.—"James and I have lost *our* horses." "James and you have lost *your* horses."

Numbers.

The **number** of a word shows whether the word refers to one object or to more than one.

There are two numbers; the *singular* and the *plural*.

124. The **singular** number denotes but one.

Ex.—Apple, knife, pin, grain, flower, I, he, one, an, this, that.

125. The **plural** number denotes more than one.

Ex.—Apples, knives, grains, mice, flowers, we, they, ones, these, those.

126. Two or more singulars connected merely by *and*, are equivalent to a plural.

Ex.—"*John, James,* and *Thomas,* are studying"—The *boys* are studying.

127. Two or more objects viewed one by one, or separately, have words referring to them in the singular number.

Ex.—" Every HEART best *knows its* own sorrows." " Neither MARY nor MARTHA *has studied her* lesson."

128. A possession or attribute relating in common to several objects, should generally be expressed by a singular word.

Ex.—" It was done for our *sake,*" not *sakes.* " Let them be content with their *lot,*" not *lots.* " You and I have the same *purpose,* but different judgments."

129. A proper noun, when pluralized, denotes a race or family, or two or more objects as having the same name or character.

Ex.—" The Dixons and the Boltons." " The twelve Cæsars." " Her Marions, Sumpters, Rutledges, and Pinkneys."

130. Abstract or material nouns, as such, are never plural, except a few that have no singular form.

Ex.—Pride, ambition, hope, motion, duration, business; gold, copper, meat, hay, straw, specie, butter, cider, beer, molasses, ivy, fire, snow, mud, water, flax, silk, dust; ashes, oats.

131. Sometimes they are pluralized to denote more *kinds* than one.

Ex.—Diseases, fevers, vices, airs, wines, teas, cottons, silks, satins, taxes.

132. Sometimes they denote two or more objects having the quality or substance, or else something as composed of parts.

Ex.—Curiosities, slates, straws, timbers, proceedings, liberties, rights. " All the sisters are *beauties.*" " The *heights* of Abraham, at Quebec." " My *marbles.*" " I had only a few *coppers* left." " I heard the *waters* roar down the cataract."

133. Some nouns that denote objects consisting of *two* parts, or conceived to consist of *many* parts or individuals, are always plural.

Ex.—Tongs, scissors, lungs, embers, ashes, pincers, breeches, trousers, drawers, hose, bowels, entrails, intestines, billiards, calends, ides, nones, annals, archives, clothes, goggles, snuffers, stairs, head-quarters, poetics, riches, victuals, assets, teens, matins, vespers, hemorrhoids, hysterics, dregs, bitters, filings, remains, obsequies, nuptials, chops, spatterdashes, statistics, folks, aborigines, antipodes, mammalia, grallæ, passeres, sporades, regalia, paraphernalia, vetches, cattle, hustings, belles-lettres (bel-let'tr). Except, however, the class, *furniture, jewelry, hosiery,* etc., which are singular.

134. Sometimes such a word may be used in the singular number to denote a part, or to denote the object as an individual, or to denote the entire collection as one thing.

Ex.—" The left *lung* was diseased." " A stair; a bellows; the annal; a valuable statistic."

135. Some nouns have the same form for either number.

Ex.—Deer, sheep, swine, grouse, series, species, superficies, corps, apparatus, means.

136. A collective noun is plural, even when singular in form yet plural in idea.

Ex.—" The American *people* are jealous and watchful of their liberties."

In a few instances, the same collective noun is used in both numbers in the same sentence, and perhaps not improperly. "Each *House* shall keep a journal of *its* proceedings, and from time to time publish the same, excepting such parts as may in *their* judgment require secrecy."—*Constitution of the United States.* "There *is a tribe* in these mountains, *who are* fairer and more intelligent than the other Indians."—*Irving.* The first view refers to the whole; and the other, to the individuals.

137. Some nouns denoting animals, and also words of number preceded by a numeral adjective, are sometimes used in the singular form to express a plural sense.

Ex.—"This creek abounds in *trout* and *perch.*"—*Exploring Expedition.* To say, "in *trouts* and *perches,*" might mean different kinds. "*Fowl* and *fish* for sale." "Two *pair;* three *dozen;* three *score;* five *hundred.*" Here the numeral adjective seems of itself sufficient to determine or express the number.

138. *Foot* and *horse,* in the sense of troops, and *sail,* in the sense of ships, are plural. Sometimes *cannon* and *shot* are plural: also *head;* as, "forty *head.*"

139. In a word, the singular form of some words is sometimes used for the plural form, though the latter may also be in good use.

Ex.—"The *foe!* they come; they come."—*Byron.* "We shall have plenty of *mackerel* this season."—*Addison.* "All *manner* of evil." "To mould *brick* and burn them." "We have caught some *fish.*"
"They had *herrings* and *mackerels.*" "*Trouts* and *salmons* swim against the stream." "*Fowls* and *fishes.*" "In *scores* and *dozens.*" "By *hundreds* and *thousands.*" "*Cannons* and *muskets.*"

140. In using the singular form, the mind dwells perhaps rather on the *nature* than on the *number* of the objects,—on *what* is meant rather than on *how many* are meant.

141. The singular form and the plural sometimes differ in sense, or are different words.

Ex.—Arm, *arms* (weapons); letter, *letters* (literature); pain, *pains* (care); color, *colors* (banner); *means, manners, morals, physics, ashes.*

142. Some nouns, though always plural in form, are considered to be either singular or plural, according as the mind conceives the thing as composed of parts, or as a single object of thought.

Ex.—News, odds, means, amends, alms, suds, mathematics, politics, ethics, physics, optics, mechanics, hydraulics, apocrypha, mumps, measles, wages. "The *measles* HAVE BROKEN out thick upon him." "The *measles* IS sometimes a dangerous disease." "There the different *politics* of the day WERE DISCUSSED." "*Politics* IS an uncertain profession." "Can all that *optics* TEACH unfold thy form to please me so?"—*Campbell's Rainbow.* The tendency rather is, to construe such words plurally, except a few of the most common ones. Writers sometimes shun the doubtful construction, by saying, for instance, "The *science of mathematics* IS"——; "*Physical science* IS"——.

It is the sense rather than the form, that determines the number; hence *molasses, jeans,* &c., are singular, though they end in *s.* A noun that makes sense with *a* or *an* before it, or *is* after it, is singular; a noun that makes sense with *two* or *these* before it, or *are* after it, is plural.

How the plural number is expressed.

143. Most nouns become plural by adding *s* to the singular

Ex.—Book, *books;* street, *streets;* hat, *hats;* river, *rivers;* village, *villages.*

140   NOUNS AND PRONOUNS.—NUMBERS.

144. When *s* alone annexed, could not be easily pronounced; and when the singular ends in *s, o, u,* or *y,* preceded each by a consonant,—the plural is formed by adding *es.*

Ex.—Church, *churches;* bench, *benches;* blush, *blushes;* miss, *misses;* atlas, *atlases;* isthmus, *isthmuses;* topaz, *topazes;* tax, *taxes;* alkali, *alkalies;* rabbi, *rabbies;* halo, *haloes;* negro, *negroes;* gnu, *gnues;* story, *stories;* "the *Winnebago-es;* the *Missouri-es.*"

145. Proper nouns, foreign nouns, and unusual nouns, are changed as little as possible, and hence often assume *s* only.

Ex.— Henry, *Henrys;* Tully, *Tullys;* Mary, *Marys;* Cicero, *Ciceros;* Scipio, *Scipios;* Nero, *Neros.* "The two Miss Foots." Teocalli (Mexican temple), "*teocallis;*" major-domo, "*major-domos.*"—*Prescott.* "The novel is full of *ohs, bys, whys, alsos,* and *noes.*"—*Review.* And, owing to their *foreign* tinge, we still find in good use, *cantos, grottos, juntos, mementos, octavos, porticos, quartos, solos, tyros, seros,* in stead of *cantoes* from *canto, grottoes* from *grotto, juntoes* from *junto,* etc., which are also coming into use.

But when words of these classes are so familiarly known as to be easily recognized in almost any form, they are often pluralized like ordinary nouns; as, *Harries, Henries, Muries, Ptolemies, Neroes, whies, noes.*

146. The following nouns change their ending into *ves:*—

Beef, *beeves;* calf, *calves;* elf, *elves;* half, *halves;* knife, *knives;* leaf, *leaves;* life, *lives;* loaf, *loaves;* self, *selves;* sheaf, *sheaves;* shelf, *shelves;* thief, *thieves;* wife, *wives;* wolf, *wolves.* *Wharf* has sometimes *wharves*—a heavier word for pronunciation. *Staff* has *staves,* when not compounded; but it should always have *staffs,* to distinguish its plural from *staves,* the plural of *stave.*

147. For forming the plural of some words, no general rule can be given, and they are therefore said to be *irregular.*

Man, men.   Foot, feet.   Ox, oxen.   Cow, cows.   I, we.
Woman, women.   Goose, geese.   Mouse, mice.   *Cow* has also *kine,*   Thou, you.
Child, children.   Tooth, teeth.   Louse, lice.   the old or poetic plural.   He, they.

The words ending in *man,* that are not compounds of *man,* are regular and take *s;* as, German, *Germans;* talisman, *talismans;* Mussulman, *Mussulmans.*

148. Some nouns have both a regular and an irregular plural, but with a difference in meaning.

Brother, *brothers* (of the same family),   *brethren* (of the same society).
Die, *dies* (stamps for coining),   *dice* (small cubes for gaming).
Fish, *fishes* (individuals),   *fish* (quantity, or the species).
Genius, *geniuses* (men of genius),   *genii* (spirits).
Index, *indexes* (tables of contents),   *indices* (algebraic signs).
Penny, *pennies* (pieces of money),   *pence* (how much in value).
Pea, *peas* (individuals—two or more),   *pease* (in distinction from other vegetables).

149. Most compound words are pluralized, by making plural only that part of the word which is described by the rest.

Ex.—"Mouse-traps, ox-carts, brothers-in-law, sisters-in-law, billets-doux, courts-martial, aids-de-camp, cupfuls, spoonfuls, coachfuls, wagon-loads, commandors-in-chief, cestuis que trust." It is generally the first part of a compound word, that is descriptive, or is used in the sense of a prefix.

150. When the compound word is a foreign term or other

phrase, of which the descriptive part is not very obvious, the whole word is generally pluralized like a simple one.

Ex.—"Piano-fortes, camera-obscuras, auto-da-fes, congé-d'-élires, louis-d'ors, flower-de-luces, tete-a-tetes, ipse-dixits, habeas-corpuses, scire-faciases, jack-a-lanterns."

151. A few compound words have both parts made plural.

Ex.—Man-servant, *men-servants;* woman-servant, *women-servants;* knight-templar, *knights-templars* (better, *knights templar*); ignis-fatuus, *ignes-fatui.*"

152. A term composed of a proper name preceded by a title, is pluralized by annexing the plural termination to either, the name or the title, but not to both.

Ex.—"The *Misses* Davidson; the Miss *Browns;* the *Drs.* Edmondson; the *Messrs.* Harper." "The *Misses* Warner."—*Morris and Willis.* "The *Misses* Smith."—*Bryant.* "The Miss *Hornecks.*"—*Irving.* "With respect to the *Miss Thompsons,* or the *Misses Thompson,* I am decidedly for the *Miss Thompsons.*—*Arnold's Grammar: London.* "Some persons would say *the Miss Thompsons,* others *the Misses Thompson:* the former mode is clearly more in keeping with the general practice of the language, and one's leaning at first would be toward it; but those who plume themselves on their accuracy adopt the latter."—*Ib.* "From Duchesses and *Lady Maries.*"—*Pope.* "I went to *the Ladies Butler.*"—*Swift.* "May there be *Sir Isaac Newtons* in every science."—*Watts.*

153. But when the title is *Mrs.,* or is preceded by a numeral, the latter noun is always made plural.

Ex.—"The Mrs. *Welbys.*" "The two Mr. *Barlows.*" "The two Miss *Scotts* had been gathering flowers."—*Irving.* "The two beautiful Miss *Clarks.*" The word *Miss,* in such phrases, bears more resemblance to an adjective than to a noun: its use is similar to that of the adjectives in such phrases as, "The stingy old miser;" "The two stingy old misers."

154. And the *title* is always pluralized, when it refers to two or more different or separate persons.

Ex.—"*Drs.* Bruns, Edwards, and Johnson;" "*Misses* Mary and Julia Harrison."

In regard to the plural of names involving titles, there has been not a little of diversity in practice and doctrine. Some always pluralize the title; others, the name; and a few venture to pluralize both. The prevailing custom is, I believe, not to pluralize that word of the term which the speaker means to use as explanatory or descriptive of the other. It would be an elegant distinction, and in the analogy of such plurals as *teas, silks, wines,* &c., to pluralize the title only, when brothers or sisters are meant; and the name only, when the persons belong to different families of the same name,—to say "*the Misses Brown*" when the ladies are sisters, and "*the Miss Browns*" when they are not. But as this distinction would sometimes perplex the writer in addressing persons whose family relations he does not know, it will probably never be adopted. To persons wishing a plain and positive rule, I would say, Always pluralize the title only, when it is *Mister, Miss, or Doctor,* not preceded by a numeral; as, "The *Messrs. Morton;*" "The *Misses Dixon;*" "The *Drs. Bolton;*" "*Drs. Bolton.*" This mode of pluralizing such terms will, I believe, ultimately prevail in this country; and I rather think it has the best right to do so. It is a law of our language to vary proper names as little as possible; some proper names can not well be pluralized; many proper names have both the singular and the plural form, yet are singular in each, and mean different persons. "Drs. Mott. Office," plainly denotes two men; but "Dr. Motts. Office," would probably be understood as denoting but one man. Besides, we always pluralize the title when but once used in speaking of several persons taken distributively; as, "The *Messrs.* John and Thomas Wharton;" "The *Messrs.* Newman and Patterson;" "The *Messrs.* Branch & Co.;" "James and William Simms, *Esquires;*" and, to add the strongest argument in conclusion, I would say that almost all the advertisements which I have seen—at least thirty or forty—of eminent schools conducted by an association of ladies or gentlemen of the same name, begin with "The *Misses*" ———, or, "The *Messrs.* ———, will recommence," &c.

Our language has many words adopted from other languages. These usually retain the same plural in ours that they have in the languages from which they were taken. Some, however, take the English plural only; some, the foreign only; and some, either. No certain rule can be given for forming such plurals, but the following may be of some assistance:—

155. The termination *us* is changed to *i*; *um* or *on*, to *a*; *is*, to *es* or *ides*; *a*, to *æ* or *ata*; and *x* or *ex*, to *ces* or *ices*,

Those nouns of the following list, which have become so far naturalized as to have also a regular plural like that of the natives, in addition to their original plural, are distinguished by Italics.

Change final ʌ *to* ᴁ:—	Sarcoph'agus,	Amanuen'sis,	*Calx*,	Va'rix.
	Hippopot'amus.	Analysis,	*Ca'lix*,	Ex *to* ices:—
Larva,	Uᴍ, ᴏɴ, *to* ᴀ:—	Antith'esis,	*Cic'atrix*,	*Apex*,
Lam'ina,	*Animal'culum*,	Basis,	*He'lix*,	*Vertex*,
Mac'ula,	Arca'num,	Crisis,	*Ma'trix*,	*Vortex*,
Minu'tia,	*Autom'aton*,	Diær'esis,	*Ra'dix*,	*Index*.
Neb'ula,	*Crite'rion*,	Ellipsis,	*Quincunx*,	Caudex.
Sil'iqua,	Corrigen'dum,	Emphasis,		
Sim'ia,	Da'tum,	O'asis,	*Phal'anx*,	phalan'gês.
Sco'ria,	*Desidera'tum*,	Borea'lis,	*Lar'ynx*,	laryn'gês.
Alumna,	Efflu'vium,	Thesis,	*Beau*,	beaux.
Alu'mina,	Ephem'eron,	Phasis,	*Cher'ub*,	cher'ubim.
Are'na,	*Enco'mium*,	Praxis,	*Ser'aph*,	ser'aphim.
Form'ula.	Erra'tum,	Fascis,	*Sta'men*,	stam'ina.
A *to* ᴀᴛᴀ:—	*Gymna'sium*,	Di'esis,	Tegmen,	teg'mina.
Dogma,	*Herba'rium*,	Metamor'phosis,	*Legu'men*,	legu'mina.
Stigma,	*Me'dium*,	Synopsis,	*Bandit*,	banditti.
Mias'ma.	*Memoran'dum*,	Paren'thesis,	*Virtuo'so*,	virtuo'si.
Us *to* ɪ:—	*Momen'tum*,	Hypoth'esis,	*Cicero'ne*,	cicero'ni.
Alumnus,	Phenom'enon,	Syn'thesis,	Litterateur',	literati.
Focus,	*Scho'lium*,	*Metrop'olis*.	Ge'nus,	gen'era.
Fungus,	Spec'ulum,	Is *to* ɪᴅᴇs:—	Monsieur,	Messieurs.
Genius,	*Stra'tum*,	Chrys'alis,	Madame,	Mesdames.
Ma'gus,	*Men'struum*,	Ephem'eris,	Mr.	Messrs.
Ob'olus,	Spectrum,	Can'tharis,	*Ignis-fat'uus*,	ignes-fatui.
Pol'ypus,	Vin'culum,	Epider'mis,	*Hia'tus*,	hiatus.
Ra'dius,	*Trape'zium*,	A'phis,	*Appara'tus*,	apparatus.
Stim'ulus,	Parhe'lion,	Apsis,	Ver'tigo,	vertig'inês.
Cal'culus,	Aphe'lion,	*Iris*,	Billet-doux,	billets-doux.
Echi'nus,	Perihe'lion.	*Proboscis*.	Ma'lum prohib'-	mala prohibita.
Nau'tilus,	Is *to* ᴇs:—	X *to* ᴄᴇs:—	itum,	
Nu'cleus,	Axis,	*Appendix*,		

I believe the tendency is, to give the preference to the English plural in familiar language; to the foreign, in technical or scientific language.

156. Letters, figures, and other characters, are pluralized by adding 's.

Ex.—"The *a's* and *n's* in the first line." "By 5's and 7's." "What mean those ♃'s and @'s?" The apostrophe is used to prevent ambiguity; thus, "Cross your *t's* and dot your *i's*," is not the same as "Cross your *ts* and dot your *is*." 5*s* might mean 5 shillings or five times *s*.

Numbers of Pronouns.

157. In editorials, speeches, and proclamations, *we, our,* etc., are frequently used to denote apparently but one.

Ex.—" *We* trust these sentiments will meet with approbation." " *We* believe provisions will be scarce." " *We* shall not yield to *our* rebellious subjects."

This manner of speaking gives generally an air of modesty or authority to the assertion; the speaker seeming to deliver his own sentiments as if they were also entertained, or could be enforced, by others as well as by himself. Let a writer in an influential periodical say, "*I* believe there is an impending crisis in the money market," and who cares for or heeds his assertion? but let him say, "*We* believe there is an impending crisis in the money market," and the expression will at once strike alarm and terror into the hearts of thousands. The one is presented as the opinion of the writer only, the other as that of the community. But the palpable use of *we* for *I*, is, like some other politeness, unsupported by nature and good sense. Some one has said, that it is as if the person were ashamed to show his face. It is generally assumed as a veil of modesty, or to avoid " the charge of egotism." Many of the greatest masters of our language, namely, Johnson, Whateley, Webster, and others, have not been afraid or ashamed to use the abhorred *I*. An author may sometimes use *we*, not in reference to his party, or the world generally, but simply in reference to his reader as going along with him,—a sort of grandpa style; but when there is no reference whatever to any others than himself, the use of *we* for *I* may be more polite, yet it is certainly less correct. Authors often avoid the dilemma, by speaking of themselves in the third person. When responsibility or an unenviable position is to be assumed, it is obviously more polite to use *I* than *we*.

To the foregoing manner of speaking, *ourself* is peculiarly adapted, and it is sometimes used accordingly; but *yourself* is strictly singular. " What then remains? *Ourself.*"—*Pope's Dunciad ; The Goddess of Dullness.*

158. *You, your, yours,* etc., are now singular as well as plural.

" It is altogether absurd to consider *you* as exclusively a plural pronoun in the modern English language. It may be a matter of *history*, that it was originally used as a plural only; and it may be a matter of *theory*, that it was first applied to individuals on a principle of flattery; but the *fact* is, that it is now our second person singular. When applied to an individual, it never excites any idea either of plurality or of adulation; but excites, precisely and exactly, the idea that was excited by *thou*, in an earlier stage of the language."—*Lord Jeffrey: Edinburgh Review.*

The Quakerism of Murray and Brown accounts for their partiality to *Thou*.

159. When a pronoun stands for two or more nouns taken together, that are equivalent in sense to a plural, or when any one of the substantives referred to is plural, the pronoun must be plural; but when it refers to a singular implying more than one object, or to several singulars taken separately or individually, it must be singular.

Ex.—" *John* and *James* are studying *their* lessons." " Neither the *father* nor the *sons* ever surrendered *their* rights." "*Every one* should have *his* own place." "*A person* should never be very sanguine in *his* expectations."

160. *Each other* applies to two only, or to pairs; *one another*, to more than two.

Ex.—" The *brother* and *sister* love *each other.*" " *Wives* and *husbands* are, indeed, incessantly complaining of *each other.*"—*Johnson.* " Put the *dozen cups* within *one another.*" " The *several* Indian *chiefs* made peace with *one another* "

7*

161. *What*, in close connection with a plural, is sometimes used in the plural number.

Ex.—" We were now at the mercy of *what* ARE CALLED guerillas."—*Travels in Mexico.* " I must now turn to the faults, or *what* APPEAR such to me."—*Byron.*
Other was formerly sometimes used for *others.*
Another—an other ; hence, singular.
None (no-one) is singular or plural, and it is generally used for *no* and a noun.

For more in regard to the Numbers of Pronouns, see page 8. See also pp. 210–211.

Cases.

The **cases** are the relations of substantives to other words, in the forming of sentences.

There are three cases; the *nominative*, the *possessive*, and the *objective*.

Some grammarians give another case,—the *independent*, or *absolute ;* but there seems to be no more propriety in distinguishing this case from the *nominative*, than there would be in dividing the differently governed objective cases into two or three classes.

162. The **nominative** case denotes the condition of a substantive that is used as the subject of a predicate.

Ex.—" The *moon* SHINES beautifully upon the garden." " *John* and *James* ARE PLAYING, but *you* and *I* ARE STUDYING." " The *murderer* WAS HANGED." " Dear ARE the *recollections* of youth." " The *sum* of five thousand dollars WAS PAID." The nominative can always be found by asking a question with *who* or *what* before the verb. " The river is deep." What is deep ? The *river.*

163. A substantive is also in the *nominative case*, when it is used *independently* or *absolutely.*

Ex.—*Independently:* "*John*, you may go for some water." " You may recite, *Mary.*" " *Mr. President*, it is natural for man to indulge in the illusions of Hope." " Rise, *fellow-men !* our country yet remains." " *Ye* flowers that cluster by eternal frosts." " And Harry's *flesh* it fell away." " *He* that hath ears to hear, let him hear." " O *Absalom !* Absalom ! my *son*, my son !" " *Reputation !* reputation ! oh, I have lost it !" " And then she died, poor *thing !*" " Webster's *Dictionary*, Unabridged." *California:* what can you say about it !" " His *bed* and *board !* he never had any !"

" The *isles* of Greece ! the isles of Greece !
Where burning Sappho loved and sung."—*Byron.*

The student can observe, that the Italicized words neither govern other words nor are they governed by other words. Such substantives generally occur in addresses or in exclamations ; or, rather, they are used to direct the attention of some one addressed, to what the speaker says, or else to draw attention to what the word denotes. Sometimes, as in the last example above, they imply that the speaker's feelings are so enkindled by the contemplation of the object, that the flood of accumulated feeling bursts forth at once, and without an effort on his part.
In the sentence, " Fiddle-sticks ! who cares for what he thinks ?" *fiddle-sticks* is simply an interjection, because it is used merely as the sign of a sudden emotion, and is not uttered to draw attention to the musical implements themselves.
Absolutely: "*Shame* being lost, all virtue is lost. " *I* being sick, the business was neglected." " *Flush* following flash, we had but little hope." " The *work* being done, we went to the river to fish"—When the work was done, &c. " His being a *foreigner*, was the cause of his defeat"—He was defeated because he was a foreigner. " No one was aware of his being a *runaway ;*" better, " No one was aware that he was a runaway." " To become a *spendthrift*, is easy"—A person may easily become a spendthrift. " To be a respectable *preacher* or *doctor*, is

easier than to be a respectable *lawyer*." "The *wolf* [being] at bay, the dogs barked the more." "What more could they do, a *youth* [being] their leader." "My luty as [being] her *instructor*." "His nomination, as [to be] *bishop* [German, 'als Bischof zu sein'—as bishop to be], was confirmed." By a more strained supply of words, Rule 7th may be applied in the last two examples: "My duty, considered as being her *instructor's*" [duty]. "His nomination, considered as to be the *bishop's*" [nomination], &c.

By carefully examining the foregoing examples, the student can observe that the phrases having substantives used absolutely, are but abridged expressions for clauses beginning with *when, while, since, because,* or *inasmuch as,* &c.; and that when they are converted into clauses, the substantives become *nominatives* according to Rule 1st or 7th.

The early tendency of our language rather was, to express substantives used absolutely, in the objective case, according to the analogy of Greek and Latin; and Milton wrote, "*Him* [being] destroyed, or won to what may work his utter loss." But modern custom is decidedly in favor of the nominative.

A noun of the first or the second person, is never used as the subject of a verb.

Ex.—"I William Smith believe," &c. "Children, obey your parents." *Believe* agrees with *I*, as its nominative; and *obey* with *ye*, or *you*, understood.

164. A word in the **possessive** case denotes an object to which something belongs or pertains.

The word in the possessive case may denote the originator, or the first owner, or the full owner, or a partial owner, or a temporary owner, or an intended owner, or the whole object comprising the thing possessed as a part. The other substantive may denote a material object, a quality, an action, or a state.

Ex.—"Irving's works; Harper's Ferry; my horse; my father; my country; my cup and saucer; men's and boys' boots for sale here; my head; my sufferings." "John's brother—happiness—haste—running—sleeping." "Nature's gifts." "He bought a place in Boone's settlement, called Kemper's farm." "The master's slave and the slave's master." "Ambition's rise may be virtue's fall." "The lily's beauty." "India's coral strand." "John's head is large."

165. The possessive case of every noun not ending in the sound of *s*, is indicated by annexing '*s*.

Ex.—"Harry's slate; the children's books; Bunyan's Pilgrim's Progress; for the Atridæ's sake." The '*s* is a contraction of the old possessive sign, *es* or *is;* as, "The *kingis* crowne;" "In widdowes habite."—*Chaucer*.

166. To plurals ending in *s*, only the apostrophe (') is added; and to nouns of the singular number, ending in the sound of *s*, '*s* is added, but sometimes the apostrophe only.

Ex.—"*Boys*' sports;" "*Mechanics*' Bank." "*Charles's* affairs."—*Prescott*. "Louis's reign."—*Macaulay*. "Mr. Brooks's integrity."—*E. Everett*. "King James's Bible."—*Geo. P. Marsh*. "Brookes's translation."—*Id*. "Morris and Willis's Office."—*N. P. Willis*. "The title of Phillips's dictionary."—*J. E. Worcester*. "Confucius's system."—*Oxford Professor: England*. "Some of Æschylus's and Euripides's plays open in this manner."—*Blair's Rhetoric*. "Demosthenes's life."—*Ib*. "From Stiles's pocket into Nokes's."—*Hudibras*. "Dennis's Works."—*Pope*. "Miss's fine lunardi."—*Burns*. "Adonis's death."—*Mrs. Browning*. "In King James' Version."—*R. G. White*. "In the Countess's speech."— *Id*. "Bullions' Grammar."—*Bullions*. "Sanders' Series of Readers."—*Sanders*. "Davies' Mathematics."—*Davies*.

The phrases "For conscience' sake," "For goodness' sake," "For Jesus' sake," are rather idiomatic exceptions than fair illustrations of a general principle. It has been said that the possessive *s* may be omitted, when each of the last two syllables of the possessive word begins with an *s*-sound, and the next word also begins with an *s*-sound; as, "Augustus' speech."

In poetry, when the singular ends in a hissing sound, the *s* may be used or omitted to suit the poet's convenience; but in prose, I think it should generally be used where it is omitted. If not too many hissing sounds come together, and if the possessive *s* would not be too far removed from an accented syllable, it should doubtless be used; and in other cases, *of* is probably always preferable. People do not hesitate to write, "The horse's heels;" "The young prince's father." And, if sound is to determine the use or the omission of the *s*, I can not see why many other words are less entitled to the *s* than such words as these. Few full possessives would be harsher or heavier than such plural words as *glasses, carcasses, atlases, duchesses, actresses,* &c., which nobody hesitates to use when needed. Besides, the *s* is often *needed to make the sense clear*. "Watt's works" and "Watts' works" are intelligible only to the eye, and should be "Wutt's works" and "Watts's works." I can not concur with Dr. Bullions, in the propriety of omitting the *s* in written language, but retaining it in spoken. Let language be written as it is spoken; at least, let us not introduce any more anomalies in this respect.

A harsh possessive may often be avoided by converting it into an adjective, or by using *of*. "A fox's tail"—A fox tail; "Bunker Hill" is now more commonly used than "Bunker's Hill;" and "Lucas Place" is quite as intelligible as "Lucas's Place;" "Hastings' trial" or "Hastings's trial"—The trial of Hastings. "Socrates's life and death"—The life and death of Socrates; "John's brother's wife's sister"—The sister of John's brother's wife. But "A summer's day" is not necessarily equivalent to "A summer day;" nor does *of* always imply possession; as, "A spring *of* clear water;" "To have some idea *of* the subject."

167. When two or more consecutive words, taken together, are used to denote but one possessor, or when the same object belongs to several in common, the possessive sign is usually annexed but once, and immediately before the name of the object possessed, but not always to the word in the possessive case.

Ex.—"William Henry Harrison's election;" "Her Majesty Queen Victoria's government;" "The Bishop of Landaff's residence;" "At Hall's, the baker." "The captain of the Fulton's wife died yesterday." Here *captain* is in the possessive case, governed by *wife*; and *Fulton* in the objective case, governed by *of*. "The Duke of Wellington's achievements." Here *Duke of Wellington's* may be parsed as one noun, so also may *Bishop of Landaff's*, and most such expressions. "Barton, Hutchinson, and Spotswood's store." Here *Barton, Hutchinson,* and *Spotswood's*, are each in the possessive case, governed by *store*. "Barton's, Hutchinson's, and Spotswood's store"—Barton's store, Hutchinson's store, and Spotswood's store; or, *Barton's* and *Hutchinson's* are governed by *store* understood.

The various sorts of terms or phrases that may denote possessors, and the best modes of expressing the sense of the possessive case wherever difficulties present themselves, may be briefly noticed as follows:—

Monosyllables ending with the sound of *s*,—*'s ; dissyllables*,—*'s* or *of*, rarely '; *words of more syllables*,—*of*, rarely ', or else *'s*, when the last syllable thus formed is not too far from the primary or the secondary accent.

Ex.—"Sparks's Washington;" "Edwards's West Indies;" "The landing of Cornwallis;" "Euphrates' banks."

Compound names,—sign to the last word. "Edward Everett's Works."

Complex names, or single terms with single adjuncts,—sign to the last word, or use *of*; with adjuncts or compound adjuncts,—*of*.

Ex.—"The Duke of Wellington's residence;" "The Report of the Secretary of the Navy;" "The wife of a member of Congress;" "An Act of the Legislature of the State of New York."

Apposition, the two terms used like one name,—sign at the end; principal term, with explanatory part short,—sign to either, but not to both; explanatory part long, or consisting of two or more nouns,—sign to the first, or use of.

Ex.—"The Emperor Napoleon's grave;" "At Smith's, the bookseller;" "At Smith the bookseller's;" "Mr. Crawford's Report, the Secretary of the Treasury;" better, "The Report of Mr. Crawford, the Secretary of the Treasury;" "The psalms of David, the king, priest, and poet of the Jews;" "From the death of Edward the Third to the reign of Queen Elizabeth;" "The residence of George Clinton, ex-governor of New York, and vice-president of the United States."

Series of terms, and common possession,—sign to the last term; but not common possession,—sign to each term.

Ex.—"Belton, Dixon, and Glover's farm;" "Bolton's, Dixon's, and Glover's farm." "Bolton, Dixon, and Glover's farms," rather implies joint or common possession. "Bolton's, Dixon's, and Glover's farms," implies that each man owns two or more farms.

168. The **objective** case denotes the condition of a substantive that is used as the object of a verb or preposition.

Ex.—"Mary PLUCKED a fresh *rose*." "I saw Mary PLUCKING a fresh *rose*." "Mary went to PLUCK a fresh *rose*." "A clear stream FROM the *mountain* flowed DOWN the *valley*." "*Whom* do you see?" "I saw *him* gathering *apples*." "I came TO HEAR *him*, or WITH the *expectation* of HEARING *him*." The word in the objective case can be readily found by asking a question with *whom* or *what* after the verb or preposition. Thus, "The soldiers carried their bleeding companion to the river." Carried whom? *Companion*. To what? *River*.

169. The object may be a verbal noun, or consist of an entire phrase or clause.

Ex.—"My brother likes *to study*, but I like *running* and *jumping* better than *studying*." "He knew *to build* the lofty rhyme." "You do not consider *how little most people care for what is not to their interest*." "I ordered *the horse to be brought*." To determine whether a verb followed by a clause or a phrase is transitive, we must consider whether a noun or a pronoun put in the place of the phrase or clause, would be governed by the verb or preposition.

As an entire clause may be the object of a verb or preposition, so may an entire phrase beginning with a substantive followed by an infinitive. The governing word does not govern the noun or pronoun alone, yet it has sufficient influence over it, as a part of its object, (a part otherwise uncontrolled.) *to determine its case;* and *this influence* is *sufficient* for the application of Rule 4th or 5th.

Ex.—"Let *me finish the problem*." "I desire *you to go*." "I supposed *him to be your brother*." "He commanded *the horse to be brought*." "One word is too often profaned for *me to profane it*."

The effort has been made several times, to implant from the Latin into the English, a Rule for "the subject of the infinitive;" but most grammarians have discarded the innovation without even deigning to give it a critical notice or a formal rejection. I too incline to reject it. "Rule XI. The infinitive has sometimes a subject in the objective case."— *Butler's Grammar*. OBJECTIONS:—1. The English language never allows an object before an infinitive, unless there is at the same time *a governing word before the object;* but the Latin sometimes allows an *intransitive* verb before such an object, and therefore *differs* from our language, and *requires* a Rule for the subject of the infinitive. We can say, "Gaudeo te valere;" but not, "I rejoice thee to be well." 2. Though Mr. Butler's few examples are plain and plausible enough, as examples made or selected for a Rule usually are, yet it is impossible to tell, in every instance, whether the object should be parsed as the "subject" of the infinitive or as the "object" of the preceding verb. 3. The participle has sometimes as good a right to such a subject as the infinitive; thus, "I saw the sun *rise*" and "I saw the sun *rising*," differ no more than "The sun *rises*" and "The sun *is rising*."

170. A passive verb, since it converts its object into its subject, can not have an object.

171. A few verbs may have two different objects at once, provided they can govern them as well separately.

Ex.—"He asked me a question"—"He asked me" and "He asked a question;" but "He gave me a question," is not equivalent to "He gave me" and "He gave a question."

When a verb governing two objects is made passive, either object, but not both, may be made the nominative. The other object remains in the objective case; but as a passive verb can not govern an object, the other object, if it denotes the person, is governed by a preposition expressed or understood; and if it denotes the thing, it may be referred to Rule 6th.

Ex.—"My mother taught me arithmetic"—I was taught arithmetic by my mother, or, Arithmetic was taught (to) me by my mother. *Observe the difference:* "James struck *him* a *blow*;" "James wrote *him* a *letter*;" "James called *him* his *friend*."

172. A substantive is also in the *objective case*, when it is used without a governing word, yet modifies like an adjunct or adverb some other word. The suppressed governing word is a preposition.

Ex.—"I do not care a *straw!*" Care not how much? "The wall was 1200 *feet* long, and 40 *feet* high." How long? how high? "It was richly worth a *dollar*." Worth how much? "We went *home*." Whither? "The slippered pantaloon, a *world* too wide."—*Shak.* How much too wide? "He is *head* and *heels* in debt." To what extent? "He wore his coat cloak *fashion*." How? "I was taught *grammar*." Taught as to what?—Sometimes a substantive may be referred to the foregoing principle, or parsed at once as an adverb. Some grammarians prefer to consider every such expression elliptical, and to supply a preposition, which can generally be done without straining the matter very far.

173. There are expressions, however, obviously elliptical.

Ex.—"Dr. Rush, No. 840, Pine Street, Philadelphia, Penn."—*To* Dr. Rush, *at* No. 840, *on* Pine Street, *in* Philadelphia, *in* Pennsylvania. "Jan. 1st, 1860"—*On* the first day *of* January, *in* the year 1860. "Ah me!"—Ah, what has happened *to* me! So, "*Me* miserable!" or else it may be considered simply a Latinism, used by Milton for the nominative absolute.

Same Case.

174. A substantive that does not bring another person or thing into the sentence, and is used merely for explanation, emphasis, or description, must be in the *same case* as the one denoting the person or thing.

Ex.—"COMPANY, villainous *company*, has been the ruin of me." "I *Joseph Walter*, a *justice* of the peace, certify," &c. "CORTES, the *conqueror* of Mexico, was a brave *man*." "I, also *I*, am an *American*." "The Emperor *Napoleon's* grave." "This book is John's, my *classmate*." "It was *I*." "We will go *ourselves*." "They crowned him *king*." "His purse was *wealth*, his word a *bond*." "Will sneaks a *scrivener*, an exceeding *knave*." The one substantive may be called the *principal term;* and the other, the *explanatory term*.

175. Frequently, the explanatory term is predicated or assumed of the other, by means of some neuter, intransitive, or passive verb. The explanatory term is then usually called a *predicate-substantive*. The verb, if any other than *be*, shows how the title or characteristic is acquired or made known.

Ex.—"The world is but a *stage*, and all the men and women [are] merely *players*." "My friend was appointed *judge*." "She walks a *queen*"—She is a queen, and displays it in her walk; or, She is not a queen, but affects the airs of one. The latter sense would seem to require Rule 6th, but the analogy of foreign languages rather requires Rule 7th in either sense. "Tom struts a *soldier*." "The soldiers sent a petition requesting him to become their *leader*—a petition for him to become their *leader*." Such a predicate-substantive after verbs not finite, is in the nominative case whenever there is no preceding object to control its case.

176. When not attached to the other term by means of a verb, the explanatory term is said to be in *apposition*, and is called the *appositive*.

Ex.—" WEBSTER, the *orator* and *statesman*, was related to WEBSTER the *lexicographer*." " At Smith's, the *bookseller*." " A firth, or *frith*." " As a *statesman*, he had great ability."

Predication and apposition are fundamentally the same. When the explanatory term is predicated, it seems to be first made known that such an attribute belongs to the person or thing. *Afterwards* we use *apposition;* or when the attribute is already well known or easily perceived, and we wish to assert something else. Thus, " Mr. Jones was a *saddler*, but now he is a *merchant*." Afterwards we may say, " Mr. Jones the *merchant* is a bankrupt."

Apposition frequently enables us to distinguish different persons of the same name, by means of their profession, occupation, or character.

177. Sometimes two objects follow certain verbs: the one simply denoting the person or thing; and the other, as affected by the act.

Ex.—" They named *her Mary*." " They elected *him Mayor*."

That the latter substantive is rather in apposition with the former than governed by the verb, seems evident to me from the following consideration: " They named her Mary"— Make *her* the nominative, and *Mary* at once becomes a nominative too, so as to agree with it; as, "*She* was named *Mary*." But, " He taught me grammar"—Make *me* the nominative, and *grammar* still remains in the objective case;—as, "*I* was taught *grammar*."

178. The explanatory term sometimes precedes the other, or the verb.

Ex.—"*Child* of the Sun, refulgent Summer comes." " *Who* is he ?" " A *man* he was to all the country dear." " *Who* is his friend ?" This last is an ambiguous expression. If *friend* is the explanatory term, the sentence means, " Is any one friendly to him ? has he any friends at all ?" If *who* is explanatory, the meaning is, " What sort of man is his friend ?"

179. It is not always necessary that the explanatory term should agree with the other in any thing else than case.

Ex.—"Our *liberties*, our greatest *blessing*, we shall not give up so easily." " His *meat* was *locusts* and wild *honey*." " *Eyes* was *I* to the blind, and *feet* to the lame." " The streams ran *nectar*."

180. The whole is sometimes again mentioned by a distributive word, or by words denoting the parts; and sometimes the separate persons or things are summed up in one emphatic word denoting the whole.

Ex.—" THEY bore *each* a banner." " The WORDS *pleasure* and *pain*." " The two love *each* [loves the] other." (See Pronouns, p. 132.) " Time, labor, money, *all* were lost." Or else Rule 7th may be applied to *time, labor*, and *money*, and Rule 1st to *all*.

" But those that sleep, and think not of their sins,
Pinch THEM, *arms, legs, backs, shoulders, sides*, and *shins*."—*Shakespeare.*

To this head, also such expressions as " The stars disappeared *one* by one," "They perished *man* by man," may sometimes be more properly referred.—See Adverb, p. 240.

150 NOUNS AND PRONOUNS.—CASES.

181. The principal or the explanatory term may be any ordinary noun, a verbal noun, a pronoun, a phrase, or a clause.

Ex.—"O *Music*, sphere-descended *maid.*" "*It* was my *pride | to govern* justly." "*Promising* is not *paying.*" "*It* is an admitted *truth*, [*that honesty is the best policy.*" " *Who* is *he ?* " "The *phrase*, | '*not at all*', is an *idiom.*" " Our *doom is*, ' *Earth to earth, and dust to dust ?* " "*I resolved to pay as I go,—a resolution* which I have ever kept."

182. The explanatory term is sometimes cut off from the other by a governing word, and may then be different in case.

Ex.—"In the MONTH of *September.*" " Yonder is the city of *St. Louis.*" " He was sent with us for a *guide.*" " I hurt *myself.*"

183. The explanatory term is essentially an adjective element.

Ex.—"He was a *hero*"—He was *heroic.* " Every heart was *joy*"—Every heart was *joyful.* " They called him *a patriot ;*" " They called him *patriotic.*" "*Sluggish* in youth, he," &c.—A *sluggard* in youth, he, &c.

Cases of Pronouns.
For the Declension of Pronouns, see p. 8.

Ours, yours, hers, and *theirs,* should always, and *mine* and *thine* should generally, be considered equivalent to the other possessive pronoun and the name of the object possessed, and then be parsed accordingly.

Ex.—" He ate his apple, you ate *yours* [your apple], and I ate *mine*" [my apple]. *Yours* is not governed by a noun understood, for the noun could not be put after it; but it is equivalent to *your* and a noun.

In familiar language, these words are sometimes used in a peculiar idiomatic way: thus, " This law of yours," may mean, " This law of your laws;" but, " This head of yours," " That father of yours," " This poor self of mine," are not equivalent to " This head of your heads," " This father of your fathers," " This poor self of my selves." Perhaps we may, in parsing, treat such phrases thus: " This head of *yours*"—" This head of *your possession ;*" or in some other similar way.

184. Before vowel sounds or the aspirate *h*, *mine* and *thine* are sometimes preferred, in the solemn style, to *my* and *thy*.

Ex.—" Blot out all *mine* iniquities."—*Bible.* " *Thine* altar."—*Whittier.*

185. The compound personal pronouns are used only in the nominative and the objective case; and for both they have the same form.

186. To express emphatic distinction in the possessive case, we use the word *own* instead of *self* or *selves*.

Ex.—" Let every man attend to *his own* business, and every woman gossip about *her own* faults." " Selfish men always take care of themselves, and *their own* property."

In the objective case, the simple pronoun is sometimes used for the compound, especially in poetry.

Ex.—" I thither went, and laid *me* down on the green bank."—*Milton.* " I set *me* down a pensive hour to spend."—*Goldsmith.*

It is worthy of notice, that the compound pronouns of the first and second persons take the *possessive* simple pronoun; and those of the third person, the *objective.*

Who and *which* are declined, and have the same form in both numbers.

187. *Whose* may be used as the possessive of *which* or *that*, when needed.

Ex.—" A party *whose* leaders are corrupt"—A party *of which* the leaders are corrupt. " It is the same man *whose* horse we caught."

188. *What, that,* and *as,* are used in two cases only; the nominative and the objective.

189. *What* is never changed in form.

190. *What,* used as a common relative pronoun, and other expressions of the same kind, may have a twofold construction in regard to case.

This is the substance of Rule 8th, which applies to *what,* its *compounds,* to some nouns preceded by such adjectives as *what* or *which,* and to any other relative *whenever the sense requires two cases, and the* FORM *of the word does* NOT *prevent it from being adapted to express both.*

Should Rule 8th seem a *peculiar* one, we answer that it applies to a class of *peculiar* expressions. There is not room here to present an array of arguments in favor of our position. Suffice it to say, that we endeavor to accept the language, so far as possible, as we find it; and that what such expressions were in former or ancient times, is no proof of what they are now. There was a time when every steamboat-engine had a balance-wheel, but now the water-wheel performs the office of that wheel too; and who would think of putting a balance-wheel into a drawing of such an engine, when the wheel is no longer needed or used? Besides, the kindred words, *when, where,* and *while,* are usually parsed as modifying a word in each of two different clauses; and participial nouns are frequently parsed as performing a double office. Furthermore, the parsing is much simplified.

191. When *what* is interrogative or responsive, it is needed in but one case, depending in construction on some word in its own clause. When the form of the relative prevents it from furnishing two cases, it must take the form required for its own clause, and a suitable antecedent must be supplied for the other clause; but then the *ever* or *soever* must be omitted. See Compound Relatives, p. 130.

Remember, in parsing, that the antecedent never relates to a word in the relative clause, but frequently refers to one beyond it.

Ex.—" The boy who trifles away his time, will be wretched in manhood." *Boy* is in the nominative case, not to *trifles,* but to *will be.*

192. *One, other,* and *another,* are declined like nouns.

EXERCISES.
Examples to be Analyzed and Parsed.

Parse the nouns and the pronouns:—

1.

A fisherman's[2] boat[1] carried the passengers[4] to a small island[5]. Napoleon Bonaparte defeated the allies at the battle of Austerlitz. Milton's Paradise Lost and Young's Night Thoughts are great poems[7]. Fifty painted Indians from Minnesota went down the Mississippi, on the Black Hawk Education expands and elevates the mind. Religion refines and purifies the affections. Spices are brought from the East Indies.

2.

I will use John's book, and you may use Mary's. Great hypocrisy characterized a part of Louis XIV's reign. John's wife's sister is in town. I have read Charles de Moor's Remorse, and the Introduction to Loomis's

Legendre's Geometry. The literati of Europe are famous for profound erudition. Mexico lies between the Pacific Ocean° and the Gulf of Mexico°. The little company then sailed to the Azores. I have just heard a lecture on the useful°. Rome from her throne of beauty ruled the world. The clouds² dispersing, we renewed our journey. Scotland²! there is magic in the sound.

Prefer, my son², the toils of Hercules,
To dalliance, banquets, and ignoble ease.

3.

I¹ will never forsake you⁴. We should always prefer our² duty to our pleasure. He is not content with his situation. I seated myself next¹⁰ to the window. Joseph bought the book for himself°ᵃ°. Man²l know thyself°ᵃ⁴: all wisdom centres there. The Indians often paint themselves. The party reposed themselves on the shady lawn.

4.

The poor widow lost her°ᵃ² only son. John and James know their°ᵃ² lessons. Neither John nor James knows his°ᵃ² lesson. Where confidence has been destroyed, it seldom revives. The deer waved its branchy head. It is wicked to scoff⁷ at religion. It is too early for flowers. It happened on a lovely summer's day. It rains. It went hard with him. She is handsome, and she knows it°ᵃ⁴. My heart beats yet, but hersᵗ I can not feel!

5. Antecedent Expressed.

The man who⁹ᵃ¹ neglects his°ᵃ² business, will soon be without business. That² man is enslaved who can not govern himself. How beautiful are yonder willows, which overshadow the little river! Sarah has plucked the prettiest rose that°ᵃ¹ bloomed in the garden. The traveler described very accurately such things as he remembered. She has already as many troubles as she can bear. The sister has the same traits of character asᵉ her brothers.

6. Antecedent not Expressed.

Many blessings has the world derived from those whose origin was humble. Assist suchᵈ as need thy assistance. Who⁶ has not virtue, is not truly wise. I saw whom⁸ I wanted to see. I love whoever¹ loves me. Whoever⁸ violates this rule, shall pay a fine. Whomsoever⁸ you send, I will cheerfully instruct.

7.

I remember what⁶ was said. He reads whatever⁸ is instructive. Fops are more attentive to what⁸ is showy, than mindful of what⁸ is necessary. Whatever purifies the heart, also fortifies it. Whatever he found, he took. Whatsoever he doeth, shall prosper. Whatever money⁸ I had, I spent. Conscience wakes the bitter memory of *what⁷ he¹ was, what he is, and what must be.

8.

Who¹ first crossed the Alps?—Hannibal¹. What constitutes a State? M ⁊ countrymen, oh what¹⁰ a fall was there! What⁴ means this martial array? Which belongs to you? Do you know *who¹ said so? I know not who said so. Who can tell *whom⁴ he meant? What⁷ is it¹ that°ᵃ⁴ you want? I never heard what° it was that brought him here. What country is better than oursᵇ?—None¹. Which man was hurt? What¹⁰ man⁸ but enters, dies. Take whichever horse⁸ you like. On whichsoever side we cast our eyes, we saw nothing but¹⁴ ruins.

9.

Gentle reader, whoever[7] thou[1] art, remember this. I believe no other author whatever[10] would advance the same doctrines. I tell you what[f], my son, those friends of ours have forgotten us. My son, whatever[4] the world may say, adhere to what[6] is right. Whatever you undertake, do it well. Whomsoever he finds, him he will send.

10.

She took the good ones, and left the others. None are perfectly good. Mankind slay one another in cruel wars. They deemed each other[4] oracles[7] of law. Pity from you is dearer than that from another. Who is there to mourn for Logan? Not one.

11.

Johnson the doctor[7] is a brother[7] of Johnson the lawyer[7]. Wait for me at Barnum's, the barber. Shakespeare lived in Queen Elizabeth's reign. The Misses Lewis are amiable young ladies. Messrs.[7] Lucas[1] and Simonds[1] are bankers in St. Louis. Ah! Warwick, Warwick, wert thou as we are. The Spanish general presented the young prince to them as their future sovereign[7], and as the true heir to the Peruvian sceptre. My wife, the sweet soother of my cares, fell a victim[7] to despair. The inferior animals are divided into five classes; quadrupeds[7], fowls, fishes, reptiles, and insects. Officer, soldier, friend, and foe, were all[f] shoveled into a common grave. It was I, your friend, that[h] became his protector. He led the troops himself. She is modest and virtuous; [and modesty and virtue are] qualities ever to be esteemed.

12.

And all our knowledge is ourselves[4] to know[7]. "To be good is to be happy," is a truth[7] never to be forgotten by those commencing the journey of life. Far other scene was Thrasemene now. This life is the springtime of eternity,—the time to sow[12] the seeds of woe or the seeds of bliss. She walks [has become] a queen. Queen[7] of flowers the fair lily blooms. Now, what[7] is your text? I see you what[7] you are. Whom do you take him to be? He made us wiser[10]—made us walk[12]—made us scholars[7]. An elm, says the poet Holmes, is a forest waving on a single stem. Such a one[4] as[7] I was, this picture presents. Death is the wages of sin. That Louis XIV was crafty, does not make him a great ruler.

See the blind beggar[4] dance[12], the cripple sing,
The sot[4] a hero[7], lunatic a king.—*Pope.*

13.

Friends[2], Romans[2], countrymen[2]! lend me your ears.—*Shakespeare.*

Young ladies, put not your trust in money, but put your money in trust.—*O. W. Holmes.*

His praise, ye[j] winds[k], that from four quarters blow,
Breathe soft or loud; and wave your tops, ye pines.—*Milton*

My friends, do they now and then send
A wish or a thought after me.—*Cowper.*

To arms! they come! the Greek[l]! the Greek!—*Halleck.*

"Come back! come back!" he cried in grief,
  "Across this stormy water;
And I'll forgive your Highland chief,—
  My daughter! oh, my daughter!"—*Campbell.*

14.

The sun having risen, we began our journey.
Bonaparte being banished, peace was restored to Europe.
Forth he walked, the Spirit² leading and his deep thoughts².
He² being a boy⁷, the Indians spared him. He¹, being a boy⁷, was not killed.
  Her wheel at rest, the matron thrills no more
  With treasured tales, and legendary lore.—*Rogers.*
To be a great historian, is easier than to be a great poet.
His being a foreigner, should not induce us to underrate him.

15.

The sailors, in wandering over the island, found several trees bearing delicious fruit⁴. I forgot to tell⁴ [to] him the story. Boys like to play⁴. I was about to express⁵ my opinion, when he spoke to suggest¹² to me to remain⁴ silent. I can not permit him⁴ to go¹². He taught us⁴ arithmetic⁴, reading⁴, and writing⁴. He taught us to cipher, to read, and to write. He was taught to walk¹² on the rope. The horse I bought, is five years old. We were taught arithmetic, reading, and writing. The profit is hardly worth¹⁰ the trouble⁶. The Atlantic Ocean is three thousand miles wide.

(*a.*) "*Loomis's*" limits the meaning, not of "*Geometry,*" but of "*Legendre's Geometry.*" (*b.*) "*Hers*"=*her heart.* (*c.*) "*As*" is the object of *have,* understood: when the governing word is expressed, "*as*" should be *that.* (*d.*) "*Such*"=*such persons.* (*e.*) "*What he was,*" is a substantive clause, of the neuter gender, third person, singular number, and in the objective case—being the object of the preposition "*of*"—according to Rule V. Now parse each word as before. (*f.*) After "*what,*" supply *I think,* or something equivalent. (*g.*) "*All,*" as here used, is usually parsed as a pronoun; but it may perhaps be as well considered an adjective. (*h.*) "*That*" properly refers to "*It*" as its antecedent. (*i.*) Not Rule VII, for each subsequent term is meant to be more comprehensive. (*j.*) Rule VII may be applied to either word; but some grammarians think, better to *ye,* as being the strengthening word. (*k.*) A noun is never the subject of an imperative verb; and a pronoun is the subject, only when it comes immediately after the verb and is joined to it. (*l.*) Rule VII is sometimes not inapplicable, and may be preferred.

Examples to be Corrected.

All the liabilities to error in regard to nouns and pronouns, may be reduced to the following heads:—

I. 1. *Usurpation by the adverb.* 2. *Genders.* 3. *Persons.* 4. *Numbers.* 5. *Nominative case.* 6. *Possessive case.* 7. *Objective case.* 8. *Same case.* 9. *Position in regard to case.*

II. 1. *Choice of pronouns.* 2. *Agreement of pronouns with antecedents, in gender, person, and number.* 3. *Position of pronoun in regard to antecedent.* 4. *Pronoun inadequate to represent antecedent.* 5. *Inelegant insertion of pronoun.* 6. *Inelegant omission of pronoun.* 7. *Relative pronoun improperly used in its conjunctive capacity only.*

Nouns and Pronouns.

1. *Usurpation by the Adverb.*

We should avoid the inelegant use of adverbs in the place of nouns or pronouns.

NOUNS AND PRONOUNS.—EXERCISES. 155

A diphthong is where two vowels are united in one sound. —*the union of*— A diphthong is when two vowels are united in one sound. Fusion is while a solid is converted into a liquid by heat. When a letter or a syllable is transposed, it is called Metathesis. *The transposition of a letter*, &c. Personification is when we ascribe life, sentiments, or actions, to inanimate beings, or to abstract qualities. —*is a figure by which*— A deed of trust is a deed where the lender has power to sell to secure himself. —*is a deed giving*— Manslaughter is where a man is killed without malice or previous ill-will. He drew up a petition where he too freely represented his own merits. The occasions where a man has the right to take the law into his own hands, are but few. The manner how it was done, I never could ascertain. The plural of these nouns is formed as in the languages whence they are derived.

2. *Genders.*

Substantives should be properly used in gender, according to the sex, the general nature of the object, or the particular view of the author.

a. Unworthy objects should not be personified as male or female.

b. Care should be taken to ascribe to a personified object the most appropriate sex.

She is administrator. The marquess was celebrated for her wit and beauty. He was married to a most beautiful Jew. She was the tallest woman I ever saw: she was really a giant. Mrs. Lydia Smith, the editor, lately turned actor, at Memphis. She is considered the best bakeress in the establishment. She is not so great a prophet as to scare me into belief. (Is a governess the wife of a governor, or is she a woman that governs?) The tiger broke from its cage. A weasel put his head out from an old stone wall. How can a calf distinguish his mother's lowing from that of a thousand other cows? How timidly the rabbit looks out from his bushy covert, and how briskly the squirrel chatters on the limb near her nest in a hole of some tall tree. The sun, in its bright career round the world, does not look down upon a lovelier or livelier land; nor does the moon throw, anywhere else, its silver mantle more softly or beautifully upon the slumbering world below. Alas! we know only that the ship sailed from England, but that to England it never returned again. They who seek wisdom, will certainly find her. (Not personified.) His form had not yet lost all her original brightness.—*Milton.* Her sway extends o'er all things that have breath; a cruel tyrant, and her name is Death.—*Sheffield.* While Spring shall pour his showers.—*Collins.*

3. *Persons.*

Politeness usually requires that the speaker shall mention the addressed person first, and himself last.

I, Mary, and you, are to go next Sunday. If James and you take the horses, I and Martha shall have nothing to ride. Mother said that I and you must stay at home. We and they studied Latin together. When he and you are married, I will come to see you. This law, fellow-citizens, bears hard upon me, upon you, and upon every other laboring man. (Proper or not proper, depending on the sense.)

4. *Numbers.*

Nouns and pronouns should be correctly used in number, according to the sense, and the proper form of the word.

The room is eighteen foot long, and sixteen foot wide. I measured the log with a pole ten foot long—with a ten-feet pole. The lot has 25 foot front, and

NOUNS AND PRONOUNS.—EXERCISES.

is 8 rod deep. The teamster hauled four cord of wood, and three ton of hay, in nine hour. St. Louis is seven mile long and two mile wide. Five quintillion, six quadrillion, seven trillion, eight billion, nine million, two thousand, three hundred and forty-five. Five billions six millions twenty-five thousands two hundred and three. For this dog he paid five pound and ten shilling. She gathered a few handful of flowers. The corpse of the Mexicans were left to the wolf and the vulture. The work embraces every minutiæ—all the minutia of the science. If six apples cost three pence, two apples will cost one pence. The prairie-hens were sold by score and dozen. I bought two pairs of socks. The Swede are a patriotic people, as well as the Swiss. The whole fleet consists of twelve sail. —*ships*. Of his oxens, he had just sold six or seven heads. He used his influence as a mean for destroying the party. In the early settlement of Missouri, beaver and water-fowl were abundant about the rivers and creeks. He never took two shot at a deer. A bag of shots will last us a year.

We now came to a region where buffalo, turkeys, elk, and bear, were to be found. Several chimnies were blown down by the last storm. The vermins were so numerous that we could raise no fowl. As we emerged from the woods, we saw three deers standing on a small eminence in the prairie. These are desideratas not found every day. I will take no more of his nostra, be the consequences what they may. Of these plants, there are several genuses. The garden of Eden contained all kind of fruit. The heathen are those people who worship idols. He is a chemist, and has many apparatuses in his office. —*much apparatus*— or, *many kinds of apparatus*— The Mussulmen are Mahometans, but the Germans are not. The *ay's* and *nay's* were then taken. How many 6s in nine 8s? Your *zs* and *ys* are not well shaped. (Write out in words $\frac{7}{4\frac{1}{T}}$ and $\frac{9}{2\frac{1}{3}}$.) No familys stand higher than the Winthrop's, Webster's, and Everett's, of New England. The fowls were sold at nine pennies a piece. Byron was one of the greatest poetic genii that ever lived. The sheafs were carried away by thiefs. The cargos consisted chiefly of calicos, mangos, and potatos. Two folioes. The angelic Peri's. Two of his aid-de-camps were killed. His brother-in-laws were educated at the same university. The deserters were tried by court-martials.

The Doctors Stevensons and the Misses Arnolds seem to be on very good terms. The two Misses Cheevers, the Misses Boltons, the Messrs. Hays, and the Mrs. Talbots, were all at the party. The second, third, and fifth story, were filled with goods. The Old and the New Testaments—the Old and New Testament, in one large volume, called the Bible. You may learn the ninth and tenth page—the ninth and the tenth pages, and review the first or second pages. The English, French, and German nation—the English, the French, and the German nations, are the most enlightened. Nouns have the nominative, the possessive, and the objective cases; the singular and the plural numbers; the masculine, feminine, common, and neuter gender; and the first, second, and third person. Bushnell's, Halsall's, and Woodward's stores occupy the next three buildings. *Bushnell's store, Halsall's*, &c. He and I were neither of us any great talkers. The sermon produced a deep impression on the hearts of every hearer. We shall give but a short Preface. (There was but one author.) It was for our sakes that Jesus died upon the cross. Very few persons are contented with their lots. They were trained together in their childhoods. The members will regard their reputations, and not demand exorbitant wages. It is not worth our whiles, to study stenography. —*our time*— Let us drive on, and get our suppers at the next house. The directors did little on their parts, to relieve the bank. We shall advocate these measures, not in the names of our constituents, but on our own responsibilities. All these uses send their tap-roots deep into the ground. —*the tap-root*—

6. Nominative Case.

A noun or a pronoun must be in the *nominative* case,—
1. When it *is* the subject of a finite verb.
2. When it is used absolutely or independently.
   a. The object of the active verb, and not of the preposition, should be made the subject of the passive verb.

7. Objective Case.

A noun or a pronoun must be in the *objective* case,—
1. When it is the object of a verb.
2. When it is the object of a preposition.

8. Same Case.

A noun or a pronoun used to explain or identify another, must be in the *same* case.

Him and me went to the same church. Them that seek wisdom, will find it. You and him are of the same age. Gentle reader, let you and I, in like manner, walk in the paths of virtue. Them are not worth having. Let there be none but thee and I. The whole need not a physician, but them that are sick. He can not write as well as me. I sorrowed as them that have no hope. He is taller than me, but I am as tall as her. I do not think such persons as him competent to judge. You did fully as well as me. It is not fit for such as us to sit with the rulers of the land. You can find no better man than him. We are as good arithmeticians as them, but they are better grammarians than us. Few persons would do as much for him as he and me have done. This is a small matter between you and I. All, save I, wore at rest and enjoyment. There was no one in the room except she. Her price is paid, and she is sold like thou. The Lee's were distinguished officers in the Revolution. Such a man, in the sight of angels, is more illustrious than all the Alexander's, Cæsar's, and Bonaparte's, that ever lived. He and they we know, but who art thou? Esteeming theirselves wise, they became fools. Let each one help hisself. He said so hisself.

If people will put theirselves into danger, they should be willing to bear the consequences. She that is idle and mischievous, reprove sharply. Ye only have I known. Who should I meet the other day but my old friend! Who did she marry? Tell me, in sadness, whom is she you love?—*Shakespeare.* To poor we, thine enmity is most capital.—*Shakespeare's Coriolanus.* Him I accuse, has entered. Who spilt this ink?—Not me; it wasn't me. Who can work this sum?—Me. Who rode in the buggy?—Him and her. Who broke this pitcher?—Not her; it was me. Who is that boy speaking to? *To whom,* &c. Who did you send for? Who did you buy it of? They who much is given to, will have much to answer for. He who committed the offense, thou shouldst correct; not I, who am innocent. Who shall we send?— Whomsoever will go. Whom do you think stands head in our class? That is the boy whom we think deserves the prize. I should like to assist a young man who I think to be so worthy of assistance. Can not a gentleman take into his buggy, to ride with him, whosoever he pleases? Never tie yourself to any one, before knowing whom the person is you are choosing. But, first, I must show who I mean by the administration.—*Benton.* He offered his daughter in marriage to whomsoever might subdue the place.—*Irving.* This excited the curiosity of the Recorder as to whom the consequential darkey might be.—*Mo. Republican.* Let the people elect whom they think is best qualified to lead them—whomsoever is best qualified to lead them—whosoever they know to be best qualified to lead them. He supported those whom he thought were of his party—who he thought true to his party. He attacked the enemy, whom he saw were crossing the river—who he saw crossing the river.

I was offered a seat. He was offered the control of the entire school. He was left a large estate by his uncle. We were shown a sweet-potato that weighed 15 pounds. I was shown into the parlor. (Allowable.) Let him be shown the method we have adopted. I have been promised a better situation in the South. You were paid a high compliment by the young lady. Pupils expelled from other colleges, will not be allowed admittance here. By such a course of proceeding, I am refused that protection which every citizen has a right to expect. We were allowed the use of a large pasture near the mansion. These documents were had recourse to in the course of the debate.

Him losing the way, we were obliged to remain in the woods till morning. Me being absent, the young folks lived high. Their refusing to comply, I withdrew. Oh! happy us, surrounded by so many blessings. And me, what shall I do? Him who had led them to battle being killed, they immediately retreated. The whole family believed in spiritual rappings, us excepted. Her being the only daughter, no expense had been spared in her education. Whose gray top shall tremble, Him descending. The bleating sheep with my complaints agree; them parched with heat, and me inflamed by thee. I mean Noah Webster, he who wrote the dictionary. The man has just arrived, him whom we expected yesterday. Believing the man to be a doctor, or he who had cured the others, we applied to him for assistance. We will go at once,—him and me. And do you thus speak to me, I who have so often befriended you? These are the volunteers from Texas, them who fought so bravely in Mexico. Christ, and him crucified, is the corner-stone of our Faith. Let the pupils be divided into several classes; especially they who read, they who study grammar, and they who study arithmetic. —*especially those*— I dread this man, being he that has so often injured me. —*because he is the one who*— To John and James, they who had misspent their time at school, their father left nothing. (Omit *they*.) Whom being dead, there was no one to check him in his wild career. I would say so, were it he or any other person whomsoever. —*whatsoever*.

It was not me; it was them or her. Is it me you mean? Was it him, or me, that you called? If I were him, I would send for the doctor. If it were me, I would act differently. 'Twas thee I sought. I knew it was him—it to be he. But whom say ye that I am? It is him whom you said it was. Who did you take us to be? She is the person who I understood it to have been. —*that I*— He is a man who I am far from considering happy. I would not be the man whom he now is. It was not me, that said so. I care not, let him be whom he may. No matter where the vanquished be, nor whom. What you saw was but a picture of him, and not him. It was not us, that made the noise. I knew it to be they. It is them and their posterity who are to be the sufferers. He did not prove to be the man whom he was recommended to be. Its being me should make no difference in your determination. (Better: *That it is I,* &c.) There was no doubt of its being him.

6. *Possessive Case.*

1. The relation of possession or property should be expressed in the most appropriate manner, according to custom and euphony.

2. The possessive sign should be used but once, to express one possession, whatever number of words denote the possessor.

His misfortunes awaken nobody's pity, though no ones ability ever went farther for others good. A mothers tenderness and a fathers care are natures gifts for mans advantage. John Norton his book. We used Pierce' Trigonometry, Loomis' Geometry, and Wells' Grammar. How do you like Douglas' bill? Achaia's sons at Ilium slain for the Atridæ' sake. Your's, our's, her's, their's, who's, hisself, theirselves, yourn, hern, ourn, his'n. Adams' Administration. Essex' death haunted the conscience of Queen Elizabeth. Five year's interest remained unpaid. Three days grace was given to the debtors. Six months wages will then be due. I will not destroy the city for ten sake. Rubens' pictures. Horace' satires—Horace's satires—. (Find a different but equivalent expression.) Terence' plays—Terence's plays—. Socrates's death—. Demosthenes' orations—Demosthenes's orations. Hortensius' wonderful memory. For Herodias' sake, his brother Philip's wife. The Governor of Missouri's message. Marcy's letter, the Secretary of War, is a masterly reply—. John's brother's wife's sister married a mechanic—. Was it your book, or somebody else's? The wife of the captain of the Tropic—. (Allowable.)

The Commons' House represents the yeomanry; and the Lords', the nobility. Sunday is also called the day of the Lord. God's love—. The world's government is not left to chance. The extent of the prerogative of the king of England. A list of some of the books of each of the classes of literature will be given. —*in each.* Daniel Boone of Kentucky's adventures. Edward the Second of England s queen. He is Clay the great orator's youngest son. Geo. McDuffie was nominated by John Calhoun the Senator's request. These works are Cicero's, the most eloquent of men's. The opinionative man thinks his opinions better than any one's else opinions—any one else's opinions. This picture of your mother's is a very good likeness. This last work of Longfellow will add little to his reputation. Jack's the Giant-killer's wonderful exploits. We deposited our money at Wiggins's, the banker's and commission merchant's. It was the men's, women's, and children's lot, to suffer great calamities. Linton's, Pope's, and Company's library is large—. Allen's, Thomson's, and Hardcastle's store is opposite to ours. Allen, Thomson, and Hardcastle's stores, are not joint possessions. Albert's and Samuel's heads are shaped like teapots. Peter's and Andrew's occupation was that of fisherman.

Morrison's and Fletcher's farms are the next two on the road. Morrison's *farm and Fletcher's are,* &c. Morrison and Fletcher's farm will be occupied by the respective owners. I have no time to listen to either John or Joseph's lesson. It was necessary to have both the surgeon and the physician's advice. Neither the lawyer nor the doctor's aid was ever needed in this happy valley. Louis the Fourteenth and Bonaparte's reign are distinguished periods in the history of France. He disobeyed his father as well as his mother's advice. Brown, Smith, and Jones' wife, usually went shopping together. The bill had the cashier, but not the president's, signature. Whose dictionary do you prefer,—Johnson, Webster, or Worcester? The horse got away in consequence of me neglecting to fasten the gate. —*my neglecting*— or, *because I had neglected*— He was averse to the nation involving itself in war. There is some talk of us getting into a war. Much depends on the pupil composing frequently. —*on how frequently*— He being a rich man, did not make him a happy man. *That he was a rich,* &c. The time for us beginning to plough, is at hand. *The time for us to begin,* &c. The time for him making the speech, had nearly passed away. What is the reason of you not having gone to school? —*that you have not gone*— There is nothing to prevent him going—his going— your going. —*him from going;* or,—*you from going.* Such will ever be the consequences of youth associating with vicious companions. —*when young persons associate*— From him having always assisted me, I again applied to him for help. *Because he*— or, *Inasmuch as he,* &c. The situation enabled him to

8

earn something, without him losing too much time from his studies. —*without losing*—

9. *Position in regard to Case.*

Nouns and pronouns should be so construed with other words, as not to leave the case uncertain or ambiguous.

The settler here the savage slew. (Which slew the other?) I do not love him better than you. And thus the son the fervent sire addressed. And all the air a solemn stillness holds. Our hunters caught the orang-outangs themselves. He suffered himself to betray his friend. Poetry has a measure as well as music. Forrest plays these pieces better than all others. She acted her part better than any other one. I would rather give her to thee than another.

Pronouns.

1. *Choice of Pronouns.*

In the use of pronouns, great care should be taken to select the most appropriate.

a. In the selection of pronouns, we are governed by the sense, rather than by the nouns which they are to represent.

b. It is inelegant to use pronouns of different kinds for the same object, and in the same connection, when we naturally expect uniformity.

I gave all what I had. I sent every thing what you ordered. I am the boy what is not afraid to go. There is the same man whom we saw a while ago. There is the same wagon of apples which was at the market. In her looks, she is the same as she always was. The same objects which pleased the boy, will not always please the man. *The objects which,* &c. We prepared us to die. —*ourselves*— Give that which you can spare to the poor. —*what you*— We speak that we do know. I am that I am. I am happy in the friend which I have long proved. Those which are rich, should assist the poor and helpless. The heroic souls which defended the Alamo. She was a conspicuous flower, which he had sensibility to love, ambition to attempt, and skill to win. My dogs now came upon the tracks of the lion, who had caught and eaten the man during the night. So I gave the reins to my horse, who knew the way much better than I knew it. Who of those ladies do you like best?
Moses was the meekest man whom we read of in the Old Testament. Humility is one of the most amiable virtues which we can possess. He was the first man who came. This is the most fertile part of the State which we have as yet seen. Marcy was perhaps the ablest secretary who ever was in this department. He sold his best horse, which had been given to him. (Proper; the relative clause not being restrictive.) Who who has the feelings of a man, would submit to such treatment? Who is she who comes clothed in a robe of light green? By this speculation he lost all which he had promised to his daughter. All who ever knew him, spoke well of him. A most ungrateful return for all which I have done for him. Of all the congregations whom I ever saw, this was certainly the largest. The very night as suits a melancholy temperament. He was devoured by the very dogs which he had reared. They are such persons that I do not like to associate with. These are the same sums as we had before. He is like a beast of prey who destroys without pity. In a street in Cincinnati is a parrot who has been taught to repeat a line of a song which many of you have heard. The monkey which had been appointed as

NOUNS AND PRONOUNS.—EXERCISES.

the orator on the occasion, then addressed the assembly. There was a little dog whose name was Fido, and who was very fond of his master. —*dog named Fido, that*— Yarico soon became a general favorite, who never failed to receive the crumbs from the breakfast-table. The little ant, which had a plentiful store, thus spoke to the little cricket: " We ants never borrow, we ants never lend."

With the return of spring came four martins, who were evidently the same which had been bred under those eaves the previous year. The witnesses and documents which we wanted, have been obtained. The passengers and steamer which we saw yesterday, are now buried in the ocean. Was it the wind, or you, who shut the door? The land on the east side of the river, was claimed by the chiefs and tribes who inhabited the land on the other side. Even the corpses who were found, could not be recognized. The character whom he represented, was by much the best in the play. This lubberly boy we usually call Falstaff, who is but another name for fat and fun. It is I, who will go with you. That man is wisest——keeps his own secrets. It is this alone, which has induced me to accept the office. Was it you, or he, who made so much noise? Is it I, or he, whom you want to see? It was the frankness and nobleness of his disposition, which I admired. Would any man who cares for himself, accept such a situation? Let us not mingle in every dissipation, nor enjoy every excitement, which we can.

He is a man who is very wealthy. —*that is*— or, *He is a very wealthy man.* She is a woman who is never contented. The misfortunes of a man who would not listen to his wife. I hate persons who never do a generous action. Nouns of the common gender denote objects which are males or females. People who are always denouncing others, are often no better themselves. Principles which have been long established, are not easily eradicated. The tribes whom we have described, inhabited the Mississippi Valley. The nations who have good governments, are happy. I joined a large crowd who was moving towards the capitol. He was a member of the legislature who passed this bill. He instructed and fed the crowds who surrounded him. The committee which was appointed to examine the students, was hardly competent to do so. Wilt thou help me drive these horses to the pasture? *Will you*, &c. Do you be careful that all thy actions be honest and honorable. *Do thou*— or, *that all your actions*— Thou shouldst never forsake the friend who has ever been faithful to you. Ere you remark another's fault, bid thy own conscience look within. You have mine, but I have thine. O Thou, who hast preserved us, and that wilt continue to preserve us. There is the same boat that came last evening, and which will go away again this morning.

The poor man who can read, and that possesses a taste for reading, can find entertainment at home. The man who came with us, and that is dressed in black, is the preacher. Is it possible that he should know what he is, and be that he is? But what we saw last, and which pleased us most, was the character of the old miser in the farce. It is such a method as has never been thought of before, and which, we believe, will be generally adopted. They are such apples as ours, or which you bought. —*or such as you*— Policy keeps coining truth in her mints—such truth as it can tolerate; and every die except its own, she breaks, and casts away. Learning has its infancy, when it is luxuriant and juvenile; and lastly his old age, when it waxeth dry and exhaust.— *Bacon.* Is reputable, national, and present use, which, for brevity's sake, I shall simply denominate good use, always uniform in her decisions? One does not like to have one's self disparaged by those who know one not. *A person*... *himself*   *know him not.*

2. Agreement of Pronouns with Antecedents.

Pronouns must agree with their antecedents, in gender, person, and number.

a. When the pronoun can not strictly or fully represent its antecedent in gender, it prefers the masculine.

b. The person and number of the antecedent to a pronoun, are always what they would be if the antecedent were the subject of a finite verb.

Every person should try to improve their mind and heart. Each of our party carried a knapsack with them, for their private convenience. Not one of the boys should come without their books. Many a man looks back on the days of their youth, with melancholy regret. A person who is resolute, energetic, and watchful, will be apt to succeed in their undertakings. An orator's tongue should be agreeable to the ears of their hearers. I do not think any one should incur censure for being tender of their reputation. If we deprive an animal of instinct, he will no longer be able to take care of himself. When a bird is caught in a trap, they of course try to get out. Scarcely any person is so stupid as not to know when they are made sport of. If any member of the congregation wishes to connect themselves with [to] this church, they will please [to] come forward, while the brethren sing. Take up the ashes, and put it into the large tub behind the kitchen. If you have any victuals left, we will help you to eat it. His pulse did not beat so fast as they should beat. Grains of sand they might be, those hoarded moments, but it was golden sand. I like those molasses, for they are almost as good as honey.

I have sowed all my oats, and it is growing finely. Our language is not less refined than those of Italy, France, or Spain. There lay the paraphernalia of her toilet, just as she had left it. The simiæ can stand erect on its hind feet. Where the early blue-bird sung its lay. (The male among birds, and not the female, usually sings.) The heron built its nest among the reeds. The peacock is fond of displaying its gorgeous plumage. The hen looked very disconsolate, when it saw its whole brood rush into the pond. The Earth is my mother, and I will recline upon its bosom. John studies;—*John* denotes the agent or doer, and he is therefore in the nominative case. *Horses* is of the plural number, because they denote more than one. To persecute a truly religious denomination, will only make them flourish the better. The people can not be long deceived by its demagogues and selfish politicians. The mob soon dispersed, after their leaders were captured. Egypt was glad at their departure, for they were afraid of them. The first object of the multitude was, to organize itself into a body. The Society will hold their meetings in the highest room of the building. Each tribe is governed by a chief whom they have chosen. (Perhaps allowable.)

The government will have cause to change their orders. The cabinet seemed to be divided in its sentiments. The cabinet was distinguished for their wise and vigorous measures. The corps of teachers should have its duties properly distributed and arranged. The board of directors, for its own emolument, located the road through this part of the country. The board of directors should have their powers defined and limited by a charter. The regiment was much reduced in their number. The court, in their wisdom, decided otherwise. Send the multitude away, that it may go and buy itself food. The army, being abandoned by its chief, pursued meanwhile their miserable march. (Let the construction be either singular thoughout, or plural throughout, but not both.) The party, though disgraced by the selfishness and corruption of its leaders, made nevertheless a vigorous and successful struggle to regain their former ascendency. The Almighty cut off the family of Eli the high priest, for its transgressions. The twins resemble one another so much as to be scarcely distinguishable. People should be kind to each other.

Neither of us is willing to give up our claim. (Say, "*his claim*," if not possessed in common; "*our claim*," if denoting common possession.) He and I love their parents. If none of you will bring your horses to the camp, I will let mine stay too. I did not notice which of the men finished their work first. The tongue is like a race-horse, which runs the faster, the less weight it carries. —*he carries*— or, *race-horse: it runs*, &c. John, thou, and I, are attached to their country. You and your playmates must learn their lessons. Two or three of us have lost our hats. The sister, as well as the brother, should perform their share of the household duties. The industrious boy, and the indolent one too, shall find their proper reward. Every soldier and every officer remained awake at their station during the night. Every herb, every flower, and every animal, shows the wisdom of Him who made them. Let every governor and legislature do as it thinks best. Every half a dozen boys should have its own bench. If any boy or girl be absent, they will have to go to the foot of the class. I borrow one peck, or eight quarts, and add—— to the upper term. Discontent and sorrow manifested itself in his countenance. No man or woman ever got rid of their vices, without a struggle. One or the other must relinquish their claim. John or James will favor us with their company.

Neither the father nor the son had ever been distinguished for their business qualifications. A man may see a metaphor or an allegory in a picture, as well as read them in a description. Poverty and wealth have each their own temptations. No thought, no word, no action, whether they be good or evil, can escape the notice of God. Both minister and magistrate are sometimes compelled to choose between his duty and his reputation. Coffee and sugar are imported from the Indies; and great quantities of it are consumed annually. Avoid self-conceit and insolence: it will never increase your wealth or your happiness. If you should see my horse or mule, I wish you would have them turned into your pasture. If any gentleman or lady wish [wishes] to have their fortune told, they now have an opportunity. —*his or her . . . . he or she now has*— I do not see why I or any other man should not have a [the] right to express our—his—my opinions of public affairs. (Avoid the use of the pronoun altogether; say, "*the opinion which either of us may*," &c.) My horse is a little darker than yours; but, in every other respect, they are exactly alike. —*he is exactly like him*; or, —*your horse . . . . he . . . . yours.* My horse is a little darker than yours; but, in every other respect, they are a perfect match. (Allowable. Parse *they*.) Notice is hereby given to every person to pay their taxes. (Change the antecedent; say, "*to all persons*", &c.) Our teacher does not let any one of us do as they please. If any person thinks it is easy to write books, let them try it. Neither the negro boy nor the coach was ever restored to his owner. —*to the owner ;* or, *Both the negro . . . . were never . . . . their owner.* Every person and thing had its proper place assigned to it. —*the proper*—

3. *Position of Pronoun in regard to Antecedent.*
4. *Inadequacy of Pronoun to represent Antecedent.*

A pronoun should not be so used as to leave it obscure or doubtful what antecedent it represents.

It is generally inelegant to make a pronoun needlessly represent an adjective, a phrase, or a sentence.

The king dismissed his minister, without any inquiry, who had never before done so unjust an action. P ɔ should not marry a woman in high life, that has no money Where there is nothing in the sense which requires the last sound to be elevated, a pause will be proper. A man has no right to judge another, who is a party concerned. I am the jailor who have come to take you. The jailor am I, who will guard you safely. Lysias promised his father, that he would never forsake his friends. Thou art a friend indeed, who hast often relieved me. We admire the beauty of the rainbow, and are led to consider the cause of it. John told James that his horse had run away. The lord can not refuse to admit the heir of his tenant upon his death; nor can he remove his present tenant so long as he lives.

The law is inoperative, which is not right. —*and that it is so, is not right.* Some men are too ignorant to be humble, without which there can be no docility. —*and without humility*— An old man, bent with years, was languidly digging, or attempting it. —*to dig.* A bird is that which has feathers. —*an animal that*— Every seat is to be occupied by the one before it. —*by the person*— A compound sentence is one composed of two or more others. —*is a sentence*— This rule is not strictly true, and a few examples will show it. —*as a few examples will show.* When a man kills another from malice, it is called murder. —*the deed is called murder.* The servant took away the horse, which was unnecessary. The accent is laid upon the last syllable of a word, which is favorable to the melody. The man brought the whole package, which was more than we expected. The prisoners rebelled against the regulations of the establishment, of which we shall presently give an account. There is among all people a belief of immortality, arising from the natural desire of living, and strengthened by uniform tradition, which has certainly some influence on practice.

5. *Inelegant Insertion of Pronoun.*

When a pronoun can add nothing to the sense, it should not be needlessly inserted to usurp the place of a better word.

Henry Holmes his book. These lots, if they had been sold sooner, they would have brought more money. *If these lots had been,* &c. John he went, James he went, and Mary she went; but the rest they all staid at home. Two nouns, when they come together, and signify the same thing, they must be put in the same case. The Latin and the Greek, though they are much neglected, yet competent judges know that our language can hardly be perfectly understood without them. The river rising very rapidly, it overflowed its banks. These wild horses having been once captured, they were soon tamed. I would like to have it now, what I had then. (Omit "*it.*") Whatsoever you learn perfectly, you will never forget it. It is not to the point, what he said. Whatsoever she found, she took it with her. Whoever thinks so, he judges erroneously. Whom, when she had seen, she invited him to dinner. —*seen him.... invited to dinner.* It is indisputably true, his assertion, though it seems erroneous. *His assertion is,* &c. It is marvelous what tricks jugglers sometimes play. —*to observe what*— Every thing whatsoever he could spare, he gave away. (Omit "*every thing.*")

6. *Inelegant Omission of Pronoun.*

1. The omission of the relative adjunct, or of the relative in the nominative case, is generally inelegant.
2. Parts that are to be contrasted, emphatically distinguished, or kept distinct in thought, must usually be expressed with fullness.
3. The omission of the nominative is inelegant, unless the verb is in the imperative mood, or in the same connection with another finite verb.

He is not now in the condition he was. Yonder is the place I saw it. A few remarks as to the manner it should be done, must suffice. The money

has not been used for the purpose it was appropriated. There is Miss Liddy can dance a jig, raise paste, write a good letter, keep an account, give a reasonable answer, and do as she is bid. He was a man had no influence. Whose own example strengthens all his laws, and is himself the great sublime he draws. Will martial flames for ever fire thy mind, and never, never be to heaven resigned? —*and will thou never*— There is not a man here, would not do the same thing. There is no man knows better how to make money. It was the man sat next to you. It was this induced me to send for you. Who is there so base that would be a bondman? —*that he*— The word depends on what precedes and follows. There are who can not bear to see their friends surpass them. If there are any have been omitted, they must say so. They were rich once, but are poor now. He is a man of corrupt principles, but has great talents. This is a style of dress to which I am partial; but is not now fashionable. I approve your plan so far as relates to our friend. The arrangement is very good; at least, so far as relates to my convenience. If the privileges to which he was entitled, and had been so long enjoying, should now, &c. All the young trees which I planted last year, and were growing finely, have been destroyed by rabbits. Any of these prisoners knowing the facts of the case, and will give his testimony in full to the court, shall be pardoned by the State. Why do ye that which is not lawful to do on the Sabbath-days? —*which it is not*— The show-bread, which is not lawful to eat but for the priests only. From these proceedings may be readily inferred, how such men become rich. (Perhaps allowable.)
Neither my poverty nor ambition could induce me to accept such an office. —*nor my*— This part of California is the loveliest country in the world, whether we regard its climate or soil. He was related to some of the first families of the State, both by his father's and mother's side. God punishes the vices of parents in themselves or children. The future should excite not only our hopes, but fears too. Dr. Jones and wife occupy the front room. His own and father's farm were adjacent to each other. My inability to get employment, and destitute condition, pressed heavily upon my feelings. My duty, my interest, and inclinations, all urge me to the undertaking. This is a position I condemn, and must be better established to gain the faith of any one. The mail came this morning, and will leave again this evening. (Allowable; also "*leave*," which begins to be generally used, as a less formal word, for *depart*.)
  Dear Sir,
  Have received your manuscript, but not had time to examine it; will do so in a few days, and may have it published if good.   Yours, &c.

7. *Pronoun Improperly Used as a Connective.*

A relative pronoun should never be used as a mere connective.

These evils were caused by Catiline, who, if he had been punished, the republic would not have been exposed to so great dangers. —*the punishment of whom would have prevented the republic from being exposed to dangers so great.* There is no doubt but what he is mistaken. —*that*— There are few things so difficult but what they may be overcome by perseverance and zeal. —*that they may not*— There was no profit, though ever so small, in any thing, but what he took the pains to obtain it. He lived in the same house that we now live. —*in which*— The boat will leave at the same time that the cars do. —*will leave with the cars.* The passive verb will always be of the same mood, tense, person, and number, that the verb *to be* is, before it is incorporated with the participle. Sir Alexander arrived at Charleston, about the time that Governor Burrington reached Edenton. At the same time that men are giving their orders, God is also giving his. *While men*, &c. He has never preached, that I have heard of. *I have never heard*, &c. He has never gone to see her that I know of.

OBSERVATIONS.

The Observations should always be read over carefully by the student, in connection with the preceding Exercises.

1. *Where* may be used in place of *which* and a preposition, when *place* is the predominant idea. "The grave *where* [in which] our hero was buried."—*Wolfe.* "The ancient house *where* I was born."—*O. W. Holmes.* But to say, "The battle *where* he was killed," would be less elegant than to say, "The battle *in which* he was killed." In poetry and in the familiar style, greater indulgence is generally allowed; and words of time or cause are sometimes used in connection with adverbs exactly corresponding in sense. Such compounds as *hereof, thereof, whereof, therewith, wherewith,* are not so common as they were formerly.

2. Terms of masculine terminations, or terms that have been formed to denote males, and that are usually applied so, may occasionally be applied also to females, when there are no peculiar terms for these, or when we wish to include the females with the males, and do not speak of them especially in regard to sex. It would be correct to say, "She is a better *farmer,* and *manager,* and *penman* than her husband was." Also, "She is my *accuser,*" although our language has the uncommon word *accuseress.* "The poets of America" may include the poetesses. When I say, "She is the best *poetess,*" I compare her with female poets only; but when I say, "She is the best *poet,*" I compare her with both male and female poets. To brute animals and even to spiritual beings we sometimes apply *it* or *its,* when we speak of them as things, or when the sex is unimportant or not obvious. "Every *creature* loves *its* like." Here neither *his* nor *her* would express the sense so well. "Lo! there *it* [a ghost] comes!"—*Shakespeare.*

There is a peculiar nature or disposition that belongs to each sex, and on the analogy of this we ascribe life and sex to abstract qualities or to inanimate objects, which, in reality, have no sex. Even *it* and *its* are sometimes used in slight personifications, in a sense analogous to that which they have when applied to animals or other living objects. In accordance with the foregoing principles, we sometimes speak of a mannish woman as of a man, and of an effeminate man as of a woman; and of a hare, for instance, in the feminine gender; of a fox, in the masculine; &c.

The following examples may serve as further illustrations of the subject: "When *War* to Britain bent *his* iron car." "*Peace* rears *her* olive for industrious brows." "In the *monarch Thought's* dominions." "*Remorse,* that tortures with *his* scorpion lash." "Or if *Virtue* feeble were, Heaven itself would stoop to *her.*" "Why peeps your coward *sword* half afraid from *its* sheath." "While *Vengeance* in the lurid air lifts *her* red arm, exposed and bare."—*Collins.* This last sentence is allowable, as alluding to the Furies.

In personifications, we are sometimes aided in ascribing the proper sex by reference to the gender of the corresponding terms in the Classic languages. But this is not always a safe rule. The principles mentioned above, should also be taken into consideration. The sex to be ascribed in personification, is sometimes a matter of great nicety, and must be determined from the peculiar glow or sentimental color of the writer's conceptions.

3. For a person to speak of himself before speaking of others, is much the same as if he should help himself first at table, and then wait upon others. Instances, however, may occur, in which it would be proper, or even polite, to mention himself first; as when the parties differ much in rank, or when the assertion implies something burdensome or not desirable.

To address others and speak of them and ourselves in the third person, usually implies greater reserve, courtesy, and politeness; as in cards of invitation, and the like: but where no such reserve or courtesy can be meant, as in business letters between familiar acquaintances, the style of writing in the third person may rather tend to suggest contempt.

Just here may as well be said a few words about titles. *Sir,* applied to strangers, and also when used after such words as *yes, no, well, why, O,* &c., is rather *respectful;* but when it is applied to friends or familiars, it may seem to disown the friendship or familiarity, and to request the person to keep at a proper or respectful distance: it is apt to be in the spirit of the young lady's remark to her long-wooing and finally rejected lover, "I know nothing about you, sir." *Mister,* without the name, is rather contemptuous—it is similar to the contemptuous *Sir;* with the name of a stranger, it is rather respectful. When it is omitted from a name, the expression may imply that a very ordinary fellow is meant—a fellow of little importance—of no high respectability—of rather low standing in society,—it is somewhat similar in spirit to the word *Jack;* or it may imply that the person is a very well-known, intimate, and familiar acquaintance or favorite, not only to the speaker, but to all present,—suggesting that great cordiality, and entire want of formality, which are peculiar to the family circle; or else it may imply that the person is of general or universal fame. Dr. Johnson spoke very contemptuously of a certain man's taste, who had indexed his "Lives of the Poets" thus: "Milton, Mr. John; Shakespeare, Mr. William." It also indicates sometimes a better state of feelings, to address a person by the Christian name than by the surname. So, if I am on very intimate terms with *Prof. Mitchel,* for instance, I should rather prefer to call him, in familiar and private conversation, *Mr. Mitchel.* To write one's name with *Mr.* before it, would be self-conceited and ridiculous, but to title oneself as in the following expressions,—" I have no card; please to tell Gov. Ed wards that Mr. Richardson—Mr. Phelps from Springfield—Capt. Mitchell—called to see him," would be more appropriate and polite than to give the name simply. See above.

The same remarks apply, in general, to the titles *Miss* and *Mrs.* To mention a woman by her surname only, is apt to have a very contemptuous air: it usually presents her as an insignificant or masculine personage. At parties, balls, &c., we always say, "gentleman and *lady,*" and we generally call the *mistress* of the house "the *lady* of the house;" but a family that should send out cards with "Mr. and *Mrs.* Morgan send their compliments," &c., would, I think, show better taste than if the words were, "Mr. Morgan and *lady* send," &c.

Should we give to a married lady or to a widow her own Christian name, or that of her husband? I think the lady's name should be preferred, unless there is some special reason for using the husband's. The husband's Christian name may sometimes be more definite, better known, or better suited to the end in view. When there are two or more Catharine Johnsons, they may be best distinguished by using their husbands' Christian names. Our merchants, I believe, nearly always use the husband's Christian name, in directing parcels to married ladies; not merely, I suppose, because the husband is better known, but also because the responsibility usually rests upon him. In England, it is more common, I am told, than in the United States, to use the husband's Christian name.

Never, in addressing a person, put a title both before and after the name.

4. It is not always necessary to make a noun plural, merely because it denotes something belonging to more than one, or that it may agree in number with the governing word. "God has given us our *reasons* for our own good." This sentence hardly expresses the intended meaning. Better: "God has given us Reason for our own good." Who would say, "It was for *their goods* that I did it," instead of "It was for *their good* that I did it"? To say, "These plants have their flowers at the tops," is ambiguous: it may mean that each plant has but one top with but one flower, or, that it has a plurality of either or of both. Better: "These plants have *the flower* at *the top,*" or—"*the flower* at *the tops,*" or—"*the flowers* at *the top,*" according to the sense. Language is not a perfect instrument; at least, we can not always find expressions that are exact or satisfactory; and therefore must content ourselves when we have the best expression the language affords. Writers generally aim to make substantives that must vary alike in number, agree in this respect. Mr. Goold Brown writes, "Proper *names,* of every description, should always begin with *capitals;*" *i. e.,* each name with but *one* capital. Lord Jeffrey writes, "These same circumstances have also perverted *our judgments* with respect to *their characters;*" for we have different judgments, and they different characters. But, "Iambic lines may occasionally begin with trochees," may suggest that each line begins with two or more trochees; therefore say, "Occasionally, *an iambic line* may begin with *a trochee.*"

Two nouns making one term, should never be both made plural, unless the idea of *apposition* is very prominent; as, "The lords proprietors," "Knights Templars," ("*Knights Templar*"—MITCHELL'S HISTORY OF FREEMASONRY,) "men-servants, women-servants." We sometimes find such condensed plurals as these: "The *governors* of Virginia, South Carolina, and Missouri;" "The *earls* of Arundel and Buckingham," *i. e.,* the earl of Arundel and the earl of Buckingham. The

8*

sense is obvious, and hence the expressions are allowable; but "Prescott's and Bancroft's *Histories*" is not necessarily equivalent to "Prescott's History and Bancroft's History," and is hardly allowable. "Prescott and Bancroft's Histories" is as good a phrase as "The Old and New Testaments," and is perhaps allowable.

In imitation of an idiom in the Classic languages, we sometimes prefer the plural to the singular, in order to give the expression the greatest comprehensiveness possible, and hence greater force; as, "He gained her *affections*," *i. e.*, her whole heart. Sometimes there is also a variation in sense. "When it was asked whether a wealthy lawyer had acquired his riches by his *practice*, there was a terrible satire in the answer: 'Yes, by his *practices*.' "—*G. P. Marsh.*

The plural, in some instances, guards us against ambiguity; thus, "The *outpouring* of the heart," may suggest either the *act* of pouring or the *thing* poured, but "*outpourings*" is apt to suggest "*the things poured*," and nothing else.

Such expressions as "A ten-*foot* pole," "A twenty-*cent* piece," &c., are proper; but a hyphen should always be used to connect the parts. The noun, in such expressions, being used as an adjective, loses the properties of a noun. If these singulars should be plural, then it would not seem unreasonable to require *he* to be *him* or *them* in the following example: "They brought *he*-goats."

The singular is usually preferred in forming compounds, but sometimes the plural; as, "A *watch*-maker (—a maker of *watches*), a *horse*-stealer;" but, "A *sales*-man, a *draughts*-man, a *savings*-bank."

Since we say *two-thirds*, *three-fourths*, *four-fifths*, &c., it is more in accordance with analogy, and also best, to read such fractions as $\frac{5}{21}$, $\frac{7}{32}$, *five twenty-firsts, seven thirty-seconds*. (Unhyphened: so are large ordinals; as, "*One hundred and twenty-five*.")

As to the mode of expressing certain numeral terms, especially if long and composite, there is not a little diversity of practice. "Five *thousand* seven hundred and two."—*Davies.* "Fifty-nine *millions* three hundred and ten."—*Id.* "Five million."—*R. R. Report.* "Five *millions*."—*Ib.* The sense of nouns and that of adjectives meet, in such terms, like the colors of the rainbow: it is almost impossible to tell where one ends or the other begins. The form of the term must evidently depend on whether the number is conceived *adjectively* or *substantively*, that is, whether in reference to a noun, or abstractly. "Eighty *thousand*, two *hundred* and one."—*Ray.* "Four *hundreds*, three *tens*, and five units."—*Id.* "Forty-two *millions* two *thousand* and five."—*Greenleaf.* "*Tens* of *Thousands* of *Trillions*." —*Id.* To decide the matter briefly, I would say, Let the words be singular in form, when the whole is conceived as one numeral, or has no intermediate commas or points; but let them be plural in form, when the number is broken into parts, and the phrase has commas or points. "Five hundred and thirty-six *million* three hundred and forty-seven *thousand* nine hundred and seventy-two."— *Robinson's Mathematics.* "Forty-seven *quadrillions*, sixty-nine *billions*, four hundred and sixty-five *thousands*, two hundred and seven" [*units*].—*Davies.* "The number of his subjects must have been about five *million* two hundred *thousand*." —*Macaulay.* "To enslave five *millions* of Englishmen."—*Id.* "The population of China in 1743 was fifteen *millions* twenty-nine *thousand* eight *hundred* and fifty-five."—*Wilson's Treatise on Punctuation.* Custom, in the United States, perhaps prefers *s* from millions up, but not down; especially in round numbers. "The Croton Aqueduct cost nine *millions*." "His house cost him five *thousand*."

The plural of words that are spoken of merely as words, is sometimes written with the apostrophe; as, "Your composition has too many and's, therefore's, and wherefore's." But all such words are better expressed by pluralizing them regularly, and Italicizing them; as, "Your composition has too many *ands*, *therefores*, and *wherefores*." Here the meaning is sufficiently obvious. Yet if the regular plural should render the word or its meaning liable to be mistaken, then I see no good reason for not using the apostrophe, or any other means, to avoid the difficulty. "The extract is full of *bies*." Full of what? Perhaps *bys* or *by's* would have been more intelligible. "The poem is full of *flies* and *cries*," is perhaps not so obvious in sense as, "The poem is full of *fly's* and *cry's*."

Words ending in *i* or *o* preceded by a consonant, if they are native, perfectly naturalized, or well known, always take *es* to express the plural; as, Wo, *woes*, hero, *heroes;* alkali, *alkalies:* but if the words are foreign rather than English, good writers have, in many instances, added *s* only, to form the plural; as, Teocalli, *teocallis;* mufti, *muftis;* stiletto, *stilettos*. This mode of pluralizing has this advantage: The word not being generally known, by annexing simply *s*, the reader at once sees what the singular is. Yet I think the regular plural is always preferable, when there is no liability of mistaking the singular form, or when the word is so far naturalized as to have already found its way into our dictionaries. We Americans do not begrudge an *e* to *mulattoes,* yet clip *musquitos;* but the English are more consistent, and treat *mulattoes* and "*mosquitoes*" alike, not even regarding *toes.*

5 & 7. As there is sometimes an ellipsis of the finite verb, it is necessary to bear in mind what verb is omitted, in order to determine readily what the case should be. "He is wiser than I" [*am*]. "She is as good as he" [*is*]. "Who will go? I" [*will go*]. "Who was it? Not I"—*It was* not I.

6. The sense of the possessive case is usually expressed either by giving a certain form to the word denoting the possessor, or by using *of* and the objective case. These two forms should be interchanged in such a way as to relieve each other, and avoid the inadequacy and inelegance of either. I should always endeavor to use, in prose, '*s* with singular possessive nouns, or else *of*. Though, "The defeat of *Xerxes*' army was the downfall of Persia," for instance, could hardly be improved.

A noun or pronoun, before a participle, may be put in the possessive case, when the sense requires it, and a better expression can not be readily found. Such a phrase is sometimes a very convenient one, if not the most appropriate that can be used to convey the sense. Much depends on which word conveys the idea uppermost in the speaker's mind. "What do you think of *my* PLANTING corn?" Is it roper? You being a farmer as well as I, would you plant? "What do you think of ME *planting* corn?" Am I not out of my proper line of business? What sort of farmer do I, or would I, make? "I well remember *Peyton Randolph's* INFORMING me of the crossing of our messengers."—*Jefferson.* "But what gave it most interest, was *its* BEING in some way CONNECTED with the pirate ship."—*Irving* "There is no doubt of *my* SEEING him." But such uncouth possessives as, "One of them's falling into a ditch was an accident"—*Greenleaf's Grammar;* "A place's being at a distance"—*Ib.;* "Instead of the mind's being made to go through with this tedious process"—*Ib.,*—should be avoided: say, "That one of them fell"——; "The distance of a place"——; "Instead of making the mind go through"——.

Finally, the possessive sign should be used wherever there is a noun expressed or understood denoting the thing possessed; and a phrase explanatory of the possessor, should never be placed between the possessing and the governing noun. Sense, custom, and euphony, should be carefully consulted.

"They praised the farmer's, as they called him, excellent understanding, should be, "They praised the excellent understanding of the farmer, as they called him." The "Lord's Day" is Sunday, but "the day of the Lord" sometimes means the Judgment Day; "A picture of Washington" is a likeness of him; but "A picture of Washington's" is one of the pictures belonging to him. "Lee's and Allen's store"—Lee's store and Allen's store; "Lee's and Allen's stores"—Lee's stores and Allen's stores; Lee and Allen's stores," is ambiguous, as it may signify either joint or separate possessions. "At Halsall's, the bookseller's, and stationer's," may suggest three different places; but, "At Halsall's, the bookseller and stationer," can suggest but one place.

Poets write—"Shiraz' walls," "Pelides' wrath," "Ajax' seven-fold shield," "Douglas's command," "Providence's sway," "The lance's crash," "Thebes's streets."

9. The nominative most frequently precedes its verb; and the objective most frequently follows the governing word. Both should be so placed as to avoid ambiguity, and promote elegance and force. "I love him as well as you," may mean either "I love him as well as I love you," or, "I love him as well as you love him."

Pronouns.

The use of *you* for *thou* is said to have originated in this, that it was formerly a custom and an honor for persons of rank and respectability to have attendants about them, and to be addressed accordingly.

1. *Thou, thy, thine, thee, thyself, ye,* and *you, your, yours,* &c., should never be intermingled, or used promiscuously in the same sentence. The same remark applies to the different relatives. But when one relative clause is subordinate to another, the relatives may differ. "*Thou* must take care of *thyself;*" "*You* must take care of *yourself.*" "They worship 'the Great Spirit,' *who* has created them, *who* preserves them, and to *whom* they expect to go after death." But, "There are men *that* have nothing, *who* are happier than he."

The predominant sense of *who* is, to suggest *persons* or other objects viewed as having the *reason, sympathy,* and *individuality* of human beings; of *which,* brute animals, or things, or other objects viewed as *things. That* is usually restrictive. Whether it is to be preferred to *who* or *which,* may sometimes be determined by some preceding word that fixes the application of the antecedent, but more frequently by the sense. *Who* and *which* are generic; *that* is specific. *Who* and *which* may sometimes suggest the entire class of objects; *that* perhaps never does, but only the part described by its own clause. "I do not like men *who* do mean little actions," may imply that *all* men do mean little actions; but, "I do not like men *that* do mean little actions," expresses the intended meaning. "I took the pigeons *which* were white," "He is like a beast of prey *which* destroys without pity," "He is a man *who* is rich," are not equivalent to—"I took the pigeons *that* were white," "He is like a beast of prey that destroys without pity," "He is a man *that* is rich," better, "He is a rich man." In general, *that* is preferable when it is doubtful whether *who* or *which* should be used; also, when the intention is, to show that a preceding word is restricted to something particular, or to something viewed in a particular light. But when the adjective or the conjunction *that* stands near, euphony may sometimes exclude the relative *that.* Whether *as* or *that* should be used after *same,* depends often on whether the verb of the latter clause is omitted or expressed. "Yours is the same *as* mine;" "You have the same *that* I have."

The doctrine of the relative *that,* in reference to *who* and *which,* as taught in our grammars, seems to rest on a rather sandy foundation, if we appeal to the practice of our best writers. I have met with well-read people "*who*" contend that *who* should *always* be used in speaking of persons. And Lord Macaulay, a remarkably accurate writer, nearly always uses it so, regardless of grammar. "A strange question was raised by the very LAST PERSON *who* ought to have raised it."—*Macaulay.* "The HIGHEST CHURCHMEN *who* still remained were Doctor William Beveridge, Archdeacon of Colchester, who many years later became bishop of St. Asaph .... and Doctor John Scott, the SAME *who* had prayed by the deathbed of Jeffreys."—*Id.* "No MAN *that* ever lived was," &c.—*Id.* "'The Bishop of Salisbury,' said Tillotson, 'is one of the BEST and WORST FRIENDS *that* I know.'"—*Id.* "The FIRST WORDS *which* he spoke," &c.—*Id.* "The SAME ATROCITIES *which* had," &c.—*Id.*

The relative *which* was formerly applied to persons as well as to things. "I know that ye seek JESUS, *which* was crucified."—*Bible.*

Whether was formerly used as an interrogative pronoun, in referring to one of two; but, in this sense, *which* or *whichever* supplies its place now, and it is employed only as a conjunction that usually corresponds to *or.* "*Whether* of the twain"—*Which* of the two. "*Whether* he will OR not."

A very practical rule in regard to personification is the following: "Objects represented as persons, take pronouns denoting persons." When a pronoun refers to a figurative antecedent, great care should be taken to ascertain whether the literal or the figurative sense prevails, and to select the pronoun accordingly. "He was the SOUL *which* animated the party." "Brave SOULS! *who* died for liberty." Wordsworth says, of a Highland beauty, "She was a conspicuous FLOWER, *whom* he had sensibility to love, ambition to attempt, and skill to win." Macaulay writes, "Several epigrams were written on the double-faced JANUS [the name of a statue, applied to a man], *who,* having got a professorship by looking one way, hoped to get a bishopric by looking another."

2. A collective noun, when used to denote a group of persons or other beings as one whole, is of the neuter gender, and singular number. Such nouns are properly represented by the pronouns applicable to things; as, "The MOB *which* assailed the palace, soon lost *its* leader."

Our language is defective in not having, in the third person, a singular pronoun for the common gender. This often leads to an improper use of the plural pronouns *they, their.* &c.; as, "Every *member* of the church should have *their* own pews." In such cases, we must use either the singular masculine pronoun for both sexes, or both the masculine and the feminine, or the neuter, (if we are speaking of small animals,) or we must pluralize the antecedent. "Every *servant* knew *his* duty." "Every *member* of the church should have *his* or *her* own pew." "Every *animal* loves *its* like." "The *child* loves *its* mother." "All the *members* should have *their* pews," &c. To avoid difficulties of construction, it may sometimes be best to recast gnarly sentences, and express the meaning in some other way.

"Full *many a flower* is born to blush unseen, and waste *its* sweetness on the desert air."—*Gray's Elegy*. "In Hawick twinkled *many a light*, behind him soon *they* set in night."—*Scott*. "Full *many a lady* have I eyed with best regard; and many a time the harmony of *their* tongues hath into bondage brought my too diligent ear."—*Shakespeare: Tempest, Act* iii, *Scene* 1. Hence, grammarians have said, that when *many a*, and the pronoun relating to it, occur in the same clause, the latter *should* be singular; "if in different clauses, the latter should [*may*] be plural." The plural structure seems to violate the general principle that governs the syntax of *every*, *each*, *no*, *nor*, &c.: but the example quoted from Shakespeare, stands doubtless best as it is; for the singular pronoun would seem to refer to *one particular lady*, and "*many ladies*" would not suggest that the person "fell in love" from time to time. In the following example, however, quoted and justified by Mr. Goold Brown, I should rather use the singular structure throughout: "Hard has been the fate of *many a great genius*, that [,] while *they have* conferred immortality on others, *they have* wanted *themselves* some friend to embalm *their names* to posterity."—*Wellwood*. I should prefer the plural pronoun, only when it obviously conveys the sense better.

3 & 4. The relative properly relates to the nearest substantive, before it, that it can represent so as to make sense; and it should generally stand as near as possible to its antecedent. "There was very little theory in the discourse that pleased me." "The man forsook his wife, who had always been kind and affectionate." The ambiguity of these sentences might have been avoided by a different arrangement of the parts. "There was, in the discourse, very little theory that pleased me;" "There was very little theory that pleased me, in the discourse;" "In the discourse that pleased me, there was very little theory." "The man, who had always been kind and affectionate, forsook his wife;" "His wife, who had always been kind and affectionate, the man forsook." When ambiguity can not be avoided by the arrangement of the words, the noun itself must be used, or the meaning must be expressed by a different sentence. "The lad can not leave his *father;* for if he should leave his *father*, the *father* would die." When two or more antecedents are introduced into a sentence, which denote different objects, and are not capable of being distinguished by the pronouns relating to them, it is sometimes difficult to avoid the entangling of the pronouns, or to make the structure satisfactory. By judicious arrangement and repetition, the difficulty may generally be avoided; and rather than make the sentence clumsy by repetition, I think it may sometimes be better even to let the pronouns stand, provided the meaning, though liable to *grammatical* ambiguity, is yet sufficiently obvious to ordinary *common sense*. To avoid obscurity, it is sometimes better to use a suitable noun, than a pronoun representing the noun as suggested by the use of an adjective, a phrase, or a clause. "I admit he is sagacious in trouble, but *it* can not save him now." Say, "but his *sagacity*," &c.

In such expressions as "It was not I, that said so," "It was he, that said so," the genuine antecedent of *that* is undoubtedly "*It*." But sometimes, by a sort of *attraction*, the relative agrees with the nearest substantive. "'Tis these *that* early *taint* the female mind." "It is THEY and their POSTERITY *who are* to suffer." Sometimes, however, there is evidently a difference in sense: as, "It is not I, *that does* it; "It is not I *that do* it."

The following sentences differ in meaning: "I am the general, who give orders to-day;" "I am the general, who gives orders to-day." By the first, you learn *that I am the general;* by the second, *that it is my business to give the orders*. Mr. Butler's Remark, "A relative pronoun which modifies the subject, should not be placed after a noun in the predicate," is too stringent on the liberty of writers, and would condemn sentences that are good English. At least, Spenser's "Fairy Queen" condemns the doctrine.

The position of pronouns is sometimes rather troublesome. Suppose I wish to say, "In the Athens of America," with an emphasis, on "Athens," expressed by "*itself*." I can not say, "In the Athens itself of America," nor, "In the Athens of America itself," but must avoid the expression, and say, "In the very Athens of America."

5. The pronoun may sometimes be elegantly used with the noun, when we wish first to draw the attention emphatically to the object itself, and then to say something of it. "Beautiful Mary Porter,—where is she now!" "My banks they are furnished with bees." "Harry's flesh it fell away." This phraseology is more allowable in poetry or impassioned discourse than in any other kind.

Compound relatives suggest by means of their termination an indefinite or universal antecedent, and hence they are not usually accompanied by an antecedent; as, "*Whoever* lives temperately, will be apt to live long." Even the simple relative sometimes sufficiently suggests the antecedent; as, "*Who* steals my purse, steals trash." A relative pronoun, in the objective case, may sometimes be elegantly omitted; as, "There is the man I want to see," for, "There is the man *whom* I want to see." "I have brought a basket to carry it *in*." "There is nothing to judge *by*." But to omit the preposition and the relative, is inelegant or improper; as, "In the condition I was then," better, "In the condition *in which* I was then." The relative *that* is frequently used improperly, without a governing word, as a mere connective. "At the same time that the meat was roasting, the bread was baking;" better, "While the meat was roasting," &c. *What* or *but what* should not be used in the place of *that*. "I could not believe but what [otherwise than that] you had been sick;" "I have no doubt but what [that] you will succeed."

Some grammarians condemn such use of the personal pronouns as is shown in the following sentence: "*Falstaff*. It [sack] ascends *me* into the brain; dries *me* there all the foolish, and dull, and crudy vapors which environ it; makes it apprehensive, quick, and inventive,— full of nimble, fiery, and delectable shapes."—*Shakespeare*. But I think such sentences should not be disturbed. The usage was good in its time, and the pronoun imparts a peculiar earnestness and quaintness, that could not be expressed so well by any other means.

6. Poets sometimes omit the nominative relative; as, "It was a tall young oysterman ⌃ lived by the river-side"—*O. W. Holmes;* and in certain kinds of sentences, the nominative pronoun is usually omitted after *but* or *than;* as, "There is not a child but knows the way," "You have brought more than is needed."

It is not necessary to repeat the subject before the second of two connected verbs that differ in mood or tense, or imply contrast, unless the parts are unusually long, or the contrast is marked and emphatic. "Many of them *were* of good families, and *had held* commissions in the civil war. Their pay *was* far higher than that of the most favored regiment of our time, and *would* in that age *have been thought* a respectable provision for the son of a country gentleman."—*Macaulay*. "So large a sum was expended, but expended in vain."—*Id*.

We sometimes find hasty letters, especially from business men, written without personal pronouns in the nominative case, wherever these can be inferred from the context. This style is condemned by all grammarians, and therefore should be avoided. Yet in favor of it may be urged—1. Some foreign languages usually omit the nominative pronouns from their verbs; 2. Tiresome repetition and an egotistical air are somewhat avoided, without leaving the sense obscure; 3. Good authors sometimes use this style, or what is equivalent to it, when their discourse is fragmentary, and designed to appear hasty, or full of sprightliness and vivacity.

Ex.—"Tender-eyed blonde. Long ringlets. Cameo pin. Locket. Bracelet. Album. *Reads* Byron, Tupper, and Sylvanus Cobb, junior, while her mother makes the puddings. *Says*, 'Yes!' when you tell her anything."—*O. W. Holmes*.

6. ARTICLES.

193. An **article** is a word placed before a substantive, to show how the latter is applied.

Ex.—Horses; *the* horse, *a* horse, *the* horses. *A* good one; *the* others.
"From liberty each nobler science sprung,
A Bacon brightened, and *a* Spenser sung."—*Savage*.

Article literally means *joint*. The Greeks, who gave the name, frequently used nouns with an article on each side; just as we might say, "I saw *that* STEAMBOAT *that* came last night!" a noun thus used, is not unlike the part of a limb between two *joints*.

Only two words in our language are called articles: THE, the *definite* article; and A or AN, the *indefinite.*

194. The points out a particular object or class, or a particular one or portion of a class.

Ex.—The man, the men; the large wagon. "The sun and the moon." "The fowls of the air and the fishes of the sea." "The lion is nobler than the hyena." "The statesman should be honored, as well as the soldier." "The Delawares and the Cherokees are Indians almost civilized." "The poor and the rich, the wise and the ignorant."

195. It sometimes precedes a proper noun, to render it sufficiently definite; or else it points out a certain object as already known or heard of, or as preëminently distinguished.

Ex.—"*Missouri* and *Ohio* mean States; but *the Missouri* and *the Ohio* mean rivers." "The Fulton went up the river this morning." "The Turk was dreaming of the hour." "The generous Lafayette and the noble Washington."

196. *The* may relate to either a singular or a plural word.

Ex.—The river, the rivers; the four men, the fourth man; the one, the others.

197. **A** or **an** shows that no particular one of a class is meant.

Ex.—A man, a bird, a wagon, an owl, a plum; a small picture. "He was a merchant." It suggests that there are others of the same kind, and also that there are other kinds of objects.

198. Sometimes the predominant idea is *any*, sometimes *one.*

Ex.—"*A* man may lose all his property in *a* year"—*Any* man may lose all his property in *one* year.

199. *A* or *an* can be used to point out one only, or one aggregate. Sometimes more are spoken of, but they are still considered one by one.

Ex.—" A *pen*;" not, A *pens.* "An idler; a large orange; a dozen apples; a wealthy people; a few dimes." "I gave for the marbles a dime a dozen." "We paid for the mules a hundred dollars a head."

When a noun is limited by other words, the indefinite article affects not the noun alone, but the noun thus limited. "A young man," "A man of fine sense," do not mean no particular *man;* but, no particular *young man*, no particular *man of fine sense.*

A and *an* are both called the *indefinite* article, because they are but a later and an earlier form of the same word, have the same meaning, and differ in use only.

200 Before words beginning with a vowel sound, *an* should be used. Before *a, e, i, o, u* not equivalent to *yu, y* articulated with a consonant after it, silent *h*, and *h* faintly sounded when the next syllable has the chief accent.

Ex.—"*An* arm; *an* ear of corn; *an* idle boy; *an* orange; *an* urn; *an* hour, *an* heroic deed."

201. Before words beginning with a consonant sound, *a* should be used. *U* long, *eu, w, o* in *one*, and *y* articulated with a vowel after it, have each a consonant sound.

Ex.—"*A* brother, *a* cup, *a* union; *a* eulogy; *a* yearling; *a* word; *a* one-horse carriage."

202. No article is used when we refer chiefly to the nature of the object, to the class generally, or to only a part indefinitely; also when the substantive is sufficiently definite itself, or is rendered so by other words.

Ex.—"*Meat* is dearer than *bread*." "*Gold* is heavier than *silver*." "He took *water*, and changed it into *wine*." "*Peaches* are better than *apples*." "*Virtue* and *vice* are *opposites*." "*Working* is better than *stealing* or *starving*." "*Man* is endowed with *reason*." "There are *fishes* with *wings*." "John, George, '76; that tree; this tree; every tree; some trees; all trees; Post Office." "*Words* that breathe." "*They* were the means by *which*;" not, *the which*.

GENERAL ILLUSTRATION.—" From the beginning of the world, an uninterrupted series of predictions had announced and prepared the long-expected coming of the Messiah, who, in compliance with the gross apprehensions of the Jews, had been more frequently represented under the character of a king and conqueror, than under that of a prophet, a martyr, or the son of God."—*Gibbon's Rome*.

Articles, being used to aid nouns, are said to belong to them. When the article stands only before the first of two or more connected nouns, it belongs to them jointly, if they denote but one person or thing, or more viewed as one; if not, it belongs to the first noun, and is understood before the others.

Ex.—"I saw Webster, the great statesman and orator." "Of books I am a borrower and lender." "A man and horse passed by the house and lot." "A man, a woman, and a child were drowned."

The is sometimes an adverb; *a*, a preposition; and *an*, a conjunction.

Ex.—"*The* stronger, *the* better." " To go *a* [at] hunting." "FALSTAFF. *An* I have not songs made on you all, and sung to fifty tunes, may a cup of sack be my poison."—*Shakespeare*.

EXERCISES.

Examples to be Analyzed and Parsed.

Parse the articles:—

The cat caught a mouse. A crow flew over the valley. The oxen are grazing on the meadow. The[a] lion roams in Africa. The lion killed his keeper. The[b] Gasconade is exceedingly clear and beautiful. The Highland Mary leaves St. Louis to-day. The ancients did not know the use of the compass. A[c] beautiful white house gleamed from the summit of the adjacent hill. A free people should be jealous of their liberties. I have bought a[d] dozen chickens. The lambs were sold for a dollar a head[f]. The[e] bright stars without number adorn the sky. We send exports to the Sandwich Islands.

(a.) ——*definite*, it refers to "*lion*" as denoting a particular kind of animals; and belongs to "*lion*," &c. (b.) ——*definite*, it refers to "*Gasconade*" as denoting a particular river; and belongs to it, &c. (c.) ——*indefinite*, it does not refer to "*beautiful white house*" as denoting a particular one of the kind; and belongs to "*house*," according to Rule X. (d.) —— *indefinite*, no particular "dozen chickens" are meant; &c. (e.) —— *definite*, the reference is to "*stars*" as denoting a particular class of things.

Examples to be Corrected.

All the liabilities to error in regard to articles, may be reduced to the following heads:—
1. *When not used.* 2. *When the* DEFINITE *article should be used.* 3. *When the* INDEFINITE *article should be used.* 4. *Whether* A *or* AN *should be used.* 5. *Improper use of* A *or* AN *before plurals.* 6. *When the article should not be repeated.* 7. *When the article should be repeated.*

1. *When not Used.*

No article is used,—
1. When the mind considers an object in reference to its nature or character, rather than as an individual to be distinguished from others, or from something else. Or: When the noun answers to *what* rather than to *who* or *which*.
2. When the mind refers to the whole species generally, or to only a part indefinitely.
3. When the substantive is sufficiently definite by itself, or is rendered so by other limiting words.
   a. The article is sometimes elegantly omitted from titular phrases or from other familiar expressions, when the omission can lead to no misconception of the meaning.

What sort of a man is he? He is a different sort of a man. What kind of an article, then, would you call a? We found him a very worthy good sort of an old man. —*a very worthy good old man.* Such a man does not deserve the name of a gentleman. The highest officer of a State is styled a Governor. They hated the name of a Stuart. Santa Anna ruled over the nation, under the title of a Dictator. The original signification of *knave* was a boy. The pink, the rose, and the lily, are the names of certain species of a flower. The weather is getting cool enough for a fire. Of these twins, I never can tell the one from the other. He was drowned in the attempting to cross the Mississippi. A wise man will avoid the showing any excellence in trifles. This tree is worth the planting—the being planted. The stray horses are posted at this place. (Of course not all; nor can they be contrasted with any other class of horses.) Reason was given to a man to control his passions. (Of course to more than one.) I had a reference to the other. You may avoid offensive expressions by a circumlocution. These foreigners, in the general, are peaceful and industrious. You may send the letter by the mail. (No particular mail was meant.) The whites of America are the descendants of the Europeans; but the blacks are the descendants of the Africans. A neuter verb can not become a passive. These sketches are not imaginary, but taken from the life. The law by the which they were condemned. It would take a half a day to do it. The ancients believed the fire, the air, the earth, and the water, to be the elements of all other material things.

2. *When the Definite Article should be Used.*

The *definite* article is used,—
1. To make the following noun sufficiently definite for denoting a particular object as distinguished from others of the same kind, or from something else.
2. To show that the whole is meant, or that all of the kind are meant.

Women who never take any exercise, necessarily become invalids. *The women who*— or, *Women that*, &c. Persons who have been instructed in colleges, are said to have a collegiate education. The work is designed for the use of persons who may think it merits a place in their libraries. No account is given of such an event by historians who lived at that time. Modes of traveling in the last century were far inferior to ours. Wisest and best men sometimes commit errors. John Simonds [a boat] left for Now Orleans yesterday. They forbid wearing of rings and jewels. Convert sinners without shedding of blood. Great benefit may be derived from reading of good books. A neglecting of our own affairs, and a meddling with those of others, are the sources of many troubles. The Indians are descendants of the aborigines of this country. A pronoun is a part of speech used as a substitute for a noun. A violet is an emblem of modesty. A lion is bold, a cat is treacherous, and a dog is faithful. Sometimes one article is improperly used for another. Who breaks a butterfly upon a wheel? (*Wheel* here means a peculiar engine for torturing. There is also reference to other kinds of punishment.) I have a right to do it. (The universal abstract was meant.)

3. *When the Indefinite Article should be Used.*

The *indefinite* article is used—
To show that no particular one is meant, implying that there are or may be others. Its various meanings range through the substitutes *one, any, all, each, every*, and the phrase—*this, and not any thing else.*

a. When *a* is used before *few* or *little*, the meaning is, *some at least.*

b. When no article is used before *few* or *little*, the meaning is, *none*, or *almost none.*

The profligate man is seldom or never found to be the good husband, the good father, or the beneficent neighbor. In Holland, great part of the land has been rescued from the sea. He received only the fourth part of the estate. The interest is the tenth part of the sum. A pronoun is the word used for a noun. A librarian is the person who has charge of a library. Avoid the too frequent repetition of the same word. Sometimes the adjective becomes a substantive, and has another adjective joined to it. An articulate sound is the sound of the human voice, formed by the organs of speech. Contrast makes each of the contrasted objects appear in the stronger light. To the business of others I give but a little attention. A little respect should be paid to those who deserve none. Are not my days a few? A few men of his age enjoy so good health So bold a breach of conduct called for little severity in punishing the offender.

4. *Whether* A *or* An *should be Used.*

1. *A* should be used before *consonant* sounds.
2. *An* should be used before *vowel* sounds.

a. A word beginning with the consonant sound of *w* or of *y*, is to be treated as if beginning with a consonant; as, *One, union, eulogy.*

b. A word beginning with *h* sounded, and having the accent on the second syllable, is usually treated as if beginning with a vowel; as, *Heroic, hyena, hiatus, hereditary.*

He had a interest in the matter. It was a humble and dutiful petition to the throne. Argus is said to have had an hundred eyes. An African or an European. An heretic; a heretical opinion. A harangue. A hyena. A hiatus. A harmonious flow of words. Is it an *i* or an *u*? An history; a historical account; a historian. A heroic poem. A hyperbole. A hypothesis

An hexagon; a hexagonal figure. There was not an human being on the place. An hopeful young man. An unity of interest. I would not make such an use of it. It was not such an one as I wanted.

5. *Improper Use of* A *or* An *before Plurals.*

The indefinite article should never be so used as to appear to have a plural signification. Insert words, omit words, or change the term.

A winding stairs led us to the Senate Chamber. *A flight of,* &c. I saw her trim her nails with a scissors. —*a pair of*— The next object was, to provide a head-quarters. The farm was a long ways from town. The right wing en camped behind a small woods. I saw a snuffers lying on the mantel-piece. This idiom is a remains of the Saxon dialect. Let us make a little memoranda of it. A few miles from the river is a large swamp, or flats. The problem can not be solved from such a data. A long minutiæ of detail made the story very tedious. About a two days afterwards the legates returned to Cæsar. The child was not a three weeks old, when it died. The Jews were permitted to return to their country, after a seventy years of captivity at Babylon. —*a captivity of seventy years*— An eight years' war was the consequence. With such a spirit and intrigues was the war carried on. —*and such intrigues*— The cottage was fringed by a very handsome eaves. A mother and children were captured by the Indians. —*and her children*— A neat house and gardens were thus sold for a trifle. My friend bought a house and lots in the suburbs of St. Louis.

Remark.—*Allowable:* "Never did a set of rascals travel further to find *a gallows.*"—*Irving.* "The draught of air performed the function of *a bellows.*"—*Dr Robertson.* Irving also has the phrase "a tongs." See Numbers, p. 188.

6. *When the Article should not be Repeated.*
7. *When the Article should be Repeated.*

1. When the repetition of the article would suggest more objects than are meant, the article should be omitted.
2. When the omission of the article would not suggest all the objects meant, the article should be repeated.
3. The article is *elegantly omitted* to show that the objects are joined, or comprehended in one view.
4. The article is *elegantly inserted* to show that the objects are separate, distinct, or opposite; or that they are viewed so.
5. When the article relates to a series of terms, it should precede the whole series, or else each term of the series.

The forsaken may find another and a better friend. My friend was married to a sensible and an amiable woman. The matter deserves an impartial, a careful, and a thorough investigation. Everett, the scholar, the statesman, and the orator, should be invited. The white and black inhabitants amount to several thousands. A hot and cold spring issued from the same mountain The sick and wounded were left at this place. The Eastern and the Western Continents. The Eastern and Western Continent. The first and the last payments are the two in dispute. Give the possessive and the objective cases of *who*—the possessive and objective case of *who.* The Old and New Testament. The Old and the New Testaments. Macaulay is not so good a poet as an historian. He is not so good a statesman as a soldier. She is not so good a cook as a washerwoman. I am a better arithmetician than a grammarian. The figure is a globe, a ball, or a sphere. Is this a *v, a,* or *u?* A Philosophical Inquiry into the Origin of our Ideas on the Sublime and Beautiful. The Latin introduced between the Conquest and reign of Henry the Eighth. ("*Conquest*" refers to William the Conqueror, not to Henry.) In my last lecture I treated of the concise and diffuse, the nervous and feeble manner. The black and red soil will produce the best crops. (Two kinds of soil were meant.) A horse and a buggy went up to the house. Here, at different times, the parents had buried a son and daughter. He understands neither the Latin or Greek languages. —*neither the Latin language nor the Greek.* (Parts compared, contrasted, or distinctly noticed, should be expressed with equal fullness.) The poor as well as rich, the high and low, the wise and ignorant, would be benefited by such a law. Both the house and barn were consumed by fire. He as distinguished himself both as a teacher and scholar. Neither the poor nor ich are completely happy. You must shoot a bear either through the heart or brain. —*or through the brain.* Let us make a distinction between the loss and expense. There is little difference between a catamount and leopard-cat. It is not difficult to distinguish the demagogue from statesman. Not the use, but abuse, of worldly things, is sinful. The young, as well as old, may sicken and die. It was not the loss, but dishonor, that grieved him. We are the friends, not enemies, of the Institution. I would rather pluck a lily than rose. I would rather hear the whippoorwill than katydid. The one or other of the two. There is not a tree in the yard, nor flower in the garden. The hum of bees, and songs of birds, fell sweetly upon my ear. Was the man fined, and damage paid? The oak, ash, maple, elm, and the hickory, are the principal trees of this State. Such a law would be injurious to the farmer, mechanic, and the merchant. *Come* is an irregular transitive verb; found in the indicative mood, the present tense, third person, and singular number.

Remark.—Avoid such an arrangement of terms as will make the article relate to some to which you do not mean to apply it. EXAMPLE: "I was thinking of the solar system, time, and space;" *i. e.*, the solar system, the solar time, and the solar space. But the author meant to say. "I was thinking of time, space, and the solar system."

Miscellaneous Examples.

I have had a dull sort of a headache all day. The Tennessee, the Mississippi, and the Missouri, are all the names derived from the Indian languages. The violation of this rule never fails to displease a reader. *A* or *an* is sometimes used to convey an idea of unity. By adding *s* to *dove*, we make it a plural. When a whole is put for the part, or the part for a whole; a genus for the species, or the species for a genus; a singular for a plural, or a plural for a singular, the figure is called a *synecdoche.* Surely there is little satisfaction in the having caused another's ruin. She contributed a thousand dollars to building of a college edifice. The virtues like his are not easily acquired: such qualities honor the nature of a man. I bought a vest-pattern and trimmings, for five dollars. This caused an universal consternation throughout the colonies.—*Burke.* We stopped at a hotel on Broadway. Apostrophe ['] is used in the place of a letter left out. The day and night succeed each other. All the chief priests and elders took counsel against Jesus, to put him to death. You may measure the time by a watch, clock, or dial. Beware of drunkenness: it impairs understanding, wastes an estate, destroys a reputation, consumes the body, and renders the man of the brightest parts the common jest of the meanest clown. True charity is not the meteor which occasionally glares, but the luminary which, in its orderly and regular course, dispenses benignant influence. Purity has its seat in the heart, but extends its influence over so much of the outward conduct, as to form the great and material part of a character

OBSERVATIONS.

From the Saxon *ane* are derived our *an*, *a*, and *one*. Hence *an* is the older for n, which has become *a* for the sake of euphony. Even in English written in the last century, we not unfrequently find *an* used where *a* would now be preferred. *An* or *a* is now sometimes equivalent to *one*; but generally it differs from it by a shade of meaning. "It weighs *a* pound, or *one* pound;" but when I say, "The whole community rose like *one* man, and built *a* bridge over the river," *one* and *a* are not interchangeable. "Will you take *a* horse?"—or *something else?* " Will you take *one* horse?"—*or two?* *The* is akin to *that*, but less emphatic; and formerly it was sometimes used even before relative pronouns. "Northumberland, thou ladder, by *the which* my cousin Bolingbroke ascends my throne."—*Shakespeare*.

As a general thing, substantives must have or assume meaning, or must have meaning liable to be widened or contracted, before the articles can be applied to them; and substantives must be without meaning, or have meaning not liable to be widened or contracted, or must be fixed in application, before they can dispense with the articles. Substantives denoting material or abstract substances *sui generis*, or having themselves the accessory idea of distinction from other things, do not require the article. The article generally has a double reference: the one, to other objects of the same kind; and the other, to other kinds. "Give me *an* apple," refers not only to other apples, but also, by way of exclusion, to oranges, peaches, plums, cakes, or other objects.

The often suggests that there is but one object or group of the kind, supposed, by the speaker, to be generally known; *a* or *an* always implies that there are or may be other similar objects. *The* implies that the speaker and the hearer have in common a knowledge of the individual as well as of the class,—such a knowledge as enables the speaker to suggest at once to the hearer, by means of the article, the object meant; but *a* or *an* does not necessarily require that they have in common more than a knowledge of the class.

The article may be *definite*, *indefinite*, or *omitted*, according to many different views:—

1. *Definite*, as referring to the general knowledge of mankind. " *The* sun, *the* earth, *the* Messiah, *the* dyspepsy, *the* sword, *the* Sabbath."
2. *Definite*, as referring to the general knowledge of a community,—to things often noticed, or often thought of. "*The* Missouri Compromise." "*The* Legislature." "*The* never-failing brook, *the* busy mill, *the* decent church that topped *the* neighboring hill."
3. *Definite*, as referring to the knowledge of the family circle. "Go to *the* well —to *the* barn." "Where is *the* washbowl?" "*The* old oaken bucket."
4. *Definite*, as referring to the knowledge of the person addressed. "Give me *the* letter."
5. *Definite*, as referring to what has been mentioned, spoken of, or already brought to the notice of the person addressed. "Go along till you come to *a* bridge; and just beyond *the* bridge, turn to the right." These last two principles are often violated; speakers or writers presuming too much on the knowledge of their hearers or readers, or speaking of objects unknown as if other people were as well acquainted with them as they themselves are. "I will now give you an account of *the* great hurricane, which passed over our village when I was a boy." Say, " *a* great."
6. *Definite*, as referring to the class to which the object belongs. "*The* [boat] Fulton went up *the* Hudson" [river]. " Alexander *the* Great." " Bolivar was *the* Washington of South America."
7. *Definite*, by way of preëminence. (See the preceding paragraph.) "*The* man of men." " The Bible is *the* book of books." "*The* generous Lafayette."
8. *Definite*, as comprehending the whole class, or as referring to other classes of objects. "*The* horse is a useful animal." "*The* letters are divided," &c. "*The* beautiful." " *The* Stuarts." " One or *the* other of two."
9. *Definite*, as referring to the other parts associated with the object. " *The* neck connects *the* head and *the* trunk."
10. *Definite*, as being a necessary part or accompaniment, and as being therefore known to some extent to the hearer. "*The* weather was fine." " *The* fare was good: *the* coffee and rolls were particularly excellent." " Andre stood beside *the* coffin." " The enemy were on *the* other side."

ARTICLES.—OBSERVATIONS.

11. *Definite*, as being alone, or all, and known to be so. "*The* earth is somewhat flat at *the* poles." "*The* first and *the* last."
12. *Definite*, as being made so by some accompanying descriptive words. "*The* BLUE-EYED damsel." "*The* winds OF AUTUMN." "*The* man WHO IS UPRIGHT."

1. *Indefinite*, as first introducing an object of a known class, or as implying that there are or may be other objects of the same kind. "*An* old manuscript, found in Rome, has," &c. "He is *a* saddler." "*A* Homer." In this sense, the noun may be even to some extent made definite by other words.
2. *Indefinite*, as being used in the sense of *any*, *each*, or *every*. "*A* conjunction connects words." "*A* dollar *a* pair."
3. *Indefinite*, to exclude the ambiguous sense which *the* would give. "She received *a* third of the estate." "*The* third" might suggest a particular third. "A librarian is *a* person who has charge of a library." "*The* person" might suggest that "*person*" is the subject-nominative.

1. *Omitted*, because the mind does not individualize the object, or conceive it with definite limits. "*Orthography* treats of the forms of *letters* and *words*." "The oak is a species of *tree*."
2. *Omitted*, because, by frequent notice of the object, the word has acquired almost the definiteness of a proper name, or because it is merely descriptive. "Where is *father?*" "At *table*." "With *body* and *soul*." "On *foot*." "Go to *bed*." "Boston *Common*."
3. *Omitted*, because if used it might imply too much importance or emphasis. "Notice." "*A* Notice" might suggest, Now look here; for this is a notice that is a notice.
4. *Omitted*, because it might give a wrong impression. "He was then *sheriff*." "Use *essence* of peppermint." "She is *heir* to a little fortune."
5. *Omitted*, for the sake of poetic measure. "The why is plain as *way* to parish church."—*Shakespeare*.

Always consider carefully, in the use of words, what the sense requires. "A pine is a species of a tree," is improper; because one tree is not a class, nor is a whole class a part of one tree. *The pine is a species of tree*. But when *a* is needed to express the meaning, it is perhaps allowable. "What kind of *paper* [the *material*] have you?" differs from "What kind of *a paper* [*document*] have you?" "Bear Worcester to the death."—*Shak.* Improper, because no particular kind of death was meant. — *to death—to his death*. "A half eagle," and "half an eagle," are not necessarily equivalent. What is true of all, is usually true of each : hence we can say, "*A* wise man may be more useful than *a* rich man;" "*A* good pupil never disobeys his instructor;"—or, "*The* wise man may be more useful than *the* rich man;" "*The* good pupil never disobeys his instructor." There are some things that may be conceived either in the gross or as individuals ; and hence the article may be either omitted or used. "It fell with loud *noise*," "It fell with *a* loud *noise*." "I see *a* farm." First observance; just enough knowledge of it to tell what it is. "I see *the* farm." Previous knowledge. "Cæsar, a Cæsar;" "From liberty each nobler science sprung, *a* Bacon brightened, and *a* Spenser sung." Meaning assumed, application extended. "Dar'st thou, then, to beard the lion in his den,—*the* Douglas in his hall?"—*Scott*. "These are the sacred feelings of thy heart, O Lyttleton, *the* friend."—*Thomson*. "I never knew any other man so much *the* gentleman." Preëminence. *The* is sometimes an elegant substitute for the possessive pronoun. "He took me by *the* hand"—*my* hand. "Judge the tree by *the* fruit"—*its* fruit. "They had never bowed *the* knee to a tyrant."

"There are few mistakes in his composition"—*almost none*. "There are a few mistakes in his composition"—*some*—*many*. "There are not a few mistakes in his composition"—*very many*. So, "She has *little* vanity;" "She has *a little* vanity;" "She has *not a little* vanity." A noun limited by the indefinite article, may often be made plural in the same sense, by omitting the article: as, "He was *a representative* from St. Louis;" "They were *representatives* from St. Louis." Elegance requires,—"He paid neither *the* principal nor *the* interest—both *the* principal and *the* interest—*the* principal as well as *the* interest—*the* principal, but not *the* interest—principal and interest. We usually say, "Too good a man," "Too large an apple," &c.; accordingly, it is better to say, "Too nice a woman," "Too frequent a repetition," than, "A too nice woman," "A too frequent repetition." "He is a better poet than painter." He is not so good a painter. "He is a better painter than a poet." In painting, he excels poets. "The black and white calf"—*one calf*. "The black and the white calf"—*two*. "He wrote for a light and a strong wagon"—*two*. "He wrote for a light and strong wagon"—*one*.

"He married *a* handsome, *a* sensible, and *an* accomplished woman"—*married three.* Say, "*a* handsome, sensible, and accomplished woman." "A farmer, lawyer, and politician, addressed the assembly"—*one person.* "I saw the editor, the printer, and the proprietor of the paper"—*three persons.* But, for the sake of emphasis, and when the meaning can not be misconceived, the article is sometimes repeated; as, "There sat *the* wise, *the* eloquent, and *the* patriotic Chatham." 'Give **me** the fourth and the last," may not be equivalent to "Give me the fourth and last." We can not say, "The definite and the indefinite articles," nor, "The definite and indefinite article;" but we must say, "The definite and the indefinite article," "The definite and indefinite articles," or, "The definite article and the indefinite." The last is generally the best mode of expression. The omission of the article sometimes implies a unity in the objects, or in the view taken; the repetition of it, separation. "The soul and body." Viewed as one. "The soul and the body." Viewed separately and distinctly. "The day, the hour, and the minute, were specified." Emphasis. "I have just sold a house and lot—a horse and buggy." One belonged to the other. "I have just sold a house and a lot— a horse and a buggy." One did not belong to the other. "He is a poet and a mathematician." Qualifications seldom found in the same person. "He is a physician and surgeon—a lawyer and politician." Qualifications usually found in the same person. "A singular and plural antecedent require a plural verb."— *Wells. Require,* in the plural number, shows the sense; but the article should rather have been repeated. "There are three persons; *the* first, second, and third." Mr. Brown contends that this should be, "There are three persons: *the* first, *the* second, and *the* third." I think he is hypercritical in regard to such expressions. QUERY.—Should the indefinite article be repeated before each one of a series of substantives, merely because a different form of the article is required ? Mr. Murray thinks it should; the other grammarians treat the difficulty with characteristic evasion. I should not hesitate to omit the article to avoid a clumsier expression. I should rather say, "A preposition shows the relation of *a* noun, adjective, verb, or adverb, to *an* objective," than, "A preposition shows the relation of *a* noun, *an* adjective, *a* verb, or *an* adverb, to *an* objective." Some of the best authors favor the former mode of expression. Such expressions as "A historian," "A harmonic scale," have occasionally been countenanced by the best writers and critics; and it would seem that euphony sometimes allows the *a,* when the first syllable is closed by a consonant sound, or when the *h* is heard with considerable distinctness.

7. ADJECTIVES.

203. An **adjective** is a word used to qualify or limit the meaning of a substantive.

Ex.—"A *mellow* apple; a *beautiful* woman; a *brilliant* star; *five* carriages; *yonder* mountains; *brass* buttons; *hoary-headed* men; a *large, red,* and *juicy* apple; eyes *bright, blue,* and *affectionate.*" "He is *industrious* and *frugal.*" "To slight the poor is *mean.*"

Our language has about 7,000 adjectives; and they give to it not a little of its beauty, energy, and precision.

204. Words from other parts of speech are frequently used as adjectives.

Ex.—"A *gold* ring; a *mahogany* table; *state* revenue; *California* gold; *she* politicians; a *would-be* scholar; *parsing* exercises; *rolling* prairies; the *far-off* future; the *above* remarks; a *farewell* address." "The lightnings flashed *vermilion.*"—*Dante.* ("The rose looks *red.*") "The West is as truly American, as genuinely *Jonathan,* as any other part of our country."—*Wise.*

205. Adjectives may be divided into two chief classes; *descriptive* and *definitive.*

206. A **descriptive** adjective describes or qualifies.

Ex.—Good, white, square. "The *green* forest was bathed in *golden* light."

207. A **definitive** adjective merely limits or modifies.

Ex.—" There are *many* wealthy farmers in *this* country."

Adjectives may be divided also into several smaller classes: namely, *common; participial; compound; numeral*, comprising *cardinal, ordinal*, and *multiplicative;* and *pronominal*, comprising *distributive, demonstrative,* and *indefinite*.

208. A **common** adjective is any ordinary epithet of the language; as, *Good, upper.*

209. A **proper** adjective is an adjective derived from a proper noun; as, *American, English, Newtonian.*

210. A **participial** adjective is a participle ascribing the act or state to its subject as a quality; as, "*Twinkling* stars."

In the phrase " his dying day," *dying* is a mere adjective; and it is plain, for instance, that *unepitaphed*—"without epitaph," and *unhorsed*—"deprived of horse," differ radically in sense. A *participial* adjective is derived directly from a verb, is nearly always placed before its noun, and generally expresses a permanent or habitual act or state.

211. A **compound** adjective is a compound word used as an adjective; as, "*Thick-warbled* songs."

212. A **numeral** adjective expresses number definitely; as, *Two, second, twofold.*

The *cardinal* numerals tell how many, as *one, two;* the *ordinal*, which one, as *first, second;* and the *multiplicative*, how many fold, as *single, double, twofold*. A long or composite numeral is parsed as one word.

213. The **pronominal** adjectives are a class of definitive adjectives of which some are occasionally used as pronouns; as, *That, this, other.*

The *distributive* point out objects as taken separately; as, *Each, every, either, neither, many a.*

The *demonstrative*, or *definite*, point out objects *definitely;* as, *This, yonder*

The *indefinite* point out objects *indefinitely;* as, *Any, some.*

Degrees of Comparison.

Since the same quality may exist in different objects and in different degrees, adjectives are modified to express higher or lower degrees, or the highest or the lowest degrees, of the quality. Hence adjectives have what are called the *degrees of comparison.*

Ex.—" Lime is *white;* milk is *whiter;* but snow is the *whitest* of all."

Adjectives have three degrees of comparison; the *positive*, the *comparative*, and the *superlative.*

214. *a.* The **positive** degree expresses the quality simply.

Ex.—" A *young* orchard; a *large* farm." " The fields look *green* and *fresh.*"

215. *b.* It ascribes an equal degree of the quality, without reference to lower or higher degrees of the same quality.

Ex.—" She is as *good* as he." " A woman as *modest* as she is *beautiful.*"

216. *a.* The **comparative** degree ascribes the quality in a

higher or a lower degree to one object, or set of objects, than to another.

Ex.—"A *younger* brother; *more important* affairs; a boy *less studious*."

217. *b.* It expresses the quality in a higher or a lower degree, as reckoned from some other condition or quality of the same object or of a different object.

Ex.—"A nation is *happier* in peace than in war." "I am *better* than I was." "She is *more accomplished* than wise." "My horse is *whiter* than yours is black."

The comparative degree always implies *two* considered distinct from each other; and it either refers to the same quality in two different objects or in two different conditions of the same object, or it refers to one quality as contrasted with a different one. That from which it is reckoned, is sometimes understood, or exists only in the mind.

Ex.—"A *more eligible* situation" [than some other one]. "What is *better* is always preferred."

The comparative degree may be construed with *than* after it; therefore such words as *superior, inferior, interior, preferable, previous,* &c., are not in the comparative degree. And I doubt very much whether such words as *inner, outer, upper, hinder,* can be properly said to be in the comparative degree. They do not admit *than* after them, and they refer to an *opposite* rather than to a *positive* state: thus, *upper* refers to *lower,* rather than to *up; inner,* to *outer. Inner* and *outer* differ very little from *internal* and *external.*

218. *a.* The **superlative** degree expresses the quality in the highest or the lowest degree in which such objects have it.

Ex.—"The *loveliest* flowers were there." "The *most skillful* rider could do no better." "The *least skillful* rider could do no worse." "Two *kindest* souls alone must meet; 'tis friendship makes the bondage sweet."—*Watts.*

219. *b.* It ascribes the quality in the highest or the lowest degree to one object, or group of objects, as compared with the rest, or with other conditions of the same object.

Ex.—"The *largest* sycamore on the river." "The *best* peaches are taken from the tree." "He sat *highest* on Parnassus." "I am *happiest* at home."

The superlative degree implies three or more objects classed together; or else it implies other similar conditions of the same object.

220. An adjective can not be compared with propriety, when it denotes a quality or property that can not exist in different degrees.

Ex.—Equal, level, perpendicular, square, naked, round, straight, first, second, one, two, blind, deaf, dead, empty, perfect, right, honest, sincere, hollow, four-footed.

221. Good writers, however, sometimes use such adjectives in the comparative or the superlative degree; but then they do not take them in their full sense.

Ex.—"Our sight is the *most perfect* of our senses."—*Addison.* This means that it approaches nearer, than the rest, to perfection. "And love is still an *emptier* name."—*Goldsmith.* Almost all descriptive or qualifying adjectives may be used either as *absolute,* in their meaning, or as *relative.* And hence the comparative and superlative degrees may sometimes express even less of the quality than the positive degree expresses. "John's apple may be *better* than mine, and William may have the *best* apple, yet not one of them may be really *good.*" "Your *largest* horse is a mere pony."

222. A little of the quality may be expressed by adding *ish* to the positive, or by placing before it such words as *rather, somewhat*, &c.

Ex.—Black, *blackish; saltish; yellowish; somewhat* disagreeable; *rather* young.

223. A high degree of the quality, without implying direct comparison, is expressed by *very, exceedingly, a most*, &c.

Ex.—"Very respectful; exceedingly polite; a most distinguished soldier."

How adjectives are compared.

224. To express inferiority, we use *less* and *least*.

Ex.—Pos. *good*, comp. *less good*, superl. *least good;* important, *less important, least important*.

225. To express superiority, the comparison is formed by adding *er* and *est* to the positive, or by placing *more* and *most* before it.

Ex.—Pos. *large*, comp. *larger*, superl. *largest;* rich, *richer, richest;* cheerful, *more cheerful, most cheerful*. See Rules for Spelling.

Which of these methods should be used, depends chiefly on the sound of the word, or on the number of its syllables.

226. Adjectives of one syllable are compared by adding *er* for the comparative, and *est* for the superlative.

Ex.—Deep, *deeper, deepest;* wise, *wiser, wisest;* sad, *sadder, saddest;* dry, *drier, driest*.

227. Adjectives of three or more syllables must always be compared by *more* and *most*.

Ex.—Beautiful, *more beautiful, most beautiful*.

Adjectives of two syllables follow some of them one method, and some the other.

228. Adjectives of two syllables ending in *y*, or in *le* after a consonant, or accented on the second syllable, are generally compared by *er* and *est*.

Ex.—Happy, *happier, happiest;* feeble, *feebler, feeblest;* polite, *politer, politest*.

229. Some other adjectives of two syllables are sometimes compared in like manner; especially if they end in a vowel or a liquid sound.

Ex.—"Narrow, *narrower, narrowest;* handsome, *handsomer, handsomest;* tender, *tenderer, tenderest*." "The metaphor is the *commonest* figure."—*Blair's Rhetoric*. "Philosophers are but a *soberer* sort of madmen."—*Irving*.

230. Some words are expressed in the superlative degree, by annexing *most* to them.

Ex.—Foremost, utmost, inmost, innermost, hindmost, nethermost.

231. To express superiority, any adjective may sometimes be compared by *more* and *most*.

Ex.— "A foot *more light*, a step *more true*,
  Ne'er from the heath-flower dashed the dew."—*Scott*.

232. When two or more adjectives come together, of which some are properly compared by *er* and *est*, and others by *more* and *most*, the smaller are generally placed first, and all are compared as one, by *more* and *most*.

Ex.—" The *more nice* and *elegant parts*."—*Johnson*. " Homer's imagination was by far the *most rich* and *copious*."—*Pope*.

More, most, less, and *least,* when used to compare other words, should be parsed separately, and as adverbs.

The adjectives whose comparison can not be learned by means of a general rule, are said to be *irregular*.

Ex.—" Good, *better, best;* bad, *worse, worst*." See p. 11.

Number.

Some adjectives express number.

Ex.—This, these; that, those; few; many.

One, first, second, etc.; *each, every, either, neither; this, that, another; much, all* (the whole), *whole* (all the),—denote but one object or one aggregate.

Ex.—"The *first* MAN." "The *first* TEN MEN." "*Every* CREATURE loves its like." "*Neither* COMBATANT recovered from HIS wounds."

The numerals above *one,* (as *two, three,* etc.,) and *these, those, all* (number), *few, several, many, divers, sundry,* refer to more objects than one.

233. Adjectives implying number, must agree in this respect with the substantives to which they relate.

Ex.—" Four *feet;*" not, " Four *foot*." " *That* KIND of trees," or, " Trees of *that* KIND;" not, " *Those* KIND of trees."

Pronominal and other definitive adjectives.

All takes in the whole number spoken of, or the entire object or class. "*All* men." "*All* the *years* of man's life." " If *all* the *year* were playing holidays." " He is the best of *them all*."

Any strongly denotes an indefinite object. It denotes it as opposed to a particular one or to none. " There is little honor in what *any body* can do." " Have you *any foreigners* in your county ?"

Both means *the two*. It is usually emphatic, implying *not only the one, but the other also*. "*Both* horses are lame." " His *father* and *mother* are *both* dead."

Certain indefinitely describes what the speaker more definitely knows. "*A certain* man planted a vineyard." " I will not vote for a *certain* candidate."

Divers—*several* or *many* + *different.* " *Divers* philosophers hold that the lips are part and parcel of the mind."—*Shak.* Everso many different philosophers, etc.

Each means both or all considered separately. It implies two or more. "*Each* one of the twins has a horse." "*Each* pupil must use his own books."

Either means one or the other of two, but not both. Sometimes it denotes the two in the sense of *each,* but with greater distinctness. " I will sell *either* one of my two horses." "*Either* road leads to town." " On *either* side they found impassable barriers."—*Irving*. That is, if they turned to one side, they found them there; and if they turned to the other side, they also found them there.

Either is sometimes applied to more than two, but with very questionable propriety. "*Either* or *neither,* applied to any number greater than one of two objects,

is a mere solecism,* and one of late introduction."—*Harrison's English Language.*
"The pronominal adjectives *either* and *neither*, in strict propriety of syntax, relate to two only; when more are referred to, *any* and *none*, or *any one* and *no one*, should be used in stead of them."—*Goold Brown.* The following senten ce from Geo. P. Marsh, however, could hardly be improved: "Dryden, Pope, and Wordsworth have not scrupled to lay a profane hand upon Chaucer, a mightier genius than *either.*"

Else excludes what is ascertained, from something indefinite. "What *else?*" "Any one *else.*" "Who *else* have seen him?"

Every means all considered separately. It implies several or many. "*Every* apple in the basket is frozen." "Pick up *every* one."

Few denotes a comparatively small number. "*Few* shall part where many meet."

Former. See *This* and *That.*
Latter. See *This* and *That.*
Many denotes a comparatively large number.
Many a means many considered separately. It differs from *every*, only in not denoting all. *Many a* is to *many*, as *every* is to *all.* "*Many a* man has been ruined by intemperance."

Much denotes a comparatively large quantity. "*Much* money."

Neither means *not the one nor the other.* It is opposed to *each* denoting two, or to *either* in this sense; sometimes to *both.* "*Each* of yours is good, but *neither* of mine is." "Shall I take *both, one,* or *neither?*"

No means *not any*, or *not a*, or it denies of all separately. Sometimes it denies a certain character of an object. "*No* man knows his destiny." "She is *no* friend of mine." "Even Sunday shines *no* Sabbath-day to me."—*Pope.*

One may be applied indefinitely to any person or other object.

One corresponds to *another*, when the meaning is not that there are but two; one or *the one*, to *the other* of two. *One—either of two; the one—a particular one of two.* "First came *one* daughter, and then *another.*" "They marched *one* after *another.*" "He went from *one* extreme to *the other.*" *One* sometimes denotes a person as not well known, or as of not much importance. Hence it is sometimes very contemptuous. "*One* Peter Simmons was the defendant." "An attack upon me by *one* Reid."—*Benton.*

Other or **another** denotes something different or distinct from something else, yet of the same class or name. With allusion to something known or mentioned, it denotes something else. "An *other* overflow." "Take the *other.*" "They are meant for us; they can be meant for no *other.*"—*P. Henry.*

Own implies possession, with emphasis or distinction. "My *own.*" "Use your *own* book." "Our *own* Webster."

Same means *not another* or *not different.* It denotes the identical object or a similar object. "It is the *same* boat that we saw an hour ago." "This church is built of the *same* stones as the other."

Several denotes more than *two* and fewer than *many.* "*Several* boys."

Some denotes one or a portion indefinitely. It is opposed to *all, a particular one,* or *the whole.* "*Some* of the robbers were caught." "*Some* one said so." "*Some* of his money was stolen." When two indefinite portions are spoken of or are contrasted, *some* is often applied to one, and *others* to the other; when more than two are spoken of, *some* is generally used throughout. Sometimes *others* is used to continue the sentence after the first *some.* "*Some* of the men were without coats, and *others* without shoes." "*Some* of the pupils are indolent, *some* are mischievous, and *some* are stupid."

---

* Errors of grammar are commonly called *solecisms*, from *Soli*, the name of a Grecian colony, noted for the misuse of their mother-tongue. "The *barbarism* is an offence against etymology, the *solecism* against syntax, and the *impropriety* against lexicography."—*Campbell's Rhetoric.*

Such refers to an object as being of the same nature, character, or description as something else. " Modesty, meekness, and *such* virtues." "*Such* men as he is." "*Such* principles as we approve." It is sometimes so used as to include both the objects or classes to which the comparison relates. " It is so used by *such* writers as Swift and Addison ;" *i. e.*, by Swift and Addison, and other writers like them. Sometimes it denotes identity in stead of similarity, and is then generally in the way of a better expression. "*Such* nouns as end in *x* assume *es* :" say, "*The* nouns *which*," &c.

Sundry—*divers*, but it is not quite so emphatic. " So teach *sundry* grammarians."—*Brown.*

This (plu. *these*) strongly and distinctly points out something as near the speaker, in place or time. " *This* house and *these* fields, are they not yours ?" "*This* subject has been frequently discussed."

That (plu. *those*) strongly and distinctly points out something as not near the speaker, or as not so near as something else. Hence, in speaking of two, *that* may be applied to the former, and *this* to the latter. "*That* cloud is exceedingly beautiful." " *These* roses will bloom longer than *those.*" · " *That* question which we were yesterday discussing."

"*Some* put the bliss in action, *some* in ease :
Those call it pleasure ; and contentment, *these*."—*Pope.*

In such cases, *former* and *latter, one* and *other, ones* and *others*, may also frequently be used. *Former* and *latter* are the most obvious in their reference. " The cry of danger to the *Union* was raised to divert their assaults upon the *Constitution.* It was the *latter*, and not the *former*, that was in danger."—*Benton.* In the explanatory phrase "*that is*," *that* often seems to be used in the sense of *this.* Sometimes *that* is simply more forcible than *the.* "*That* man who said so, is mistaken." " I trust I have none of *that* other spirit which would drag angels down."—*Webster.*

Very is nearly equivalent to a compound personal pronoun, or to the word *even* " Our *very* existence depends upon it"—Our existence *itself,* etc.

What and **which,** whether *interrogative* or *responsive*, and also their compounds, point out objects *definitely,* and sometimes *indefinitely.* "*What* man among you ?" "*Whatever* motives govern him." "All persons *whatsoever.*" "*What* money he earned, she spent." " By *which* charter, certain rights were secured to us."

Yon or **yonder** strongly points out something in sight. ' *Yon* hawthorn bush." "*Yonder* hills, robed in misty blue, were the haunts of my childhood."

---

234. Since every quality or attribute must belong to some object, adjectives are said to belong to the substantives which they qualify or limit.

235. When an adjective relates equally to two or more substantives, it should be parsed accordingly.

Ex.—" The APPLES, PEARS, and PEACHES, are *ripe.*" "A man of *great* SENSIBILITY and GENIUS." " *That* HOUSE and LOT." " The cow and CALF are *white.*" " A *white* cow and CALF." But, "A *white* cow and *a* calf," "A *white* cow and *her* calf," do not mean that the calf is *white* too. " He is a venerable old man." Here *venerable* qualifies *old man,* rather than *man* only.

236. When two or more adjectives come between an article and a plural noun, they sometimes qualify each only a part of what the noun denotes.

Ex.—" The *New* and *Old* TESTAMENTS"—The New Testament and the Old Testament ; not, The New Testaments and the Old Testaments.

237. An adjective is sometimes used without a substantive, to complete the sense of a preceding participle or infinitive. The adjective relates in sense to the object suggested by a previous possessive; or else it relates indefinitely to some being, or to all beings whatsoever.

Ex.—" To BE *good* is TO BE *happy*." " These are the consequences of BEING too *fond* of glory." " His BEING *rich* was the cause of his ruin." " There is nothing lost by BEING *careful*." The phrase is equivalent to a noun, or to an adjective and noun: also, a noun that will preserve the sense, can generally be supplied. "*Goodness* is *happiness*." " These are the consequences of too *much fondness* for glory." " His *riches* were the cause of his ruin." " To be a *good person*, is, to be a *happy person*;" or, " To be *good people*, is, to be *happy people*." " These are the consequences of being a *nation* too *fond* of glory." " His being a *rich young man*, was the cause of his ruin." " There is nothing lost by being a *careful person* —by being *careful persons*."

A word that is usually an adjective, has sometimes the sense or modifications of a noun or a pronoun, and may then be parsed accordingly.

Ex.—" Burke wrote on the *beautiful* and the *sublime*." " O'er the vast *abrupt*."—*Milton*. " We crossed the mighty *deep*." " In the *dead* of night." " Companion of the *dead*."—*Campbell*. " Children are afraid to go into the *dark*." " I prefer *green* to *red*." " The *past*, at least, is secure."—*Webster*. " These *primitives* have no *derivatives*." " Between the *noble's* palace and the hut." " Where *either's* fall determines both their fates." " Every *one* must have heard of the tragical fate of Emmett."—*Irving*.

Such a word, when used as a noun, expresses the quality by a general reference to some or all objects possessing it; or it sets forth some particular object or class as characterized by it.

When an adverb is joined to such a word, the word must be parsed as an adjective, belonging to such a substantive understood as will make sense; namely, *thing, things, persons, people, place, style, one, ones,* &c. : as, " The *truly wise* are not avaricious;" " *How much* have you got?" " *Nearly all* were captured;" " A fine instance of the *truly sublime*," better,—" of *true sublimity*."

So, indeed, should every such word be parsed, when the word denoting the person or thing referred to, is obviously understood, or can be supplied without injuring the sense; as, " Of the apples he took the *larger* [ones] and left the *smaller* [ones]. " Turn to the *left*" [hand or side]. It is generally better to parse the adjective as a substantive, only when it has so far usurped the character of one that the expression with the most suitable word supplied, would not exactly convey the same sense, or else would be tedious and clumsy. Many grammarians, though perhaps needlessly, parse as pronouns most of the definitive adjectives above described, when the modified substantive is omitted. Such parsing is objectionable, furthermore, inasmuch as the words generally may be, and frequently are, modified by adverbs.

When an adjective is used substantively, it is sometimes difficult to tell whether it should be parsed as a noun or as a pronoun. This will depend on whether the word is descriptive of a class, like a common noun, or is merely designative— belonging to the class called form-words, and applicable to objects that differ in kind.

An adjective sometimes becomes an adverb, without a change of form.

Ex.—" I like it *best*." " Go, get you to my lady's chamber; and tell her that if she PAINT an inch *thick*, yet to this favor will she come at last."—*Shakspeare*.

EXERCISES.
Examples to be Analyzed and Parsed.

Parse the adjectives:—

1.

*A dark cloud came over the city. The summer[a] breezes blow soft[1] and cool[10]. The annual, autumnal, desolating[b] fires have almost destroyed this well-timbered country. Horses are as[12] valuable[c] as[14] mules [are]. Homer was a greater[d] poet than Virgil. Here the valleys are more[12] beautiful, and the mountains [are] less[14] rugged[10] and more fertile. Then comes an elevated rolling prairie country. The sweetest[e] flowers fringed the little stream. The river is highest in June. The cedars highest on the mountain, are the smallest [cedars]. The last blow was more fatal. The foremost horse is superior to the rest.

2.

Up[12] springs the lark, shrill-voiced and loud, the messenger[f] of morn. He treated poor[g] and rich alike. To be[1] poor[h] is more honorable[h] than to be dishonorably rich [is honorable].

The beautiful[i] fields and forests now in view, were very extensive[10], and governed[11] by some Peruvian prince or princess.—*Prescott.*

On the grassy bank stood a tall waving ash, sound to the very top.—*Dickens.*

How brilliant and mirthful the light[1] of her eye,
Like[10] a star[a] glancing[12] out[13] from the blue[e] of the sky!—*Whittier.*
There brighter suns dispense serener light,
And milder moons imparadise the night.—*Montgomery.*
Where smiling spring[1] its earliest visit[4] paid,
And parting summer's lingering blooms[1] delayed.—*Goldsmith.*

3.

There are two[j] pear-trees in the second row. Any man can carry the whole limb with all its apples. Would any man defend infidelity by such or any other arguments? No man is perfectly independent of all others[a]. There is a horse for each man. Many a fine intellect is buried in poverty. Neither course is proper. This chair is nearer to me than that[10]. Who else came? One story is good until another[10] is told. Silver and gold have I none[k]. These resolutions reasserted the sole right of the colonies to tax themselves in all cases whatsoever[10].

---

[a] It may be well, when time allows it, for the pupil to descend, in parsing, according to our classification of adjectives: thus, —— *adjective*; *descriptive* or *definitive*; *common, proper, compound, pronominal,* &c.; *distributive, demonstrative,* &c. It may also be well to say, in parsing some descriptive adjectives, —— " it can not be compared with propriety· and belongs," etc.

(*a.*) "*Summer*" is an adjective,—a word * * * *definitive*, etc. (*b.*) " *Desolating*" is an *adjective,* —a word * * * *participial*, it is a participle ascribing * * * and belongs, etc. (*c.*) —— in the *positive* degree, it ascribes an equal degree of the quality; and belongs, etc. (*d.*) —— *comparative* degree, it ascribes the quality in a higher degree to one object as compared with another; and belongs, etc. (*e.*) —— in the *superlative* degree, it ascribes the quality, etc. (See definitions of the superlative degree.) (*f.*) —— and belongs to *people* understood, according to Rule X. (*g.*) —— and belongs to *person* or *persons* understood, according to Rule X. Or *say,* "—— is here used without a substantive, according to Note X." (*h.*) —— and it belongs to the phrase "*To be poor*," according to Rule X. (*i.*) —— and belongs to "*fields and forests,*" according to Rule X. (*j.*) "*Two*" is an *adjective* * * * *definitive* * * * *numeral* * * * *cardinal* * * * and belongs, etc. (*k.*) "*None*" is here perhaps more best as an adjective belonging to "*silver*" and "*gold*," notwithstanding it can not be placed next to them. " We shall have *none* END."—*Bacon.* It is not essential that an adjective must always be capable of standing next to its substantive.

Examples to be Corrected.

All the liabilities to error in regard to adjectives, may be reduced to the following heads:—

1. *Choice.* 2. *Number.* 3. *Comparison.* 4. *Position.*

1. *Choice.*

1. In the use of adjectives, care should be taken to select the most appropriate for the meaning intended.
2. Adverbs should not be unnecessarily used as adjectives.
3. *Them* should not be used for *those.*

Them boys are very idle. What do you ask for them apples? Let some of them boys sit on them other benches. I have three horses, and you may ride either of them. Neither of my dozen razors is worth a cent. Further information may be obtained from either of the [eight] professors. Neither of the [six] hats is large enough for my head. None of the two pleases me. Any one of the two roads will take you to town. Tall pines grew on either side of the river. Each one of the thousand soldiers received a guinea. You may take e'er a one or ne'er a one, just as you please. That very point which we are now discussing, was lately decided in Kentucky. These very men with whom you traveled yesterday, are now in jail. There seems to be little glory in doing what every body can do. —*any body*— Memory and forecast just returns engage; this pointing back to youth, that on t> age.—*Pope.* The whole school were at play; some at marbles, others at ball, these at racing, those at jumping the rope, and some few at mumble-peg. (Use *some*, and lastly say, "*and a few at mumble-peg.*") Such capers are unbefitting a man of his age. —*unsuitable to*— Such verbs as assume *ed*, are regular. Such persons as are unprovided, will please to apply at the office. *All persons that are,* &c.

There are not less than fifteen banks in the city of New York that suspended to-day. I have caught less fish than you. A proper fraction is less than one, because it expresses less parts than it takes to make a unit.—*D. P. Colburn.* The summit of the hill was covered with stinted trees. (Say "*stunted,*" for *stinted* is usually restricted to eating and drinking.) It all tends to show, that our whole plans had been discovered. *The whole tends . . . . that all our,* &c. We stand the last, and, if we fall, the latest, experiment of self-government. His now wife is a cousin of his former wife. The then minister was unusually talented. Our bullets glanced harmlessly from the alligator's back. Open the door widely. We were all sitting quietly and comfortably round the fire. The shutters were painted greenly. We arrived safely, after all our misfortunes. This rose blooms most fairly. Velvet feels smoothly. I live freely from care. John reads too loudly, and James reads too lowly. (*I. e.*, John is too loud, when . . . . James is too low in voice, when—) Yet often touching will wear gold. —*frequent*— It is the often doing of a thing, that makes it a habit. He makes seldom mention of his relatives. *He seldom mentions,* &c. Motion upwards is more agreeable than motion downwards. *Upward motion,* &c. He made a soon and prosperous voyage. You jump too highly when you dance. I thought she looked very beautifully in her new silk dress. When a noun stands independently or absolutely of the rest of the sentence, it is in the nominative case. The relative should be placed as nearly as possible to its antecedent. A regularly and well-constructed sentence. The symptoms are two-fold, inwards and outwards. Apples are more plenty than peaches.—*N. Webster.*

2. Number.

Adjectives implying number, must agree in this respect with the substantives to which they belong.

a. The nouns which are not changed in form to express number, are singular when they denote one object, and plural when they denote more.

You have been playing this two hours. This oats, I fear, will never come up. Give him this memoranda. How do you like these sort of things? You will always see those kind of men sitting and loafering about taverns —*men of that kind*— I never wear those sort of hoops. Take up this ashes. These molasses I bought yesterday. That tongs should be left in the kitchen That victuals will last us to-day and to-morrow. We have not much provisions for the journey. —*not many provisions*— or, *not much provision*— She was very extravagant in dressing, and by these means became poor. He was indolent and extravagant, and by that means became a pauper. He had no other thoughts than that of amassing money and hoarding it. There are no thoughts more painful than that of suspense and disappointment. If that be the facts of the case, he shall not escape from punishment. Every reasonable amends have been made. *All reasonable amends,* &c.

3. Comparison.

a. The mode of comparing. *b.* Double comparison. *c.* Adjectives that should not be compared. *d.* The terms denoting the objects compared.

a. Adjectives should be compared in the best manner according to usage and euphony.

It was the powerfullest speech I ever heard. I think the rose is the beautifullest of flowers. Omar was the faithfullest of his followers.—*Irving.* The fox is the cunningest of animals. There are few bachelors soberer than he is. A cleverer man is not to be found. You are welcomer now than you were then. He is the awkwardest, backwardest fellow we have ever had. This is a reasonabler proposition than the other. By silence, many a dunderpate, like the owl, the stupidest of birds, comes to be considered the very type of wisdom.—*Irving.* They unfortunately escaped to the insecurest places. I never was at a pleasanter party. This pink is more red than the other. Young folks never had a more merry time. This is the baddest accident that ever happened to us. The furthermost and the hindermost wagons are in the greatest danger. The upmost room was occupied by the gentlemen, and the lowermost by the ladies. He is a profoundest philosopher. (Observe that the idiom of our language allows us to say, "*a most profound,*" but not, "*a profoundest.*") A clearer, more rapid and impetuous stream, flows from no other part of these mountains. *A more clear, rapid, and impetuous,* &c. The commissioners selected the firmest, narrowest, and shallowest part of the river, for the bridge.

b. Adjectives should not be doubly compared.

More greater calamities yet await us. After the most strictest sect of our religion I lived a Pharisee. The duke of Milan, and his more braver daughter. —*Shak.* This was the most unkindest cut of all. How much more are ye better than the fowls. There are few more politer men than he. The Most Highest shall judge between me and thee. Worser misfortunes yet await us. If he told that tale on me, he is the most meanest boy that ever was. I never heard a more truer saying. I think her less fairer than her sister. You came more earlier than I expected. A firmer's life is the most happiest of all.

Those were the least happiest days of my life. The worst may become more worse. —*still worse.* The most hindmost man was captured by the Indians. He was the most unluckiest of the speculators. The lesser quantity I remove to the other side of the equation. This was the most unwisest thing you could have done. She always dressed in the most costliest and finest silks. He fished at the most quiet and deepest place. —*the deepest and most quiet place;* or, —*the most deep and quiet place.*

c. A word that usually has an absolute meaning, should never be used in a limited sense, unless the language does not afford a better expression for the intended meaning.

His performance was the most perfect of all. —*best*— These artificial flowers are the most perfect I ever saw. (Perhaps allowable.) Virtue confers supremest dignity on man, and should be his chiefest desire. —*supreme . . . . chief desire.* A more rectangular figure would hold more. *A rectangular*— or, *A figure more nearly rectangular,* &c. I would rather have a squarer box. The roundest pebbles are found on the extremest part of the sand-bar. The heath-peach is more preferable than the Indian-peach. The report was not so universally spread as was supposed. —*not so generally or widely*— The most universal customs are apt to last longest. He has a most spotless reputation. Cotton and sugar are most principally raised in the Southern States. —*mostly raised*— or, *principally raised*— Her insolence is most insufferable. —*almost insufferable.* Aristides was the least unjust of the Athenians. Angelina is the least imperfect of her sex. I trust the people are more uncorrupted than their leaders. —*less corrupted*— I hope they will be more undeceivable in future. The side of a hill is more ineligible for a house, than the summit.

d. 1. The superlative must be used, when three or more are compared; and the comparative is usually required, when but two are compared.

The oldest of the two boys was sent to college. The youngest of the two sisters is the handsomest. He is the stouter of all the boys in our school. Which is the largest number,—the minuend or the subtrahend? Selim is the liveliest horse of the pair. The latter one of the three had forgotten his books. The house has but two stories, and the uppermost rooms are not yet finished. Women are the weakest sex. Which can run the fastest,—your horse or mine? His wife is the best manager; therefore let her rule him. Of the two Latin poets, Virgil and Horace, the first is the most celebrated. A trochee has the former syllable accented, and the latter unaccented.

2. The superlative degree represents the described objects as being a part of the others.

3. All comparisons without the superlative degree, do not strictly represent the objects denoted by one term, as being a part of those denoted by the other.

a. The word *other*, and similar terms, imply two distinct parts, and but one kind or general class.

That boy is the brightest of all his classmates. China has the greatest population of any nation on earth. Solomon was wiser than any of the ancient kings. Jacob loved Joseph more than all his children. Webster's spelling-book is the most popular of any yet published. Youth is the most important period of any in life. That grove is the shadiest and coolest place of any—of any others—of all others. Webster is one of the greatest orators of any country. —*may well be ranked among the greatest orators of any country.* Our grammar lessons are the hardest of any we have. This is a better-furnished room than any in the house. This is the best-furnished room of any in the house. There is nothing so good for a sprain as cold water. —*nothing else*—. He was less partial than any historian that ever wrote. —*any other*— It is a better treatise on this subject than any that ever was written. (The treatise could not be better than itself.) None of our magazines is so interesting to me as Harper's. *No other one of*, &c. Natural scenery pleases me the best of any thing else. Nothing pleases me so much as natural scenery. In no case is man so apt to act unjustly, as where his love or hatred interferes. Noah and his family outlived all the people who lived before the flood.—*N. Webster*. (They did not outlive themselves.) That tree overtops all the trees in the forest.

<blockquote>
Adam, the goodliest of men since born,
His sons; the fairest of her daughters, Eve.—*Milton*.
</blockquote>

4. *Position.*

1. Adjectives should be placed where they will show clearly what word or words they are to qualify or limit. The sense is the best guide.

a. Such an arrangement of words should be avoided, as will make the adjective modify any other than its proper word.

b. Of a series of coördinate adjectives that may be differently compared, it is generally more elegant to place the shorter ones before the longer.

Remark.—A noun with its adjective may be limited or qualified by another adjective, and these again by another, and so on. In such cases, the adjectives denoting the more casual qualities, usually precede the others. "An old man;" "A good old man;" "A venerable good old man;" "A stout venerable good old man;" "Two stout venerable good old men;" "The first two stout venerable good old men."

The congregation will please to sing the three first and the two last stanzas of the hymn. The four first benches are reserved for pupils; the others are for visitors. The three last mails brought me no letter. I have just bought a new pair of gloves. —*a pair of new gloves*. This is an excellent tract of land. The heads of the horses were all adorned with ribbons. He is a very young tall man. All were drowned except the captain and other three officers. If I be served such another trick, I'll have my brains taken out.—*Shak*. In a few more years, not even an Indian burial mound will be left untouched. The dress had a row of silk fancy green buttons, and strings of satin pink ribbon. He is one of the most influential and richest men in the city. There is not a more fertile, fairer, and more delightful valley west of the Mississippi. The eagle soared above the mountain high. He is the apparent heir to the crown. The convent is surrounded by a fifteen feet high and a three feet thick wall. —*a wall fifteen*— A large reward and pardon will be offered to the informer. *Pardon and a large reward,* &c.

OBSERVATIONS.

All and *whole* are sometimes misapplied, one for the other; and *less* is frequently misused for *fewer*. "The whole world"—All the world : but the plural phrases "All the apples," "The whole apples," are not equivalent; *all* being opposed to a part of the number, and *whole* to a part of each object. "The bear received no less than six balls." Say, "no fewer," or, "not fewer." *Less* is apt to suggest *quantity*, while *fewer* can suggest *number* only. Such phrases as "*one or more persons*" which Murray said should be "*one person, or more than one,*" are now considered allowable. "Every village or garrison has *one or more scape-goats* of this kind."—*Irving*.

Much that we now consider erroneous English, is merely old English that was once in fashion and in good repute. Of this kind are such forms as "*beautifuler, powerfulest, virtuousest.*" "Benedict is not the *unhopefullest* husband that I know."—*Shakespeare*.

Most adjectives may be taken either in an absolute or in a relative sense. In the former they suggest that the object has the quality in full, or, in what is usually considered the full state; in the latter, that it merely has *of the quality*. The latter sense must often be inferred from certain uses of the comparative or the superlative degree; and when these degrees are not used, it is usually expressed by the ending *ish*, or by means of such limiting terms as *somewhat, a little, partly, as—as*, &c. "My *worst* horse is *better* than your *best*, though neither one is really good." "I feel somewhat *better* to-day, though I am by no means *well*." "*Sadder* than the *saddest* night."—*Byron*. "Who canst the *wisest wiser* make, and babes as *wise* as they."—*Cowper*. "The poor man that loves Christ, is *richer* than the *richest* man that hates him."—*Bunyan*. "It is almost as *thin* as the *thinnest* paper."—*Chambers*. "And in the *lowest* deep a *lower* deep, still threatening to devour me, opens wide."—*Milton*. From these examples, which are all correct, we may infer that the comparative may sometimes be estimated from the superlative or the comparative; and that these degrees may occasionally be considered equal to or even below the positive, as well as above it.

1. The *comparative* may be estimated from the positive taken in the full or absolute sense; as, "Girard is *rich*, but Astor is still *richer*." "The pipers *loud* and *louder* blew, the dancers *quick* and *quicker* flew."—*Burns*. 2. It may imply a positive taken in a relative, or not in the full, sense; as, "If you have but five dollars, you are *richer* than I am." "A *fuller* explanation;" "A *less thorough* investigation;" "A *more perfect* system;" "A *less perfect* system." 3. Sometimes it is estimated from the comparative or the superlative; as, "My kite rose *higher, higher, higher*, and *higher*, until it was *highest*, and far *higher* than the *highest* of all the other kites." 4. The comparative may be estimated from the positive of some other quality or state; as, "He is *more intelligent* than *rich*." "They are *better clothed* than *fed*." 5. Sometimes it seems to be estimated from the comparative of the opposite quality; as, "The *wealthier* citizens were disposed to make peace, but the *poorer* were not." "The *higher* classes are generally well educated, but the *lower* are not." 6. Sometimes it implies that the increase or decrease of one quality proceeds uniformly with that of another; as, "The *older* the wine, the *better* it is." "The *sooner*, the *better*."

1. *Superlative* estimated from the positive absolute; as, "The *bravest* of the *brave*." 2. Superlative estimated from the positive taken in a relative or limited sense; as, "The creek was too shallow for dipping with a bucket, even where it was *deepest*." 3. Superlative estimated from the comparative or the superlative; as, "The *ripest* of the *riper* peaches were delicious." "The *finest* of the *finest* horses took the sweepstakes." (I think that the last two sentences are proper.)

The superlative degree seems not always to imply an intervening comparative, but sometimes to be estimated directly from the positive of the same quality; as, "The *last* years of his practice were more lucrative than the *first*." "The *highest* classes are generally rich and haughty" [but the *lowest* classes are poor and humble]. "He sold the *largest* apples, and made the others into cider." In fact, this degree seems to be allowable in speaking of two, when the design is not so much to show that one is superior to the other, as to suggest that there is none above it or beyond it that is superior to it; in other words, when we do not look back to the inferior objects, but rather look for superior objects and find none. "The *farthest* house on the peninsula is my residence," could be said if there were but two houses on the peninsula. "An iambus has the *first* syllable unaccented, and the *last* accented." "*This* refers to the *nearest* object; *that*, to something more distant." "His antagonist made the *ablest* speech;" *i. e.*, I heard none that was better. Sometimes, also, the comparative tends to suggest proportion.

It is worthy of notice, that many qualities or attributes exist in more degrees, or in much greater variety, than the degrees of comparison can express. Other modes of expression are therefore often used to show degrees or varieties of the quality, and frequently with fine effect. "A *light*-green—*dark*-green—*emerald*-green—*pea*-green color." "*Pink* red, *crimson* red, *saffron* red, *strawberry* red, *bluish* re-

ADJECTIVES.—OBSERVATIONS.

(—purple)." "*Boiling* hot, *stark* mad, *stone* dead, *dead* drunk." "She is *most* beautiful—*incomparably* beautiful—*angelic*." "She appeared in a *snow*-white dress, and a rich *saffron*-colored shawl." Poets take greater liberty, in the use of adjectives, than is allowed to prose writers; as, "That *heavenliest* hour of Heaven is worthiest thee!"—*Byron.* "And you shall see who has the *properest* notion."—*Id.* "A foot *more light*, a step *more true.*"—*Scott.* Perhaps in light literature, such expressions as the following are quite proper: "Her husband was none of the *soberest.*"—*Dickens.* "None of the *most sober*," would here, I think, sound rather stiff and affected. *More* and *most* are sometimes preferred in prose, for greater emphasis, or to express the degree of a shorter and a longer adjective in the briefest uniform manner; as, "He is *more bold* and *active*," for, "He is *bolder* and *more active.*" "She is a most bright, polished, and amiable young lady." *Most* is usually required after *a* or *an*, or to express the superlative of eminence; s, "A most polite gentleman;" "A most queer sight." Such adjectives as *perfect, round, extreme, correct, blind,* and *still,* are sometimes compared when not used in their full sense. "More perfect"—*nearer to perfection;* "most perfect"—*nearest to perfection:* both implying less than *perfect.* It has been well argued, that if "*greater perfection*" is an allowable phrase, why should not "*more perfect*" be *allowable*. To say, "She is the least imperfect of her sex," would imply that the whole sex is quite imperfect. "Aristides was the least unjust of the Athenians," is as much as to say, "The Athenians were all unjust,—a set of knaves, of whom Aristides was only not the worst one." The adjectives should have been. "most perfect," "most just." Such expressions as "the most unconquerable," "the less imperfect," "the least imperfect," "the more unnecessary," "the most unbecoming," "the most unnatural," "most uncertain," "a most superior," "a most inferior," "the most blameless," "the most worthless," "a fuller," "the most complete," "the completest," "a most thorough," "the straightest," "a straighter," "a more reddish," "a less yellowish," &c., are all, in certain cases, allowable.

Many, more, most, have for their opposites *few, fewer, fewest; much, more, most,* have *little, less, least; great, greater, greatest,* have *little, small, less, lesser* (implying dignity), *smaller, least, smallest. Lesser* should generally be rejected; though it is sometimes used, by good writers, in opposition to *greater.* Also the phrase "Lesser Asia," is sometimes used for the more elegant phrase "Asia Minor." *Worse* is itself a comparative, therefore *worser* must be a double comparative, which is improper. So is "most happiest," for instance, a double superlative, and therefore improper. Adjectives should not even seem to be doubly compared; thus, "A more elegant and simpler method," might be supposed to mean, "A more elegant and *more simpler* method." It should be, "A simpler and more elegant method," or, "A more simple and elegant method."

"A tobacco-seed is the least of any other seed—of all other seeds—of any seed —less than any seed;" "There is no seed so small as a tobacco-seed." That is, a tobacco-seed is a seed of some other kind of seed, or it is smaller than itself—absurdities. "The *weakest* of the two." That is, one is weaker than the other; therefore say, "The *weaker* of the two."

"An old pair of shoes." The meaning is not that the pair is old, but that the shoes are old; hence say, "A pair of old shoes." There are some ambiguities in regard to adjectives, that must be left to the discernment of common sense, for they can not be well avoided unless we use the hyphen; and this mark would generally make the expressions too uncouth. Said a gentleman to a lady, "That is a *beautiful* child's cap;" and she replied, "If it is not bought for an *ugly* one." "*Large* Bread Bakery." Is the *bread* large, or the *bakery?* "*Cincinnati* Boys' School." A critical wag said, that only the boys belonging to Cincinnati could attend the school. "A child's *beautiful* cap," seems affected, and may imply that every child has also an *ugly* cap; though we must say, "A child's *black* cap." When I say, "*Five* thousand *two* hundred and thirty-five dollars," each small numeral relates to the larger next to it, and the entire phrase to the noun; and when I say, "That distinguished venerable old man," each adjective modifies all that follows it: hence an adjective may relate either to the next word or to the next two or more words. "The American Artificial Teeth Company." And even, "I have just bought a fine suit of clothes," is perhaps allowable; for *fine* may relate to the *fit, correspondence,* and *cloth.* "A fine collection of gems."—*Macaulay.*

When such words as *first* and *last* are used with plural numerals, the sense usually requires them before the plurals; as, "The first three," "The last four," not, "The three first," "The four last." So, "The first six men," "The last two men," "The last ten rows," even if there should not be enough for twice the number, or for "A last six," "A first two," "A first ten." But usage, or the state of things, may sometimes allow a different arrangement; for instance, it would certainly be correct to say, "The four first trees of the four rows." If "The first six French kings," should suggest the idea of six kings ruling at once, I would rather say, "The six first French kings;" but, if this phrase should express the meaning no better than the other, I would prefer the other. We usually say, "For the next five years," "The last two out of three," "The best six out of eleven;" and not, "For the five next years," "The two last," &c. But we say, "The two hindmost wheels;" for one is as far back as the other. "The two foremost horses," is also correct. We would hardly say, "The laziest two boys," but, "The two laziest boys;" for the former phrase would suggest that they are in some way united as a pair, which is not our meaning.

In favor of "The first two—three—five," "The last four—six," &c., may be urged—1. *Analogy:* we always say, in speaking of large numbers, "The first twenty—last twenty," &c.; not, "The twenty first—thirty last;" we also say, "The next five." 2. *Authority:* grammarians, and good writers generally, give this form the preference. *Against:* The expressions may suggest that the entire number is divided into at least two such groups, which may be neither true nor possible; as, "The first four acts of the play." (The whole play having but five acts.) *In favor of* "The two first," "The last four," &c., may be urged—1. That they avoid the grouping; 2. That many good writers not unfrequently use them. *Against:* That the phraseology is apt to suggest, that there can be more firsts or lasts than one when this is not strictly true. In short, all other things being equal, I should prefer the first form given above; but, if the latter would express my meaning better, I should not hesitate to use it. The German language, I believe, favors the latter form.

Adjectives may either precede or follow the substantives, but their position has sometimes a great influence on the energy of the sentence; as, "*Excellent* as the present version of the Bible is, still we believe," &c. "*Great* is Diana of the Ephesians." "*Bright* flashed the clouds, and loud the thunder rolled." "*Young* she was, and *rich*, and *beautiful*." "*Sublime* on radiant spheres he trod." "It was a *clear* morning, *bright* and *balmy*." "So that our whole company, *young* and *old*, *rotten* and *sound*, did not amount to more than fifty men." "The scattered clouds *tumultuous* rove." "The interminable sky *sublimer* swells." "Goodness *infinite*." "Woe *unutterable*." "She was a woman *heartless*, *talented*, and *ambitious*." "*Sagacious* in policy and *prompt* in action, his whole life was a brilliant career." Observe that the adjective, preceded by *the* and not followed by a noun, sometimes denotes persons, and sometimes the abstract quality; as, "The *humorous* may please us more than the *witty*." This may mean, "The humorous man, or humorous people in general, may please," &c.; or, "Humor may please us better than wit."

An adjective immediately preceding two or more nouns in the same construction, is usually understood as qualifying them all; hence, "His luncheon was a small biscuit and cheese," was perhaps meant for, "His luncheon was cheese and a small biscuit."

8. VERBS.

238. A **verb** is a word used to affirm something of a subject.

239. The **verb** is the part of speech whose chief use is, to make the predicates of propositions. Almost every verb denotes some kind of action or state. And *affirmations*, with grammarians, mean all kinds of assertions; also commands and questions.

Ex.—"The horse *ran* up the street." "The thunder *rolls*." "Sweet *blooms* the rose." "Sodom and Gomorrah *were destroyed* by fire from heaven." "Troy *was*, but *is* no more." "Fairies *are* beings of the fancy." "The clouds *parting*, the moon *shone* through." "Some *are born to creep.*" "I *saw* her *weeping.*" "He *did* not *order* the carriage *to be sent* away." "I *said, Go;* and he *went.*" "Who *would* not *have resisted,* if he *had been* thus *attacked ?*"

The essential or chief characteristic of the verb is, to *predicate,* or to *say* something of something; and hence the Germans call it the *say-word.*

240. The verb *be,* then, when used affirmatively, to bind together a subject and an attribute, must be the *purest* and *greatest* or *fundamental* verb. If I say, "God love," "The world beautiful," the words are lifeless; but the moment *is* is inserted, it indicates at once the presence of an observing and rational being, animates the lifeless parts, and a thought, *judgment,* or TRUTH, is born! "God *is* love." "The world *is* beautiful."

241. The verb *be,* when used to bind together the subject and its attribute into a proposition, is called the *copula.*

As we can not well conceive an abstract relation between two objects, without adding to it something else belonging to them, or forming a *complex* idea, most verbs comprise the sense of the verb *be,* and something additional, that is, some kind of *action* or *state.*

When a verb is actually used to express affirmation, it is called a *finite* verb; but there are two forms of the verb which do not express affirmations, and are called the *participle* and the *infinitive.* For we may also conceive an act or state abstractly, or else without predicating it. And it is chiefly by means of these two forms, or parts, that the verb passes out into other parts of speech; that is, not only retains, to some extent, the nature of a verb, but also participates that of an adjective, an adverb, or a noun.

242. The **participle** is a form of the verb, that merely assumes the act or state, and is generally construed like an adjective.

Ex.—"I saw the oak WHITE with snow; "I saw the oak *riven* by a thunderbolt." "The grass is GREEN;" "The grass is *growing.*" "John *being struck.*"

243. The **infinitive** is a form of the verb that begins generally with *to,* and expressing no affirmation.

Ex.—"The farm is *to be sold.*" "The jailor is supposed *to have let* the prisoner [to] *escape.*"

Classes.

Verbs are classified, according to their form, and their construction in sentences,—

Into *regular* and *irregular.*

Into *transitive* and *intransitive;* and the transitive verbs are often used as *passive,* and some of the intransitive are always *neuter.*

244. A **regular** verb takes the ending *ed* to form its preterit and its perfect participle.

Ex.—"Plant, *planted, planted;* carry, *carried, carried;* rebel, *rebelled, rebelled*

245. An **irregular** verb does not take the ending *ed,* to form its preterit and its perfect participle. See pp. 13-16.

Ex.—"Sweep, *swept, swept;* cling, *clung, clung;* cut, *cut, cut.*"

The **principal parts** of a verb are the *present,* or the simplest form as registered in a dictionary; the *preterit,* or the simplest form of the past indicative; and the *perfect participle,* or the form that will make sense with the word *having* or *being* before it. To these may be added the *present participle*, which, as it ends always in *ing*, is too well known to need mentioning.

By means of these parts and the auxiliary verbs, all the other parts of verbs are formed.

The *present*, if traced back in dictionaries, is the present infinitive or the present indicative form; but it would perhaps be as well to consider it the present imperative.

The irregular verbs are the oldest, and perhaps the heart of the language.

Regular verbs never become irregular, except that *ed* is sometimes shortened nto *t*.

Irregular verbs sometimes become regular.

All newly made verbs brought into the language, assume the regular ending.

246. A prefix, joined to a verb, does not change the form of the principal parts.

Ex.—" Go, *undergo, underwent, undergone;* give, *misgive, forgive;* do, *undo;* hold, *withhold;* act, *counteract;* say, *gainsay. Exception:* Welcome.

247. A **transitive** verb has an object, or requires one to complete the sense.

Ex.—"The lightning *struck* the OAK." "WHOM *did* you *see?*" "The garden *has* FLOWERS." "I *knew* HIM well, and every truant *knew.*" "*Avoid* GIVING OFFENSE." "I *dislike* TO DO it." "He *commanded* | the soldier to be brought." "I *know* | how deeply liberty is rooted in the hearts of these people."

248. A **passive** verb is a transitive verb so used that it represents its subject as acted upon, or has the object for its subject.

Ex.—" James killed a snake; "A snake *was killed* by James." "I will plant a cedar over her grave;" "A cedar *shall be planted* over her grave."

249. An **intransitive** verb does not require an object to complete the sense.

Ex.—" Birds *fly.*" " Roses *bloom.*" " Martha *learns* fast." "*Acquire* in youth, that you *may enjoy* in age." " Gamblers *cheat.*"

250. A **neuter** verb is an intransitive verb that does not imply action or exertion.

Ex.—"The ocean *is* deep." "The book *lies* on the table." "Here *sleep* the brave." Since existence is a more general idea than action or motion, the *neuter* verbs, though few in number, range farther than all the *active* verbs.

251. The same word is sometimes used as a transitive, and sometimes as an intransitive, verb.

Ex.—" The prince SUCCEEDS the *king;*" "In every undertaking he *succeeds.*" "To SET *trees* in a row;" " The sun *sets.*"

252. A verb usually *transitive*, sometimes becomes *intransitive*. The intention, in such cases, is, to ascribe simply a certain act or state, and to leave the object designedly unknown or indefinite: the mind dwells upon the act, rather than upon the object affected by it.

Ex.—" She *reads* well." " He *studies* in the morning, and *rides* in the evening." "I keep his house, and I *wash, wring, brew, bake, scour,* dress meat, and make the beds, and do all myself."—*Shakespeare.*

253. A verb usually *intransitive*, sometimes becomes *transitive*.

This occurs, when the verb is used in a causative sense; when the object is like the verb in meaning; and in certain poetic expressions.

Ex.—" *To march* armies ;" *i. e.*, to cause them to march. "*To live* a righteous life." "*To die* a miserable death." "*To blow* a louder blast." "*To look* daggers." (See also Rule VI.) " Eyes *looked* love—*looked* pity." ."Death *grinned* a ghastly smile." " The lightnings *flashed* a brighter curve." In many such instances, the verb shows how the object is expressed or made; or else the object characterizes the verb.

From some intransitive verbs are derived corresponding transitive verbs.

Ex.—Lie, *lay;* sit, *set, seat;* fall, *fell;* rise, *raise;* drink, *drench.*

254. Sometimes the object is combined with the verb so closely as to make in sense almost a part of it; and sometimes the object is identical with the subject, merely completes the sense, and implies no transfer of the act.

Ex.—" To take *care* of; to lose *sight* of; to lay *hold* of." " To bestir *oneself;* to bethink *oneself;* to conduct *oneself* well; to feign *oneself* sick; to laugh *oneself* hoarse ;" " He slept *himself* weary ;" " He drank *himself* dead drunk."

Properties.

VERBS have **voices, moods, tenses, persons,** and **numbers.**

Voices, in general, relate to action ; *moods*, to reality ; *tenses*, to time; and *persons* and *numbers* show the nominative, wherever in the sentence it may be.

Voices.

The *voices* are rather absorbed in the foregoing classification of verbs; yet, considering the importance of the subject, and its treatment in the grammars of other languages, I have retained them.

The **voices** are two modes of expressing transitive verbs.

They are called the *active* voice and the *passive.*

255. The **active** voice represents the subject as acting, or the verb as relating to an object.

Ex.—"The laborers *gather* corn." " The frost *broke* the pitcher." " The girls *are learning* their lessons." " John *resembles* his father." "The house *has* a portico."

256. The **passive** voice represents the subject as acted upon, or the verb as having the object for its subject.

Ex.—" The pitcher *was broken.*" "Many hogs *are driven* to market." " The bridge *is building.*" "*To be ridiculed* is unpleasant."

257. Transitive verbs may sometimes be used as passive verbs, even in the active form. Such verbs often denote, not so much the receiving of the act, as the capacity to receive it in a certain way.

Ex.—" This timber *saws* well." " Sycamore *splits* badly." "This field *ploughs* well." " Linen *wears* better than cotton." "Your poem *reads* smoothly." "Wheat *sells—is selling—is sold* for a dollar a bushel." "I could easily see what *was doing* on the other side of the river." "Virgil describes some spirits as *bleaching* in the winds, others as *cleansing* under great falls of water, and others as *purging* in fire, to recover the primitive beauty and purity of their nature."—*Ad-*

dison. "Be assured he has an ax *to grind.*" "There is no work *to do.*" Such infinitive expressions, however, may be considered elliptical; as, "There is no work [for us] *to do.*"

258. The *present participle*, when not combined with any other verbal form, is generally active; and the *perfect participle*, passive.

Ex.—"Close beside her, faintly *moaning*, fair and young, a soldier lay, *Torn* with shot and *pierced* with lances, *bleeding* slow his life away."
Whittier.

259. A few intransitive verbs are sometimes used in the passive form. This is a French idiom; and the verbs are not passive.

Ex.—"He *is fallen.*" "She *is gone.*" "The melancholy days *are come.*" Equivalent to *has fallen, has gone, have come;* but, "John *is struck,*" is not the same as, "John *has struck.*" The passive form seems to differ from the active, by an elegant shade of meaning: in the former, the mind dwells rather on *the state of things after the act;* in the latter, *on the act itself.*

260. A few intransitive verbs may be made passive, when their meaning is combined with a following preposition or other word. Such a verb with the modification may be termed a *compound passive verb.*

Ex.—"Col. Butler *was* accordingly *written to*, and ordered to hasten forward with the volunteers."—*Irving.* "*Had* Monmouth really *been sent for* to the Hague?"—*Macaulay.* "An honest man *will be* well *thought of*, and *looked* up *to.*" "If you wear such a coat, you *will be laughed at*"—*ridiculed.* "He *was smiled on* by fortune"—*favored.* "He *was* justly *dealt with*"—*treated.* "My claim *was lost sight of.*" The modification is so closely combined in sense with the verb, that it seems to make a part of it.

261. Hence we see that the object of the active verb, sometimes that of the preposition, is made the subject of the passive verb.

But when the object of the preposition or that of the infinitive is made the subject, the expression is sometimes too inelegant to be allowed. "WEIGHTS and MEASURES *were now attempted to be established.*"—*Carlyle.*

262. Transitive verbs may be used, at pleasure, either *actively* or *passively*. By having both forms, language is enriched in variety of expression. The active voice, however, sets forth chiefly the doer with the kind of action performed by him; the passive voice, the object with the kind of action affecting it, and also enables us to avoid changing the subject. The active can be used without the object, the passive without the agent; each of which it is sometimes not possible, not important, or not desirable, to mention.

Ex.—"WASHINGTON *defended* our country;" "Our COUNTRY *was defended* by Washington." "BASCOM *preached* in Kentucky, and CAMPBELL *disputed* in Virginia?" (Who did? and did what?) "The WORK *was done*, notwithstanding BE *refused* to touch it." "I *went* to the river, *was ferried* over, and *saw* the procession." "My MOTIVES *were slandered.*" "The ship *was stranded.*"

Moods.

The **moods** are certain modes of expressing the verb in regard to its subject. MOOD expresses the *manner* of assertion.

There are five moods; the *indicative*, the *subjunctive*, the *potential*, the *imperative*, and the *infinitive*.

263. The **indicative** mood affirms something as an actual occurrence or fact.

Ex.—"Columbus *discovered* America." "The bank *has failed*." "The trees *are budding*." "The peaches *will be* ripe." "If the bank *has failed*." "If the peaches *shall be* ripe." "*Are* you sick?" "Who never *fasts*, no banquet e'er enjoys." "Then, if thou *fall'st*, thou *fall'st* a blessed martyr."

A proposition, having a verb in the indicative mood, may be *declarative, interrogative*, or *negative*. It may also express a *condition* or an *inference;* for what is not known as being actually in existence, may nevertheless be assumed as matter of fact.

---

264. The **subjunctive** mood affirms something as a future contingency, or as a mere supposition, wish, or conclusion. See p. 207.

Ex.—"If he *be* studious, he will excel." "If he *were* studious, he would excel." "If he *had been* studious, he would have excelled." "If you *be* rich"— *a condition not improbable*. "If you *were* rich"—*a supposition without fact.* "O, that you *were* rich"—*a mere wish.* "Though he *deceive* me, yet will I trust in him." It is not certain that he will deceive me. "Till the owner *present* himself, I will keep it." I do not think it certain that he will. "Except ye *be born* again, ye can not enter the kingdom of heaven." Ye may be born again, or ye may not. "Beware, lest thou *be led* into temptation." There is not a certainty, yet a liability. So, "See that no one *go* astray—*be forgotten*." "If a common bottle *were filled* with water, and *plunged* under the oil until it *reached* . . . . it would remain." &c.—*Dr. Arnot*. It may be done, or it may not; the actual occurrence is not denied. "The wicked sometimes conduct themselves in such a manner as if they *expected* no punishment for their sins."—*Addison*. They may expect it, or they may not; the author does not positively deny that they do. "If all *knew* their duty, and *appreciated* their responsibilities, there would be less calamity in the world."—*Dr. Shannon*. The author denies that they do. "O, that I *were* as when my mother pressed me to her bosom, and sung the warlike deeds of the Mohawks." But I am not. "*Had* I *heard* of the affair sooner, this accident *had* not *happened*." But I did not, and it happened. "I *had* rather pay [infinitive] the debt at once, than be his security." An ideal view: it is not said that I do pay. ("I *had* [*subjunctive*] rather [to] have lost [infinitive] my money, than my manuscript," is not elegant English, though perhaps hardly incorrect.) "*Were* it so, I would consent." A mere supposition. "It *were* useless," &c. "It *had been* useless," &c. A mere conclusion. "If it *rains*," is *indicative*, and implies that the speaker does not know whether it is *now* actually raining or not. "If it *rain*," is *subjunctive*, and implies that the speaker does not know whether it *will* rain or not. "If it *was raining*," is *indicative*, referring to a past fact, and implies that the speaker does not know whether it did actually rain or not. "If it *were raining*," is *subjunctive*, referring to a present act denied, and implies that the speaker is merely supposing a case. "If this *is* treason, make the most of it," is *indicative*, and decides the matter *now*, or supposes it decided. "If this *be* treason, make the most of it," is *subjunctive*, and refers the matter to *future* decision or judicial investigation.

The subjunctive mood has three tenses: the *present*, the *past* or *aorist* (=indefinite), and the *pluperfect;* generally equivalent in time to a future, a present, and a past tense,—tenses sufficient, yet needed, for all the purposes of this mood. See pp. 20 and 26.

It remains almost entirely unchanged throughout the same tense, and shows its peculiarity of form chiefly in the verb *be*. See p. 26.

265. In its form, it is most like the indicative mood; in sense, more like the potential, with which it is also most frequently associated, and into which it may often be converted. See above, also pp. 25–26.

When a verb in this mood refers to past or present time, it generally, but not always, implies a denial of the fact; when to future time, that the fact is uncertain or contingent. See the examples above.

266. To a verb in this mood, some auxiliary verb—*shall, will, may, should*—may in most instances be understood, without materially varying the sense; provided the auxiliary be conceived as expressing time or contingence, and not resolution, necessity, obligation, &c.

Ex.—" If he *be* at home, I shall go to see him"—If he *shall be* at home, &c. " If thou ever *return*, thou shouldst be thankful"—If thou *shouldst* ever *return* &c. " Beware that thou *come* not to poverty ;" *i. e.*, that thou *mayst* not *come* to poverty.

267 A verb in the subjunctive mood generally has, or may have, *if, though, unless, except, whether, that, till,* or some equivalent word before t. The clause perhaps always implies another. expressed or understood; nd hence the mood is called *subjunctive*, which means *joined to*.

It should not be supposed, however, that these preceding words produce the mood, or change the form of the verb. It is rather the state of mind, under which the verb is set forth, that produces the mood, and requires or allows the conditional word before it.

268. The **potential** mood affirms merely the power, liberty, liability, necessity, will, duty, or a similar relation of the subject in regard to the act or state.

Ex.—" It *may* rain." " You *can go—could go—must go—should go—would go—might go*." " I *would go* with you, if I *could spare* the time." " When John Gilpin rides again, *may* I *be* there to see."

When an act or state is expressed in this mood, it may take place, or not. It is not the business of the mood to show whether it does or not, but merely what relation the subject bears to it.

269. To express this mood, we combine with the verb—the infinitive form without the sign *to*—the word *may, can, must, might, could, would,* or *should,* and sometimes perhaps *shall* in the sense of *must,* or *will* in the sense of *would* or *to be willing.*

This mood is, in fact, *composite ;* its forms being composed of indicative and infinitive, of subjunctive and infinitive, or of imperative and infinitive, elements. The sign *to* of the infinitive being omitted in combination. *Indic.* + *infin.:* "I knew he *could* | *learn* it ;" "He *would* | *go* then ;" " We *must* | *endure* it ;" " I *can* | *pay* him." *Subjunc.* + *infin.* : " She *could* | *sing* if she *would ;*" " I *might* | *learn* the lesson ;" " I *should* | hardly *believe* you even then ;" " I *might* | *have written* to him, had I known it ;" " Study, that you *may* | *learn.*" *Imper.* + *infin.:* "*May* you | *prosper ;*" "*May* it | *please* your honors." When the auxiliary element adheres to the time usually given to its tense, it is *indicative;* but when it does not, or, like *subjuntives*, moves forward in time, or becomes indefinite in time, it is *subjunctive.*

270. The **imperative** mood expresses command, exhortation, entreaty, or permission.

Ex.—" *Charge*, Chester, *charge !*" " *Do* nothing that your heart tells you is wrong." "*Do come* to see us." "*Depart* in peace."

The act or state may or may not take place. If it takes place, it must be after the command itself, which is always expressed in present time, or in what is considered so at the time referred to. As we always speak to some person or thing when we command, this mood has the second person only; and the subject of the verb is *thou, you,* or *ye,* which is nearly always understood. But sometimes this mood is used in other persons or in the perfect tense.

Ex.—" *Have done* thy charms, thou hateful, withered hag."—*Shakespeare.* "Somebody *call* my wife."—*Id.* " This mortal house I'll ruin, *do* Cæsar what he can."—*Id.* "*Laugh* those who can, *weep* those who may."—*Scott.* " ' Now *tread* we a measure !' said young Lochinvar."—*Id.* (Now *let* us *tread*, etc.) " *Fall* he that must, beneath his rival's arms."—*Pope.* " Whoever comes this way—*behold* and tremble."—*Pollok.* "*Be* it this day *enacted.*" "*Be* it so."—*Webster.* "*Perish* my name, and *perish* my memory, provided Switzerland may be free."—*Tell.*

"Ruin *seize* thee, ruthless king; confusion on thy banners *wait.*"—*Gray.* Whether such verbs as some of the last should be parsed as imperative, or as potential having *may* understood, it is not always easy to decide. Perhaps it is best to parse them as IMPERATIVES *expressing a mingled wish and command.* The speaker commands in what he proposes to bear a part himself; or he commands, so far as he can, what is absent, inanimate, unknown to him, or not under his absolute control. The expressions are all rather poetical or rhetorical.

271. The imperative mood is sometimes used when there is but a slight or no reference to a person addressed, to express more modestly the intention or will of the speaker.

Ex.—God said, "*Let* there be light." "*Allow* me to congratulate you."

272. The **infinitive** mood expresses the act or state without affirming it. It comprises the participle and the infinitive.

Ex.—To slay; to have slain; to be slain; to have been slain. Slaying; having slain; being slain; having been slain. "*Having spoken,* he arose." "*He arose speaking.*" "He arose *to speak.*" "The deer, *having seen* me, tried *to escape.*"

"The infinitive mode so called is the crude-form of the verb. It is the verb divested of all modality. It is no mode at all."—*J. W. Gibbs.* Again, "The infinitive and participle have no claim to be considered as modes. They are participials."—*Id.* And, "Under the general name of *participial* we include the participles, the infinitive mode, the gerund, and the supine."—*Id.*

The following reasons why I have classed participles and infinitives together, must suffice: 1. They are both without affirmation. 2. They are similarly combined with the auxiliary verbs to form the compound tenses. 3. They may both be used as substantives. 4. They are sometimes interchangeable. 5. They both express time relatively, and not, like finite verbs, absolutely. 6. The infinitive sometimes supplies the place of a future participle. 7. Other languages sometimes use one form where we would use the other. 8. The remarks of eminent grammarians and scholars, on the subject. See Kühner, Whately, Anthon, Becker.

273. Almost the same sense may sometimes be expressed by a different mood.

Ex.—"I came that I *might assist* you—*to assist* you." "*May* you always *love* virtue;" "*Do* always *love* virtue." "You *will* not *hurt* him?" "*Do* not *hurt* him." Mild imperatives. "It *would be* useless;" "It *were* useless." "*Deny* us pleasure, and you unfit us for business;" "*If* you deny us," etc. Emphatic condition.

Should the subjunctive mood ever disappear entirely from our language, then the best classification of moods will be into three; the *indicative,* the *imperative,* and the *infinitive.*

Tenses.

The **tenses** are the forms and meanings of the verb in regard to time.

There are six tenses; the *present,* the *past,* the *future,* the *perfect,* the *pluperfect,* and the *future-perfect.*

TIME may be divided into *present, past,* and *future. Present time,* strictly speaking, can denote but a moment of duration; yet longer periods, extending into both the future and the past, are often considered present; as when we say, *this day, this week, this year, this century, in our lifetime. Past time* begins from the present, and extends back as far as our thoughts can wander; *future time* begins from the same point, and goes forward to a similar extent. In each of these periods, an act may be considered as merely occurring or continuing, or as completed or ended,—thus making *six tenses.* To each period belongs also a sort of future tense, expressed by *about* and the infinitive, and sometimes called the *periphrastic future;* as, "I *was about to study.*" But the following—to be read both down and across the page—may be more intelligible to the learner:—

204   VERBS.—TENSES.

PRESENT.	PAST.	FUTURE.
I write	I wrote	I shall write
I have written	I had written	I shall have written
I am about to write	I was about to write	I shall be about to write
I am writing	I was writing	I shall be writing
I have been writing	I had been writing	I shall have been writing.

It seems best to define the tenses according to their *forms*, and in *every mood*.

274. The **present indicative** denotes what now exists, or is going on.

Ex.—" This *is* a warm day." " The grass *is growing* in the meadow."

What is now habitual or customary.

Ex.—" He *chews* tobacco." " People *go* to church on Sunday."

Universal truths.

Ex.—" Heat *melts* snow." "Virtue *produces* happiness." "Drunkards seldom *reform*."

Past or future transactions with greater vividness or certainty.

Ex.—" The combat *deepens*. On, ye brave!" " Do this, and thou *diest!*"

Future events, in connection with words that carry the scene into future time. Generally after relatives, *when, as soon as*, &c.

Ex.—" When he *comes*, I will go." " Catch whatever *comes*."

The actions or qualities of authors as observed in their works now existing.

Ex.—" Seneca *reasons* and *moralizes* well." " Milton *is* sublime."

275. The **present subjunctive** implies future time.

Ex.—" If it *rain*, our flowers will live." Physical. " If this *be* true." Mental.

276. The **present potential** is present or future in regard to both the mood and the act or state.

Ex.—" He *may | be coming*." " I *can | pay* you next Christmas."

277. The **present imperative** is present in regard to the mood, and future in regard to the act or state.

Ex.—"*Return* soon." "*Pour* out the rich juices still bright with the sun." " I said, *Go*." So vivid is this mood, that it can easily and readily set forth a scene as present in any period of time.

278. The **present participle** denotes continuance of the act or state, at the time referred to.

Ex.—" Before us lay the lake *glittering* in the sun."

279. The **present infinitive** denotes simply the act or state, or as present or future at the time referred to.

Ex.—" A lesson hard *to learn*." " She seems *to sleep*." " I intended *to say* less."

280. The **past indicative** denotes simply what occurred in past time.

Ex.—" He *was fishing* when I saw him." " If he ever *was* there."

What was habitual or customary.

Ex.—" The good times, when the farmer *entertained* the traveler without pay,' &c.—*Benton*.

281. The **past subjunctive** denotes present or indefinite time, seldom past or future; and it generally denies the act or state.

Ex.—" If I *were* rich, I would give freely." " He ran as if he *were running* for life." " If I *were* to admit the pledge, he would then say," &c. See p. 20.

282. The **past potential** may be present, past, or future in regard to both the mood and the act or state. It presents the act or state as real, contingent, or denied.

Ex.—" He *would* | *go*." " I *should* | then *buy* it." " If I *could* | *buy* it, I *would*."

It denotes what was habitual or customary.

Ex.—" There *would* she *sit* and *weep* for hours."

When this tense does not denote past time, it may be called *aorist*, which means *indefinite*.

283. The **future** tense denotes simply what will take place hereafter.

Ex.—" The snow *will melt*." " I *shall be* at home this evening."

What will be habitual or customary.

Ex.—" You *will* then *beg*." " The steer and lion at one crib *shall meet*."

284. The **perfect indicative** represents something as past, but still connected with present time.

Ex.—" I *have lost* my knife." " They *have been married* twenty years."

a. It implies that the doer, or what the subject denotes, yet exists, and that the act or state may be repeated.

Ex.—" I *have read* Virgil many times." " Gen. Scott *has gained* several victories."

b. That the act or state (begun in the past), and of course that to which it belongs, yet exist.

Ex.—" This house *has stood* twelve years." " Thus *has* it *flowed* for ages."

c. That the result yet exists, though the actor or act may be no more.

Ex.—" Cicero *has written* orations." " Washington *has left* his example to the world."

This tense is peculiarly well adapted to express many of the relations which past things have to present things. It shows that past events, without any thing intervening, come down to us in their consequences, causes, or circumstances. It usually implies that the time in which the act occurred or began, and the present time, with perhaps some of the future, are viewed as one unbroken period. " Many who *have been saluted* with the huzzas of the crowd one day, *have received* its execrations the next; and many, who, by the popularity of their own times, *have been held* up as spotless patriots, *have*, nevertheless, *appeared* on the historian's page, when truth *has triumphed* over delusion, the assassins of liberty."— *Mansfield*. That is to say, Things have always been so, and will continue to be so, while human nature remains what it is. " And where the Atlantic rolls, wide continents *have bloomed*."—*Beattie*. That is to say, In the great chain of events extending through all time, this remarkable one actually occurred; and who shall say what strange things may yet happen ? In stead of taking a day, a year, or a lifetime, as present time, the poet grasps, and glances over, all duration as one unbroken period in which he speaks. Or the sentences may imply that these things have been handed down historically or traditionally to even the present time.

285. This tense, preceded by relatives, *when, as soon as,* &c., may sometimes express future events.
Ex.—" When you *have seen* Niagara Falls, write to me."
The **perfect imperative** commands the ending of something begun.
Ex.—" *Have done* thy charms."—*Shak.* "*Do*"= Begin and do. "*Have done*"= Make an end of what you are now doing. This perfect is very seldom used.

286. The **perfect potential** is present or future in regard to the mood, and presents the act or state as relatively past.
Ex.—" The child *may | have fallen* into the well." " Then he *may | have gone* ahead of you."

287. The **perfect participle** and the **compound** denote the completion, sometimes the continuance, of the act or state, at the time referred to.
Ex.—" This is a coat *made* by the machine." " He lives *loved* by all." "*Being* already *enlisted*, and *having bought* my outfit, I refused to turn back."

The **compound participle** which has the auxiliary *having*, is generally equivalent in time to the pluperfect, the perfect, or the future-perfect indicative.
Ex.—" The sun *having risen*, we departed"='When the sun *had risen*, we departed. "*Having found* a pleasant home, he is content and happy." "*Having succeeded* in this speculation, you will then of course venture upon a greater."

288. The **perfect infinitive** represents the act or state as past at the time referred to.
Ex.—" My business shall appear *to have been* well *conducted.*"
The *perfect* and the *future-perfect subjunctive* also occur in old or antique English.

289. The **pluperfect indicative** represents something as finished or ended by a certain past time.
Ex.—" Here a small cabin *had been erected.*" " The cars *had started* when we came there."

It is not always necessary to use this tense, merely because the act or state was finished or ended by a certain past time.
Ex.—" Little John *was* up before daylight;" " The horse *jumped* into the field, and soon afterwards *began* to eat the corn,"—are proper, and not the same as,——" *had been up*"——, ——" *had jumped*"——

290. The **pluperfect subjunctive** or **potential** denotes simply past time, and denies the act or state.
Ex.—" We *might have sailed.*" " If I *had been* at home, I *should have gone.*"
The illiterate, whose sagacity is sometimes greater than that of philosophers, frequently endeavor to express this mood in pluperfect time; thus, "*Had I ov [have] known* it;" "*Had* he *ov touched* me." Observe also that we can say, " The tree bears better fruit than if it *had been grafted*;" and, having gone into the past, we still say, " The tree bore better fruit than if it *had been grafted.*"

291. The **future-perfect** tense represents something as finished or ended by a certain future time.
Ex.—" The house, when finished, *will have cost* a fortune."

A tense is sometimes used emphatically, to deny the same state or act of the person or thing in a neighboring tense.
Ex.—" He *has been* rich." But he is not so now. " He *had been* rich." But he was not so then. " But you *will come* to this." Though you are not in such a state now.

The present, the past, and the future, are sometimes called the *absolute tenses;* and the perfect, the pluperfect and the future-perfect, the *relative tenses,* for these generally relate from one point of time to another.

Sometimes the prominent idea in the absolute tenses is, the *existence* of a certain act or state; in the relative tenses, the *completion* of the act or state.

Since the perfect passive participle generally implies completion, a passive verb, in the absolute tenses, is often equivalent in time to the corresponding relative tenses of the active voice.

Ex.—My rose-bush *is destroyed;*" "Some one *has destroyed* my rose-bush "· "My coat *will* then *be finished;*" "The tailor *will* then *have finished* my coat." "Corn appears *to be gathered;*" "The farmers appear *to have gathered* their corn." Hence such forms as *may be loved, may be taken, must be loved, must be taken, is taught,* &c., are ambiguous. "He *is* well *taught*"—He has been well educated, or, He is now receiving good instruction. "The fleet *must be captured*"—It is now necessary to believe it has been captured, or, It is necessary to capture it. Hence, too, the present passive is often used to express the present results of past actions. "The church *is built* of granite." "This book *is* well *printed.*"

The **forms** may properly be considered subdivisions to the tenses. See p. 20.

Moods and Tenses.—The subject of moods and tenses, though apparently a mystery, has perhaps a beautiful philosophy running through it, that well shows man may sometimes be wiser in his instincts than in his reason or learning. I have room for but a few and therefore incoherent remarks, which are designed to bear chiefly upon the subjunctive mood, and the apparent incongruity of the tenses in regard to time. According to Mr. Bancroft, the verbs, in some rude Indian languages, express, by means of inflections, entire propositions. It is known, too, that the Emperor Augustus sometimes required, in his documents, *in aliquem* in preference to *alicui,* alleging that it was "more definite." The natural growth, then, of a language, in simplicity and improvement, is from inflections to particles; for a separate word arrests the attention better to an idea than if the idea were expressed along with the idea of another word. Our subjunctive mood, accordingly, has been well-nigh absorbed by *conjunctions, adverbs,* and *auxiliaries.* Again, there are two worlds,—the *mental* and the *material.* What is of the former, is *subjective;* of the latter, *objective.* The mind, though dependent on matter, is still, as poets say, "its own kingdom," in which "an eternal *now* does always last." The mental, therefore, often predominates over the material; and hence the moods often prevail over the tenses. The moods properly relate to the mind of the speaker, and express what is *real, ideal, contingent,* or *willed;* the infinitive mood being tolerated only as we tolerate a *neuter* gender. About our affairs we are continually reasoning and conjecturing; and, consequently, language abounds with sentences having *conditions* and *conclusions.* A *condition* may be assumed as a fact, as that which may become a fact, as a mere supposition without regard to fact, or as a mere supposition contrary to fact; and the conclusion is about as variable. (See p. 201.) Such sentences require something like our SUBJUNCTIVE MOOD. But shall we make the mood depend on the *conjunction?* or on the *subjective* sense of the verb? If on the *conjunction,* we then have the novelty of making mood a property of conjunctions, the forms of the verb are disregarded, and our mood floods the two other declarative moods. But if on the *subjective* sense of the verb, and on the peculiar forms, then we shall at least be in the analogy of all the sister languages, and readily find a province for our mood. It will then have two peculiar forms,—the *present* tense and the *past,* which furnish a beautiful distinction where there is an obvious and important difference, and which have been regarded, by our best writers, at least in the proportion of nine to one. "If love *be* rough with you, be rough with love."—*Shakespeare.* "If all the year *were* playing holidays, to play would be as tedious as to work."—*Id.* "He brags as if he *were* of note." —*Id.* "If thou *warn* the wicked, and he *turn* not from his wickedness, he shall die in his iniquity."—*Bible.* "If the husbandman *relax* his labors, and his fields *be left* untilled," &c.—*E. Everett.* "It I *were* to repeat the names . . . . I should,"

&c.—*Id.* "If I *were* to doubt .... I should," &c.—*D. Webster.* "If it *were* ... I would say," &c.—*Id.* "If it *be proved* that he also was an accomplice," &c.—*Id.* "If the question *were*," &c.—*Jeffrey.* "If the natural course of a stream *be obstructed*," &c.—*Id.* Lord Macaulay, I believe, *never* fails to distinguish the subjunctive forms from the indicative. Some grammarians, however, would abolish them, or merge them into the indicative; but, since our language is already barren of inflections, it were a pity that these few important ones should also be dropped. I am aware that the subjunctive mood is often disregarded in popular usage; yet, because people often overlook or blur in the bustle of worldly pursuits the delicate logic which runs through language, is it a sufficient reason to degrade the language itself to a level with their practice or ignorance? To the two tenses of this mood, already given, may be added the pluperfect, which has the same form as in the indicative mood, yet differs from it so much in sense that it is often parsed as *potential* BY EQUIVALENCE!

"Oh! *had* your fate *been joined* with mine,
As once this pledge appeared the token;
These follies *had* not then *been* mine,—
My early vows *had* not *been broken.*"—*Byron.*

Compare with—" Thy name is princely: though no poet's magic
Could make Red Jacket grace an English rhyme;
Unless he *had* a genius for the tragic,
And *introduced* it into pantomime."—*Halleck: Old Edition.*

The latter pluperfect above is *subjunctive,* and NOT *indicative:* Because it is construed like the admitted forms of the subjunctive; it is equivalent to a potential form; in time, it is NOT *antecedent,* but *concomitant* or *subsequent;* a conclusion, even if more certain than a supposition, is still mental, and not matter of fact; literally put into German, the form would be an unquestioned subjunctive; the two languages are precisely analogous in this construction. It is surprising that, for two or three centuries, more than 500 grammarians have overlooked this point.

Now, as to the tenses. The moods often prevail over them; and any deviation from the strict time of the latter, may be considered *modal.* Let us suppose that we have the *present* and the *past* indicative. These will express whatever is now taking place, and whatever has taken place; and these are all the events that we know with certainty. Now, suppose that our chief concern is, to express, not time, but the nature of the act or state, and mood, or modality, from reality or the greatest certainty as far as pure ideality,—how shall we get forms of the verb? We are surest of what we are now witnessing; and hence the present indicative expresses not only present events, but also the greatest certainty. Suppose we wish to express past or future events with greater than ordinary certainty, of course the present tense is the best form we can find. What depends on the organization or inherent nature of things, not only exists now, but has a high degree of certainty; therefore the present tense expresses also universal truths. Suppose now that we wish to state future or contingent events; what can be more natural than to express with the act the *will, authority, obligation, power, necessity,* etc., on which its development into reality depends? and hence, *will, shall, can, may, must,* etc., is adopted as a part of the verb. Now suppose that we wish to exclude the auxiliary sense, but to retain that of uncertainty. By dropping the auxiliary, we get a new form, which will answer for this purpose, and may be called the *present subjunctive.* Since doing precedes having, and since striving is apt to cease with possession, *have* was naturally adapted to express completion; and so we get the *perfect tenses.* Lastly, suppose that we wish to express acts or states as merely ideal. None of the forms that we have made, will answer. But we can not now, or in future, do a past act. So what could be more ingenious or natural than that the mind should go back, and take the past tense and the pluperfect, and convert them into the needed tenses?—the past tense to denote merely the act or state, and present or indefinite time; and the pluperfect to denote the completed act or state, and past time. The participles and the infinitives express but the state of the act as relatively continuing, finished, or purposed. This seems to me to be the general philosophy of the tenses; the minor shades of expression being but figurative accommodations to the necessities of language.

Persons and Numbers.

The **person** and **number** of a verb are its form as being suitable to the person and number of its subject.

Ex.—I *am.* Thou *art.* He *is.* We *are.* They *are.*

Excepting the verb *be* and some auxiliaries, English verbs have but few variations to express persons and numbers; and hence these properties must generally be inferred from the subject. It is worthy of notice, too, that only the first part of the verb, or that which predicates, expresses the person and number.

A finite verb must agree with its subject in person and number.

That is, it must be expressed according to the Conjugation, pp. 24–29, which shows how the best writers and speakers express the verb in regard to its subject.

The subject of every finite verb, in regard to person and number, either is, or may be represented by, *I, thou, he, she, it, we, you,* or *they.*

294. *Thou* generally requires the verb, or the first auxiliary, to end in *est, st,* or *t.*

Ex.—"Thou *knowest—wast—hast—sitst.*" "Thou *art* the man." "Thou *shalt* not *kill.*" *Wert* is used as well as *wast,* and is analogous to *art.* "That riches rarely purchase friends, thou didst soon discover, when thou *wert left* to stand thy trial uncountenanced and alone."—*Johnson.* "To her who sits where thou *wert* laid."—*Bryant.* "'Tis all too late—thou *wert,* thou *art,* the cherished madness of my heart."—*Byron.*

295. As the termination required by *thou,* is sometimes harsh, there is some tendency to drop it, especially in poetry.

Ex.—"O thou my voice inspire who *touched* Isaiah's hallowed lips with fire."—*Pope.* "Perhaps thou *noticed* on thy way a little orb, attended by one moon—her lamp by night."—*Pollok.* "But thou . . . . *shall bind.*"—*Sprague.*

296. *He, she,* or *it,* often requires the verb or the first auxiliary to end in *s* or *th.* See pp. 24–29 & 212.

Ex.—"He *writes;*" "He *writeth.*" "She *controls;*" "She *controlleth.*" "It *does become* you;" "It *doth become* you."

297. *We, you,* or *they,* never allows *s* or *th* to be annexed to the verb. In other words, plural verbs never assume *s* or *th,* and have the same form for all the persons.

Ex.—"We *learn,*" not *learns.* "They *learn,*" not *learns.* "You *learn.*" "John, James, and William, [—they,] *learn.*"

Since it is not always easy to determine the person and number of the subject when it is variable in sense or complicated in its words, let us consider, first, the person of the entire subject; secondly, the number of the entire subject; and, lastly, what terms do not affect the form of the verb.

298. **Person.**—When two or more nominatives, differing in person, are taken collectively, or are connected merely by *and,* the verb prefers the first person to the second, and the second to the third; when they are taken separately, or are connected by *or* or *nor,* it prefers that of the nominative next to it. "*You* and *I,*" or, "*You, he,* and *I*"= *We.* "*You* and *he*"= *You.*

Ex.—"*You, he,* and *I,* | *have* to recite our lessons." "*You* and *he* | *have* to recite your lessons." "*You* or *I am* mistaken;" better, "Either you are mistaken, or I am." "*Thou* or thy *friends are* to make reparation." Courtesy usually requires the first place to be given to the second person, and the last to the first. "*You, he, and I;*" "*You* and *I;*" "*She* and *I.*"

299. Singular.—A single object denoted by a singular nominative; a united group of objects viewed as one thing, and denoted by a singular collective or other noun; an object conceived as a whole or unit, though denoted by a plural nominative, or by several nominatives or words which may be connected by *and;* two or more distinct or different objects taken individually, and denoted by a singular nominative, or by several nominatives,—require the verb to be in the *singular* number. The word, or phrase, *each, every, no, many a, or, nor, and not, but not, as well as,* &c., commonly makes a part of such a subject, and modifies its sense.

Ex.—"Fire | burns." "The *army* of Xerxes *was vanquished* by the Greeks." "His *family* | *is* large.". "The '*Pleasures* of Hope' *was written* by Campbell." "Goldsmith's '*Edwin* and *Angelina*' *is* a fine little poem." "In yonder house *lives* a great *scholar* and celebrated *writer.*" "The *saint,* the *father,* and the *husband, prays.*" —*Burns.* "Why *is* | *dust* and *ashes* [man] proud?" "The twenty *dollars* [a twenty-dollar bill] *has been* duly *received.*" "Fifty *feet* of the second square *was* reserved for a church." The last two verbs should probably be plural; and yet the singular implies a unity—a compactness in one—which the plural would not necessarily express. "*Descent* and *fall* to us *is* adverse."—*Milton.* Here *is* is more expressive than *are* would be. It implies that the *fall* is so connected with the *descent,* or follows it so closely, that the two may be considered *one* thing. *And* unites the two in *form,* but *is* strengthens the union by uniting them also in *sense.* "*Wooing, wedding,* and *repenting, is* a Scotch jig, a measure, and a cinque-pace." —*Shakespeare.* Here *is* seems to be proper as referring to the three things taken in a certain order as one whole. "Down *comes* the *tree, nest, eagles,* and all."— *Fontaine.* "*To turn* and *fly* | *was* now too late."—*Washington Irving.* But I question whether even poetic license can protect the following couplet: "*Here's* no war-steed's *neigh* and *champing,* shouting clans or squadrons stamping."—*Scott.* "Every *house* | *was burned;*" and every *man, woman,* and *child, was killed.*" "Tuesday, Wednesday, or Thursday, *was* the appointed day." "*To forsake* a friend, or *to divulge* his secrets, *is* mean." "Neither *precept* nor *discipline* | *is* so forcible as example." "No *house* and no *fence* | *was left.*" "Many a *man* | *has fallen* a victim to intemperance." "There *is* Concord, and Lexington, and Bunker Hill,— and there they will remain for ever."—*Webster.* Emphatic arrangement. "For thine *is* the *kingdom,* and the power, and the glory."—*Bible.*

300. Plural.—Two or more objects denoted by a plural nominative; a single object or group conceived as to its parts or individuals, even when denoted by a collective or other noun singular in form; objects denoted by a plural nominative in company with singular nominatives, taken separately, or connected by *or* or *nor;* two or more distinct or different objects taken collectively, and denoted by different nominatives connected by *and,*—require the verb to be in the *plural* number.

Ex.—"The *fires* | *burn.*" "The *ashes* | *are* hot." "The *council* | *were divided* in opinion." "The *multitude* eagerly *pursue* pleasure." "Forty *head* of cattle | *are grazing* on yonder meadow." "*John, James,* and *William, are studying*"—The boys are studying. "*You, he,* and *I, are allowed* to go." "*To love* our enemies, *to mind* our own business, and *to relieve* the distressed, are things oftener praised than practised." "Either the magistrate or the *laws* are at fault." The plural nominative should generally be placed nearest to the verb; or else each nominative should have its own verb expressed or understood. "Either the *laws are* at fault, or else the magistrate" [*is*]. Sometimes the verb agrees with the nearest nominative. "When there *is* an *infant* or *infants who* | *are* yet," &c.—*Mo. Salutes.*

Terms that do not affect the form of the verb.—Adjuncts to the nominative, explanatory terms, parenthetical terms, terms to which others are compared, terms excluded or excepted, terms apparently set aside for a more expressive or important one, and terms mentioned as if the objects had not been thought of till one assertion was already made,—do not affect the form of the verb.

Ex.—"The long row *of elms* was luxuriantly green." "Star *after star* appears." "Death is *the wages* of sin." "The wages of sin are *death.*" "Peace and honor are the *crown* of virtue." "His *pavilion* were dark waters and thick clouds." Which term is explanatory, will depend on the sense, or on the conception of the person using the expression.

Consider carefully what is chiefly to be said, and of which thing it is to be said. "The Bible, or *Holy Scriptures*, is the best book." "This man (and indeed all such *men*) deserves death." "Our statesmen, especially *John Adams*, have reached a good old age." "The carriage, as well as the *horses*, was much injured." "Industry, and not mean *savings*, produces wealth." "Since none but *thou* can end it."—*Milton.* "What black *despair*, what horror fills his mind." —*Thomson.* "*Honor* and *virtue*, nay, even interest demands a different course." "Not only the *father*, but the son also, was imprisoned." "Well, there is Bardolph, and *Smith*, and *Jones*, and *who* else?"

It is sometimes difficult to determine whether a collective noun that is singular in form, expresses unity or plurality of idea, or whether its verb should be singular or plural. This will depend, in most instances, on the particular view or conception of the speaker. In the plural sense, a collective noun may be compared to a rope having its strands or threads untwisted; in the singular, to the same in a twisted state. Collective nouns denoting persons, are more commonly made plural than those denoting things; and we may say, as a general rule for all cases, that whenever the term implies a separation, or distribution, or diversity, in regard to the place, the time, the action, or the state, the verb should be plural, but not in other cases. Hence I should say, "The *public are* respectfully *invited;*" "My *family are* in the country"—*some here, some there;* "My *family is* in the country"—*all in one place;* "The *committee was* large;" "The *committee were* not unanimous;" "Congress has adjourned;" "A *number* of boats [from time to time] *have passed* up the river this spring, and the *number* [as a whole] *is* daily *increasing.*" This last example shows the distinction of unity and plurality of idea, in its greatest nicety.

301. It is sometimes necessary to supply a substantive, to complete the entire subject.

Ex.—"Little and often fills the purse"—*To put in* little and often, etc. "Poor and content is rich, and rich enough"—*To be* poor and content, etc. "Slow and steady often outtravels haste"—*What is* slow and steady, etc. "Upwards of forty houses were burned"—*A group*, amounting to, etc.

302. Most verbs in the imperative mood are in the second person, agreeing with *thou, you,* or *ye,* understood, and sometimes expressed.

Ex.—"Go where glory waits thee"—*Go thou*, etc. "Strike—for the green graves of your sires"—*Strike ye*, etc. "*Guard thou* the pass." "Girls, *do you gather* the strawberries."

Verbs of this mood are sometimes found, especially in poetry, of the first or the third person. When thus used, the nominative is always expressed. See p. 202.

303. A verb is sometimes made to agree with *it*, in order to express a well-known act or state of something not easily discerned or named, or named by several words in the subsequent part of the sentence.

Ex.—"It snows." "It rains." "It cleared off." "*It behooves* us to improve our time." "What *shall it profit* a man *if he gain the whole world and lose his own soul?*" When such verbs denote states of the weather, or the fitness of things, they are usually called *impersonal* or *unipersonal* verbs, though rather unnecessarily so; for the difficulty lies in the import of *it*, and not in the agreement of the verb. Only such expressions as *meseems, meseemed, methinks, methought*, should be termed impersonal, or rather, *anomalous;* because they have no nominatives with which they can properly agree. So, "Forthwith on all sides to his aid *was run* by angels many and strong,"—*Milton ;* (a Latinism;) and perhaps, "God said, *Let* there be light; and there was light," for the verb *Let* hardly refers to any being addressed. *Meseems* is abridged from "To me it seems;" and *methinks* perhaps from "To me it thinks," *i. e.*, it causes me to think. "*Prince.* Where shall we sojourne till our coronation? *Gloucester.* Where *it thinks* best unto your royal self."—*Shakespeare: Old Edition.* In the sentence, "*Thinks* I to myself, I'll stop" —Jane Taylor, *thinks* may be parsed according to Note XI, or as put for *think* by *enallage*.

Person-and-number inflections belong to the indicative mood and the potential, mostly to the in licative. The subjunctive mood is varied, only to agree with *thou*, and then not always. Whether *s* or *es* should be added, should always be determined in accordance with the regular mode of forming the plural of nouns; hence the forms "wooes," "cooes," &c., which are sometimes found, should be *woos, coos*. Most auxiliaries are not varied in the third person singular. *Thou* requires the termination *t, st,* or *est. Are, were, shall,* and *will,* take *t;* the other auxiliaries, *st.* Other verbs take, in the indicative present, *st* or *est,* according as they require *s* or *es* in the third person singular; though sometimes *est* is preferred even to *st.* A few verbs, which end in vowel sounds, always assume *est ;* as, *wooest.* In the past tense, the verbs assume *st* only, if it will coalesce in sound; if not, *est.* Poets and preachers sometimes reject either, to avoid harsh or difficult pronunciation. In general, *st* only should be added, when this is sufficient; and when the verb already ends in the sound of *st,* or in a cluster of consonants not coalescing well with *st,* the termination may be rejected. In the solemn style, in stead of *s* or *es, th* is added, if it will coalesce in sound; if not, *eth.*

AUXILIARY VERBS.

An **auxiliary** verb helps another verb to express its meaning in a certain manner or time. Verbs, not auxiliary, are called *principal* verbs.

The auxiliary verbs are *be* and all its variations; *do, did ; can, could ; have, had ; may, might ; must ; shall, should ; will, would.* See p. 16.

304. Sometimes *be, do, have, will, would,* or even *can,* is used as a principal verb. When so used, it is not combined with a principal verb expressed or understood. Do—*act, perform ;* have—*own, possess ;* will —*wish, bequeath.*

Ex.—" It *is* easy *to be* idle." " He *has done* the work." " He *willed* his property to his sister." " I *would* I could please you." " In evil, the best condition is, not *to will ;* the second, not *to can.*"—*Bacon.*

305. Auxiliary verbs are often convenient when we wish to express the verb interrogatively, negatively, or elliptically.

Ex.—" *Do* you *know* Lydia Flare ?" Placed before the nominative. "*Can* you *go ?*" "I *do* not *want* his company." " If man will not do justice, God *will*" [do justice]. " He could have done it, and so *could* you." "They herd cattle and raise corn, just as we used *to do ;*" *i. e.*, to herd cattle and raise corn. *Do* is frequently thus used as a sort of *pro-verb,* to represent an active verb already mentioned. Some grammarians condemn this use of it; yet, as it often enables us to avoid the repetition of a long and tedious phrase, our language can not well spare it.

Be primarily signifies predication or existence; *do*, action in general, which is limited to a particular kind by the principal verb; *can*, to know; *have*, to possess; *may*, ability; *must*, necessity; *shall*, proceeding from another's will or from our circumstances; and *will*, proceeding from our own will. But the primitive or literal sense can not always be traced.

Ex.—" The corn *is* planted." " He *does* study." " I *can* [know how to] read." (To *con* a lesson—to study it. Out of *ken*—beyond perception.) " I *have* been hurt." " I *may* buy it;" " You *might* help us." (A *mighty* storm.) " He *shall* study." " He *will* study."

306. **Be** is used chiefly to express the verb in the passive and progressive forms. See p. 216.

Ex.—" The house *is built*." " The leaves *are falling*." It shows when and how the person or thing exists in the state denoted by the rest of the verb.

307. **Do** or **did** generally adds force to the predicate, or expresses the emphatic form. See p. 216.

Ex.—" I *do* really *believe* it." "*Do* you *treat* him well, nevertheless."

308. **Can** or **could** expresses *ability* or *possibility*,—physical mental, or moral.

Ex.—" I *can carry* the bucket." "*Can* you *write* a composition !" " I *can* not *break* my promise." " It *can* not *snow* here in July." " It *can* not *be*." " Such a man *could* not *live* in our neighborhood." It is morally impossible.

309. **Have** or **had** makes a part of every perfect tense.

310. **May** or **might** expresses *ability, possibility, probability, permission, wishing.*

Ex.—" I *might have bought* this valuable lot then." " It *might be answered* thus." " It *may* rain this evening." " We *may* not *live* to see it." " You *may* all *go* out to play." "*May* you *prosper*." " O, that he *might return !*"

311. **Must** expresses *necessity*,—physical, mental, or moral.

Ex.—"*Die* I *must*." " But for a little tube of mercury, the whole crew *must have sunk*." " There *must have been* a heavy rain in these parts." It is necessary to believe there was. " Your promise *must be kept*." " My vote *must* not *be registered* in favor of such a bill." It ought not to be, and shall not be.

When we look into the world, we can readily observe that the acts or states ascribed to objects, proceed either from their own will or nature, or else are caused by other agents or things. The former province is chiefly that for *will* and *would*, the latter for *shall* and *should*.

312. **Shall** or **should** sets forth the act or state, not as depending on the doer's will, but on that of another; or as proceeding from authority, influence, or circumstances perhaps out of his control. Hence, *shall* often implies *compulsion;* and *should, duty* or *obligation.* Frequently, they denote something as simply future or subsequent, or an assertion modestly set forth as being somewhat a condition or inference.

Ex.—" You *shall stay* at home to-day." " Thou *shalt love* thy neighbor as thyself." " I *shall be drowned*; for nobody will help me." " I resolved that he *should go*." " He vowed that I *should repent* of it." " Whoever *shall violate* this law, *shall be punished*." " Our children *shall celebrate* this day with bonfires and illuminations." It will come to pass. " Yes, my son; you *shall* often find the richest men the meanest." In your course through life, this will necessarily obtrude itself upon your notice. (A use somewhat obsolescent, but good.) " Go and see him, and you *shall* never *want* to see him again." "*Should* you *find* any papaws, halloo to us." " I *should be obliged* to him, if he would gratify me." " I *should be pleased* to have his company" [if he would condescend to wait upon me].

"Do you think the book will sell?—I *should think* so" [judging from its qualities, and the wants of the public].

314. Will or **would** sets forth the act or state as depending on the will or the nature of what is denoted by the subject of the verb. Hence this auxiliary often implies repetition of the act. Frequently, it denotes the act or state as simply future or subsequent.

Ex.—"If he *will go* to California in spite of remonstrance, I *will furnish* him an outfit; but I fear he *will find* but little gold there, and *will* never *bring* back as much as he took with him." "The cause *will raise* up armies." "He *would* not *go* without his father's word." "This *would answer* our purpose." "He knew that this *would have been* wrong." "There *will* she *sit* and *weep* for hours." "But still the house affairs *would draw* her thence."

315. In a dependent proposition, *shall* or *should* must nearly always be used to express simple futurity or contingence; for, in such a proposition, *will* or *would* generally refers to the *will* of what the subject denotes.

Ex.—"If I *shall have been.*" "If you *shall have been.*" "When he *shall go.*" "Whoever *shall say* so."

Since *shall* and *will* are often misapplied, the following rules may all be found useful:—

1. Our own voluntary actions are denoted by *will*, and our contingent ones by *shall*; the contingent actions of others are expressed by *will*, and their compulsory ones by *shall*.

2. *Shall*, in the first person of independent propositions, and *will*, in the second and third persons, foretell. *Will*, in the first person, implies volition or promise; and *shall*, in the second and third persons, implies compulsion or force. *Shall*, in dependent propositions, foretells; and *will* implies volition. *Should* is generally preferable to *would*, where *shall* would be preferable to *will*; and *vice versa*.

3. *Will* or *would* excludes the volition or control of the speaker over the act or state, unless he is also what the subject of the verb denotes. *Shall* or *should* excludes the volition or control of what the subject denotes, over the act or state.

The first and second rules are simple but inadequate; the last reaches all cases.

The auxiliaries *may, can, must, will,* and *shall,* generally accord best with one another, and with the present tenses; the auxiliaries *might, could, would,* and *should,* generally accord best with one another, and with the past tenses.

PARTICIPLES AND INFINITIVES.

What is a participle? What is an infinitive? See p. 197.

Participles and *infinitives* also express the acts or states expressed by other forms of the verb.

They likewise have voices.

They do not have moods; or rather, they are themselves a mood

316. They express tense relatively and in any period of time, and not absolutely, like finite verbs, in fixed periods of time.

Ex.—"He CAME *wounded;*" "He CAME *wounding;*" "He CAME *to wound.*" "He COMES—WILL COME *wounded.*" "I INTEND *to go;*" "I INTENDED *to go.*"

They do not have person and number, and therefore do **not** express affirmation.

317. While they have the general meaning of verbs, they also partake of the nature of nouns, adjectives, and adverbs.

They form a circuit of expressions between predicate-verbs, and other parts of speech; and hence they enrich language in variety and power of expression.

318. Since they have not person or number, or do not predicate, they ascribe acts or states to substantives, and yet leave them free in their case construction with other words; thus enabling us to abridge clauses, condense the sentence, and give suitable prominence to each of its parts.

Ex.—"The man, *turning* round as if *to seek* a passenger of whom *to make* inquiry, beheld, on the other side of the way, another man apparently *engaged* in the same search." "The man, when he turned round as if he sought a passenger of whom he might make inquiry, beheld, on the other side of the way, another man who was apparently engaged in the same search," is more tedious than the preceding sentence, and does not even express precisely the same sense. "His body, *dropping* from the horse, was found, after several days, *stretched* upon the ground, with the faithful animal still *standing* at its side." Observe here how the finding of the body is made most prominent, and how all other parts become duly subordinate.

Their brevity gives force; besides, participles are often the most vivid and expressive of terms.

Ex.—"The *rising* sun, o'er Galston moors, with glorious light was *glinting*."

There are three participles; the *present*, the *perfect*, and the *compound*.

There are two infinitives; the *present* and the *perfect*.

319. The **present participle** ends in *ing*, and denotes continuance of the act or state. It is active, if from an active verb; sometimes passive.

320. The **perfect participle** ends in *ed*, or is formed as shown in the list of irregular verbs; and it denotes completion, sometimes continuance. It is passive, except when combined with the auxiliary *have*.

321. The **compound participle** consists of *being*, *having*, or *having been*, and some present or perfect participle placed after it.

The words *being*, *having*, *having been*, are needed and inserted to exclude predication; to express voice, time, cause, &c.; or to bring out the sense of the participle more exactly, clearly, or forcibly.

Ex.—"This *proved*, the conclusion is irresistible." *Proved* is apparently finite, and the sense is obscure or ambiguous. "This *being proved*, the conclusion is irresistible." "The old chief, *warned* by these few words, departed immediately." Passive. "The old chief, *having warned* by these few words, departed immediately." Active. "He comes *attended* by his friends." Present. "He comes, *having been attended* by his friends." Past. "The army did not march ill *provided*." State. "The army did not march, *being* ill *provided*." Cause. "I saw the man *admitted*," is not equivalent to "I saw the man, *being admitted*." "The man *skilled* in the business, was appointed." Restrictive. "The man, *being skilled* in the business, was appointed." Not restrictive. The compound participle is never restrictive. "Santa Anna kept no prisoners; it *having been decreed* so." Voice, time, and cause.

The nature of our compound participles is misunderstood in all the English grammars I have seen.

322. The **present infinitive** begins with *to*, and is relatively present or future in time.

323. The **perfect infinitive** begins with *to have*, and denotes completion, or past time.

Ex.—"I hoped *to see* you." "He appears *to be* rich." "He appears *to have been* rich."

We may consider participles and infinitives, *first*, as combined with auxiliaries to make finite or other verbs; *secondly*, as being participles and infinitives proper; and, *thirdly*, as having become words of other parts of speech.

324. *Participles* are combined with *participles* to make *compound participles*.

Ex.—Having been; being worn; having been standing. "Being standing;" rarely used.

325. The *present participle* is combined with the auxiliary *be* and its variations, to make the *progressive form*.

Ex.—To be writing; to have been writing. "The bells *are tolling*."

326. The *perfect participle* is combined with the auxiliary *be* and its variations, to make the *passive form* or *voice*.

Ex.—To be written; to have been written. "He *is gone*." "He *was struck*."

327. The *perfect participle* is combined with the auxiliary *have* and its variations, to express the *perfect tenses*. It is then active, if from a transitive verb.

Ex.—To have written; to have been writing. I *had written*.

328. The *compound participle* is not properly combined, with any auxiliary, as a part of a finite verb. But see p. 236.

Ex.—"A new party *is* now *being formed*," should be, "A new party *is* now *forming*." "The church *was* then *being built*," should be, "The church *was* then *building*."

329. The *present infinitive*, without the sign *to*, is combined with the auxiliaries *do, can, may, must, will*, and *shall*, and with their past forms, to express absolute tenses.

Ex.—"He *does* [to] *study*." "I *can* | *study*—I am able to study." "I *shall* | *study*." "I *would* | *study*."

The original infinitive properly has not *to;* the form with *to* is made from the other, and is needed, in construction, to distinguish the infinitive from the present indicative or imperative. Thus the preposition *to* has become a sort of *auxiliary* to the infinitive, though not an auxiliary verb; for the infinitive, not expressing affirmation, needed not a verb for its auxiliary.

330. The infinitive is also construed, without the sign *to*, after the active verbs *bid, make, need, hear,* | *let, see, feel,* and *dare;* sometimes after *find, have, help, please,* and equivalents of *see;* and sometimes after a conjunction or in colloquial expressions.

Ex.—"Let us *sing*." "I heard him *say* it." "You had better *go*." "They learn to read and [to] write [It is] " Better [to] lose than [to] be disgraced."

331. The *participle* may express something subordinate—
As the *cause*. "John, *being tired*, went to bed." [fore feet.
As the *means*. "The horse charged upon the wolves, *striking* them with his
As the *manner*. "The cars came *rattling*." See Southey's Lodore.
As the *time*. "*Having taken* shelter here, he saw an ant," &c.
As the *state*. "He became *attached* to us."
As the *accompaniment*. "She sat near, *reading* a book."
As the *condition*. "*Circling* round, you may approach on the other side."
As the *respect wherein*. "I consider him as *having* lost his right."

332. It is sometimes used—
Absolutely with a substantive. "The bells *having rung*, we went to church.
Absolutely after an infinitive. "To go *prepared*, is necessary."

333. The *infinitive* may express something—
As the *cause*. "I grieve *to hear* of your bad conduct."
As the *purpose*. "And they who came *to scoff*, remained *to pray*."
As simply a *future* or *subsequent event*. "He fell *to rise* no more."
As the *respect wherein*. "Willing *to wound* and yet afraid *to strike*."
As a *determination* or *obligation*. "I am *to go*." "It is *to be deplored* that," &c.
As the *manner*. "All things went *to suit* me."
As the *supplement of a comparison*. "Good enough *to sell*." "So high as *to be* invisible." "He knows better than *to venture*."

334. It is sometimes used—
As a *subject*. "*To cultivate* the earth is the most pleasant occupation."
As an *object*. "He is learning *to read*." "The ship is about *to sail*."
As a *predicate-nominative*. "To sin is *to suffer*."
As an *appositive*. "Delightful task! *to rear* the tender thought."

There are several less important uses of participles and infinitives.

335. The *infinitive* may be construed with—
A *noun*. "He has the courage *to venture*."
A *pronoun*. "Hear *him* speak."
An *adjective*. "He is *anxious* to start."
A *verb*. "He *seems* to prosper." "I *came* to remain."
An *adverb*. "He knows *when* to purchase."
A *preposition*. "He is *about* to sell his farm."
A *conjunction*. "He is wiser *than* to believe it."
An *interjection*, elliptically. "*O*, to be in such a condition!"

The participle leans to the adjective, and the infinitive to the noun.

Ex.—"I am *studying*"—I am *in the state of studying*; but, "I can *study*"—I am able to do *the thing called studying*.

336. Since every act or state must belong to some object, participles and infinitives relate to substantives; and since they partake of the nature of other parts of speech, they may, especially the infinitive, modify other words besides.

Ex.—" The Passions oft, to hear her shell, thronged around her magic cell." *To hear* relates to *Passions*, and also modifies *thronged*, by showing the purpose. Sometimes the principal verb is omitted. "To tell the truth, [I *must confess*] I was in fault." Sometimes participles and infinitives are used absolutely or independently; though words by which we may avoid this construction, can often be supplied. "To become *disheartened*, is ruinous." [We] "*Considering* his youth, [think] he is very prudent." See p. 47.

The foregoing paragraph is substantially Rule XII. In the syntax of verbs, the most obvious distinction is into verbs finite and verbs not finite. Since finite verbs are always referred to subjects, since every act or state must belong to some object, and since participles and infinitives "partake the nature of verbs," why should their relation to a subject be disregarded, or less regarded in one than in the other? To the participle combined with the copula, or used abverbially after the verb,—as, "He is *writing*," "He spoke *standing*,"—the last part of the Rule is also applicable; but since the former makes with the copula the verb, and since the latter is construed like the adjective in such sentences as "The apples boiled *soft*," the first part of the Rule seems sufficient for participles.

---

337. Participles and infinitives become *nouns*, when they assume cases; and they may then be used in any case except the possessive.

Ex.—" *To love* is natural." "Mary is learning *to read*." "There is little glory in *having been detected* in a mean action." "It is better *to suffer* than *to injure*." " No sooner has he peeped into the world than he has done his *do*."—*Hudibras*. Here the infinitive has become entirely a noun.

338. By virtue of their verbal sense, verbal nouns may govern other substantives in the objective case, or be modified adverbially; and by virtue of its substantive sense, the participle may govern another substantive in the possessive case.

Ex—" To love our *neighbors*, is our duty." "*His* having *sometimes* written to me, is no evidence of *Mary's* corresponding with him." Such possessives are authorized by good writers: it is often better, however, to use an ordinary noun, or a clause beginning with *that*.

339. The infinitive always remains abstract, and is never governed by a preposition, except sometimes by *about, but,* or *except.*

340. The participle may so far lose the nature of the verb as to assume the modifications of a noun, or become even concrete.

Ex.—" *Painting* and sculpture." " Good *lodgings.*" " In the *arranging* of his affairs"—In the *arrangement* of his affairs. The participle, with an article before it and *of* after it, is always a noun; and, as such, converts adverbs into adjectives, or is compounded with them. " By *carefully reading* your composition;" " By the *careful reading* of your composition." " In *setting forth* his system;" " In the *setting-forth* of his system."

Participles and infinitives lose, with their verbal nature, the .dea of time.

341. The participle sometimes becomes a *participial adjective*, that is, it ascribes the act or state to its subject as a quality.

Ex.—"A *shattered* oak." " Life's *fleeting* moments." Sometimes it becomes a mere adjective. " This is *surprising*"—*wonderful.*

Participles sometimes become *adverbs, prepositions,* or *conjunctions.*

Ex.—" It is freezing cold." Concerning, respecting. Provided.

CONJUGATION.

The **conjugation** of a verb is the proper combination and regular arrangement of its parts, to express voices, moods, tenses, persons, and numbers.

342. Most forms of the verb consist of auxiliaries combined with participles or infinitives. See the preceding section.

343. Only the present, the preterit, and a few other forms, can be used without auxiliaries.

344. The preterit can not be properly combined with any other part of the verb.

Ex.—"I had *went*," "He was *took*," should be, "I had *gone*," "He was *taken*."

A verb that has assumed an auxiliary, is sometimes called *compound*, or *composite*.

A few verbs want most of their parts, or have no participles, and are therefore termed *defective*.

These are *beware, methinks, ought, quoth, wit*, and most of the auxiliary verbs.

Beware, derived from *be* and *aware*, may be used wherever *be* would occur in the conjugation of the verb *be*. "*Beware* of pickpockets." "'Tis wisdom *to beware*, and better to avoid the bait than struggle in the snare."—*Dryden.* "If angels fell, why *should* not men *beware*."—*Young.*

Ought, said to be an old preterit of *owe*, is, without regard to the infinitive after it, in the present tense when it refers to present time, and in the past tense when it refers to past time. So is also *must. Present:* "I know he *ought* to go;" "I know he *ought* to have gone." No *s* is added. *Past:* "I knew he *ought* to surrender" [then]; "I knew he *ought* to have surrendered."

Quoth is sometimes used, in familiar or humorous language, for *said.* "'Not I,' *quoth* Sancho."

Wit, in the sense of *know*, is yet used in the phrase *to wit—namely*. The other forms are nearly obsolete. See p. 16.

---

345. The **forms** are certain modes of expressing the verb, which may be considered subdivisions to the tenses.

In general, verbs branch out thus: They have moods; moods have tenses; tenses have forms; and forms have persons and numbers.

There are five forms; the *common*, the *emphatic*, the *progressive*, the *passive*, and the *ancient*, or *solemn style*. See pp. 20-29.

Define the forms. See p. 20.

The *common form* should be used in familiar discourse.

The *emphatic form* often implies an opposite opinion which it aims to remove. When *do* or *did* is excluded by some other auxiliary, we simply lay a greater stress on the latter.

The *progressive form* can generally be applied only to acts or states that may have intermissions and renewals. Permanent mental acts or states can therefore be seldom expressed in it. "I *respect* him;" not, "I am *respecting* him." This form is sometimes highly vivid and expressive.

The *ancient form*, or *solemn style*, is used in the Bible, by the religious denomination called Friends, frequently in religious worship, sometimes in poetry, and sometimes in burlesque.

Since the chief purpose of Conjugation is the making of predicates, we may add the following :—

346. *Be* is often combined with *about* and the infinitive, to express something as future or impending at the time referred to.
Ex.—" We *were about to start*."

347. *Be*, in some of the tenses, may be combined with the infinitive to express determination or design.
Ex.—"I *was to go* early." "They *are to be sold*."

348. *Have* is often combined with the infinitive to express obligation or necessity.
Ex.—"I *have to go*." "I *had to do* every thing."

349. The verbs *seem, appear, suppose*, &c., are often combined with the infinitive to modify or soften the assertion.
Ex.—"She *seems to know* but little."

350. A proposition is made *interrogative*, generally by placing the verb or some part of it after the nominative.
Ex.—"*Know ye* the land?". "*Have* you *seen* him?"

351. A verb is made *negative*, by placing *not* after it or after the first auxiliary. Participles and infinitives generally require *not* to be placed before them.
Ex.—"I *know not*." "I *did not know* it." "*Not to know* some things, is an honor." "*Not finding* me, he went away."

352. Some propositions are both interrogative and negative. Negative questions imply something adverse to the speaker's belief, or ask for confirmation; affirmative questions ask for information. The former often suppose an affirmative answer in the hearer; and the latter, a negative answer. Both kinds are answered by *yes* or *no* alike.

Ex.—"*Has* the carriage *not come* yet?" "*Is not* Philip master of Thermopylæ?" &c. "*Shall* we *gather* strength by irresolution and inaction?" &c. "*Did* you *go?* —No." "*Did* you *not go?*—No." "And *did* they *not catch* you?—No, thank Heaven.—You were not kicked, then?—No, sir.—Nor caned?—No, sir.—Nor dragged through a horse-pond?—O Lord! no, sir."—*Garrick*.

EXERCISES.

Examples to be Analyzed and Parsed.

Parse the verbs, including participles and infinitives:—

1.

A fierce dog caught[a] the robber. A cloud is[b] passing over us. The place was covered with a profusion of flowers. Misers hoard money. Money is hoarded by misers. That noisy marsh is now draining. Man becomes indolent in a warm climate. Thou didst create this wondrous world.

2.

You do not understand me. We have learned our lessons. The hunters had killed a bear. I shall remain at home when it rains. When I have completed this grammar, I will visit you. The turkeys will have left the field, before you can get there. I will not beg favors of you, as others have done. "Will you walk into my parlor?" said a Spider to a Fly.

3.

You may walk[c] into the garden, but you must not pluck[c] the flowers. The storm may have broken down the old apple-tree. I could not carry the trunk. A good resolution should not be broken. If a horse could have been procured, we would have sent him. If you should write to her, it might appear that I had requested it.

4.

Who would refuse to reward[d] them[d]? Does any man believe that this giant aggregate of states can be preserved by force? Shall we submit to chains and slavery? If he be chosen, he will become insolent. I would I were with him. If he valued it highly, he would not sell it so cheap. He smiled as if he knew me. He was spoken[e] of for Congress. The victory had been ours, had they fought more bravely.

5.

Revere thyself, and yet thyself despise. Do not give a poor man a stone, after he has died for want of bread. Go, wash your face, and get ready for school. Seek we now some deeper shade. Lead he the way who knows the spot. Hallowed be thy name; thy kingdom come.

6.

He was born to be[f] great. I came here to work[g], not to play. The poem was to be published. We like to please our teacher. You behave too badly to go into company. The house is estimated to have cost fifty thousand dollars. To work[h] is better than to starve[i]. He is afraid, methinks[k], to hear you tell it. There let the laurel spread[12], the cypress wave.

7.

James ran fast, pursuing[i] John, and pursued by us. The machinery, being oiled[j], runs well. Having written his letter, he sealed it. Spring comes robed in silken green. Truth, crushed to earth, shall rise again. A word can send the crimson color hurrying to the cheek with many meanings. The falling[10] leaves remind us of declining years. There tyrants, uncrowned[19], unepitaphed[10], shall rot.

8.

Considering[a] his age, he is far advanced. To conclude, I shall oppose the sending of the navy there. By fearing to attempt something, you will do nothing. There is much to do. She was punished for having torn her book. I wept a last adieu.

9.

The flax often failed, and the sheep were destroyed by wolves. The mansion, with its gardens and groves, extends over a large area. The seasons, each in its turn, cheer the soul. Every twenty-four hours make a day. Every people have some kind of religion. Each private family pays a tax of five dollars for water. A remnant of cloth was left[11]. A remnant of the tribe were left[11]. 5 from 7 leave 2. 5 from 7 leaves 2. Two-fifths are greater than one-fourth [is]. A portion of these Indians have some education.

10.

The Rhine[1] and the Rhone rise[m] in Switzerland. Lofty mountains, enormous glaciers, and wild, romantic valleys, successively appear. Tower and temple, hut and palace, were consumed by fire. A log-rolling, a quilting, or a wedding, was a time of general festivity. Every horse and every ox was stolen. You[n] or he is in fault. You, he, and I, [we,] are[o] invited. Continued exertion, and not hasty efforts, leads to success. Every doubtful or chimerical speculation was forbidden.

11.

The howling of the wolf, and the shrill screaming of the panther, were mingled in nightly concert with the war-whoop of the savages. Where now is peace, sobriety, order, and love? To have suffered the inhabitants to escape, would have prolonged the evils of war. That[p] Cortes with but a handful of adventurers should have conquered so great an empire, is a fact little short of the miraculous.

[To have] All work and no play makes Jack a dull boy[r].
All play and no work makes Jack a mere toy.

The sun hath set in folded clouds,—
Its twilight rays are gone;
And, gathered in the shades of night,
The storm is rolling on.

12.

We ought not to sacrifice the sentiments of the soul, to gratify the appetites of the body. The conclusion, [r]that this river must be the outpouring of a continent, was acute and striking. She does not spend her time in making herself look more advantageously what she really is.

Observe also the effect on the mind of Richard, of Palmer's being arrested, and committed to prison.—*D. Webster.*

Delightful task! to rear[r] the tender thought,
To teach[r] the young idea how to shoot[12].—*Thomson.*

(*a.*) "*Caught*" is a *verb*, it affirms something of a subject; *principal parts,—catch, caught, catching, caught; irregular*, it does not assume *ed; transitive*, it has an object; *active*, it represents the dog as acting; *indicative mood*, it declares something as an actual occurrence or fact; *past tense*, it refers the act simply to past time; and of the 3*d person, singular number*, to agree with its nominative, or subject, "*dog*," according to Rule XI. (Repeat it.) (*b.*) "*Is*" is an *auxiliary verb,*—a verb that helps another to express the act in a certain manner or time; it here expresses the *affirmation, indicative mood*, and *present tense*, of the verb "*is passing.*" "*Is passing*" is a *verb*, etc. (*c.*) Say,——*potential mood*, it expresses the permission to walk. ——*potential mood,* it expresses the moral necessity of plucking. (*d.*) "*To reward*" is a *transitive, active, present infinitive,* from the verb *reward, rewarded, rewarded.* It is here used as a noun of the *neuter gender,* 3d *person, singular number;* and in the *objective case*—being the object of the verb "*would refuse*"—according to Rule IV. (*e.*) "*Was spoken of*" is a *verb,* it affirms * * * *compound,* it is composed of a verb and a preposition; *prin. pts.,* etc. (*f.*) "*To be*" is an *infinitive,*—a form of the verb * * * *neuter,* it does not imply action; *present,* it does not express completion at the time referred to; and it relates to "*he,*" and modifies "*was born,*" according to Rule XII. (*g.*) —— it relates to "*I,*" and modifies "*came*" by expressing the purpose, according to Rule XII. (*h.*) ——principal parts,—*methinks, methought; defective,* it has not all the parts of a full verb * * * and *impersonal,* being used only in the 3d *person, singular number,* without a suitable subject, according to Note XI. (*i.*) "*Pursuing*" is a *participle,*—an inflected form * * * *transitive,* it has an object; *active,* it represents James as acting; *present,* it expresses the continuance of the act at the time referred to; and it relates to "*James,*" according to Rule XII. (*j.*) "*Being oiled*" is a *participle,* * * * *compound,* it is composed of the auxiliary participle "*being*" and the perfect participle "*oiled;*" *passive,* it assumes the act of the object acted upon, etc. (*k.*) Equivalent to "*We,* considering his age, *think,*" etc.; or apply Note XII. (*l.*) ——and one of the nominatives to "*rise,*" according to Rule I. (*m.*) ——and of the 3d *person, plural number,* to agree with "*Rhine and Rhone*"—a plural subject—according to Rule XI. (*n.*) —— and in the nominative case to *are* understood, etc. (*o.*) ——and of the 1st *person, plural number,* to agree with "*You, he, and I,*"—equivalent to *we,* a plural subject,—according to Rule XI. (*p.*) "*That Cortes with,*" etc., is a clause used as a noun of the *neuter gender,* 3d *person* * * * and in the *nominative case* to "*is,*" according to Rule I. (Now parse the words separately.)

Examples to be Corrected.

All the liabilities to error in regard to verbs, may be reduced to the following heads:—

1. *Choice of verbs.* 2. *Choice of forms.* 3. *Choice of auxiliaries.* 4. *Promiscuous use of different forms in the same connection.* 5. *Improper omissions or substitutions.* 6. *Verbs improperly made transitive, intransitive, or passive.* 7. *Moods and tenses.* 8. *Persons and numbers.* 9. *Participles and infinitives.*

In correcting the following examples, the principles already given should also be applied; and sometimes an example will occur that must be referred to the first precepts of this entire section.

1. *Choice of Verbs.*

The true or most appropriate verb should always be selected.

We were all setting round the fire. At the last setting of our legislature. He set up a short time, then lay himself down again. After laying a while, he raised up. He laid down to take a nap. He flew with his family to America. They shall fly from the wrath to come. All the lands near the Mississippi were overflown. Can you learn me to write? I waked early. The thief illuded the police. He was much effected by the news. I spent much time to advance my interest, but affected nothing. I expect it rained yesterday. We suspect the trip will afford us great pleasure. I love milk better than coffee. —*like*— Morse discovered the telegraph, and Harvey invented the circulation of the blood. The garment was neatly sown. A verb ought to agree with its subject, in person and number. (Say, "*should agree,*" for *ought* implies moral obligation.) Carry the horse to water. He was raised in the South. What large rivers from the west empty into the Mississippi? After dilating a while on the subject, the learned judge took his seat. —*expatiating*— With Mr. Headley, an event always "transpires."—*Poe.* The queen, whom it highly imported that the monarch should be at peace, acted the part of a mediator. I calculate to invest my money in something else. —*intend*— or, *expect*— I didn't go to do it. I have made a thousand bushels of potatoes this year. I am necessitated to go. We were falling trees to build a house. His property was forfeited to the State. —*confiscated*— (Suppose you are away from home, would you, in your letters, speak of *going* or of *coming* home?) Write for me no more, for I will certainly——. If I can absent myself, I will——to see you. She is now getting the better of her sickness. He was taken hold of by a ruffian. —*seized*— We were found fault with. —*censured*— One of the ships was lost sight of. And resolutely keep its laws, uncaring consequences.—*Burns*. —*not heeding*— or, *not fearing*— So and so got among horses, and it was all up with him.—*Tattler*. —*began to trade in horses, and lost all he had;* or, —*kept a coach, and soon became a bankrupt*.

2. Choice of Forms.

The true or most appropriate form of the verb should always be selected.

a. The past indicative should not be used as a participle.
b. The perfect participle should not be used for the past indicative.
c. A compound participle should not be used as a part of a finite verb.

He knowed more than he said. The blacksmith shoed my horse yesterday. He shewed me his library. I clomb the tree, and my brother holp me. What he writ, I never read.—*Byron*. A line was drawed under it. She is possessed of a large estate. —*possesses*— or, *owns*— She is possessed of a very amiable disposition. —*has*— I have this day parted possession with my finest horse. —*dispossessed myself of*— The accident was not taken notice of. —*was not noticed*. The young aspirant made use of every expedient to insure success. The warning was not taken heed of. The landlady says, our nocturnal carousings must be put a stop to. Troubles in Kansas have not as yet been put an end to. The book was give to me. Had I have known his design, I should not have let him have my horse. *Had I known ....I would not have loaned,* &c. Had I but have staid at home. You had not ought to have done so. —*You ought not to have*—or, *should not have*—

Loud quackt the ducks. It is a fixt fact. The hay was stackt. The goods were shipt yesterday. The want of money has checkt trade, and, in some instances, entirely stopt it. Grog is whiskey mixt with water. John alit from his horse. The wind swepped by. I stept in. Dipt, equipt, whipt, annext, attackt, dropt, stript, crusht, nurst, elapst, absorpt, linkt, distrest. Bedropt with azure, jet, and gold.—*Gay*. Rather than thus be overtopt, would you not wish their laurels cropt?—*Swift*.

Thou didd'st adore him. —*didst*— Spirit of freedom! once on Phyle's brow thou satt'st.—*Byron*. Thou mayest—mightest depart. How well thou reas'nest—reason'st, time alone can show. Thou rememberest—preservst. Thou noticedst. —*didst notice*. Thou indulgedst—indulged'st—indulg'dst. And long he try'd, but try'd in vain. —*tried*—

Wast thou chopping wood? (Say, "*Were you,*" &c.; for, in familiar language, the grave forms are not becoming.) Knowest thou where my books are? *Do you know,* &c. Learns she her lesson? He readeth pretty well. A drive into the country delighteth and invigorates us. The child had just been falling over board. —*had just fallen*— She is loving him. We be all of us from York State. I do not think you be in need of silk.

You might have went yourself. Mary has tore her book. My coat is completely wore out. Having swam the river, he was took by some Indians.

He begun well, but ended badly. I never seen any thing of it. The wine was all drank up, though I drank but little. Our candidate run well, though he was beat. The tree had fell, and all its branches were broke. The apples were shook off by the wind. They done the best they could. I have done written. —*already written.* I have done done it. She was chose on my side. Somebody has took my book. The deer had ran into the bottom, and swam across the river. The language spoke in this section of country, is not the best of English. I seen the limb tore off by the wind.

Wheat is now being sold for a dollar a bushel. —*is now selling*— The new capitol is now being completed. He gave me an account of all the books now being written or published in Europe. My predictions are now being fulfilled. He knew nothing of what was then being done. The timbers are now being hewed for a new bridge. Another Methodist church is now being built in the upper part of the city. The statutes were then being revised. My coat is now being made by the tailor. *The tailor is now making,* &c. His anticipations are now being realized. Dramshops are now being closed on Sundays. —*are closed*— Here certain chemical mysteries are being secretly carried on by some engineers.—*Harper's Magazine.* More than 20,000 children are being gratuitously educated in this city. —*are receiving gratuitous education*— The daughter is being accomplished at one of the most fashionable schools. Two Irishmen are being tried for fighting. —*are on trial*— Such a poem as this is worth being committed to memory. —*committing*— Whatever is worth being done, is worth being done well. The apple-tree will bear being pruned more. —*more pruning.* Such a body can not be overthrown without the centre of gravity being lifted. —*without lifting*—

3. *Choice of Auxiliaries.*

(The following examples come under both the foregoing heads, and may be corrected according to either.)

We will suffer from cold, unless we go better protected. The drowning foreigner said, "I will be drowned; nobody shall help me." Will I find you at home? You——find me there. Queen Isabella promised a pension to the first seaman that would discover land. (As if he could discover it at pleasure.) I left orders that every one would remain at his station. Shall he find any gold there? (As if it were in your power to grant the finding.) Will we find any? Would we hear a good lecture, if we would go? Surely goodness and mercy shall follow me all the days of my life, and I will dwell in the house of the Lord forever. Death was threatened to the first man who would rebel. (The overt act was meant.) I would have been much obliged to him, if he had have sent it. —*had sent it.* He should be obliged to you, if you would assist him. On the other hand, would they consult their safety, and turn back, who should blame them? We would be ruined, would they disappoint us. Whoever will marry that woman, will find her a Tartar. You may be sure that we will be paid, when it will be in his power. You might have known that we would have been paid, if the treasurer should have allowed it. We believed all the workmen should be paid, when our employer should have received his money. (Perhaps better, —"*had received*"—) I had much rather do it myself. —*would*— I desired the lady should walk in. Be that as it will, I shall not despair yet. —*as it is*— or, *as it may be*— I would not be surprised to see him any day. I would think no reasonable man could object to such a proposition. I was thinking what a happy life we would lead together. Were I to go with you, I would get a whipping. In that other world, what reflections shall not probably arise! By relieving him, we will do him a great favor. I was afraid I would lose all the capital I had invested.

4. *Promiscuous Use of Different Forms in the Same Connection.*

The promiscuous use of different forms of verbs, in the same connection, is inelegant.

Educating is to develop the faculties of the mind. To refrain from luxuries, is better than going in debt for them. To strip off old habits, is being flayed alive. To profess regard, and acting differently, discovers a base mind. Professing regard, and to act differently, discovers a base mind. So much explanation tends to obscure instead of elucidating the subject. —*rather than to elucidate*— or, *and not to elucidate*— ("It tended rather to confuse than to enlighten his understanding."—*Macaulay*.) This had served to increase instead of lleviating the inflammation.—*Murray*. We can find the product of two numbers, by multiplying one of them by the parts into which we choose to separate the other, and then add the products together. Fierce as he moved. his silver shafts resound. Spelling is easier than to parse or cipher. Scanning is to divide poetic lines into their feet. To scan is the dividing of poetic lines into their feet.

He giveth, and he takes away.—*Harper's Magazine*. He was playing, and does yet play. Does he not behave well, and gets his lessons as well as any other boy in school? Did you not borrow so much of me, and promised to repay it the next day? If these remedies be applied, and the patient improves not, the case may be considered hopeless. If the signature or indorsement be in the usual form, but the party receiving it knows that it is given by way of suretyship, he must prove the assent of the parties.—*Parsons on Contracts*. Thou who didst call the Furies from the abyss, and round Orestes bade them howl and hiss.—*Byron*. He comforteth the widow, and becomes a father to the orphan. For their sake, human law hath interposed in some countries, and has endeavored to make good the deficiency of nature. He was either misunderstood, or represented in a false light. —*or misrepresented.*

5. *Improper Omissions or Substitutions.*

When the omission of a verb, or the representing of it by an auxiliary word, would lead to impropriety or obscurity, the verb itself should be used.

The winter is departing, and the wild-geese flying northward. —*are flying*— Be quiet; for neither he nor I am disposed to harm you. —*neither is he, nor am I*— A room has been secured, and all other preparations made. Money is scarce, and times hard. The extremes of heat and cold are great; but the climate, nevertheless, salubrious. Our breakfast was ready, and our horses saddled. A dollar was offered for it, but five dollars asked. The ground was covered with forests, and the ravines completely hidden. I never have and never will assist such a man. —*have assisted*— All those who have or do purchase any of these books, shall receive a present.

As you have made the first, so you may do the rest. —*may make*— The intentions of some of these philosophers might, and probably were, good. His sermons must have and certainly should produce a reformation. Neither does he nor any other persons suspect so much dissimulation. No man can be more wretched than I. —*than I am.* I can not go, but I want to. —*to go.* (Such expressions, I think, are sometimes allowable, in light colloquial language; at least, the best authors sometimes use them.) Such a law, I believe, has been enacted; but if it has not, I think it ought to. I have not subscribed, nor do I intend to. This must be my excuse for seeing a letter which neither inclination nor time prompted me to.—*Washington*. He does pursue the course many others have done. —*have pursued.* No one ever sustained such mortifications as I have done to-day. I shall persuade others to take the same remedies for their cure that I have. A shower of rain refreshes vegetation more than can be done by ever so much watering.

6. *Verbs Improperly made Transitive, Intransitive, or Passive.*

Verbs should not be needlessly made transitive, intransitive, or passive, contrary to their general use, or contrary to analogy.

He had fled his native land. And Pharaoh and his host pursued after them. San Francisco connects with the sea, by an entrance one mile wide. A verb signifying actively, governs the accusative.—*Adam's Lat. Gram.* Any word that will conjugate, is a verb. I must premise with two or three circumstances. Go, flee thee away into the land of Judea. It now repents me that I did not go. They finally agreed the matter among themselves. Well, I suppose, we are agreed on this point. Such as prefer, may rise from their seats. —*prefer to do so*— Sit thee down, and rest thee. We had just entered into the house. He is entered on the duties of his office.

We are swerved far from the policy of our fathers. My friend is returned—is arrived. All the flowers are perished. His time of imprisonment was nearly elapsed. He is possessed of great talents. The tumult was then entirely ceased. A few were deserted, and more killed. This is true power: it approaches men to Gods. She is become more fretful than she used to be. Brutus and Cassius are rid, like madmen, through the gates of Rome. His profits will diminish from yours. She sat herself down on the sofa. He ingratiates with some by traducing others. His estate will not allow of such extravagance. You shall not want for any thing while I have it. The carriage is so full as not to admit of another passenger. I will consider of the matter, and let you know by morning. *What is the difference of meaning?* "To eat an apple;" "To eat of an apple."

7. *Moods and Tenses.*

1. Every verb should be in the mood and tense best adapted to express the meaning intended.

2. In mood and tense, all the verbs of a sentence should be consistent with one another, and also with the other words of the sentence.

a. The indicative mood expresses matter of fact, or what is assumed as such.

b. The subjunctive mood is used to express what is both doubtful and future, or a mere wish, supposition, or conclusion.

c. The subjunctive mood sometimes has the sense of the past or the pluperfect potential, but it should not take the place of these forms where they would be more elegant.

d. The infinitive leans to the noun, and most frequently expresses the purpose, or shows the respect wherein; the participle rather resembles the adjective in sense and construction.

e. Universal truths are expressed in the present tense, regardless of the construction, or the other words used.

She were as good buried, as married to him. —*might as well be*— I had better staid where I was. —*might have better*— You had better have let those wasps alone. —*might better*— He had better remain on the small farm. *It would be,* &c. Bad boys had better be without too much money. —*should not be indulged with—* The Glenn family will try and requite the favor. If he acquires riches, they will corrupt his mind. I shall go into the country to-day, unless it rains. If he speak only to display his talents, he is unworthy of attention. I wish I was at home. He talked to me as if I was a widow. Should you come up this way, and I am still here, you need not be assured how glad I shall be to see you.—*Byron's Letters.* I would be surprised if this marriage will take place. Make haste, lest the dinner cools. Beware that thou sinnest not. If I am at home, I will go with you. If he be safe, I am content. If the book be in my library, I will send it immediately. If the book is found in my library, I will send it immediately. If the book was in my library, I would send it. If the book were in my library, some one must have borrowed it. See that every thing is put in the right place. (Right or wrong, depending on the sense.) I can not tell whether the opossum be dead or alive. Will you tell us who they be? Try I will, whatsoever oppose. (Say, "*opposes,*" if opposition is considered certain; "*may oppose,*" if doubtful.) He indeed would be a useful policeman, that should detect all the rogues that were found in every part of this city.

If the hand is removed, the air immediately fills the vessel. *If....be.... will immediately fill—* or, *When the hand is removed....fills,* &c. (I think that "*fills*" might also be allowed to stand with "*be removed,*" and that it would make the expression merely a little more spirited.) If a man smites his servant, and he dies, he shall surely be put to death. —*smite....and the servant die, the man shall—* Though he be poor and helpless now, you may rest assured that he will not remain so. He will maintain his suit, though it costs him his whole estate. (Here the latter verb implies, or should imply, both doubt and future time.) Though a liar speaks the truth, he will hardly be believed. If he was to be elected, he would disgrace the party. —*were elected—* Suppose only one side with the adjacent angles were given, how would you find the other parts? I will keep this, provided there be no better one in your store. The work will be carried on vigorously, until it be completed. These hypocrites would deceive, if it was possible, the Deity himself. If any member absents himself, he shall pay a dollar for the use of the Society. The mother hurried her little children up a ladder for safety, in case she was overcome by the bear.—*Pioneer History.*

Saxony was left defenceless, and, if it was conquered, might be plundered. —*if it should be conquered—* Nay, Father Abraham, but if one went unto them from the dead, &c. If they did not believe Moses, they will not believe, though one rose from the dead. —*rise—* Though self-government produce some uneasiness, it is light when compared with the consequences of vicious indulgence. No one engages in that business, unless he aim at reputation, or hopes for some singular advantage. Micaiah said, If thou certainly return in peace, then hath not the Lord spoken by me. —*thou return—* In moving bodies, if the quantities of matter are equal, the momenta will be as the velocities. If the body A be equal to the body B, but A has twice the velocity of B, then A has twice as much motion as B. If a telescope is inverted, objects seen through it will be diminished. If a telescope be inverted, objects seen through it are diminished. If the two mirrors were separated, it is obvious that the number of images will be increased. Was there not another evil, I would object.—*P. Henry.* If the new Constitution takes place, the duties on imported articles will go into the general treasury.—*A. Hamilton.* A corporation is liable for the tortuous acts of its agent, though he were not appointed under seal.—*Parsons on Contracts.* (Perhaps allowable; though I should rather have said, "*even if he was not appointed,*" or, "*though he may not have been appointed,*" &c.) If the debtor pays the debt, he shall be discharged.—*Id.* But, if he have moved out of the State, the demand may be made at his former residence.—*Id.*

The Lord hath given, and the Lord hath taken away. I know the family more than twenty years. Knowing him for many years, I confidently recommend him. They continue with us now three days. All the family have been much indebted for their present greatness, to their noble ancestor. In the city of Mexico are preserved, for hundreds of years, relics of the Aztec monarchy. I am now two years in St. Louis. He has lately lost his only daughter. (Allowable, if there is also reference to the existing bereavement.) This style has been formerly much in fashion. He that was dead, sat up, and began to speak. I will pay him what I have promised him when I was with him. The workmen will finish the work by midsummer. Next Christmas I shall be at school a year. This was four years ago next August.—*Report of Normal School Convention.* It has been a common prejudice, that persons thus instructed had their attention too much divided, and could know nothing perfectly.—*Ib.* I have been frequently asked what we teachers did at our meetings.—*Ib.* (*I. e.,* at all times.) I should be obliged to him, if he will gratify me. Ye will not come unto me, that ye might have life. It is proper and humane to wear a habit suitable to mourning, while those we loved and honored are mouldering in the grave. It will be useless for you to raise so many grapes, unless you knew how to make wine.

The most glorious hero that ever desolated nations might have mouldered into oblivion, did not some historian take him into favor.—*Irving.* If I lend you my horse, I should have to borrow one myself. I thought it had been you that was bidding. Yet, if I should pay his debts, and get employment for him, he will not do any better in future. (Say, "*would do,*" if you refer simply to your own conclusion; but I think "*will do*" may stand, if you mean to express greater certainty in regard to his conduct.) To-morrow——Saturday. If we would examine into the springs of action in the prudent and the imprudent, we shall find that they move upon very different principles. I was going out to tea at dear mother's to-morrow.—*Mrs. Caudle.* (Allowable; for it expresses merely a past determination.) I told him that the cars leave in half an hour—left in half an hour. —*would leave*— (The first expression is probably allowable, as referring to an established order of things,—to a certain, punctual, daily occurrence.) As I never saw a play before, it was very entertaining to me. All church members should be pure in heart, that they might not be a reproach to Christianity. When I shall have heard from you, I will write immediately. As soon as he shall bring the horses, we shall leave. When the workmen completed our new house, we removed into it. As soon as our new house had been completed, we removed into it.

Our teacher told us that the air had weight. Prof. Silliman's experiments plainly proved that the gas was combustible. He showed clearly what powers belonged to Congress. He insisted that the Constitution was certain and fixed, and contained the permanent will of the people, and was the supreme law, and could be revoked only by the authority that made it.—*Kent.* Keats said, that beauty was truth, and truth was beauty. The doctor said that fever always produced thirst. Plato maintained that the Deity was the soul of the world. He remarked that the word had several different meanings. He insisted that the article was a mere adjective. If I should use the clause, "When spring returns," you would perceive that something more was wanting to make a statement. Without the name, I could not have told that this was a picture of him. I asked the quack whether calomel was not his remedy for every disease. He knew not that I was a foreigner. When I studied the classics, I observed that many a moral lurked in the mythology of the ancients. I have always thought that little was ever gained by marrying for wealth. A late writer on horses supposed that a horse could perform the labor of six men. He said it was a great misfortune, that men of letters seldom looked on the practical side of life. He said it was 125 miles from St. Louis to Jefferson City. Where did you say the church was? for I wish to hear its minister.

At Athens, he who killed another accidentally, was not deemed guilty. He is supposed to be born about three centuries ago. To be disappointed by him now, would have broken her heart. I very much wished to have gone, but mother could not spare me. We hoped to have had the pleasure of a visit from you. I intended to have sent your horse home yesterday, that you might not have been obliged to send for him yourself. I feared I should have lost it before I reached home. We have done no more than it was our duty to have done. It would have given me great pleasure to see you. (Allowable.) How could you forbear to have punished him? It was a pity I was the only child; for my mother had fondness of heart enough to have spoiled a dozen — *Irving*. I was then disposed to have given twice as much. I was under no obligation to have adhered to a party that deserted its own principles. The furniture was to have been sold at auction. When I saw into her coquetry, thinks I to myself I will let you know that you are not the only woman in the world. (Say, "*thought I to myself;*" yet "*thinks,*" as a light, colloquial expression, is not without good authority to sustain it.) Well, says I, there is, after all, much genuine goodness and solid happiness in the world. *What is the difference in meaning?* "Achilles is said to be buried at the foot of this hill." "Achilles is said to have been buried at the foot of this hill."

8. *Persons and Numbers.*

Every finite verb must agree with its subject, in person and number.

I called, but you was not at home. Was you there? My outlays is greater than my income. I says to him, Be your own friend. He dare not say it to my face. Such a temper need to be corrected. You who has earned it, is best entitled to it. Thou who are the author of life, can restore it. O thou pale orb that silent shines.—*Burns.* Thou art the friend that hast often relieved me. Thou art a friend indeed that has so often relieved me. Thou can pardon us if thou will. That which yourself has asked. 'Tis so; myself has seen it. I, who has done most of the work, should receive most of the pay. The molasses are excellent. His pulse are beating too fast. If a man have built a house, the house is his. Unless better bail have been given, he shall not be set at liberty. There are not many children in this city whose education have been entirely neglected. Has the horses been fed? What signifies fair words without good deeds? What have become of your promises? What avails the best maxims if we do not live suitably to them? On each side of the river was ridges of hills. Not more than one man was hurt. From this Indian girl has sprung some of the first families of Virginia. Six is too many to ride in the canoe at one time. Hence comes so many unhappy marriages.

There seems to be no others included. There was more than one of us. There's two or three of us. There appears to have been some buffaloes here last night. There was no memoranda kept of the sales. The victuals was cold. The wages was paid. There is no tidings. *Th* have two sounds. *Ph* are pronounced like *f*. In the following words, *sion* are pronounced *zhun*. *Boys* are a common noun. Here *as well as* are used in the sense of a conjunction.

Every one of the witnesses testify to the same thing. Every body are disposed to help him. Every twenty-four hours affords to us day and night. Every ten tens makes one hundred. Many an Indian were laid low on that day. Not one of them whom thou sees clothed in purple, are completely happy. One, added to nineteen, make twenty. Nothing but vain and foolish pursuits delight some persons. Enough of the corn and potatoes have been sold, to pay the debt. The derivation of these words are uncertain. Each one of us have as much as he can do. Each one of the vowels represent several sounds. Either one of the schools afford facilities sufficiently good. Neither of us have a dollar left. Neither of these hypotheses are well founded, though they have each of them their advocates. Which one of these soldiers were wounded at Monterey? A variety of pleasing objects charm the eye. Six months' interest are due on the bonds. The sum of twenty thousand dollars have been expended on this bridge. A hundred thousand dollars of revenue is now in the treasury. The spirit of our forefathers still animate their descendants. The expense for repairs render it necessary to raise the tuition. This poem, together with those which accompany it, were written several years ago. The mother, with her daughter, have spent the summer here. The captain, with most of the other officers, were killed. *The captain and, &c.*

You are not the first one that have been deceived in the same way. She is one of the women that is always hankering after towns, crowds, and parties. He is one of the preachers that belongs to the church militant, and takes considerable interest in politics. The book is one of the best that ever was written. Such accommodations as was necessary, was provided. Goethe and Schiller are men of such genius as have but seldom appeared in the human race. It is either the rain or the sun that cause this corn to grow so fast. It is the rain and the sun that——this corn to grow so fast.

A committee were appointed to examine the accounts. The committee disagrees. In France, the peasantry goes barefoot, while the middle sort makes use of wooden shoes. The greater part of the audience was pleased. The greater part of the exports consist of cotton. The public is respectfully invited. The fleet were seen sailing up the channel. The jury was not unanimous. All the world is spectators of your conduct. The regiment consist of a thousand men. There go a gang of deer. The legislature have adjourned. Never were any other nation so infatuated as the Jewish people. Generation after generation pass away. The company were chartered last winter. (Always consider carefully whether the reference is to the individuals composing the group, or to the group itself. There is plainly a difference between the two in regard to states or actions.) The corporation is individually responsible. At least half of the members was absent. The higher class looks with scorn on those below them. Our youth is not everywhere properly educated. The number of inhabitants in the United States now amount to thirty-two millions. The Society hold their meetings on Fridays. The House were called to order. The railroad company was rather uneasy—were rather unsafe. The multitude eagerly pursues pleasure. This sort of men is always sensitive. *Men of this sort,* &c. Five pair was sold. Fifty head was drowned. Our horse was routed with great slaughter by the Russian foot. *Our cavalry....infantry.* An exploring party that was sent to the north, were appalled by the aspect of the Appalachian chain, and pronounced the mountains impassable.—*Geo. Bancroft.* (Structure seldom found, but allowable, I think; for the one verb refers to the party as a whole, and the other refers rather to the individuals composing it.)

8 apples is no part of 12 pears. 8 are what part of 12? (If such a subject is viewed as an abstract whole, the verb should be singular; if viewed in reference to the composing units, or to concrete individuals, the verb should be plural.) As 2 are to 4, so 4 are to 8. 4 times 8 is 32.—*Bullions.* If $\frac{1}{4}$ of a sheep is worth $\frac{2}{3}$ of a calf, and if $\frac{1}{2}$ of a calf is worth $\frac{3}{5}$ of a hog, how many sheep are 8 hogs worth? (When a numeral subject must be read *plurally,* I should prefer the plural verb.) What part of 1 A. is 18 R. 18 P. 3 sq. yds.?—*D. P Colburn.* (I should rather say, "*are;*" for, though such a subject must be viewed as a

whole, it does not therefore necessarily require the verb to be singular; as, 'The mule, horse, and cow, | were sold for $200." Furthermore, the subject must be read plurally.

Mary and her cousin was at our house last week. Neither Mary nor her cousin were at our house last week. When sickness, infirmity, or misfortune, afflict us, the sincerity of friendship is proved. So much of ability and merit are seldom found. Enough ingenuity and labor has been bestowed, to make the machine a good one. When the memories and hopes of youth is embittered by past misfortunes, future happiness and usefulness becomes uncertain. Man's happiness or misery are, in a great measure, put into his own hands. Time and tide waits for no man. What signifies the care and counsel of preceptors, when youth think they have no need of assistance? Wisdom, virtue, and happiness, dwells with the golden mediocrity. The planetary system, boundless space, and immense ocean, affects the mind with sensations of astonishment. In all her movements, there is grace and dignity. And so was also you and I. Her beauty, intelligence, and amiability, was praised even by her own sex. Four and two is six, and one is seven. John, you, and I, am going to visit my uncle. The legality and utility of this law has never been called in question. Hill and dale doth boast thy blessing. What is the gender, person, and number of the following words? In unity consists the welfare and happiness of every society.

There was not a little wit and sarcasm in his reply. There is a right and a wrong in human actions. There was a man and a woman on our ship, who were natives of Borneo. There seems to be war and disturbance in Kansas. Out of the same mouth proceedeth blessing and cursing. On the same square has since been built a large hotel and a museum—a large warehouse and store. Hence comes the early decay and misery of such persons. Both vocal and instrumental music was heard every night. . This and that house belongs to him. In every room there was a large and a small bed. In him were happily blended true dignity with gentleness of manner.

Either Thomas or George have to stay at home. The violin or the banjo, played by some merry old negro, beguile the summer evenings. Neither the syntax nor the general scope of the paragraph are obvious. Neither Holmes, Forbes, nor Jenkins, were classmates of mine. When or, nor, or as well as, connect the nominatives, &c. The vanity, the ambition, the pride, or the sensitiveness of some men, keep them always in trouble. Luxurious living and excessive pleasure begets a languor and satiety that destroys all enjoyment "The Sword, the Needle, and the Pen," have been selected by her as the subject of her composition. It is honor, false honor, that produce so many quarrels. What black despair, what horror fill his mind!—*Murray.* That distinguished patriot and statesman have retired from public life. To be moderate in our views, and to proceed temporately——the best ways to insure success. To be of pure and humble mind, to exercise benevolence toward others, and to cultivate piety toward God, is the sure means of becoming happy. To live soberly, righteously, and piously, are required of all men. To do unto all men as we would that they, under similar circumstances, should do unto us, constitute the great principle of virtue. To be old and destitute, are truly deplorable. To possess true merit and yet be humble and obliging, are the true way to gain the esteem of the world. To buy such a lot, and build such a house upon it, require money. That it is our duty to relieve wretchedness and check oppression, admit not of any doubt. That a belle should be vain, or a fop ignorant, are not to be wondered at.

Every person are hereby notified to pay his or her taxes. *All persons.... their taxes.* (It is sometimes better to change the subject than to change the verb.) The horse, saddle, and bridle, was sold for $100. *The horse, with the*

VERBS.—EXERCISES. 233

saddle, &c. Every one of these houses have been lately built. Great pains has been taken to make the work accurate. *Great care*, &c. The sagacity and learning of that boy surpasses the rest. *In sagacity and learning, that boy*, &c. At the camp-meeting were all manner of folks and viands. —*all kinds*— The doctors' and mothers' giving calomel for every little illness, is one cause of so many puny women and children. *The practice of giving calomel*, &c. There is an elegance and simplicity in Addison's style, that will always please. —*an elegance, as well as a simplicity*— or, *an elegance, a simplicity, in*— The clerk, as well as the captain, own the entire boat. —*and*— He, and not I, am responsible. I, and not he, is responsible. Not honor, but emolument, have induced him to accept the offer. Economy, as well as industry, are necessary to make us wealthy. The land, as well as the personal property, were sold at auction.

Books, and not pleasure, occupies his mind. Pleasure, and not books, occupy his mind. Not honor, but emoluments, has induced him to accept the offer. Not only the sails, but also the mainmast, were torn away by the storm. He, not less than you, deserve punishment. He, and his brother too, ⎯⎯ in the battle of Buena Vista. The father, and the son also, ⎯⎯ imprisoned for many years. No one but yourself and the lecturer believe such doctrines. Nothing, save the chimneys of the boat, were visible. (*Are both the following sentences correct?* " Happiness, honor, yea, life itself, are sacrificed in the pursuit of riches;" "Happiness, honor, yea, life itself is sacrificed in the pursuit of riches." What is the difference in meaning?) Every tall tree and every steeple were blown down. Every leaf, every twig, and every drop of water, teem with delighted existence. Every man's heart and temper is productive of much inward joy or misery. Every person and every occurrence were viewed in the most unfavorable light. Every seven days makes a week. No wife, no mother, and no child, were there to comfort him. No lazy boy or girl love their books. Every skiff and canoe were loaded almost to the water's edge. Here lie buried every chief and every warrior of the tribe.

For the sake of brevity and force, one or more words is sometimes omitted. Neither beauty, wealth, nor talents, was injurious to his modesty. Whether one or more persons was concerned in the transaction, does not appear. Neither he nor you was mentioned. Either thou or I art much mistaken. Neither he nor I intends to be present. Either you or James have spilt my ink. Either they or I are responsible. Neither thou nor I art to blame. *Neither thou art to blame, nor am I.* The forest, or the hunting-grounds, was deemed the property of the tribe. (Here "*forest*" seems to be rejected for the more appropriate term "*hunting-grounds*," which, therefore, becomes the nominative to the verb "*was*," and this should accordingly be "*were*.") Lafayette Place, or Gardens, occupy several acres. (Here "*Gardens*" is merely parenthetical.) Neither the potatoes nor the corn are as good as usual. (Make the verb agree with the nearest nominative or the most important.) Riding on horseback, or rowing a skiff, are good exercises. His food were locusts and wild honey. (What am I chiefly speaking of,—his *food*, or *locusts* and *wild honey?*) The quarrels of lovers is a renewal of love. The difference between 8 and 12 are 4. Eight pples is the difference between twelve apples and twenty. Five dimes is half dollar. The timber are walnut, elm, mulberry, and linden. —*is*— or, *consists of*— A great cause of sickness in cities are filthiness and bad food.

Two parallel horizontal lines is the sign of equality. The sign of equality are two parallel horizontal lines. —*consists of*— First, ascertain what is the texture, color, and weight? The few dollars which he owes me, is a matter of small consequence. Twelve single things, viewed as an aggregate, is called a dozen. Divers philosophers hold that the lips is parcel of the mind.—*Shak.* Said the burning Candle, "My use and beauty is my death." Virtue and mutual confidence is the soul of friendship. To do good to them that hate us, and on no occasion to seek revenge——the duty of a Christian. Temperance, more than medicines, are the proper means of curing many diseases. What a fortune does the thick lips owe, if he can carry her thus.—*Shak.* (Proper; for "*thick lips*" is here put for the Moor Othello.) Here is the Republican, the Herald, and the Leader.—*Newspaper-boy.* (Proper; for the design is to keep the objects distinct.) On a sudden, off breaks the limb, and down tumbles negro, raccoon, and all. (Proper; for the design is to represent the objects as most intimately united—so intimately that they may appear as but one thing.) *Proper, or not?* "A coach and six is in our time never seen, except as a part of some pageant."—*Macaulay.* "Two thousand a year was a large revenue for a barrister."—*Id.*

9. Participles and Infinitives.

1. The participle or the infinitive should never be so used as to make the sentence clumsy, obscure, or ambiguous.
2. *To*, the sign of the infinitive, is omitted after the active verbs *bid, make, need, hear, | let, see, feel,* and *dare;* and occasionally, after a few other verbs that are like some of these in sense.
3. Since the participle and the infinitive are much alike in sense and construction, great care should always be taken to select that which is more appropriate.
4. A participial noun should never be so used that it may be mistaken for an adjective, a participle, or a part of a compound verb.
5. When a participial noun from a transitive verb is limited by a preceding article, adjective, or possessive, it generally becomes intransitive, and requires *of* after it.
6. When a participial noun from a transitive verb is not limited by a preceding word, it may generally govern the objective case.
7. Of the four modes of expression,—the ordinary noun, the participial noun, the infinitive, and the substantive clause,—great care should be taken to select the most appropriate the language affords.

We saw the lady while passing down the street. (Who passed?) He pleaded the case in such a manner as to become tedious and disagreeable. (Change the entire sentences if necessary.) I think of you alone more frequently than when surrounded by others. While sleeping under a large tree, my horse was stolen. I heard the noise of a carriage, eating my supper.

You will please send them back immediately, if you can not sell them. We ought not speak ill of others, unless there is a necessity for it. If I bid you to study, dare you to be idle? To go I could not, but to remain I would not. That old miser was never seen give a cent to the poor. Not a single complaint was heard escape the lips of any individual. We made her to believe it. She was made believe it. We durst not to approach any nearer to the elephant. His father compelled him return to his school. It is better live on a little than outlive a great deal. Will you please answer my letter immediately? I would have you read all the books on the subject. I have known young men spend more in a week than they earned in a year.

EXCEPTIONS.—" My horse bids fair to take the premium; "He was let go;" "I dared him to bet;" "I feel it to be my duty;" "How could you make out to get along?" "She needed only to have told us that she was unwell;" "I can not see to write this letter,"—are all correct or allowable. "He can show his moral courage, only by daring do right."—*G. Brown.* Mr. Brown has written this sentence for good English; but, to my ear, "*by daring to do right,*" sounds better.

I would not have let her gone to such a place. —*go*— He neglected doing his duty. —*to do*— He failed reciting his lesson. I intended giving him a piece of my mind. He chose building in another place. I preferred staying at home. You have no right meddling with my property. No nation should be allowed interfering with the domestic affairs of another. We should never undertake doing too much at once. I never desired having such a man for a friend. No one likes being in debt. It is easier asking questions than answering them. Going to law is giving the matter in dispute to the lawyers. I was about sending for you when you arrived. He said to us, "It is as sport to a fool doing mischief." There is no telling what he would do if left to himself. *It is impossible to tell what, &c.* The being branded with such a piece of iron, would make the horse run away. *To brand the horse, &c.* We considered ourselves to be badly treated. He was seen to ride along the road. Relieving misery is a pleasure to the good. Compromising conflicting opinions, will ever be necessary in a large republic. What prevents our going immediately? —*us from going*— What is to prevent us going together? I had bolted the door to prevent it being opened—its being opened. What prevents such worthless fellows passing for fine gentlemen but the good sense of other men?— *Addison.* The mother's good sense prevents the daughter's having her head made giddy by fops, beaus, and riches.

His being industrious and frugal will make him rich. *His industry, &c.* Paying visits will be losing time. Barter is exchanging different commodities. Is not this abusing the privileges of the House? The mind soon becomes weary by its being intensely applied to one subject. The most important business is determining the boundary line.

There is a strong necessity for us being more frugal. This measure is taking a bold step. This punctuation is giving the sentence a different meaning from the true one. Such a law would not be giving all the States an equal right to the territories. Scanning is dividing poetic lines into their feet. The highway of the upright is departing from evil. His whole speech was begging the question. His being acquainted with influential men was of great service to him. What is called a compound pronoun, from its usually representing two words. —*because it*— She was much opposed to him rioting with bad companions. Your being left was altogether accidental. *That you were, &c.* The common saying of every one's being the architect of his own fortune, is hardly true. Nothing that she has done, can justify your having treated her so contemptuously. —*you in having treated*— There are not many instances of creditors not being disposed to be oppressive to their debtors. —*instances in which*— Her lameness was caused by a horse's running away with her. —*by a horse that ran*— It is not proper to speak of a river's emptying itself. —*river as emptying*— We were speaking of the congregation's being so much affected by the sermon. The servant's being negligent has caused the losing of the horse. In order to our correctly understanding the subject, let us suppose, &c. The fact of he being a partner—of him being a partner, gave credit to the firm.

By speaking of truth, you will command esteem. By the obtaining wisdom, you will command esteem. By obtaining of wisdom, you will command esteem. By reading of good books, his mind became improved. Learning of languages is difficult. It is an overvaluing ourselves, to reduce every thing to our own standard of judging. Poverty turns our attention too much upon the supplying our wants; riches, upon the enjoying luxuries. This was a cowardly forsaking his party. By the vigorously pursuing his studies, he will soon be competent. *By vigorously pursuing his, &c.* We were agreeably entertained by the visiting of our friends. —*by a visit from*— or, *by a visit to*— This money was used in feathering of his own nest. Luxury, indolence, and a fantastic sense of propriety, are the chief causes which tend to the enervating and enfeebling our women. The taking things by force is apt to produce reaction. This was in fact a converting the deposits to his own use. The placing yourself in the most conspicuous situation will tend to render you contemptible. (The infinitive is sometimes preferable to the participle, and the ordinary noun is sometimes preferable to either.)

Multiplication is the repeating a number a given number of times. —*is the repetition of*— Emphasis is the laying a greater stress on some particular word or words. The cutting evergreens for Christmas was fashionable when I was a boy. The saying what we think, is not always prudent. *To say what*, &c. The inviting them will not put us to any more trouble. The not having invited them to the party, she afterwards regretted. *That she had not*, &c. There is no keeping such children in the house. —*no keeping of*— or, *It is impossible to keep*, &c. A more careful guarding the prisoners would have prevented this accident. For the better regulating our governments in the territories. This amounts to a full relinquishing her dowry. His neglecting my affairs, has been very injurious to me. The separating large numbers into periods, facilitates the reading them correctly. *Is each of the following sentences correct?* "Your building so fine a house, may excite the envy of your neighbors;" "My seeing him, will be sufficient;" "My seeing of him, will be sufficient;" "My having seen him, will be sufficient;" "My having seen of him, will be sufficient;" "The soldiers deserted on account of the captain's ordering him to be whipped;" "The soldiers deserted on account of the captain's ordering of him to be whipped."

OBSERVATIONS.

1 & 2. In Old English, *be* was often used where other parts of this verb are now used. "In other pleasures there is satiety; and, soon after they *be used*, their verdure fadeth."—*Bacon.* Verbs differing in sense, are sometimes nearly identical either in their primitive forms or in their derived forms, as *set, sit ; overflowed, overflown:* and hence they are often ridiculously misapplied. "I can but go," implies that I can do nothing more; "I can not but go," implies that I can not do otherwise, but most go: hence both forms should be retained, since they are both needed. *Dare, let, need,* and *ought*, are considered principal verbs, and not auxiliaries, though they seem to be in a middle or transition state, especially *need*, which is sometimes found without inflection. "She *need* not *make* herself uneasy."—*Irving. Can not* should rather be written as two words, unless we mean to prevent *not* from qualifying some other word than the verb; as, "You *cannot* consistently deny it."

When the ordinary passive form implies completion, habit, or custom, the word *being* is sometimes inserted to express continuance. "To other stations where the new rifle-practice *was being introduced*."—*Atlantic Monthly.* "The materials of discontent *were* gradually *being concentrated*."—*Ib.* "The evaporation dish of the the philosopher *was being used* by an irreverent sparrow."—*Harper's Magazine.* "Your friend *is being buried*."—*Ib.* Such forms are avoided by the best writers. "While these affairs *were transacting* in Europe."—*Bancroft.* "Where a new church *is* now *building*."—*E. Everett.* "The medley of monuments with which Kensing-green *is filling*."—*E. Surgent.* "The shocking neologism, 'The ship *is being caulked*.'"—*G. P. Marsh.* We should combine the simple present or perfect participle with the auxiliary, or, if neither of these forms will give the sense, use the active voice, or recast the sentence. Our language occasionally needs forms to express in the continuative passive sense those verbs whose perfect participles imply completion; and, as necessity makes slaves of us all, the foregoing uncouth passive forms are rather gaining ground. But, if the perfect participle implies completion, the compound participle also does; therefore, *is being built*, for instance, is literally the same in time as *is built*, and has the progressive sense merely by adoption. The uncouth forms are used only in the *present* and the *past* indicative; for such forms as *had been being built, might be being built, might have been being but*, die of sheer ugliness.

3. So very often are the auxiliaries needed and misapplied, that the following full explanation will perhaps not seem too lengthy to the reader. "*Shall* I go?" Is it your wish or determination? Are you willing? "*Shall* I find you when I return?" Will it come to pass? Will you have it so? "*Will* I go?" Ordinarily absurd, unless taken up and repeated as another's question. "*Shall* you go?" Is it so determined? Will it take place? "*Will* he go?" Is he willing to go? Is he likely to go? "*Shall* we be married?" Are you willing? Will it take place? (Where the plural is not given, it agrees with the corresponding singular.) "*Shall* I be elected?" "*Shall* I suffer?" Will it come to pass? Is that to be my fate? "*Will* you be elected? Are you willing? *More frequently*, Will it come to pass? "*Shall* you be elected?" Will it come to pass? (Seldom so used in the West.) "*Shall* he be elected?" "*Shall* he suffer?" Is that the determination? "*Will* he be elected?" "*Will* he suffer?" Will it come to pass?

"I *shall* go." "I *shall* be elected." "I *shall* suffer." It will come to pass—I foretell it. "I *will* go." "I *will* be elected." "I *will* suffer." I am willing; I promise it; I am resolved upon it. It is in my power, and I am determined to have it so. "You *shall* go." "You *shall* be elected." "You *shall* suffer." It is so determined. It is to be so in spite of your will or of obstacles. "He *shall* go." "He *shall* be elected." "He *shall* suffer." The same in sense as the preceding. "You *will* go." "You *will* love him." "You *will* come to this at last." It will come to pass, and probably be voluntary. "You *will* be elected." "You *will* suffer." It will come to pass. "He *will* go." "He *will* assist you." "He *will* be elected." "He *will* suffer." Same as the second person. "It *will* cost blood and treasure." "It *shall* cost neither." Determination to prevent. "Hickory *will* make a good fire." It is adapted thereto. "This *will* do." "This *will* never do." Adaptation; adequacy. "I *will* be pleased with his company." I will try to make it agreeable to myself, even if it should tend to be otherwise. "I *shall* be pleased with his company." It will be agreeable, whatever it be. *Will* may denote a future certainty, depending on ability; *shall*, a future certainty assuming the ability. "Philip *will* hang Astor, if he [Philip] takes the city."—*Ancient History*. "I *shall* then *trample* on all those forms in which wealth and dignity intrench themselves."—*Chatham*. *Shall*, being *authoritative*, is sometimes preferred in emphatic prediction. "It *shall come* in empire's groans, burning temples, trampled thrones."—*Croly*.

"If any one *shall* subscribe." "Whoever *shall* subscribe." Simply, if it take place. "If any one *will* subscribe." "Whoever *will* subscribe." "If you *will* subscribe." "When you *will* subscribe." "Unless we *will* give our consent." To be willing, and do so. In this sense, *shall* or *should* often refers to the *overt* act; and *will* or *would*, simply to the intention. I would say, "I promise that I *will*——you *shall*——he *shall*"——; "I resolved that I *would*——you *should*——he *should*"——; where I have or mean to use authority: "I believe that I *shall*——you *will*——he *will*"——; "I believe that I *should*——you *would*——he *would*"——; "I assured him that you *would*——he *would*"——; where the matter is not in my control. And so in the other persons: "You are determined that I *shall*——you *will*——he *shall*"——; "You were determined that I *should*——that you *would*——that he *should*"——. "He is determined that I *shall*——that you *shall*——that he *will*"——; "He was determined that I *should*——that you *should*——that he *would*"——. "You think I *shall* suffer——you *shall*——he *will*"——; "You thought that I *should* suffer——that you *should*——that he *would*"——. "He thinks that I *shall* be killed——that you *will*——that he *shall* or *will*——that our friend *will*"——. "He hoped that I *should* be sent——that you *should*——that he himself *should* or *would*——that our friend *would*"——. "He requested that our friend *should* be sent for."

"Do you think I *shall* go?" That it will come to pass. "Do you think I *should* go?" That I ought to go; or, that my going would take place, if certain things should happen, whether I might be willing or not. "Did you think that I *should* go?" That it would come to pass; or, that it was my duty to go. "Do you think, or did you think, that I *should* have gone?" That it would have happened; or, that it was my duty to go. "Do you think I *will*?—I *would*?" "Did you think I *would*?" refer to my will—my motives. "I am surprised that he *will* go." At his going under such circumstances. "I am surprised that he *would* go." From what I know of his general character. "I am surprised that he *shall* go." That it is so determined. "I am surprised that he *should* go." I am surprised at the mere occurrence of the a.t, without reference to any motives or necessity. "John was afraid that he *would* not succeed." "John was afraid that he *should* not succeed." The former implies a stronger reference to the adaptation of the means to the end; the latter implies more of chance. "I, you, he, it, *should*"——. It is a matter of duty, right, or propriety. "I, you, he, it, *should* .... *if*"——. Something to take place on condition; or else, the same as the preceding. "*Should* I, you, he, it .... then"——; "If I, you, he, it, *should* .... then"——. If it were to take place .... then——. "I, you, he, she, it, *would*"——. Inclination, proneness, custom, tendency; or, consequence, result. "If I *would* study." If I were willing. "If I *should* study." Were it to take place; a mere supposition. "If I *would* have written." I was unwilling, and did not. "If I *should* have written." Had I done so. "If I *would* betray him, he *should* forsake me," is very different from "If I *should* betray him, he *would* forsake me." So, "If he *should* leave you, you *would* suffer;" "If he *would* leave you, you *should* suffer." "If it *would* ruin." Wished. "If it *should* ruin." Perhaps not wished. "He was to remain until he *should* be sent for." Bare event. "Until he *might* be sent for." Greater contingency; or possibility. In a moral sense, *can* is a little stronger than *may* "I may not do so." I have not permission, or it would be improper. "I *can* not violate my oath." My conscience forbids it. "It *must* have been so." Present necessity of belief. "Had the river risen, he *must have drowned;*" pluperfect. Past necessity.

Most of the auxiliary verbs usually set forth the act or state as not absolutely certain; but as tinged with allusion to the condition, time, or circumstances, on which it depends, and as expressing, accordingly, a corresponding degree of certainty. Hence, they may sometimes be used to express softened commands or assertions. "You *will* not hurt him, will you?" for, "Do not hurt him." "It *would* seem so" [if you should examine the evidence; or rather, the evidence tends to persuade one to this belief], for, "It seems so." "It *should* seem so" [from the deference naturally due to evidence of such authority], for, "It seems so." "I *should* think not" [from what you tell me], for, "I think not." "I *should* hardly believe it" [were it told to me; or, scarcely any thing is sufficient to cause such belief], for, "I hardly believe it." Sometimes the sense of the auxiliaries in the potential mood is nearly lost, and the mood becomes almost indicative in meaning. "He knew not how far the ramifications of the conspiracy *might extend*."—*D. Webster.* —did *extend.* When the time is sufficiently indicated without the auxiliary, then the auxiliary must denote something else, or be superfluous. "When he *will come;*" "When I *shall have arrived.*" If *will* and *shall* were here inserted merely to express the time, the expressions would have been better without them. "When he *comes;*" "When I *have arrived.*" *Will*, when put into such clauses, relates directly to the will of the subject; and *shall* implies determination, resolution, contingency. "They should remember that England entered India from the sea, and that until she *shall have been subdued* on that element, it would be idle to think of dispossessing her of her Oriental supremacy."—*Atlantic Monthly*. That is, until resolved upon and accomplished. The author rather believes or intimates that this is not easy or likely to be done.

6. In imitation of a French idiom, the passive forms of such verbs as *become, arrive, rejoice, sit,* &c., were formerly much used; but the present tendency is, to prefer the active forms. Mr. Brown says, that a few verbs are yet thus used, to signify that a person's own mind is the cause that actuates him; as, "He *was resolved* on going to the city to reside;" "He *is inclined* to go;" "He *is determined* to go." When a passive sense can not be conceived, or when the active form seems equally proper, this should generally be preferred. Thus, "I *incline* to think," is now generally preferred to "I *am inclined* to think." *Mistake*, in the passive form, is still in good use; as, "I *am mistaken;*" but the active form is also used; as, "I *mistake:* it is your bull that has kil'sd one of my oxen." "You *are mistaken,*" can be sometimes conceived as being a delicate euphemism for, "I misconceive your meaning."

7. The selection of moods and tenses is sometimes a matter of great nicety, especially in argumentative discourse. The conditional present indicative expresses doubt only. The conditional present subjunctive expresses both doubt and future time; and the conclusion belonging to it, is generally expressed in the future indicative. Indicative forms are sometimes preferred as being a little sprightlier, or as relating to permanent or universal truths. "I will keep it till he *returns.*" I am sure he will return. "I will keep it till he *return.*" I doubt that he will ever return. "If Congress *have* not the granted right, it can not exercise it." Said before the Constitution was made. "If Congress *has* not the granted right, it can not exercise it." Said after the Constitution was made. "If the government of Virginia *passes* a law contrary to the bill of rights, it *is* nugatory." —*P. Henry.* At any time; and there is no doubt as to the conclusion. "If gentlemen *are* willing to run the hazard, let them run it."—*Id.* They seem to be quite willing. The orator referred to existing facts then before his mind; but had he not been aware of the existence of any such willingness at the time, and supposed it merely probable, he would have said, "If gentlemen *be* willing," etc. "If a piece of paper *be laid* on the table of the discharger, and a powerful shock *directed* through it, it *will be torn* in pieces."—*Arnot.* "*Be* laid" accords best with "*will be* torn." "If a fresh quantity of water *is thrown* upon the remaining fragments, it *is absorbed* with a hissing sound."—*Id.* "*Is* thrown" accords best with "*is* absorbed;" besides, the former verb here denotes what is often done, and the latter, what certainly follows. "If the earth *is* at H, and the planet at I, the outermost satellite *will be* in conjunction with its primary."—*Bowditch.* Allowable; for *will* expresses merely the natural consequence. "If an object *is* [or *be*] in the principal focus, it *will appear* brighter." The present subjunctive is now applied merely to future and contingent matter of fact, rather than to present matter of fact of which our knowledge is future and contingent. "If this *be* true, I shall," &c. It either is true, or is not true; but there is a mental contingency in regard to ascertaining its truth hereafter. "If this *is* true," etc., is better authorized. And, "If this *is* treason, make the most of it." The time involved in the tenses, may relate to the speaker, to the doer, to the beginning, state, or end of the act, or to any of its circumstances; and hence the many niceties in regard to tenses. The perfect infinitive is antecedent, in time, to the leading verb; hence verbs of *hoping, intending, commanding,* &c., generally require the present; but it is wrong to teach that none of them ever admit the perfect. "Dr. Rush *hopes to have laid* the foundation of a system which, if adopted, will," &c.—*G. Brown.* (Correct.)

8. Sometimes the form of the subject, but more commonly the sense, controls the form of the verb. When a verb relates to two nominatives, of which one is a predicate-nominative, it is not always easy to decide which should be considered the subject. If both stand after the verb, the nearer one is its subject. When the arrangement is otherwise, the student, if he has been well drilled in Analysis, will generally be able to determine without much difficulty. When two or more *infinitives,* or *infinitive phrases,* or *substantive clauses,* are connected by *and,* it is also sometimes difficult to decide whether the verb should be singular or plural. The writer or speaker best knows his own meaning: let him consider whether he refers *to all as one thing,* or whether he refers to *each,* and accordingly make the verb *singular* or *plural.* The phrases "as follows," "as regards," "as appears," "as concerns," should generally be used as they are here given, unless they occur so closely in connection with a plural substantive as to be influenced by it; as, "The *exceptions* are as *follow.*"—*Wilson's Punctuation.* Mr. Wilson uses this mode of expression frequently, though other writers generally prefer the singular form. Mr. Brown's doctrine of *Thou,* and its "familiar forms" of the verb, is evidently erroneous.

Nominatives involving *numbers,* or *arithmetical nominatives,* are not yet well settled in regard to their syntactical structure. Most of them may be classed with *collective* nouns. In *addition,* the verb must of course be *plural;* in *subtraction, division,* or *proportion,* it may be *singular* or *plural,* according to the view taken; in *fractions* and *compound numbers* that must be read *plurally,* the verb should, I hink, be generally *plural,* though the principle that a plural term sometimes denotes a single object, or that two or more singular nominatives connected by *and* denote but one person or thing, sometimes operates in favor of the *singular* verb. As to *multiplication,* I believe the prevailing custom is this: When the word *times* is used, it controls the form of the verb; when *once, twice,* or *thrice,* is used, the verb should be singular or plural, according as the expression involves the idea of *time* or *times.* Mr. Brown says, that the *multiplicand* should be considered the nominative; and that when this is *one, naught,* or any other singular, the verb should be *singular;* and when it rises above *one,* the verb should be *plural.* This is certainly the most rational view, and can be best sustained by the grammatical analysis of the subject, and also by analogy. It accords best with such expressions as, "Twice the sum is insufficient to pay my debts;" "Four times the son's age is equal to the father's;" "Ten times the amount was refused;" "Five times the quantity was sold;" which are perhaps too well established to be condemned. The German language also confirms this latter opinion, except, I believe, that it more frequently regards the multiplicand a singular collective noun.

9. It is sometimes difficult to determine whether the participle or the infinitive should be preferred. Sometimes either may be used. The present participle denotes an act or state as accompanying that of the principal verb, while the infinitive commonly implies that the acts or states are successive. The infinitive is generally better adapted, than the participle, to express the act or state substantively. When a substantive participle or infinitive is to be used in connection with the substantive denoting the object to which the act or state belongs, it is often better to use the clause beginning with *that*. When a verbal appositive relates to an initial *it*, it should rather be the infinitive than the participle; as, "It is useless *trying*," should be, "It is useless *to try*." After verbs of *trying* or *intending*, the infinitive should be used. After the verbs *hear*, *see*, and *feel*, either may be used. After verbs of *omitting*, *avoiding*, or *preventing*, the participle should generally be used. After verbs of *beginning*, *continuing*, or *desisting*, the participle may generally be used, though the infinitive is sometimes more elegant. Whether a substantive associated with a participle should be made possessive, depends on which term conveys the more prominent idea. "The fair wind is the cause of the vessel's sailing;" not, "The fair wind is the cause of the vessel sailing." When a participle is limited by such a preceding word as usually requires *of* after the participle, the *of* may sometimes be omitted before pronouns, when it rather affects the sense of the participle than corresponds to the antecedent limiting word. "Your eating of it made you sick," is not equivalent to "Your eating it made you sick." "He said it in hearing his father," "He said it in the hearing of his father," differ in sense: the word *hearing*, in the former, relates to *He*; in the latter, to *father*. "He was killed by galloping a horse." He himself rode the horse. "He was killed by the galloping of a horse." Some other person, or else no one, rode the horse.

9. ADVERBS.

353. An **adverb** is a word used to modify the meaning of a verb, an adjective, or an adverb. Sometimes an adverb modifies a phrase or an entire proposition.

Ex.—"She is homely, but she sings *beautifully*." "The lake is *very* deep." "*Yonder* lies your book." "I will write *to-morrow*." "He speaks *tolerably well*." "He sailed *nearly* round the world." *Nearly* modifies not the preposition *round*, but the adjunct *round the world*, for an adjunct—an adjective or an adverb. "The book is soiled *only* ON THE OUTSIDE." "He was *so* young, *so* intelligent, *so* | every thing that we are apt to like in a young man."—*Irving*. Here the entire part of the sentence after the last *so*, has the sense of an adjective modified by *so*. "Have you seen him?—*No*." Here it is simplest to regard *No* as modifying the question. Words from other parts of speech are also occasionally used as adverbs. "*Carnation* red; *marble* cold; *somewhat* better; *none the* worse; *passing* strange; *dripping* wet; *scalding* hot." "It fell *down*." "*Above, around, beneath, within,* the lurid fires gleamed." "You have paid *dear* for the whistle." "*Tramp, tramp,* across the laud they speed; *splash, splash,* across the sea."—*Scott*. "*The* stronger the mind, *the* greater its ambition."—*Addison*. Degree. "His heart went *pit-a-pat*, but hers went *pity Zekle.*"—*Lowell*. How?

354. Some entire phrases are customarily used as adverbs. Such are termed *adverbial phrases*, and parsed like adverbs.

Ex.—"In general"—*generally* ; "by and by"—*soon, shortly;* "at all"—*in any degree.* "At least; in short; on high; in fine; at present; at last; on the contrary; out and out; through and through; no more; at most; for the most part; three times; four times; man by man—Lat. *viritim;* foot by foot; glass to glass." "He said it *again and again.*" "Whose brisk awakening sound he loved *the best.*"

"Representation and taxation should go *hand in hand*." "The argument was carried against him *all hollow*."—*Irving*. A phrase should not be parsed as a whole, when its words can be parsed separately with as much propriety.

355. An adverb *modifies* by expressing *manner, degree, place, time,* or some other circumstance. See above.

356. Sometimes an adverb modifies its word, in relation to a substantive in the same clause or proposition.

Ex.—"*Not only* he must go, but you *too*." "And *chiefly* thou, O Spirit, instruct me."—*Milton*. "'Twas better so to close, than longer wait to part *entirely* foes."—*Byron*. "John *only* | borrowed the horse." No other person assisted. "John | *only* borrowed the horse." He did not buy him. "John borrowed the horse *only*;" "John borrowed | *only* the horse." He borrowed nothing more. "And leave the world for me to bustle *in*."

357. Some adverbs connect two clauses, and modify a word in each. Such are called *conjunctive adverbs*. The clause with the adverb has the sense of an adverb, an adjective, or a noun.

Ex.—"Make hay *while* the sun shines." When. "He rode the horse *before* he bought him." "You speak of it *as* you understand it." How? "Go *where* glory waits thee." Whither? "In the grave *where* our hero was buried." In what grave? "The reason *why* it has been negected, is obvious." What reason? "I saw *how* a pin is made." I saw what? Sometimes the antecedent or correlative adverb is expressed, and then the latter adverb merely joins on and modifies its own part. "I was *there* | *where* it happened." *Where it happened* is explanatory of *there* somewhat like an appositive.

358. Sometimes adverbs so little affect the sentence that it would not seem improper to say they are used *independently*.

Ex.—Yes, no, ay, amen, accordingly, consequently, &c. "*Nay*, such was the general clamor, that," &c. "*Why*, you must be crazy." "*Well*, I hardly know what to say." "*So, so*, and this is the way you have spent your time." "There were three in all; *namely*, John, James, and Joseph." "*Secondly*, he could go there if he would." "There is none righteous, *no*, not one." "*Thus*, in France, common carriers are not liable for robbery."—*Kent*. Adverbs thus used partake of the nature of conjunctions or interjections. Most of them may be parsed as adverbs modifying the entire proposition, or the preceding sentence or discourse, or else something understood; and some of them are always best parsed as conjunctions.

359. Adverbs, like adjectives, may be divided into classes, and they have also comparison. Many adverbs may be compared like adjectives; but derivative adverbs ending in *ly*, are nearly always compared by *more* and *most*, or by *less* and *least*. See pp. 30–32.

Ex.—Soon, *sooner, soonest;* early, *earlier, earliest;* wisely, *more wisely, most wisely*.

Frequently, an adverb denotes *manner*, when it modifies a *verb;* and *degree*, when it modifies an *adjective* or an *adverb:* as, "He thinks *so;*" "He writes *so* awkwardly." "*How* did you do it?" "I know not *how* deep it is."

360. Most adverbs are formed by annexing *ly* to adjectives or participles. Sometimes *s* is annexed.

Ex.—Firm. *firmly;* noble, *nobly;* united, *unitedly;* sparing, *sparingly;* outward, *outwards*. *Ly* (Saxon *lic*, Germ. *lich*) is originally the same as *like*, or simply another form of *like*. Gentleman, *gentleman-like, gentlemanly*

361. Some adverbs are compounded of two or more words and adverbs are often used to form other compound words.

Ex.—*In*deed, *for*ever, *here*upon, where*with*al, aboard—on board, ahead—at the head, *here*after, *for*evermore, whithersoever, helter-skelter. *Well*-bred, *far*-fetched *down*trodden; *un*punished, *un*true, *im*pure. The common prefix *un*, and its equivalents, are adverbial, signifying *not*.

362. Adverbs promote brevity. The sense of almost every adverb can be conveyed by an adjunct or some other expression. A conjunctive adverb is nearly always equivalent to two adjuncts; and most adverbial phrases and some adverbs are but imperfect adjuncts.

Ex.—*Wisely*—in a wise manner, with wisdom; *rapidly*—with rapidity; *here*—at or in this place; *thus*—in this manner; *very*—in a high degree; *why*—for what reason; *never*—at no time. " *Whence* [*from what place*] is he?" "She was buried *when* the sun was setting"—She was buried *at the time in which* the sun was setting. The seed grew up *where* it fell; *i. e., from the place on which* it fell. *When* may stand for *then when; where*, for *there where; as*, for *so as*. *At present*—at the present time; *yesterday*—on yesterday; *in vain*—in a vain manner; *long ago*—at a time long gone by. Sometimes it is better to use the adjunct. " In a silly manner," is a better expression than *sillily ;* " in a small way or degree," than *smally ;* "in concord," than *concordantly ;* " by which," " with which," than *wherewith.*

363. Adverbs supply the inadequacy of tenses, and they have also some affinity with moods.

Ex.—" I will study | *presently*—*by* and *by*—*to-morrow*—*henceforth.*" " He will *certainly* come." Indicative mood strengthened. "*Perhaps* he will come"—He *may* come. Some adverbs need not the verb, to express commands in the most forcible manner. "*On*, Stanley, *on !*"—March *on*, &c. *Up*, warder, ho ! "*Away* with it." *Down* with tyranny. *Out* with him. "*Hence*, or thou diest."

364. It is sometimes difficult to distinguish adverbs from adjectives.

Some words retain the same form in either sense; but, generally, the ending *ly* or *s* is made the sign of the adverb.

Ex.—No, well, better, best, much, more, most, very, wide (—*ajar*), long, first, all, even, just, like, right (—very, directly), else, next, pretty (—tolerably), little, less, least, still, ill, worse, worst, enough, full (—very), only, hard (—laboriously), fast, yonder, early, late, likely, daily, weakly, weekly, monthly, yearly, gentlemanly, manly, comely, princely, deadly, kingly, nightly; " *no* man," *adj. ;* " *no* deeper," *adv.* Brave, *bravely ;* witty, *wittily ;* able, *ably ;* upward, *upwards*.

365. In poetry and in compound words, the adjective form of the word, or the adjective mode of comparison, is allowed to a greater extent than elsewhere.

Ex.—" The swallow sings *sweet* from her nest in the wall."—*Dimond*. " Drink *deep*, or taste not the Pierian spring."—*Pope*. " Ten censure *wrong* for one that writes amiss."—*Id*. " Though thou wert *firmlier* fastened than a rock."—*Milton*. *High*-colored, *smooth*-gliding : yet, even in most such compounds, the reference is still to a noun rather than to a verb ; as, *sweet-scented*—of sweet scent; *high-soaring* —high in soaring ; and we can not say *high-polished*, but must say *highly polished*.

366. An adjective may be affected by a verb, and still remain an adjective, provided the verb shows merely how the quality is acquired or made known. The quality may often be conceived as belonging to the person or thing, regardless of the act; or else as belonging to the former in the way shown by the verb.

Ex.—"Who PAINTS the lily *white*, the violet *blue?*" "The clay burns *white*." "The waves dashed *high*." "The fields look *pleasant*." "I *feel cold*;" *i. e.*, I am *cold*. State or quality. "She looks *coldly* on him." Manner. "The rose smells *sweet*." "Mary appears *neat*." She is always so, or in regard to every thing: neatness is a trait in her character. "Mary dresses *neatly*." She is *neat*, so far as dressing is concerned. "The apple tastes *sour*." Here we could not say, "*in a sour manner*." "The trees stand *thick*;" *i. e.*, they are thick, dense, or numerous. "He stood *firm*." "We arrived *safe*." "He made *merry* over his loss;" *i. e.*, *was merry*, or made *himself merry*, etc. "*Soft* blows the breeze." ("*Soft* is the breeze that blows o'er Ceylon's isle.") "Velvet feels *smooth*." "His hummock wung *loose* at the sport of the wind." "The wind blew the *colder*, the longer it blew." So, when the word expresses state or condition in relation to the subject, rather than manner, place, or time in relation to the verb; as, *athirst*, and commonly *asleep, alone, alike, ablaze, afoot, afloat, adrift*.

367. Generally speaking, the adverb approaches the adjective as the verb approaches a neuter signification, or that of the verb *be*.

Ex.—"He spoke *better*;" *adv*. "He seemed *better*;" "He felt *better*;" *adj*.

368. *Ever*=at any time, at all times. It is often a very expressive word, and is much used in composition; as, *evergreen, everlasting*. *Now—now*=sometimes—sometimes. *Then* sometimes implies rather condition than time. *There* does not always denote place, but sometimes elegantly introduces the sentence, or makes a convenient handle to it. *Thus* and *so* may each sometimes represent a preceding or a following word, phrase, or sentence. *So* occasionally represents a noun, though not always elegantly. *Yes* and *no* are each equivalent to a sentence.

Ex.—"Did you *ever* see the like?" "*Now* loud, *now* low; *now* swift, *now* slow, o'er hill and vale they winding go." "Suppose your parents should die; how would you make a living *then?*"—*in that condition*. "*There* came to the beach a poor exile of Erin." "*There* was nothing there that I wanted." "*Thus* has it ever been." "He is a great scholar.—*So* I was told." "The lord treasurer was often a bishop. The lord chancellor was almost always *so*."—*Macaulay*. "You saw him?—*Yes*"—I saw him.

369. Adverbs are sometimes used as nouns.

Ex.—"For *once*." "By *far* the best." "And closed for *aye* the sparkling glance." "We have caught *enough*." "We have played *enough*;" *adv*. Such words as *much, more, enough, little*, are nouns when used after transitive verbs.

370. Adverbs are said to belong to whatever they modify. See p. 47.

EXERCISES.

Examples to be Analyzed and Parsed.

Parse the adverbs and adjectives.

1.

The clouds move *slowly*. *Now* came still evening *on*. She gazed *long* upon the clouds in the west, *while* they were *slowly* passing *away*. As the year blooms and fades, so does human life. So great a man could not be always kept in obscurity. Having duly arranged his affairs, he departed immediately. You are yet young enough to learn the French language very easily. The most worthless things are sometimes most esteemed. Where was there ever an army that had served their country more faithfully?

2.

Night's candles are burnt out, and jocund day stands tiptoe on the misty mountain's top. In vain we seek for perfect happiness. We lived there long ago. The more I study grammar, the better I like it. Man by man, and foot by foot, did the soldiers proceed over the Alps. It was not at all strange, that he should at last defend himself. Only the young men were sent to war. The field had only been ploughed. The wretched fugitives were pursued even to the churches. Briefly, we rely on you alone. Finally, the war is already begun, and we must either[15] conquer or perish. Shall this colossal Union be broken asunder? No; never, never! They are most firmly good that best know why.

3.

Friends, but[12] few on earth, and therefore[12] dear;
Sought oft, and sought almost as[12] oft in vain.—*Pollok.*
Now they wax, and now they dwindle,
  Whirling with the whirling spindle;
Twist ye, twine ye! even so
  Mingle human bliss and woe.—*W. Scott.*
The piper loud and louder blew,
The dancers quick and quicker flew.—*Burns.*

Examples to be Corrected.

All the liabilities to error in regard to adverbs, may be reduced to the following heads:—

1. *Choice.* 2. *Form.* 3. *Position.*

1. *Choice.*

The most appropriate adverb should be selected to express the meaning intended.

A wicked man is not happy, be he never so hardened in conscience. We do not want the sound of these charmers [organ-grinders], charm they never so sweetly.—*Harper's Magazine.* Snow seldom or ever falls in the southern part of Texas. Whether you are willing or no, you will have to pay the debt. The road is so muddy that we can proceed no further. Nothing farther was said about the matter. It rains most every day. This wheat stands most too thick. He is a mighty insignificant fellow. Where shall I flee? Who brought me here, will also take me from hence. We remained a week at Galveston, and proceeded from thence to Indianola. Such cloaks were in fashion about five years since. —*ago.* About two weeks since, two grocery-keepers at Doniphan had a fight. Related not only by blood, but likewise by marriage —*but also*— James is studious, but Thomas is studious also. —*too.* I am some better than I was. —*somewhat*— He felt something encouraged on receiving the news. No other tree, in its old age, is as beautiful as the elm. Have you done like he directed you? —*as*— Directly he comes, we shall go. (Say, "*As soon as*," for *directly* is not a conjunctive adverb.) Immediately when they arrive, we shall go. I never before saw such large trees. —*trees that were so large.* She is such a good woman. —*so good a woman.*

2. Form.

Adverbs should be expressed in their true or most appropriate form.

Speak slow and distinct. You have behaved very bad. This pen does not write good. He behaved manlily. She behaved very sillily. At this place, the mountains are extraordinary high and steep.—*History of Virginia.* He lived an extreme hard life. She is a remarkable pretty girl. An abominable ugly little woman officiated at the table. I am only tolerable well, sir. It is wonderful to see how preposterous the affairs of this world are sometimes managed. The fox is an exceeding artful animal. He is doing fine. She was dressed as fi—— as silk could make her. People say he is independent rich. He struggled manful, and became independent. You have been wrong informed on the subject. Sure he is as fine a gentleman as can be found anywhere. She dresses suitable to her station and means. We went direct to the cave.

I shall first notice why we should worship God; and, second, how we should worship him. Fifth and last, I would remark that he never succeeded at any thing. Agreeable to the present arrangement, I shall have to recite my Greek during the first hour. Previous to our arrival, the captain was taken ill. The insolent proud soon acquire enemies. We have near finished our work. You did the work as good as I could expect. The Irishman was so bruised that he said he scarce knew himself again. As like as not you love her yourself. Push the wagon backward. —*backwards.* Come hitherward. I received the gift with pleasure, but I shall now gladlier resign it. —*more gladly*— These are the things highliest important. I can easier raise a crop of hemp than a crop of tobacco. Abstract principles are easiest learned when clearest illustrated.

3. Position.

Adverbs should be so placed in the sentence as to make it correct, clear, and elegant.

This precept is also applicable to adjuncts and to some conjunctions.

Every man can not afford to keep a coach. *Not every man,* &c. All their neighbors were not invited. All that we hear, we should not believe. There could not be found one man that was willing to enlist. They became even grinders of knives and razors. The two young ladies came to the party, nearly dressed alike. I only recited one lesson during the whole day. In promoting the public good, we only discharge our duty. Theism can only be opposed to polytheism. He is only so when he is drunk. I only bought the horse, and not the buggy. I have borrowed this horse only, yet I intend to buy him. Such prices are only paid in times of great scarcity. These words were not only uttered by a mortal man, but by one who was constantly exposed to death, and expecting it. The word *couple* can only be properly applied to objects in connection. The interest not only had been paid, but the greater part of the principal also. Bibulus could only escape outrage, by not only avoiding all assemblies of the people, but every solemn and important meeting of the senate. If you have only learned to spend money extravagantly at college, you may stay at home. *If you have learned, at college, only to spend money extravagantly,* &c. The future tense simply expresses future time. Corn should be generally planted in April. He is thought to be generally honest. For beginners and generally young men. The farmers sell their produce generally to the merchants.

In other countries, where the fate of the poor is wretched indeed, offices are merely created for the emolument of certain classes. How much would the difficulty be increased, were we solely to depend upon their generosity! I am not as attentive to the studies I even like, as I should be. Most nations, not even excepting the Jews, were prone to idolatry. He can not show me where ever I voted different. No man has ever so much that he does not wish to accumulate more. We do those things frequently which we repent of afterwards. There was another man still, who had lost his horse also. —*was still another man*— There is still a shorter method. —*a still shorter*— My opinion was given after rather a cursory perusal of the book. Such conduct rather will make him sulky and stupid than amiable and sprightly. I myself was a little inclined to visit her once. Having lost once a thousand dollars by speculation, he would never venture again. Having almost lost a thousand dollars by the speculation, he was able only to pay a part of the debt. Sextus the Fourth, if I mistake not, was a great collector of books, at least. By hasty composition, we shall acquire certainly a very bad style. The argument is very plausible, certainly, if not conclusive. Having not known, or having not considered the measures proposed, he failed of success. Our boat had fortunately left the ship, previous to the explosion. He promised to send to me as much again as he had borrowed, the next day. They were almost cut off to a man. There is nothing more pleases him than to praise his performances. *There is nothing that pleases him more, than for others to praise*, &c. We may happily live, though our possessions are small. Not only he found her employed, but pleased and tranquil also. She will be always discontented. The following bet is said actually to have been made between an Adams man and a Jackson man. —*is said to have actually been made*—

I occupy the same political position nearly, that I occupied five years ago. The words should be arranged so that harmony may be promoted. —*so arranged*— The law does not undertake to compel him so to do, or punish him for not so doing.—*Kent*. The front part of the house was very differently built from the back part. The goods could not be possibly shipped any sooner. He seems clearly to have understood this part of the Constitution. —*seems to have clearly*— He seems early to have applied himself to the study of law. We should not be overcome totally by present events. It can not be impertinent or ridiculous therefore to remonstrate. It is impossible continually to be at work. We have often opportunities to do good. It seems but three miles distant, and yet it perhaps is twenty. He determined to invite back the king, and to call together his friends. Nature mixes the elements variously and curiously sometimes, it is true. The Secretary was soon expected to resign—was expected daily to resign. A school must carefully be conducted to please such patrons. They managed so as completely to elude their pursuers. We are not inclined to unnecessarily place ourselves in so perilous a situation. You are to slowly raise the trap, while I hold the sack. The sealing of the documents up, also delayed me. *The sealing-up of*, &c. Spelling is the putting of letters together, so as to make words.

Negatives.

When two negatives contradict each other, they can not express a egation.

It is hardly proper, though according to custom, to place this class of errors under Adverbs; for sometimes neither one of the negatives is an adverb.

I will never do so no more. We didn't find nobody at home. I don't know nothing about your affairs. There can not be nothing more contemptible than hypocrisy. The scene was truly terrific; nothing never affected me so much. But, O! the greedy thirst of royal crown, that knows no kindred, nor regards no right.—*Spenser*. Congress has not, nor never had, the Constitutional power to intermeddle thus. He wondered that none of the members had never thought of it. Be honest, nor take no shape nor semblance of disguise. Do not let no one disturb me. Never was a fleet more completely equipped, nor never had a nation more sanguine hopes of success. Neither that nor no such thing was said in my hearing. There was no bench, nor no seat of any kind, that was not crowded with people. Neither he, nor nobody else, ever raised, in one year, so many bushels of potatoes on one acre. She will never grow no taller. For hence I will not, can not, no, nor must not. Death never spared no one. "And yet say nothing neither;" "And yet say nothing either." (Usage is unsettled as to this phraseology.)

OBSERVATIONS.

1. *No*, in such expressions as "whether or no," should be *not*. *Ever so* properly expresses indefinite or unlimited degree; its place, therefore, should not be usurped by *never so*. *Most* means *in the highest degree*, and it is often improperly used for *almost* or *rather*, or as a contraction of the former. *Nearly* should rather be applied to quantity, time, or space; and *almost*, to degree. So, *entirely* and *scarcely* rather imply quantity; *completely* and *hardly*, degree. *Hither, thither,* and *whither*, are now preferred, only in the grave style, to *here, there,* and *where*, when the principal idea is motion to or from a place. *Hence, thence,* and *whence*, imply the idea of *from* something; hence, to place *from* before them, makes the expressions tautological and generally inelegant. *Likewise* strictly implies *something more in like manner; also, something more;* and *too, something more of the same act, state, or kind of things.* But these distinctions are not always observed. "I have done *like* he directed," should be, "I have done *as* he directed." *Like* suggests a similarity of manner in the two actions; but *as* properly expresses their connection and correspondence. *So*, with a modifying word, expresses degree; and, in this sense, *such* or *as* is sometimes incorrectly or inelegantly used in the place of it. "She is not *such* an amiable woman as her sister;" *i. e.*, not an amiable woman of the same kind as her sister. "She is not *so* amiable a woman as her sister;" *i. e.*, not amiable in the same degree. But, since different grades are often the same as different kinds, the two modes of expression are often equivalent, and are so used by many good writers. The same remark applies to sentences of this kind: "She is not *as* amiable as her sister." Better: "She is not *so* amiable as her sister." But, without the preceding negative, we might properly say, "She is *as* amiable as her sister;" "It is *as* good as the other." *Further—beyond this place; further—in addition,* and is not usually applied to place.

2. Adjectives and adverbs are often confounded, because they resemble in signification; because some words are used in either capacity, while others are not; because most adverbs are derived from adjectives, and because they are sometimes really interchangeable without injuring the sense, for the nature of every act is intimately connected with the objects on which it depends. Grammarians have tried to guard pupils against errors, by the precept, "*Adjectives should be used to qualify nouns, or pronouns; but adverbs, to qualify verbs, adjectives, or adverbs.*"

DIFFERENT FORMS: *Well*, for instance, is the adverb corresponding to the adjective *good*. SAME FORMS: *Better, best, worse, worst,* &c., are used either as adverbs or as adjectives. DERIVED FORMS: Previous, *previously;* easier, *more easily;* &c. The ending *ly* or *s* should be preferred, when it will distinguish the adverb from the corresponding adjective; as, *scarcely, upwards, downwards.* LICENSED FORMS: The adjective may sometimes be used in stead of the adverb; or rather, the form of the adjective, especially the comparative or the superlative preceded by an article, may be used as an adverb. "He lives best who acts *the noblest.*" "*Swift* to the breach his comrades fly"—They *are swift* in flying to the breach. "*Swiftly* to the breach his comrades fly"—They *fly swiftly* to the breach. Perhaps the adjective in most such expressions implies a fixed and permanent quality or attribute, and the adverb only a temporary state. "*Soft* sighed the flute;" *i. e.*, with that sweetness and softness which are peculiar to it,—which it always has. "*Softly* sighed the flute" [in that particular instance]. When the adverbial ending would change the meaning, the adjective form must be used. "To stop *short*," differs from "To stop *shortly.*" "He came *contrary* to my expectations;" not, *contrarily.*

"For gentlemen who speak me *fair*." Sometimes the adjective form is proper, because the expression is, in thought at least, elliptical, or is but the adjective remnant of an adjunct or other phrase that performed the office of an adverb. "Though she paint an inch *thick*;" *i. e.*, paint her face with rouge an inch thick. "You have paid *dear* for the whistle;" *i. e.*, a dear price for the whistle. "You work *late*;" *i. e.*, till a late hour. "It happened, *contrary* to my expectations"—It happened; which thing was *contrary* to my expectations. "He hit the tree *wide* from the mark;" *i. e.*, a wide distance. "Speak *true*," *i. e.*, what is true. If I say, "The machinery works *smoothly*," I refer simply to its operation; but if I say, "It works *smooth*, I refer to its parts as affected by its operation. So, "The mahogany polishes *finely*," expresses the sense better than "The mahogany polishes *fine*;" for the meaning is, that it not only becomes fine, but admits polish better than most other things. Should we say, "I feel *bad*, or *badly?*" Butler and Clark have decided in favor of *bad*. Our best writers seem to have avoided the expression altogether. We say, "I feel *cold*," "I felt *mean*;" but the best popular usage seems to be in favor of saying, "I feel *badly*," which, moreover, is not equivalent to "I am bad." We say, too, "I suffered *severely*."

When the meaning is a mongrel of adjective and adverb, I believe general usage, in most instances, prefers the adjective form.

To avoid the disagreeable termination *lily*, we sometimes use a synonymous word; as, *piously* for *holily:* sometimes we use the corresponding adjunct; as, "In a *wily* manner," for *wilily:* and there is some tendency to use the adjective form for both the adjective and the adverb; as, "A *manly act* it was;" "He acted *manly*."

To poets is allowed great liberty in the use of adverbs; especially in the *form*. But neither poets nor any other persons are allowed to use them so as to pervert their meaning. A poet may say, "The swallow sings *sweet* from her nest in the wall;" or, "*To slowly trace* the forest's shady scenes;" or, "*From* thence to other scenes he passed;" for we understand him. But, "His visage to the view was only bare," does not convey the meaning intended; and should be, "His visage only to the view was bare."

3. The position of adverbs is regulated, in the first place, by the sense; and next, by emphasis and melody.

Adverbs are generally placed after the verb, or after the first auxiliary, before or after participles, and before adjectives or adverbs.

Enough follows its adjective or adverb; as, "A place *good enough*." *Ever, never, sometimes, often, always*, most frequently precede the verb. Such adverbs as *only, merely, solely, chiefly, at least*, &c., may be used to limit almost any part of the sentence, and should therefore be placed near to the parts which they are intended to modify. Some of the most common adverbs are very diffusive in their shades of meaning, and their capability of modifying. "He is *generally* at home"—*time*. "Crops are *generally* good"—*time* or *place*. "The sermon was *generally* interesting." Were most of its parts good? or did it please most of the people? or did the person often preach good sermons? The effect of inserting such adverbs can not be too carefully scrutinized. *The* is sometimes elegantly required before a comparative or a superlative adverb, to express emphasis; as, "Whose sweet entrancing tones he loved *the best*."—*Collins.*

EMPHATIC POSITION: "Then *never* saw I charity before." "In their prosperity, my friends shall *never* hear of me; in their adversity, *always*."

METRICAL POSITION: "Peeping from *forth* their alleys green;" "To *swiftly* glide o'er hill and dale."

4. Two negatives make an affirmation, as in the following sentence: "I *never* said *nothing* to him about it"—I said something to him about it. The sentence should have been, "I never said any thing to him about it;" or, "I said nothing to him about it." *Not*, followed by *only*, or by some equivalent word, modifies this, and does not affect the negative coming after it; so that a sentence with two negatives thus situated, is still negative; as, "I *not* only *never* said so, but never thought so." Two negatives independent of each other, a negative repeated, or a negative strengthened by its correlative, do not destroy the negation; as, "*No, never*." "I will *never, never* give my consent." "There was *no* peace, *no* happiness, in the family." "I have seen Christians that had *neither* love *nor* charity."

"It may *not* be popular *neither* to take away any of the privileges of Parliament."—*Mansfield.* "I do not understand this business.—*Nor* I *neither.*"—*Garrick.* Here *either*, I think, would be incorrect; for *neither* is the proper correlative of *nor.*

Two negatives are sometimes preferred to express a modest, an elegant, or a forcible affirmaton; as, "He is *not unschooled* in the ways of the world;" *i. e.*, he is shrewd enough. "I mean the riding-habit, which some have *not injudiciously* tyled the hermaphroditical, by reason of its masculine and feminine composition." —*Gay.* "There is *no* climate that is *not* a witness of their toils."—*Burke.*

"*Nor* did they *not* perceive the evil plight
In which they were, *or* the fierce pain *not* feel."—*Milton.*

10. PREPOSITIONS.

371. A **preposition** is a word used to govern a noun or pronoun, and show its relation to some other word.

Ex.—"A rabbit *in* a hollow tree." What in what *l* "How sweetly bloom the violets *on* yonder bank!" "The wind glides *in* waves *over* the bristling barley."

Two prepositions are sometimes combined and used as one, and some phrases are customarily used as prepositions.

Ex.—Upon, according to, as to, as for. "The river flowed *from under* the palaces." "*Over against* the church stood the hospital." "The lady sits genteelly, the more *because of* company."

372. Prepositions subjoin the place, time, doer, possessor, cause, source, purpose, means, manner, condition, or some other circumstance. They show *where, whither, whence, when, how long, by what means, to what extent, in what way, of what kind,* &c.

Ex.—"The fox was caught *under* a bluff, *before* sunrise, *by* the dogs *of* our neighbor." "To be punished *for* mischief." "The light *of* the sun." "To work *for* pay." "To chop *with* an ax." "To write *with* elegance." "To be *in* poverty." "Done *against* law."

373. An **adjunct** is a preposition with its object, or with the words required after it to complete the sense.

Ex.—"This large melon grew *on a slender vine.*" "He was shot *in his cabin,* | *on Wednesday,* | *with an arrow,* | *by an Indian* | *of the Comanche tribe.*" "The same man *that* I came *with;*" *i. e.*, with whom. "The ship was *about to be wrecked.*" "Anxious *for him to be caught.*" "The labor *of clearing* land depends on how much timber there is growing *on it.*" "Reason and justice have been jurymen *since before Noah was a sailor.*"—*Shakespeare.*

374. Some adjuncts may be inverted or parted, especially in poetry.

Ex.—"*Whom* was it given *to?*" better, "*To whom* was it given?" "From crag to crag, *the rattling peaks among;*" *i. e., among* the rattling *peaks.* "Come, walk with me *the jungle through.*"—*Heber.*

375. Two or more prepositions may govern the same substantive; two or more substantives may be governed by the same preposition; and two or more adjuncts are often combined into one.

Ex.—"He walked *up* and *down* the hall." "He approved *of*, and voted *for*, the measure;" better, "He approved *of the measure*, and voted *for it.*" "A battle between the *Sioux* and the *Comanches.*" "He bequeathed his estate to his *wife, children,* and *friends.*" "The gold | *in a piece of quartz from the mines of California.*"

376. An adjunct may relate to an object, an act or state, or a quality; that is, it may modify a substantive, an adjective, a verb, or an adverb.

Ex.—"*Caves* in the mountains." "The river *rises* in the mountains." "The river is *clear* in the mountains.

The modified term, which commonly precedes, is called the *antecedent term;* and the governed substantive, the *subsequent term,* which may sometimes be even a participle, an infinitive, a phrase, or a clause. See adjuncts, above.

377. Adjuncts extend over nearly all the ground occupied by adjectives, adverbs, and the possessive case, and even beyond, supplying their deficiencies.

Ex.—"A man *of wisdom and virtue*"—A *wise* and *virtuous* man. "A ship *without motion*"—A *motionless* ship." "To stand *here*"—To stand *in this place.* "*Absalom's* beauty"—The beauty *of Absalom.* "A land *of liberty.*" No adjective. "To stand *on the shores of New England.*" No adverb.

478. When a preposition has no word to govern, it becomes an adverb, and sometimes perhaps an adjective.

Ex.—" The eagle flew *up*, then *around*, then *down* again." "It fell *from above;*" "It came *from within—from without.*" Here *above, within,* and *without,* are perhaps best parsed as nouns. " It overlooked the PLAINS *below.*" *Below* is equivalent to the adjective adjunct " *below it.*"

379. Sometimes the object is merely omitted; and sometimes the antecedent term is omitted, or there is none.

Ex.—" The man you spoke *of;*" *i. e., of whom* you spoke. " Vengeance *on* whoever has killed him ;" *i. e., on him* who. " Industrious all, *from* the youngest to the oldest;" *i. e., reckoning from* the youngest. "*As for* riches, they are not worth so much care and anxiety." " Sold at the rate *of* from fifty cents to a dollar ;" *i. e., of prices varying* from fifty cents to a dollar : or, when but one indefinite thing is meant, the first preposition may be parsed as governing all the rest of the phrase, and the second as having no antecedent term.

380. The preposition itself is sometimes omitted; especially *for, to,* or *unto.* These prepositions are usually omitted after *like, unlike, near, nigh, opposite,* or such verbs as may be followed in the active voice by two objects; the one governed by the verb, and the other denoting the person to whom the act refers,—sometimes called, for distinction, the *direct* object, and the *indirect.*

Ex.—" The house was near [*to*] the river—nearer [*to*] the river—next *to* ours." "The son is like [*to* or *unto*] his father." " Opposite [*to*] the market." " Lend him *your knife*"—Lend *your knife to him.*

381. Prepositions, as modifying or qualifying words, make in part hundreds of our most expressive compound words.

Ex.—*Over*shoot, *over*spread, *over*throw ; *under*mine, *under*brush, *under*strapper; *up*hold, *up*heave ; *by*-stander; *after*thought; implant (*in*-).

Some prepositions show WHERE: In, on, under, over, above, before, behind, below, around, between, among, by, beyond, at. *Some show* WHITHER: To, toward, into, up, down, for. *Some show* WHENCE: Out of, from, of. *Some show* WHEN : At, in, on, after, before. *Some show* HOW LONG: During, for, till. *Some imply* CONTACT *or* UNION : On, upon, with. *Some refer to* INNER *parts :* In, into, within, among, amid, through. *Some, to* OUTER *parts:* On, around, about, over, to. *Some have* OPPOSITES : To—from ; over, on—under; above—below, beneath; with—without· up—down; for—against; along—across

PREPOSITIONS. 251

through—around; before—behind; on—off; before—after, since (*time*); till—after; within—without. Some are ALLIED *in* MEANING: Over, above; on, upon; under, below, beneath; from, of, out of; behind, after; across, athwart; about, around; in, within; at, by (*place*); by, with (*means*); to, for.

The prepositions have been too superficially treated by most of our grammarians. There is no object, act, quality, or condition, not exclusively described by other words that may not be described by adjuncts in any conceivable way; and hence the correctness, clearness, and vigor of discourse, depend not a little upon them. There are a few grand ideas, namely, those of space, time, cause, means, purpose, manner, &c., which control and limit the mind in its acquisitions, encompass and pervade all its other knowledge, and tincture speech universally, but especially prepositions. Hence, nearly all the prepositions may express relations of *place;* a smaller number may be applied to *time;* and a still smaller number to *cause, purpose, means, manner,* &c. Some relations are of the external world, but many others rather lie in the judgments or views taken by the mind. Prepositions are often extended from the most obvious relations of place, to the most abstruse and delicate maneuvres of the mind itself; but, as they are generally extended *figuratively* (see pp. 298–300) from relations of *place* to relations of *time, cause, means, manner,* &c., any meaning apparently different from the primitive, generally resembles it, is readily suggested by it, or can be traced to it. The following exposition of prepositions will be valuable to the studious learner.

Most of the examples are taken from Lord Macaulay.

A, said to be from *at, on,* or *in,* is now rarely used as a separate word, except sometimes before a participial noun; as, "Towards evening we went *a* fishing.'

Aboard. "To go or be *aboard* a ship."

About is less precise than *around* or *at.* It is applicable to *place, time, quantity, number, acts,* and *states.* "A girdle *about* the waist;" "To be *about* the house;" "To go *about* the country, making speeches;" "*About* noon;" "Costs *about* so much;" "*About* a dozen;" "Engaged *about* one's business;" "Angry *about* something;" "*About* to be hanged"—*nearness* to an act not yet done.

Above. "The room—the stars *above* us;" "A tree rising *above* the house;" "A city *above* another on the same river;" "To be *above* in rank—*above* suspicion;" "To feel oneself *above* others—*above* labor;" "To be *above* reach—*above* comprehension."

According to, taken from music, means *harmonizing with.* "*According to* reason—law—rules;" "*According to* the dictates of conscience;" "*According to* weight—value."

Across— *at cross, in a cross.* "*Across* the road—river;" "Arms *across* each other."

After. "To come *after* another;" "A day *after* the time;" "*After* the debate;" "Dogs *after* a fox;" "A hankering *after* pleasure;" "To inquire *after* some one;" "To write *after* a copy."

Against. "To sit over *against* another;" "A ladder *against* a wall;" "Be ready *against* to-morrow morning;" "Ants provide *against* winter;" "To set one account *against* another;" "To tug *against* the stream;" "To be *against* nature;" "*Against* one's feelings;" "*Against* law."

Along, following the length of. "Trees *along* the river;" "Fringed *along* the edges;" "To drive cattle *along* the road." "*Along* with"—in company with.

Amid, amidst, akin to *middle.* "A lark reared her brood *amid* the corn;" "Oranges gleaming *amidst* leaves and blossoms," or *among;* "Firm *amidst* the

PREPOSITIONS.

storm," not *among;* "Undaunted *amidst* insults and mockeries." *Amid* usually implies quantity, and something more overwhelming than *in; among,* number. "*In* the flames;" "*Amid* the flames."

Among, amongst, akin to *mingle* and *many.* "Flowers *among* weeds," "The fools *among* men;" "A tradition *among* the Indians." See *Between.*

Around, round—encompassing like a ring or like a globe. It is local, and more precise than *about.* "*Around* the neck;" "*Around* the fire;" "*Around* the kernel;" "He went *round* the country, making speeches;" "He sailed *round* the world."

As to—respecting, concerning, in reference to. "*As to* the law itself, I have nothing to say."

At. "*At* the door"—*nearness* in *place;* "*At* church;" "*At* nine o'clock"—*nearness* in *time;* "*At* the election"—*nearness* in both or either; "*At* work"—*act; "At* war," "*At* best,"—*state;* "To be *at* the expense"—*nearness* and *burden;* "To be *at* one's service"—*nearness* and *control;* "Attorney *at* law;" "To estimate *at* a certain price"—*nearness* in thought, for judging; "Sold *at* a dollar per bushel"—*nearness* and *exchange;* "To take offense *at* what is said"—*nearness,* in time, of the saying and the offense,—thence, *cause;* "To come *at* a wink;" "To laugh *at* some one;" "To aim *at* a mark." See *In.*

Athwart—across + opposition. "Thou that dar'st advance thy miscreated front *athwart* my way."—*Milton.*

Before—*by* and *fore.* "*Before* the house"—*place;* "*Before* night"—*time* "*Before* the war"—*action;* "To be *before* another in rank;" "To appear *before* court"—*place,* and something more.

Behind. "*Behind* the house"—*place;* "To be *behind* the curtains"—*place* +; "He died, and left no property *behind* him"—*place* and *time;* "*Behind* in excellence;" "The ministry *behind* the throne"—*place* and *inferiority* or *influence.*

Below implies *under,* in place, rank, or quantity. "*Below* the eaves," "*Below* another;" "*Below* fifty." We can say, "A city *below* another on the same river," but not *beneath,*—"*Below* fifty," not *beneath.* "To be *below* consideration," is very different from "To be *under* consideration."

Beneath often implies greater distance, and less possibility of approach, than *below.* "A horrid chasm *beneath* us;" "He is *beneath* notice."

Beside, besides. "A tree *beside* the river;" "Something *besides* accomplishments;" "It is *beside* my purpose;" "He is *beside* himself"—*out of* his wits.

Between, from *by* and *twain,* has a twofold reference; *among,* a manifold. "*Between* the house and the river;" "*Between* one and the rest;" "*Between* dawn and sunrise;" "*Between* hope and fear;" "Two travelers, with but one dollar *between* them;" "To distinguish *between* good and bad." "To divide *between* one and another," is correct: "To divide *among* one another"—*one among another;* therefore say, "*among themselves:*" "To divide *between themselves,*" not *each other.* "A combat *between* twenty English *against* forty French;" say, "*between*....*and,* or, *of*....*against.*" "*Between* the intellectual and moral worlds" —*Professors Fowler & Gibbs;* better, "*Between* the intellectual and the moral world," or, "the intellectual world and the moral."

Betwixt is rather local; and it is not so widely extended in significations as *between.* This word shows remarkably how variable English orthography has been. Its genealogy runs thus: *Betwuh, betuh, betwy, betwih, betwyh, betweoh, betweohs, betux, betweox, betwuxt,* BETWIXT.

Beyond. "The hills *beyond* the river;" "To look *beyond* the present;" "*Beyond* a hundred;" "*Beyond* the evidence;" "*Beyond* temptation;" "*Beyond* reach;" "*Beyond* comprehension."

But is a preposition when equivalent to *except*, and construed with the objective case; as, "The boy stood on the burning deck whence all *but* him had fled."—*Hemans*. It is sometimes, however, construed with the nominative case, and is then a conjunction. "Should all the race of mortals die, and none be left *but* he and I."—*Scott*.

By. "A flower *by* a rivulet"—*nearness* in *place*; "To come *by* sea"—*place* and *means*; "Related *by* marriage," "Achieved *by* valor,"—*means*; "To work *by* day," "To be ready *by* morning,"—*time*. "To take *by* the hand"—*place* and *manner*; hence, "To demolish *by* cities." "One *by* one," "*By* pairs," "*By* degrees," "*By* little and little,"—*manner*. "*By* oneself"—alone; "It makes sense *by* itself—*of itself*—is complete *in itself*." "To hew a log *by* a line," "To travel *by* moonlight," "To prove *by* the Scriptures,"—*nearness* to something for judging or sanction; thence, "To try *by* law," "To swear *by* the gods," "Too heavy *by* six pounds." An act received is naturally ascribed to something near, and hence *by* is used in reference to the agent; as, "He was kicked *by* a horse." *By* and *with* are often confounded. *By* rather directs the mind to the cause or the indirect means; *with* frequently implies accompaniment: *by* annexes the agent or the remoter means; *with*, the immediate means or the manner. "I was favorably impressed *by* his remarks;" "I was impressed *with* great esteem for him;" "It was *with* great difficulty that we succeeded;" "He walks *with* a staff *by* moonlight;" "Punished *with* death"—*Macaulay*; "The vermin which he could not kill *with* his sword, he killed *by* poison"—*Johnson*. "Killed *with* a limb," implies an agent not mentioned; "Killed *by* a limb," implies no other agent, unless it denotes place merely; "Struck *with* a palsy," implies that the disease has become a part of the person. When *with* would not express the *means*, *by* must be used: "To burst *with* violence"—*manner*; "To burst *by* violence"—*means*. "*By* the stream," does not denote so close a union as "*With* the stream;" *by* also implies authority, as, "Condemned *by* the law:" hence, "*By* these [swords] we gained our liberties, and *with* these we will defend them." *With* here refers to the immediate and instrumental use. Our school geographies have "*distinguished for*;" *i. e.*, the distinction is caused by the following things: but Macaulay writes, "*distinguished by*;" *i. e.*, the distinction lies in the following particulars.

Concerning. "A law *concerning* religion;" "He spoke *concerning* virtue." *According*, *bating*, *excepting*, *respecting*, *regarding*, *pending*, *touching*, etc., generally show their participial tinge, and may sometimes be parsed as participles.

Down. "To come *down* the tree—the river;" "To live *down* town," hardly elegant.

During. "*During* the summer;" said to be an inverted mode of expression for "The summer² *during*," *i. e.*, while the summer lasts.

Except and **save** are primarily imperative verbs. *Save* belongs rather to poetry; and *except* seems to be stronger and more definite than *but*.

For. "Muddy *for* several miles"—*place*; "In jail *for* life"—*time*; "To give money *for* provisions"—*exchange*; "Sold *for* sound;" "To inquire *for* information"—*something in view*; "Done *for* him;" "To send *for* a doctor;" "Sent *for* a guide," better *as*; "Wise *for* his age;" "Fit *for* service;" "Some were *for* the law"—*in favor of*; "Honored *for* his services"—*cause*, past time; "Equipped *for* battle"—*purpose*, future time; "A man's a man *for* all that"—*notwithstanding*; "As *for* me," &c.; "*For* me to go," &c.

From. "A part *from* the whole;" "A wind *from* the mountains;" "*From* morning till night;" "To judge *from* the description;" "Secure *from* winds and waves"—*out of their reach*; "Secure *against* winds and waves"—*able to withstand them*; "Disabled *from* voting," prospective; "Disheartened *from* seeing the obstacles"—*on account of*, retrospective

In. "*In* a meadow"—*circular surrounding;* "*In* the dumpling"—*globular surrounding;* "*In* a chair—corner"—*angular surrounding;* "*In* the morning;" "*In* debt;" "*In* haste;" "*In* pairs;" "One *in* a dozen;" "*In* reach;" "Pleasure *in* studying;" "*In* all probability;" "Warms *in* the sun, refreshes *in* the breeze" —*by means of,* a Grecism. *In* and *at* are often used in speaking of places or residences. *In* is more generally applied to countries and large cities; and *at* to single houses, small places, or foreign cities. *In* implies enclosure, or something surrounding; *at* rather implies nearness to a point or border. "To touch, arrive, or land *at* Boston;" "To live *in* St. Louis—*in* New York—*at* Saratoga—*at* or *on* the next farm;" "To stay *at* the tavern;" "To stop *at* or *in* the next town;" "To have a store *on* Broadway, *at* No. 40." "This produced a great sensation, not only *in* England, but also *at* Paris, *at* Vienna, and *at* the Hague."—*Macaulay.* The choice often depends on the distance: remote places dwindle, in the mental vision, to a mere point; so that *at* becomes sufficiently definite. *In* is more definite than *at*: it vouches for an exact knowledge of the relation. When I say, "He is *in* the tavern—*in* Constantinople," I assume to know that he is within these places, and not outside of them; but when I say, "He is *at* the tavern— *at* Constantinople," I suggest simply that he is somewhere about these places— occasionally within them.

Into is an inverted expression for *to-in.* The natural order is *to, into, in; to* approaches a boundary, *into* passes a boundary, and *in* does not pass out of a boundary. "To step *into* a carriage, and then ride *in* it;" "To flow *into* the sea;" "Made *into* cloth;" "Driven *into* opposition;" "Adopted *in* my school," or, "*into* my school," according to the sense. "To cut *in* two;" "To get *on* a horse;" "To dash *to* pieces;" "Office *up* stairs,"—are all allowable as being figurative (see Metonymy and Synecdoche, p. 299).

Notwithstanding implies unsuccessful opposition, and is milder than *despite.*

Of is used nearly as much as all the other prepositions together. It generally serves to limit the antecedent term by a subsequent term whose meaning is not exhausted or expressed by the former. It is the most general word for showing whence something comes, or else to what it belongs or pertains. "The rivers *of* America"—*place;* "Within ten feet *of* me;" "The first month *of* the year —*time;*" "Days *of* yore;" "A pitcher made *of* silver"—*material;* "The exploits *of* Don Quixote"—*source;* "The house *of* my father"—My father's house;" "The brother *of* the senator;" "A man *of* wealth"—*encompassed by;* "A man *of* wisdom;" "The pleasure *of* thinking *of* home"—*drawn from;* "It makes sense *of* itself"—*out of;* "The city of London"—*consisting of.*

On. "*On* the floor"—*place;* "*On* the wall;" "*On* the ceiling;" "A boat *on* the river;" "A city *on* the river;" "*On* the left—right;" "To stand *on* pillars;" "Blow *on* blow;" "To play *on* the flute"—*place+* ; "*On* New-Year's Day"— *time;*" "To pay *on* sight;" "She wept *on* hearing the report"—*time* and *cause;* "To keep the eye—the mind *on* something;" "Chitty *on* Contracts;" "To be *on* the wing"—*support;* "To rely *on* a person's veracity"—*support;* "To take *on* oath;" "To live *on* fruits—*by* sewing;" "To go *on* a voyage;" "To be *on* fire:" "My blessing *on* you;" "To take pity *on* some one;" "To have *on* trial;" "To wait *on* some one;" "To be *on* hand;" "To be *on* the alert;" "*On* a sudden."

Out of. "Drawn *out of* a well;" "*Out of* joint;" "*Out of* tune;" "*Out of* taste;" "Made *out of* wax;" "Done *out of* spite."

Over is allied to *cover.* It is sometimes to *on* as a surface is to a point. "*Over* my head;" "*Over* logs and creeks;" "*Over* a spell of sickness"—an obstacle, as it were, in the journey of life; "To look *over* a book;" "*Over* a month;" "*Over* a dozen;" "To grieve *over* calamities;" "To rule *over* a nation." A higher position generally gives advantage; hence superiority is often compared to height, and inferiority *to* lowness.

Since reckons from a point of time. "*Since* last Christmas."
Till reckons to a point of time. "*Till* next Christmas."
Through. "*Through* the woods"—*place;* "*Through* many ages"—*time;* "To escape *through* a crevice"—*place* and *means;* and thus, *cause,* as, "To fly *through* fear." Hence *through* approaches *by* and *with* so nearly as to be often used for suggesting the intermediate or appointed channel for effecting something. "I will send you the money *through* the bank."
Throughout is a little more forcible than *through;* signifying through in every part, through to the very end, or through and passing out. "*Throughout* the universe—the entire process—the day."
To implies tendency or approach. *To, toward,* and *into,* have something in view; *along, up,* and *down,* do not. "*To* the river"—an *object;* "From morn *to* noon"—*time;* "*To* a dozen"—*number;* "*To* a bushel"—*quantity;* "Reduced *to* poverty"—*state;* "Led *to* slaughter"—*act;* "Anxious *to* learn"—*in what respect;* "To dance *to* the violin"—*cause* or *agreement.* (See p. 216.) *To,* with the infinitive, implies a closer connection than *in order to.* "Politicians endeavor *to* please, *in order to* obtain as many votes as possible." Here *to* and *in order to* are not interchangeable. To a question asked me by a surveyor, I answer: "Is parallel *to,* runs parallel *with;*" "At right angles *with.*"
Toward, towards, less direct than *to.* "*Towards* me;" "*Toward* noon;" "*Toward* the close of the war;" "To contribute *toward* a sufficient sum."
Under. "*Under* foot—water;" "They crept along *under* the walls of the fort;" "*Under* a dozen;" "*Under* age;" "To pass *under* inspection;" "To groan *under* a burden;" hence power over,—"To be *under* restraint—*under* afflictions;" "Given *under* my signature"—*by my authority;* sometimes, "*Over* my signature." "*Under* the garb of friendship;" "Innocence presented *under* the figure of a dove."
Up. *Up, upon, on,* are analogous to *to, into, in.* The prominent idea of *up* is elevation; of *on,* place: *upon* unites both meanings, and is sometimes used as a stronger term for *on.* "*Up* the ladder—river." See *On.*
With. See *By* and *In.* "The ship *with* its cargo;" "Girls *with* sparkling eyes;" "A soldier *with* a musket;" "Enameled *with* flowers;" "To act *with* firmness." "He died *with* a fever," implies that both died: say, "*of.*" "To dwell *in* security," not *with.* "To grow rich *by* working," not *with.* "To end *with* a consonant;" "To end *in* a consonant, &c.:" the former is perhaps better authorized.
Within. "*Within* or *in* the house." "*Within* six months," differs from "*In* six months." "*Within* a year ago," not *in.*
Without. "*Without* money—friends—beauty—hope."
The longer or fuller prepositions are often merely a little more forcible than the short ones, or slightly modify the sense; as, *Until, amongst, alongside, underneath, unto, excepting.*
The remaining prepositions are most of them either poetic, antique, technical, or comic.

The teacher may interrogate his pupils thus: *Abandoned?* Ans. *To.*

A.—Abandoned *to;* abatement *of;* abhorrent *to, from;* abhorrence *of;* abide *in, at, with, by;* abominable *to;* abound *in, with;* abridge *from;* abridgment *of;* absent *from;* abstain *from;* abut *on, upon;* accede *to;* acceptable *to;* access *to;* accommodate *to, with* lodgings; accord *with,* a thing *to;* accordance *with;* accountable *to* a person, *for* a thing; accuse *of;* acquaint *with;* acquiesce *in;* acquit *of;* adapted *to;* add *to;* address *to;* adhere *to;* adjacent *to;* adjourn *to;* adjudge *to;* adjust *to;* admonish *of;* admission *to* (access), *into* (entrance); advantage *over, of;* advise *of, to;* advocate *for;* affection *for;* affinity *to, with,* *between*; affection *for*; agree *with* a person, *to* what is proposed, *upon* something determined; agreeable *to*; alienate, alien, *from*; allude *to*; alter *to*, alteration *in*; amenable *to*; analogous *to*; analogy *to*, *between*; angry *with* a person, *at* a thing; annex *to*; animadvert *on*, *upon*; answer *for*, *to*; antecedent *to*; antipathy *to*, *against*; anxious *about*, *for*; apology, apologize, *for*; appeal *to*; apply, applicable, *to*; apprehensive *of*; appropriate *to*; approve *of*; argue *with*, *against*; array *with*, *in*; arrive *at*; ask *of* a person, *for* what is wanted; aspire *to*; assent *to*; assimilate *to*; associate *with*; assure *of*; atone *for*; attach *to*; attain *to*; attend, attentive, *to*; averse, aversion, *to*, *from*.

B.—Banish *from* one place—*to* another; bare *of*; based *on*, *upon*; beguile *of*, *with* (the means); believe, belief, *in*, *on*; bereave *of*; bestow *on*, *upon*; betray *to* a person, *into* a thing; betroth *to*; bigoted *to*; bind *to*, *in*, *upon*; blame *for*; blush *at*; boast, brag, *of*; border *on*, *upon*.

C.—Call *on*, *upon*, or *for* a person, *at* a house, *for* something; capable *of*; capacity *for*; careless, careful, *of*, *in*, *about*; carp *at*; catch *at*; caution *against*; certify *to*; change *for*, *to*, *into*; charge *on* or *against* a person, *with* a thing; clear *of*; coalesce *with*; coincide *with*; commune *with*; commute (a punishment) *to for*; commit *to*; communicate *to*, *with*; compare *to* (to liken unto), *with* (to view in connection with); compelled *to*; comply, compliance, *with*; concede *to*; conceive *of*; concur *with* a person, *in* a measure, *to* an effect; condemned *for* a crime, *to* a punishment; condescend *to*; conduce *to*; confer *on*, *upon*; confide *in*; conform, conformable, *to*, *with*; congenial *to*, *with*; congratulate *on*, *upon*; consecrate *to*; consent *to*; consign *to*; consist *of* (composed of), *in* (comprised in), *with* (to agree); consistent *with*; consonant *with*; contend *with*, *against*; contest *with*; contiguous *to*; contrast *with*; contrary *to*; contradistinction *to*; conversant *with* persons, *in* things (*about* and *among* are inelegant); convert *to*, *into*; convict *of*; convince *of*; copy *after* actions, *from* things; correspond *with* (consistent), *to* (answering); correspondence *with*, *to*; cured *of*.

D.—Deal *in*, *by*, *with*; debar *from*, *of*; decide *on*, *upon*; defend (others) *from*, (ourselves) *against*; deficient *in*; defraud *of*; demand *of*; denounce *against* a person; depend, dependent, *on*, *upon*; deprive *of*; derived *from*; derogate *from*; derogatory *to*; derogation *from*, *to*; descended *from*; desirous *of*; desist *from*; despair *of*; despoil *of*; destined *to*; destitute *of*; detach *from*; detract *from*; deviate *from*; devolve *on*, *upon*; devote *to*; dictate *to*; die *of* a disease, *by* an instrument, or *by* violence, *for* another; differ *with* a person *in* opinion; differ, different, *from*; difficulty *in*; diminish *from*; diminution *of*; disagree *with*, *to* something proposed; disagreeable *to*; disabled *from*; disappointed *of* what I failed to get, *in* something obtained; disapprove *of*; discourage *from*; discouragement *to*; disengaged *from*; disgusted *at*, *with*; dislike *to*; dismission *from*; disparagement *to*; dispose *of*; disposed *to* (inclined), *for*; dispossess *of*; disqualify *for*, *from*; dispute *with*; dissatisfied *with*; dissent *from*; distinct, in distinction, *from*; distinguish *from*, *between*; distrustful *of*; divested *of*; divide *between* two, *among* more; dote *on*; doubt *of*, *about*; dwell *in*, *at*, *on*.

E.—Eager *in*, *for*, *after*; embark *in*, *for*; embellished *with*; emerged *from*; employ *in*, *on*, *upon*, *about*; enamored *of*, *with*; encounter *with*; encouragement *to*; encroach *on*, *upon*; endeared *to*; endeavor *after* a thing; endowed, endued, *with*; engaged *in* (work), *with*, *for*; enjoin *on*, *upon*; enter, entrance, *on*, *upon*, *into*; envious *of*, *at*; equal *to*, *with*; equivalent *to*; espouse *to*; estimated *at*; estranged *from*; exception *from*, *to*, *against*; exclude, exclusion, *from*; exclusive *of*; expelled *from*; expert *in*, *at*; extracted *from*; expressive *of*.

F.—Fall *under* notice, &c.; familiar *to* me, I am familiar *with*; fawn *on*, *upon*; feed *on*, *upon*; fight *with*, *against*, *for*; filled *with*; followed *by*; fond *of*; fondness *for*; foreign *to*, *from*; formed *from* (another word); founded *upon*, *on*, *in*; free *from*; friendly *to*, *towards*; frightened *at*; frown *at*, *upon*; fruitful *in*, *of*; full *of*.

G.—Glad *of, at*—applied sometimes to what concerns another; glance *at, upon*; glow *with*; grapple *with*; grateful *to* a person, *for* a favor; grieve *at, for* guard *against.*

H.—Hanker *after*; happen *to, on*; healed *of*; hinder *from*; hiss *at*; hold *on, of, in.*

I.—Immersed *in*; impatient *at, for, of*; impenetrable *to, by*; impervious *to*; impose *on, upon*; inaccessible *to*; incentive *to*; incorporate *with, into*; inconsistent *with*; inculcate *on, upon*; independent, independently, *of*; indulge *with* occasionally, *in* habitually; indulgent *to*; influence *over, on, with*; inform *of, about, concerning*; initiate *into, in*; inquire *of, after, for, into*; inroad *into*; insensible *to, of*; inseparable *from*; insinuate *into*; insist *on, upon*; inspection *into, over*; instruct *in*; intent *on, upon*; interfere, intermeddle, *with*; intermediate *between*; intervene *between*; introduce *into* a place, *to* a person; intrude *on, upon, into* something enclosed; inured *to*; invested *with, in.*

J.—Jealous *of*; join *with, to.*

K.—Knock *at, on*; known, unknown, *to.*

L.—Laden *with*; lame *of*; land *at*; lean *on, upon, against*; level *with*; liberal *of, to*; liken *to*; live *in, at, with, on, upon*; long *for, after*; look *on* (in order to see), *for* (in order to find), *after*—to follow with the *eye*; long *for, after.*

M.—Made *of*; marry *to*; meddle *with*; mediate *between*; meditate *on, upon*; martyr *for*; militate *against*; mingle *with*; minister *to*; mistrustful *of*; mix *with.*

N.—Necessary *to, for*; need *of*; neglectful *of*; negotiate *with.*

O.—Obedient *to*; object *to, against*; observant, observation, *of*; obtrude *on, upon*; offend *against*; offensive *to*; omitted *from*; operate *on, upon*; opposition *to*; overwhelmed *with, by.*

P.—Part *from, with*; partake *of*; participate *in, of*; partial *to*; partiality *to, for*; patient *in, with, of*; pay *for, to, with*; peculiar *to*; penetrate *into*; persevere *in*; pertinent *to*; pitch *upon, on*; pleasant *to*; pleased *with*; plunge *into*; possessed *of*; prefer *to, before, above*; preferable *to*; preference *to, over, before, above*; prefix *to*; prejudice *against*; prejudicial *to*; preserve *from*; preside *over*; press *on, upon*; presume *on, upon*; present things *to* a person; pretend *to*; prevail *on, upon, with*, (to persuade,) *over* or *against* (to overcome); prevent *from*; prey *on, upon*; prior *to*; productive *of*; profit *by*; profitable *to*; prone *to*; pronounce *against* a person, *on* a thing; protect others *from*, ourselves *against*; protest *against*; proud *of*; provide *with, for, against*; purge *of, from*; pursuant *to*; pursuance *of.*

Q.—Quarrel *with*; quarter *on, upon, among*; questioned *on, upon, by.*

R.—Reckon *on, upon, with*; recline *on, upon*; reconcile *to* (friendship), *with* (consistency); recover *from*; reduce *to, under* (subjection); reflect *on, upon*; refrain *from*; to have regard *for*, to pay regard *to, in* or *with* regard *to*; rejoice *at, in*; relation *to*; relish *of, for*; (see *taste*;) release, relieve, *from*; rely *on, upon*; remark *on, upon*; remit *to*; remove *from*; repent *of*; replete *with*; reproached *for*; resemblance *to, between*; resolve *on, upon*; rest *in, at, on, upon*; respect *to, in* or *with* respect *to*; restore *to*; restrain *from*; retire *from*; return *to*; rise *above*; rich, poor, *in*; rid *of*; rob *of*; rove *about, over*; rub *against*; rule *over.*

S.—Satiate, saturate, *with*; save *from*; seek *for, after*; share *in, of, with* another; send *to, for*; sick *of*; significant *of*; similar *to*; sink *into, in, beneath*; sit *on, upon, in*; skillful *in*; smile *at, on, upon*; snap, snatch, sneer, *at*; solicitude *about, for*; sorry *for*; stay *in, at, with*; stick *to, by*; strip *of*; strive *with, against*; subject *to*; submit, submissive, *to*; substitute *for*; subtract *from*; subside *into* suitable *to*; surprised *at*; suspected *of, by*; swerve *from*; sympathize *with.*

T.—Taste *of* something enjoyed, taste (—desire or capacity) *for*; tax *with* something done, *for* something in view; tend *to, towards*; thankful *of, about, upon, on*; touch *at, on, upon*; transmit *to*; troublesome *to*; true *to*; trust *in, to.*

U.—Unite *with*, something *to*; unison *with*; useful *for, to*.

V.—Value *upon, on*; variation *in* a plan; vest *in* a person, *with, in,* a thing void *of*.

W.—Wait *on, upon, for, at*; want *of*; weary *of*; weep *at, for*; witness *of* worthy, unworthy, *of*.

Y.—Yearn *for, towards*; yield *to*; yoke *with, to*.

The same preposition that is required after a primitive word, is generally required after its derivatives; as, "To comply *with*," "In compliance *with*;" but, "Dependent *on*," "Independent *of*." What preposition should be used, often depends on the following word, as well as on the preceding; as, "To speak *to* an audience;" "To speak *about* the war;" "To speak *with* eloquence."

EXERCISES.
Examples to be Analyzed and Parsed.

Parse the prepositions and the adverbs:—

1.

The waters issued from[a] a cave, and spread into a liquid plain. The stars retire at the approach of day. We searched for violets on yonder hill. A plain path leads through the bottom, between the river and the bluffs. The Rhone flows out[13] from[b] among the Alps. As to the expenses, we will help to defray them. From virtue to vice, the progress is gradual.

2.

Washington died at his residence, on the 14th of December, 1799, and was buried near the Potomac, among his relatives. The robin and the wren are flown, and from the shrub the jay. From crag to crag, the rattling peaks among, leaps the live thunder. Hold up[13] the flag. Turn over[13] another leaf.

The window jingled in its crumbled frame;
And, through its many gaps of destitution,
Dolorous moans and hollow sighings came,
Like those of dissolution.—*Hood.*

Overhead the dismal hiss
Of fiery darts in flaming volleys flew—*Milton.*

(*a.*) *Ques.* What from? *Ans.* Issued from. *Ques.* From *what? Ans.* From a cave. Etc. (*b.*) "*From among*" is a complex preposition, it consists of two prepositions combined and used to show the complex relation between "*flows*" and "*Alps.*"

Examples to be Corrected.

All the liabilities to error in regard to prepositions, may be reduced to the following heads:—

1. *Choice.* 2. *Position.* 3. *Insertion or omission.* 4. *Repetition.*

1. *Choice.*

In the use of prepositions, great care should be taken to select the most appropriate.

The sultry evening was followed, at night, with a heavy storm of rain. The soil is adapted for hemp and tobacco. Congress consists in a Senate and a

House of Representatives. Of what does happiness consist? Not any syllable in a word may take the accent. In some derivative words the *e* is omitted. The *e* is left out in some of the derivative words. The government is based in republican principles. The Saxons reduced the Britons to their own power. Said client believes that said judge is prejudiced to his cause. The case has no resemblance with the other. Some of the warriors wore an extra tuft of feathers, in distinction to those who had brought in no scalps. In contradistinction from the other. Religion and membership may differ widely with each other. The judge is disqualified from deciding in this case. —*disqualified for*— He was accused with having acted unfairly. He died for thirst—with the bilious fever. Col. Washington was very ill with a fever.—*Irving.* You may rely in what I say, and confide on his honesty. I have little influence with him. —*over him.* These bonnets were brought in fashion last year. This is a very different dinner to what we had yesterday. The bird flew up in the tree. Charles let his dollar drop in the creek. The persecutions of these wretched people were truly barbarous. —*against these*— It is an affair on which I am not interested. Above this, who shall fix a limit to his cares?

He made the order in authority of the instructions he had received. —*by authority of*— But what is my grief in comparison of that which she bears? He ended with a panegyric of modern sciences. I have an abhorrence to such politicians. It was no diminution to his greatness. He came of a sudden. About two months ago, he went out of a fine morning with a bundle in his hand. —*Irving.* I take a walk of evenings. —*a walk every evening;* or,—*a walk almost every evening.* He swerved out of the true course. He does not aspire at political distinction. I was disappointed in the pleasure of meeting you. There is no need for so much preparation. His hardships produced little change on his appearance. I have been to New Orleans, and I am now going for New York. We remained at the South, in a little village. You will find me in No. 25, at Olive Street. He was eager of making a display. —*eager to make*— I find no difficulty of keeping up with my class. —*in keeping up*—or, *find it no difficulty to keep up*— Among every class of people, self-interest prevails. They quarreled amongst one another. —*with*— There is constant hostility between these several tribes. He divided his estate between his son, daughter, and nephew. Such a series of words generally have a comma between each. —*after each word.* A combat between twenty Texans against fifty Mexicans. —*of . . . against*—or, *between . . . and*— The space between the three lines is the area of the triangle. —*within*—

2. Position.

1. Adjuncts should be so placed in the sentence as to make it correct, clear, and elegant.

2. A needless separation of the preposition from the word which it governs, is generally inelegant.

3. Terms that express time or measure, should not be joined, by a preposition, to a word which they are not designed to limit.

There we saw some fellows digging gold from China. A Lecture on the methods of teaching Geography at 10 o'clock. He obtained a situation of great profit, in the beginning of his career. These verses were written by a young man who has long since lain in the grave, for his amusement. *Wanted*—A young man to take care of some horses, of a religious turn of mind. He went to see his friends on horseback. Habits must be acquired of temperance and self-denial. In every church it must be admitted there are some unworthy members. The customs and laws are very different from ours in some countries. Many act so directly contrary to this method, that, from a habit of sup-ing time and paper, which they acquired at the university, they write in so diminutive a character that they can hardly read what they have written. Are these designs which any man who is born a Briton, in any circumstances or in any situation, ought to be ashamed or afraid to avow? · Such boatman may recover, against such master or commander, the wages justly due him, according to the service rendered, notwithstanding such contract may be entire, in any court having jurisdiction.—*R. S. of Mo.*

Whom did he give it to? *To whom did he,* &c. I never could ascertain what it was useful for. Whom was the message directed to? Which of the books can I find it in? How much did you send him to market with? He rushed into, and expired in, the flames. —*rushed into the flames, and expired in them.* The first law is different from, and much inferior to, the second. The cost of the carriage was added to, and greatly increased, my account.

My mistress had a daughter of nine years old.—*Swift.* (Omit "*of;*" for "*nine years*" limits "*old,*" and not "*daughter.*") Almost any boy of twelve years old knows as much. They enclosed the garden with a wall of six feet high. A monument of several centuries old. A room of twenty feet long and eighteen feet wide.

3. *Insertion or Omission.*

1. We should not insert or omit prepositions so as to destroy the proper connection between other words. Prepositions should not be omitted, when required by the sense.

2. Prepositions should not be inserted or omitted contrary to long and general usage.

It was to your brother to whom I was mostly indebted. *It was your brother,* &c. It was in vain to remonstrate. Allow me to present you with a gold watch. —*to you a*—or, *you a*— I will now present you with a synopsis.—*Smith's Gram.* The performance was approved of by all who saw it. Women are governed by fancy in stead of by reason. It stands in the proposition introduced by *toi,* in stead of in a preceding sentence. —*and not in*—or else allowable. The proper course of action, in this case, is by assumpsit. —*is assumpsit.* By a deed of trust there will be a less troublesome security than by a mortgage. *A deed of trust will,* &c. What went ye out for to see? At about what time will you come again? What use is it to me? The horned frog is nearly the size of a lizard. The sycamore was fifteen feet diameter. From having heard of his distress, I sent him relief. From abusing his constitution in youth, he became prematurely old. *Having abused,* &c. My business prevented me attending the last meeting of the Society. He refused taking any further notice of it. —*refused to take*— She could not refrain shedding tears. I shall oppose the granting this company any more privileges. *I shall oppose the granting of any more privileges to,* &c. There was no disputing the point.—*Irving.*

The remark is worthy the fool that made it. The attack is unworthy your notice. San Francisco is the other side the Rocky Mountains. The spring is near to the house. She sat next us. He was banished the country—expelled the college. Many talented men have deserted from the party. The court of France or England was to be the umpire. I will consider of your proposition. I admit of what you say. You have anticipated on what I was going to say. It was rather the want of customers than money that induced him to abandon his business. —*than that of money*— Ignorance is the mother of fear as well as admiration. I put some apples into the buggy and my hat. California is not more noted for its gold than bears. The calf followed on after its mother. The passion of anger leads tc repentance. *Anger leads,*

&c. *Wanted*—A young man of from 16 to 21 years of age. The distance from before one ear to before the other, is 15 inches. (Change the sentence.) He was right in that which you blame him. —*for which*— She took it more to heart than I thought for. —*than I thought she would.* Let us consider the works of nature and art, with proper attention. An event so unexpected to my mind and many others. One should not be omitted without the other. *They should be either both omitted or both inserted.* You will seldom find a dull fellow of good education, but (if he happen to have some leisure on his hands) will turn his head to one of those two amusements for all fools of eminence, politics or poetry.—*British Essayists.* —*to politics or to poetry.*

4. Repetition.

A preposition, relating to a series of objects, must be used but once before the entire series, or be repeated before each term of the series.

He is a man of sagacity, experience, and of honesty. By industry, by economy, and good luck, he soon accumulated a fortune. Their hearts are torn by the worst, most troublesome and insatiable of all passions,—by avarice, by ambition, by fear, and jealousy.—*Burke.*

OBSERVATIONS.

1. What preposition is most appropriate in any given instance, does not always depend on the preceding or on the following term, but on the relation of the terms, or on the view that is taken of them. A different preposition may sometimes express the meaning as well, or more forcibly; or it may be sufficiently definite by the aid of some principle in the Figures, to suggest the relation intended. To be able to use prepositions and conjunctions rightly, requires not only a thorough knowledge of them, but also an extensive and sagacious insight into the whole fabric of language.

2. Adjuncts may often be variously placed in sentences, though they should generally be placed as near as possible to the words to which they relate. A troublesome adjunct is sometimes placed most advantageously at the beginning, seldom at the end. Adjuncts should not be needlessly inverted. "*Of whom* did you buy it?" is a better expression than "*Whom* did you buy it *of?*" But when the relative is omitted, the preposition must be put at the end; as, "I have nothing to tie him *with,*" i. e., I have nothing *with which* to tie him. To place an object common to both, after a transitive verb and a preposition, or after two or more prepositions separated by several intervening words, sometimes produces a disagreeable hiatus in the sense. When the objective term is short, it is better to place it after the first governing word, and its pronoun after the second; but when it is long, it may be allowed to stand after all the governing words. "Here he *saw,* and was soon after surrounded *by,* several *Indians;*" better, "Here he *saw* several *Indians, by whom* he was soon afterwards surrounded." "The second proposal was different *from,* and inferior *to,* the *first;*" better, "The second proposal was different *from* the *first,* and inferior *to it.*" "He has quarrelled *with* and *betrayed* every *friend* that he ever had." "He was descended *from,* and allied *to,* some of the best families of the State."

We may say, "A child of six years," or, "A child of six years of age," or rather, "A child six years old;" but not, "A child of six years old," for "six years" should modify "old," and not "child." A necessary modifying phrase or clause may sometimes be allowed to separate the adjunct from the preceding term; as, "In this dialect we find written nearly the whole of what remains to us of ancient Greek literature."—*Crosby.* Adjuncts, in regard to position as well as signification, are much like adverbs and adjectives.

When not emphatically distinguished, the indirect object usually precedes the other; as, "Give *me* the knife:" but when placed after the other, the preposition must be expressed; as, "Give the knife *to me*" [not to some other person].

3. When the insertion or the omission of the preposition would cause a slight variation in the sense, we should be very careful to select the most appropriate expression. *To know* differs from *to know of;* and *to meet,* from *to meet with.* "I *met with* an old friend, who showed me all the curiosities of the city." "I *met* the stranger, but passed on without stopping." *For* can not, according to modern usage, be properly used before the infinitive. "What went ye out *for to see?*" should be, "What went ye out *to see?*" When the antecedent term relates to two or more adjuncts after it, the preposition must, in many cases, be repeated, to show this common relation; as, "Religion is a comfort in youth as well as old age." —*as in old age.* "Wealth is more conducive to wickedness than piety." —*than to piety.*

4. Judicious repetition adds sometimes much to the vigor and solemnity of the sentence. "This bill, though rejected here, will make its way *to* the public, *to* the nation, *to* the remotest wilds of America."—*Chatham.* "All his talents and virtues did not save him *from* unpopularity—*from* civil war—*from* a prison—*from* a bar—*from* a scaffold!"—*Macaulay.* To avoid the tediousness caused by placing many objects after the same preposition, or by repeating the same preposition very often, a long series of terms is sometimes elegantly separated into groups, as in the following sentence: "I could demonstrate that the whole of your political conduct has been one continued series of weakness, temerity, and despotism; of blundering ignorance and wanton negligence; and of the most notorious servility incapacity, and corruption."—*Chatham.*

11. CONJUNCTIONS.

382. A **conjunction** is a word used to connect clauses or sentences, or else words or phrases in the same construction, and to show in what sense the parts are connected.

Ex.—"The chain will gall, *though* wreathed with roses." "*If* you would enjoy the fruit, pluck not the blossom." " John *and* James are happy, *because* they are good."

383. Two conjunctions are sometimes combined, and some phrases are customarily used as conjunctions.

Ex.—"*And yet* I would not get riches thus, *even if* I were a beggar." " John, *as well as* Arthur, must be punished, *inasmuch as* they have both been disobedient." But when the words of a phrase can be parsed as well according to their literal meaning, or when the conjunctions have each a separate influence over the sentence, they should be parsed separately. "A man's a man *for all that.*" "*But, if* he fails, all is lost"—*But* all is lost, *if* he fails.

Conjunctions may be divided into three chief classes; *coördinate, subordinate,* and *corresponding.*

384. A **coördinate** conjunction connects parts of equal rank, or parts of which one does not modify the other.

385. A **subordinate** conjunction connects parts of unequal rank, or parts of which one modifies the other.

386. A **corresponding** conjunction suggests another conjunction, and assists it in connecting the same parts.

Ex.—And, but, or, nor; if, that, because, therefore; *either—or, neither—nor* The corresponding conjunctions are included in the other classes, and are easily distinguished; the coördinate conjunctions are all the others, except the subordinate; and the subordinate are those which join on parts that have the sense of substantives, adjectives, or adverbs, or that answer to the questions implying these elements. "*That* he is strictly honest, is true." *What* is true? "The belief *that* the soul is immortal." *What* belief? "I came *that* I might hear him." Came *why?*

387. *And, or,* and *nor,* are the conjunctions most frequently

used for connecting single words. *And* takes all together; *or*, one at a time, or else any one to the exclusion of the rest; and *nor*, one at a time, and negatively.

Ex.—"Bring your book, slate, *and* atlas." "Bring your book, slate, *or* atlas." "God bids the ocean roar, *or* bids its roaring cease." "The house has neither doors *nor* windows."

388. *But, if,* and *that,* are the next most important conjunctions, and they are mostly used in connecting propositions. *But* implies opposition of meaning; *if,* something conditional; and *that* is often a sort of handle to a group of words conceived as a whole.

Ex.—"Milton has fine descriptions of morning; *but* not so many as Shakespeare." "*If* spring has no blossoms, autumn will have no fruit.." "It is strange *that* he never writes to us."

389. One conjunction may sometimes be used in place of another; but never when a meaning different from the one intended, can be inferred.

Ex.—"I know him, *for* I went to school with him." "I know him, *because* I went to school with him." "God bids the ocean roar, *or* bids its roaring cease." "God bids the ocean roar, *and* bids its roaring cease." "He sowed little, *and* reaped much." "He sowed little, *but* reaped much." "Conjunctions connect words *and* sentences together," should be, "Conjunctions connect words *or* sentences."

390. For the sake of brevity, elegance, or vigor, conjunctions are sometimes omitted, when the mind can connect the parts and see their dependence.

Ex.—"'Twas certain [*that*] he could write, and cipher too." "Had I been at home, you should have staid".—*If* I had been at home, you should have staid.

"The woods are hushed, [*and*] the waters rest,
[*And*] The lake is dark and still."—*Mrs. Hemans.*

" The king to Oxford sent a troop of horse ;
[*For*] The Tories own no argument but force."

391. Conjunctions are usually first omitted, and then expressed; other words are usually first expressed, and then omitted.

Ex.—John, [*and*] James, *and* Thomas, were drowned. You *may go,* or [*you may*] stay.

392. The conjunction is sometimes used where it is usually omitted.

1. At the beginning of a sentence, to make its introduction less abrupt; 2. In the body of a sentence, when the speaker means to dwell on particulars, in order that the hearer may duly appreciate what he says.

Ex.— "*And* tell me, I charge you, ye clan of my spouse,
Why fold ye your mantles, why cloud ye your brows ?"—*Campbell.*

' Italy teems with recollections of every kind ; for courage, *and* wisdom, *and* power, *and* arts, *and* science, *and* beauty, *and* music, and desolation, have all made it their dwelling-place." See also p. 266.

393. When conjunctions connect words or phrases, these are nearly always in the same construction.

Ex.—"*Mary, Jane,* and *Alice,* | *went* into the garden, and *brought* some *large, ripe,* and *juicy* peaches." Here the connected nouns are nominatives to the same verbs, the connected verbs or phrases have the same subject, and the connected adjectives qualify the same noun.

Most of the conjunctions have evidently emigrated from other parts of speech.

Ex.—Both, either, that, *adj.;* then, yet, as, *adv.;* except, if (—give), provided, seeing, *verbs.*

———

Connectives may, in general, be divided into *pure conjunctions, conjunctive adverbs, conjunctive phrases,* and *conjunctive* or *relative pronouns.*

And is the chief conjunction, and implies addition. It either connects parts that may be referred *separately* to a third, or it connects parts that must be referred *conjointly* to a third. To avoid this latter sense, we must sometimes use *or* or some other connective. "John and James study"—John studies, and James studies. "John *and* Kate are a smiling couple;" not, John is a smiling couple, and Kate is a smiling couple. "Conjunctions connect words *and* sentences," may mean, "Conjunctions connect words to sentences;" hence we should say, "Conjunctions connect words *or* sentences."

As. "*As* you have come, I will go with you"—*since.* "You are welcome *as* flowers in May"—*comparison.* "A letter represents an elementary sound; *as, a, b, c;*" *i. e.,* such a sound as *a, b,* or *c,* represents. "This is your duty *as* an instructor"—*apposition.* And so, perhaps, in this somewhat anomalous sentence, "England can spare such men *as* him"—*Brougham,* it is best to parse *him* as in apposition with *men,* being comprised in it. *As* should be used after *such* implying similarity or comparison, and sometimes after *same* used in the sense of *such. As* should be used before the infinitive expressing a consequence. "He behaved so badly *as* to be expelled"—*that* he was expelled. *As,* before a participle, sometimes implies cause, or points to the special view to be taken. "He was tried *as* having passed counterfeit money." "He was represented to us *as* being well educated in mathematics." "The soldiers were unprovided, *as* were also the officers"—*and so. As—as, as—so, so—as, such—as,* imply comparison. In some of the foregoing examples, *as* is rather a *conjunctive adverb* than pure *conjunction.*

Although. See *Though.*

Because—*by cause* of. "The water is cool, *because* I put ice into the pitcher"—*natural cause.* "The water is cool, *because* there is moisture on the pitcher"—*logical cause, reason.* The one shows why it is so, and the other why I know it. "A man should not be despised *because* he is poor."

As is most incidental, or takes the slightest notice of an admitted cause; *since* is more formal and serious, and invites attention to the alleged cause or reason; *for* is less formal than *because; because* is the most formal and expressive word; *inasmuch as* implies an inference drawn only to the extent of a limited cause.

Both—*and*—the one as well as the other; not only the one, but also the other.

But. "Wide will wear, *but* narrow will tear"—*on the contrary.* "He never could have been elected, *but* by my exertions in his behalf"—*except.* "I could not *but* notice how much he was confused"—*do otherwise than.* "The postboy is not so tired *but that* he can whistle"(—G. BROWN)—*that....not.*

But is either a pure adversative or a reserving adversative; *however* is milder, takes the least notice of objections, or simply waives them; *yet* admits to some extent, but holds on to some weighty offset or obstacle; *still* implies that the position is unmoved after all; *notwithstanding* braves all opposition; and *nevertheless* is the strongest term, implying that the position is not weakened in the least.

Either corresponds to *or;* and *neither,* to *nor.* It is sometimes necessary to apply them to more than two. The connected parts should be equally full, and as nearly alike as they can conveniently be. This last remark applies also to *both,* and sometimes to *whether.*

Except. "He took no further notice of him, *except* when he happened to meet him"—*take out.* "*Except* a man be born again, he can not enter the kingdom of heaven"—*unless.*

For has all the meanings of *because,* except the last. See *Because.*

If, derived from *give*—grant, allow. "*If* it continue to rain, the river will rise"—*natural consequence.* "*If* Virgil was the better artist, Homer was the greater genius"—*logical consequence.* "It has not been decided *if* the war is to continue or not;" better, *whether.* If the condition is granted, the inference is established; thus, "*If* A=B, C=D; A=B, therefore C=D." "*If* Æschines joined in the public rejoicing, he is inconsistent; *if* he did not, he is unpatriotic; but he either joined or did not join, therefore he is either inconsistent or unpatriotic."—*Demosthenes.* Such an argument is called a *dilemma.* There is sometimes nice choosing between *if* and *when.* *When* always has a tincture of time; *if,* never. "A diphthong is proper *if* both the vowels are sounded;" not, "A diphthong is proper *when* both the vowels are sounded;" for the latter may imply that the same diphthong is sometimes proper, and sometimes improper.

Lest. "I will write to him, *lest* he neglect my business"—*that not.* "Cain's apprehensions were excited, *lest* he should meet the retribution of his crime"—*for fear that.* "Afraid *lest*"—JOHNSON; "Fearful *lest*"—PRESCOTT; better, *that.*

"**Moreover** and **furthermore** appear to connect only paragraphs."—*G. W. Gibbs.* "*Moreover,* by them is thy servant warned."—*Bible.* This is generally, though not always, true.

Nevertheless. "It is true that Homer sometimes nods; *nevertheless,* he is still the greatest of ancient poets."

Notwithstanding. "Great quantities of grain were raised, *notwithstanding* the soil is so poor."

Or is either *exclusive* or *distributive.* "The punishment is $100, *or* imprisonment in jail for three months;" not both. "Sheep are white *or* black;" *i. e.,* some are white, and some are black. "The relative pronoun is resumptive *or* restrictive; *i. e.,* sometimes resumptive, and sometimes restrictive. *Or* may imply either a difference in things, or merely a difference in words. "In a cabin *or* in a palace;" "In an Indian hut, *or* wigwam." In this latter sense, *either* can not be used; and hence *either* is often used or needed to exclude this latter sense. Sometimes *else* is added to *or,* for the same purpose. To avoid the ambiguous sense of *or,* lawyers use *alias,* when there is a mere change of names See *Whereas.*

Neither is the proper correlative of *nor;* sometimes it is used as a correlative to other negatives, and sometimes it is used as an independent conjunction. "She is *neither* handsome *nor* amiable." "My brows become *nothing* else, *nor* that well *neither.*"—*Shak.* "Be *not* too tame *neither.*"—*Shak.* "He had *no* money, *neither* could he find any employment." Whether, in two of the foregoing examples, *either* or *neither* should be used after *nor,* custom has not decided as yet, though I incline to think *neither* should be considered the proper strengthening or correlative word.

Nor. It is sometimes difficult to determine whether *or* or *nor* should be used to continue a negative sense after a preceding negative. Usage seems to give the preference to *nor;* especially when the parts connected are long, or emphatically distinguished, or do not have a common dependence on the first negative. "The King has *no* arbitrary power to give him; your Lordships have *not; nor* the Commons; *nor* the whole Legislature."—*Burke.* "Never cal·mniate any man, *nor* give the least encouragement to calumniators." Here *or* could not have been used. "Yet Paul did not waste all his hours in this idle vaporing, *nor* in the pleasures of the table."—*Prescott.* "But not thieves; *nor* robbers; *nor* mobs; *nor* rioters, insurgents, *or* rebels."—*Parsons on Contracts.* "I can not see better than another, *nor* walk so well."—*Garrick.* "I can not tell which way his Majesty went, *nor* whether there is any one with him."—*Fielding.*

But *or* may be preferable to *nor*, when the parts are short and closely connected, or when the preceding negative plainly affects all the parts, or when the parts are not emphatically distinguished, or when the latter part is merely explanatory or alternative. "*No* senator *or* representative shall be appointed to," &c. "This was *not* to be ascribed chiefly *or* solely to political animosity."—*Macaulay.* "*No* tie of gratitude *or* of honor could bind him."—*Id.* "So long as they did not meddle with politics *or* religion."—*Prescott.* "*No* special words, *or* form, are necessary to make the contract binding."—*Parsons.* *Nor* sometimes cuts off preceding, modifying, or other words, and then *or* must be used; as, "You can *not* be too exact *or* honest in your business," *i. e., nor* too honest. "You can *not* be too exact *nor* honest in your business," implies that it is impossible to be honest. "These syllables are *not* always sounded *or* accented in the same way." "There was *no* excess of fraud *or* cruelty, of which he was not capable."—*Macaulay.* Here *nor* would suggest "no cruelty," and not, "no excess of cruelty." *Nor* sometimes allows the word after it to have the widest application; as, "There is *no* person *nor* law to prevent him," *i. e.,* nor law in general. Better: "There is *no* person, *no* law," etc., or, "There is *no* person *or* law," etc., or, "There is *no* person *nor any* law," etc. When *or* would suggest that the latter part is merely alternative when it really is not so, *nor* must be used, or else some other mode of expression; as, "*No* dependent proposition, *nor* clause," &c., or, "*No* dependent proposition, or *other* clause," &c.

"Seasons return, but not to me returns Seasons return, but not to me returns
Day, *or* the sweet approach of even *or* morn, Day, *nor* the sweet approach of even *or* morn,
Or sight of vernal bloom, *or* summer's rose, *Nor* sight of vernal bloom, or summer's rose,
Or flocks, *or* herds, *or* human face divine." Or flocks, or herds, or human face divine."
    Milton.   *Goold Brown's Emendation.*

Or and *nor* are sometimes used by poets in stead of *either* and *neither*. "*Or* floating loose, *or* stiff with mazy gold."—*Milton.* "*Nor* in sheet *nor* in shroud we wound him."—*Wolfe.*

Provided. "At the father's death the property is divided equally, *provided* there is no will to the contrary."

Since. The cause or motive always precedes in time; hence *since* may be used as a conjunction. "*Since* you have brought your hounds, we will take a hunt."

Still. "Though their homes were laid waste, *still* the spirit of the people was invincible"—*yet even then.*

Than should be used after comparatives, and after *other, else, otherwise, rather,* and words of similar meaning. *Besides* may also be used after *else* or *other,* when the sense requires it. It joins on something as additional, or to be included with what has been previously mentioned. "He will hold the land against all others *than* the king;" *i. e.,* but not against him. "He will hold the land against all others *besides* the king;" *i. e.,* not merely against him, but against all others too.

That properly introduces a consequence or purpose; sometimes it heads a group of words that form an expanded explanation in reference to some other word. "There was such a noise *that* we could not study." "I came *that* I might assist you." "The Bible is such *that* a child can understand it, and yet a philosopher may study it all his life." After words of *fearing, doubting, denying,* and some others, *but, but what, but that, lest,* or *lest that,* should not be used for *that.* "I do not doubt *but that* you will succeed," seems to except the very thing not excepted: say, "I do not doubt *that* you will succeed."

Therefore. "It has rained, *therefore* the grass will grow"—*natural consequence.* "The dust is laid, *therefore* it has rained"—*logical consequence, conclusion.*

Then is less formal than *therefore,* and *so* is still less formal; *hence* refers to a cause near at hand; *thence* to a remoter one; *wherefore* to something immediately preceding; *therefore* deduces an important conclusion, and often refers to a series of causes or reasons; *accordingly* introduces what chimes in with nature and reason or some admitted statement; and *consequently* sums up matters in the most formal style.

Though, although, imply admission or opposition. (See the preceding paragraph.) "The Spaniards pushed on, *although* the barbarians clambered up, and broke in upon their ranks"—*notwithstanding.* —"*though* the barbarians"—the barbarians, *however*— *As though* is often improperly used for *as if.*

Unless attaches to a clause the exception which would establish the opposite clause. "A man can not be convicted, *unless* he is guilty"—*if not.* "The accused is set at liberty, *unless* he has been convicted"—*but not....if.*

Whereas. "*Whereas* it doth appear that one Isaac Bertram, alias William Burton," &c.—*since,* or, *inasmuch as.* "His good deeds are never thought of, *whereas* his evil ones are everywhere told and exaggerated"—*while, on the contrary.*

Whether. See *If* and *Either.*

Yet. "Though resistance to the tyrant spread desolation over our lands, *yet* future industry may repair them"—future industry, *however,* may, &c.

Again, also, however, now, nay, even, further, furthermore, namely, therefore, wherefore, otherwise, likewise, so, still, thus, else, accordingly, consequently, and a few other such words, though originally adverbs, are considered by many grammarians conjunctions when they stand near the beginning of a clause or sentence, or when they introduce something. Most of them have acquired their conjunctive sense by ellipsis. The pupil should consider whether they modify according to their usual meaning, or connect like conjunctions, and then parse them accordingly. It may sometimes be a matter of little consequence to which class they are referred, provided their meaning, or force in the sentence, is fully understood.

Some of these words are occasionally used to avoid a too frequent repetition of some very common conjunctions; such as *and, or, but.* Sometimes they merely assist or strengthen the conjunction. "He has a laborious profession; *but* it is very lucrative." "He has a laborious profession; *however,* it is very lucrative." "The corn was sold, *and also* delivered, before we saw it, *or even* heard of it."

Conjunctive adverbs have already been considered. See p. 241.

Conjunctive phrases are such as, *on the contrary, on the other hand, the moment that, as well as.* Most of them are often used to relieve or strengthen the ordinary connectives. Some clauses are connected simply by having a correlative sense; and the phrases which give them this sense, may also be termed *conjunctive phrases.* "*The more* we have, *the more* we want."

The longer conjunctions or expressions are sometimes merely a little more emphatic or forcible.

All the relative pronouns attach clauses in the sense of adjectives or nouns. (See pp. 128–31.) Hence *and* is often improperly used before relative clauses. "The windmill on the hill, *and* which was built last year, has been blown down." Omit *and.* "Here lies buried Thomas Brown, who founded this city, *and who* died in 1797." Here *and* is proper, for it joins the relative clause to the one preceding it, while *who* joins it to the antecedent.

EXERCISES.

Examples to be Analyzed and Parsed.

Parse the conjunctions, prepositions, and adverbs:—

1.

Her eyes are bright and[a] blue. The ship carried off a load of ice, and[b] brought back sugar, coffee, and spices. Never show your teeth, unless you can bite. Talk not too much, nor of thyself. Fear God, and keep his commandments; for this comprehends the whole duty of man. To learn in youth, is less painful than to be ignorant in old age. No other persons are so[12] blind as[13] those[10] who will not see.

2.

He supposed that his defeat gave us hope that he would yield to our forces, inasmuch[c] as he believed we were sure that he could now receive no reënforcements.—*Washington.*

However, since the best of us have too many infirmities to answer for, we ought not to be too severe upon those of others; and therefore, if our brother is in trouble, we ought to help him, without inquiring over seriously what produced it.—*Swift.*

We are annoyed either[d] by our own follies, vices, and misfortunes, or by those of others; so that the greater part of life, with the many, consists of suffering and sorrow.—*Johnson.*

(*a.*)——is a *conjunction* (def.); *coördinate*, it connects parts of which one does not modify the other; *copulative*, it implies addition; and here connects "*bright*" and "*blue*," according to Rule XV. (*b.*) ——is a *conjunction*, etc.; it implies addition; and here connects two phrases, according to Rule XV. (*c.*) "*Inasmuch as*" is a *conjunctive phrase*, or simply a *conjunction*, etc.; it implies cause or reason; and here connects clauses or sentences, according to Rule XV. (*d.*)——is a *corresponding conjunction*, it assists another conjunction, etc.

Examples to be Corrected.

All the liabilities to error in regard to conjunctions or connectives, may be reduced to the following heads:—

1. *Choice.* 2. *Position.* 3. *Insertion or omission.* 4. *The parts connected.*

1. *Choice.*

1. The simplest and most appropriate connective should always be selected.

2. Two or more connectives occupying different places in the sentence, and serving to unite the same parts, should exactly correspond:

Your notions are too refined, so as we are not likely to agree. —*so that*— He was dismissed, not so much because he was too young, but because he was too unskillful. —*as because*— A conjunction connects words, phrases, and clauses. The land is equally adapted to farming or to pasturage. To borrow or to lend may be equally imprudent. Proportion is simple and compound. —*either....or*— I can not conceive how my horse got away, without somebody untied him. —*unless*— I do not know why he should have bought the lot, without he bought it for speculation. The report is the same with that which I heard. —*the same as that*— I have the same opinion of the matter with my friend. A man of great ability, but for all that he is not successful. —*and yet*— They told us how that it happened. —*how it*— He is too reckless and indolent that we should put confidence in him. —*for us to put*— The multitude rebuked them, because they should hold their peace. The donation was the more acceptable, that it was given without solicitation. I will see if it snows or not. —*whether*— Do you know if the mail has arrived? If a body moves in a curve, the curve is in one plane. *When*, &c. The last of the horses had scarcely crossed the bridge, than the head of the third battalion appeared on the other side —*Harper's Magazine*. I will go, except I should be ill. I saw them all unless two or three. So as that his doctrines were embraced by great numbers. To go by water will be equally as expensive as to go by land.

He looked as though he could eat up an ox, and pick his teeth with the horns. —*Irving*. —*as if*— I will assist you, if that you can not do the work yourself. Some useful maxims, and which I shall never forget, I learned from him. —*maxims, which*— Some of the land, and for which he paid the highest price, was subject to overflow. He soon discovered some qualities in her, of a disagreeable nature, and which gradually implanted aversion. The money was stolen at the time that the boat was landing. At the time that I saw her, she was young and beautiful. Cæsar wrote in the same manner that he fought. This is one reason that he will not comply. —*why*— A wise man will be contented that his glory shall be deferred till such a time as he shall be truly glorified. —*till the time at which*— He holds no opinion but what is supported by authority and reason.—*Kent*. This passion arises from much the same cause as sympathy.—*Burke*. Bruce spoke of himself and his compeers as being neither Scottish or English, but Norman, barons.—*Scott*. I could not buy it nor borrow it. —*neither ... nor*— His life is neither tossed in boisterous seas or the vexatious world, or lost in slothful ease. He has no love nor veneration for his superiors. Neither flatter or contemn the rich or the great. There was no place so hidden nor remote as the plague did not find it. We need not, nor do not, confine the purposes of God. —*and*— I will defraud nobody, nor nobody shall defraud me. No problem is so difficult which he can not solve. —*that he can not solve it.* No occupation is so easy and simple, but it requires some care and cultivation.

He could not deny but what he borrowed the money. —*deny that*— There is no question but the universe has certain bounds to it.—*Addison*. I have no doubt but that the pistol is a relic of the buccaneers.—*Irving*. A corrupt governor is nothing else but a reigning sin. —*than a*— She thinks of little else but dressing and visiting. He is fond of nothing else but play and mischief. This is none other but the gate of Paradise. O fairest flower, no sooner blown but blasted!—*Milton*. Unaccommodated man is no more but such a poor, bare, forked animal as thou art.—*Shak*. I can not otherwise reduce these fractions but by multiplying by the denominators. There is no other umbrella here but mine. The book is not as accurate as I wished it to be. —*so accurate*— He is, as far as I can judge, well qualified. So still he sat as those who wait till judgment speak the doom of fate. His weakness is such as that he can not sit up. Do your work so as that you will not be obliged to do it again. There is no disposition naturally so good as that it does not require cultivation. I will not go away till your brother returns. (Perhaps allowable; though *before* seems preferable to *till.*) The loafer seems to be created for no other purpose but to keep up the ancient and honorable order of idleness.—*Irving*. —*other .... than*— or, *no purpose .... except*— Such writers have no other standard but what appears to be fashionable and popular.—*Blair's Rhetoric*.

2. Position.

(See page 245.)
He is unqualified for either teaching mathematics or languages. I shall neither depend on you nor on him. —*neither on you nor on him.* The farm will then either be rented or sold. Some nouns are either used in the singular or in the plural number. Some nouns are used either in the singular or the plural number. Mules are both imported from Kentucky and Missouri. Mules are imported both from Kentucky and Missouri. Mules are imported from both Kentucky and from Missouri.

3. Insertion or Omission.

1. Connectives should not be used so frequently as to encumber the sentence.
2. Connectives should not be used so seldom that the discourse is rendered too fragmentary, or the connection between the parts obscure.

John, and Mary, and William, and Susan, went to visit their uncle. He is a man of visionary notions, unacquainted with the world, unfit to live in it. The important relations of masters and servants, and husbands and wives, and brothers and sisters, and friends and citizens. While the earth remaineth, seed-time and harvest, cold, heat, summer, winter, day and night, shall not cease. It happened one day he went out of curiosity to see the great Duke's lions.—*Addison.* Surely no man is so infatuated to wish for a government different from that which we have.

4. The Parts Connected.

1. To vary connected or related parts needlessly, in kind or form, is generally inelegant.
2. When a part has a common dependence on two connected parts before it or after it, it should be proper when construed with each.

He managed the affair wisely and with caution. —*wisely and cautiously*—or, *with wisdom and caution.* In the morning of life we set out with joy and hopefully, but we soon pursue our journey sorrowfully and with despondence. . Enjoying health, and to live in peace, are great blessings. You may take some or all the apples in the basket. (Hardly allowable; say rather, " *You may take some of the apples in the basket,* or *all of them.*") He either could not, nor wished, to refute the argument. It is grammatically independent, but referring logically to some indefinite person. To borrow is easier than paying. —*than to pay.* She was a young lady of great beauty, and possessing an ample fortune. —*and an ample fortune.* The author is more remarkable for strength of sentiment than harmonious language. —*than for harmony of language.* He did not mention Leonora, nor that her father was dead. —*nor her father's death.* He can bribe, but he is not able to seduce; he can buy, but he has not the power of gaining; he can lie, but no one is deceived by him. —*but he can not*— He embraced the cause of liberty faintly, and pursued it without resolution; he grew tired of it when he had much to hope, and gave it up when there was no ground of apprehension.

He ought and will go this evening. —*ought to go and will go*— He can and ought to give more attention to his business. Cedar is not so hard but more durable than oak. —*so hard as oak, but more durable.* She is fairer, but not so amiable, as her sister. It is different but better than the old. The court of chancery frequently mitigates and breaks the teeth of the common law.

—*Addison.* We could not find the place nor the persons by whom the goods had been concealed. That lot is preferable and cheaper than the other. The opinions of the few must be overruled and submit to the opinions of the many. Into this cave we luckily found the way, and a comfortable shelter. —*and it afforded us a comfortable shelter.* The comparison depends on the sound or the number of syllables composing the word. Whatever we do, shall be displayed and heard in the clearest light.

OBSERVATIONS.

1. By means of conjunctions, the speaker or writer intimates that his discourse is to be continued, and generally how he means what he is about to say to be regarded in reference to what he has already said. They serve to unite, or bind together, the several parts of sentences, or to attach additional sentences to the preceding discourse. It has been said that they are to other parts of discourse what nails and mortar are to other building materials.

Conjunctions depend perhaps more on the mind than on the external world, or less on the outward world than most other words; and hence those of one language can perhaps never be all precisely translated by those of another. If I say to you, "Our tea is brought from China, *and* our coffee from the Indies," I bring together, into one sentence, things not necessarily connected by nature: if I suspect that you believe both are brought from China, I would be apt to say, "Our tea is brought from China, *but* our coffee is brought from the Indies;" or, "*Though* our tea is brought from China, *yet* our coffee is brought from the Indies." The speaker or writer has always something in view, or supposes a certain tendency in the minds of those whom he addresses; and he selects his conjunctions accordingly. As the number of conjunctions is comparatively small for all the windings and labyrinths of thought, we may infer that conjunctions are used with considerable vagueness, and have various shades of meaning, which must often be inferred rather from the parts connected, than from any definition that can be given. In reasoning, the effect of the conjunctions, and the meaning of the parts connected, should always be very carefully examined.

2. *That, if,* and some other conjunctions, are frequently omitted to avoid heaviness or harshness of expression, or when the connection and dependence of the parts is sufficiently obvious. "I am satisfied that is the proper plan"—I am satisfied *that* that is the proper plan. "Were it so"—*If* it were so. The judicious insertion or omission of conjunctions sometimes contributes much to the elegance or expressiveness of sentences. Repetition implies deliberation, or a desire to make the most of the matter. The omission of the conjunction usually implies rapidity, haste, or so deep an interest, on the part of the speaker, in what is uttered, that he can not pay attention to connectives or unimportant words. A series of terms are sometimes elegantly connected in pairs or groups. See pp. 347, 358.

The following paragraphs exhibit, the one, frugality, the other, profusion, in the use of connectives, carried perhaps to the furthest point of endurance :—

"Morning came: we rushed to the fight; from wing to wing is the rolling strife. They fell like the thistle's head beneath the autumnal winds. In armor came a stately form: I mixed my strokes with the chief. By turns our shields are pierced: loud rung our steely mails. His helmet fell to the ground. In brightness shone the foe. His eyes, two pleasant flames, rolled between his wandering locks. I knew Cathmor of Atha; I threw my spear on the earth. Dark we turned, and silent passed to mix with other foes."—*Ossian.*

"And the three companies blew the trumpets, and brake the pitchers, and held the lamps in their hands, and the trumpets in their right hands to blow withal: and they cried, The sword of the Lord, and of Gideon. And they stood every man in his place round about the camp; and all the host ran, and cried, and fled."—*Bible.*

4. When the mind naturally expects uniformity of structure, a deviation is generally harsh, and should be avoided. Hence, for instance, "He went *to plunder,* instead of *governing,* the colony," though a mode of expression used by good writers, would probably be better expressed by saying, "*to plunder,* and not *to govern,*" or, "rather *to plunder* than *to govern.*" But when the sense or even the melody of the sentence requires a difference of structure, a deviation is allowable; as, "He has merely strung together words grammatically, and without absurdity." To say, "He has merely strung together words grammatically, and not absurdly," might convey a different meaning.

A part relating to two or more connected parts, is usually construed in the mind with each, and hence it should make sense with each. "He *can* and *ought to* go this evening"—He *can to* and *ought to* go this evening. "It is *different* and *inferior* to the second"—It is *different to* and *inferior to* the second. Therefore say, "He *can go* and *ought to go* this evening;" 'It is *different from* the second, and *inferior to* it." "He was as much belov'ed, but less admired, than his brother"—He was as much beloved than his brother, but less admired than his brother: say, "He was as much beloved as his brother, but less admired." In such sentences, it is customary to make the third part relate to only one of the connected parts, by completing the construction with the first connected part, and requiring the reader to supply the third part, in a suitable form, after the second connected part. When the two connected parts are very short, and the other part is very long, I question the impropriety of placing the latter after the other two, and requiring the reader to supply it in its proper form after the first of the connected parts. Why not supply a proper expression after the first, as well as after the second, of the connected parts? "An improper fraction is equal to, or greater than, 1, because it expresses *as many or more parts than it takes to equal a unit.*"— *D. P. Colburn.* To put the latter part of this sentence in a different form, would make the sentence rather stiff, affected, and pedantic. Besides, the construction seems to be no worse than that of such well-established expressions as, "Preceded by *one or more consonants.*"

12. INTERJECTIONS.

394. An **interjection** is a word that expresses an emotion only, and is not connected in construction with any other word.

Ex.—"'*O,* stay,' the maiden said, 'and rest.'" "*Alas, alas!* fair Inés." "*Poh!* never trouble thy head with such fancies."

"Few, few, shall part where many meet!
The snow shall be their winding-sheet,
And every clod beneath their feet
Shall be a soldier's sepulchre!"

"*Ah!* few shall part where many meet!
The snow shall be their winding-sheet,
And every clod beneath their feet
Shall be a soldier's sepulchre!"

The latter stanza is the first as it was afterwards improved. *Ah* indicates much better the transition from the storm of battle to the wail of woe. See also p. 56.

395. Words from almost every other part of speech, and sometimes entire phrases, when abruptly uttered to express emotion, may become interjections.

Ex.—Strange! behold! what! why! indeed! mercy! away! "Why, *there, there, there!*" "*Fire and brimstone!* what have you been doing?"

396. But when it is not the chief purpose of the word to express emotion, and when the omitted words are obvious, it may be better to parse the word as usual.

Ex.—"*Patience,* good lady! *comfort,* gentle *Constance!*"—*Shakespeare.*
Have patience, good lady! *receive* comfort, [—be consoled,] gentle Constance.

397. Words used in speaking to the inferior animals, and imitative words that are uttered with emotion, are generally interjections.

Ex.—Haw! gee! whoh! scat! whist! 'st, 'st! "The words are fine, but as to the sense—*b-a-h!*"—*Newspaper.* "Up comes a man on a sudden, *slap! dash!*

snuffs out the candle, and carries away all the cash." Interjections. " When, *click !* the string the latch did draw, and, *jee !* the door went to the wa'." —*Burns.* Interjections rather than adverbs. " The lark that *tirra-lirra* chants."—*Shak.* Adverb, showing how. " With a lengthened, loud halloo, *tu-who, tu-whit, tu-whoo-o-o.*"—*Tennyson.* A noun, descriptive of *halloo.*

"Go, get you to bed and repose—
To sit up so late is a scandal;
But, ere you have ta'en off your clothes,
Be sure that you blow out the candle.
Ri fol de rol tol de rol lol."—*Horace Smith.*

If such an expression can be parsed at all, it must be parsed as an interjection; it may be said to indicate pleasurable emotions.

398. The case of a substantive after an interjection, often depends on some word understood.

Ex.—" Ah *me !*"—Ah ! *pity me;* or, Ah ! what has happened *to me !* or, Ah ! wo is *to me !* or, Ah ! it *grieves me.* "Ah ! luckless *I*"—Ah ! luckless *am I !* " O, happy *we !*"—O, happy *are we !* See also p. 144.

399. When an interjection is used, it is generally placed at the beginning of the sentence; but sometimes within the sentence, or even at the end; and sometimes it stands alone. In its syntax, it is always independent of other words.

EXERCISES.

Examples to be Analyzed and Parsed.

Parse all the words :—

Alas! the way is wearisome and long. Adieu, and let me hear from you soon again. Gods[a]! if I could but paint a dying groan. Ah me! Hist! hush! within the gloom of yonder trees, methought a figure passed. Ha, ha, ha[b]! well[c] said. Welcome, [d]welcome, Lafayette! Out upon her[d]! thou torturest me, Tubal.

THE ARMORY.—Ah! what a sound will rise, how wild and dreary,
When the Death Angel touches those swift keys!

(*a.*) "*Gods*" is here used as an *interjection*, it is abruptly uttered to express an emotion, etc. (*b.*) "*Ha, ha, ha !*" is an *interjection*, etc. (*c.*) *That thing was* " well said." (*d.*) "*Out upon her !*" is an *interjectional phrase*, it is abruptly uttered to express an emotion; it denotes anger, etc.

OBSERVATIONS.

Some interjections may be uttered by the speaker when alone, as *alas;* others always have reference to another being, as *farewell.* Some denote painful emotions, as *pish ;* others pleasurable emotions, as *hurrah.* Some indicate intense feeling, as *oh ;* others, slight emotion, as *eh.* Some, depressed feelings, as *alas ;* others, buoyant emotions, as *heigho.* Some of them, as *O, ah,* are, like laughter and weeping, universal expressions for certain feelings: they are found in all languages.

Interjections are most apt to occur when the mind is agitated or suddenly excited ; and hence we meet with them most frequently in poems, orations, novels, and dramatic writings. They do not imply thought or reflection, like other words ; but spring instantaneously from the sensibilities or the will, with but little reference, if any, to the intellect; and hence they are more capricious or less logical than other words, and not so fixed in form and signification. Thus, O and oh denote a variety of emotions, and are used by some writers indifferently, one for the other. Perhaps it would be better to make O denote only such emotions as are lively and joyful; and oh, such as are violent and sorrowful. "Peace be with thee, O our brother."—*Whittier.* " Oh my heart's love! oh my dear one! .... mercy! mercy! all is o'er!"—*Id.* Some writers recommend that O should always be preferred when an address is made. This is a plain and convenient distinction, but it is not always observed. Some of the very common emotions, as wonder, anger, or joy, we find expressed interjectionally by everso many different words. In fact, interjections being to some extent instinctive sounds, their propriety does not always depend on conventional usage, but often somewhat on the peculiar character and condition of the person using them. Frequently, a speaker takes merely some word or words of the previous speaker,—those which chiefly excited the surprise, approbation, or indignation,—and uses them interjectionally. " Consider, Sir Charles is upon a visit to his bride.—*Bride!* he is fitter for the gallows."—*British Drama.* As a general thing, however, interjections should be selected with great care, and not used too frequently nor too seldom. When properly used, they have sometimes a fine effect; but it must not be inferred that they alone can make discourse sprightly or pathetic. They must grow naturally out of the subject or the sentiment. They may, like the overspreading vine, deepen the shade of feeling, but they can not supply the place of the tree. When I see them standing thick on a page, I am generally reminded of the well-known line of Dryden:—

"He whistled, as he went, for want of thought."

It is perhaps needless to add that the words of swearing or cursing, which rowdies use for grace and emphasis, are interjections as superfluous as ungentlemanly.

WORDS BELONGING TO TWO OR MORE PARTS OF SPEECH.

400. The part of speech to which a given word belongs, should always be determined by the sense in which the word is used. When I say, " Our *well* is deep," *well* is a noun; " The man is *well*," *well* is an adjective; "John writes *well*," *well* is an adverb; " The waters *well* from the ground," *well* is a verb.

All is used—
    As an *adjective.* "*All* flowers must fade."
    As a *noun.* "Not *all* that glistens, is gold."
    As an *adverb.* "*All* [*altogether*] listless roamed a shepherd swain."
As is used—   ["*As* cold as ice"—*degree.*
    As an *adverb.* " Skate *as* I skate"—*manner.* " It fell *as* I entered"—*time.*
    As a *conjunction.* "*As* [*since*] we all must die, why not be charitable?"
    As a *pronoun.* " Let such *as* hear, take heed."
Before is used—
    As an *adverb.* "I came *before* it rained."
    As a *preposition.* " He stood *before* me."
    So are also used *above, after, below, ere,* etc.
Both is used—
    As an *adjective.* " *Both* trees are in blossom."
    As a *conjunction.* "She is *both* handsome and intelligent."
    So are also used *either, neither,* etc.

But is used—
  As a *conjunction.* " Sin may gratify, *but* repentance stings."
  As a *preposition.* " Whence all *but* [*except*] him had fled."
  As an *adverb.* " Words are *but* [*only*] leaves."
For is used—
  As a *preposition.* " He works *for* me."
  As a *conjunction.* " Improve each day, *for* life is short."
  So is also used *notwithstanding.*
Much is used—
  As an *adjective.* "*Much* money is often an evil."
  As an *adverb.* " He is *much* better than he was."
  As a *noun.* " Where *much* is given, *much* will be required."
  So are also used *more, little, less,* etc.
Since is used—
  As a *preposition.* "*Since* last year."
  As an *adverb.* " It happened long *since.*"
  As a *conjunction.* "*Since* no one claims it, I will keep it."
That is used—
  As an *adjective.* "*That* book belongs to me." [years."
  As a *conjunction.* " Few people know *that* some crows live a hundred
  As a *relative pronoun.* " The same flag *that* [*which*] we saw before."
  As a *demonstrative pronoun.* " The court of England or *that* [*the court*] of
What is used— [France."
  As an *interrogative pronoun.* "*What* ails you ?"
  As a *relative pronoun* with one case. " I know *what* ails you."
  As a *relative pronoun* with two cases. " Take *what* I offer."
  As an *adjective.* "*What* news from Genoa ?"
  As an *adverb.* "*What* [*partly*] by entreaty, and *what* by threatening, I succeeded." *What,* I think, for *somewhat ;* an unusual and inelegant expression.
  As an *interjection.* "*What !* take my money, and my life too ?"

When doubtful cases occur, a large dictionary may be consulted ; and the teacher may sometimes translate the expression literally into some foreign language, and decide accordingly.

GENERAL EXERCISES.

All the remaining errors in regard to grammar, may be summed up under the three following heads:—

1. *Sentences having too many words.* 2. *Sentences wanting words.*
  3. *Sentences in any other respect faulty.*

1. *Sentences having too many Words.*

No word should be used that is not needed to express the meaning correctly, clearly, and forcibly.

The first qualification required, is a genius.—*Pope.* Old age will prove a joyless and a dreary season, if we arrive at it with an unimproved or with a corrupted mind. These counsels were the dictates of virtue, and the dictates of true honor. Avarice and cunning may gain an estate, but avarice and cunning can not gain friends. His two sisters were both of them handsome. Thought and language act and react upon each other mutually. The neck connects the head and trunk together. These savage people seemed to have no other element but that of war. The more that you give him, the more will he want. They returned back to the city from whence they had come forth. If I mistake not, I think I have seen you before. Whenever he sees me, he always inquires concerning my health. These are rights that Congress can not infringe upon. Our debts and our sins are generally greater than we think for.—*Franklin.* Their situation can scarcely be conceived of at the present day. The continental army moved down to Charleston in the latter end of the year.—*Ramsay.* These things had great and politic ends in their being established. That there snath will not fit this here scythe.

Such have no other law but the will of their prince.—*Kent.* How different is the conduct of the prosecutors from that of yours! The passion of anger, the passion of envy, and the passion of avarice. And he pursued after the children of Israel. Those nice shades by which virtues and vices approach each one another.—*Murray.* The other book is equally as good. All of my time. These examples serve to explain both the parts of the rule. He died in less than two hours' time. Failing in his first effort, he again repeated it. James is tall, but Henry is taller than he. We sought in vain to find the path. He succeeded in gaining the universal love of all men. Let us be ready according as opportunities present themselves, to make a prudent investment of our means. The umbrageous shade of the woody forest. He is temperate, he is disinterested, and he is benevolent; he is an ornament to his family, and a credit to his profession. Perseverance, in laudable pursuits, will reward all our toils, and will produce effects beyond our calculation. The Incas, or kings of Peru, and all those partaking of, or being within a certain degree of consanguinity to them ... were allowed this privilege. —*all those within a certain degree*— Being content with deserving a triumph, he refused the honor of it. Having been reared in affluence, he could not endure poverty. (Allowable; though "*having been*" may be omitted.)

His happy, cheerful temper, remote from discontent, keeps up a kind of daylight in his mind, excludes every gloomy prospect, and fills it with a perpetual serenity. [By a multiplicity and variety of words, the thoughts and sentiments are not set off and accommodated; but, like David dressed out and equipped in Saul's armor, they are encumbered and oppressed. There is a sweetness and sacred holiness in a mother's tears, when they are dropped and fall on the face of her dying and expiring babe, which no eye can see, and no one can behold, with a heart untouched and unaffected.

2. *Sentences wanting Words.*

No word should be omitted that is needed to express the meaning correctly, clearly, and forcibly.

How shall we, any other way, account for it? It is not only the duty, but interest, of young persons, to be studious and virtuous. Such a law would involve the good and bad, the innocent and guilty, in the same calamity. It is education which almost entirely forms the character, the freedom or slavery, the happiness or misery, of the world. Let us avoid the making such amendments as will be needless. As much propriety must be observed in the dress of the old as young.—*Addison.* Chancery will treat it as a personal matter, so far as respects the rights of creditors. Transitive verbs have an active and passive participle. The speculation will produce great gain or loss. —*or great* loss. The people of this country possess a healthy climate and soil. By these happy labors, they who sow and reap, will rejoice together. The court of France or England was to be the umpire. He regards his word, but you do not. The natural abilities of some men much exceed others. I think his works more classical than all our other historians. We were at the fair, and saw every thing there. —*that was there.* We speak that we do know, and testify to that we have seen. A servant whose duty was to take care of the children. —*duty it was*— Which road should be taken, was not easy to determine. This is what best became us to do.—*Swift.* He met with such a reception as those only deserve who are content to take.—*Id.*

I do not remember any place where he said so. —*he ever said so.* It is foreign to the present purpose, to more than allude to these facts. You can not read too much of the classics, nor too well. —*nor read it*— Simon, son of Jonah, lovest thou me more than these? (Ambiguous.) At that place we were neither well paid nor fed. Not a fence or fruit-tree was to be seen.— *Irving.* —*nor a*— Groves, fields, and meadows, are at any season of the year pleasant to look upon, but never so much as in the opening of spring.— *Addison.* —*so much so*— I am inclined to adopt your book, and encourage others to do likewise. —*and to encourage*— The scribes made it their profession to study and teach the laws of Moses. The sale of one farm or several will take place to-day. English verse is regulated rather by the number of syllables than of feet. There is no situation so good anywhere. —*is not anywhere else a*— How can I distinguish the good from bad? He was a warrior by necessity, if not choice. I believe that when things are at worst they will certainly mend; and when they are at best, they will soon deteriorate.

His honor, interest, and religion, were all embarked in the undertaking. (Repeat *his*.) I suppose he prefers her, because she possesses more beauty, more accomplishments, and wealth, than the other. By this habitual indelicacy, the virgins smiled at what they blushed before. —*blushed at*— By such a course, the progress of the pupil will be greatly facilitated, and many difficulties avoided. Such were the first settlements in Texas, claiming to be civilized, but have now passed away. It was neither the buying lands, nor dealing in mules, but extravagance of his wife, that made him a bankrupt. Neither my brother nor sister went to the fair. He did not know whether it would be best to sell his lot or farm. The hawk was chased by the martins, as well as crows. Whether we take the upper or lower route, we can not get there in two days. The cholera is said to be in New Orleans and vicinity. He is eminent both as a lawyer and politician. Not only the peace of the family was broken, but their dignity considerably diminished, by this alliance.

3. *Sentences faulty in Thought or Expression.*

1. The words, the modes of expression, and the arrangement, should be the best the language affords for the author's meaning.

2. We should always think with clearness, vigor, and a full comprehension of the subject, and speak or write accordingly.

3. What is said or written, should be sensible and becoming,—or in accordance with nature, truth, and reason.

"All the parts of a sentence should correspond with one another: a regular and dependent construction, throughout, should be carefully preserved."—*Murray.*

You may as well spend the balance of the evening with us. I do not, however, imagine that the water-spout would have endangered the loss of the ship.

Will you fix the clock so that it will run? The business will suit any one who enjoys bad health. Religion will afford us pleasure, when others forsake us. I am willing to pay a hundred or two dollars. The more I see of his conduct, I like him better. Form your measures with prudence, but all anxiety about the issue divest yourself of. Though virtue borrows no assistance from, yet it may be accompanied by, the advantages of fortune. The Greeks, fearing to be surrounded on all sides, wheeled about and halted, with the river on their backs.—*Goldsmith*. Replevin is when suit is brought to recover property in the possession of another.[a] The mill stood between the old and new bridges. He wrote the recommendations both of the first and last editions. The manner of these authors' writing books so fast, I will now explain. I can not find one of my books.[b] We have not the least right to your protection. I want to see what he wants. When *if* precedes a verb, it is in the subjunctive mood. Porter, however, fired some three or four times at Jones, before he fell. The Romans stipulated with the Carthaginians, to furnish them with ships for transport and war.—*Arbuthnot*. Solomon, the son of David, who built the temple of Jerusalem, was the richest monarch that ever reigned over the Jewish people.

He has little regard for your and my friend's welfare. White sheep are much more common than black. The heads of a panther and a cat are similar in shape. He is not rich,[c] and incompetent for business. The furniture is more showy than useful; but that, I suppose, was not taken into consideration.[d] He came on the boat, which his friends expected.[e] He sent me the books, which he had promised.[f] The magistrate punished him for some misdemeanor, which was approved.[g] Be honest, for it certainly is the best policy.[h] He was thought to be very polite, which indeed he was to those of whom he expected favors.[i] He is always still and grave, which makes him to be thought wise.[j] I was thinking of the best place for an office.[k] This can be made an objection against one government as well as another. The valley of the Amazon is perhaps as large as the Mississippi; but more of it is overflown. I have that that will keep you. There is not a harder part in human nature, than becoming wealth and greatness. This letter being too long for the present paper, I intend to print it by itself. It mattered little what the nature of the task was; whether it were organizing an opposition to a political faction, or a troop of cavalry to resist invasion.—*Prescott*.

The acceptance must also be absolute, and not in any respect differing from the bill. A participle is a word derived from a verb, and which denotes action, or a state of being. There is no vice which mankind carry to such wild extremes as that of avarice. It had been better for us to serve the Egyptians, than that we should die in the wilderness.[l]—*Bible*. This victory seemed to be like a resurrection from the dead, to the Eastern States. John Rutledge and John Jay were nearly of an age. The people had not the wherewith to pay their debts. The supplying an army by contractors, Gen. Jackson had objected to, as highly objectionable. Here it is rare for three fair days to follow each other. The pretenders to polish and refine the English language, have chiefly multiplied abuses and absurdities. God heapeth favors on his servants, ever liberal and faithful. The work, in its full extent, being now afflicted with an asthma, and finding the powers of life gradually declining, he had no longer courage to undertake.— *Johnson*. Dryden makes a very handsome observation on Ovid's writing a letter from Dido to Æneas, in the following words. The perplexity that attends

---

[a] is a mode of trial for the recovery of
[b] even one of, *or*, can find all but one
[c] nor is he competent, *or*, and *he is* incompetent
[d] but its utility, I spppose, was not taken into consideration
[e] according to the expectation
[f] as he had promised to do, *or*, according to promise
[g] and the punishment
[h] for honesty is
[i] and indeed he was so to those
[j] and therefore he is thought
[k] what place would be best
[l] than to die in

a multiplicity of criticisms by various hands, many of which are sure to be futile, many of them ill-founded, and some of them contradictory to others, is inconceivable.^m

It is an acknowledged fact by some of our most experienced teachers, &c.^n I never heard mentioned that fellow's being a poet before.^o The long, undisturbed possession implies the title to be good.^p The hyena, they pretend, to have been brought from Abyssinia. By analyzing is meant the resolving of a sentence into its elements. The book is meant to be adapted to the capacity of children. (A clumsy mode of expression; change the sentence.) The hosts stood still. (Want of euphony.) We were exceedingly kindly treated. They died and fought for liberty. (Unnatural arrangement.) Intemperance produces death, misery, and want. The merciful are blessed, for they shall obtain mercy. The family treated me in the same way that they treat their own sons.^q What is the reason that you are here yet?^r By agitating and discussion, the truth is elicited. Some governments forfeit the property of outlaws. When there is no heir, the estate of course forfeits to the state.^s I wish to cultivate a farther acquaintance with you. Thursday is set aside for thanksgiving day.^t And this is it men mean by distributive justice, and is properly termed equity.^u It was an unsuccessful undertaking, which, although it has failed, is no objection to an enterprise so well concerted. And he entered into a certain man's house named Justus, one that worshiped God. At the same time, there are some defects which must be acknowledged, in his Odyssey. —*Blair.* They were refused entrance into, and forcibly driven from, the house. As the denominator is greater, the value must be less.

Between grammar, logic, and rhetoric, there exists a close and happy connection; which reigns through all science, and extends to all the powers of eloquence.^v —*Mahan.* (Observe that *which* here can not properly represent the identical connection mentioned before it.) No other employment beside a bookseller suited his inclinations. There is no talent so useful toward rising in the world, or which puts men more out of the reach of fortune, than that quality generally possessed by the dullest sort of people, and is, in common language, called discretion.^w Many would gladly exchange riches and honors for that more quiet and humbler station which you are now dissatisfied with. As the guilt of an officer will be greater than that of a common servant, if he prove negligent; so the reward of his fidelity will prove proportionably greater. At first, he was received with great favorableness, but his stupidness soon appeared. The greatest masters of critical learning differ among one another. An eloquent speaker may give more, but not more convincing arguments, than this plain man offered. I favored him, because in looks he favored my brother.

The wealthy merchant and the journeyman tradesman were seen marching side by side, and often exchanged the contents of their canteens with each other.^x —*Hist. of U. S.* In seeking to dig up one fact, it is incredible the number of facts I unearthed.—*Irving.* The asylum was founded upwards of two centuries since, on an old monastic establishment.—*Id.* By this system, money became plenty —such as it was.—*Id.* A letter written by an inhabitant of that place, speaks of the sudden apparition of the enemy.—*Irving's Washington.* The blunder was detected on an order being issued for a new supply of cartridges.^y —*Id.* If his army were demoralized, or was badly whipped, such deliberation would not have been seen on either side.—*Boston Post.* I know

---

^m of which many   ^n a fact acknowledged   ^o heard that fellow mentioned
as being a poet, *or*, heard it mentioned that that fellow is   that the title is good
^q 1ne as they   ^r Why are you   ^s escheats   ^t set apart   ^u is what
men mean .... and what   ^v Grammar .... have .... and such a connection reigns, indeed
through   ^w which is generally , ... and which is   ^x shared the contents
when an order was issued.

that all words which are signs of complex ideas furnish matter of mistake a.ıd
cavil.—*Locke.*   No nation can or have any right to look for respect abroad as
being just, that is not first honest at home.—*Swift.*   Which when Beëlzebub
perceived, than whom none higher sat. (An uncouth knarl; rather say, "*than
who,*" or, "*than he,*" or, "*none higher sat than he.*")

I beg the favor of your acceptance of a copy of a view of the manufactories of the
West Riding of the county of York.   When one gives one's self the liberty to
range and run over in one's thoughts the different geniuses of men which one
meets in the world, one can not but observe, that most of the indirection and
artifice, which is used among men, does not proceed so much from a degeneracy
in nature, as an affectation of appearing men of consequence by such practices.[a]
—*British Essayists.* (Too many *ones;* there are also other faults.)   The awful
distance which we bear towards her in all our thoughts of her, and that cheerful
familiarity with which we approach her, are certain instances of her being the
truest object of love of any of her sex.—*Ib.*   Never delay till to-morrow, (for
to-morrow is not yours; and, though you should live to enjoy it, you must not
overload it with a burden not its own,) what reason and conscience tell you
ought to be performed to-day. (Take out the parenthesis, and put it after the
rest of the sentence, in a separate, distinct sentence.)   The discontented man
(as his spleen irritates and sours his temper, and leads him to discharge his venom
on all with whom he stands connected) is never without a great share of malignity.

Last Saturday a gang of highwaymen broke into an empty house, and stripped it of all its furniture.—*Newspaper.* It is always objectionable to use the
same word too often.   In familiar conversation we frequently make use of ellipsis.[aa]   (To make use of a nonentity, or of the absence of a thing, is absurd.)   A
vest which from a naked Pict his grandsire had won.   When a person is
spoken to, he is of the second person.[bb]   The use of which accents [Greek and
Roman] we have now entirely lost.[cc]—*Blair.* (We never had them to lose.)
Our modern pronunciation must have appeared to them [the Greeks and Romans]
a lifeless monotony.[dd]—*Id.* (They never heard it.)   To be convicted of bribery,
was then a crime altogether unpardonable.[ee]   Orthography means word-making, or spelling.[ff]—*Smith's Grammar.*   Abercrombie had still nearly four times
the number of the enemy.[gg]—*Irving.*   The Latin tongue, in its purity, never
was in this country.[hh]   The notions of Lord Sunderland were always good;
but he was a man of extravagant habits.

The following erroneous sentences, which are taken from Whateley's *Logic*,
belong to the class called *fallacies.* Most fallacies arise because the same word
has often several different meanings, or because it may be applied to objects
of the same general class, with greater or less comprehensiveness.

None but whites are civilized: the ancient Germans were whites: therefore
they were civilized. (Observe here that the whites referred to in the second
proposition are none of the whites referred to in the first proposition.)   Nothing
is heavier than platina: feathers are heavier than nothing: therefore feathers
are heavier than platina. (My dog has more legs than no dog: no dog has
twelve legs: therefore my dog has more than twelve legs.)   All cold is expelled by heat: this person's disorder is a cold: therefore it is to be expelled
by heat.   He who is most hungry, eats most: he who eats least, is most hungry:
therefore he who eats least, eats most. Whatever body is in motion, must move
either in the place where it is, or in a place where it is not: neither of these
is possible: therefore there is no such thing as motion.

---

[a] When a person, &c.   [aa] ellipses are frequently allowed   [bb] When a person is spoken to, the noun or pronoun used for addressing him is lost   [cc] is ....   [dd] would have appeared   [ee] Bribery was   [ff] means, literally, correct writing   [gg] four times as many men   [hh] was never spoken, in its purity, in.

Miscellaneous Examples to be Corrected.

Honor or reputation are dearer than life.—*Bouvier.*
Mr. Burke was offered a very important and lucrative office.—*Goodrich.*
The protest laid quietly on the table.—*Irving.*
To this, in a great measure, has been attributed the successes of the Moslems.—*Id.*
You have chose the worse.—*Id.*
The greater part of the forces were retired into winter-quarters.—*Id.*
Washington was given the command of a division partly composed of his own men.—*Id.*
She doubted whether this were not all delusion, and whether she was not still in the palace.—*Id.*
The Indian chief and his son, being a small distance from the line of march, was surrounded and taken.—*Id.*
Where will we find such merry groups now-a-days?—*Id.*
Sir Walter speaks to every one as if they were his blood relations.—*Id.*
The right wing was composed of Glover's, Mason's, and Patterson's regiments.—*Id.*
Burgoyne was stated as being arrived at Quebec to command the forces in an invasion from Canada.—*Id.*
Were Aristotle or Plato to come among us, they would find no contrast more complete than between the workshops of their Athens and those of New York.—*Bancroft.*
On rather a narrow strip of land.—*E. Everett.*
We had fortunately engaged rooms at the only decent inn at Melrose, and after supper went out at nine o'clock to see the abbey.—*Id.*
To the antiquary and artist, these columns are a source of inexhaustible observations and designs.—*Byron.*
That fortune, fame, power, life, hath named themselves a star.—*Id.*

He knew not what it was to die.—*Id.*
And goodly sons grew by his side,
But none so lovely and so brave
As him who withered in the grave.—*Id.*

Sir Henry Wotton used to say that critics were like brushers of noblemen's clothes.—*Bacon.*

Let them the state adorn, and he defend.—*Cowley.*
He is, indeed, more of an antiquary than an historian.—*Craik.*
Lingard brings forward good reasons for differing with Wright.—*Id.*
His curse be on him. He who knoweth where
The lightnings hide.—*Mrs. Sigourney.*

My robe, and my integrity to Heaven, is all I now dare call my own.—*Shakespeare.*
A silk dress or a flowered bonnet were then great rarities.—*History of Pennsylvania.*
Thomas Penn, soon after his arrival, aided by seven special commissioners, entered upon the adjustment of the southern boundary, and running the line between the proprietaries and Lord Baltimore.—*Ib.* (Recast the sentence.)
Mr. Dana asked Mr. Gore's leave to say a few words, which he did; after which he retired from the Convention.—*Elliot's Debates.*
What is seventy-five cents, or even a dollar, an acre?—*Ib.*
The miller was bound to have returned the flour.—*Kent.*
The true rule was stated to be that the seller was liable to an action of deceit, if he fraudulently misrepresent the thing sold.—*Id.*

To inquire whether or no the party be an idiot or lunatic.— *Mo. Statutes.*
The constable shall execute such jury summons fairly and impartially, and shall not summon any person whom he has reason to believe is biased or prejudiced for or against either of the parties.—*Ib.*
It is a full two hours to dinner.—*Harper's Magazine.*
The two electric fluids neutralized each others' effects.—*Ib.*
My suspicions were being more and more confirmed every minute.—*Ib.*
Now, then, what should you think water was composed of?—*Ib.*
Of the other two there exists only the first book, and the plan of the second.—*Ib.*

It is a little child of two years old.—*Ib.*
He knew not which to most admire.—*Ib.*
We have other two remarks to offer.—*Ib.*

Barnabas and his brother became, as companions in crime usually do, suspicious of one another.—*Ib.*
In England, every one is free as soon as they touch the land.—*Ib.*
There was the house and out-buildings, all of an unfashionable kind.—*Ib.*
It was I who destroyed Ehrenberg's theory that the *volvox globator* was an animal.—*Atlantic Monthly.*
Which phrase, if it mean anything, means paper money.—*Ib.*
Some virtues are only seen in adversity.—*Eclectic Magazine.*
I shall be happy always to see my friends.—*Ib.*
He not only watched a good opportunity to liberate his prisoner, but swam with him across the river on his back.—*Religious Memoirs.*
The queen bore all her duties stoutly, as she expected others to bear them.—*Hist. of Netherlands.*
Each occupied their several premises, and farmed their own land.—*Jefferson.*
New York, with several posts in the neighborhood, were in possession of the enemy.—*Id.*
My residence is at present at his lordship's, where I might, was my heart disengaged, pass my time very agreeably, as there is a very amiable young lady lives at the same house.—*Washington's Letters.*
We have much to say on the subject of this Life, and will often find ourselves to dissent from the opinions of the biographer.—*Macaulay.*
If we examine with minuteness the falling snow, we will observe that each flake consists of a number of exceedingly delicate particles of ice.—*E. Sargent.*
But we will fail of our conviction, if we have not made it evident, &c.—*Critique on Worcester.*
A squirrel can climb a tree quicker than a boy.—*Webster.*
Parents are of all other people the very worst judges of their children's merits; for what they reckon such, is seldom any thing else but a repetition of their own faults.—*Addison.*
The having a grammar of our mother-tongue first taught, would facilitate our youths learning their Latin and Greek grammars.—*Id.*
We have the power of retaining, altering, and compounding those images which we have received, into all the varieties of picture and vision.—*Id.*
Eye hath not seen, nor ear heard, neither have entered into the heart of man, the things which God hath prepared for them that love him.—*Murray's Gram.*
By intercourse with wise and experienced persons, who know the world, we may improve and rub off the rust of a private education.—*Ib.*
Prepositions, you recollect, connect words, as well as conjunctions; how, then, can you tell the one from the other?—*Smith.*

PRECEPT 1. Avoid low and provincial expressions. PRECEPT 8. Observe the natural order of things or events, and do not *put the cart before the horse.*—*Goold Brown.*

GENERAL OBSERVATIONS.

In speaking or writing, we should avoid *redundancy, deficiency, tautology, ambiguity, obscurity, affectation, pedantry, vulgarity, silliness, falseness, absurdity, nonsense, self-contradiction,* and any phraseology that is not the best the language affords.

In general, the fewer the words we use to express our meaning, the better. Many of the most esteemed and durable paragraphs in our literature, are such as tell much in very few words. It is easy to multiply words; but it is disagreeable to be obliged to read through a large volume, to get what might have been told us as well in a small pamphlet.

To the abundant or excessive use of words, we commonly apply the terms *verbosity, pleonasm, redundancy,* and *tautology*. *Verbosity* implies the use of circuitous expressions, or it is the telling of things in a round-about way: it is opposed to *sententiousness* or *conciseness*. "They who first settled in the country, made choice of the most desirable lands;" better, "The first settlers took the best lands." *Pleonasm* is the use of some word or expression that is not essential, but still adds to the vigor of the sentence; as, "I saw it with my own eyes;" "Busk ye, busk ye, my bonny, bonny bride;" "One of the few, the immortal names, that were not born to die." *Redundancy* is a needless repetition of words, or a needless fullness of expression; as, "We both of us went on the same day, and, besides, moreover, we both of us returned back on the same day;" corrected, "Both of us went and returned the same day." *Tautology* is the telling of the same thing, or nearly the same thing, again and again, in other ways. "The dawn is overcast, the morning lowers, and heavily in clouds brings on the day."—*Addison, as quoted and criticised by Johnson*. "Let observation, with extensive view, survey mankind from China to Peru."—*Johnson himself*. As much as to say, "Let *observation*, with extensive *observation*, *observe* mankind from China to Peru. Law and lawyers abound in tautology and redundancy, and sometimes in needless technical terms.

It is generally much easier to find other ways of telling the same thing, than to add more new thoughts to what is already said; hence it very often happens, that persons, in order to fill up the time or paper, add new words and expressions without adding new ideas: they string together synonymous terms and expressions, just as if they meant to repeat what they have learned in some dictionary. It is said that Daniel Webster resolved—"Never to use a word that does not add some new idea, or modify some idea already expressed." Those words may in general be omitted, which are readily inferred, by the hearer or reader, from the words that are given; and those thoughts may be left unexpressed, which are readily inferred from the thoughts that are expressed. The chief faults to be guarded against in seeking for brevity of expression, are *obscurity* and *deficiency;* which frequently arise from the use of very general and comprehensive terms, and from the omission of words. The allowable or elegant omission of words is termed *ellipsis*. Dialogue, and discourse uttered under the influence of great excitement, are most frequently elliptical.

Coleridge, to give his notion of a perfect style, once said that he had lately read, of Southey's prose, several pages so well written that nothing in them presented itself to his mind except the author's meaning,—that no word, no mode of expression, and no jar in the train of thought, diverted or drew his attention. A perfect style, then, is so transparent a medium for the thought as to become itself invisible,—a train of words presenting the meaning so well and impressively that it passes by itself unobserved. It has been truly said, "Nature's chief masterpiece is writing-well." A person's skill in style depends chiefly on his knowledge, judgment, and taste, and his practice in composition. His discourse should be, throughout, one entire, consistent, congruous, and perfect picture of all that is pertinent to the subject, his aim, and the reader's capacity·

presenting neither too much nor too little. Nothing important should be left out, and nothing useless should be allowed to come in. In short, the piece should be such that no word, phrase, clause, sentence, or paragraph, can be omitted, inserted, transposed, or changed, without injuring the excellence of the whole. The natural order of things should be observed, or such an order as will make the greatest impression. If thoughtful of what we are saying, we would hardly say, "He dressed and washed himself;" "He tumbled, head over heels, into the river;" "He will kill, steal, cheat, and lie, for gold." Things that have no connection, should not be jumbled together; as, "I am well, and hope you have got my last letter." We should not be so flighty as to say something on one topic, then pass to another topic, then come again to the first topic: nor should we, in a subsequent part of the discourse, tell, as if we had not told, what we have already told; nor make any statement inconsistent with some other statement at some distance before it.

The transition from one topic to another should be natural and easy. Not so many different subjects should be introduced into one sentence as will make it confused. The most important parts should be placed where they will make the strongest impression. Modifying parts should be so placed or distributed as to encumber the discourse as little as possible, and to show clearly and readily what they are intended to modify. The longer and more important parts of a sentence should generally follow the shorter and less important parts. To conclude a sentence with an insignificant word or phrase, is always inelegant.

When a serial structure has been adopted, it is generally disagreeable to discontinue or to change it, before the entire enumeration is made. Parts contrasted or emphatically distinguished, should generally be expressed with fullness. "It is not by indolence, but by diligence, that you will succeed." "Spring borrowed a new charm from its undulating grounds, *its* luxuriant woodlands, *its* sportive streams, *its* vocal birds, and *its* blushing flowers." Parts connected by correlative words, and parts implying contrast or comparison, must generally be expressed so nearly alike as possible. Observe the elegance of arrangement and expresssion in the following sentence: "Homer hurries us with a commanding impetuosity; Virgil leads us with an attractive majesty: Homer scatters with a generous profusion; Virgil bestows with a careful magnificence." —*Pope.*

Short sentences and long ones should be properly intermixed. Many short sentences, in succession, are apt to have a disagreeable hitching or jerking effect; and long-winded sentences also displease, by becoming tiresome or tedious. Most of the best modern writers rather prefer short sentences and simple structure, to long and complicated sentences. Long and involved sentences should generally be avoided, by expressing the same meaning in two or more shorter sentences. A long parenthesis within a sentence is generally better expressed by taking it out, and putting it after or before the other part, as a distinct sentence. It is sometimes better to recast a disagreeable sentence altogether; or to dismiss it, and to express the meaning in some other way. Mr. *Bancroft* says, in his History, "Private interest, directed to the culture of a valuable staple, was more productive than the patronage of England; and tobacco enriched Virginia." Here the tobacco clause is hitched on very abruptly and awkwardly; just as if the author did not know what to do with it. Perhaps *Macaulay* would have said: "Private interest, directed to the culture of a valuable staple, was more productive than the patronage of England. The Virginians turned their attention to tobacco; and tobacco enriched them."

In selecting words, or modes of expression, the question is not whether they are perfectly adapted to express the meaning, but whether they are the best the language affords for the meaning; if they are, then they are proper. The preference should, in general, be given to those words and expressions which are most popular, or understood by the greatest number of people; and whose fundamental meaning, when they are analyzed, or traced to their etymology, accords best with the sense in which we mean to use them.

Our little words of one or two syllables, and our pithy idioms, are generally the best. A great master of language says: "Saxon words can not be used too frequently. They abridge and condense, and smack of life and experience, and form the nerve and sinew of the best writings of the day; while the Latin is the fat. The Saxon puts small and convenient handles to things, handles that are easy to grasp; while your ponderous Johnsonian phraseology extends and exaggerates, and never peels the chaff from the wheat." Dr. Johnson said, "The Rehearsal has not life enough to keep it sweet;" but immediately recollecting himself, he added, "It possesses not sufficient vitality to preserve it from putrefaction." He defines *net-work* so that no lady can fail to have a clearer idea of it than she ever had before: "Any thing reticulated or decussated, with interstices at equal distances between the intersections."

We should never use foreign words, expressions, or idioms, when we have native ones that will express the meaning as well. Such a use of languages is nonsensical, affected, and pedantic. "Is Lizzie on the carpet *adhuc?* Are things still in *statu quo?* I shall put out in a few days, and go *quo animus fert;*—you know where."—*From a Letter.* "Tres humble serviteur. Et comment sa porte, Mademoiselle? Why you look divinely. But, mon enfant, they have dressed you out most diabolically. Why, what a coiffure must you have! and, oh mon Dieu! a total absence of rouge. But perhaps you are out."—*Foote: Englishman returned from Paris.*

The following paragraph is composed in the French idiom: "I no sooner found myself here than I visited my new apartments, which are composed of five pieces; the small room, which gives upon the garden, is practised through the great one, and there is no other issue. As I was exceeded with fatigue, I no sooner made my toilette than I let myself fall upon a bed of repose, where sleep came to surprise me."

It is not always easy to determine what is genuine English idiom. Our language, being formed from several others, *has idioms from them all.* To what extent foreign idioms may be allowed in our poetry, it is not easy to determine. I incline to think, that in the whole of our poetry—English, Welsh, Scotch, Irish, and American—may be found all the naturally intelligible idioms from all the foreign languages that our writers ever studied.

It is possible to make discourse out of words merely; that is, without having vivid ideas of things themselves. Words are often strung together grammatically, and with just enough sense or propriety to avoid absurdity. Such emptiness of expression may be termed *nonsense.* It comes from dull minds, or from indolent or vacant states of the mind. Thus it happened that a certain Spanish poet could not tell what his own sonnet meant, and thus have been produced hundreds of unmeaning paragraphs in our literature. Hence we can not be too careful, or use too great efforts, in getting at clear and distinct ideas. Indeed, *vivid, statuesque* ideas are the greatest charm, or that which, above all things else, enchains the hearer or reader. *Truth—truth* worth learning and remembering, is the first quality; and the next is *beauty.*

A common species of nonsense and pedantry is the grandiloquent use of learned language, when the speaker or writer has nothing to say, or does not himself comprehend, or only in a shadowy way, what he pretends to explain or prove to others.

Ex.—"The thinkable, even when compelled by analysis to make the nearest approach that is possible to a negation of intelligibility, thus implies phenomena objectified by thought, and conceived to exist in space and time." ("If thou hast any tidings," says Falstaff to Pistol, "prithee, deliver them like a man of this world.")

Language of this kind is mostly found in spiritual or transcendental writers and speakers; especially divines and metaphysicians. In fact, we are all liable to use language thus, whenever we attempt to draw forth into light what is beyond the reach of the limited faculties of the soul.

Another species of pedantry or affectation is the excessive or needless use of technical language. "Lay in your oars, my lads; step the short mast—close-reef the storm-lug, and beach the galley under canvas."—*From a Novel.* None but a seaman knows what is meant here. Most people are too indolent to search out the meanings of the words they do not understand, nor is it always convenient to do so. In writing a scientific treatise, or in addressing scientific persons, technical language may sometimes be necessary or most appropriate.

Another species of pedantry, or rather, of affectation, is the ridiculous aping, in fine or pompous language, of those people who are deemed worthy of imitation.

Ex.—"Administer your proposition; you will have my concurrence, sir, in any thing that does not derogate from the regulations of conduct; for it would be most preposterous in one of my character to deviate from the strictest attention. Nor would there, Sir Gregory, did circumstances concur as you insinuate, be so absolute a certitude, that I, who have rejected so many matches, should instantaneously succumb. And had not Penelope Trifle framed irrefragable resolutions, she need not so long have retained her family name."—*Foote, ridiculing an old prude.*

Much akin to the foregoing fault is *silliness*, which also should be carefully avoided.

A popular book on physic, thus describes the process of eating:—

"Prehension, or the taking of food into the mouth, is performed mainly by the hand, assisted by the lips and cheeks, as well as the anterior teeth and the tongue. The contact of the solid food with the interior of the mouth, excites the act of mastication, performed by alternating contractions of the muscles which pull the lower jaw upward, downward, backward, forward, and laterally, by acting on the bone in which they are implanted."

To defer the main subject in order to define the meaning of words, borders frequently upon silliness; and so does most of the unbecomingly florid or figurative language. These two faults may be termed the *sophomoric style*, as being naturally and generally found in the half-green and half-ripe age of college sophomores. Similar to silliness of expression is another fault, which I have often noticed, and which sometimes affects whole communities as well as individuals. It is the hackneyed use of some particular word, phrase, or sentence.

Some people are always *guessing*; some, *reckoning*; some, *calculating*; and some, *'sposing*: some find every thing *sweet*; some, *first-rate*; some, *mighty good*; some, *mighty bad*; and others have all things in the superlative degree: some always respond with a "That's so," "Did you ever!" "Yes?" "Well, to be sure!" or, "That's a fact." A certain politician was never known to make a speech without having "our great and glorious Union" in it. Some speeches are flooded with "my fellow-citizens." In England, whatever pleases, is "*nice*;" in the United States, "*fine*." Poets often exhibit this fault in their use of rhymes. In fact, the fault seems to be a natural infirmity of the human mind, whenever it becomes morbid or indolent, or when it comes to a stand in the growth of its knowledge. We are often annoyed by remembered scraps buzzing in the head, like gadflies, especially if they find there something of a Pegasus.

Low, vulgar, or provincial expressions should be avoided. Such are, "To get into a scrape," "To play the 'possum," "To acknowledge the corn," "To cut shines," "To bark up the wrong tree," "To get the hang of," "To have a fair shake at," and many others, which we decline to quote for fear the learner should catch them. Some of these low yet current expressions are so well founded and so energetic that they should rather be regarded as gold in bullion, that has not yet received the stamp; and there are many of them which our people, especially the politicians, could hardly spare.

A departure from grammatical accuracy, or from elegance, is sometimes allowed, in order to represent more faithfully the language or character of another. "*Child.* Once, when I sat upon her lap, I felt a beating at her side; and she told me 'twas her heart that beat, and bade me feel for mine, and they both beat alike, only mine beat *the quickest.* And I feel my heart beating yet—but hers I can not feel!" Had the author here said "*more quickly,*" he would have shown at once, not the pathetic prattle of the child over its dead mother, but his own counterfeiting, and thus spoiled the dramatic effect. Hence, too, Cowper makes Mrs. Gilpin say: "So you must ride on horseback after *we.* To this head may also be referred the imitations of *brogues* and *dialects.*

All uncouth, harsh, antiquated, obsolete, unauthorized, or new-fangled terms should generally be avoided, unless they are meant to be imitative, or are peculiarly appropriate and expressive.

Ignorant people often pervert words, or confound words that resemble in sound, or imagine that words belong to the language that are not in it, or not authorized; as, *critter* for *creature*; *disgracious* for *ungracious*; *prehaps* for *perhaps*; *con'igious* for *contiguous.* "He was much *effected* by the operation." "They got out a *capeas horpus.*" A certain man "meant to run a *revenue* up to his house, build a *pizarro* in front, a *portorico* behind, a *conservatory* on top, and treat his friends in the most *hospital* manner."

The same word or the same mode of expression should not be so often used as to indicate poverty of language; nor in so many different senses as to render the meaning doubtful, or disappoint disagreeably the expectation of the reader.

When there are several synonymous words or expressions, great care should be taken to select the most appropriate one. "An *idle* boy is unwilling to be employed:" say rather, "A *lazy* boy," &c. *Idle* means *not doing,* or *not effecting much*; *lazy* means *unwilling to do.* "The proud pile is of great magnitude, and *soars* grandly up with its numerous towers and splendid terraces."—*Travels in Europe.* I believe *soars* is applied only to what leaves its support; therefore it can not be applied to an edifice: say, "*rises.*" If our language had no word nearer to the meaning than *soars,* then *soars* would be proper. In order to discriminate words, it may be useful to the student to keep in mind the three following observations:—

1. Learn the principles of language, or of synonymy, and endeavor to apply them judiciously. For example: Some words are more comprehensive or less specific than others. Every *river* is a stream, but not every *stream* is a river. Some words are active, and others are passive. *Force* affects, *strength* sustains; fickle men *waver,* prices *fluctuate*; *reasonable* men exercise reason, *rational* men have reason. Some words are positive, and others are negative. A *fault* is something positively bad; a *defect* is a mere want of something needed. Some words differ in degree; as, *damp, moist, wet*; *delicacy. dainty.* Some words relate more directly to nature; others, to art. *Gentleness* may be the gift of nature but *tameness* is the result of art. Some words are rather spiritual or heavenly; others, worldly or material: *soul, mind; spirit, vigor; delightful, delicious.* Some words rather have reference to something inward; and others, to something outward; as, *dignity, decorum.* Some words are the names of things themselves; others are but the names of the signs of things; as, *idea, word.*

2. Consider what distinctions the differences in things require; look through your knowledge, look into the world around you—into other men's knowledge and practice, and into the relations of things, and discriminate accordingly. For example: *Genius* is rather inward, creative, and angelic; *talent,* outward, practical, and worldly. *Genius* disdains and defies imitation; *talent* is often the result of imitation in respect to every thing that may contribute to the desired

excellence. *Genius* has quick and strong sympathies, and is sometimes given to revery and vision; *talent* is cool and wise, seldom losing sight of "common sense." *Genius* is born for a particular pursuit, in which it surpasses; *talent* is versatile, and may make a respectable figure at almost any thing. To *genius* are due about all the achievements that distinguish enlightened from savage life; *talent* has merely preserved, polished, and enjoyed the productions of *genius,* but created nothing. Men of *talent* are but time-servers: they usually carry on the world, and get the best of it while they are in it; but their glory generally ends at the grave. Men of *genius* sometimes starve for want of bread; though they are generally appreciated and honored by posterity.

Discriminate words as you find them used in sentences written by good authors. If I say, "When the disciples saw the Savior arisen on the morning of the resurrection, they *gazed* upon him with astonishment and rapture;" "I have often seen impudent fellows station themselves at the doors of churches, and *stare* at the women;" you can easily see the difference between *gaze* and *stare.*

Every word has a peculiar set of associations belonging to it; and in the proper discrimination of words with reference to their secondary ideas, lie chiefly the precision and elegance of language.

We should rather choose the words and expressions already in common use, and employ them in their ordinary signification, than coin new words or expressions, or use old ones in a peculiar sense; for, if we were at liberty in these respects, soon every man's writings would need a glossary. Ex.—" We may recognize this construction by the name of the accusative and infinitive contracted objective accessory."—*Mulligan.*

Another fault is *ambiguity,* which arises chiefly from the several different meanings which some words have, from the position of words, and from the omission of words. "He is *mad.*" "The governor had several *fast* friends in the Territory."—*Burnet's Northwest Territory.* What sort of friends does he mean? "*firm* friends," I suppose. "The rising tomb a lofty column bore." Which bore the other? "While the sun was gently sinking below the horizon in the west, with much beauty, the bright moon rose serenely above it in the east."

Rhymes, poetical words, and poetic structure, should be avoided in prose:—

Ex.—"He pulled out his *purse* to reïm*burse* the unfortunate man." "The *morn* was cloudy and dark*some,* but the *eve* was serenely beautiful."

"The gállant wárrior stárts from sóft repóse, from gólden vísions ánd volúptuous éase; where, in the dulcet piping time of peace, he sought sweet solace after all his toils. No more in beauty's siren lap reclined, he weaves fair garlands for his lady's brows; no more entwines with flowers his shining sword, nor through the livelong lazy summer's day chants forth his love-sick soul in madrigals. To manhood roused, he spurns the amorous flute; doffs from his brawny back the robes of peace, and clothes his pampered limbs in panoply of steel. O'er his dark brow where late the myrtle waved, where wanton roses breathed enervate love, he rears the beaming casque and nodding plume; grasps the bright shield and shakes the ponderous lance; or mounts, with eager pride, his fiery steed, and burns for deeds of glorious chivalry."—*Irving: Knickerbocker.* Possibly, the foregoing was meant in ridicule of the turgid or bombastic style. The golden-mouthed author, however, not unfrequently transgresses, by passing into poetic grounds.

In accordance with Dr. Blair's system of rhetoric, we may briefly sum up the most important qualities of style, in the six following terms: *purity, propriety,* and *precision,* chiefly in regard to words and phrases; and *perspicuity, unity,* and *strength,* in regard to sentences. He who writes with *purity,* avoids all phraseology that is foreign, uncouth, or ill-derived; he who writes with *propriety,* selects the most appropriate, the very best expressions, and generally displays sound judgment and good taste; he who writes with *precision*, is careful to state exactly what he means—all that he means or that is necessary, and nothing more; he who writes with *perspicuity*, aims to present his meaning so clearly and obviously that no one can fail to understand him at once; he who observes *unity*, follows carefully the most agreeable order of nature, and does not jumble together incongruous things, nor throw out his thoughts in a confused or chaotic mass; and he who writes with *strength*, so disposes or marshals all the parts of each sentence, and all the parts of the discourse, as to make the strongest impression. A person's style, according as it is influenced by taste and imagination, may be *dry, plain, neat, elegant, ornamental, florid,* or *turgid*. The most common faulty style is that which may be described as being stiff, cramped, labored, heavy, and tiresome; its opposite is the easy, flowing, graceful, sprightly, and interesting style. One of the greatest beauties of style, one too little regarded, is simplicity or naturalness; that easy, unaffected, earnest, and highly impressive language which indicates a total ignorance, or rather, innocence, of all the trickery of art. It seems to consist of the pure promptings of nature; though, in most instances, it is not so much a natural gift as it is *the perfection of art.*

Dr. Campbell gives the following excellent laws of language, which should be ever kept in mind, and which will best exemplify themselves in the course of the student's life and experience:—

1. When the usage is divided as to any particular words or phrases, and when one of the expressions is susceptible of different meanings, while the other admits of only one signification, the expression which is strictly univocal should be preferred.

2. In doubtful cases, analogy should be regarded.

3. When expressions are in other respects equal, that should be preferred which is most agreeable to the ear.

4. When none of the preceding rules takes place, regard should be had to simplicity.

a. All words and phrases, particularly harsh and not absolutely necessary, should be dismissed.

b. When the etymology plainly points to a different signification from what the word bears, propriety and simplicity require its dismission.

c. When words become obsolete, or are never used but in particular phrases, they should be repudiated, as they give the style an air of vulgarity and cant, when this general disuse renders them obscure.

d. All words and phrases which, analyzed grammatically, include a solecism, should be dismissed.

e. All expressions which, according to the established rules of language, either have no meaning, or involve a contradiction, or, according to the fair construction of the words, convey a meaning different from the intention of the speaker, should be dismissed.

NOTE.—The remaining pages of this book, beyond the questions, might be termed Part Third. In the foregoing pages, we have shown what the most ordinary language must have; in most of the following pages, we shall endeavor to show how language acquires force and beauty.

QUESTIONS FOR REVIEW.
Parts of Speech.

122. What is a Part of Speech? How many and what parts of speech has the English language? Why are not participles made a separate part of speech? Why are not the articles classed with adjectives? Which of the parts of speech are inflected? What is said of inflections?

Nouns and Pronouns.

123. Nouns.—What is a Noun? Give examples. (Always give examples with the answers, where examples are given in the book.) What is said of phrases and clauses? **Classes.**—Into what classes are nouns divided? What is a proper noun? What more is said of proper nouns? **124.** When do common nouns become proper nouns? What is a common noun? What more is said of common nouns? What is a collective noun? **125.** What is said of such words as *furniture, jewelry,* and *clothing?* What is an abstract noun? A material noun? What is said of verbal nouns? Of correlative nouns? Of diminutive nouns? **126. Pronouns.**—What is a Pronoun? What is said of the three great classes of names? What is the advantage of having pronouns? What is the antecedent of a pronoun? What kind of term may it be? **127.** How do pronouns represent their antecedents? When may pronouns be parsed without referring them to antecedents? **Classes.**—How are pronouns divided? What is a personal pronoun? Which are the personal pronouns? What is said of *you, your, yours,* etc.? Of *thou, thy, thine,* etc.? Of *he, she,* and *they?* Of *it?* **128.** What is said of compound personal pronouns? How are they formed? What is a relative pronoun? In what sense is a relative clause used? Which are the relative pronouns? What is said of *who?* Of *which?* **129.** Of *what?* Of *that?* When is the relative clause restrictive? **130.** What is said of *as?* Of the compound relative pronouns? What is an interrogative pronoun? Which are the interrogative pronouns? How are they applied? **131.** Define their uses more definitely? What is said of responsive relative pronouns? What other words are sometimes used as pronouns? What is said of *one?* Of *each other* and *one another?* **132.** What is said of substituting nouns for pronouns, especially for relatives? What is said of omitted pronouns and antecedents?

Properties.—What properties have nouns and pronouns? **133. Genders.**—What is gender? How many and what genders are there? Define each. What is said of nouns strictly applicable to one sex only, yet applied to both? What is said of objects regarded as male or female from their general character? **134.** What is said of objects personified? What is said of the gender of collective nouns? How many methods has the English language of distinguishing the two sexes? Define and exemplify each. **135.** What is said of the genders of pronouns? **136. Persons.**—What is person? How many and what persons are there? Define each. What else is said of the third person? **137.** What is said of the persons of pronouns? **Numbers.**—What is number? How many and what numbers are there? Define each. **138.** What nouns are generally singular? and when are they made plural? What is said of nouns that are always plural? Of nouns that have the same form for either number? What is said about the number of collective nouns? **139.** What is said of *news, odds, means,* etc.? How is the plural number of nouns most commonly formed? **140.** When do we add *es?* What is said of proper names? Of *beef, calf, knife,* etc.? Of *man, woman, child,* etc.? Of *brother, die, fish,* etc.? How are compound words made plural? **141.** How are names with titles made plural? Would you rather say, The Misses Brown? or, The Miss Browns? **142.** What is said of words adopted from foreign languages? Of letters, figures, and other characters? **143.** What is said of the numbers of pronouns? Of the editorial *we?* **144. Cases.**—What are cases? How many and what cases are there? What is said of the nominative case? **145.** Of the possessive case? How is the possessive case of nouns formed? **147.** What is said of the objective case? **148.** When must substantives agree in case? What is said of predication and apposition? **149.** Must substantives that agree in case, necessarily agree in person and number? **150, 151.**—What may the explanatory term be? What is said of the cases of pronouns? How do you parse *yours?—what?—whoever?* What is said of *what?*

QUESTIONS FOR REVIEW.

Repeat all the Rules of Syntax for nouns and pronouns, beginning with the first Rule. Decline *cousin,—gipsy,—Thomas,—I,—thou* or *you,—he,—she,—it,—who,—which,— —that,—what,—whoever,—one,—other.* **154—65.** The errors, in regard to nouns and pronouns, may be reduced to what heads? Give the precept or precepts under each head, and also correct some examples. **166.** When is it proper to speak of ourselves first, in connection with others? **168.** What is said of plural composite numbers? **169.** What is said of possessives governed by participial nouns? **170.** How was *which* used in Old English? Show how our language is defective, in needing a common-gender pronoun of the third person, singular number. **172.** What is said of repeating the nominative, when verbs differ in mood and tense?

Articles.

172. What is an Article? **173.** What two words are called articles? and how are they distinguished? What is said of *the?* Of *a* or *un?* Why are *a* and *an* called the same article? Where should *a* be used? Where should *an* be used? **174.** When is the article not used? How are articles construed with nouns? **175—8.** To what heads may the liabilities to error, in regard to articles, be reduced? Give the precepts under each head, and correct some examples.

Adjectives.

181. What is an Adjective? Into what two great classes may adjectives be divided? What is a descriptive adjective? **182.** What is a definitive adjective? Into what smaller classes may adjectives be divided? What is a common adjective? A proper adjective? A participial adjective? A compound adjective? A numeral adjective? The kinds? A pronominal adjective? The kinds? What are the degrees of comparison? How many and which are they? Define fully the positive degree, and give examples. **183.** The comparative. The superlative. What is said of such adjectives as *perfect, round, still, straight,* etc.? **184.** What is said of the ending *ish?* Of *very, a most,* etc.? Explain fully how adjectives are compared, and give examples. Compare *rich,—wise,— red,—sly,— muddy,— able,— profound,—cautious, — negligent,— necessary,— good,— but,—much,—many,—little,—far,—near,—hind,—fore,—late,—low,—up,—in,—out.* **185.** What is said of number, in connection with adjectives? Mention some adjectives of the singular number. Some of the plural. What is said of *all?* Of *any?* Of *both?* Of *each?* Of *either?* **186.** Of *every?* Of *few?* Of *many?* Of *many a?* Of *much?* Of *neither?* Of *no?* Of *one?* Of *other* or *another?* Of *own?* Of *same?* Of *several?* Of *some?* **187.** Of *such?* Of *this?* Of *that?* Of *former* and *latter?* Of *very?* Of *what* and *which?* Of *yon* or *yonder?* How do you dispose of adjectives in parsing? **188.** How, when the noun is not expressed? What is the Rule of Syntax for articles and adjectives? When do adjectives become nouns? **190.** The liabilities to error, in the use of adjectives, may be reduced to what heads? **190-3.** Give the precepts under each head, and correct some examples. **195.** What is said of the position of adjectives in regard to the sense? **196.** What is said of *first two, last five,* etc.? What is said of the rhetorical position of adjectives?

Verbs.

196. What is a Verb? What is said of affirmations? **197.** What is said of the verb *be?* What is said of verbs, with reference to their being finite or not finite? What is a participle? An infinitive? **Classes.**—Into what classes are verbs divided? What is a regular verb? An irregular verb? Which are the principal parts of the verb. **198.** Why called the principal parts? What is said of irregular verbs? When is a verb called defective? and when redundant? (See p. 16.) What is a transitive verb? A passive verb? An intransitive verb? A neuter verb? What is said of verbs used both as transitive and as intransitive? Of transitive verbs becoming intransitive? Of intransitive verbs becoming transitive? **199.** Of objects blended, in sense, with their verbs?

199. Properties.—What properties have verbs? **Voices.**—What is said of voices? Define the active voice. The passive voice. What is said of verbs that are active in form, yet passive in sense? **200.** Of verbs passive in form, yet active in sense? Of present and of perfect participles? Of compound passive verbs? How can verbs in the passive voice be changed into the active? What is the advantage of having the passive voice? **Moods.**—What are moods?

QUESTIONS FOR REVIEW.

How many and which are the moods? **201.** What is said of the indicative mood? Of the subjunctive? **202.** Of the potential? Of the imperative? **203.** Of the infinitive? **Tenses.**—What are tenses? How many and which are they? **204.** Give a synopsis of *write*, showing the general divisions of time. Define the present tense fully, through all the moods, and give examples. Define the past tense in like manner. **205.** The future. The perfect. **206.** The pluperfect. The future-perfect. What is said of such expressions as, "He *has been* rich?" **207.** What is said of the divisions of the tenses into absolute and relative? Of the agreement in time between active and passive verbs in the two classes of tenses? Define the "forms." What is the great law of growth in a language, toward simplicity and improvement? How has this law affected our subjunctive mood? **208.** What tenses should be given to the subjunctive mood? What two great tenses are verbs naturally adapted to express? Show how the other tenses are composite forms, and how they naturally acquired their present meanings. How many and what tenses has the indicative mood? (See pp. 24–8.) The subjunctive? The potential? The imperative? The infinitive?
209. Persons and Numbers.—What are the person and number of a verb? How many persons and numbers, then, must verbs have? Have English verbs many variations to express person and number? Why are only the personal pronouns used in the conjugation? What is the ending required by *thou?* By *he, she,* or *it?* By *we, you,* or *they?* What is said of the persons of verbs? **210.** When must the verb be singular? When plural? What terms do not affect the form of the verb? **211.** What is said of the agreement of verbs with collective nouns? What is said of omitted subjects? Of verbs agreeing with *it?* To what mood do person-and-number endings chiefly belong? **212.** What is said of the ending *t, st,* or *est?* Of *s* or *es, th* or *eth?*
212. Auxiliary Verbs.—What is an auxiliary verb? Which are the auxiliary verbs? Which are sometimes used as principal verbs? When are auxiliary verbs convenient, and sometimes perhaps necessary? **213.** What is said of their primitive meanings? What is said of *be?* Of *do* and *did?* Of *can* and *could?* Of *have* and *had?* Of *may* and *might?* Of *must?* Of *shall* and *should?* **214.** Of *will* and *would?* Of *shall* and *should* in dependent propositions? What rules are given for the use of *shall, should, will,* and *would?*
214. Participles and Infinitives.—In what respects do participles and infinitives agree with finite verbs? and in what respects do they differ? **215.** What are the advantages of having them in language? How many participles are there, and what are they? How many and what infinitives? What is said of the present participle? Of the perfect? Of the compound? Why do we have the compound participles, or in what respects do these differ from the others? **216.** What is said of the present infinitive? Of the perfect? In what three different ways are participles and infinitives used? How are compound participles formed? How is the progressive form made? The passive form? How are the perfect tenses made? Of what do the composite absolute tenses consist? Can you tell why *to* was adopted as a part of the infinitive? After what verbs is *to* omitted? **217.** Participles are construed in what various senses with other words? Infinitives are construed in what various senses with other words? Infinitives can be construed with words of what classes? To what parts of speech do participles and infinitives lean? **218.** When do participles and infinitives become nouns? How may verbal nouns be construed with other words? Show how the participle does not so strictly retain the sense of an abstract noun as the infinite does. What is said of participles and infinitives, with reference to time?
219. Conjugation.—What is the conjugation of a verb? Of what do most forms of the verb consist? What tenses can be expressed without auxiliaries? What is said of defective verbs? What tenses do they lack? What is said of *beware?* Of *ought?* Of *quoth?* Of *wit?* What is said of the "forms" of the verb? **220.** What is said of *be,* as to its combination with other words? Of *have?* Of *seem, appear, suppose,* etc.? How are propositions made interrogative? How, negative? What is said of negative and of affirmative questions? **24.** Conjugate together, as shown in the Conjugation, the verbs *be, rule,* and *drive.* **46.** What are the Rules and Notes of Syntax that apply to verbs? **223.** The liabilities to error, in regard to verbs, may be reduced to what heads? **223–36.** Give the precepts under each head, and correct some examples. **236.** What is said of such sentences as, "The new rifle-practice *was being introduced.*" **238.** What is said of certain passive forms made in imitation of a French idiom. **240.**

What is said of choosing participles or infinitives after certain verbs? When should a substantive, with a participle, be construed in the possessive case?

Adverbs.

240. What is an Adverb? What is said of adverbial phrases? **241.** Adverbs modify, by expressing what? Mention some of each class. Do adverbs ever affect substantives? What are conjunctive adverbs? What is said of adverbs used independently? How are adverbs compared? How are most adverbs formed? **242.** What is said of adverbs, in connection with compound words? What relation between adverbs and adjuncts? What is said of adjectives or adjective forms that are used in an adverbial sense? **243.** When should the adjective be preferred to the adverb? What is said of *there, ever, thus, so, yes,* and *no?* Compare *well, badly* or *ill, much, little, wisely*. **47.** What are the Rule and Notes of Syntax relating to adverbs? **244.** The liabilities to error, in the use of adverbs, may be reduced to what heads? **244-7.** Give the precepts, and correct some examples? **247.** When should we use adjectives? and when adverbs? **248.** What is said of *cold, badly,* etc.? Of the position of adverbs? Of poetic licenses? **249.** Of two negatives, designedly used to express an affirmation?

Prepositions.

249. What is a Preposition? The list? What is said of phrases used as prepositions? What is an adjunct? In what senses are adjuncts used? What is said of inverted adjuncts? Of compound and complex? **250.** To what may adjuncts relate? How are adjuncts related to adverbs, adjectives, and possessives? What does a preposition, when used without an object, become? What is said about the omission of the object, of the antecedent term, and of the preposition itself? What is said of direct objects and of indirect? Are prepositions much used in making compound words? **251.** What few great ideas are expressed by most adjuncts? **252-5.** What is said of *between* and *among?* Of *betwixt?* Of *but?* Of *at* and *in?* Of *in* and *into?* Of *by* and *with?* Of *except* and *save?* Of *according, excepting,* etc? Of *of?* Of *through?* Of *to?* **47.** What is the Rule of Syntax for prepositions? **258.** To what heads may the liabilities to error, in regard to prepositions, be reduced? **258-61.** Give the precepts, and correct some examples. **261.** What is said of the position of adjuncts? **262.** What is said of repetition and grouping?

Conjunctions.

262. What is a Conjunction? What is said of phrases so used? Into what chief classes may conjunctions be divided? Define each class? What is said of *and, or,* and *nor?* Of *but, if,* and *that?* Of the omission of conjunctions? Of their repetition? (See also p. 171) **264.** What is said of conjunctions, as being derived from words of other parts of speech? Into what general classes may connectives be divided? **264-7.** What is said of *and?* Of *either* and *neither?* Of *when* and *if?* Of *or?* Of *nor?* **47.** What is the Rule of Syntax for conjunctions? **268.** The liabilities to error, in regard to conjunctions, may be reduced to what heads? **268-71.** Give the precepts, and correct some examples. **271.** What is said of making similar the parts connected? **272.** What is said about two or more connected parts that relate in common to a third?

Interjections.

272. What is an Interjection? What is said of using as interjections words from other parts of speech? When should such words not be parsed as interjections? **47.** Rule for interjections? **273.** How do you parse a noun or pronoun used after an interjection?

General Principles.

274. What is said of words used as different parts of speech? Give some examples. **275.** To what heads may the remaining errors, in the use of language, be reduced? **275-82.** Give the precepts, and correct some examples. What faults should we avoid in writing or speaking? What excellent thought on style has Coleridge given? **284.** What is said of transitions? Of short sentences and long ones? Of the selection of expressions? **285.** Of the preference that should be given to Saxon words? Of foreign expressions and idioms? Of using words without attaching definite ideas to them, or without having distinct and worthy thoughts? **286.** Of technical or pedantic expressions? Of silliness? Of hackneyed and low expressions? **287.** Of uncouth, obsolete, or new-fangled terms? Of expressions used too frequently, or in different senses? Of departures from grammatical accuracy, for the sake of dramatic effect? Of confounding words? Of synonyms? **288.** Of the secondary ideas attached to words? Of poetic expressions used in prose? Can you give some of Dr. Blair's ideas about style? **289.** Some of Dr. Campbell's laws of language?

13. RHETORICAL DEVICES.
EQUIVALENT EXPRESSIONS.

An expression is equivalent to another, when it conveys the same meaning in different words.

Language often affords us the choice of either a single word, a phrase, or an entire clause.

Ex.—"*Pleasant* scenes"—Scenes *of pleasure*—Scenes *that please*. Now—at the present time. Sharp-edged—having a sharp edge. "The book, *containing the story*, is in my library"—The book *which contains the story*, is in my library. "We expected *him to make a speech*"—We expected *that he would make a speech*. "The river was so deep *as to be impassable—that it was impassable—that it could not be passed over*."

Transitive verbs may be used in either voice.

Ex.—"Cain *killed* Abel"—Abel *was killed* by Cain.

We may sometimes express an assertion modestly by substituting a denial of the opposite.

Ex.—"I *remember* your promise"—I *have not forgotten* your promise. "He is wise;" "He is not ignorant;" "He is no fool." "She is handsome;" "She is not homely."

It or *there* is often used to introduce a sentence more elegantly.

Ex.—"*It* is not probable that those who are vicious in youth, will become virtuous in old age." "*There* never was a time when labor was more in demand or better rewarded."

Frequently, we may use an entirely different word, or mode of expression, with equal or even greater propriety.

Ex.—"The gentleman does not possess the necessary qualifications"—He is unfit for the business. "She died;" "God released her from her pain." "The one was a horse, *named Pound-cake*; the other, a mule *that wagged his long ears to the call of 'John'*." "My opponent does perhaps not see that he has contradicted himself;" "The honorable Senator does not seem to know that he is caught tight and fast in the fixed fact of a killing contradiction."

The shortest and most familiar expressions are generally the best. The longer or more unusual ones are more ceremonious, and, to be appropriate, should imply greater importance of matter, or greater accuracy, clearness, or elegance.

The use of one part of speech, or form, for another, is called *enal'lagè*.

Ex.—"The swallow sings *sweet* from her nest in the wall."—*Dimond*. So, *we* sed for *I*.

ARRANGEMENT.

"Forth rushed with whirlwind sound
The chariot of paternal Deity."—*Milton*.
"Up rose the sun, and up rose Emilie."—*Chaucer*.
"Silver and gold have I none."—*Bible*.
"We set him loose, and away he ran."—*Swift's Gulliver's Travels*.

How spirited does the arrangement of the words make the foregoing sentences.

Arrangement may be considered with reference to words, phrases, and clauses.

The place most important in a sentence, is usually its beginning; the next most important is the ending.

Hence the subject, which is the germ or source of the whole sentence, naturally takes the first place; and, in some languages, the verb is generally reserved for the end.

Ex.—"*He* maintained a large army at his own expense." "*Rome* was an ocean of flame."—*Croly.* "Him the Almighty *hurled.*"—*Milton.*

An adjective, an adverb, a verb, or a substantive, may sometimes usurp the place of the subject, or be brought out at the close of the sentence; especially when it sets forth what is most striking, or what is uppermost in the speaker's mind.

Ex.—"*Louder* and *louder* the deep thunder rolled, as through the myriad halls of some vast temple in the sky; *fiercer* and *brighter* became the lightning; *more and more heavily* the rain *poured down.*"—*Dickens.* "What a sentence! "Then *never* saw I charity before." "Then *rushed* the steed to battle driven." "The *goods* he sent away, and the *money* he put into his pocket." "*Strait* is the gate, and *narrow* is the way, that lead to life *eternal.*" "*Long* was the way and *dreary.*" —*Milton.* (Slightly changed.) By placing *long* at the beginning, and *dreary* at the end, how admirably has Milton expressed what must have been most striking and disheartening to Satan, who was about to undertake his journey over Chaos.

Frequently, an adjunct, a participial phrase, or an infinitive phrase, may be transposed.

Ex.—"*In proportion to the increase of luxury*, the Roman state evidently declined"—The Roman state, *in proportion to the increase of luxury*, evidently declined —The Roman state evidently declined *in proportion to the increase of luxury.*

Frequently, the clauses may change places, or one be placed within another.

Ex.—"*If you desire it*, I will accompany you;" "I will accompany you, *if you desire it;*" "I will, *if you desire it,* accompany you."

Some regard should be paid to the importance and the natural order of things.

Ex.—   "The cloud-capt towers, the gorgeous palaces,
        The solemn temples, the great globe itself,
        Yea, all that it inherit, shall dissolve;
        And, like the baseless fabric of a vision,
        Leave not a rack behind."—*Shakespeare.*

But the mind sometimes disregards the natural order of time or place, and puts forth first what is first or most thought of.

Ex.—"Where I was *bred* and *born.*"—*Shakespeare.*

A sentence so constructed that the meaning is suspended till the close, is called a *period.*

Ex.—"When, in the course of human events, it becomes necessary for one people to dissolve the political bands which have connected them with another * * * a decent respect to the opinion of mankind requires, that they should declare the causes which impel them to separation."—*Jefferson.*

The transposition of words, grammarians call *hyper'baton.*

Ex.—"From crag to crag, the rattling peaks among, leaps the live thunder."— *Byron.*

ELLIPSIS, OR OMISSION OF WORDS.

For the sake of brevity and force, words not necessary to convey the meaning are sometimes omitted.

Ex.—"A horse! a horse! my kingdom for a horse!" is much more forcible than, Fetch me a horse! fetch me a horse! I would now give my kingdom for a horse. "A boy and [a] girl." "The old bridge and the new [bridge]." "Sweet [is] the pleasure, rich [is] the treasure."—*Dryden.*

In the following stanza, the omission of *which* is quite elegant:—

"I hear a voice—thou canst not hear,
  Which says I must not stay;
 I see a hand—thou canst not see,
  Which beckons me away."—*Tickell.*

Omitted words are such as have already been mentioned, or else such as may be readily inferred from the words used.

Suppose you should see merely a horse's head projecting from behind a stable, would you not, from your knowledge, know what animal is there even without seeing him? The same principle allows ellipsis, or the omission of words.

In analyzing and parsing, only such words should be supplied as are necessary to complete the construction.

PLEONASM, OR REPETITION OF WORDS.

Sometimes more words may be used than are absolutely necessary.

Ex.—"I saw it *with my own eyes.*" "The vessel sailed for Cuba, *and not for New York.*" "Our boat sunk down to the very bottom."

"One of the few, the immortal names,
 That were not born to die."—*Halleck.*

The same word or the same construction may sometimes be repeated.

"Strike—till the last arm foe expires!
 Strike—for your altars and your fires!
 Strike—for the green graves of your sires!
  God, and your native land!"—*Halleck.*

"No employment for industry—no demand for labor—no sale of the produce of the farm—no sound of the hammer, but that of the auctioneer knocking down property!"—*Benton.* How well here does *no* indicate the utter prostration of business and prosperity.

"The endless sands yield nothing but small stunted shrubs—even these fail after the first two or three days; and from that time you pass over broad plains—you pass over newly reared hills—you pass through valleys that the storm of the last week has dug—and the hills and the valleys are sand, sand, still sand, and only sand, and sand, and sand again."—*Eothen: Crossing the Desert.* How well here does repetition indicate the tediousness and weariness felt by the traveler.

"Howbeit, the door I opened, or so I dreamed;
 Which slowly, slowly gaped."—*Hood's Haunted House.*

Here *slowly*, repeated, very ingeniously intimates the fear and hesitation of the opener.

"Mourn, hapless Caledonia, mourn." "Fal'n, fal'n, fal'n, fal'n, fal'n from his high estate, and weltering in his blood." "Our lives, our fortunes, and our sacred honors." "There is but one, one Mary in the world for me."

"She winks, and giggles, and simpers,
 And simpers, and giggles, and winks;
 And though she talks but little,
 'Tis a great deal more than she thinks."—*Stark.*

"Explain upon a thing till all men doubt it;
And write about it, and about it."—*Pope's Dunciad.*
" By foreign hands thy dying eyes were closed;
By foreign hands thy decent limbs composed;
By foreign hands thy humble grave adorned;
By strangers honored, and by strangers mourned."—*Pope.*
"Must I then leave you? Must I needs forego
So good, so noble, and so true a master?
The king shall have my service, but my prayers
For ever and for ever shall be yours."—*Shakespeare.*

Authors sometimes consider it a beauty to begin two or more words of the same line, or in the same construction, with the same letter. This is called *alliteration.*

" In friendship false, implacable in hate,
Resolved to *ruin* or to *rule* the state."—*Dryden.*
" *Fields* forever *fresh,* and *groves* forever *green.*"
" *Round rugged rocks, rude ragged rascals ran.*"
" Alike for *feast* and *fight* prepared,
Battle and *banquet* both they shared."—*W. Scott.*

EXERCISES.

Change the voice:—
John fed the horse. Cornwallis was defeated by Washington. He made it. His friends will recommend him. I offered him a situation.

Change the participial and the infinitive phrases into clauses:—
The teacher being in sight, all the boys ran to their books. He came to examine the matter himself. His views are so extravagant as to be ridiculous. Having paid his clerk, he dismissed him.

Use IT:—
To devise any apology for such conduct, is utterly impossible.

Use THERE:—
Not one man was in the country, unwilling to defend it. Thorns are to roses.

Change into compound adjectives:—
My boots with red tops. Violets of sweet scent fringed the bank. The live-oaks of the South, that are curtained with moss.

Change the words, or the mode of expression:—
Every one who hunts after pleasure, or fame, or fortune, is still restless and uneasy till he has hunted down his game.—*Swift.* I bore the diminution of my riches without any outrages of sorrow, or pusillanimity of dejection.—*Johnson.* Suspenders were abandoned with the first intimation of the present summer solstice.—*Willis.*

Change the arrangement, and occasionally the mode of expression:—
A person gains more by obliging his inferior, than by disobliging him. The murmurs of the people were loud, as their sufferings increased. Various, sincere, and constant are the efforts of men, to produce that happiness which the mind requires. The necessary ingredients of friendship are confidence and benevolence. If beasts could talk, they might often tell us a cruel story. For many a returning autumn, a lone Indian was seen standing at the consecrated spot we have mentioned; but, just thirty years after the death of Soonseetah, he was noticed for the last time.

Beneath those rugged elms, that yew-tree's shade,
Where heaves the turf with many a mouldering heap,
Each in his narrow cell forever laid,
The rude forefathers of the hamlet sleep.—*Gray.*

Change to prose:—
> For see, ah! see, while yet her ways,
> With doubtful steps, I tread,
> A hostile world its terrors raise,
> Its snares delusive spread.—*Merrick.*

Supply all the omitted words:—
The large and the little man were great friends. Stay longer. Arm, soldiers! Vain—vain—give o'er. How now, Tubal, what news from Genoa? A diamond gone, cost me three thousand ducats in Frankfort! The combat deepens.—On, ye brave. But gone was every Indian we had seen. The more, the better. Heaven hides from brutes what men, from men what spirits, know. He offered a reward to whoever could solve the problem. He has behaved as well as you. He has behaved better than you. The honor, and not the profits, is what he values most. Quick at meals, quick at work. Better long something, than soon nothing. Soon ripe, soon rotten.

> When pain and sorrow wring the brow,
> A ministering angel thou.—*Scott.*

14. RHETORICAL FIGURES.

The expressiveness of language may be increased or extended, by the judicious use of the rhetorical figures. They promote *clearness, beauty, brevity,* and *force.*

Some Southern orator has thus extolled the moral influence of woman:—

"Woman wields the Archimedean lever whose fulcrum is childhood, whose weight is the world, whose length is all time, and whose sweep—is eternity!"

"Burns thus laments the vanished happy days of youth:—

> "Still o'er these scenes my memory wakes,
> And fondly broods with miser care;
> Time but the impression deeper makes,
> As streams their channels deeper wear."

Dryden speaks thus of the inventress of the church-organ:—

> "He raised a mortal to the skies,
> She drew an angel down."

That is, the organ, at divine service, is as an angel that has just hastened down from heaven, to instruct and lead the choir in praising God.

Grattan closes his character of Chatham with this sublime sentence:—

"He struck a blow in the world, that resounded through the universe."

All these examples owe their beauty and vigor chiefly to the figures which they contain. A perfect classification of the rhetorical figures is perhaps impossible; for sometimes several set the same expression aglow at once. Some rhetoricians pretend to have seen more than 250 different ones; the following classification, however, will about exhaust the subject.

---

1. A simile is an express comparison.

Ex.—"The music of Carryl was, *like the memory of joys that are past,* sweet and mournful to the soul."—*Ossian.* "The child reclined on its mother's bosom *as some infant blossom on its parent stem.*"—*Mrs. Sigourney.* "He [the steed] looked as if the speed of thought were in his limbs."—*Byron.* "Too much government may be a greater evil than no government. *The sheep are happier among themselves than under the care of the wolves.*"—*Jefferson.* Sometimes we find such condensed similes as this: "*A false friend* and *a shadow* attend only while the sun shines."

2. A metaphor is an implied comparison. It is a word or an expression applied from one object or attribute to another, on account of some resemblance. It sometimes comprises several words.

Ex.—" Life is an *isthmus* between two eternities." " Her disdain *stung* him to the heart." " Bonaparte called burning Moscow an *ocean* of flame." " The *morning* of life." " The *storms* of life." "Some mute, inglorious *Milton* here may rest."—*Gray.* " Man! thou *pendulum* betwixt a smile and tear."—*Byron.* " You are always *putting your nose* into my affairs." " A heart! *a cushion to stick pins into.* For so the world has it."—*Jerrold.* " Sin is a *bitter sweet,* and *the fine colors of the serpent by no means make amends for the poison of his sting.*"—*South.*

3. An allegory is a fictitious discourse on one thing, suggestive of a train of thoughts, usually instructive, on another. It has been called *continued metaphor.*

Ex.—" Thou hast brought a vine [the Jewish nation] out of Egypt: thou hast cast out the heathen, and planted it. Thou preparedst room before it, and didst cause it to take deep root, and it filled the land. The hills were covered with the shadow of it, and the boughs thereof were like the goodly cedars."—*Bible.* See Bunyan's Pilgrim's Progress, Addison's Vision of Mirza, Johnson's Journey of a Day, Fontenelle's Empire of Poetry, Poe's Haunted Palace, Milton's Sin and Death.

The allegory includes parables and fables. *Similes, metaphors,* and *allegories,* are all founded on *resemblance;* but some allegories imply personification. Resemblance may be either in the *appearance* of objects, or in their *relations* or *effects.* The latter is commonly called *analogy.* " Far through the *rosy depths ;*" i. e., sunset sky. Appearance. " Have you a *key* to this arithmetic?" Analogy.

4. Personification represents as persons, or as rational or living beings, objects that are not such in reality.

Ex.—" How sweet the Moonlight sleeps upon this bank!"—*Shakespeare.* " Cheered with the grateful smell, old Ocean smiles."—*Milton.* " There Honor comes a pilgrim gray."—*Collins.* " Greece cries to us from the convulsed lips of her poisoned Demosthenes; and Rome pleads with us in the mute persuasion of her mangled Tully."—*Everett.* " How does God reveal himself in nature? She answers thee with loud voices, and a thousand tongues: 'God is love.' "—*Sherlock.*

SPRING.—" And buds that yet the blasts of winter fear,
Stand at the door of life, and ask to clothe the year."—*Dryden.*

The slight personification which merely represents a noun naturally neuter as masculine or feminine, is sometimes called *syllepsis.* " The *ship* was delayed on *her* voyage."

Personification is probably the noblest, the most creative, of all the figures; being the very soul of poetry. It is closely allied to metaphor, and sometimes it is based on metonymy or synecdoche.

5. A meton'ymy is the proper word or expression for one thing, applied to another, different in kind, but so related that the mind readily perceives what is meant. It is founded on the relations of cause, effect, contiguity in place, and contiguity in time. The cause, the effect, and the circumstances; the container, and the thing contained; the sign, and the thing signified; the whole and its parts,— are naturally associated in the memory, and readily suggest one another.

Ex.—"They have *Moses* and the *prophets*;" i. e., their writings. "I have read *Homer* and *Virgil*." "The women and children were put to the *sword*;" i. e., to death. "The husbandman has lost his *sweat*;" i. e., the reward of his labor. "*Gray hairs* should be respected;" i. e., old age. "He was the *sigh* of her secret soul;" i. e., the youth for whom she sighed in secret. "We drank but one *bottle*." "*Pennsylvania* passed certain resolutions." "He assumed the *sceptre*;" i. e., the regal authority. Sign for thing signified. We often use this figure to avoid disagreeable circumlocution. When a grammarian says, "The predicate is that which is affirmed of the subject," he means, "The predicate denotes that which is affirmed of what the subject denotes."
"My *adventurous* song." Attribute transferred from one object to an accompanying object. "*Drowsy* night; *musing* midnight; *jovial* wine; *giddy* heights; the *artful, dizzy* brink; *bleating* mountains." "The ploughman homeward plods his *weary* way." "You have a very *impudent* mule," said a young man to another who had just rode between him and a young lady.

6. A synec'doche is a term or an expression applied to more or less than it strictly denotes. Some grammarians say, "Synecdoche is the naming of a part for the whole, or of the whole for a part."

Ex.—" Give us our daily *bread*;" i. e., food. "We bought a hundred *head* of sheep." "The same day were added unto them three thousand *souls*." Observe that the preaching was to save *souls*, and hence the selection of this part for the whole. "I am glad we are under *roof*." "Stay thy avenging *steel*;" i. e., sword. "Here lies buried *William Jones*;" i. e., the body. "The *Assyrian* came down like the wolf on the fold." "So thought the countries of Demosthenes and the Spartan, yet *Leonidas* is trampled by the timid slave." " *Youth* and *beauty* shall be laid in dust." The character, quality, or attribute of a person, is of course a part of him. "To his *Excellency* the Governor." "'Crate'rus,' said Alexander, 'loves the *king*; but Hephæstion loves Alexander.'" "He remained silent, and thus wisely kept the *fool* within." "Ten thousand *fleets* sweep over thee in vain;" i. e., a large number. "The thirsty Texan pointed his finger down his open mouth, and said to the Mexican woman, '*Rio Grande! Rio Grande!*'"

Metonymy and *synecdoche* are founded, not on resemblance, but on *relation*; and they sometimes approach each other so nearly as not to be readily distinguished. They enable the speaker to be more definite, by confining the attention to that only which is most obvious or intelligible, or to that which necessarily implies the rest; they enable him to be more impressive, by drawing the attention especially to that on which the fact or action immediately depends; and frequently they enable him to avoid circumlocution.

Ex.—"He addressed the *Chair*," is more definite than, "He addressed the *President*;" for it must mean, "He addressed the President *in his official capacity*." "We descried a *sail*" [a ship]; but, "Our *keels* [ships] ploughed the deep;" because the former accords better with seeing; and the latter, with ploughing. "The fruit of that *forbidden* tree, whose *mortal* TASTE," is a very artful expression. Eve had an unconquerable curiosity to *taste* the fruit which was *forbidden* under the penalty of *death*.

7. 'Antith'esis sets different objects or attributes in contrast.

Ex.—" *Sink* or *swim, live* or *die, survive* or *perish*, I give my hand and heart to this vote."—*Webster*. "Though *deep*, yet *clear*." "At his touch, crowns crumbled, beggars reigned, systems vanished."—*Phillips*. "As when a husband or a lapdog dies."—*Pope*. "The notions of Dryden were formed by comprehensive speculation; those of Pope, by minute observation. Dryden is read with frequent astonishment; Pope, with perpetual delight."—*Johnson*. See the first two stanzas of Halleck's Bozzaris.

"To-day man's dressed in gold and silver bright,
  Wrapped in a shroud before to-morrow night."
"They heard the clarion's iron clang,
  The breeze which through the roses sang."—*Croly*.

8. Irony sneeringly means the reverse of what the words literally denote. It is usually mockery uttered for the sake of ridicule or sarcasm. It has the finest effect when the speaker seems to fall into the real sentiments of those whom he attacks.

Ex.—To call a fool a Solomon, or to praise what we mean to disparage, is irony. "Have not the Indians been kindly and justly treated? Have not the temporal things, the vain baubles and filthy lucre of this world, which were too apt to engage their worldly and selfish thoughts, been benevolently taken from them; and have they not instead thereof, been taught to set their affections on things above?" *—Irving.*

9. Paralip'sis pretends to conceal or omit what it really expresses or suggests.

Ex.—"*I will not call him villain*, because it would be unparliamentary. *I will not call him fool*, because he happens to be Chancellor of the Exchequer."—*Grattan.*

"Boys, you would not throw stones at the Police,—would you?"—*O'Connell,* thus putting into their heads what he wants them to do,—inciting the mob to a riot.

"Mr. President, I shall enter on no encomium upon Massachusetts: she needs none. There she is,—behold her and judge for yourselves. There is her history,—the world knows it by heart. The past, at least, is secure. There is Boston, and Concord, and Lexington, and Bunker Hill,—and there they will remain for ever."—*Webster.*

"Must I remember? Why, she would hang on him
As if increase of appetite had grown
By what it fed on; and yet, within a month—
Let me think on it— Frailty, thy name is woman."—*Shakespeare.*

10. Hyper'bole greatly exaggerates what is founded in truth. To be proper, it should imply strong emotion in the speaker, or the apprehension that the hearer would not otherwise attach sufficient importance to what is said.

Ex.—"Brougham is a *thunderbolt.*" "He was the owner of a piece of land not larger than a *Lacedemonian letter.*" "That fellow is so tall that he does n't know when his feet are cold."

"Some Curran, who, when thrones were crumbled, and dynasties forgotten, might stand the landmark of his country's genius, rearing himself amid regal ruins and national dissolution, a mental pyramid in the solitude of time, beneath whose shade things might moulder, and around whose summit eternity must play."—*Phillips.*

"Falstaff, thou globe of flesh, spotted o'er with continents of sin."—*Shakespeare.*

"Here Orpheus sings; trees, moving to the sound,
Start from their roots, and form a shade around."—*Pope.*

11. Climax means *ladder*. It is a gradual climbing, or rise of thought, from things inferior to greater or better. When reversed, it is called *anticlimax*.

Ex.—"The stream of literature has swollen into a torrent—augmented into a river—expanded into a sea."—*Irving.* "Here I stand for impeachment or trial! I dare accusation! I defy the honorable gentleman! I defy the government! I defy their whole phalanx!"—*Grattan.*

"A Scotch mist becomes a shower; and a shower, a flood; and a flood, a storm; and a storm, a tempest; and a tempest, thunder and lightning; and thunder and lightning, heaven-quake and earthquake."—*Prof. Wilson.*

ANTICLIMAX: "Great men—such as Washington, Adams, Jefferson, Aaron Burr, Stephen Arnold, and the friend of my worthy opponent."—*Political Speech.* See Irony.

12. Allusion is such a use of some word or words as will recall some interesting fact, custom, writing, or saying. It is usually founded on resemblance or contrast.

Ex.—"Give them *Saratoga* in New York, and we'll give them *Yorktown* in Virginia."—*Political Speech.* "When you go into the museum, be Argus, but not Briareus." "The excesses of our youth are drafts upon our old age, payable about thirty years after date."

"Hands that the rod of empire might have swayed,
Close at my elbow stir their lemonade."—*Holmes*.

A continued allusion or resemblance in style, is termed *parody*. There may, at the same time, be a contrast in sentiment. A play on the sound or meanings of a word, is termed a *pun*.

Ex.— "'Tis the last rose of summer, left blooming alone;
All her lovely companions are faded and gone;
No flower of her kindred, no rosebud is nigh,
To reflect back her blushes, or give sigh for sigh.
I'll not leave thee, thou lone one, to pine on the stem;
Since the lovely are sleeping, go, sleep thou with them.
Thus kindly I scatter thy leaves o'er the bed
Where thy mates of the garden lie scentless and dead," &c.

Parody: "'Tis the last golden dollar, left shining alone;
All its brilliant companions are squandered and gone.
No coin of its mintage reflects back its hue,
They went in mint-juleps, and this will go too!
I'll not keep thee, thou lone one, too long in suspense;
Thy brothers were melted, and melt thou, to pence!
I'll ask for no quarter, I'll spend and not spare,
Till my old tattered pocket hangs centless and bare," &c.

Pun: "Ancient maiden lady anxiously remarks,
That there must be peril 'mong so many *sparks*; [fire ;]
Roguish-looking fellow, turning to the stranger,
Says it's his opinion she is out of danger."—*Saxe*.

13. Eu'phemism is a softened mode of speech for what would be offensive or disagreeable if told in downright plain language. It is often based on other figures, but it is effected most frequently by circumlocution; that is, by a round-about mode of expression.

Ex.—"You labor under a mistake," for, "You lie." "He does not keep very exact accounts;" "He cheats when he can." "She certainly displays as little vanity, in regard to her personal appearance, as any young lady I ever saw;" "She is an intolerable slattern." "Slaves are often called *servants*." "Sweet child! lovely child! your parents *are no more*." Cushi did not say to David, "Absalom *is killed*;" but he avoided wounding his feelings as much as possible, by saying, "*May all the enemies of the king be as that young man is*."

14. Interrogation is an animated mode of speech, by which the speaker prefers to put forth, in the form of question, what he neither doubts, nor expects to be answered.

Ex.—"But when shall we be stronger? Will it be the next week, or the next year? Will it be when we are totally disarmed, and when a British guard shall be stationed in every house? * * * Is life so dear, or peace so sweet, as to be purchased at the price of chains and slavery?"—*P. Henry.*

"Can storied urn or animated bust
Back to its mansion call the fleeting breath?
Can Honor's voice provoke the silent dust,
Or Flattery soothe the dull, cold ear of death?"—*Gray.*

This figure fixes the attention more strongly on some important point, than a simple declaration would; and sometimes it implies a defiance to the adversary or hearer, to deny if he can.

15. Exclamation is usually an abrupt or broken mode of speech, designed to express more strongly the emotions of the speaker.

Ex.—"*Dr. Caius.* What business could the honest man have in my room!" for, "The honest man could have no business in my room."

"Oh! that I could return once more to peace and innocence! that I hung an infant on the breast! that I were born a beggar—a peasant of the field! I would toil till the sweat of blood dropped from my brow, to purchase the luxury of one sound sleep, the rapture of a single tear!"—*Schiller.*

" How poor, how rich, how abject, how august,
How complicate, how wonderful is man !
Distinguished link in being's endless chain !
Midway from nothing to the Deity !
A beam ethereal, sullied, and absorbed !
Though sullied and dishonored, still divine !
An heir of glory ! a frail child of dust !
A worm ! a god ! I tremble at myself,
And in myself am lost."—*Young.* See Antithesis.

There seems to be a peculiar elegance in the use of this figure, when the speaker means to show that the object produces at least some interest or excitement in his own feelings, though others may not appreciate it so fully.

Ex.—   "How sweet from the green mossy brim to receive it,
    As poised on the curb it inclined to my lips!"

Here the author slyly intimates that there are persons who underrate the excellence of water, as a beverage.

16. Apos'trophe is a sudden turning-away in the fullness of emotion, to *address* some person or other object.

Ex.—"Death is swallowed up in victory. *O Death! where is thy sting? O Grave! where is thy victory?*"—*Bible.* "But—ah!—him! the first great martyr in this great cause! him! the premature victim of his own self-devoting heart! * * * him! cut off by Providence, in the hour of overwhelming anxiety and thick gloom, falling ere he saw the star of his country rise! *how shall I struggle with the emotions that stifle the utterance of thy name!*—Our work may perish; *but thine shall endure!* this monument may moulder away, *but thy memory shall not fail!*"—*Webster.*

        " Thou ling'ring star, with less'ning ray,
            That lov'st to greet the early morn,
        Again thou usher'st in the day
            My Mary from my soul was torn.
        O Mary! dear departed shade!" etc.—*Burns.* See Vision.

17. Vision represents something that is past, future, absent, or simply imagined, as if it were really present.

Ex.—" One morning, while they were at breakfast, up *gallops* a troop of horse, and *presents* an order for the arrest of the whole party."—*Jeffrey.*

"Frederick immediately sent relief; and, in an instant, all Saxony *is overflowed* with armed men."—*Macaulay.*

"Advance, then, ye future generations! We would hail you as you rise in your long succession! * * * We bid you welcome in this pleasant land of the Fathers."—*Webster.*

"Soldiers! from the tops of yonder pyramids, forty centuries look down upon you!"—*Bonaparte.*

18. Onomatopœia is such an imitation by the sound of the words, as may correspond to or suggest the sense. Sound, motion, and even sentiment, may be imitated by this figure.

Ex.—"Away they went, pell-mell, hurry-skurry, wild buffalo, wild horse, wild huntsman, with clang and clatter, and whoop and halloo, that made the forests ring!"—*Irving.*

"On a sudden open fly,
With impetuous recoil and jarring sound,
Th' infernal doors, and on their hinges grate
Harsh thunder."—*Milton.*

"Heaven opened wide
Her ever-during gates, harmonious sound
On golden hinges turning."—*Milton.*

"When Ajax strives some rock's vast weight to throw,
The line too labors, and the words move slow."—*Pope.*

To this figure may also be referred such new-coined expressions as these: "He was *bamboozled.*" "He offered me the whole *capoodle* for three hundred dollars." "Now she *gallivants* it with another." "I mean that curve, flash, flourish,—or *circumbendibus*—if you please—which he always sticks to his name."

Two or more figures are sometimes involved in the same expression.

METON. AND META.: "Here the *sword* and *sceptre rust;*
Earth to earth, and dust to dust."—*Croly.*
METON. AND PERSON.: "All *Switzerland* is in the field;
She will not fly, she can not yield."—*Montgomery.*
EXCLAMATION, INTERROGATION, CLIMAX, AND ANTITHESIS: "I—a foreigner! Yes, gentlemen! But who was De Kalb? Who was McDonald? Who was Pulaski? Who was La Fayette? and—*who* was Arnold!"—*Dr. Shannon.*

The figures underlie the entire fabric of language. The principles which they involve, have produced, and continue to produce, most of the various meanings or applications of words, and often, the words themselves. Nearly one half of the meanings of words, as given in our dictionaries, are but *faded* figures,—*faded* metaphors, *faded* metonymies, and *faded* synecdoches.

Ex.—"The *blooming* rose," is *literal;* "The *blooming* damsel," is *metaphorical.* "A *clear* brook," *literal;* "A *clear* sky," *metaphor;* "A *clear* demonstration," *metaphor;* "A *clear* head," *metaphor* or *metonymy.* "A *hard* rock," *literal;* "A *hard* lesson," *metaphor;* "A *hard* heart," *metaphor.* "To *apprehend* a thief," *literal;* "To *apprehend* the meaning," *metaphor;* "To *apprehend* [*fear*] danger," *metaphor* and *motonymy.* "*Imagination*"—"the making of images or idols," *literal* and *obsolete;* "the making of images in the mind," *metaphor;* "the faculty," *metonymy* (cause); "the result" (as, "strange *imaginations*"), *metonymy.*

The faculty, its action, the manner of its action, the result of its action, and whatever exhibits or concerns any of these, have all, frequently, but one name in common.

From the material world around us, or from the world of the senses, the mind has borrowed nearly all the words in which it has clothed its own or peculiar possessions; that is, many words, applied first to material things, have been extended to things intellectual or abstract.

"The *spirit* in its literal import is *breath* or *wind*. Its *states* are *standings*, its *emotions* are *movements*, its *sensibilities* are *feelings*, its *views* and *ideas* are *sights*, its *conceptions* and *perceptions* are *takings*, its *apprehension* and *comprehension* are a *holding*, its *reflection* is a *turning back*, its *purpose* is an *exhibition*, its *inference* is a *bringing in*, and its *conclusion* is a *shutting up*."—*Prof. Gibbs.* "*Rectitude* is *straightness*, error is a *wandering*, transgression is a *going over*, education is a *drawing out*, a *language* is a *tongue*, and *heaven* is what is *heaved* or *arched*."—*Id.* "*Bright* hopes, *unshaken* confidence, *corroding* cares."—*Id.*

By frequent use, the figurative sense of words and phrases becomes literal, or is considered so.

EXERCISES.

Point out the figures, and define them:—
Ambition often puts men upon performing the meanest offices: so climbing and creeping are performed in the same posture.—*Swift.* No, Orlando; men are April when they woo, December when they are wed; and maids are May while they are maids, but the sky changes when they are wives.—*Shakespeare.* What a piece of work is man! how noble in reason! how infinite in faculties! in action, how like an angel! in apprehension, how like a God!—*Id.* Honor travels in a way so narrow, where but one goes abreast.—*Id.* What's this? a sleeve? 'Tis like a demi-cannon. Here's snip, and nip, and cut, and slish, and slash.—*Id.* The lover can see a Helen in a brow of Egypt.—*Id.* When sorrows come, they come not single spies, but in battalions.—*Id.* Where Midnight listens to the lion's roar. Must I leave thee, Paradise?—*Milton.* One, with God on his side, is a majority. He sells, he buys, he steals, he kills, for gold. Humbled, but not dispirited; disappointed, but not despairing. But when they shook the thirty pieces of silver at you, you took them. A life on the ocean wave, a home on the rolling deep. Yes, this [a skull] was once ambition's airy hall, the dome of thought, the palace of the soul.—*Byron.* Canst thou send the Lightnings, that they may go, and say unto thee, "Here we are!"—*Bible.* Moses the lawgiver and God's first pen.—*Bacon.*

1. Figures should be well founded, becoming, striking, congruous throughout, not too numerous, and not overstrained or carried too far.
2. Figurative language should be preferred to plain language, only when it will express the meaning better, or improve the discourse.

IMPROPRIETIES.—" The colonies were not yet *ripe to bid adieu* to British connection."—*Jefferson.* Incongruous; mixed metaphor. "There is not a single view of human nature that is not sufficient to extinguish the seeds of pride."—*Addison.* How can a view extinguish,—and worse, extinguish *seeds.* "The commercial liberties of rising states were shackled by paper chains."—*Bancroft.* The phrase *paper chains* suggests nothing formidable. "When the mustang is caught in a lasso, all his struggles serve only to rivet his chains, and deprive him of breath."—*Hist. of Texas.* Where did the author get the "chains?" "Flowers are the sweetest things that God ever made, and forgot to put a soul into."—*Rev. H. W. Beecher.* Quite fanciful, though rather puerile and fantastic. "We kneeled for the last time by that wonderful old furnace [a volcano], where the hand of God works the bellows."—*Rev. Geo. Cheever.* A figure that represents God as a bellows-blower, seems to me undignified and unbecoming. "A shower had just parenthesized the way before us."—*Willis.* The resemblance is not so obvious as it should be. "He had as numerous an offspring as a Greek verb."—*Travels.* Farfetched and obscure. "O maid! thou art so beauteous that yon bright sun is rising all in haste, to gaze upon thee."—*Novel.* Overstrained.

"Why, beautiful nymph, do you close the curtain that fringes your eyes?"—*Newspaper Poem.* Worse. "Up to the stars the sprawling mastiffs fly, and add new monsters to the frighted sky."—*Blacklock.* Terrible dog-barking, truly! "And Heaven peep through the blanket of the dark."—*Shakespeare.* The idea of representing Heaven as peeping through a blanket, is ridiculous. "Thy image on its wing before my Fancy's eyes shall Memory bring." All this ragfair glitter simply means, "I will remember thee." "Let's grasp the forelock of this apt occasion, to greet the victor in his flow of glory."—*British Drama.* Could this sentence be expressed by a congruous picture? To conceive all the imagery as grouped into one visible picture, is often the best way to judge of its accuracy, propriety, or beauty.

Point out the errors:—
No human happiness is so serene as not to contain some alloy. These are the first fruits of my unfledged eloquence, of which thou hast often complained that it was buried in the shade. Since the time that reason began to bud, and put forth her shoots, thought during our waking hours has been active in every breast. The current of ideas has been always moving. The wheels of the spiritual ocean have been exerting themselves with perpetual motion. (Buds, currents, and wheels, are all jumbled together.) At length Erasmus, that great injured name.... curbed the wild torrent of a barbarous age. —*stemmed*—

> On the wide sea of letters, 'twas thy boast,
> To crowd each sail, and touch at every coast;
> From that rich mine, how often hast thou brought
> The pure and precious pearls of splendid thought.

OBSERVATIONS.

A figure may be contained in a single *word;* or it may comprise a *phrase,* a *clause,* a *sentence,* or the *entire discourse.* Sometimes the literal and the figurative language are interwoven throughout the sentence; sometimes each occupies a distinct part of the sentence; sometimes they are consecutive in distinct sentences; and sometimes the figurative takes up the entire sentence or discourse, leaving the literal to be inferred.

Most figures are a sort of emblems or pictures,—a universal language, favorably received, readily understood, and easily remembered. All literature, especially that which has lived longest and delighted the world most, abounds in figures. Figures, however, should be used sparingly and judiciously. An abuse of them is very apt to render the person so using them ridiculous, and thus to diminish at once the dignity and effect of his entire discourse. He that forsakes the common path to show his superior adroitness by walking on the wire, naturally raises our laughter if he falls. Figures are designed to *adorn,* to *illustrate,* or to *abridge* discourse; and particular regard should therefore be had to the subject of the discourse, and to the persons for whom it is meant. Some of our Indian agents have very properly addressed Indians in a figurative style that would be quite ridiculous if used in addressing their own countrymen. Poetry too, being founded in æsthetic principles, admits of much more ornament than prose. The figures used, should be such as would naturally arise to a person whose mind and heart have fully grasped the subject in all its bearings. They should never indicate that he left the main subject to search for them. Not the cheek that is daubed over with glaring cosmetics is the one to please us, but that which glows with a native, healthy, roseate beauty of its own. The briefer a figure is, and the more it expresses that is to the point, the better it is. How excellent is that figure of Dean Swift's, in which he compares the holding of high public offices to dancing on a wire! It suggests at once the vanity of worldly glory, the hankering and folly of ambition, the tact and labor required to sustain oneself, the liability to a fall, the stare and huzza of the crowd, and their contempt and mockery after a fall.

Figures should be not only graphic, and in harmony with the sentiment, but they should be so perfect as to bear study or criticism. The very use of figures implies an aim to express some thought or sentiment with more adequate and becoming simplicity, clearness, beauty, and force. They can therefore be considered hardly proper, or preferable to plain language, unless they express the meaning better.

Figures should be new, if possible. When they are already well known, they are not striking, and will generally appear stale and insipid. But figures should not be drawn from arts or sciences not well known, or from any knowledge remote from common observation; for when so derived, they generally indicate pedantry, and are seldom understood or fully appreciated. Sometimes, however, a figure can be veiled in a certain indirectness, or in a little obscurity, with a very happy effect. A single word may sometimes show a delicate and highly expressive figure lurking along the entire sentence.

As the same object may often be compared to several different things, care must be taken, in using metaphors, not to represent it partly by one comparison and partly by another. Thus,—

"I *bridle* in my struggling muse in vain,
That longs to *launch* into a bolder strain."—*Addison*.

That is, his muse is a monster, partly horse and partly ship.

When several consecutive metaphors are used, they must be congruous with one another, or make a perfect picture. Different perfect pictures may, however, be successively presented to the mind. Hence different similes or metaphors are sometimes used in succession, to illustrate the same subject; as,—

"But pleasures are like poppies spread,—
You seize the flower, its bloom is shed;
Or like the snow-falls in the river,—
A moment white, then melt forever," &c.—*Burns: Tam O'Shanter*.

But the same picture must not be monstrous,—partly one thing and partly another. The same thought should not be expressed partly figurative and partly literal; unless the figurative words are mere tropes, or unless a complete and proper figure at once suggests itself throughout the entire sentence or paragraph. Such a mixture of figurative and of plain language, or of concrete and of abstract objects, as is contained in the following sentences, is inelegant: "Her cheeks were blooming with *roses* and *health;*" "The *harvest* early, but mature the *praise.*"

Style should not be overloaded with figures; especially if they do not form an allegorical picture throughout. Young, imaginative speakers and writers are sometimes ridiculously extravagant in the use of figurative language, and thus acquire a habit of fustianizing, spouting, or frothing, which they never entirely lose. The following is a specimen:—

"The marble-hearted marauder might seize the throne of civil authority, and hurl into thraldom the votaries of rational liberty. Crash after crash would be heard in quick succession, as the strong pillars of the republic give way, and Despotism would shout in hellish triumph among the crumbling ruins. Anarchy would wave her bloody sceptre over the devoted land, and the bloodhounds of civil war would lap the gore of our most worthy citizens. The shrieks of women and the screams of children would be drowned amid the clash of swords and the cannon's peal; and Liberty, mantling her face from the horrid scene, would spread her golden-tinted pinions, and wing her flight to some far-distant land, never again to revisit our peaceful shores!"—*From a Fourth-of-July Oration*. This is the ranting, bombastic, or Asiatic style. The proper and opposite quality is *terseness*. A *terse* style indicates sound common sense. It is not too adorned or elaborate, nor extravagant in any respect; but manly, correct, neat, and expressive.

15. VERSIFICATION.

Poetry,[*] in its highest perfection, is thought, feeling, imagery, and music, expressed in language.

The spirit of music in the poet causes not only the selection of words agreeable in sound, but makes the language *metrical*.

Deficiency in any of these must be compensated by greater excellence in the rest.

Versification is either the *act* or the *art* of making verse. Sometimes it denotes the *result*, or that peculiar structure of language which distinguishes poetry from prose.

Verse has rhythm and rhyme.

Rhythm is essential, but rhyme is not.

"Thou árt, O Gód, the lífe and líght
Of áll this wóndrous wórld we sée."—*Moore.*

"The Assýrian came dówn like the wólf on the fóld,
And his cóhorts were gléaming in púrple and gold."—*Byron.*

"Líves of gréat men áll remínd us
Wé can máke our líves sublíme."—*Longfellow.*

"Cóme as the wínds come when fórests are rénded;
Cóme as the wáves come when návies are stránded."—*Scott.*

"O'nce upón a mídnight *dréary*, while I póndered, wéak and *wéary*,
O'ver mánȳ ă quáint and cúrious vólume óf forgótten *lóre*—
While I nodded, nearly *napping*, suddenly there came a *tapping*,
As of some one gently *rapping, rapping* at my chamber *dòor.*
' 'Tis some visitor,' I muttered, '*tapping* at my chamber *dòor*—
Only this, and nothing *móre.*' "—*E. A. Poe.*

From these lines it is easy to see, that in poetry the voice or the mind passes along the words by a sort of regular pulsations, which constitute the *rhythm, metre,* or *measure.* The correspondence or similarity of sound at equal or proportionate intervals, or in immediate succession, is termed *rhyme.*

Verse is beautiful language, keeping time like music; or, syllables arranged according to accent, quantity, and, generally, rhyme; and so divided into lines as to promote harmony.

Feet.

Feet are the smallest rhythmical divisions of the lines.

---

[*] POETRY means, literally, *a making*; VERSE, *a turning,* i. e., at the end of a line to make another line; IAMBUS, *attacking*, being first used in satire; TROCHEE, *tripping, running*; DACTYL, *finger*; ANAPEST, *reversed*, i. e., reversed *dactyl*; CÆSURA, *cutting, dividing*; SPONDEE, *solemn*; PYRRHIC, *a war-dance,* thence, *lively*; HYPERMETER, *a measure over.* ELLIPSIS, *a leaving-out*; PLEONASM, *more than enough.* FIGURE, *a FORM of language*; SIMILE, *likeness*; METAPHOR, *transfer*; ALLEGORY, *speaking in another thing*; METONYMY, *change of names*; SYNECDOCHE, *understanding one thing with another*; ANTITHESIS, *setting against*; IRONY, *dissembling*; PARALIPSIS, *passing by or over*; HYPERBOLE, *throwing beyond, overshooting*; EUPHEMISM, *speaking well*; APOSTROPHE, *turning away*; ONOMATOPŒIA, *making or coining words.*

VERSIFICATION.—FEET.

Grammarians say they are called *feet*, because they show how the voice "*steps*" along the lines. I rather think the name was at first given from the fact that men, especially in a primitive state of society, naturally use the *foot*, to mark or beat time in music.

Feet, in the English language, are formed according to accent *and* quantity.

A simple foot comprises not more than three syllables.

There are four principal feet,—the *iambus*, the *anapest*, the *trochee*, and the *dactyl;* and three secondary feet,—the *cæsura*, the *spondee*, and the *pyrrhic*.

An **iambus** consists of *two* syllables, and has the poetic accent on the second.

Ex.— "The cúrfew tólls the knéll of párting dáy."
"The fíeld is héaped with bléeding stéeds, and flágs, and clóven máil."

An **anapest** consists of *three* syllables, and has the poetic accent on the last.

Ex.— "O'er the lánd of the frée and the hóme of the bráve."

A **trochee** consists of *two* syllables, and has the poetic accent on the first.

Ex.— "Sée the distant fórest dárk and wáving."

A **dactyl** consists of *three* syllables, and has the poetic accent on the first.

Ex.— "Báchelor's háll,—what a quéer-looking pláce it is!"

The *iambus* and the *anapest* are kindred feet, and hence they are sometimes used promiscuously.

Ex.— "Fŏr thĕ winds ănd thĕ wāves ăre ăbsĕnt thére,
And thĕ sánds ăre bright ăs thĕ stárs thăt glów."

The *trochee* and the *dactyl* are kindred feet, and hence they are sometimes used promiscuously.

Ex.— "Bóundĭng ăwáy ŏvĕr hĭll ănd vállĕy."

A **cæsu'ra** is a long or accented syllable used as one foot.

Ex.— "Réstless mórtals tóil for *náught*."

"Thou wást that áll to mé, *lŏve*,
 For which my sóul did pine—
A green isle in the sea, *lŏve*,
 A fountain and a shrine."—*Poe*.

"Góld! góld! góld! góld!   (4 feet) } (time equal.)
Héavў tŏ gét ănd light tŏ hóld."—*Hood*. (4 feet) }

A **spondee** consists of two long syllables about equally accented. Sometimes only the first syllable is a long one.

Ex.— "Néar the láke where dróoped the wíllow,
 Lŏng tīme ăgó!"—*Morris*.

"O'er mány a frózen, mány a fíery Álp,
 Rócks, cáves, lákes, fēns, bōgs, dēns, ănd shādes ŏf déath."—*Milton*.

A **pyrrhic** is a foot of two syllables left unaccented. Sometimes the accent in iambic verse, to avoid resting on a short syllable, passes to the first syllable (if long) of the next foot, making this foot a spondee, and leaving the other unaccented.

Ex.— "Of thĕ lŏw sŭnset clŏuds, ănd thĕ blūe skȳ."—*Willis.*
"Prĕsĕntly in the ĕdge ŏf thĕ lăst tint."—*Id.*
"Tŏ thĕ făint gōlden mēllowness, a stār."—*Id.*

Pyrrhics and spondees are not always thus produced; but they are generally best when made on the *compensation* principle.

The secondary feet are sometimes allowed to break the regular measure, in order to avoid a tedious sameness in the rhythm, or for the sake of onomatopœia.

Poetic Pauses.

To improve the rhythm or the verse still further, there are also two pauses; the *final* and the *cæsural.*

The **final pause** is a slight pause made at the *end* of each line even when the grammatical sense does not require it.

Ex.— "Ye who have anxiously and fondly *watched*
Beside a fading friend, unconscious *that*
The cheek's bright crimson, lovely to the view,
Like nightshade, with unwholesome beauty bloomed."

The **cæsural pause** occurs *within* the line; most frequently about the middle of it. It belongs chiefly to long lines. It not only improves the rhythm, but, like emphasis, it often serves to arrest, with fine effect, the attention to the meaning. Sometimes a line has two or more cæsural pauses, one of which is commonly greater than the rest.

Ex.— "But nŏt to mĕ retŭrns
Dăy, | ŏr thĕ swĕet appróach of ĕvĕn ŏr mŏrn."—*Milton.*

"Then her cheek | was pale, and thinner | | than should be | for one so young;
And her eyes, | on all my motions, | | with a mute observance hung."—*Tennyson.*

"Warms | in the sun, | | refreshes | in the breeze,
Glows | in the stars, | | and blossoms | in the trees."—*Pope.*

"No sooner had the Almighty ceased, | than all
The multitude of angels, | with a shout
Loud | as from numbers without number, | sweet
As from blest voices | uttering joy," etc.—*Milton.*

What a fine effect on the sense have the pauses after *loud* and *sweet.* Milton has generally shown remarkable skill in his management of the poetic pauses.

Good poets generally aim to construct their verse in such a way that the final and cæsural pauses may properly fall where the sense, in expressive common speech, naturally requires pauses. The same is true in regard to poetic accent, with reference to common accent and to emphasis. See stanza 22, p. 317.

This is a very important principle; for natural, smooth, and easy versification depends mainly upon it.

Quantity.

The **quantity** of a syllable is its relative quantity of sound, or, what is equivalent to the same thing, it is the relative time occupied in uttering it.

Quantity and *accent* are two different things, and should never be, as they usually are, confounded. Not every long syllable is accented, nor is every short syllable unaccented.

In respect to quantity, all the syllables in the language may be divided into three classes; *long, short*, and *variable*.

The quantity of many syllables depends *on the manner of uttering them, and on their association with other syllables;* yet we may safely say, that some syllables are *always* long, and others *always* short.

A syllable having a long vowel or diphthongal sound, especially when closed by one or more consonant sounds, is *long*.

Ex.—Dry, warm, proud, flashed. "Round us roars the tempest louder."

A syllable having a short vowel sound, but closed or followed by consonants in such a way as to retard pronunciation, is generally *long*

Ex.—"When Ajax strives some rock's vast weight to throw."

A syllable ending with a short vowel sound, is *short.*

Ex.—The, a, to, quan*ti*ty, sala*ry*.

A syllable next to an accented syllable of the same word, is often made *short* by the greater stress on the accented syllable.

Ex.—Hóme*ward*, púni*sh*ment.

An unimportant monosyllable, ending with a single consonant preceded by a single short vowel, and joined immediately to the more important word to which it relates, is *short;* as, "*at* war."

A few syllables in the language may be pronounced either as one syllable or as two.

Ex.—Hour, our, fire, lyre, choir.

Two syllables may sometimes be contracted into one, either by the pronunciation or by omission.

Ex.—*Fie-ry* for *fi-e-ry*, *'tis* for *it is, threat'ning* for *threatening*.

Poetic Accent.

The **poetic accent**, which divides the lines into feet, corresponds to the *beat* in music. It controls the position of words according to quantity and word-accent.

There is perhaps no word so long or so uncouth, that it may not by some arrangement, be brought into some kind of verse.

Any monosyllable may receive the poetic accent.

Ex.— "Blue wás the láke, the clóuds were góne."
"Gone wére the clóuds, the láke was blúe."

But it is generally inelegant, and sometimes perhaps incorrect, to place it on a short syllable.

Ex.—We can not read, "As á friend thánk him, ánd with jóy see him." But we may read, "Seé him with jóy, and thánk him ás a friénd."

Monosyllables, being unencumbered by word-accent, are the words most easily reduced to feet.

When words of more than one syllable are introduced into verse, the poetic accent must take the place of the primary or the secondary accent.

Should the poetic accent fall on a different syllable, the word must be rejected, or the arrangement must be so varied as to admit it. (To this rule we find in our poets a very few exceptions; chiefly in the use of compound words.)

 Ex.— "Perháps like mé he floúnders oút a líne,
   And begíns anóther—there stops——" (Erroneous.)

A long syllable of a word, next to an accented syllable, never receives the poetic accent, or it is made short. (There are a very few exceptions.)

 Ex.—" Wést*ward* the coúrse of é*mpire* tákes its wáy."

It should not, however, be inferred, that every syllable having the word-accent, must also receive the poetic accent. Only this is necessary,—that the poetic accent, in its proper march through the verse, shall never supersede the other accent, by resting on a different syllable of the same word.

 Ex.—" Whilst our máidens shall dánce with their white *wáving* árms,
  Sínging jóy to the bráve that delivered their chárms.—*Campbell*.

The poetic accent generally passes in some regular order through the entire poem. Accented syllables demand it; long syllables naturally tend to draw it upon themselves; and short syllables incline to refuse it.

When it comes in collision with the common accent, the harshness is generally greater than when it rests on a short syllable. It sometimes accommodates itself to the common accent, where the sense and melody allow a considerable pause; that is, at the end, at the beginning, or near the middle of the line, though rarely the last. It seems, indeed, to be a general principle, to allow the poet most liberty at these places, not only as to accent, but also as to extra short syllables. (See pp. 313,314). To accommodate itself to quantity, the poetic accent may sometimes vary from its regular stations, either by preferring the previous or the subsequent syllable, or by passing over one more syllable than the regular number, or by resting on each of several successive long syllables. See pp. 313,314.

Verse is generally most melodious when the regularly accented syllables are long, and the unaccented short.

 Ex.—" At the clóse of the dáy when the hámlet is stíll."

Lines, or Verses.

A **line**, or **verse**, is the shortest finished portion from which the poet may *turn* to make another.

A line, according to its number of feet, is sometimes called a *monom'eter* (one foot), a *dim'eter*, a *trim'eter*, a *tetram'eter*, a *pentam'eter*, a *hexam'eter*, a *heptam'eter*, or an *octom'eter*.

Iambic or *anapestic* lines sometimes end with one or two additional unaccented short syllables, called *supernumerary* or *hypermeter* syllables. Such lines are called *hypermeters*.

Trochaic or *dactylic* lines often end with the cæsura.

Iambic lines may occasionally begin with a trochee, a dactyl, or a spondee.

 Ex.— "*Búrsts thĕ* wĭld crȳ of térror ănd dismáy."—*Campbell*.
   "*Hŏvĕring* a spáce till wĭnds the sígnal blów."—*Milton*.
   "*Lĭbĕrăl*, not lávish, ĭs kĭnd Náture's hănd."—*Beattie*.
 "*Wĕep, wĕep*, and rĕnd your háir for thóse who néver shăll retúrn."—*Macaulay*.

A trochee may sometimes be admitted within an iambic line, where the rhythm and sense allow a considerable pause.

 Ex.— "Of góodlĭest trées *lŏadĕn* with fáirest frúit."—*Milton*.
   "These [prairies] áre the gárdens ŏf the désert, thése
   Thĕ únshŏrn fĭelds, *boúndlĕes* ănd beaútifúl."—*Bryant*.
   "The sóng is húshed, the láughing nýmphs are flówn;
   And hĕ is léft, *músing* of blĭss, alóne."—*T. Moore*.

Iambic lines occasionally admit an anapest, provided it is such a one as might be contracted, or one that has no consonant between the unaccented syllables, or only a liquid, or such a consonant as very little obstructs utterance.

 Ex.— "With Héavĕn's *ărtĭllĕry fraúght*, come ráttling ŏn."—*Milton*.
   "And mány ă *yoúth*, and mány ă *máid*."—*Id*.
   "That bĭnds hĭm tŏ a wŏman's *délĭcăte lŏve*."—*Willis*.

It is sometimes a beauty to lengthen out a line a little by short, tripping syllables.

 Ex.—"Where érst the jăy withĭn the élm's tăll crĕst,
   Măde *gărrŭloŭs* troúble roúnd her únfledged yoúng."—*T. B. Read*.
   "And my native land! whose magical name
   Thrills to my heart like electric flame."—*Pringle*.

Anapestic lines may occasionally begin with an iambus or a spondee.

 Ex.— "*Their swórds* are a thoúsand,—their bósoms are óne."—*Campbell*.
   "*Ō! flȳ* tŏ thĕ práirie, sweet máiden, with mé;
   'Tis as gréen, and as wĭde, and as wild, as the séa."

Some anapestic verse occasionally admits a spondee or an iambus.

 Ex.— "The póplars are félled, *fărewĕll* to the sháde, [the poem.
   And the whispering soúnds of the cóol colonnáde."—*Cowper*. See

A pleasant rhythm is sometimes produced by throwing one anapest, or even two, into each iambic line.

 Ex.— "I cóme! I cóme! yĕ hăve cálled mĕ lóng;
   I cóme ŏ'er thĕ moúntăins wĭth light ănd sóng."—*Mrs. Hemans*.
   "Afăr ĭn thĕ désĕrt I lóve tŏ ride,
   With thĕ sĭlĕnt Búsh-bŏy ălóne bў mȳ side."—*Pringle*

To preserve equality or proportion in time, seems to be a governing principle in versification; and variations in the position of the poetic accent or in the number of unaccented syllables, are allowable where the chief poetic pauses occur,—at the beginnings or the ends of lines, and at the cæsural pause.

Ex.— " And give me fŏr my búshel sŏwn
   Twice ten for one."   (Prolong the sound as you read.)
" Kéeping time, time, time,
   In a sórt of Rúnic rhýme."—*Poe.*
" Ye've tráiled me through the *forest;* | ye've tráiled me ó'er the stréam;
And strúggling through the éverglade | your brístling báyonets gléam."—*Patton.*

This is a very important principle; for by means of it most of the apparent irregularities in versification may be explained.

Stanzas.

Lines are formed into *stanzas.*

A **stanza** is a complete group of lines constructed in a certain way with respect to one another.

Two consecutive lines form a *couplet* or *distich ;* three, a *triplet.* Such lines are usually understood as rhyming together.

Short lines are seldom formed into stanzas, unless in combination with long lines.

The greater portion of our poetry consists of lines of medium length.

Long lines are sometimes broken at the cæsural pause, and written in two lines each.

Rhymes must begin with different letters, but end with the same or nearly the same sound.

Rhymes that are not exact, yet authorized, are called *allowable* rhymes.

Rhymes may run back into the lines as far as three syllables. Hence they are classified thus: *Single* rhymes, *double* rhymes, and *triple* rhymes.

A rhyming element usually corresponds to but one other one; but sometimes to more.

Lines are sometimes so formed as to have rhyming syllables within them, as well as at the end.   See p. 308.

Some verse has no rhyme.   Such is styled *blank verse.*

Blank verse, being without the music of rhyme, must usually, to sustain the dignity of poetry, excel in other respects.

Verse.

The word **verse** is properly applicable to any single line of poetry; but, by synecdoche, it may be applied to a stanza, or to poetry in general, as a modest term, meaning something that has at least the form, if not the spirit, of poetry.

Verse, according to what foot prevails in it, is usually divided into four kinds; *iambic, anapestic, trochaic,* and *dactylic*.

Verse that is very irregular in its feet, or in the combination of its lines, has been styled *composite*.

SCANNING.

To **scan** verse is to show how it is formed in respect to its feet, —to analyze its versification.

Each line is usually scanned by itself; but it seems best to scan continuously from one line into another, when we can thus avoid irregularities.

Ex.—
"'Tis the lást rose of súmmer
   Left blóoming alóne;   (4 feet.)
All its lóvely compánions
   Are fáded and góne."   (4 feet.)

Sometimes more than one mode of scanning, may be applied to the same poem.

That mode is always preferable which is simplest or most musical.

THE ELEMENTARY COMBINATIONS OF LINES IN ENGLISH POETRY.

To a person wishing to write verse, perhaps nothing can be presented more useful than a general circuit of the combinations of poetic lines, with their scansion; especially if so selected as to embrace all the various deviations, or licenses, of which poets may avail themselves.

☞ The letters *f, i, a, t, d,* and *c,* placed on the left of the stanzas, denote respectively *feet, iambics, anapests, trochees, dactyls,* and *cæsuras*; the letters above the stanzas show the rhyme; the sign *plus* (+) denotes hypermeter syllables; accentual marks are used to aid in showing the versification, and sometimes they show irregular versification; and upright dashes are sometimes used to show cæsural pauses.

1. IAMBIC VERSE.

1.
a b a b

i   "His wít,
    With smárt,
  Has hít
    My heárt."—*Newspaper.*

2.
a a b c c b

i +   "The lósses,
    The crósses,
3 *i* That áctive mén engáge;
    The fears all,
    The tears all,
Of dim declíning áge."—*Burn.*

3.
a b a b

2 *i* "Love múst, in shórt,
    Keep fónd and trúe,
  Through good repórt,
    And evil too."—*T. Moore.*

4.
a b a b

2 *i* + "To hálls of spléndor,
2 *i*   Let gréat ones híe;
   Through light more tender,
    Our pathways lie."—*Moore.*

5.
a a b c c b

2 *i* "O précious óne,
   Let thy tongue run
    In a sweet frét;
   And this will give
   A chance to live
    A long time yet."
         Newspaper.

6.
a a b c c b

2 *i* "The píbroch ráng
    With bólder cláng
3 *i* + Alóng the hills of héather;
    And fresh and strong
    The thistle sprung,
That had begun to wither."—*Hogg.*

7.
a b b a

2 *i* "His gifts divine
Through all appear,
And round the year
His glories shine."—*Songster.*

8.
a b b a

3 *f* "No:—'Tis a fast to dole
2 *i* Thy sheaf of wheat,
i And meat,
3 *f* Unto the hungry soul."—*Herrick.*

10.
a a b c c b

2 *i* "The soul refined
Is most inclined
4 *f* To every moral excellence;
All vice is dull,
A knave's a fool;
4 *i* And Virtue is the child of Sense."
Young.

12.
a b a b

3 *i* "When thou art nigh, it seems
A new creation round;
The sun has fairest beams,
The lute a softer sound."—*Moore.*

14.
a b c c b

3 *i* "Tread softly,—bow the head,—
3 *f* In reverent silence bow;
No passing bell doth toll,—
Yet an immortal soul
2 *i* Is passing now."—*Mrs. Southey.*

16.
a a b c c b

3 *f* "Freeze, freeze, thou bitter sky,
3 *i* Thou dost not bite so nigh
As benefits forgot;
Though thou the waters warp,
Thy sting is not so sharp
As friends rememb'ring not."
Shakespeare.

18.
a a b b

4 *i* "Whene'er a noble deed is wrought,
4 *f* Whene'er is spoken a noble thought,
Our hearts, with glad surprise,
3 *i* To higher levels rise."—*Atlantic Monthly.*

19.
a b a b c d d c

4 *i* "An infant on its mother's breast—
3 *i* A bouncing boy at play—
A youth by maiden fair caressed—
An old man silver gray—
3 *i* Is all of life we know:
2 *i* A joy—a fear;
A smile—a tear;—
4 *i* And all is o'er below !—*Shaw.*

9.
a a a b c c c b

2 *i* + "Could love forever
Run like a river,
And Time's endeavor
2 *i* Be tried in vain,—
No other pleasure
With this could measure;
And like a treasure
We'd hug the chain."—*Byron.*

11.
a b a b c c c b

2 *f* "Dream, baby, dream !
2 *i* + Thine eyelids quiver.
Know'st thou the theme
Of yon bright river ?
It saith, 'Be calm, be sure,
3 *i* Unfailing, gentle, pure :
So shall thy life endure,
Like mine, for ever.' "—*Cornwall.*

13. GAY'S STANZA.
a b a b

3 *i* + "From Greenland's icy mountains,
From India's coral strand,
Where Afric's sunny fountains
3 *f* Roll down their golden sand."
Heber.

15.
a b c b

3 *i* + "'Tis sweet to love in childhood,
3 *f* When the souls that we bequeath,
3 *i* + Are beautiful in freshness,
3 *f* As the coronals we wreathe."

This stanza may also be scanned continuously, without irregularity; and it may be written as well in two lines.

17.
a b a b

3 *i* "Fly swift, my light gazelle,
3 *i* + To her who now lies waking
To hear thy silver bell
The midnight silence breaking.
Moore.

20.
a b a b c c

3 *f* "Go, Soul, the body's guest,
3 *i* + Upon a thankless errand ;
Fear not to touch the best,
The truth shall be thy warrant
3 *f* Go, since I needs must die,
3 *i* And give the world the lie.***
3 *i* + Tell arts they have not soundness,
3 *i* + But vary by esteeming ;
Tell schools they want profoundness,
And stand too much on seeming.
If arts and schools reply,
Give arts and schools the lie.
Barnfield.

21. See 18.
a a b b

8 i "What scénes of glóry rise
    Before my dazzled eyes !
4 i Young zéphyrs wáve their wánton wings,
    And melody celestial rings."—*Croly.*

23. SHORT-METRE STANZA.
a b a b

8 i "The húrricáne hath might
    Along the Indian shore;
4 i And fár, by Gánges' bánks, at night,
    Is heard the tíger's roar."
    Hemans.

25.
a a b c c b

4 i "If sólid háppinéss we príze,
    Within our bréast the jéwel lies;
8 i And théy are foóls who róam:
    The wórld has nothing to bestow;
    From our own selves our joys must flow,
    And that dear hut—our home."
    Cotton.

27. COMMON-METRE STANZA. (Mártial.)
a b c b

4 i "To húnt the déer with hoúnd and hórn,
8 i Earl Pércy toók his wáy;
    The child that's yet unborn, may rue
    The hunting of that day."
    Chevy Chase.

Or thus:—
"To hunt the deer with hound and horn, Earl Percy took his way;
The child that's yet unborn, may rue the hunting of that day."

28.
a b c b

4 f "Fáir scénes for chíldoód's ópening blóom,
8 i + For spórtive yoúth to strây in;
    For manhood to enjoy his strength,
    And age to wear away in."
    Wordsworth.

30. LONG-METRE STANZA.
a b a b

4 i "So blúe yon wínding river flóws,
    It séems an oútlet fróm the skỳ,
    Where, waiting till the west-wind blown,
    The freighted clouds at anchor lie."—*Longfellow.*

32.
a a a

4 i "Aroúnd Sebágo's lónely láke,
    There lingers not a breeze to break
    The mirror which its waters make."
    Whittier.

22.
a b a b

2 f "Gó, lóvelý róse !
4 i Tell hér that wástes her tíme and mé,
2 i That nów she knóws,
4 i When I resemble her to thee,
4 i How sweet and fair she seems to be."
    Waller.

This stanza forcibly illustrates several of the chief principles laid down under Versification.

24.
a b a b

2 f "Gáy, guíltléss páir,
4 i + What séek ye fróm the fíelds of héaven ?
8 i + Ye have no need of prayer,
    Ye have no sins to be forgiven."
    Sprague.

26.
a b c b d d

8 i + "It wás a súmmer évening,—
8 i Old Káspar's wórk was dóne,
4 i And he, before his cottage door,
    Was sitting in the sun ;
    And by him sported on the green,
    His little grandchild Wilhelmine."
    Southey.

a b a b. (Sentimental.)

4 f "A víolét bý a móssy stóne,
8 i Half-hidden fróm the eýe,
    Fair as a star, when only one
    Is shining in the sky."
    Wordsworth.

29.
a b a b

4 i + "The Ócean loóketh úp to héaven,
8 i As 'twére a líving thíng;
    The homage of its waves is given,
    In ceaseless worshiping."
    Whittier.

31.
a b a b

4 i + "Her heárt is like a fáded flówer,
4 i Whose beaúty's lóst and sweetness flówn;
    Forgot, neglected in the bower,
    And left by all to die alone."
    Songster.

33.
a b a b

4 i "There is a cálm for thóse who wéep,
    A rést for weáry pílgrims foúnd;
    They softly lie, and sweetly sleep,
2 f Low in the ground."—*Montgom.*

VERSIFICATION.—SCANNING.—IAMBIC VERSE.

34.
a a b b

4 í "Those évening bélls! those évening bélls!
How mány a tále their músic télls
Of youth and home, and that sweet time
When last I heard their soothing chime."—*Moore.*

36.
a a a b

4 í "Who féd me fróm her géntle bréast,
And hushed me in her arms to rest,
And on my cheeks sweet kisses pressed?
í + My Mother."—*Thomson.*

The expression "My Mother," closes each stanza of the poem. A part thus repeated, or making the burden of the poem, is called a *refrain.*

39. BURNS'S STANZA.
a a a b a b

4 í "When rípened fiélds and ázure skies
Call forth the reaper's rustling noise,
I saw thee leave their evening joys,
2 í And lónely stálk,
To vent thy bosom's swelling rise
In peusive walk."—*Burns.*

41.
a a b c c b

4 í + "Two spirits réached this wórld of óurs:
The lightning's locomotive powers
8 í + or 4 í Were slow to their agility:
In broad daylight they moved incog.,
Enjóying, withoût mist or fóg,
Entire invisibility."
Campbell.

43.
a a a b

4 í "When máidens súch as Héster die,
Their place ye may not well supply,
Though ye among a thousand try,
í + With váin endéavor."
Lamb.

44.

4 í "By tórch and trúmpet fást arráyed,
Each horseman drew his battle-blade,
4 f And fúrioús évery chárger néighed
8 í + To join the dreadful revelry."
Campbell.

35.
a b c b

4 í "All thoúghts, all pássions, all delights,
Whatever stirs this mortal frame,
Are all but ministers of love,
3 í And feed his sacred flame."
Coleridge.

37.

4 f "Óh, néver tálk agáin to mé
4 í + Of nórthern clímes and Brítish ládies;
It has not been your lot to see,
Like me, the charming girl of Cadiz."—*Byron.*

38.
a b c c b

4 í "To hórse! to hórse! the stándard flies,
3 í The búgles soúnd the cáll;
The Gallic navy stems the seas,
The voice of battle's on the breeze,—
Arouse ye, one and all!"—*Scott.*

40.
a b a b c c

4 í "You háve the Pýrrhic dánce as yét,
4 f Where is the Pyrrhic phalanx gone?
Of two such lessons why forget
The nobler and the manlier óne?
4 í You have the letters Cadmus gave—
Think you he meant them for a slave?"—*Byron.*

42.

4 í + "Thou árt not fálse, but thóu art fickle,
4 í To those thyself so fondly sought;
The tears that thou hast forced to trickle,
Are doubly bitter from that thought:
4 í + 'Tis this which breáks the heárt thou griévest,—
Too well thou lov'st, too soon thou leavest."—*Byron.*

45.
a a b c c b

4 f "Thou gréwĕst a góodly trée, with shóots [róots
4 f Fánning thĕ ský, and éarth-bound
2 í ± So grappled únder,
4 í That thóu, whom pérching bírds could swing,
And zephyrs rock with lightest wing,
From thy firm trunk unmoved didst fling
2 f + Témpĕst ánd thúnder."
Magazine: Charter-oak.
Observe how the change of feet in the last line, improves the vigor of the stanza.

46.
a a b b c

4 í "His brŏw was sád ; his eýe benéath
4 ƒ   Flashed like a falchĭŏn from its sheath ;
      And like a silver clárĭŏn rúng
4+ or 2 í   The accents of that mountain tongue,
            Excelsior !"—*Longfellow*.

47.
a a b b c c, &c.

4 ƒ "Swift tŏ thĕ bréach his cómrades flý,—
4 í 'Make way for liberty !' they cry,
    And through the Aŭstrĭăn phalanx dárt
    As rushed the spears through Arnold's heart ;
    While, instantaneous as his fall,
    Rout, ruin, panic, seized them all."—*Montgomery*.

4 í + "The túrkman láy beside the river ;
    The wind played loose through bow and quiver ;
4 í The chárger ŏn the bánk fed frée ;
4 ƒ The shield hung glittering from the trée. * * *
    Wild burst the burning element
    O'er man and courser, flood and tent !
    And through the blaze the Greeks outsprang,
    Like tigers,—bloody, foot and fang !
    With dagger-stab and falchion-sweep,
    Délving thĕ stúnned and stággĕrĭng heap,
    Till lay the slave by chief and Khan,
    And all was gone that once was man !"—*Croly*.

The iambic tetrameter is a sprightly, vigorous measure, in which much of our poetry is written. See Scott, Byron, Moore, Butler, Swift, Gay, Mrs. Hemans.

48.
a b a b

3 ƒ "Léaves hăve their time to fáll,
5 ƒ And flŏwĕrs tŏ wither ăt the nŏrth-wind's bréath,
3 í And stars to sét ; but all—
5 ƒ Thou hast all seasons for thine own, O Death !"—*Hemans*.

49.
a b a b c c

3 ƒ "'Tis swéet, ĭn thĕ grĕen spring
5 ƒ To gaze upŏn the wakĕnĭng fĭelds around ;
    Birds in the thicket sing,
5 í Winds whisper, waters prattle from the ground ;
3 í A thousand odors rise,
    Breathed up from blossoms of a thousand dyes."—*Bryant*.

50.
a b b a c c

3 ƒ "Ăh ! thĕre 's a déathless náme !—
5 ƒ A spirit that the smothĕrĭng vault shall spurn,
5 í And like a steadfast planet mount and burn—
3 í And though its crown of flame
5 í + Consumed my brain to ashes as it won me,
    By all the fiery stars ! I'd pluck it on me !"—*Willis*.

51.
a b a b

5 ƒ "We mourn for thée when blind blănk night
2 í The chamber fills ;
5 í We pine for thee when morn's first light
2 ƒ Reddĕns thĕ hills."

52.

a b b a

5í
2ƒ
2í
"A long way off Lucinda strikes the men;
   As she draws near,
   And one sees clear,—
A long way off one wishes her again."

53.

a b a b

5ƒ+
3í
" It is the Rhine! our mountain vineyards laving;
   I see the proud flood shine.
Sing on the march, with every banner waving,
   Sing, brothers! 'tis the Rhine."—*Hemans.*

54.

a b a b

5ƒ
4í
5í
" Westward the course of empire takes its way;
   The first four acts already passed,
A fifth shall close the drama with the day;—
   Time's noblest offspring is the last."—*Berkeley.*

55. Pentameters, or Heroic Measure. 5í or 5í+.

In this measure, by far the greatest and most valuable part of our poetry is written. It comprises nearly all our *blank verse* and *epic poetry*, and all our *dramatic poetry*. See Chaucer, Spenser, Shakespeare, Milton, Dryden, Pope, Thomson, Cowper, Pollok, Rogers, Byron, Campbell, Crabbe, etc.

Blank.

5ƒ+

5í
"The poet's eye, in a fine frenzy rolling,
Doth glance from heaven to earth, from earth to heaven;
And, as imagination bodies forth
The forms of things unknown, the poet's pen
Turns them to shape, and gives to airy nothing
A local habitation and a name."—*Shakespeare.*

5ƒ

5ƒ
5í
   " Yet, higher than their tops
The verdurous walls of Paradise upsprung,
Which to our general sire gave prospect large,
Into his nether empire neighboring round.
And higher than that wall, a circling row
Of goodliest trees, loaden with fairest fruit,
Blossoms and fruits at once of golden hue,
Appeared, with gay enamelled colors mixed;
Of which the sun more glad impressed his beams
Than in fair evening cloud, or humid bow,
When God hath showered earth."—*Milton.*

a a b b c c d d, &c.

5ƒ
" Oh! had he been content to serve the crown,
   With virtues proper only for the gown;
Or had the rankness of the soil been freed,
   From cockle that oppressed the noble seed;
David for him his tuneful harp had strung,
And heaven had wanted one immortal song."—*Dryden.*

56. Elegiac Stanza.

a b a b

5í
" The breezy call of incense-breathing morn,
The swallow twittering from the straw-built shed,
The cock's shrill clarion, or the echoing horn,
No more shall rouse them from their lowly bed."—*Gray*

VERSIFICATION.—SCANNING.—IAMBIC VERSE. 321

57.

5 i +
5 i
"For thou wast monarch born. Tradition's pages
   Tell not the planting of thy parent tree,
But that the forest tribes have bent for ages
   To thee, and to thy sires, the subject knee."—*Halleck.*

58.

5,'
5 i
"Harp of the North, farewell! the hills grow dark,
   On purple peaks a deeper shade descending;
In twilight copse the glowworm lights her spark,
   The deer half-seen are to the covert wending."—*Scott.*

59.

5 i +
5 i +
"Philosophers may teach thy whereabouts and nature;
   But wise, as all of us, perforce, must think 'em,
The schoolboy best has fixed thy nomenclature;
   And poets, too, must call thee Bob-o-linkum."—*Hoffman.*

60.
a b a b c c

5 i +
5 i
"And thou hast walked about—how strange a story—
   In Thebes's streets, three thousand years ago;
When the Memnonium was in all its glory,
   And time had not begun to overthrow
Those monuments and piles stupendous,
Of which the very ruins are tremendous."—*H. Smith.*

61. BYRON'S STANZA.
a b a b a b c c

5 i +
"O, that I had the art of easy writing,
   What should be easy reading! could I scale
Parnassus, where the Muses sit inditing
   Those pretty poems never known to fail,
How quickly would I print (the world delighting)
   A Grecian, Syrian, or Assyrian tale;
And sell you, mixed with Western sentimentalism,
Some samples of the finest orientalism."—*Byron.*

When iambic hypermeters of moderate length occur only now and then in the poem, they are more commonly humorous than serious.

62. THE SONNET.
a b b a a c c a d e e d f f

5 i
"And canst thou, Mother, for a moment think
   That we, thy children, when old age shall shed
   Its blanching honors on thy weary head,
Could from our best of duties ever shrink?
Sooner the sun from his high sphere should sink,
   Than we, ungrateful, leave thee in that day,
   To pine in solitude thy life away,
Or shun thee tottering on the grave's cold brink.
Banish the thought!—where'er our steps may roam,
   O'er smiling plains, or wastes without a tree,
   Still will fond memory point our hearts to thee,
And paint the pleasures of thy peaceful home;
   While duty bids us all thy griefs assuage,
   And smooth the pillow of thy sinking age."—*H. K. White.*

63. SPENSERIAN STANZA.
a b a b b c b c c

5 i
"There is a pleasure in the pathless woods,
   There is a rapture on the lonely shore,
There is society, where none intrudes,

By the deep sea, and music in its roar.
I love not Man the less, but Nature more,
From these our interviews, in which I steal
From all I may be, or have been before,
To mingle with the universe, and feel
What I can ne'er express, | yet can not all conceal."—*Byron.*

An iambic hexameter is usually called an *Alexandrine.*

64.
a a b b

"The déw was fálling fást, | the stárs begán to blínk,—
I heard a voice; it said, | 'Drink, pretty creature, drink!'
And looking o'er the hedge, | before me I espied
A snów-white móuntain lámb | with á máiden át its síde."—*Wordsworth.*

65.
a b a b c c

"For áges, ón the sílent fórest hére,
Thy beams did fall before the red man came
To dwell beneath them; in their shade the deer
Féd ánd féared nót the árrow's déadly áim.
Nor tree was felled, | in all that world of woods,
Save by the beaver's tooth, | or winds, or rush of floods."—*Bryant.*

66.
a a b b

"I sée the válleys, Spáin! | whére thý míghty rívers rún,
And thé hills that lift thy hárvésts | ánd vineyards tó the sún,
And the flocks that drink thy brooks | and sprinkle all the green,
Where lie thy pláins, | with shéep-wálks séamed, | and ólive shádes
[betwéen."—*Bryant.*

67. LINES DIVISIBLE.

"The mélanchóly dáys are cóme, | The sáddest óf the yéar,
Of wailing winds and naked woods, | And meadows brown and sear."
Bryant.

"O, bétter thát her sháttered húlk | Should sínk benéath the wáve!
Her thunder shook the mighty deep, | And there should be her grave!
Náil tó thé mást her hóly flág,—sét évery thréadbare sáil,
And give her to the god of storms,— | the lightning and the gale!"
Holmes.

68.*

"No;—the jóke has béen a góod one, | Bút I'm gétting fónd of quíet;
And 1 don't like deviations | from my customary diet;
So I think I will not go with you | to hear the toasts and speeches,
But stick to old Montgomery Place, | and have some pig and peaches."
Holmes.

"Fáthér ánd Í went dówn to tówn | Alóng with Cáptain Góoding,
And thére we sée the mén and bóys | As thick as hasty púdding."
Dr. Shackburg: Yankee Doodle.

The quantity of iambic verse in English literature, far exceeds that of all the other kinds of verse.

---

* There is also a sort of doggerel stanza, usually iambic, ending with a long prosy line, and frequently found in newspapers; as,—

"Now Reúben wás a nice young mán
As ány in the tówn;
And Phœbe loved him very dear,
But, on account of his being obliged to work for a living, he never could make himself agreeable to old Mr. and Mrs. Brown.

2. ANAPESTIC VERSE.

1.

a b a b

s "Móve your féet   Or, *t c*   Móve your féet   Or, *d*   Móve your féet
     To our soúnd,   Tó our sóund,   Tó our sound,
     Whilst we gréet   Whilst we gréet   Whilst we greet
     All the gróund."—*Fletcher.*   All the gróund.   All the ground.

2.

a b a c d b d c

2*f*   "Now, mórtal, prepáre,
2*a*   For thy fáte is at hánd;
       Now, mortal, prepare
s+   And surrender.
       For Love shall arise,
       Whom no pow'r can withstand,
       Who rules from the skies
       To the centre."—*Granville.*

3.

a b a b c c d e d e

2*a*   "When, in ráge, he came thére,
2*f*   Behólding how stéep
2*f*   The sídes did appéar,
2*a*   And the bóttom how déep;
2*f*+   His tórments projécting,
        And sadly refléctíng,
2*a*+   That a lover forsaken,
2*f*   A néw love may gét;
        But a neck, when once broken,
        Can never be set," etc.—*Walsh.*

4.

a b a b

2*f*+   The aútumn winds rúshing
2*a*+   Waft the léaves that are séarest;
       But our flow'r was in flushing,
       When blighting was nearest.
                       Scott.

5.

a a b b

2*a*   "Our life is a dréam,
2*a*   Our time, as a stream,
2*f*   Glides swiftly awáy;
4*a*   And the fúgitive móment refúses to
                     [stáy."—*Wesley.*

6.

a a b c c b

2*a*   "Come, my mátes, let us wórk,
       And all hánds to the fórk,
3*a*   While the sún shines, our háycocks
       to máke:
2*f*   So fine is the day,
       And so fragrant the hay,
       That the meadow's as blithe as the
       wake."—*Smart.*

7.

a a b b

2*a*   "Let the stúpid be gráve,
       'Tis the vice of the slave;
       But can never agree
       With a maiden like me,
4*a*   Who is born in a country that's happy
       and free."

8.

a b a b

3*a*   "I am mónarch of áll I survéy,
3*f*   My right there is nóne to dispúte;
           From the centre all rour 1 to the sea,
           I am lord of the fowl and the brute."—*Cowper.*

9.

3*a*+   "Though the dáy of my déstiny's óver,
2*a*   And the stár of my fáte has declíned,
           Thy soft heart refused to discover,
           The faults which so many could find."—*Byron.*

10.

3*f*+*s*   "The stráwberries grów in the mówing, Mill Máy,
3*a*   And the bob-o-link sings on the tree;
           On the knolls the red clover is growing, Mill Máy,
           Then come to the meadows with me."—*Eastman.*

11.

4*f*+   "How fáir is the róse! what a beaútiful flówer!
3*f*   The glóry of A'pril and Máy!
4*a*+   But the leaves are beginning to fade in an hour,
3*a*   And they wither and die in a day."—*Watts.*

12.
a b a b b

3*f*   "To Ríches ! Alás ! 'tis in váin ;
3*f*   Who híd in their túrns have been híd ;
         Their treasures are squandered again ;
4*f*   And hére in the gráve are all métals forbíd
4*a*   Save the tinsel that shines on the dark coffin-lid."—*Knowles.*

13.
a b a b c c

3*f*   "The músic of stréam and of bírd
3*a*   Shall come báck when the winter is ó'er ;
4*a*   But the vóice that was déarest to ús, shall be héard
         In our desolate chambers no more !
4*f*   The súnlight of Máy on the wáters shall quíver—
4*a*   But the líght of her éye hath depárted foréver !"—*Burdett.*

14.
a a b b

4*a*   "When the flówers of friéndship or lóve have decáyed
         In the heart that has trusted and once been betrayed,
4*f*   Nó súnshine of kíndness their blóom can restóre ;
         For the verdure of feeling will quicken no more !"—*Hoffman.*

4*a*+   "So I hópe, from hencefórward you né'er will ask, cán I maul
4*f*+   This téasing, concéited, rude, ínsolent ánimal.
         And if this rebúke might be túrned to his bénefit,
         (For I píty the mán,) I should be glad thén of it."—*Swift.*

a b a a b

4*f*   "A wárrior so bóld, and a vírgin so bríght,
3*f*   Convérsed as they sát on the gréen ;
         They gázed on each óther with ténder delíght,—
         Alonzo the Brave was the name of the knight,
         The maid—was the fair Imogene."—*Lewis.*

15.
a a b b c c d d e e

3*f*+   "A breáth of submíssion we bréathe not ;
         The swórd that we've dráwn we will shéathe not ;
4*f*   Its scábbard is léft where our mártyrs are láid,
         And the vengeance of ages has whetted its blade.
3*a*+   Earth may hide, waves ingulf, fire consume us ;
         But they shall not to slavery doom us :
4*a*   If they rule, it shall be o'er our ashes and graves ;
         But we've smote them already with fire on the waves,
3*a*+   And new triumphs on land are before us ;
         To the charge !—Heaven's banner is o'er us."—*Campbell.*

16.
a b a b

4*a*+   "When the bláck-lettered líst to the góds was presénted,
4*f*   (The list of what Fáte for each mórtal inténds,)
         At the long string of ills a kind goddess relented,
         And slipped in three blessings—wife, children, and friends."
                                                                Spencer.

17.

4*a*   "Should the témpest of wár overshádow our lánd,
4*f*+   Its bólts could ne'er rénd Freedom's témple asúnder ;
         For unmoved at its portals would Washington stand,
         And repulse with his breast the assaults of the thunder."—*Paine.*

18.

a b a b c c c b

4 a + "When a prince to the fáte of the peásant has yiélded,
4 f   The tap'stry waves dark round the dim-lighted hall;
              With 'scutcheons of silver the coffin is shielded,
4 f +   And páges stand múte by the cánopied páll:
4 a +   Through the cóurts, at deep mídnight, the tórches are gléaming;
              In the proudly-arched chapél the banners are beaming;
              Far adown the long isle sacred music is streaming,
              Lamenting a chief of the people should fall."—*Scott.*

19. LINES DIVISIBLE.

a b a b

4 f   "The cáptive usúrper, | Hurled dówn from the thróne,
         Lay buried in torpor, | Forgotten and lone."—*Byron.*

3. TROCHAIC VERSE.

1.

a a b b c

Túrning,
Búrning,
Chánging,
Ránging,
8 t c   "Fúll of grief and fúll of páin."
—*Addison.*

2.

a a b b c c, &c.

t c   "Sée him stríde
         Válleys wíde,
         Over woods,
         Over floods;
         So shall I
8 t c (Lófty póet !) toúch the skỳ."—*Swift.*

3.

a a b c c b

2 t   " 'Tis most cértain,
           Bý their flirting,
8 t c Wómen háve most énvy shówn;
           Pleased to ruin
           Others' wooing,
Never happy in their own."

4.

a b c b

8 t "Whizzing through the mountains,
2 t c   Búzzing ó'er the vále;
           Bless me! this is pleasant,
           Ríding on a ráil."—*Saxe.*

5.

a a a b c c c b

2 t   "Cléar wells spring not,
         . Swéet birds sing not,
           Loud bells ring not
d   Cheerfully;
           Herds stand weeping,
           Flocks all sleeping,
           Nymphs back creeping
               Fearfully."—*Shakespeare.*

6.

a b a b

2 t c   "Cán I céase to cáre,
8 t   Cán I céase to lánguish,
6 f   While my dárling fáir
              Is ón the coúch of ánguish?"
—*Burns.*

7.

4 t   "Thóugh we chárge to-dáy with
           fléetness,
8 t c   Though we dréad to-mórrow's
              skỳ,
           There 's a melancholy sweetness
           In the name of days gone by."
—*Tupper.*

8.

8 t c "Woò the fáir one, whén around
8 t   Eárly birds are sínging;
           When o'er all the fragrant ground
           Early herbs are springing."
—*Bryant.*

9.

           "Húsband, húsband, céase your strife,
7 f   Nor lónger idly ráve, sir;
         Though I ám your wédded wife,
7 f   Yét I'm nót your sláve, sir."—*Burns.*

10.

8 t c   "Nów the pine-tree's wáving tóp
8 t c   Géntly gréets the mórning gále;
     Kidlings now begin to crop
      Daisies in the dewy vale."
                      Cunningham.

12.

4 t   "Cáll not this the mónth of róses—
2 t o   Thére are nóne to blóom;
     Morning light, alas! discloses
8 t o   But the winter of the tomb."
                        Dewey.

13.

a a b c c b, &c.

8 t c   "Scóts who háve with Wállace bléd,
     Scots whom Bruce has often led,
     Welcome to the gory bed,
2 t o   Or to victory."—*Burns.*

Compare 8 t o with 4 i, 318, st. 44.

15.

a a b b c a, &c.

8 t o   "It shall cóme in émpire's gróans,
     Burning témples, trámpled thrónes!
     Then, Ambition, rue thy lust.—
     Earth to earth! and dust to dust!"
                        Croly.

17.

a b a b c d c d

4 t   "In the gréenest óf our válleys
8 t o   By good angels tenanted,
     Once a fair and stately palace
     (Snow-white palace) reared its héad;
     In the monarch Thought's dominion,
      It stóod thére;
     Never seraph spread a pinion
     Óver fábric hálf so fáir"—*Poe.*

19.

a b a b c c

2 t o   "Póet óf the heárt,
     Delving in its mine,
     From mankind apart,
     Yet where jewels shine;
3 t o   Héaving úpwards tó the líght,
     Precious wealth that charms the
      sight."—*Locke.*

20.

8 t o   "Hé that lóves a rósy chéek,
     Or a coral lip admires,
     Or from starlike eyes doth seek
     Fuel to maintain his fires;
     As old time makes these decay,
     So his flames must melt away."
                        Carew.

11.

8 t c   "Sóldier, rést! thy wárfare ó'er,
4 t   Sléep the sléep that knóws not
      breaking;
     Dream of battle-fields no more,
     Days of danger, nights of wak-
      ing."—*Scott.*

14.

a a b c c b

8 t   "Óft as súmmer clóses,
     When thine eye reposes
     On its lingering roses,
2 t o   Once so loved by thée,
     Think of her who wove them,
     Her who made thee love them;
8 f   Oh! thén remémber mé."
                        Moore.

16.

a a a b refrain

d 2 t o   "Whén the Alhámbra wálls re
      gáined,
8 t o   On the moment he ordained
     That the trumpet straight should
      sound
     With the silver clarion round.
8 t   Wó is mé, Alháma!"
                        Byron.

18.

a b a a a b c c d d

8 t o   "In a válley thát I knów,
t o   Happy scéne!
8 t o   Thére are méadows slóping
      lów,
     There the fairest flowers blow,
     And the brightest waters flow,
     All serene;
     But the sweetest thing to see,
     If you ask the dripping tree,
     Or the harvest-hoping swain,
     Is the rain."—*Hoyt.*

21.

a a b b

4 t   "Sée the rúddy mórning smiling,
     Hear the grove to bliss beguiling;
     Zephyrs through the woodland
      playing,
     Streams along the valleys stray-
      ing."—*Goldsmith.*

VERSIFICATION.—SCANNING.—TROCHAIC VERSE.   327

22.
a a b a b

4 *t* "Néver wédding, éver wóoing,
   Still a lovelorn heart pursuing,
   Read you not the wrong you're doing,
2 *t o* In my cheek's pale hue?
   All my life with sorrow strewing,—
   Wed, or cease to woo."
                            Campbell.

13.
a b c c a b a b

4 *t* "Ah! my heárt is éver wáiting,
2 *t o* Waiting for the May,—
   Waiting for the pleasant rambles
   Where the fragrant hawthorn brambles,
   With the woodbine alternating,
   Scent the dewy way.
   Ah! my heart is weary waiting,
   Waiting for the May."
                            Dublin Magazine

24.
a a b b

4 *t*   "Thén, methóught, I héard a hóllow soúnd,
4 *f*   Gáthering úp from áll the lówer groúnd;
        Nárrowing in to where they sát assémbled,
        Low volúptuoús músic, winding, trémbled."—*Tennyson.*

25.
a b a b

5 *t*   "Mountain-winds! oh! whither do ye cáll me,
4 *t o* Vainly, vainly, would my steps pursue:
        Chains of care to lower earth enthrall me,—
        Wherefore thus my weary spirit woo."—*Hemans.*

26. LINES DIVISIBLE.

a a, &c.

"Where the wood is waving, | Steady, green, and high,
Fauns and dryads, nightly, | Watch the starry sky."

27.
a b a b

6 *t*   "Up the déwy móuntain, | Héalth is bóunding lightly;
        On her brow a garland, | twined with richest posies:
        Gay is she, | elate with hope, | and smiling sprightly;
        Redder is her cheek | and sweeter than the rose is."—*G. Brown.*

28.
a a b b, &c.

7 *t*   "Thén in theé let thóse rejóice, | who séek thee, sélf-denýing,
        All who thy salvation love, | thy name be glorifying."

29.

7 *t o* "Cóme, and téll us, oúr Xiména, | loóking nórthward fár awáy
         O'er the camp of the invaders, | o'er the Mexican array."—*Whittier.*

        "Sóftly blów the évening bréezes, | Sóftly fáll the déws of níght;
         Yonder walks the Moor Alcanzor, | Shunning every glare of light."—*Percy*

30.

8 *t*   "Béams of nóon, like búrning lánces, | through the tree-tops fláah and glisten
         As she stands before her lover | with raised eyes to look and listen."
                                                              Whittier.

15

4. DACTYLIC VERSE.

Our literature has but little regular or pure dactylic verse.

1.
a a a b

2 d "Land of the Pilgrim's pride,
Land where my fathers died,
From ev'ry mountain-side
2 t Let freedom ring."—*Smith.*

2.
a a a b

2 d "Free from satiety
Care and anxiety,
Charms in variety,
d c Fall to his share."

3.
a a a b c c c b

2 d "Bright in her father's hall
Shields gleamed upon the wall,
Loud sang the minstrels all,
d t Chanting his glory;
When of old Hildebrand
I asked his daughter's hand,
Mute did the minstrel stand
2 i +or d t To hear my story."
Longfellow.

4.
a b a b

2 d "Take her up tenderly,
d e Lift her with care;
Fashioned so slenderly,
Young, and so fair!"—*Hood.*

5.

2 d "Where shall the lover rest,
d t Whom the fates sever
From his true maiden's breast—
Parted forever."—*Scott.*

6.
a a b c c b

2 d   "Bird of the wilderness
3 d e Blithesome and cumberless,
Light be thy matin o'er moorland and lea,
Emblem of happiness,
Blest is thy dwelling-place—
O, to abide in the desert with thee!"—*Hogg.*

7.
a b a b

2 d t e "Come from the mount of the leopard, spouse,
2 d t   Come from the den of the lion;
Come to the tent of thy shepherd, spouse,
Come to the mountain of Zion."—*G. Brown.*

8.
a a a b c c c b

3 d   "Boys will anticipate, | lavish, and dissipate
3 d e   All that your busy pate | hoarded with care;
And, in their foolishness, | passion, and mulishness,
Charge you with churlishness, | spurning your prayer."

9.
a a a b c c c b

3 d t 'Pause not to dream of the future before us;
Pause not to weep the wild cares that come o'er us;
Hark, how Creation's deep, musical chorus,
Unintermitting, goes up into heaven!
Never the ocean-wave falters in flowing;
Never the little seed stops in its growing;
More and more richly the rose-heart keeps glowing,
Till from its nourishing stem it is riven,"—*Osgood.*

10. LINES DIVISIBLE.

a a b b

8 d *l*
"Sée, in his wáywardness, Hów his fist doúbles;
Thus pugilistical, during life's troubles:
Strange, that the neophyte enters existence,
In such an attitude, feigning resistance."—*Hood.*

11

a a b b, &c.

4 d *c*
"Óften had moúntain-side, moúntain-side, bróad lake and strěam,
Gleamed on my waking thought, waking thought, crowded my dream."

12.

a b a b c c d e e d

8 d *t*
"Gréen be the gráves where her mártyrs are lýing!
8 d *c*
Shróudless and tómbless they súnk to their rést,
While o'er their ashes the starry fold flying
Wrapt the proud eagle they roused from his nest.
2 d
Bórne on her nórthern pine,
Long o'er the foaming brine
Spread her broad banner to storm and to sun;
Héav'n keep her éver free,
Wide as o'er lánd and sea
Floats the fair emblem her heroes have won."—*Holmes.*

13. LINES DIVISIBLE.

a b a b

5 d *t*
"Time, thou art éver in mótion | On wheéls of the dáys, years, and ágos;
Restless as waves of the ocean, | when Eurus or Boreas rages."
G. Brown's Gram.

14.

a a b b

7 d
"Oút of the kingdom of Christ shall be gáthered, by ángels o'er Sátan victórious,
All that offendeth, that lieth, that faileth to honor his name ever glorious."
Ib.

15.

7 d *c*
"Nimrod the húnter was mighty in húnting, and fámed as the rúler of cíties of yóre:
Babel, and Erech, and Accad, and Calneh, from Shinar's fair region his name afar bore."—*Ib.*

5. COMPOSITE VERSE.

IAMBICS AND ANAPESTS.

1.
"Our frée flág is dáncing
In the frée mountain áir,
And búrnished árms are gláncing,
And wárriŏrs gathĕring thére."
Bryant.

2.
"With a láugh and sóng we glide alóng,
Acróss the fleéting snów;
With friénds beside, how swift we ride
On the beaútiful tráck belów."
Fields.

Throughout this composite verse, show what feet compose each of the lines.

3.
"We búried him dárkly, at déad of night,
The sóds with our báyonets túrning;
By the strúggling moónbeams' misty light,
And the lántern dimly búrning."—*Wolfe.*

"'Twas the báttle-fiéld; and the cóld, pale moon
Looked dówn on the déad and dýing;
And the wind passed ó'er with a dirge and a wáil,
Where the yoúng and bráve were lýing."—*Landon.*

4.

"I knów where the yoúng May víolet gróws,
   In its lóne and lówly nóok;
On its mossy bank, where the large tree throws
   Its bróad dark boúghs, in sólemn repóse,
Far óver the silver bróok."—*Bryant.*

5.

"Thy heárt was a river | Withoút a máin—
Would I had lóved thee néver, | Flórence Váne.'—*Pendleton Cooke.*

6.

"There was ónce a little foúntain | That flówed awáy unseén
In the bosom of a mountain, | Where man had never been."—*C. Young.*

7.

"Let us gó, lassie, gó to the bráes of Bálquhither,
Where the bláe-berries gŕow 'mong the bónny híghland héather."—*Tannahill.*

8.

"O, the óld, old clóck, of the hoúsehold stóck, | Was the brightest thing and néatest;
The hánds, though óld, had a toúch of góld, | And its chime rang still the swéetest."

9.

"It was mány and mány a yéar agó, | In a kingdom bý the séa,
That a máiden there lived whom yoú may knów, | By the náme of Ánnabal Lée;
And this maiden she lived with no other thought | Than to love and be loved
by me."—*Poe.*

ALL THE FEET.

10.

"Night sinks on the wáve;
   Hóllow gústs are sighing;
Séa-birds, to their cáve,
   Throúgh the glóom are flýing."—*Hemans.*

11.

"Gó where glóry wáits thee,
But when fáme elátes thee,
Oh! still remémber mé," etc.
Moore.

12.

"It is written ón the róse,
   In its glóry's fúll arráy,—
Read whát those búds disclóse—
   Pássing awáy."—*Hemans.*

13.

"The depárted! the depárted!
They vísit ús in dréams;
And they glíde abóve our mémories
Like shadows over streams."

14.

"Óft in the stíllý níght,
   Ere slúmber's cháin has boúnd
      me,
Fond Mémorý brings the light
   Of óther dáys aróund me;
The smiles, the téars,
   Of bóyhood's yeárs,
The words of love then spoken;
   The eyes that shone,
   Now dim and gone,
The cheerful hearts now broken."
                                Moore.

15.

"Géntle and lóvely fórm,
   What didst thou hére?" &c.

16.

"Néar the láke where dróoped the willow,
   Long time ágó;
Where the rock threw back the billow
   Brightĕr thán snów;
Dwelt a maid beloved and cherished
   Bý high ănd lów;
But with autumn's leaf she perished,
   Long time ágó."—*Morris.*

17.

Or: "Mány áre the thóughts that cóme to mé | In my lónely músing;
      Mány áre the thóughts thăt cóme tŏ mé | In mỹ lónelỹ músing;
And they drift so stránge and swift, | There's no time for chóosing
Which to follow, for to leave any seems a losing."—*Cranch.*

18.

"Márch—márch—márch! Earth gróans as they tréad!
Each cárries a skúll; going dówn to the déad."—*Coxe.*

19.

" Knów ye the lánd where the cýpress and mýrtle
Are émblems of déeds that are dóne in their clíme—
Where the ráge of the vúlture, the lóve of the túrtle,
Now mélt into sóftness, now mádden to crime !
Knów ye the lánd of the cédar and víne,
Where the flowers ever blossom, the beams ever shine," etc.—*Byron*

20.

" Búsk ye, búsk ye, my bónny, bónny bride,
Busk ye, busk ye, my winsome marrow !
Busk ye, busk ye, my bonny bride,
And think nō mōre ŏn thĕ bráes of Yárrow."—*Hamilton.*

21.

" Wĭld rōved ăn Ĭndĭăn gĭrl, | Brĭght Ālfărātă.
Whĕre swĕep thĕ wátĕrs | Of thĕ blŭe Jŭnĭată.
Swĭft ăs ăn ăntĕlōpe | Through thĕ fŏrĕst góing,
Lōose wĕre hĕr jĕttў lŏcks | In wávy trésses flówing."

22.

" Mérrily swinging on brier and wĕed,
Néar to the nĕst of his little dàme,
Óver the moúntain-side or méad,
Róbert of Lincoln is télling his nāme—
Bób-o-link, Bób-o-link ;
Spink, spànk, spink ;
Snŭg and sáfe is that nĕst of oúrs
Hĭdden amóng the súmmer flówers.
Chĕe, chĕe, chĕe !"—*Bryant.*

This beautiful stanza is remarkable for a skillful combination of nearly all the feet.

Many songs are composite in their versification; and odes are frequently not only composite in metre, but very irregular in the length and rhyming of the lines.

Ex.— " 'Twas àt the róyal féast for Pérsĭă wón
  By Philip's warlike són ;
 Alóft, in áwful státe,
 The gódlike héro sáte
 On his impérial thróne :
 His váliant peérs were plăced aróund,
 Their bróws with róses and with mýrtle bóund ;
 So should desért in árms be crówned.
 The lóvely Tháis bý his síde
 Sat like a bloóming Eástern bride,
 In flówĕr ŏf yoúth and beaúty's príde.
  Háppy, háppy, háppy páir ;
   Nŏne bŭt thĕ bràve,
   Nŏne bŭt thĕ bràve,
 Nŏne bŭt thĕ bràve desérves the fáir," etc.—*Dryden.*

See Dryden's Ode on St. Cecilia's Day, Poe's Bells, Collins's Ode on the Passions, and Gray's Odes.

We sometimes meet with scraps of verse, formed chiefly with the design of being mechanically ingenious.

" She *drove* her *flock* o'er *mountains,*
 By *grove,* or *rock,* or *fountains.*"
" *Lightly* and *brightly* breaks away
 The morning from her mantle gray."—*Byron.*

" Now, O, now I needs must *part,*
 Parting though I *absent* mourn ;
 Absence can no *joy* impart,
 Joy once fled can ne'er return."

This is *line-rhyming* or *word-matching.*

"*T oward* yon *t owered* castle,
T ime-and-*rhyme*-renowned,
L ightly l et thy waves then
L ap the *steepy l* edges,
P our in *p urest* silver
P roudly, l oudly over,
D ancing d own with laughter,
D ashing, flashing onward," etc.
     Marsh's Lectures.

This is *line-rhyming* and *alliteration* combined. See page 261.

"*E* vening draws her rosy veil
L ovely o'er the western sky;
L ingering clouds in beauty sail
E re the night withdraws their dye.
N ot a wavelet," etc.

Such verse makes what is called an *acrostic.*

"Such sharpness shows the sweetest *friend,*
Such cuttings rather heal than *rend,*
And such beginnings touch their *end.*"

 cur- f- w- d- dis- and p-
A -sed -iend -rought -eath -ease -ain.
 bles- fr- b- br- and ag-

"A cursed fiend wrought death, disease, and pain;
A blessed friend brought breath and ease again."

Such verses have been called *task poetry.*

Faulty Lines.

Point out the errors:—

FAULTY MEASURE: "And the mountains will echo industry's glad song."

"Low shall they lie while ages after ages flee,
But their tomb shall stand a proud Thermopylæ."

FAULTY RHYME: "Should every hopeful prospect fade on life's uncertain way;
Should every tie that love has made, be rudely torn **away.**"

"Another story all the town will tell;
Phillis paints fair to look like an angeL."

BOTH: "And now, where shade and fountain meet,
Herds of horses and cattle feed."

INELEGANT RHYME: "Above the woody vales, on high
The eagle soars in majesty."

TOO MANY EPITHETS: "Dark-rolling, high in eddying wreaths uprising,
Awfully grand, majestically awful."

BAD IMAGERY: "Balmy zephyr, lightly flitting,
Shade me with your azure wing."

FAULTY THOUGHTS: "The smiles of joy, the tears of woe,
Deceitful shine, deceitful flow—
There's nothing true but Heaven."—*T. Moore.*

Smiles and tears may be deceitful; but smiles of joy, and tears of woe, are never so.

"Back from Miami, like a star he flies,
Meigs to assist to hurry the supplies."—*Fredoniad.*

What a sad falling-off, in the second line, from the epic grandeur assumed in the first!

"All the congregation arose in the pews that were numbered.
But, with a cordial look to the right hand and the left hand, the old man,
Nodding all hail and peace, disappeared in the innermost chancel.
Simply and solemnly now proceeded the Christian service;
Singing and prayer, and at last an ardent discourse from the old man."
                 Longfellow.

This is downright prose, and rather poor prose at that. "The pews *that were numbered*"—what a poetical idea!

OBSERVATIONS.

1. Poetry is closely allied to music, painting, statuary, and, indeed, to all the fine arts, of which it is the greatest. Its master passion is love, in the most enlarged sense of the term. In some poetry, thought predominates, as in Pope's Essay on Man; in some, feeling, as in Wolfe's Burial of Sir John Moore; in some the imagery, as in Moore's Lalla Rookh; in some the music, as in songs, which often have but little to recommend them, except that they are good vehicles for pretty tunes or airs. In some poetry are happily combined all the excellencies.

2. Poetry must be composed in accordance with the principles of correctness, and the traits of excellence, required in good prose; that is, it must possess fundamentally all the good qualities of good prose, and all deviations must be such, as make it poetry, and elevate it above prose, or such as impart to it some peculiar poetic excellence.

3. Poetry should be composed in a lofty or ardent glow of spirit; and a deficiency allowed in any of its essential qualities, should generally be atoned for by superior excellence in the other qualities.

4. Poetry, in its feet, cæsural pauses, rhymes, words, modes of expression, arrangement of words, and licenses, should be in accordance with the usage of the best poets, or in accordance with the principles in which the art itself is founded.

---

5. Such a mode of versification should always be chosen, as will best correspond with the sentiments of the intended poem.

6. When a certain stanza, or a certain mode of versification, has been adopted, there should not be, throughout the same poem, any departure from it, either in the kind of feet, in the number of feet to the respective lines, or in the mode of arranging the lines that rhyme. Regularity is one of the chief beauties of poetry.

Rhyming lines should not be allowed to come occasionally into blank verse; nor should lines of blank verse be occasionally interspersed among rhyming lines.

7. Rhymes should exactly correspond, or at least be allowable; that is, correspond sufficiently to be authorized by the usage of good poets.

8. When the merit of poetry is to depend on its structure as to quantity and accent alone, there must be regularity and great melody, or great excellence of thought, sentiment, and expression, to atone for the qualities that are wanting. Therefore most of our "Sapphics," "hexameters," and other fantastic imitations of what is found in ancient or in foreign languages, are hardly poetry according to the genius of our literature.

9. Songs are not always so regular as other poems. To write a good song requires great art, unless the mind happens to be one of those rare and fine ones in which nature has combined the poet and the musical composer. The best songs are written by learning the air, tune, or music first, and then setting it to words, or, rather, *wedding* it to words.

10. In the composition of odes, the poet may, in general, pursue whatever variety of versification he pleases, in order that he may express a varying train of feelings in rhythm suiting the different parts, and thus produce a much richer and better harmony than unvaried regularity could afford.

11. It seems to be a prevailing opinion among the people of western and of southern Asia, that poems—especially long ones—should be *varied* in versification, in order to produce the highest degree of pleasure. Scott, Byron, and Moore, have written many of their cantos thus, and successfully. The privilege, however, of using different feet promiscuously, or of varying the versification, can be allowed only to relieve monotony, or when such diversity will make the verse more expressive, or decidedly more agreeable than regular structure would make it.

12. We sometimes find, even in shorter poems that are not odes, a sort of wayward irregularity in the length and rhyming of lines. The propriety of such structure must, I suppose, be judged by the effect; and if it proves to be really the *inborn music of genius*, of course it is allowable. But perhaps the reader would rather hear a poet's opinion of it:—

"He [Halleck] is familiar with those general rules and principles which are the basis of metrical harmony; and his own unerring taste has taught him the exceptions which a proper attention to variety demands. He understands that the rivulet is made musical by obstructions in its channel. In no poet can be found passages which flow with more sweet and liquid smoothness; but he knows very well that to make this smoothness perceived, and to prevent it from degenerating into monotony, occasional roughness must be interposed."—*Bryant.*

13. Poets take unusual liberties with language, which are called *poetic licenses*. Greater liberty is allowed to them than to prose writers, chiefly in the choice of words, in the number of words, and in the arrangement of words. They sometimes use antiquated words, spelling, or pronunciation; they often shorten words, sometimes lengthen them, and sometimes exchange them for kindred words or forms. They sometimes adopt obsolete or foreign idioms. They allow unusual ellipses, unusual pleonasms, and frequent and sometimes violent inversions. In general, any arrangement of words is allowed that will preserve the sense.

14. Poetry may be faulty in the measure, in the rhyme, in the imagery, in the modes of expression, in the quality of the thoughts. But the worst and most common fault is that of making poetry out of gaudy language merely, or out of remembered poetic scraps and phrases. Such is most of the newspaper poetry, in which we have often been obliged to see the waves of the Pacific rolling about in the Mississippi Valley; rose-bushes blooming in January; buds, violets, roses, juicy peaches, golden apples, and twinkling stars, all flourishing promiscuously together. We have also heard nightingales sing on the Ohio river, and larks where surely they never were. True poetry does not consist in a jumbling-together of the images, words, and poetic expressions of other poets, but in exact copies or daguerreotypes of interesting parts of the world of nature or the world of soul, as conceived with a warm heart, a sprightly intellect, and a glowing imagination.

15. The ancients said, "The poet is born, not made." From his very infancy the beauties and melodies of earth impress themselves divinely on his soul. To him, the earth and the heavens seem full of spirituality and beauty; and, as he gazes upon them, his mind runs into delicious reveries, and revels in heavenly musings, perhaps long ere he lays his hand upon the enchanting lyre. With him, that train of thought which every person is said to have when awake, "runs to melody," or trips in poetic measures—in iambics, trochees, anapests, and dactyls. His knowledge is therefore all laid up poetically; and when a proper subject is held in the enkindling glow of his feelings, his thoughts come forth with the genuine poetic aroma, or crystallize around his theme in divine and imperishable lustre. Although we see new rhymes almost daily, there is but little of them that is real poetry; and there is no danger that the world will ever be overloaded with excellent poetry; for it is only now and then that a piece comes forth with so much divinity in it, that mankind are not willing ever to let it die.

17 PUNCTUATION.*

Punctuation is the art of applying certain points or marks to literary composition, in such a way as will present the sense and delivery to the best advantage. The chief use of points is to denote pauses.

The division into sentences, and parts of sentences, is made chiefly according to the *grammatical sense*, though it is sometimes influenced by delivery; as, "Approach, and behold, while I lift from his sepulchre its covering!"—*Dr. Nott.*

It may be well to remark, at the outset, that punctuation must necessarily vary with all the varieties of style; and that sometimes the same paragraph may be differently punctuated, and correctly too, according to the view that is taken of it. Indeed, it seems that capitals, Italics, and punctuation-marks generally, have acquired, like words, various meanings; so that we are at liberty to use them, and do use them, much in the same way as we use words; every person presenting his thoughts by their aid, of course with more or less advantage, according to his knowledge of their various meanings and uses. Uniformity, however, is a primary law; and the entire subject of punctuation is certainly something more than "a matter of taste." We should at least be careful not to use any notation unnecessarily, not to use one notation where a different one would express the sense better, and not to use the same notation—as the dash is sometimes used—in contradictory senses.

The principal marks of punctuation are the following *twelve* :—

The period............(.), | The dash..................(—),
The colon.............(:), | The curves................(( )),
The semicolon.........(;), | The brackets..............([ ]),
The comma.............(,), | The hyphen................(-),
The interrogation-point.(?), | The quotation-marks...(" " or ' '),
The exclamation-point..(!), | The underscore..(_____).

In applying these marks, discourse may be viewed as composed of paragraphs, sentences, clauses, phrases, words, and parts of words; all of which may be briefly termed *parts*.

The pauses are relative rather than absolute. The semicolon requires a pause double that of the comma; the colon, double that of the semicolon; and the period, double that of the colon, and sometimes even longer. Most of the other points require pauses that depend chiefly on the sense. Grave or solemn discourse requires longer pauses than that which is lively and spirited.

The division of his discourse into volumes, books, parts, cantos, verses, chapters, sections, paragraphs, and sentences, is left chiefly to every writer's own taste and judgment.

---

* It is said that Aldus Manutius and his grandson, two printers of Venice, devised Italics and the four principal points, about the beginning of the fifteenth century. The interrogation and exclamation points are ascribed to Spanish printers, and the dash has been ascribed to the French.—PERIOD means, literally, *a circuit of words;* COLON, *a member;* SEMICOLON *half a member;* and COMMA, *a part cut off.* See Metonymy, p. 299.

15*

A paragraph always begins anew, and consists of one or more sentences, comprising usually all that relates to one subject. Paragraphs are commonly kept apart by short breaks, or blank spaces.

A sentence must be complete, in sense and construction, with reference to what precedes it or follows it. It is, in general, so much of the author's discourse as he chooses to present as one thought.

1. PERIOD.

1. The **period** is put at the end of every complete sentence that is not interrogative or exclamatory.

    Ex.—" Begin and end with God."
    " If the counsel is good, no matter who gave it."
    " As yet, the forests stand clothed in their dress of undecayed magnificence. The winds, that rustle through their tops, scarcely disturb the silence of the shades below. The mountains and the valleys glow in warm green, of lively russet."—*J. Story.*

    Exercises.*—" He that wants health, wants every thing"
    " Give, then, generously and freely recollect, that, in so doing, you are exercising one of the most godlike qualities in your nature go home, and look at your families, smiling in rosy health, and then think of the pale, famine-pinched cheeks of the poor children of Ireland"—*S. S. Prentiss.*

2. It is sometimes used to separate sentences closely allied in sense and construction.

    Ex.—" The character of Washington is among the most cherished contemplations of my life. It is a fixed star in the firmament of great names, shining without twinkling or obscuration, with clear, steady, beneficent light. It is associated with all our reflections on things near and dear to us."— *Webster.*

Such sentences were formerly often separated by the colon, and are now sometimes separated by the semicolon.

    Exercises.—" No man ever lived under a more abiding sense of responsibility no man strove more faithfully to use time and talent as ever in the great Taskmaster's eye no man, so richly endowed, was ever less ready to trust in his own powers, or more prompt to own his dependence on his Maker"—*Review : Milton*

3. It sometimes separates sentences even when connected by conjunctions.

    Ex.—" It may be that the submissive loyalty of our fathers was preferable to that inquiring, censuring, resisting spirit that is abroad. And so it may be that infancy is a happier period than manhood, and manhood than old age. But God has decreed that old age shall succeed to manhood, and manhood to infancy. Even so societies have their law of growth."—*Macaulay.*

Sentences of this structure are also sometimes separated by the semicolon, or, where a greater point is needed, by the colon.

    Exercises.—" This scene is worth a voyage across the Atlantic yet here, as in the neighborhood of the Natural Bridge, are people who have passed their lives within half a dozen miles, and have never been to survey these monuments of a war between rivers and mountains, which must have shaken the earth itself to its centre"—*Jefferson*

---

* Insert points and capital letters, or whatever is needed to make the examples correct.

4. It is sometimes put modestly after a sentence that is expressed, for the sake of greater force, in the interrogative or exclamatory form, though declarative in sense; or when the interrogation or exclamation point would be too forcible.

Ex.—"To be a rebel or a schismatic, was surely not all that ought to be required of a man in high employment. What would become of the finances, what of the marine, if the Whigs who could not understand the plainest balance-sheet were to manage the revenue, and Whigs who had never walked over a dock-yard to fit out the fleet."—*Macaulay.*

Exercises.—" I thought my new acquirements would enable me to see the ladies with tolerable intrepidity; but, alas! how vain are all the hopes of theory, when unsupported by habitual practice"—*Eclectic Magazine*

5. It is used to separate words and phrases, when put for such entire sentences as any of the foregoing.

Ex.—"Æt. 19 +. Tender-eyed blonde. Long ringlets. Cameo pin. Gold pencil-case on a chain. Locket. Bracelet. Album. Autograph book. Accordion. Reads Byron, Tupper, and Sylvanus Cobb, junior, while her mother makes the puddings. Says, 'Yes?' when you tell her anything."—*O. W. Holmes.*

Exercises.—" Out with the boat here to the left that will do"

6. It is put after any word or phrase complete by itself, or sufficiently significant alone; as, headings, signatures, titles, directions, imprints, advertisements, etc.

Ex.—" For Sale." " Opinions of the Press." " Dr. B. Bruns, Chairman." " To the Honorable the Legislature of Virginia." " St. Louis, Aug. 1st, 1857." " The History of England, from the Accession of James the Second. By Thomas Babington Macaulay. Volume L Philadelphia: E. H. Butler & Co. 1860."

Exercises.—" Contents" " Apollo Garden" " From Punch" " Yours, truly, John Griscom" " To the Hon Edward Bates" " H Clay, Select Speeches of 8vo Price $1 00" " Popular Astronomy By O M Mitchell, LLD New York: Phinney, Blakeman, and Mason 1860"

" *Archbishop* What is your business, friend?

" *Gil Blas* I am the young man who was recommended to you"

7. The period is put after every abbreviation, and then supersedes no point except itself.

Ex.—" Albany, N. Y., Sept., 1860." " Henry Holmes, Esq., addressed the assembly." " Sir David Brewster, K. H., LL.D., F.R.S., L. & E."

Exercises.—" T S Glover, Esq , was called to the chair" " To Mr and Mrs Lindsay" " Dr I P Vaughan" " At 7 o'clock, P M" " To the Hon Wm B Clark, Sup't of Com Schools" " On the 4th inst he disappeared"

a. In compound numbers, the period usually supersedes the comma.

Ex.—"; T. 3 cwt. 2 qr. 8 lb. 3 oz."—*D. P. Colburn.* " £1. 10s. 6d."—*Wilson.*

b. When the abbreviation becomes itself a word, the period is not used.

Ex.—" Will Hardman had three sons; Tom, Ned, and George."—*Hawkesworth.* " 20 per cent advance."

Exercises.—" Rare Ben Johnson" "Gen Tom Thumb" "Pants were made for gents" " On the 1st inst, stocks were 5 per cent below par"

Such expressions as 1st, 2d, 2dly, 4th, 5th, do not take the abbreviating period; for they are not so much abbreviations as they are cardinal numbers made ordinal.

8. The period is put at the end of figures or letters that introduce enumerated parts.

Ex.—" 125. The Discontented Pendulum." "Lesson LXI.—On the Government of the Tongue." "I have two good reasons: . 1. I can not give my attention to it; 2. I have no money to invest in it." "Of this species there are two varieties: (a.) The preposition and present participle; (b.) The preposition and perfect participle."—*S. S. Greene.*

Exercises.—" 118 Practical Jokes" "Let us consider—1 Its soil; 2 Its climate "

a. The period is generally preferred, for the sake of neatness, after Roman or Arabic numerals, though the comma or the semicolon would often be more accurate; as, " Isa. lv. 3 ; Ezek. xviii. 20."

9. The period separates decimals from whole numbers.

Ex.—" 42.75 yds., for $9.055 +."

Exercises.—"The young lady at the blackboard answered, that 40 chickens, at 12 cents each, cost $480."

2. COLON.

1. The **colon** is the intermediate point between the period and the semicolon.

Ex.—" Some books are to be tasted, others to be swallowed, and some few to be chewed and digested: that is, some books are to be read only in parts; others to be read, but not curiously; and some few to be read wholly and with diligence."—*Bacon.*

Exercises.—A wicked man, in his iniquitous plans, either fails or succeeds if he fails, disappointment is embittered by reproach ; if he succeeds, success is without pleasure, for, when he looks around, he sees no smile of congratulation.—*Harper's Magazine.*

We have but faith we can not know;
For knowledge is of things we see;
And yet we trust it comes from thee
A beam in darkness let it grow.—*Tennyson.*

2. It is put at the end of a sentence, complete in sense, to which is annexed some additional remark or further explanation ; especially when the conjunction is omitted. In this sense it answers to How so ? Why so ? Explain more fully what you mean.

Ex.—" Our good and evil proceed from ourselves: death appeared terrible to Cicero, indifferent to Socrates, desirable to Cato."—*British Essayists*
' Princes have courtiers, and merchants have partners; the voluptuous have companions, and the wicked have accomplices: none but the virtuous can have friends."—*Johnson.*

"With diadem and sceptre high advanced,
The lower still I fall; only supreme
In misery: such joy ambition finds."—*Milton.*

Exercises.—What a fool am I to drudge any more at this woollen trade! for a lawyer I was born, and a lawyer I will be one is never too old to learn. —*Arbuthnot.* With regard to the faults of others, however, we say 'fear' "I fear he may be led into such and such an action."—*Whately.*

Dear Welsted, mark, in dirty hole,
That painful animal, the mole
Above ground never born to grow,
What mighty stir he keeps below !—*Pope.*

3. It is put at the end of whatever formally promises or introduces something, and ends with *as follows, the following, this, these, thus,* or suggests such a meaning.

Ex.—" Of cruelty to animals let the reader take the following specimen :— Running an iron hook into the intestines of a live animal; presenting this animal to another as his food; and then pulling up this second creature, and susending him by the barb in his stomach."—*Sydney Smith.*

" There are two questions which grow out of this subject: 1st. How far is any sort of classical education useful? 2dly, How far is that particular classical education adopted in this country useful?"—*Id.*

Exercises.—This is the state of man to-day he puts forth
The tender leaves of hope; to-morrow blossoms,
And bears his blushing honors thick upon him;
The third day comes a frost, a killing frost.—*Shakespeare.*

Mr. Wirt then rose, and began thus
"*Alumni of the University, ladies, and gentlemen*
" The occasion," etc.

4. Hence it is generally used to introduce a quoted paragraph or discourse.

Ex.— " ' The Press!—What is the Press?' I cried;
When thus a wondrous voice replied:
' In me all human knowledge dwells,
The oracle of oracles,' " etc.—*Montgomery.*

"He said to the men who carried away his trunk to the boat: 'Go, and fetch back my trunk; I will not go if my mother is to be made unhappy by it.' "—*Irving's Washington.*

The comma should be preferred, when there is a close dependence, and but a single quoted sentence; as, " He said, ' I will abide the consequences.' "

Exercises.—But Douglas round him drew his cloak,
Folded his arms, and thus he spoke
My manors, halls, and towers, shall still
Be open at my sovereign's will, etc.—*Scott.*

5. It has been frequently used to separate a figure from what it illustrates.

Ex.—" Ambition often puts men upon performing the meanest offices: so climbing and creeping are performed in the same posture."—*Swift.*

Exercises.—Small service is true service while it lasts;
Of friends, however humble, scorn not one
The daisy, by the shadow that it casts,
Protects the lingering dew-drop from the sun.—*Wordsworth.*

6. It was formerly much used, and is now sometimes used, to separate complete sentences that are more closely allied to one another than to what precedes or follows them. In this sense, the semicolon or the period is now often preferred.

Ex.—" Property is private, individual, absolute. Trade is an extended and complicated consideration: it reaches as far as ships can sail or winds can blow, it is a great and various machine. To regulate the numberless movements,' etc.—*Chatham.*

"That was enough: the spark had fallen: the train was ready: the explosion was immediate and terrible."—*Macaulay.*

"It is an intensely cold climate that is sufficient to freeze quicksilver: the climate of Siberia is sufficient to freeze quicksilver: therefore the climate of Siberia is intensely cold."—*Whately.*

But Sir William Hamilton writes, "He who conscientiously performs his duty is a truly good man; Socrates conscientiously performs his duty; therefore Socrates is a good man."

Exercises.—Lightning takes the readiest and best conductor; so does the electrical fluid lightning burns; so does electricity lightning sometimes destroys life animals have also been killed by lightning.—*Eclectic Magazine.*

7. In the grave or formal style, it is used after the address which stands next to the beginning of a letter or other writing.

Ex.—" HON. EDWARD EVERETT.
" *Dear Sir:*
" I thank you for your, etc.
" JOSEPH STORY."

In the familiar style, the comma, or the comma with the dash, is often preferred.
Ex.—" DEAR SIR,
"The latest news from Boston, giving information, etc.
" JAMES MADISON."

There is great diversity as to the mode of punctuating such phrases. When the period is put after the first address, it shows simply to whom the letter is sent, which then begins with the next address; but when an inferior point is placed after the first phrase, the person is addressed by name as if he were present to the writer. The neatest form seems to be that of putting a period after the first address, and a comma after the second, if the phrases occupy different lines; and a period with a dash after the first, and a colon after the second, if they are in the same line with the beginning of the letter.

" GEORGE W. TAYLOR, ESQ.
" *Dear Sir*,
" As you write me to give," etc.

" GEORGE W. TAYLOR, ESQ.—*Dear Sir:* As you write me to give my opinion," etc.—*The Printer.*

8. It is used after words or phrases that stand at the beginning of sentences, and have the sense referred to in the third rule of this section. Indeed, the chief use of the colon is, to show that the part before it is incomplete and promissory, and that the part after it contains the main thought, or an important appendage to it.

Ex.—" For example: 'When the verb is *a* passive, the agent and object change places.' Better: When the verb is *passive*, the agent and the object change places."—*G. Brown.*

"No: this is not learning: it is chemistry or political economy—not learning."—*Eclectic Magazine.*

Exercises.—To sum up all If we must, etc.
Terms Three Dollars a Year, invariably in Advance.

It is sometimes put between a subject and what is said of it.

Ex.—"Kansas: what can you say of it?"—*School Geography.* This usage does not seem to be well established.

9. It is sometimes used to separate the name of a person or thing from that of the locality; or a second reference from a first.

Ex.—"A layer of Slate in Hornblende: Cornwall, England."—*Hitchcock.*

Exercises.—"London   Partridge & Co."   "EDGAR A. POE   *The Pioneer.*"

But, in phrases like the following, the comma is used: "To Wm. Holmes, No 25, Spruce Street."

It is sometimes used, though improperly, as a mark of abbreviation.

Ex.—"To Chas: D. Drake, Esq."; better, "To Chas. D Drake, Esq."

10. It is used as the sign of proportion.

Ex.—2 : 4 : : 3 : 6 — As two is to four, so three is to six.

The colon, in most of its senses, is akin to the dash; and hence, when the ause which accompanies the colon would be too long, the dash is sometimes referred.

3. SEMICOLON.

1. The **semicolon** is used as the next greater point than the comma, or as intermediate between the comma and the colon or period.

It is often used when related parts already have the comma, and a greater point is needed.

Ex.—"Without dividing, he destroyed party; without corrupting, he made a venal age unanimous."—*Grattan.*

"The Indians are taken by surprise: some are shot down in their cabins; others rush to the river, and are drowned; others push from the shore in their birchen canoes, and are hurried down the cataract."—*Bancroft.*

Exercises.—If it was intended for us as well as for you, why has not the Great Spirit given it to us and not only to us, but why did he not give to our forefathers the knowledge of that book with the means of rightly understanding it?—*E. Everett.*

A love of equality is another strong principle in a republic therefore it does not tolerate hereditary honor or wealth and all the effect produced on the minds of the people by this fictitious power is lost, and the government weakened but, in proportion as the government is less able to command, the people should be more willing to obey.—*British Essayists.*

2. It frequently separates two clauses, connected by *but, for, and,* or some other connective, when they are not very closely dependent on each other.

Ex.—"That the world is overrun with vice, can not be denied; but vice, however predominant, has not yet gained unlimited dominion."—*Johnson.*

"Keep thine heart with all diligence; for out of it are the issues of life."—*Bible.*

"He is, indeed, a horse; and all other jades you may call beasts."—*Shakespeare.*

a. The conjunction or connective is sometimes omitted.

Ex.—"The miser grows rich by seeming poor; an extravagant man grows poor by seeming rich."—*Proverb.*

Exercises.—"The town was set on fire and a witness of the scene relates that two thousand Indians were slain, suffocated, or burned."—*Bancroft.*

Napoleon was an early riser so were Frederick the Great, Charles the Twelfth, and Washington.

When the latter part is a mere phrase, the comma is preferred before it, even when the part itself is subdivided by the comma.

Ex.—"And therefore will I take the Nevil's part, and, when I spy advantage, claim the crown."—*Shakespeare.*

3. It is used to separate short related sentences, when two or more of these are gathered into one sentence.

Ex.—"Listen to the advice of your parents; treasure up their precepts; respect their riper judgment; and endeavor to merit the approbation of the wise and good."

"On the land were large flocks of magpies and American robins; whole fleets of ducks and geese navigated the river, or flew off in long streaming files; while the frequent establishment of the pains-taking beaver showed that the solitudes of these waters were seldom disturbed even by the all-pervading savage."—*Irving.*

Exercises.—He suffered much oppression he was often imprisoned he was finally compelled to go into exile.—*Macaulay.*

Epic poetry recites the exploits of heroes tragedy represents disastrous events comedy ridicules the vices and follies of mankind pastoral poetry describes rural life and elegy displays the tender emotions of the heart.

4. Either of the principal elements, and, generally, any of the modifying elements, can be so extended as to make a loose series, whose parts may be separated by the semicolon, especially if any of them are subdivided by the comma. This has been called the *enumerative sense.* The dash is sometimes used, though less properly.

Ex.—"To give an early preference to honor above gain, when they stand in competition; to despise every advantage which can not be gained without dishonest arts; to brook no meanness, and stoop to no dissimulation,—are the indications of a great mind."

"As a traveler, Smith had roamed over France; had visited the shores of Egypt; had returned to Italy; and, panting for glory, had sought the borders of Hungary, where had long existed an hereditary warfare with the followers of Mahomet."—*Bancroft.*

"'I have always,' says Ledyard, 'remarked that women in all countries are civil and obliging, tender and humane; that they are ever inclined to be gay and cheerful, timorous and modest; and that they do not hesitate, like men, to perform a generous action.'"

Exercises.—The disposition to insult and mockery is awakened by the softness of foppery, the swell of insolence, the liveliness of levity, or the solemnity of grandeur by the sprightly trip, the stately stalk, the formal strut, and the lofty mien by gestures intended to catch the eye, and looks elaborately formed as evidence of importance.—*Johnson.*

A salad should be, as to its contents, multifarious as to its proportions, an artistic harmony as to its flavor, of a certain pungent taste.—*Ec. Magazine.*

False in institutions, for he retrograded false in policy, for he debased false in morals, for he corrupted false in civilization, for he debased.—*Lamartine.*

5. An explanatory or appositive phrase, an adjective phrase, a participial phrase, or any other phrase, especially when elliptical, or ubdivided by the comma, is often set off by the semicolon.

Ex.—"It was a voyage of discovery; a circumnavigation of charity."—*Burke.*

"Mercer was upright, intelligent, and brave; esteemed as a soldier and beloved as a man, and by none more so than by Washington."—*Irving.*

"Charles the Twelfth, of Sweden; born, 1682; killed by a cannon-ball, 1718."

Exercises.—Eloquence is action noble, sublime, godlike action.—*Webster.*

I assure you I will never go to see her no, not I.—*Edgeworth.*

There are three persons the first, the second, and the third.—*G. Brown.*

This lovely land, this glorious liberty, these benign institutions, are ours ours to enjoy, ours to preserve, ours to transmit.—*Webster.*

I will never give my consent to such an undertaking never, never, never!—*Chatham.*

He is my major-domo that is, my steward, or superintendent over household affairs.—*Prescott.*

Among the oaks, I observed many of the most diminutive size some not above a foot high, yet bearing bunches of small acorns.—*Irving.*

6. It is generally used before *as*, introducing an example.

Ex.—" *Can* signifies ability; as, 'I can read.'"

Exercises.—Not wet as, " Dry hay" " Dry wood."—*Worcester.*

7. The semicolon, considered simply as a greater point than the comma, is much applied to phrases, or series of phrases, that are not emotional.

Ex.—"The Minstrel; or, The Progress of Genius."—*Beattie.*

"State vs. John O'Neal, larceny; dismissed."—*Newspaper.*

"INESTIMABLE. Too valuable or excellent to be rated; being above all price; as, 'inestimable rights.'"—*N. Webster.*

"A dress of blue silk; plain, high body; the waist and point of a moderate length; the skirt long and full, with two broad flounces pinked at the edge."—*Harper's Magazine.*

"Contents: Fate; Power; Wealth; Culture; Behavior; Worship; Considerations by the Way; Beauty; Illusion."—*Atlantic Monthly.* Here the comma would have slurred over the matter too lightly, or not given it the desired importance.

Exercises.—Rio, 9 cents Maracaibo, 12 cents Java, 15 cents.

In sight of Santa Fé made an early start came to a fine spring shot an antelope saw a herd of wild horses, etc., etc.

Contributors Dr. O. W. Holmes Mrs. Sigourney Gilmore Sims, Esq.

4. COMMA.

1. The **comma** is generally used where the sense requires a short pause, but not sufficiently great for the semicolon.

Ex.—"It was supposed to be an island, and received the name of Florida from the day on which it was discovered, and from the aspect of the forests, which were then brilliant with a profusion of blossoms, and gay with the fresh verdure of early spring."—*Bancroft.*

Exercises.—There upon a point of land at the entrance of the haven a lofty cross was erected bearing a shred with the lilies of France and an appropriate inscription.—*Id.*

From the hills in his jurisdiction he could behold across the clear waters of a placid sea the magnificent vegetation of Porto Rico which distance rendered still more admirable as it was seen through the transparent atmosphere of the tropics.—*Id.*

Perhaps almost all punctuation in regard to the comma, might be reduced to the four following heads:—

1. The **serial sense.** Two parts, connective,—no comma; more parts, or
2. The **parenthetic sense.** Comma. [two without connective,—comma.
3. The **explanatory sense.** Comma.
4. The **restrictive sense.** No comma.

If any one will examine the punctuation of a well-pointed book, he will probably be surprised to see how far these four principles reach. We might easily enlarge on this view of the subject, but, to make as little innovation as possible, we shall consider the comma,—

First, with reference to compound sentences.
Secondly, with reference to simple sentences, and smaller parts.

2. The comma is used to separate the clauses of a compound sentence, when they are too closely connected for the semicolon.

Ex.—"There mountains rise, and circling oceans flow."—*Pope.* "How wretched, were I mortal, were my state."—*Id.* "The beautiful fern lies in rusty patches on the open hill-side, though within the woods it is still fresh and green.' —*Cooper.* "Columbus, who discovered America, was a Genoese." "But occasions are past, the hour of their reckoning is nigh at hand, even now my twilight is coming on, and my hopes are darkening into regrets."—*Ec. Magazine.*

Exercises.—Since life is short let us not be too solicitous about the future. I can not succeed unless my friends assist me. Where the carcass is there will the buzzards be gathered. Either a sterner course must be pursued with him or he must be sent to some other school. What you leave at your death let it be without controversy else the lawyers will be your heirs. Wealth is of no real use except it be well employed. Such was the terrible explosion of the boat that not a life was saved. So violent were the wind and rain that our wheat was destroyed. I go but I return. Whatever we ardently wish to gain we must in the same degree be afraid to lose. Her mouth costs her nothing for she never opens it but at others' expense. And yet after all it is man it is mind it is intelligent spirit that gives to this grand theatre of the material universe al. its worth all its glory. The farmer who had never been in a city before and who was therefore most easily duped at once bid on the watch. When public bodies are to be addressed on momentous occasions when great interests are at stake and strong passions excited nothing is valuable in speech farther than it is connected with high moral and intellectual endowments. If it be in the spring of the year and the young grass has just covered the ground with a carpet of delicate green and especially if the sun is rising from behind a distant swell of the plain no scene can be more lovely to the eye.

a. The clauses are sometimes elliptical, but punctuated as if they were not so.

Ex.—"The wind was the keenest, and the snow the deepest, that ever annoyed a traveler." "Husbands were torn from their wives, and children from their parents." "Say, shall my bark attendant sail?" "A peal of gunpowder was heard on the water, and another, and another."

Exercises.—If so the worst might well be expected. My pen diverged to the right then to the left. And there was now no talk no sport no rest but dig gold wash gold refine gold load gold. There was a greater variety of colors in the embroidery of the meadows a more lively green in the leaves and grass a brighter crystal in the streams than I met with elsewhere.

3. A clause is not set off when restrictive, or when it depends closely on something else, and has the sense of a noun, an adjective, or an adverb. Such are—

a. Restrictive relative clauses.

Ex.—"He was a man whom nothing could turn aside from the path which duty pointed out." "I plucked such plums as were ripe." "I will sell you whatever you wish to buy."

b. Clauses beginning with *as, because, how, if, lest, than, that, when, where, whether, while, why,* or other adverbs of time, place, or manner, and closely depending on the preceding clause.

Ex.—" He has acted as an honorable man should act." " He is not the less a gentleman because he is poor." " Edwin saw how happy the old bird was with her nestlings." " Tell me when it was that you saw him." " There is nothing humbler than ambition when it is about to climb." " Do you know whether he is at home." " Come as the waves come when navies are stranded."

c. Clauses from which the antecedent or the relative is omitted, or the conjunction *that,* to make the connection still closer. Indeed, restrictive clauses, like other clauses, are frequently elliptical.

Ex.—" Take which you like." " I saw the book you mentioned." " He thought he had never seen any thing quite so beautiful before." "A good name is rather to be chosen than great riches."

Exercises.—He deserved neither the reproaches which had been cast upon him while the event was doubtful nor the praises which he received when it had proved successful. It is such men as he is that bring the party into disrepute. Avoid a slanderer as you would a scorpion. Tory writers have with justice remarked that the language of these compositions was as servile as any thing that could be found in the most florid eulogies pronounced by bishops on the Stuarts. He informed them whence we came whither we were going who we were. The rain fell in sheets the thunder rolled the lightning flashed fierce and lurid and the wind swept in gusts over the thicket as if it would uproot it altogether. We weep over the dead because they have no life and over the living because they have no perfection. The variety of wild fruits and flowering shrubs is so great and such the profusion of blossoms with which they are bowed down that the eye is regaled almost to satiety.

4. **A word or phrase having the sense of a clause that would be set off by the comma, is also set off by the comma.**

Such are frequently participial or adjective phrases, when they are explanatory, or not restrictive.

Ex.—" By assisting him, you will benefit yourself;" i. e., " If you assist him," etc. " Ores are natural compounds, being produced by nature." " I dislike all misery, voluntary or involuntary."

Exercises.—No child's play to make a breach here. Some Cromwell guiltless of his country's blood. It is morning and a morning sweet fresh and beautiful. There was a Grecian liberty bold and powerful full of spirit eloquence and fire. The blast seemed to bear away the sound of the voice permitting nothing to be heard but its own wild howling mingled with the creaking and rattling of the cordage and the hoarse thunder of the surges striving like savage beasts for our destruction.

5. **Simple sentences do not usually require the comma.**

Ex.—" The real security of Christianity is to be found in its benevolent moral ity." " Perhaps in this neglected spot is laid some heart once pregnant with celestial fire."—*Gray.*

Exercises.—To be, contents his natural desire. The blossoms of spring and the fruits of autumn, give pleasure to the soul.

6. **When the entire subject is a clause, or a long participial or infinitive phrase; when it has a clause, a long adjunct or other similar phrase, or parts requiring the comma; when it ends with a verb, or with a noun that might improperly be read as the nominative;**

or when a word precedes the verb, that would otherwise be of doubtful character or reference,—it seems best to separate the subject from its predicate.

Ex.—"That one bad example spoils many good precepts, is well known.' "He that has much nose, thinks every one speaks of it." "Whatever improves him, delights him." "To be totally indifferent to praise or censure, is a real defect in character." "For me to furnish him so large and expensive an outfit, is utterly impossible." "His having been seen in the neighborhood, was the ground of suspicion." "Honor, affluence, and pleasure, seduce the heart." "Necessity, that great excuse for human frailty, breaks through all law."

There is a strong tendency to omit the comma from before the predicate of such sentences as the first seven of the foregoing.

Exercises.—He who falls in love with himself will have no rivals. Whatever is is right. Who does nothing knows nothing. To maintain a steady course amid all the adversities of life marks a great mind. What the design of these men was has never been ascertained. Family feuds violated friendships and litigations with neighbors are the banes of society. Flames above around beneath and within devour the edifice. Divide and conquer is a principle equally just in science and in policy.

7. When the predicate-nominative is a long clause or infinitive phrase, and immediately follows the verb *be*, it is usually set off, especially when it has the air of importance, and might be made the subject.

Ex.—"One of the greatest secrets in composition is, to know when to be simple."—*Blair.* "Their service was, to grind the corn and carry the baggage."—*Irving.* "But the question is, are the examples correct in syntax?"—*G. Brown.* "The consequence is, that most animals have acquired a fear of man."—*Nat. History.*

Exercises.—The great mystery about the theft was that the door was found still locked as before. All that a man gets by lying is that he is not believed when he speaks the truth. The question that is to be discussed to-night by the speakers is "Would the Extension of our Territory endanger our Liberties?"

8. Three or more serial terms, or two without their connective, are separated by the comma.

An adjective qualifying others after it with a noun, is not set off; as, "Two large black horses." "The little, round buds unfolded into broad white blossoms."

Ex.—"No virtue, no eminence, conferred security."

"Hedges, trees, groves, gardens, orchards, woods, farm-houses, huts, halls, mansions, palaces, spires, steeples, towers, and temples, all go wavering by, as the steed skims along, to the swelling or sinking music of the hounds, now loud as a regimental band, now faint as an echo."—*Prof. Wilson.*

"Far above us towered an iron-bound coast, dark, desolate, barren, precipitous, against which the long, rolling swell of the Pacific broke with a dull, disheartening roar."—*California.*

Exercises.—A virgin of eighteen tall and straight bright blooming and balmy seems to our old age a very beautiful and delightful object.—*Prof. Wilson.* But in truth that amplitude and acuteness of intellect that vivacity of fancy that terse and energetic style that placid dignity half courtly half philosophical which the utmost excitement of conflict could not for a moment derange belonged to Halifax and to Halifax alone.—*Macaulay.*

9. When the terms of a series are joined in pairs, they should be separated in pairs by the comma.

Ex.—" I inquired and rejected, consulted and deliberated, till the sixty-second year made me ashamed of wishing to marry."—*Johnson.*

Exercises.—The poor and the rich the weak and the strong have all one Father. Neither time nor distance neither weal nor woe can separate us.

10. Two terms connected by *and, or,* or *nor,* are not separated by the comma.

Ex.—" Seed-time and harvest shall not fail." " Did a father or a mother ever watch over him ?" " To feel no guilt and to fear no accusation, is the prerogative of innocence."

Exercises.—Here thy temple was, and is. The proper authorities were overlooked, or slightly regarded. Neither the love of fame, nor the fear of shame can make him stoop to an unjust action.

11. But when a part of one of the terms might improperly be referred to the other; when *or* adds a substantive in the explanatory sense merely; when the terms are unusually long; or when the latter term is strongly emphatic or parenthetic,—the two are separated by the comma.

Ex.—" The gleam of the ocean, and vast prairies of verdure, were before us." " The skull, or cranium, protects the brain." " That the king would retreat, or that the people would lay down their arms, was not to be expected." " Approach, and behold, while I lift from his sepulchre its covering !"

Exercises.—'Twas certain he could write and cipher too. He went and addressed the crowd. The English dove or cushat is also noted for its cooing or murmuring. Othello and Prince Hamlet. "There was now no way left but to retreat and load his gun."—*Willson's Readers.*

12. Repeated words or expressions are generally separated by the comma.

Ex.—" Home, home! sweet, sweet home!" " Verily, verily, I say unto you."

Exercises.—I I I am the man. Quickly quickly come away
The old oaken bucket the iron-bound bucket
The moss-covered bucket which hung in the well!

13. Two terms contrasted, or emphatically distinguished, are generally separated by the comma.

Ex.—" It is used so, but erroneously." " Though poor, luxurious; though submissive, vain." " He was impulsive, yet prudent." " To soften, not to wound, the heart." " He read novels, in stead of law."

Exercises.—By honor and dishonor by evil report and good report as chastened and not killed as sorrowful yet always rejoicing as poor yet making many rich.

14. The comma often cuts off a part, to show its common dependence on two or more parts which are themselves separated by the comma.

A predicate is thus set off, when it relates to separated nominatives preceding 't; a restrictive relative clause, when it relates to separated antecedents; a substantive, when it is preceded by two adjectives or prepositions that are separated by intervening matter; and parts generally that relate to separated words from which the connective is omitted.

Ex.—"The benches, chairs, and tables, were thrown down." "The wheat, corn, and hay, which it produces, are of the best quality." "They were received without distinction in public, and consequently in private, payments."—*Macaulay.* "Such implied covenants as are annexed to, and of course run with the reversion."—*Chitty.*

Exercises.—The water was as bright and pure and seemed as precious as liquid diamonds. But no such rule had ever been or ever would be formed. And all that beauty all that wealth e'er gave. The classics possess a peculiar charm from the circumstance that they have been the models I might almost say the masters of composition and thought in all ages.

When a negative and an affirmative phrase stand loosely after another part, both are set off by the comma; if the former phrase is in close combination with the verb, only the latter phrase is set off by the comma. "The pedant was therefore heard by him, not only with weariness, but with malignity;" "The pedant was therefore heard not only with weariness, but with malignity."

15. A word, phrase, or clause, that is parenthetic, or that breaks the connection of parts closely connected, is set off by the comma.

A part thus set off stands most frequently after a conjunction, an adjective, or an adverb, between a nominative and its verb, between the parts of a verb, or between a verb and its object or adjunct.

Ex.—"They set out early, and, *before the dawn of day*, arrived at the destined place." "Prudence, *as well as courage*, is necessary to overcome obstacles." "Burns, to be rightly judged, must be estimated by the times in which he lived." "Adjectives, when something depends on them, or when they have the import of a dependent clause, should, with their adjuncts, be set off by the comma."

Exercises.—Her magnificent hair black and glossy as a raven's wing fell in thick clusters almost to her knees. Bodily exercise especially in the open air is of the greatest importance to health. No disturbance however took place. The mother to save her infant sacrificed herself. Halifax mortified by his mischances in public life began to pine for his seat in Nottinghamshire. Cover your flowers for if they are unprotected to-night the frost will kill them. They knew their powers not or as they learned to know perverted them to evil.

When such parts stand at the beginning or the end of a sentence or member, they are also generally set off by the comma.

The most common parenthetic expressions are *however, surely, indeed, perhaps, also, then, too, therefore, likewise, moreover, furthermore, consequently, nevertheless, accordingly, unquestionably, doubtless, meanwhile, lastly, finally, namely, of course, in fact, to be sure, no doubt, in short, in general, in reality, in a word, in that case, in the mean time, in the first place, in every respect, for the most part, without doubt, beyond question, now and then, on the contrary, on the other hand, generally speaking, as it were.*

The chief of those set off that usually stand at the beginning, are *yes, no, well, why, now, again, first, secondly,* etc.

When a parenthetic part is short, or but slightly interrupts the flow of other words, it is not set off; as, "It is *perhaps* true;" "Gladly would we pour *into thy bosom* the balm of consolation."

16. But when the part is restrictive, it is not set off from that which it modifies.

Ex.—"He was one day in a field near a pond in which several geese were swimming." "The work is not worth the care and labor expended upon it." "The tree fell thundering to the ground."

Exercises.—Trees growing at the base of mountains are taller than those on the summit. The carriage and horses necessary to conduct you there will be here early in the morning. The horse ran two miles, in five minutes and thirty seconds. How dare you breathe that air, which wafted to Heaven the curses of those who fell a sacrifice to your ambition? When statesmen heroes kings in dust repose. Our recruits stood, shivering and rubbing their hands.

17. An adjunct, an adjective phrase, a participial phrase, an infinitive phrase, or a clause, that stands by inversion at the beginning of a sentence or member, is generally set off by the comma.

The comma is also placed after a surname when it precedes the Christian name; as, "Pope, Alexander; a British poet." "Smith, John H."

Ex.—"To her, many a soldier, on the point of accomplishing his ambition, sacrifices the opportunity." "On that plain, in rosy youth, they had fed their father's flocks." "Calm, attentive, and cheerful, he confutes more gracefully than others compliment." "Having nothing else to do, I went." "To make this clear, I must tell you an old story." "When spring returns, the flowers will bloom."

Exercises.—Of making many books there is no end. Large ripe and delicious were the plums. Large ripe delicious were the plums. Tired of his toilsome flight and parched with heat he spied at length a cavern's cool retreat. To meet to check to curb to stand up against him we want arms of the same kind. Whether he is the man I do not know.

If the extremities are related, or if the adjunct is short and unemphatic, or stands next to the verb, the comma is generally omitted; as, "*Such a horse* I would not *buy.*" "*What* is now called a ministry he did not think of *forming.*" "*For them* no more the blazing hearth shall *burn.*" "At the corner of the garden stood a tall poplar."

18. A part is often set off by the comma, that it may not affect something next to it; or to show its dependence on something remote, from which it is separated by intervening matter; or when it stands at the beginning or the end, and adds an idea rather than modifies an idea.

An adjunct, following another, or removed from what it modifies, is thus frequently set off; also an infinitive phrase, when it is removed a considerable distance from what it modifies.

Ex.—"Why, were you not there?" "He applied for the situation, without a recommendation." "No society, of which moral men are not the stamina, can exist long." "Whoever lives wickedly, must perish." "He is so young and inexperienced in the business, as to be unqualified." "He bought up all the mules he could find, to sell them again."

Exercises.—The relations of nouns verbs or modifying words to other words. The ancients separated the corn from the ear by causing an ox to trample on the sheaves. And why did you not go then? No sir never. To these bears seldom go. Is it not a melancholy thing to see a man clothed in soft raiment lodged in a public palace and endowed with a rich portion of other men's industry using all the influence of his splendid situation however unconsciously to deepen the ignorance or inflame the fury of his fellow-creatures?

19. Independent or absolute words, with what belongs to them, are generally set off by the comma.

Such parts are nominatives independent, nominatives absolute, and sometimes interjections or adverbs.

Ex.—" And so, Don Gomez, you will accompany us." "And now, sir, what is your conclusion?" "Nocturnal silence reigning, a nightingale began." " O, yes, I do." " Shame being lost, all virtue is lost."

Exercises.—Friend John what 's wanted? To you Osman I consign half the city to you Mustapha the remainder. Thou whining budget of quack medicines why not take up thy boarding at once in an apothecary's shop! To be a merchant the art consists more in getting paid than in making sales. The work being done we returned home. Front to front their horns locked every muscle strained they were fighting as bulls only can fight. Why what 's the matter? Again we conceive that natural theology though not a demonstrative is yet a progressive science.

20. When an appositive, or a phrase having an appositive, is affected by a preceding verb, or when it rather completes an idea than adds an idea, it is not set off; otherwise it is, especially when parenthetic or explanatory.

Of parts not separated, we have—*noun* with *noun* or *adjective*; as, "The River Hudson," "Read the artist," "Alexander the Great: *pronoun* with *pronoun*; as, "*He himself* went: *pronoun* with *noun*; as, "*Ye men* of Altorf."

Ex.—"They made him captain." "The nation regarded him as the proper chief of the administration." "I myself saw it." "His Excellency the Governor." "The terms *reason* and *instinct*." "It is foolish to lay out money in a purchase of repentance." "It is through inward health that we enjoy all outward things."

"It is related of Tecumseh, the Indian warrior, that he would keep a promise even toward an enemy." "Paul, the apostle of the Gentiles." "The greatest Roman orator, Cicero, was distinguished for his patriotism." "As a race, they have withered from the land." "This vastly more significant idea, that the earth is a globe, had by no means become incorporated into the general intelligence of the world."

Exercises.—The darkness he called night. Plutarch calls lying, the vice of slaves. At Bushnell's the bookseller. At Bushnell, the bookseller's. Walter the second son is a captain in the navy. The poet Burns. Matthew the publican. Thou traitor hence! Moses the lawgiver, and God's first pen.

21. The comma is often inserted where a finite verb is omitted.

Ex.—" From law arises security; from security, curiosity; and from curiosity, knowledge."

The comma is omitted, when the interruption is but slight, and when the elliptical clauses depend in common on a part set off by the comma; as, " The weather was fine, the sleigh new, and the road good "

Exercises.—Hamilton was more declamatory imaginative and poetical; Burr clear pointed concise and compact. Shakespeare wrote his poetry and Bacon his philosophy in the reign of Queen Elizabeth.

22. A quotation closely depending on a verb or other word, is generally set off by the comma.

Ex.—" 'Knowledge is power,' says the father of modern philosophy."

Exercises.—I say unto all Watch. Out spoke the hardy Highland wight " I'll go my chief—I'm ready." There is much truth in the proverb " Without pains no gains." It hurts a man's pride to say "I do not know."

To facilitate the reading of large numbers that are not dates, the comma is used to separate them into periods; as, " The population of the United States is 81,443,790." It is generally omitted when the numbers are expressed in words; as, " Five million six thousand four hundred and twenty."

5. INTERROGATION-POINT.

1. The **interrogation-point** is put at the end of every direct question.

Ex.—" Well, James, what have you got there ?"

Exercises.—Shall we gather strength by irresolution and inaction shall we acquire the means of effectual resistance by lying supinely upon our backs until our enemies have bound us hand and foot is life so dear or peace so sweet as to be purchased at the price of chains and slavery

2. Indirect questions are not distinguished by this point, nor by capital letters; but, when quoted, or made direct, both are used.

Ex.—" He asked me why I wept." Indirect. " He asked me, 'Why do you weep?'" Direct.

Exercises.—I do not know who he is whence he came or whither he is going Do you know who he is whence he came or whither he is going Let us consider first of what use it will be and secondly what it will cost. Let us consider first of what use will it be and secondly what will it cost Is the law constitutional is the question for discussion to-night Whether the law is constitutional is the question for discussion I said to Defamation "Who will bear thee " " When Diogenes was asked what wine he liked best? he answered, 'That which is drunk at the expense of others.' "—*Johnson's Rambler.*

3. Interrogative sentences may sometimes be closely related in sense, or be elliptical, or be declarative in form.

Ex.—" Is this reason? Is it law? Is it humanity?"—*Wirt.* " Does he hunt? Does he shoot? Is he in debt? Is he temperate? Does he attend to his parish?"—*Sydney Smith.* " They say if the bill is rejected, Government must stop. What must stop? The laws? The judicial tribunals? The legislative bodies? The institutions of the country? No, no, sir! all these will remain, and go on."—*Crittenden.* " Surely, sir, I have seen you before?"

4. The interrogation-point may supersede not only the period, but it may be used also within the sentence, so as to supersede the comma, the semicolon, or the colon.

Ex.—" Is any among you afflicted? let him pray;" " If any among you is afflicted, let him pray." " What have you to say, Charles? for I am waiting;" " Say what you have to say, Charles; for I am waiting." " Who will not cherish the following sentiment of Clay? 'I would rather be right than President;'" " Let us ever cherish the following sentiment of Clay: 'I would rather be right than President." But when the quoted sentence is needed to make the question complete, the interrogation-point is put at the end; as, " Then, why did you not say at once, 'It is a cold day'?"—*John Wilson.*

Exercises.—" Will you go " said he "or will you stay "
    What say you will you yield and this avoid
    Or guilty in defence be thus destroyed —*Shakespeare.*

5. When two or more questions admit of different or distinc answers, and have connectives; or are used elliptically, with such dependence on something in common that they can not stand alone, —they may all be gathered into one sentence, with the interrogation-point after each.

Ex.—"Is my name Talbot? and am I your son? and shall I fly?"—*Shakespeare.* "Is there no honor in generosity? nor in preferring the lessons of conscience to the impulses of passion? nor in maintaining the supremacy of moral principle, and paying reverence to Christian truth?"—*G. Brown.* "What are the interjections of joy?—of praise?—of sorrow?—of grief?"—*Id.*

Exercises.—To purchase heaven has gold the power
Can gold remove the mortal hour —*Johnson.*

As the gentleman has thus settled the definition of *aristocracy* I trust that no man will think it a term of reproach for who among us would not be wise who would not be virtuous who would not be above want —*Livingston.* Was it not a delusion had it been really accomplished and could it be done again —*Andrew Fulton.*

6. When a question is not complete before the end is reached; when the whole sentence is rather one question than several; or when the comma, the semicolon, or the colon, can as well be used within the sentence,—the interrogation-point should be put only at the end.

Ex.—"Will you go, or stay?" "Which is more,—three-fourths, or four-fifths?" "Doth thy heart heave with emotions of thankfulness to God, for making the earth so fair, so redolent of beauty in its garniture of flowers; and for having scattered these silent teachers up and down the world as orators of perfume, and links of beauty, to bind our souls to nature in all times and wheresoever we may be?"—*Parker.* Here some punctuators would have put an interrogation-point after *flowers;* but the semicolon is better.

Exercises.—Did he travel for health or for pleasure Who is worse he who cheats or he who steals Where are your gibes now your gambols your songs your flashes of merriment that were wont to set the table in roar

7. The interrogation-point is sometimes inserted with curves, to doubt the truth of something without formally saying so.

Ex.—"If the immortal Bacon—the wisest, greatest, *meanest* (?), of mankind—disgraced the judgment-seat." etc.—*Edinburgh Review.*

6. EXCLAMATION-POINT.

1. The **exclamation-point** is put after parts expressing emotion,—such as surprise, joy, grief, anger, etc.—very much as the interrogation-point is put after parts denoting inquiry.

Ex.—"Lo! Newton, priest of nature, shines afar,
Scans the wide world, and numbers every star!"—*Campbell.*

"Fair star of evening! splendor of the west!
Star of my country! on the horizon's brink
Thou hangest"

"Now press them! now, ye Trojans, steed-renowned,
Rush on! break through the Grecian rampart, hurl
At once devouring flames into the fleet!"—*Cowper's Homer.*

"Such a chirping and twittering! Such diving down from the nest, and flying up again! Such a wheeling round in circles, and talking to the young ones all the while!"—*Sydney Smith.* "O thou disconsolate widow! robbed, so cruelly robbed, and in so short a time, both of a husband and a son! what must be the plenitude of thy suffering!"—*Dr. Nott: Funeral of Hamilton.*

Hence we see that exclamatory sentences may be either declarative, interrogative or imperative in form; and they are also often elliptical or fragmentary.

Exercises.—" What was the cause of our wasting forty millions of money and sixty thousand lives The American war What was it that produced the French rescript and a French war The American war For what are we about to incur an additional debt of twelve or fourteen millions This cursed cruel diabolical American war "—*Fox.*

" Gentlemen what does this mean Chops and tomato sauce Yours Pickwick Chops Gracious heavens And tomato sauce Is the happiness of a sensitive and confiding female to be trifled away by such shallow artifices as these "

2. It is used after unusually solemn and earnest invocations or addresses.

Ex.—" O blessed Health! thou art above all gold and treasure!" " Spare me, merciful God!" " Conscript Fathers! I do not rise to spend the night in words."

Exercises.—Thy doom is sealed presumptuous slave Truth friendship my country sacred objects sentiments dear to my heart accept my last sacrifice

3. The point is generally used after an interjection.

Ex.—" Yoho! yoho! through lanes, groves, and villages."—*Dickens.*

But that the point must be placed after every interjection except *O*, *eh*, and *hey*, is not true. *O*, immediately preceding the name of something addressed, has usually no point. When interjections are spoken of as mere words, they should not be followed by the exclamation-point; as, *Ah, O, alas, ho.*

4. We often find fragments quoted and made exclamatory or interjectional; and sometimes parts are quoted with their exclamatory sense.

Ex.—" ' Tried and convicted traitor!' Who says this?" " ' Traitor!' I go; but I return." " We should realize, by act, the words ' awake! arise!' in as quick and immediate succession as they were uttered by the poet."

Exercises.—" ' To the guillotine to the guillotine ' exclaimed the female part of the rabble " " Then the first sound went forth ' They come they come '" " ' Tramp tramp ' was suddenly heard on the stairs Who could it be "

5. It is sometimes difficult to determine whether the exclamation-point should supersede other points; but the writer, knowing his own meaning, can best decide for himself. He should first consider whether the sentence is sufficiently emotional for the point; and then, in what part, or in how much of the sentence, the emotion is chiefly comprised, putting the point at the end of such part.

As to the length of the sentence, or as to how much shall be put into one exclamation, the same principles will apply here that apply to interrogative sentences.

Ex.—" Well, to be sure, how much I have fagged through!—the only wonder is, that one head can contain it all!" " And then there are my Italian songs! which every body allows I sing with taste."

" ' Strange,' murmurs the dying invalid, looking out from his window upon the world—' strange! how the beauty and mystery of all nature are heightened by the near prospect of that coming darkness which will sweep them all away!"

Exercises.—How ugly a person appears upon whose reputation some awkward aspersion hangs and how suddenly his countenance clears up with his character O home magical all powerful home how strong must have been thy influence when thy faintest memory could cause these bronzed heroes of a thousand fights to weep like tearful women

To justify the use of this point after each of the several parts of a sentence, they must be deeply emotional; as, " What! attribute the sacred sanction of God and nature to the massacres of the Indian scalping-knife! to the cannibal savage, torturing, murdering. devouring, drinking the blood of his mangled victims!"

6. When an interjection or other emotional word is to be expressive chiefly in connection with other words, it is better to defer the exclamation-point as nearly as possible to the end. When deep emotion belongs chiefly to the whole of a phrase or sentence, it is generally better expressed by one point at the end, than by the hitching and interrupting caused by a multitude of points within.

Ex.—" Charge, Chester, charge! On, Stanley, on!" " How meek, how patient, the mild creature lies!" " But, O thou best of parents! wipe thy tears." " Ah me!" not, " Ah! me." " Ha, ha, ha!" " Alas, my noble boy! that thou shouldst die!"

"Oh! you went with him, did you?"—*Goodrich.*
" O, what a sweet place grandmother's orchard is!"—*E. Sargent.*

Exercises.—Under such circumstances I never would lay down my arms never never never Macbeth Macbeth Macbeth beware Macduff Friends Romans countrymen lend me your ears William William (can't you hear me) bring the gun Alas sir how fell you beside your five wits

"Rejoice! rejoice! the summer months are coming;
Rejoice! rejoice! the birds begin to sing!"

"Gentle river, gentle river! tell us whither do you glide,
Through the green and sunny meadows, with your sweetly murmuring tide?"

In the former couplet, one exclamatory word requires as great a pause as the other, and the parts express much joy; in the latter, the second phrase requires a greater pause than the first, and the parts express less emotion than those of the other.

7. The exclamation-point is preferred to the interrogation-point, when the idea of emotion predominates over that of inquiry.

Ex.—" Where is the man, where is the philosopher, who could so live, suffer, and die, without weakness and without ostentation!"—*Rousseau.*

This is not addressed to any particular person for an answer; the author expects no answer, and means to give none himself. The sentence expresses his feelings rather than his doubts, or the interrogative arrangement is but a stronger mode of stating a declarative exclamation; hence marked !, and not ?.

There is sometimes nice choosing between these two points, and it is then a matter of little consequence which is preferred.

" Canst thou command the Lightnings, that they may go, and say unto thee, ' Here we are'?"
" Canst thou command the Lightnings, that they may go, and say unto thee, ' Here we are'!"

Perhaps the latter punctuation is preferable, for the form of the sentence is but a stronger mode of saying, You can not do this.

To make a declarative sentence a little more emphatic than usual, it is sometimes stated in the interrogative or exclamatory form, without the interrogation or exclamation point.   See p. 37.

8. To express great wonder, irony, or contempt, two or more exclamation-points are sometimes used together.

Ex.—" Selling off below cost!! great sacrifices!!!" "Arrest a gentleman!!! take a warrant out against a gentleman!—you villain! What do you mean?" " Reduce Providence to an alternative!!!"—*Sydney Smith.*

9. The exclamation-point is also used sometimes like the interrogation-point, to denote sneeringly the unbelief of the speaker.

Ex.—" The measures which he introduced to Congress, and which ought to have been carried by overwhelming majorities (?), proved him to have been in every sense a great statesman (!)."

7. DASH.

The *dash* seems to be used, in many modern books, wherever the author, from ignorance of the laws of punctuation, does not precisely know what point should be used. We sometimes find pages on which it is used so often that a lively fancy might almost conceive them to have been printed from a gridiron. But it seems that even long ago the world was very *dashy* ; for an old poet says,—

"All modern trash is
Set forth with numerous breaks and dashes."

The dash is generally a sort of graphic or emotional mark, indicating such a suspense in the sense as will have a peculiar or important effect on the memory, curiosity, or expectation of the reader. It has sometimes the force of a semi-exclamation-point used within the sentence. The Germans call it the *thought-stroke*, that is, the mark which aims to set the reader to thinking.

Dr. Mandeville says, it denotes unusual structure or significance; we should rather say, it denotes *transition* or *emotion*.

Though much abused, the dash is nevertheless an excellent point when put in its right places, all of which we shall endeavor to show.

---

1. The **dash** is often preferred to the comma, the semicolon, or the colon, to express unusual emphasis or suppressed emotion. When thus used, it appeals to the reader's reflection.

Ex. — " They conquered—but Bozzaris fell,
Bleeding at every vein."—*Halleck*.

" And the best plan to silence and admonish them,
Would be to give a ' party'—and astonish them."—*Id*.

It is thus often used to show witty transition.

Exercises. — This world 'tis true was made for Cæsar but for Titus too.

a. In this sense also, it sometimes supersedes, within the sentence, the interrogation-point or the exclamation-point, or is simply a little weaker.

Ex.—" Have I not seen you leaden-eyed—clay-pated—almost dumb with pain hammering at your temples—degraded by nausea tugging at your stomach —your hand shaking like a leaf—your mouth like the mouth of an oven—and your tongue, I'm sure of it, like burnt shoe-leather ?"—*D. Jerrold*. That is to say, Deny it, if you can! The dash here appeals with great force to the conscience of his drunken companion.

2. In its emotional sense, it is also sometimes inserted between parts too closely related for any grammatical point.

Ex.—"Yet this—is Rome, that sat on her seven hills, and from her throne of beauty ruled the world!"—*Mitford*.

" Is it like ?—like whom ?—
The things that mount the rostrum with a skip,
And then—skip down again."—*Cowper*.

Exercises.—This bond doth give thee here no jot of blood.—*Shakespeare*.
And life's piano now for me hath lost its sweetest tones sir
Since my Matilda Brown became some fellow's Mrs. Jones sir

3. In its emotional sense, it is sometimes *added* to other points

Sometimes it is added merely to lengthen the pause a little, or to mark transition.

Ex.— "He saw—whatever thou hast seen;
Enjoyed,—but his delights are fled."—*Montgomery.*
"It thunders;—but it thunders to preserve."—*Young.*

Such double points as the foregoing are now often avoided, by using simply the dash or the next greater common point. The comma with the dash is more emphatic than the semicolon; the semicolon with the dash is more emphatic than the colon; but the semicolon and the colon are neater points.

"He said; then full before their sight produced the beast, and lo!—'twas white."—*Merrick.* "I pause for a reply.—None? Then none have I offended.— I have done no more to Cæsar, than you should do to Brutus."—*Shakespeare.*

"And enterprises of great pith and moment,
With this regard their currents turn awry,
And lose the name of action.—Soft, you now!
The fair Ophelia.—Nymph, in thy orisons
Be all my sins remembered."—*Shak.: Hamlet.* (Transition.)

The dash here avoids the commencement of a new paragraph.

"Who next?—O, my little friend, you are just let loose from school, and come hither to scrub your blooming face, and drown the memory of certain taps of the ferule, and of other schoolboy troubles, in a draught from the Town Pump." —*Hawthorne.*

"The principal parts of a sentence are usually three; namely, the SUBJECT, or nominative,—the attribute, or finite VERB,—and the case put after, or the OBJECT governed by the verb: as, 'Crimes deserve punishment.'"—*Gould Brown.*

"The possessive case may denote the relation of persons; as, 'William's cousin;—or the relation of the *doer* to the thing done; as, 'Solomon's Temple;' —or the relation of a *whole* to its parts; as, 'a horse's head.'"—*Greene.*

Here Mr. Brown needed a point greater than the comma and less than the semicolon, and so he added the dash to the comma. Mr. Greene needed a point greater than the semicolon, and so he added the dash to it: he might better have used the colon. There is a tendency to avoid double points.

4. When elliptical or heterogeneous parts are brought emotionally into one sentence, they are generally separated by the dash.

Ex.—"Came home solus—very high wind—lightning—moonshine—solitary stragglers muffled in cloaks—white houses—clouds hurrying over the sky— altogether very poetical."—*Byron.*

Exercises.—But you are hungry want a breakfast turn into a restaurant call for ham eggs and coffee then your bill six dollars California.

5. It is used to show suspense or delay.

Ex.—"The pulse fluttered—stopped—went on—throbbed—stopped again— moved—stopped.—Shall I go on?—No."—*Sterne.*

Exercises.—One pressed his antagonist back back back till there was but another step of plank behind him between him and nothing.

6. It is sometimes imitative, and has, besides, the emotional sense which was first mentioned.

Ex.—"Pop! There—the cork 's drawn. *Gurgle—gurgle—gurgle—good-good—good*—No! it is in vain; there is no type—there are no printed sounds (allow me the *concetto*)—to describe the melody, the cadence, of the out-pouring bottle."—*D Jerrold.*

Exercises.—The clock went tick tick tick tick and I went nid-nod nodding nidding till suddenly the door-bell rang and startled me from my drowsiness

7. It is used to show hesitation or faltering.

Ex.—" I—I myself—was in love—with—PRISCILLA!"—*Hawthorne.*

Exercises.—He was very sorry for it was extremely concerned it should happen so but as it was necessary a

8. It is put at the end of a sentence left unfinished, whether from interruption, faltering, or any other cause.

Ex.—   " ' She was '——

'A great fool,' said a trooper."

" ' HERE LIES THE GREAT'—False marble! where?"—*Young.*

"It was to inquire by what title General—but, catching himself—Mr. Washington chose to be addressed."—*Irving.*

Exercises.—These are ah no these were the gazetteers. "*Gil Blas.* Your Grace's sermons never fail to be admired but "*Archbishop.* It lacked the strength the Do you not agree with me sir"

9. It is also used before and after each interruption, and before echoes, that is, expressions emphatically resumed.

Ex.—"I take—eh! oh!—as much exercise—eh!—as I can, Madam Gout. You know my sedentary state."—*Franklin.* "All seemed very well; but—for there was one of those dreadful 'buts' in the case—but he had a very small amount of money to provide a home." "No, sir; I always thought Robertson would be crushed by his own weight—would be buried under his own ornaments."—*Quarterly Review.*

10. In its transition sense, it is used to enclose a parenthesis, especially when this is rather long, and has other points within it.

Ex.—"Their female companion—faded, though still young—possessed, nevertheless, a face whose expression frequently drew my gaze."—*Bulwer.*

Exercises.—Tom Moore wrote politics at times pointed bitter rankling politics but he was really no politician at heart Setting aside a rare virtue in this clime her aristocratic antecedents she set up as a baker for the public

11. If the sentence is broken by the parenthesis where it required some ordinary point, this point is placed before each parenthetic dash; otherwise, simply the dashes are used.

Ex.—" If the immortal Bacon—'the wisest, greatest, *meanest* (?), of mankind'—disgraced the judgment-seat, and stained his own great name,—not, we believe, to prevent, but to expedite, justice,—was not bribery, which stained the ermine on infinitely *meaner* shoulders, also the vice of his time?—*Edinburgh Review.*

"I was an auditor—auditress, I mean—of one of his lectures."—*Hawthorne.* Here the latter dash has superseded the comma. "Though I have given eight pounds a year,—would you believe it?—I have never once succeeded."—*Jerrold.* " But the curate—alas, poor man!—he has been to college, and is a gentleman."—*Id.* The interrogation and exclamation points are not superseded.

12. It shows the transition of structure when a sentence is dropped in one form, and resumed in another.

Ex.—"The noble indignation with which Emmett repelled the charge of treason against his country, the eloquent vindication of his name, and his pathetic appeals to posterity,—all these entered deeply into every generous breast."—*Irving.*

At these culminating points of sentences, the colon was formerly often used.

Exercises.—The crisp snow and the woolly clouds the delightful rustle of the summer forest and the waving of the autumn corn the glory of the sunset and the wonder of the rainbow the world would have wanted these had not the winds been taught to do their Master's bidding *Dickens.*

13. It is generally used where *namely* or *that is* can be conceived as having been omitted.

Ex.—" The story is not deficient in that which all stories should have, to be perfectly delightful,—a fortunate conclusion."

Exercises.—On this was he willing to stake all he had character and life It had literally nothing to do beyond what I have said to flow to bubble to look limpid to murmur amid flowers and sweet perfumes

In this sense it is also often used alone ; as, " It is just what might have been expected from its author—a very juvenile performance."—*Edinburgh Review.* When the parts are long, the semicolon is often preferred.

14. It is placed, with the comma, after a loose series of nominative terms leading to an important predicate.

Ex.—" The same vigor of thought; the same form of expression ; the short sentences ; the calm, bold, and collected manner ; the air of solemn dignity ; the deep, sepulchral, unimpassioned voice,—have all been developed, not changed, even to the intenser bitterness of his irony."—*Wilde: Webster.*

15. On the same principle it is sometimes placed before a term relating to a series of others, to show its common dependence on all of them.

Ex.— "All business ceased, the towns in silence lay,
Men brooded deep in vengeance and dismay,
And naught was heard save woman's wail of woe,—
As spread the tidings from the Alamo."

Without the dash, it might seem that the last line relates only to the line preceding it. The ordinary sagacity of readers, however, renders this dash unnecessary.

a. But when the parts of a series are very long or very numerous, it may be best to use the dash after each of them, to show their common dependence on something remote.

Ex.—" When lawyers take what they would give,
And doctors give what they would take,—
When city fathers eat to live,
Save when they fast for conscience' sake,"— etc.—*Holmes.*

This stanza, with seven others like it, depends on a concluding one.

16. The dash is sometimes used at the beginning of renewed discourse viewed as the continuance of previous discourse left unfinished, or after a digression.

Ex.— ——" But to return to my mother," etc.—*See Sterne's Works; Holmes's Autocrat.* It here has its transition sense.

In imitation of a French custom, we now often see it at the left of newspaper paragraphs, to show that they are extracts or that they are new. When thus used, it has both its emotional and transition sense, or is simply a little more modest than the hand used in show-bills, etc.

17. In dialogue not having the speaker's name, nor distinguished by breaks, it is generally used to show the transition from one speaker's saying to that of another.

Ex.—"You have been my two-fisted valet these thirty years.—Hem!—Hem? What do you mean by hem?"—*Coleman.*

Exercises.—"In combustibility it agrees with cannel coal It does. Have you examined its fracture I have."

So, when but one person fictitiously represents two; as, " When arrived?—this evening. How long do I stay?—uncertain. What are my plans?—let us discuss them." (Questions of a friend anticipated and answered.)

18. Hence it is also placed between sentences which are not the consecutive thoughts of their author on the same subject.

Ex.—" 'The wound,' said Lord Bacon, 'is not dangerous, unless we poison it with our remedies.—The wrongs of the Puritans may hardly be dissembled or excused.—On subjects of religion he was always for moderate counsels.' "—*Bancroft.* "Both subjects sometimes come before the verb; as, "I know not who he is."—" Who did you say it was?"—" I know not how to tell thee who I am."—*Goold Brown.*

When examples are each enclosed by quotation-marks, I do not think they need the dash.

19. In books, it is placed after each period that separates the headings of a series; in newspapers, it is thus used without any other point.

Ex.—HEAVY RAIN.—CAMP.—BUFFALO HUNT.—OSAGE INDIANS.—*Irving.* "Arrival of the Great Eastern—News from Europe—State of the Money Market," etc.

20. It is placed after side-heads; and also before the authority or credit, when in the same line with the end of the paragraph.

Ex.—"THE ABUSE OF THE IMAGINATION.—He who can not command his thoughts, must not hope to control his actions. All mental superiority originates in habits of thinking."—*Jane Taylor.*

" Howard—*Burke.* Milton—*Quarterly Review.*"—*E. Sargent.*

In these senses it is not always needed, and is often omitted.

21. It is used after a line, or a part of a line, when connected with something begun or resumed in the line below:—

Ex.—"MY DEAR BOY,—

" Do you choose your friend, like an orange, by its golden outside, and the power of yielding much when well squeezed," etc.—*Punch.*

In this sense it is generally not needed, and is often omitted.

22. It is often used to separate the number of a lesson, chapter, or section, from the title placed after it.

Ex.—"LESSON LXII.—The Power of Music."

In this sense it is not always needed, and is sometimes omitted.

It is used to show the omission of letters or figures.

Ex.—"See pages 250—258;" i. e., all the pages, beginning with 250 to 258 inclusive. " See pp. 250-8." See p. 372.

In arithmetic, it should rather not be used, especially when it might be mistaken for the *minus* sign.

It is sometimes used when none of the four chief points, or none of the three minor points, is altogether appropriate; or so as to supply whatever point the punctuation system may happen to need.

8. CURVES.

1. **The curves** are used to enclose something hastily thrown in, which is merely incidental or explanatory, and may be omitted without injuring the grammatical construction. What is enclosed, is called a *parenthesis*. A parenthesis is like a by-path to the main road.

Ex.—" Mr. Plausible (to borrow a name from John Bunyan) wishes the Hon. Mr. Spendthrift to represent the county of ————."—*Eclectic Magazine.*

" Next day the landlord inquires (and all landlords are inquisitive), and after inquiry talks (and all landlords are talkative), concerning the private business of his new guest."—*Ib.*

"I send you, my dear child, (and you will not doubt) very sincerely, the wishes of the season"—*Chesterfield.*

The first and the last example tend to show that curves are sometimes indispensable, for setting off what might otherwise be viewed as a part of the sentence itself.

2. Letters or figures, used as marks of reference or for numbering, are often enclosed by curves, especially when their meaning might otherwise be uncertain or ambiguous.

Ex.—"(1.) By using different words; (2.) By difference of termination," etc. —*S. S. Greene.* "(a.) What it does; (b.) What it is."—*Id.* Curves thus used, are often unnecessary; and whenever they are so, they should be omitted.

3. The curves are now often preferred to brackets, for enclosing explanations or incidental remarks, whether given by the author or the copyist, especially when they stand within the paragraph. See under Brackets.

Ex —" *Orthoepy*, a word derived from the Greek *orthon* (upright) and ἔπὸ (I speak), signifies the right utterance of words."—*Sargent.* " The Comma (,) denotes," etc.—*Id.* " But it is objected by the Senator from Tennessee (Mr. Grundy), that the construction which I contend for, &c., &c. (Applause.)"—*Cong. Globe.*

" ' If they persist in reading this book to a conclusion, (*impossible!*) they will no doubt have to struggle with feelings of awkwardness; (ha! ha! ha!) they will look round for poetry, (ha! ha! ha!) and will be induced to inquire by what species of courtesy these attempts have been permitted to assume that title.' Ha! ha! ha!"—*E. A. Poe, laughing as he reads.*

The dash is now often used, and also the comma, in stead of the curves.

The *dash* should be preferred when the parenthesis coalesces rather closely, in sense and grammatical construction, with the rest of the sentence; or when it is rather emotional or emphatic.

The *curves* should be preferred when the parenthesis coalesces little or least, in sense and grammatical construction, with the rest of the sentence; or when the parenthesis is to be read in a very perceptible undertone.

The *comma* should be preferred when it will serve as well as either of the other marks.

Ex.—" I had given a third part of my wealth—four cents—for it." (Emotional or emphatic: it draws the attention strongly to how great the sum was.)

"I had given a third part of my wealth (four cents) for it." This takes the least notice of the sum; it may even imply that the person addressed, already knew how much that third was.

"I had given a third part of my wealth, four cents, for it." This is intermediate, in sense, between the other two.

4. When a parenthesis occurs within another, curves are usually applied to one, and dashes to the other; the less coalescent one taking the curves. But this rule is not always observed.

Ex'—"The little party were still lingering in the deep recess of the large bay-window—which (in itself of dimensions that would have swallowed up a moderate-sized London parlor) held the great round tea-table with all appliances and means to boot—to behold the beautiful summer moon shed on the sward so silvery a lustre, and the trees cast so quiet a shadow."—*Harper's Magazine.*

"The branches of knowledge taught in our schools,—reading—in which I include the spelling of our language—a firm, sightly, legible hand-writing, and the elemental rules of arithmetic,—are of greater value than all the rest which is taught at school."—*E. Everett.*

5. The parts enclosing a parenthesis, are punctuated as if they had it not.

Ex.—"The good man (and good men not only think good thoughts, but do good deeds) lives more in a year, than a selfish, covetous man in a century." (*The good man lives*, etc.)

"It behooves me to say that these three (who, by the way, are all dead) possessed great general ability, and had respectively received a good education."—*Harper's Magazine.*

6. If a point is required at the end of the first part, it may be placed before each curve, if the structure will allow it. Though many punctuators prefer to insert the point but once, and immediately after the latter curve.

Ex.—"This book is written, or supposed to be written, (for we would speak timidly of the mysteries of superior beings,) by the celebrated Mrs. Hannah More."—*Sydney Smith.*

"My sisters went to the best schools in town; (and here let me acknowledge, that, knowing our former position and present difficulties, everywhere friends turned up for us;) they had all they wanted, as far as books and masters were concerned."—*Eclectic Review.*

"Pride, in some disguise or other (often a secret to the proud man himself), is the most ordinary spring of action among men."—*John Wilson.*

7. But when the parenthesis is too closely related to the former part to be cut off from it by the point, then the point must be placed after the latter curve.

Ex.—"Gladiator (Lat. *gladius*, a sword); a sword-player, a prize-fighter."—*Sargent.* "The Nominative independent or absolute (absolutus, *released, free,* from grammatical structure)."—*S. S. Greene.*

8. The parenthesis is punctuated, within itself, as usual; and if it requires, at its end, an interrogation or exclamation point, or a different point from that of the part before it, each part takes its proper point and before the curve.

Ex.— "For the bee never idles, but labors all day,
And thinks (wise little bee!) work better than play."
"I gave (and who would not have given?) my last dollar to the miserable beggar."
"The Frenchman, first in literary fame,
(Mention him, if you please. Voltaire?—The same.)
With spirit, genius, eloquence, supplied,
Lived long, wrote much, laughed heartily, and died."—*Cowper.*
"My mother grew worse, and France also (Moscow—1813!); we were in extreme penury."—*Eclectic Review.* The punctuation of the foregoing sentence is questionable, yet I believe it brings out the sense to the best advantage.

9. When a dash, relating to either the first broken part or the parenthesis, is placed after the first broken part, it is also generally placed before the second broken part.

Ex.—"I received an office as junior clerk in—(one name will do as well as another)—in Her Majesty's Waste-Paper Office."—*British Review.* (Significant or emphatic dash, relating to the parts separated, and showing reiteration.)

10. When an entire and distinct sentence or phrase is made parenthetic, the period or other point should be placed before, not after, the latter curve. See the last example.

9. BRACKETS.

1. The **brackets** are properly used to enclose what one person puts into the writing of another.

Ex.—"Yours [the British] is a nation of unbounded resources,—a nation from whose empire (and it has been your proudest boast) the sun never disappears." (Explanation.)
"Do you know if [whether] he is at home?" (Correction.)
Abbotsford, May 12th, [1820]. (Omission.)
"LESSON LV.—LLEWELLYN AND HIS DOG.
"[A true story, showing the lamentable effects of hasty wrath.]
"The spearman heard the bugle sound, and cheerily smiled the morn,
And many a brach and many a hound attend Llewellyn's horn," etc.
"[Here Mr. Clay was interrupted by the Senator from Michigan.]"

2. The writer himself may sometimes use the brackets to enclose some explanation, direction, or observation; especially when it stands apart by itself, and has so little connection with the text that it can hardly be considered a part of it.

Ex.—"*Rosina.* [Between the scenes.] To work, my hearts of oak, to work
Here the sun is half an hour high, and not a stroke struck yet.
[Enters singing, followed by reapers.]"
But thus in the latest books:—
"*Don Luis.* Repose awhile, I will return with speed.
[*Exit hastily.*
"*Oliver.* (*Advancing.*) How fell Don Luis to such poverty?"—*Boker.*
Sometimes but one bracket is used, as in White's Shakespeare.
"Now, like to whelps, we crying run away.
[*A short alarum.*"
"DISMISSION, (—mish'-un,) n. [Lat. *dismissio.*]"—*N. Webster.*

3. The writer himself may sometimes use brackets to show what is digression or interpolation.

Ex.—See Dr. Holmes's "Autocrat of the Breakfast-Table."
"I never liked him, never, in my days!"
["O, yes! you did," said Ellen with a sob.]
"There always was a something in his ways—"
["So sweet—so kind," said Ellen with a throb.]—*Hood.*

Brackets are so uncouth that there is some tendency to use the curves in their stead, when the interpolated part, though within the paragraph, is not liable to be misunderstood, if distinguished by the curves.

Ex.—" Patrick Henry wound up by one of those daring flights of declamation for which he was so remarkable, and startled the House by a warning flash from history : 'Cæsar had his Brutus ; Charles, his Cromwell ; and George the Third—' ('Treason ! treason !' resounded from the neighborhood of the Chair)—' may profit by their example,' added Henry. 'Sir, if this be treason (bowing to the speaker), make the most of it.' "—*Irving.*

10. HYPHEN.

1. The **hyphen** is placed at the end of a syllable of a word so long that a part must be put into the next line. Words are divided into syllables according to their pronunciation and composition, the latter yielding to the former whenever they plainly disagree. See pp. 107, 108.

It is sometimes used to show the syllables of a word; as, *Dis-grace-ful, co-operate.*

2. The hyphen joins the parts of compound words, that do not coalesce sufficiently to be united without it.

Ex.—" Look at pretty, *ten-year-old, rosy-cheeked, golden-haired* Mary, gazing with all the blue brightness of her eyes, at that large *dew-drop.*"—*Prof. Wilson.*

The compounding of words depends on the *sense ;* the consolidation on the *pronunciation ;* and both depend somewhat on *custom.*

3. A compound word should denote one idea rather than two or more, or it should have a meaning different from that of the separated words, or it should imply a change in the part of speech, or it should be known as the familiar term for a certain object or attribute.

Ex.—" Horse-fly, orang-outang, gooseberry, to-night, wild-rose, slippery-elm, apple-orchard, sewing-machine, humming-bird ; a black-bearded man ; a *sine-qua-non* condition, 'the end-all and be-all ; a setting-forth of."

There is generally the greatest difficulty in deciding, when the former word has somewhat the nature of an adjective. If it denotes the substance, or is merely descriptive, and *not a part of the name*, there is no compounding ; as, *a gold cup, mountain billows, saltwater fish, village bells :* but, if otherwise, there is ; as, *school-room, watering-place.* When the former word may suggest either the idea of composing, or else that of belonging to, relating to, or connected with, the latter sense is usually distinguished from the former by compounding ; as, *a glass house, a glass-house.* In general, when the terms have passed into the nomenclature of some particular art, science, or occupation, the elements are compounded. There are some exceptions to this entire paragraph.

.4. A part common to two or more consecutive compounds, should either be left separate, or, to avoid ambiguity, be made a part of each.

Ex.—" Riding and dancing schools;" or, " Riding-schools and dancing-schools;" not, " Riding and dancing-schools," nor, " Riding- and dancing-schools."

An epithet already compound, is not usually joined to its noun; as, *"high-water mark;" "whalebone rod."* When there is a bunch of compounds, it is often better to separate or to consolidate some of them; as, " *master, quarter-master, quartermaster-general;" " creek, mill-creek, mill-creek coal-field, mill-creek cannel-coal, mill-creek cannelcoal-field.*"

Pronunciation relates to the letters, syllables, and accents.

5. If the parts coalesce with the smooth flow of syllables making one word if there is no liability of improperly joining letters of one to the other; if there is one chief accent, the other being no stronger than an ordinary secondary accent; if the parts are not too long; and if the parts are not too new in combination to be easily understood,—they are consolidated.

Ex.—" Everlasting, graveyard, gentleman, highwayman, forthcoming, barefaced." But, " Soul-stirring, ant-hill, peep-hole, sand-eel, remainder-man, knitting-needle, spelling-book, cheese-press." " Home/sickness," accent yielded by the longer word to the shorter ; " council-room," accent not yielded, nor next to the hyphen-place.

---

a. A phrase made an epithet, is always compounded.

Ex.—" A *two-foot* ruler;" " The *tree-and-cloud-shadowed* river."

But when the former word can not be conceived otherwise than as an adverb modifying the next word, the two are not compounded; as, " *Newly varnished* furniture;" " Love *ill requited.*"

b. Idiomatic phrases are usually not compounded.

Ex.—" By and by; to and fro; tit for tat; out and out."

c. A foreign phrase that is made an epithet, or that has so lost the meaning of its parts as to be Anglicized, is hyphened; but if its words remain separately significant as they stand, it is left uncompounded, and often expressed in Italics.

Ex.—" Piano-forte, camera-obscura, billet-doux, ex-post-facto laws ; habeas corpus ; scire facias ; nux vomica."

d. A phrase, having a possessive, and used as a proper name, remains uncompounded ; if it is a somewhat unusual common name, with a change of the original meaning, the apostrophe and hyphen are used ; and if it is a very common term, the parts are consolidated, and the hyphen is omitted.

Ex.—" Cook's Inlet, Barrow's Strait; Rupert's-drops, lamb's-wool ; ratsbane, beeswax." Capital letters are sometimes a sort of substitute for the hyphen.

e. Cardinal numerals are hyphened from *twenty* to *hundred*. With ordinals used as nouns, they are usually compounded, though sometimes needlessly.

Ex.—" One thousand two hundred and eighty-seven." " Two-thirds, three-fourths, five twenty-sixths."

f. Certain words consisting of rhymes, or of syllables combined for the sake of the sound, are generally consolidated if the parts are two monosyllables; and sometimes if they are dissyllables. They are hyphened in other cases.

Ex.—"Picnic, hodgepodge, powwow, zigzag, chitchat, huggermugger, helter-skelter, wishy-washy, hurdy-gurdy, ninny-hammer."

g. A prefix is generally consolidated with the rest of the word.

Ex.—"*Over*flow, *under*graduate, *semi*circle."

h. Prefixes, or similar parts, are not consolidated with the rest of the word, if they stand before a capital letter; if they are followed by a greater pause than ordinary syllables thus situated, or by a pause showing the separate significance of the parts; or if they should be kept apart to preserve the sense or pronunciation.

Ex.—"Anti-Benton, pre-Adamite, Anglo-Saxon, Neo-Platonic, concavo-convex, proto-sulphuret, vice-admiral, electro-magnetism, reformation, re-formation, recreation, re-creation, re-revise, co-operate (also coöperate), semi-cylindrical, co-tangent, non-essential."

i. When a writer makes a new compound, or chooses one that he supposes not well known to his reader, he should generally use the hyphen. But, by long and general usage, compound words tend to lose the hyphen.

Ex.—"Some of us have killed '*brown-backs*' and '*yellow-legs*' [birds], on the marshes." "Since *railroads* and *steamboats* have driven all the romance out of travel."—*Irving.*

In doubtful cases, especially when the parts are monosyllables, it is better to consolidate them; for the analogy of some eminent foreign languages—the German and the Greek—favors this mode of writing words.

Familiar Explanations.—*Many-colored birds* have many colors each; *many colored birds* are numerous, though they may all be of one color. A *light armed soldier* is a light soldier with arms; a *light-armed soldier* has light arms. A *live oak* is simply a living oak; a *live-oak* is a species of evergreen oak. A *sugar tree* is made of sugar; a *sugar-tree* is a maple that yields sugar. So, a *glass house* is made of glass; a *glass-house* is a house in which glass is manufactured. A *dancing master* is a master that dances; a *dancing-master* teaches dancing. A *boarding-house* has boarders; a *boarding house* may seem to board. *Lady's slipper* is a shoe; *lady's-slipper* is a plant. A *dog's-ear* is the corner of a leaf turned over; a *dog's ear* is the ear of a dog. A *bull's-eye* is a small round window; a *bull's eye* is the eye of a bull. A crow is a *black bird*, but not a *blackbird*. Six and seventeen—23; sixteen and seventeen—33. Twenty-five cent pieces—25 cents; twenty *five-cent* pieces—$1.00. A *horse racing* is a horse in the act of running; a *horse-racing* is a running of horses. "*Time tutored* age and love exalted youth," is very different from, "*Time-tutored* age and *love-exalted* youth." So is *touch me not* from *touch-me-not*. "The *deep-tangled* wildwood;" "*Battle-hymns* and dirges." Without the hyphen, *deep* would qualify *wildwood*, not *tangled;* and *Battle* would also refer to dirges. Hence when two adjectives stand before a noun, each of which might qualify it, they must be joined to show that one is used adverbially to modify the other.

Exercises.—There are four footed animals. Watch makers and glass cutters. He is a free mason. Texas abounds in humming birds and mocking birds. A red headed high tempered woman. The corn fields and the walnut trees. A paper mill is not made of paper, nor a tin peddler of tin. A white oak, a black oak, and a go cart. Five gallon kegs and three foot measures. The twenty-third and fourth trees are the best in the row. *The twenty-third and twenty-fourth trees,* &c. Steamships and boats are propelled by steam. The whet and how much. "Crops have been much injured by the cut worm."—*Newspaper.*

11. QUOTATION-MARKS.

1. **Quotation-marks** enclose what is to be presented as the identical word or words of some other person or writing.

Ex.—" I rise for information," said a member of Congress. " I am very glad to hear it," cried another sitting by; " for no one needs it more."

2. A quotation within another, is enclosed by single quotation-marks.

If I wished to represent the entire foregoing paragraph as something quoted by me, I should write it thus:—

"'I rise for information,' said a member of Congress. 'I am very glad to hear it,' cried another sitting by; 'for no one needs it more.'"

3. When the double and the single marks have both been used, they are, if needed, repeated in the same order.

4. When many quotations occur within one another, it is better to leave the inner ones undistinguished by quotation-marks; especially if capitals can be used to show the beginning of each.

Ex.—" Jesus answered the Jews, 'Is it not written in your law,—I said, Ye are gods?'"—*New Testament: John* x. 34.

Mr. Wilson very properly prefers the foregoing mode of pointing to the following: " Jesus answered the Jews, 'Is it not written in your law,—"I said, ' Ye are gods' " ?' "

5. When an extract of two or more paragraphs is quoted, the introductory quotation-marks are placed before each paragraph, and the closing ones only after the last.

Ex.—Some of Jefferson's rules of life are these :—
" Never spend your money before you have it.
" Never trouble others for what you can do yourself.
" Never put off till to-morrow what you can do to-day."

6. When something already interrogative or exclamatory is quoted, the closing quotation-marks follow the point; but when something is quoted, and made interrogative or exclamatory afterwards, the closing marks precede the point. The four common points, to avoid uncouth blank spaces, are always placed before the closing quotation-marks.

Ex.—He asked me, "Why do you weep?" Why did you not say at once, " I can not go" ?
"'Banished from Rome'! What's banished but set free
    From daily contact of the things I loathe."
Can you spell " phthisic" ?
" Went home yesterday" ? Then I must write to him.
Or : " ' Went home yesterday' ? Then I must write to him."
A quotation is punctuated within itself as if it stood alone.

7. Quotation-marks are often used in speaking of words, phrases, or sentences. Some writers, when quoting words from popular usage, insert but single quotation-marks. Italics and quotation-marks are often used arbitrarily, as means of distinguishing words or phrases.

Ex.—The phrase "not at all," is an idiom.

What is 'secret', may be accidentally or intentionally so: 'hidden' and 'concealed' imply something *intentionally* kept secret. We speak of 'a *hidden* plot,' 'a *concealed* intention'. 'Covert' is something not *avowed*. It may be *intended* to be seen; 'a *covert* allusion' is meant to be understood, but is not openly expressed.—*Whately*.

8. Quotation-marks are not needed, when we present in our own language the saying of another.

Ex.—Randolph said, " Pay as you go." Randolph said, that we should pay as we go.

Quotation-marks may be used even when the authority itself is annexed. They may also be used when an author furnishes from himself such illustrations as might be thus distinguished if taken from other writers. Quotation-marks may be omitted, when deemed unnecessary or too cumbersome. In the Bible they are generally omitted, when the quotation stands within the sentence, and begins with a capital.

12. UNDERSCORE.

1. The **underscore** is used in writing, being drawn under what should be printed in Italics or in capitals.

Italics are *slanting letters;* and they were so called because the Italians not only invented them, but immediately gave to the world an edition of Virgil printed wholly in these letters.

2. Italics denote, in general, emphasis or distinction. They direct particular attention to some word or words, or show in what part the point or pith of the sentence chiefly lies.

Ex.—" We must *fight;* I repeat it, sir, we *must* fight." " Here *I* reign king, and, to enrage thee more, *thy* king and lord."

" An hour or two, and forth she goes,
The school she brightly seeks;
She carries in her hand a rose,
And two upon her cheeks."—Southern Literary Messenger.

" Of *course* a race-*course* isn't *coarse*, a *fine* is far from *fine."—Hood*.

3. They are generally used to distinguish foreign words introduced among English.

Ex.—" He was secretary *pro tempore.*"
" My foolish heart beats pit-a-pat—*sic omnia vincit amor.*"

4. They are generally used to distinguish what is spoken of as a mere letter, word, phrase, or sentence.

Ex.— "*A* does want *ye* to make it *aye,—*
There's but one *p* in *peas."—Hood.*

"*Which* may be applied to phrases or clauses, but *that* only to nouns or pronouns." " *That he should be more careful* . . . . . . is a substantive clause, in the nominative case," etc.

5. The names of boats, ships, newspapers, and magazines, or other periodical literature, are usually printed in Italics; the names of books seldom need this mode of distinction, but they are sometimes quoted.

Ex.—" The *Neptune* sailed yesterday." " An article in the *New-York Mercury.*" " Gibbon's Decline and Fall of the Roman Empire." Thomson's " Seasons."

Credits and authorities annexed to quoted paragraphs, are also generally printed in Italics or in small capitals.

In the common English Bible, Italics show what words were not in the original.

When a sentence or paragraph is to be expressed in Italics, Roman or capital letters must be used to distinguish any part of it.

Ex.—"*Time is a measured portion of indefinite duration.*"—OLMSTED.

To denote still greater emphasis or distinction than Italics would express, capital letters should be used. Italics show what is emphatic; small capitals, what is more emphatic; and capitals, what is very emphatic. Draw the line under once, to denote *Italics*; twice, to denote SMALL CAPITALS; three times, to denote CAPITALS; and four times, to denote *ITALIC CAPITALS*, or ornamental letters.

OBSERVATIONS.

There is probably not, in the compass of human knowledge, a more chaotic subject than punctuation; and we might present many critical and useful remarks upon it, but our want of space will allow only a few.

Punctuation is influenced—1. By the sense; 2. By the delivery, or the pause required; 3. By the points elsewhere required; 4. By the connectives or suppressed words; 5. By the length of the parts to be punctuated; 6. By the position of the parts. **1.** "The troops landed and killed a hundred Indians," implies that they brought the Indians with them; "The troops landed, and killed a hundred Indians," expresses the true meaning. "Alphonso Karr, a celebrated writer, distinguished for his taste and knowledge in botany," implies taste in botany; "Alphonso Karr, a celebrated writer, distinguished for his taste, and knowledge in botany," refers only the knowledge to botany. "I said he is dishonest, it is true; and I am sorry for it," differs widely from, "I said he is dishonest; it is true, and I am sorry for it." "I can not violate my oath to support the Constitution," implies that the oath relates to the Constitution; "I can not violate my oath, to support the Constitution," implies some other oath. "Why did you not come to us in the beginning of the night?" inquires about the cause; "Why, did you not come to us in the beginning of the night?" inquires about the fact. "The great principles of government which are easily understood, are known everywhere," refers to some of the great principles only; "The great principles of government, which are easily understood, are known everywhere," refers to all of them. "O Shame! where is thy blush?" is an address to shame. "O, shame! where is thy blush?" is an address to something else. **2.** "Yes, you shall." "Yes; and for you too." "Yes: he has done all this, and yet you are not satisfied." **3.** "Since our journey began, it had rained in torrents; and now both horse and rider refused to go a step farther: the beast, because he sank up to his knees in mud; and the rider, because he was wet to the bone." **4.** "Study to promote the happiness of mankind : it is the true end of your creation;" "Study to promote the happiness of mankind; for it is the true end of your creation." "Let it appear so; make your vaunting true;" "Let it appear so, *and* make your vaunting true." "The cool, sequestered paths of life;" "The cool *and* sequestered paths of life." **5.** "There was fire *above* and *below* the house;" "Good men are not always found in union *with*, but sometimes in opposition *to*, the views and conduct of one another." "Teach, urge, threaten, lecture *him*;" "We would oppose, resist, repel, *such intrusion*." **6.** "*To God*, nothing is impossible;" "Nothing is impossible *to God*." "*To secure his election*, it is said that votes were bought;" "It is said that votes were bought *to secure his election*."

In discourse occurs frequently what is called the *rhetorical pause*,—a slight suspension in the sense, requiring no point, but often mistaken for the sense which requires a point. "The love of liberty, is in every. breast," should be, "The love of liberty is in every breast." When emphasis or the rhetorical pause coincides with the grammatical sense, it may induce the insertion of a point; as, "A sentence is *compound*, when it contains two or more clauses." There seems to be in use a redundant and also a sparing mode of punctuating called *close punctuation* and *free punctuation*, of which the difference is particularly obvious in the use of the comma. The following are extreme specimens: "He then, with great effort, did, by sheer strength, move the mass from the position, it, at first, occupied, to one, at least forty yards distant, and, but for impediments, would, had time been given him, have moved it, with ease, and precision, to the position, where, for the progress of the work, it was required."—*Punctuation made Plain*. "A cool and philosophical observer would undoubtedly have pronounced that all the evil arising from the intolerant laws which Parliament had framed was not to be compared to the evil which would be produced by a transfer of the legislative power from the Parliament to the sovereign."—*Macaulay*. The best mode is a medium between the two; but they are often improperly mixed, especially by pointing parenthetic parts on one side only. "Go, and without hesitation, pay the sum." Either insert a comma after *and*, or omit the comma after *hesitation*. "The dog having seen him, went in pursuit," should be, "The dog, having seen him, went in pursuit." ": such is war," can refer to the rest of the same sentence only; but ". Such is war," may refer to all the discourse before it. "The pride of wealth is contemptible; the pride of learning is pitiable; the pride of dignity is ridiculous; but the pride of bigotry is insupportable." Here the dash would have been too sentimental; the comma would have slurred the matter over too lightly; the colon would have suggested a different connection in thought; the period would have been too deliberate; but the semicolon gives due distinction to the parts, and the greatest energy to the whole sentence. Mr. Wilson, however, prefers the comma. "My comrade, on the contrary, made himself quite one of the family; laughed and chatted with them." Here the insertion of *and* before "laughed," would require the comma; the insertion of *he*, the colon. "The bill passed without amendment; though it never received the royal assent;" "The bill passed without amendment, though it never received the royal assent." The semicolon rather gives "though" the sense of *however;* and the comma, the sense of *notwithstanding*. "None but the brave, none but the brave, none but the brave deserves the fair."—*Dryden*. Ordinary repetition. "Arm! arm! it is—it is—the cannon's opening roar!"—*Byron*. Suspense and emotion. "Wherever he [the bobolink] goes, pop! pop! pop! the rusty firelocks of the country are cracking on every side."—*Irving*. Greater emotion. Observe how the repeated parts are differently punctuated as the emotion rises. "Another wave lifts the schooner—another fearful crash—she rolls over—her decks are rent asunder—her crew are struggling in the water—all is over!"—*Harper's Magazine*. "A dress of blue silk; plain, high body; skirt of moderate length," etc.—*Ib*. The dash, if inserted in the latter sentence, would make it a matter of wonder that there is such a thing as a blue silk dress.

The dash and the curves are generally used to set off a parenthesis between a part and its reiteration. "They call us angels—(though I am proud to say, no man ever so insulted my understanding)—angels, that they may make us slaves!"—*Jerrold*. In general, the punctuation should stand right when the entire parenthesis is omitted. "Thou idol of thy parents—(Hang the boy! there goes my ink.)" And double points should not be used needlessly. Curves and brackets so much break the connection that they have almost the force of a point. "AMID, [*i. e., at mid* or *middle*,] is from *a* and *mid*."—*Goold Brown*. "AMIDST [, *i. e., at midst,*] is from *a* and *midst*.—*Id*. I think, better thus: "AMID [*i. e., at mid* or *middle*] is from *a* and *mid;*" 'AMIDST [*i. e., at midst*] is from *a* and *midst.*" "'The *highest* classes are rich and haughty' [but the *lowest* classes are poor and humble]." "The most certain plan of success (I have it from a woman, and, I believe, an excellent authority,) is any way to *interest* them. In my own case—(I thought your poor mother had a deal of money, but—well, never mind,) —I at last affected consumption."—*Jerrold.* Here I should have omitted the comma from the latter curve; and the dashes and curves together are perhaps not both needed. The point is often better put after the latter curve only. "And the worse the case is about my companions—my fellow-paupers (for I must bear the word)—the greater are my chances of finding something for them—something which may prevent my feeling myself utterly useless in the world." Lord Macaulay, I believe, has never used a parenthesis.

A word is frequently set off by the comma, or not set off by it, according as it has the sense of a conjunction or that of an adverb. "You did not see him, *then?*" "You did not see him *then?*" "*However*, I will not shrink, *however* great the responsibility may be." "He gave the ideal, *too*, of truth and beauty;" "He is *too* bad to be sent there *too.*" "*Therefore* have I written to him;" "I have, *therefore*, written to him." "*So* pleased at first, the towering Alps we try;" "*So*, pleased at first, the towering Alps we try." The pointing sometimes depends on how smoothly the part flows with the other words. "*Perhaps* we shall never see him again." "We shall *perhaps* never see him again." "We shall never, *perhaps*, see him again." *Also, too, perhaps*, and *therefore*, often do not require a point. *Here* and *there* are sometimes set off, when emphatic or contrasted. *As well as* with a nominative, between another nominative and the verb, is set off. Parts compared or slightly contrasted, and closely depending on something after them, are often not separated; as, "It is a *small but thrifty* tree." An intermediate phrase beginning with *if not*, is always set off. When two or more modifying parts are parenthetic, the less coalescent are set off. "And her eyes on all my motions, with a mute observance, hung."—*Goold Brown*. Better: "And her eyes, on all my motions, with a mute observance hung." A restrictive relative clause seldom needs a comma before it, even when separated from its antecedent; as, "He preaches sublimely *who lives a righteous and pious life.*" "It was the scarcity of the peaches *that made them so dear.*" When *that* begins a clause depending closely on *it*, preceding it, or on a governing or controlling verb, or on *so* or *such*, the clause does not require the comma. "It is reported *that he is coming.*" "I know *that he is honest.*" "He does it *that you may praise him.*" "It was so heavy *that I could not carry it.*" When *such* or *so* begins the previous clause, the latter is set off; also, when the latter is emphatic. When two connected phrases, of moderate length, begin with articles, or are bound together by *both—and, either—or, neither—nor*, they seldom need the comma between them. When *or* connects adjectives or adverbs that are alternative in sense, they need not be separated. "Answers that are given in a careless, or indifferent manner."—*Willson's Readers.* Omit the comma. A noun qualified or governed by adjectives or verbs before it, is not usually set off from them. "It was a bright, lovely day." "He soils, tears, and loses his books; "So, adverbs. when followed by what they modify. "We are fearfully, wonderfully made." Also, the antecedents of adjuncts; as, "The leaves, blossoms, and roots of the tree." But when the connecting word is omitted before an adjunct or object, the comma is inserted; as, "He soils, tears, loses, his books." "The leaves, blossoms, roots, of the tree." But adjectives like the following, and separated nominatives, should be set off. "The former are called voluntary, and the latter involuntary muscles."—*Willson's Readers.* "Industry, honesty, and temperance are essential to happiness."—*John Wilson.* Here a comma should be placed after "involuntary," and also one after "temperance." The punctuation of the former sentence is so common an error, and that of the latter is so well authorized, that we shall quote some strong authority against both:

"I perceive one mistake in your manner of pointing. When there are several nouns of the nominative case to one verb. you admit no comma after the last of them previous to the verb. Or when there are several distinct short members of the sentence verging into one concluding one, you admit no stop between the last of them and this concluding one. In this, I am persuaded you are wrong, according to the dictates of reason, as well as the highest authority. Of the authority I am quite certain. A passage or two where you have introduced this correction, will tell what I mean. 'A new train of ideas, presenting the possible, and magnifying the certain, difficulties of the situation.' 'Though a man is obedient, and probably will be obedient, to habit,' &c. 'They are mistaken if they imagine that the influences which guide, or the moral principles which impel, this self-applauding progress,' &c. Now, I feel most certain that the comma ought to remain in all such cases, and that the contrary manner is a vulgar mode only of pointing. The authority of Gibbon is decisive, and he invariably points, in such instances, as I have shown."—*Foster's Life and Correspondence.*

Repeated parts are not usually set off when they govern an objective or qualify something immediately after them. The comma is often improperly omitted before *and*, when this connects the last two terms of a series; as, "A, B and Co." The Company does not belong more to B than to A; therefore the comma should be inserted; as, "A, B, and Co." The comma is, however, generally omitted when the short *and* (&) is used. "John, James and William are coming," implies that I am telling John what the other two boys are doing. Insert the comma, and the sense is clear. Mr. Wilson omits the comma when *and* or *nor* is inserted after each term. It is generally best to insert the comma; as, "The health, and strength, and freshness, and sweet sleep of youth, are yours." —*R. G. Parker.* The comma, however, may be so used elsewhere as to exclude the use of it in the series. "The voyages of Gosnold and Smith and Hudson, the enterprise of Raleigh and Delaware and Gorges," etc.—*Bancroft.* "Dividing and gliding and sliding, and falling and brawling and sprawling," etc.— *Southey.* Indeed, the comma is sometimes excluded within, because a greater point can not be admitted at the end. In the United States the comma is usually omitted between the number and the name of a street; as, "No. 76 Spruce Street." The sense, however, requires it; though when "No." is omitted, the figures may perhaps be conceived as an adjective, like *upper*, for instance, in the phrase, "on the upper Mississippi," which shows *on what part*, and requires no comma. In the United States, the comma is generally not inserted between the word *price* and the number, though the strict sense requires it; as, "Price $5." Dr. Bullions writes, "I, Paul, have written it." This may imply that Paul is addressed, and should therefore be, "I Paul have written it." Mr. Butler writes, "Words ending in *y*, preceded by a consonant, change," etc. This implies that the *words* are preceded by a consonant, and should therefore be, "Words ending in *y* preceded by a consonant, change," etc. Mr. Goold Brown writes, "To carve for others, is, to starve yourself." "So that the term, *language*, now signifies, an*y* *series*," etc. All these commas are superfluous or wrong. Mr. Brown frequently punctuates too closely, and sometimes contradicts himself. His system is in adequate; Dr. Mandeville's is, radically, partly sound and partly unsound; Mr. Wilson's is, upon the whole, the best extant; though it is both deficient and too voluminous.

MISCELLANEOUS MARKS.

1. Marks of Omission.

Blank space,   *Ditto*   (" or "),   *Dots*   (. . . . . . .),
Apostrophe ('),   *Long dash* (———),
Caret (▲),   *Stars* (* * * *),   *Hyphens* (- - - - - -).

Ex.— "Why do you repeat
My words, as if you feared to trust your own!" Blank space, at the beginning or the end of a line of poetry, best shows omission.
"Columbus! 'tis day, and the darkness is o'er!"
"What o'clock?" "Daniel O'Connel." "M'c Donald." "McDonald." (Contractions.)
    f ie   the evil
"Suf▲ic▲nt for the day is▲thereof." (Accidental omission.)
"10 lbs. of coffee, @ 10 cts. per pound, - - - - - - - $1.00.
 12 " " sugar, " 8½ " " " . . . . 1.00.
"No.———
   "I promise to pay to ———, or bearer, ——— dollars," etc.
"We have come into the den of a ———" (Interrupted by a tiger).
"But he married . . . . . . yet if he had married ———".
"And Mrs. S * * * *? is she as beautiful as ever? and where is H—m—d?"
    "Poor Mrs. C——— — (why should I not
    Declare her name?—her name was Cross)—
    Was one of those 'the common lot'
    Had left to mourn no 'common loss.' "—*Hood.*
"The next shall tell thee, bitterly shall tell,
Thoughts that * * * * *
 * * * * * * * *
Thoughts that—could patience hold—'twere better far,
To leave still hid and burning where they are."— *T. Moore: Fudge*
                                                 [*Family.*

To avoid the gross expression of what is offensive, indelicate, or profane, marks of omission are generally used.

Mr. Wilson seems to recommend the dash for omitted letters, the periods for omitted words, and the stars for omitted sentences. But the distinction is not always regarded.

2. Marks of Pronunciation or Utterance.

Accents;
{
 Acute   (′), *Diæresis* (··), *Webster's Notation,*
 Grave   (`), *Hyphen*   (-), (See his Dictionary,)
 Circumflex (^), *Separatrix* (|), *Worcester's Notation,*
 Macron (¯), *Cedilla* (under ç=s), (See his Dictionary.)
 Breve   (˘), *Tilde*   (over ñ=ny),
}

Ex.—"To conflíct, a cónflict." "Will you wálk, or ríde?"
"Madam, yoŭ have my father much offénded." (Stress, inflection, modulation, etc.)
    "Machîne, Mîongo, Montreâl, fête, lâ." (Long sound.)
        "Ye shépherds, so chéerful and gáy."—*Fowler.*
"Hōly, | hŏly, | hôly, | āll thĕ | sāints ă | dōre thĕĕ."—*Brown.* (Poetic accents and feet.)
"Glō-rĭ-oŭs, sōul-dĭs-ēased, ĭm-prū-dĕnt." (Quantity.)

"And hearken to the bird's love-learnèd song—love-learnèd song." "Reäppear, re-appear; coördinate, co-ordinate; aërial, Menelaüs, Antinoüs, Danaë." These marks show that a suppressed syllable must be pronounced, or they prevent two syllables from being improperly made one. The hyphen is often preferred when the first part is a prefix, or when each of the parts is significant.

"Façade, chaise, garçon, (generally placed before *a* or *o,*) señor." "Where the troop of Miñon [Mĭnyun] wheels."

3. Marks of Reference.

Star, or *asterisk* (*), 1st reference; *Paragraph* (¶);
Dagger, or *obelisk* (†), 2d " Then *doubled* (**, ††, etc.);
Double dagger, or *diesis* (‡); Then *trebled* (***, †††, etc.);
Section (§); Also *superiors—letters* or *figures* (^{a}, ^{b}
Parallels (‖); ^{c}, ^{1}, ^{2}, ^{3}).

These marks are placed, in the order we have shown, over words *from* which reference is made, and also at the head of those, in the margin, *to* which the reference is made.

4. Marks Directing Attention.

The *index*, or *hand* (☞), directs special attention to something.
Ex.—" ☞ All orders by mail must be accompanied by the cash."

The *asterism*, or *three stars* (*⁎*), precedes a note that has a general reference.

Ex.—"*⁎* The Teacher should require his pupils to spell and define the most important words in every lesson that is read."

The *brace* (}) unites two or more parts, and generally refers them in common to something else. It should open toward the more numerous parts.

Ex.—" Numbers; { Singular, Plural."

"Not that my verse should blemish all the fair;
Yet some are bad,—'tis wisdom to beware,
And better to avoid the bait, than struggle in the snare." } —*Dryden.*
(A triplet introduced among couplets.)

The *paragraph* (¶) usually marks the longer divisions of a large division: it shows where something new begins.

The *section* (§) usually marks the smaller divisions of a long division.
Both these marks are conveniently used with numbers, to abridge references.

Ex.—" ¶ 57. *Pure Verbs. Second Aorists.*"—*Crosby.*
"§ 219. A pronoun is a word used instead of a noun," etc.—*Id.*

Leaders (............) lead the eye from one part to another over a blank space.

                                                                                      PAGE
Ex.—" Naples, ... 63
Pompeii—Herculaneum,............................ 65." (Index.)
"*George*..............is a noun, it is a name," etc.
"*Has been rewarded*..........is a verb," etc.

5. Marks Used in Correcting Proof-Sheets.

    Peter Schoeffer is said to be the person who   *Caps.*
invented *cast metal types*, having learned
¶ the art of of *cutting* the letters from the Gut-   ⁎
temborgs: he is also supposed to have been   𝒢
the first who engraved on copper plates The   -!

following testimony is preserved in the family,   *r*
by Jo. Fred. Faustus of Ascheffenburg: #
Peter Schoeffer of Gernsheim, perceiving his   *S.cap*
master Fausts. design, and being himself
(desirous' ardently) to improve the art, found
out (by the good providence of God) the
method of cutting (*incidendi*) the characters   *stet.*
in a *matrix*, that the letters might easily be
singly cast - instead of being *cut*. He pri-   *ei|*
vately *cut matrices* ¶ for the whole alphabet: |
Faust was so pleased with the contrivance
that he promised Peter to give him his only   *w.f.*
daughter Christina in marriage, a promise   *Ital.*
which he soon after performed.   *No ¶*

as   (But there were many difficulties at first
Rom. with these *letters*. as there had be en before   ⌒|
Ital. with wooden ones, the metal being by mixing   *out s.c.*
tr. the a substance with metal which hardened it⸗   ⊙

*und when he showed his master the letters
cast from these matrices,*

EXPLANATIONS.

⸿   *dele*—take out the superfluous word "of."
◗   turn the reversed letter "p."
insert a space between "who" and "engraved."
⌒   less space between the words.
¶   make a new paragraph.
tr.   transpose the words "desirous" and "ardently."
stet. let *incidendi* (accidentally erased) remain.
w.f. "wrong fount" type to be changed.
out s. c. "out, see copy." The words omitted being too numerous for the margin, the compositor is referred to the original copy for them.

The other marks are self-explanatory.

CPSIA information can be obtained
at www.ICGtesting.com
Printed in the USA
BVHW082045200622
640215BV00001B/179